THE KEEPER ORIGINS BOOK 2

RAVEN'S RUIN

J.A. ANDREWS

For Jason

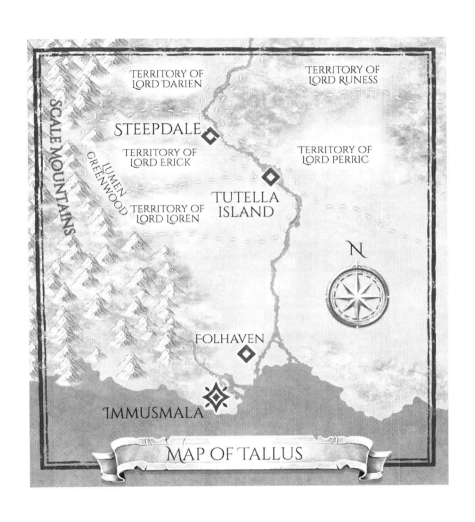

THE
CITY
OF
IMMUSMALA

LINGUA RIVER

The River Gate

The Bend

The Fallen Gate

The Spine

Docksiside

Sanctuary

THE SANCTUARY

Tol Wall

Vol Gate

PRIORY OF THE HORD

DRAGON PRIORY

PHOENIX PRIORY

GRAND STADIA

AUTHOR'S NOTE
ABOUT A FUN, LITTLE BONUS

HELLO, Most Favored Among Readers!

Before we dive back into Sable's story, I wanted to let you know about something I think is very fun.

'Round about chapter 49ish, Sable is given a book. It's a thin little volume called *Ghost of the White Wood,* and the contents of that story have ripples in Sable's story.

Now, Sable and company do discuss the tale, but I wanted you to know **that the story itself is written, in its entirety, if you're interested in reading it**.

It's short, only a few chapters, but it introduces you to some really great characters.

You can pick up **a copy for free from my website,** jaandrews.com/ghost, and the story can be read at any time:

- before Raven's Ruin
- as a little intermission when you reach the mention of it in the Raven's Ruin
- or once you're done with Raven's Ruin and hopefully wallowing in that hangover we get from a book we enjoyed.

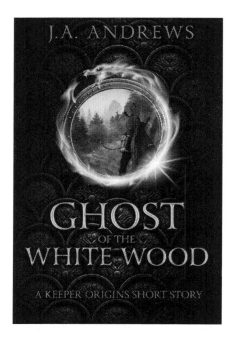

Anyway, the little story does exist, and it told me it would love to be a part of your library.

Happy Reading!

Janice

And now, on to the real reason you're here: Sable's story...

NUDGES

—Except from chapter 1 of *Interesting Beginnings* by Flibbet the Peddler

HISTORY MOVES ALONG ITS PATH, relatively straight, pointing in a certain direction with seeming inexorability until it is nudged.

These nudges can be strong—the invasion of a powerful army, for instance—or, as you will see, they can be so small they are only felt by a handful of people.

The way Issable of Shadowfall changed the course of history was filled with both kinds, but at the beginning, at least, the important nudges were intimately her own.

The First Ravens

Issable wasn't ever from Shadowfall. She went by Sable and lived contentedly with her parents and two sisters in the small town of Pelrock on the Eastern Reaches. In those early days, her unique ability to feel the truth when others spoke it was still just an interesting trick instead of a skill that her life depended on.

The first nudge came when raiders razed her town to the ground.

Through the door of the root cellar where she hid with her younger sisters, Talia and Ryah, Sable watched her father stand against the encroaching flames and the enemy, whose guttural, foreign words he inexplicably understood. She watched her mother hold her bow—the mysterious elven bow they'd never been allowed to touch—and defy the demands for surrender.

But the monsters cut them down and would have killed Sable and her sisters too, if not for the elves who emerged from the woods, their own elven bows loosing arrows like rain, destroying the enemy.

Whether the elves came of their own accord or for Sable's mother, Amelia, they disappeared into the night without saying. But their presence lent power to the nudge.

When dawn came and the nudge had faded, Sable held her sisters and stared into her new path, filled with nothing but ashes and the ravens that came to feed off the dead.

The Dragon's Reach

The second nudge came after Sable had fled with her sisters to the city of Immusmala. For years, she was trapped under the gang boss Kiva, until she finally escaped by joining Atticus, the famous playwright. Ryah made the escape as well, while Talia, deceived by Kiva, chose instead to stay and work for him.

You might suspect the nudge was when the troupe found the town of Ebenmoor burned to the ground on the Eastern Reaches, just like Sable's own home. Or when she met Andreese and discovered that all these raiders were actually soldiers of the Kalesh Empire.

Or when Sable earned the role of the beloved Dragon Prioress Vivaine in a play—a woman Atticus had known and loved early in his life. Or when Sable discovered that her ability to feel the truth had another aspect: She could fill her words with truth and make people want to believe them.

It wasn't when the play won her the chance to stand before the most powerful people in the land and convince them of the coming Kalesh threat.

Or when that attempt failed.

The second nudge wasn't even the knife that Andreese threw at that moment—the assassination of the Kalesh ambassador.

No, the second nudge, the pivotal moment, came in a small, private chapel, deep inside the Dragon Priory where the High Prioress Vivaine and her dragon cornered Sable.

It came the moment everything Sable believed about the woman shattered.

Gone was the prioress's benevolent mask. Before Sable stood a woman of cold, calculated choices. A woman who knew everything about the Kalesh attacks in the east and the coming army and had chosen to sacrifice those many lives in the hopes of securing peace for her own city.

Her facade of gentleness was gone, and only fury remained. Fury at Sable for being connected to the murder of the ambassador. Fury for destroying the treaty Vivaine had been working on with him—the safety of Immusmala in exchange for her hand in marriage.

Vivaine flicked her fingers at the hall outside the chapel and bent the very light, shifting their view until Sable could see deep below the priory to cold, stone cells where Andreese and the traveling troupe, including Ryah, were imprisoned, the troupe held as conspirators to the assassination and Andreese set to be executed at dawn.

The final push of that second nudge was Atticus's betrayal.

In a secret meeting with Vivaine, he had told her of Sable's powers to feel and convey the truth.

Sable's path turned, and to win freedom for the troupe and to save Andreese from the gallows, she pledged her loyalty to Vivaine, agreeing to gauge the truth of anyone the High Prioress negotiated with.

The next morning, Andreese stood on the gallows, and Sable performed one last role. As he watched with a look of rage and betrayal, she threw herself at Vivaine's feet, vowing her loyalty, declaring her abhorrence of what Andreese had done, and thanking Vivaine for carrying out such swift justice.

The High Prioress accepted Sable's pledge and, in an apparent act of mercy, stayed Andreese's execution, banishing him from the city instead.

───────

And so, with that second nudge, that push from Vivaine in the small chapel, unseen by most of the world, Sable was forced into servitude to the priories, and the course of history shifted ever so slightly toward a new path.

The troupe was sent away. Andreese, after one last, seething look, was dragged out of the city. Ryah was confined to serve the odious Prioress Eugessa. Talia was still firmly under Kiva's grasp, working for him, spying as the secretary of the wealthy Lady Ingred.

Sable was utterly alone. Despite her continued determination to unite the land against the Kalesh, every bit of hope and freedom she'd tasted had been stripped away.

And yet…there had been a nudge.

PART I

It has been said that I claim history moves merely by nudges. Let it be known that sometimes those nudges are on the magnitude of a rockslide nudging a tree in its path.

-Flibbet the Peddler

CHAPTER ONE

THE WARM HUES of light from the stained-glass windows did nothing to soften the cold isolation surrounding Sable as she stood inside the Dragon Priory. Past the rippled pane of glass, the gallows stood empty. The dark smudge of the crowd trickled away, taking with it the troupe and Reese.

Next to Sable, the High Prioress Vivaine stretched her fingers, and a bit of the light slipped off the glass and slid around the prioress, brightening her white robe and turning her long, straight hair to strands of silver and smoothing the irritation and small wrinkles out of her face.

What Sable had always imagined to be the blessing of Amah now looked like nothing more than thin, twisted light.

Vivaine stood with her back to the abbesses and Sanctus guards who waited for her down the hall.

"This afternoon, when you come to the council with the Kalesh," she said with a derisive look at the dirty white dress Sable had worn all night, "do attempt to look presentable."

"And you'll demand the Kalesh stop attacking towns to the east?" Sable asked.

Vivaine let out an amused breath. "Your naivety is almost refreshing. I will do what needs to be done, and you will remain silent. This is not your stage, dear. Here—in my priory—you have no voice. Your only purpose is to help me ferret out the truth so I can keep my people safe. Remember that, Issable. Or things will go badly for you and those you love."

Without waiting for a reply, Vivaine turned and called to a Sanctus guard stationed by the front door. "Please see that Issable gets to Prioress Narine."

The man bowed. "Yes, Holy Mother."

Vivaine swept away down the hall, followed by a trail of abbesses.

Sable glared after her, as though she could strip away the woman's power just by sheer fury.

The guard motioned Sable down a different hall, lined with stained-glass windows and brilliantly colored tapestries. The windows faced away from the rising sun, but the stained glass still caught enough light to glow with vibrant depictions of white-robed prioresses feeding the poor and healing the sick.

Each one flashed a glimpse of the empty gallows. Each time she could see again Reese's look of anger as she pledged herself to Vivaine.

The fury and heartbreak of the morning seethed under the surface, and Sable forced herself to focus on the door at the end of the hall. The stones around her kept trying to form themselves into cell walls, but Sable straightened her shoulders.

This was where leaders met to decide the fate of everyone she'd ever known, and countless people she would never meet. This was where the plans of the Empire would be revealed and where the leaders of the land might be convinced to unite against the Kalesh.

No, this wasn't Atticus's stage. It wasn't the stage she'd expected when she'd ridden into Immusmala only days ago, but it was a stage, nonetheless.

The true problem looming in front of her was that the role she'd been given in this grand play was small and silent. She might as well be part of the scenery.

She followed the guard down the long hallway and out into the garden tucked in the corner of the Sanctuary between the Dragon and the Phoenix Priories. The air was cooler here, fresher than the plaza had been with its crowd of people waiting to see Reese hanged. The tall Sanctuary Wall hedged in the back of the garden, almost blocking out the salty scent of the sea and the muffled crashes of waves far below. The garden itself was dotted with white-robed abbesses kneeling among neat lines of vegetables.

A flash of movement under a nearby bush caught Sable's attention. A blue face peered out at her, wide purple eyes set in a worried expression. Sable felt a tiny surge of relief. Purnicious couldn't get inside the priories, but if Sable could get to the garden, she'd at least be able to talk to Purn. Sable gave her a small wave, and the kobold drew back into the shadows.

The guard entered the Phoenix Priory through a side door into a plain stone hallway, devoid of tapestries and hollowly optimistic stained glass.

When they reached the entrance hall, they passed an intricate stone column rising up to the high, arched ceiling. Sable trailed her fingers over the shape of rippling flames, so detailed they almost flickered. The carvings were free and wild, not consuming the stone as much as bringing it to life.

The guard led her to a back hallway where a wide, wooden door was opened by an abbess. The wrinkles etched between her silver eyebrows deepened. "I suppose you must come in," she said, her voice low, "but stay quiet. The prioress is resting."

The homey smell of wood fire and mint met Sable as she entered the room. Fruit trees in the garden were visible through the window at the far end, past a tall four-poster bed. The center of the room held a large desk piled with papers. The Phoenix Prioress lay on a high-backed couch pulled up close to the hearth. Despite the mildness of the summer morning, a crackling fire warmed the room. The fireplace was a marvel of stonework.

But Sable barely glanced at the carvings, her eyes caught instead on the stunning sight next to it.

Perched on a thick beam of wood darkened with age and scarred with scratches sat the phoenix, fixing Sable with blazing orange eyes. The top of its head was crowned a deep red, brightening to orange and golden-yellow at the crest of its breast before darkening again to a cascade of ember-red tail feathers.

The bird shifted. The front edges of its wings glowed, and sparks showered down, leaving glittering trails of light.

Sable waited for the wood to smolder, but the sparks disappeared without a trace.

The abbess cleared her throat, and Sable turned back to meet the woman's hard gaze.

"So you're Issable," she said quietly, obviously unimpressed, "and even though you were part of a violent murder, the good prioress is stuck with you."

Sable opened her mouth to object, but Narine's voice came from the couch.

"Bring her over here please, Hetty."

Hetty's mouth tightened in disapproval, but she hurried toward the prioress.

Sable followed her to the front of the couch, where Phoenix Prioress arranged a thick blanket across her lap. She was dressed in the simplest robe Sable had ever seen on a holy woman, and her hair lay in a thick braid over her shoulder.

Deep lines wrinkled Narine's face, not like a woman weathered with years, but like one practiced in the art of joy. Next to Vivaine and Eugessa, Narine had always seemed like the quiet, meek prioress, but the woman's gaze was anything but weak. Narine's presence didn't hold the crushing weight that Vivaine's did, but it was more substantial than Sable had expected.

"I'm sorry she disturbed you, Holy Mother." Hetty bustled around the couch, straightening pillows and adjusting papers and medicine bottles on a nearby small table.

Unlike Narine, Hetty was the perfect example of a person whose presence carried no weight. The abbess served one of the three most powerful women in the city, and yet for all her bossing and bustle, she could be replaced with any of a hundred cross, old women, and no one would ever notice.

"I'll take her to the kitchens, where they can find something for her to do," Hetty continued.

Sable stepped forward. "No, Prioress Vivaine sent me to care for the Holy Mother."

"The High Prioress does not run this priory," Hetty said with a stern voice.

"Thank you, Hetty." Narine folded her hands on her lap. "I wish to speak to Issable alone for a few moments. Would you be so kind as to find us a bit of bread?"

Hetty frowned but nodded. "Yes, Holy Mother."

Left alone with the prioress, Sable smoothed the front of her torn and dirty white dress. There was a good chance her face paint was smudged, and from the wisps of hair hanging in her eyes, the braids Thulan had plaited for the play hadn't weathered the night well either. Sable tucked a loose lock behind her ear. "Good morning, Holy Mother. I'm sorry to come to you this…disheveled."

Narine didn't glance at her clothes or her hair but studied Sable's face. "Why are you here, Issable?"

Sable paused before stating the obvious. "Vivaine said you were ill and needed a caregiver."

"Please call her Prioress Vivaine. I did not ask what others want you to do. Why did you decide to walk into my room?"

After the way Vivaine had controlled every aspect of the morning, stripping every decision from Sable's hands, she let out a laugh at the question. "This is where that armed Sanctus guard brought me. I didn't have a choice."

"You always have a choice," Narine said, her voice still calm. "You had a choice this morning, when you turned your back on your friend while he stood on the gallows. You had a choice when you bent your knee before Prioress Vivaine and offered her your service. You had a choice last night when you stood on that stage and denounced the ambassador in front of everyone." Narine studied Sable curiously. "Which leads to an interesting question. Last night I saw a young woman stand up against people far more powerful than her. But this morning I saw her fold before everything she believed in."

"You don't know what you're talking about." Sable's words came out harsher than she'd intended.

Narine didn't blink. "Prioress Vivaine has some hold over you.

Even the young man on the gallows knew that. I assume your pledge of loyalty paid for his freedom?"

Sable took a breath, trying to get control of the swirl of anger rising in her. "I couldn't let him die."

"Of course not. The real question is, why did the High Prioress go through the effort? What use are you to her?" Before Sable could answer, Narine raised a finger. "Consider your answer carefully. It is best to speak the truth or say nothing at all. I have not decided what I'm going to do with you yet, but if you are not honest with me, I will let Hetty send you to the kitchens, and you and I will likely not speak again."

Sable shifted under the woman's gaze. A ripple of light from the phoenix caught Sable's eye. With every breath, the bird's chest glowed slightly, like someone blowing on a bed of coals.

Sable hesitated. She couldn't tell Narine the truth.

The thought stopped her.

Why not? Because Vivaine wouldn't want her to?

Everything Vivaine did relied on secrets and manipulations. All the things that had gone wrong in the past few days were because of secrets and lies.

The idea of simply telling the truth felt reckless, but freeing.

The phoenix shifted on its perch, and a trickle of sparks fluttered off the bird, glowing like tiny falling stars.

If Narine knew about Sable's skill, there'd be two prioresses wanting to take advantage of her abilities, but was that much worse than one? And it would convince Narine to keep her close.

The fact that telling Narine would probably annoy Vivaine was just an added bonus.

Sable turned back to the Phoenix Prioress, who was watching her patiently. "I can feel the truth."

The prioress considered the words. "What do you mean by that?"

"When people say something that they deeply believe to be true, I can feel it."

"And if they lie?"

"I can feel that too."

Narine paused, and Sable waited for the inevitable request for proof.

Instead, the woman merely said, "A dangerous gift."

Sable let out a short laugh. "Dangerous?"

"It is one of Amah's greatest gifts to be able to believe people."

There wasn't the slightest hint of coldness in anything the prioress had said so far, and this last statement had been the warmest of them all. Sable frowned at her. "You don't want to know if someone is lying?"

"You are missing the point of talking to people. Trusting them is the important part."

"You can't be that naïve." The words were out before Sable could stop them.

Narine raised an eyebrow. "It is not naivety to believe that people can be the best form of themselves. It is hope."

"You can't trust the Kalesh, certainly."

"Trust is given to individuals, not empires."

Sable frowned at the prioress. "Does that mean you would have believed me no matter what I said about why Vivaine wanted me?"

"*Prioress* Vivaine. And no. Only a fool believes a blatant lie. There are very few things you could have told me that the High Prioress would value enough to let that young man go unpunished, but your skill qualifies."

Narine's gaze turned to the fire as the flames chased each other across the wood. "Why did the High Prioress send you to watch me?" The words were said quietly, almost to herself.

"I'm not watching you. I'm to be your caregiver so I have a reason to attend meetings with the Kalesh."

For the first time, the look Narine cast at her showed a hint of exasperation. "If you're going to tangle with the High Prioress, child, you'll need to be sharper than that."

Narine was right. There were plenty of ways that Vivaine could have arranged for Sable to be in the meetings that were simpler and more assured than hoping Narine would agree to this idea. "Then why does she want me here?"

Narine shrugged. "Were you involved in the assassination?"

"No!" Sable took a step closer to the prioress. "All I wanted was to warn people about the Kalesh."

The prioress considered her words, then nodded. "I intend to go to the meeting with the Kalesh today, if for no other reason than to convey my sympathy. You may accompany me and serve the High Prioress if that is your wish." Sable opened her mouth to point out that none of this was her wish, but the prioress raised her hand. "On one condition."

"Anything," Sable said quickly.

Narine fixed her with a level look. "You never share with me what your gift tells you about people. I have no desire to be so restricted."

"It's not restricting," Sable objected. "It's enlightening."

Narine's look remained firm. "Do you agree to my terms?"

Sable paused, then nodded.

"Good. Then sit with me while we wait for Hetty to bring us that bread and tell me about yourself. From your speech last night, it seems you've had an interesting life."

Sable took a seat, and her eyes watched the fire dance as the prioress questioned her about the acting troupe and their travels, Sable's life in Dockside, and her parents. Sable braced herself for questions about her skills or her agreement with Vivaine, but Narine was only interested in Sable's relationships with the people in her life.

Hetty returned with some warm bread and honey, and Sable told the elderly prioress about Leonis and Thulan's endless bickering, how protective Jae and Serene were of each other, and the way Ryah had filled the role of an abbess to the people on the Eastern Reaches.

"And the young man from the gallows?" Narine asked. "Who is he?"

"Andreese is one of the only survivors of Ebenmoor," Sable said. Purnicious had survived as well, but Narine didn't need to know the kobold existed. "The Kalesh had burned the town to the ground."

Narine let out a sorrowful breath but said nothing.

The bread filled Sable's stomach with a satisfying warmth, and the cushions of the couch were so soft that she stifled a yawn.

"When was the last time you slept?" Narine asked.

Sable closed her eyes, and the room spun slowly. "It's been a while."

"Hetty," Narine called. "Take Issable to one of the open rooms down the hall. And find her something clean to wear." She turned back to Sable. "We won't meet with the Kalesh until late afternoon. You'll be of no use to Prioress Vivaine if you're falling asleep on your feet."

Sable shifted at the words. "I don't want to be of use to her."

Narine picked up a book and opened it. "Then you should have made different choices."

CHAPTER TWO

THE SCENT of soup and warm bread woke Sable what felt like moments after she'd fallen asleep. The light coming in the window of the small room she'd been given had moved far enough across the floor, though, that she must have been asleep for hours.

"You can eat once you're clean," Sister Hetty said brusquely, setting a tray down on the small table. "I've found you something more decent to wear than that rag you've got on." She held up two very plain, white servant's robes. They had long, straight sleeves and no waistline at all. "I'll show you to the baths, but there'll be no dawdling. If you're here to help the prioress, then you'll need to learn to be useful."

Sable's head was still fuzzy with sleep as she followed the woman to the baths. The room was long, with a row of pools sunk into the ground. The nearest were cold, but farther into the room, the water steamed.

Hetty pointed to the pools. "In and wash quickly. I don't have all day."

A handful of abbesses bathed in the different pools, and Sable went to the third one, which was unoccupied. She pulled the last of the braids from last night's show out of her hair and stepped into the water. It was warm, but not hot, and she took the soap Hetty offered and cleaned herself quickly.

"Don't forget your face," Hetty said. "Your powder is all smeared and smudged."

Sable scowled at the woman. "I've had a rough night."

Hetty crossed her arms. "You should be swinging from a gallows right now for playing a part in a murder. Instead you're enjoying a bath in the Phoenix Priory. You have nothing at all to complain about."

"Enjoying is an overstatement," Sable muttered, but she finished rinsing out her hair and took the towel Hetty offered.

When they returned to Narine's room, a group of abbesses filled the chairs around the fireplace, talking in muted tones with the prioress.

"Can you read?" Hetty asked quietly, motioning Sable toward the desk. At Sable's nod, the woman sniffed. "That's something. Sit."

The chair was high backed with golden, velvety cushions. The desk itself was wide and deep, its edges stacked high with letters. In the center, a map was fixed into the surface.

"You will sort through Narine's correspondence." Hetty kept her voice low. She handed Sable a stack of letters. "Most will be requests from abbeys for supplies. Note the abbey's name and the requested supplies on this list then place the letter here. Well-wishes for the Prioress's health are responded to with this exact message." She held up a small slip of paper with neatly penned words conveying the Prioress's thanks. "You will not embellish the message in any way, nor make any claims on the prioress's behalf. Nor will you seal any letters. I will review your work before it is sent." She folded her arms. "If you find mail with any other purpose, set it aside for the prioress to read. Questions?"

Sable shook her head, and Hetty moved to the fireplace, preparing cups of tea for the abbesses.

Moving some papers out of the way, Sable studied the map, running a finger over the peninsula of Immusmala. The city seemed so small compared to the vast world. At the very tip of the city, a star marked the location of the priories. Her eyes traveled north to

Folhaven, then east onto the Reaches, following the path the troupe had taken just weeks ago.

Her gaze caught on a tiny picture of a town labeled "Ebenmoor." She blinked away memories of smoke and ashes. She scanned the rest of the Eastern Reaches, wondering how many other towns had suffered the same fate.

Down near the very southeastern edge of the map, a tiny dot was marked "Pelrock."

Sable's fingers clenched on the papers in her hand, crumpling their corners as memories of her home flared to life. The smoke and ashes and swirling, screeching ravens.

"There's a rebellion brewing in the north," one of the abbesses said, dragging Sable's attention back to the room. "Sister Tanny said the people are scared. The lords aren't doing anything to protect them from the Kalesh, and towns are starting to take matters into their own hands."

"This will only lead to more violence," another tutted.

"Don't be troubled, Sisters," an older woman said. "These rebels are small, isolated farmers. Without support from people who know what's happening on a wider scale, they'll be ineffective and soon go back home."

"Instead of rumors," Narine said, "let's discuss the new garden plots on the Tremmen Hills. Have we found enough seeds?"

The abbesses glanced at each other but followed the prioress's lead.

Hetty frowned at Sable from across the room, and she returned her attention to the desk. A rebellion? If it was merely isolated farmers, they would be ineffective against the Kalesh. But why would Sister Tanny, whoever she was, have heard of the rebellion if it wasn't doing something worth noticing?

Sable pulled a piece of blank paper from the stack, an idea forming. Maybe being a small, silent player in the world of the priories wouldn't be useless. If a rebellion really was brewing, and it could be informed by someone who knew what was happening in the priories…

She looked at the map. She only knew one person who might be able to find these rebels and see if they were worth helping.

At the thought of Atticus, she tightened her hand on the quill. How could the old man have betrayed her secret to Vivaine? Sable had trusted him with the truth of what she could do. They'd all trusted him.

She stared at the blank paper, trying to think of another option, but there was no denying he'd be the one who could make contacts, and getting a letter out of the priory to him would be simple with a little help from Purnicious.

Hetty puttered near the shelves on the far wall, sorting through bowls of tea leaves and jars of herbs. The holy women's voices droned on, quiet and dull. Sable pulled a blank piece of paper out of the stack. She dipped the quill in the ink and hesitated.

Dear Leonis and Thulan,

There are rumors of a rebellion beginning in the north. They are believed to be small and unsupported, but if you could find the rebels, and if they really are resisting the spread of the Kalesh, maybe we can help them.

I'm sentenced to attend every important meeting that takes place here. I can send you what I learn.

I know the old man has connections everywhere. If anyone can find them, it's him.

But one of you write me back. I have no desire to hear from the traitor.

I miss you two already.

Tell me of your travels and

She paused. The troupe had been driven from Immusmala this morning, at the same time Reese had been banished. Undoubtedly they were traveling together. She lifted her pen to write his name, but she couldn't shake the memory of how furiously he'd glared as she knelt before Vivaine.

anyone else you pick up along the way. Maybe I can live vicariously through you and pretend I'm not trapped inside these holy walls. —Yours, S

21

. . .

Hetty was still busy, so Sable folded the paper small enough to tuck inside her sleeve. She picked up a piece of mail and turned her attention to the list of supplies requested by a small abbey far to the north.

She worked for an hour before Hetty came over, peering at her progress and motioning Sable out of the chair. The abbesses had all filed out of the room, and Narine sat quietly on her couch.

"Go help the prioress with her shoes." Hetty sat and started flipping through Sable's work.

A pair of white boots sat near the fire. Sable picked them up and brought them over to the prioress.

Narine gave her a small smile. "Could you put those on for me? Bending over that far is challenging these days."

Sable knelt and picked up Narine's foot. It was thin, bony, and alarmingly light. "What are you ill with, Holy Mother?" she asked.

"I've had too many years in my life," Narine answered with a tired sigh. The phoenix stretched its wings and flew over to the end of the couch, leaving a trail of sparks. It fixed its gaze on Narine, and she ran a finger down the feathers on its neck, leaving a line of fiery brightness. "Even Innov here is getting older, aren't you, dear?"

Sable laced the white boots up to Narine's ankle. "How can you tell?"

"Her feathers are dimmer." The prioress gave the bird a fond smile. "When she and I first met, she was as bright as the sun. But time dims us all, I suppose."

The phoenix sat, emanating light like a bed of hot coals. With every shift, embers fell harmlessly onto the couch and disappeared.

"It's time to go, Holy Mother," Hetty said briskly.

Narine sighed again. "I suppose we must. I can't imagine it won't turn political, though."

Sable slipped the second boot onto Narine's foot. "Aren't all these meetings political?"

"Unfortunately. The priories have never been political leaders," Narine said. "Never before have we presumed to make treaties with foreign powers. It is a twisting of our entire purpose. It is not my place to rule this city—it is my place to serve."

"But if you don't stop the Kalesh from spreading, who will?"

Narine's face took on a stubborn look. "I will not take on the role of political ruler. And if I refuse, perhaps the Dragon Prioress and the Prioress of the Horn will step back from this path as well. The city will raise its own political leaders to follow, and the priories can go back to our rightful role of offering spiritual guidance to the people. Amah is interested in people's hearts, not the politics of the land."

Sable kept her eyes on the laces of the second boot, hoping it wasn't obvious how much she disagreed with that sentiment. If she had the power to speak out against the Kalesh and actually curtail their actions in the city…

Narine sighed. "But let's go give our condolences and hear the new ambassador push the Empire's eternal request to quarter soldiers in the city."

"Quarter soldiers?" Sable sat back on her heels. "In Immusmala?"

"It's what they've always wanted," Narine answered, "and what the Dragon Prioress has been trying to stave off."

Sable stared at her. "We can't give them that. We can't give their army a foothold in the city."

Narine gave a short laugh and stood. "You are more like Prioress Vivaine than you may want to admit. Those are her thoughts exactly."

CHAPTER THREE

SABLE WALKED BESIDE NARINE, their steps crunching unhurried on the gravel path through the garden. The prioress paused often to inspect the vegetables, admiring their growth with the abbesses who tended them.

Sable hoped that their tortoise-like pace meant that the meeting would be half done before they reached it, but when they finally arrived at the Dragon Priory, the only people in the council room were Vivaine, two Sanctus guards, and a Mira Sable recognized from this morning at the hanging. Sable wasn't sure how many of these magic-wielding women actually worked for Vivaine, but there were always a half-dozen of them doing impressive things at the festivals. The woman's robe was long and white, draping elegantly to the floor, but her cuffs and the hem of her robe sparkled with shimmering silver.

Sable and Narine entered at the narrow end of the council chamber. Bright stained-glass windows in the far wall poured light onto the table running the length of the room. In front of the windows, two chairs, taller and more ornate than the rest, sat next to each other. Vivaine sat in one, looking over some papers.

Sable studied the dark-haired Mira standing attentively behind Vivaine's chair, wondering if she'd seen this woman before today, lighting a lantern with just a touch or ringing the festival bells without even that.

Unlike Hetty's subservient manner, or the invisible way the guards stood against the wall, this Mira's position near Vivaine held some authority. This woman wasn't merely a faceless attendant.

"Narine, dear." The High Prioress stood and swept down the room, reaching past Sable to embrace the Phoenix Prioress. "Thank you for coming. I know it's been an exhausting day."

"Hopefully this meeting will end as peacefully and mercifully as the scene at the gallows this morning," Narine answered.

"We can certainly hope." Vivaine glanced dismissively at Sable. "A comfortable seat has been prepared for the prioress near the head of the table."

The Mira pulled out the chair closest to Vivaine. Thick, red cushions lined the seat and the back.

Narine had barely reached her seat when Prioress Eugessa strode into the room, calling out orders to hurry with the wine and pastries. She came down the near side of the table, pausing at Narine's chair and patting the elderly prioress's arm. "How are you today, dear?"

Sitting on Eugessa's smallest finger was the butterfly ring, the dull blue stones glinting. The horrible, stupid ring that might have actually bought Talia's freedom from Kiva, and it was once again utterly unattainable.

"Nasty business this morning," Eugessa said. "Dreadful way to wake up." Without waiting for Narine to answer, Eugessa waved the line of abbesses behind her toward the table.

Sable dragged her gaze away from the irritating ring and froze. Standing in Eugessa's large shadow, a smaller, more familiar figure timidly held a plate of cinnamon bread.

Through the gauzy veil, Sable's gaze locked on her sister's face. Her stomach sank. "Ryah?" The word came out as a whisper.

Ryah attempted a smile, but the effort fell flat.

Eugessa snapped her fingers. "Stop dallying, girl. There are important people coming."

Ryah ducked her head and set the plate down. She hurried after the other abbesses to the far wall, tucking herself between two larger women, her arms pulled in tight, her veiled face turned toward the floor.

Sable took half a step toward her, and thick fingers closed around her arm.

The room bustled with activity, but Eugessa stood barely a pace away, her hand gripping Sable's forearm with a warm, clammy hand. The prioress's fleshy, powdered face looked down at Sable coldly, her orange painted lips twisted in disgust. "If it were up to me," she whispered, "you'd have swung on those gallows this morning alongside the traitor."

Eugessa's words pressed against Sable true and stiflingly warm, like hot sunlight on a stagnant day.

The prioress glanced at Ryah. "And the rest of your friends and family too."

Eugessa shoved Sable's arm away and strode past her, tossing a bland greeting at Vivaine and settling into the first chair on the other side of the table.

Sable rubbed her skin, trying to banish the feel of the woman's hand.

At the sight of Ryah shrunk back against the wall, the anger that had smoldered against Vivaine all day spread out to encompass Eugessa as well and fused into a thick, molten pool.

Vivaine's Mira stepped closer, the silver edges of her cuffs glimmering. She set her hand on Sable's elbow and pulled her away from the table until they stood against the wall. "Your place is here," she whispered. "The High Prioress requests that you do nothing to draw attention to yourself during the meeting."

Sable tried to yank her arm away.

The Mira didn't release her grip. "Your role is to gauge whether people are speaking truthfully. Outwardly, you will be meek and silent."

Sable's jaw clenched, and she glared at Vivaine.

The Mira's fingertips dug into Sable's arm. "That includes your facial expression. Anything you wish to convey to the Holy Mother must wait until you are alone with her. This is what you agreed to. Acknowledge that you will keep your word."

Sable clenched her hands into fists, but she gave a curt nod, and the Mira's grip loosened.

"The Holy Mother also wishes to remind you," the woman continued quietly, "that I will be standing next to you the entire time, and while I am touching you, I am aware of your thoughts."

Sable focused on the feel of the woman's hand on her elbow. There was nothing unusual in the woman's touch. *So,* Sable thought loudly, *I'm to have a nameless leech on my arm?*

The Mira gave a humorless smile. "My name is Gwen, and you don't need to shout."

Sable stiffened. She'd sensed...nothing. The thought of Gwen inside her mind made her feel terribly exposed, and she tried again to pull her arm away.

The Mira shot her an annoyed look. "Yes, I can hear your thoughts," Gwen whispered. "And no, you can't feel it."

Sable stared at her. Gwen was about Sable's age, but taller, her face smooth and serious. Her hair was long and dark, almost black. The similarity to Sable's hair was striking, except Gwen's was combed perfectly straight, hanging down her back with far more elegance than Sable's managed.

Gwen glanced at Sable's head. "At least yours looks better than it did this morning at the gallows. You looked dreadful."

The chill from Gwen's invasive talent shifted to annoyance. *I had been up all night, detained by your Most Holy High Prioress who was threatening my friends with death.*

"Yes, you are an innocent victim. It's truly heartbreaking," Gwen murmured dryly. "Do you always whine this much?"

Vivaine, Eugessa, and Narine sat discussing the upcoming Red Shield Festival. More white-robed women filed in, placing plates and cups at each seat of the table. Prioress Narine selected a piece of cinnamon bread from a passing abbess and took a large bite.

How often do I have to stand here with you? Sable put some effort into constructing a mental image of tearing her arm out of Gwen's grasp.

"As often as Prioress Vivaine desires," the Mira told her. "The Holy Mother has named you witness for the Phoenix Priory. In addition to caring for Narine, you will come to the Dragon Priory to witness meetings that don't require Prioress Narine's attendance but that the Phoenix Priory should be aware of. You'll come on the first and fourth days of the week during the hours when the High Prioress receives petitioners, and any other time you're sent for. I doubt you'll be here more than four times per week."

"Four times a week?" Sable whispered.

Gwen shushed her. "Don't speak."

Being here that often is going to make it difficult to care for Narine, Sable finished silently.

"You're there to help the Phoenix Prioress with small tasks. You're hardly essential. Prioress Narine will understand."

Sable glanced at the prioress, who had already eaten half the cinnamon bread. *I think the Prioress Narine understands the situation completely.*

Gwen shot her a narrow look. "The High Prioress also expects detailed updates on the Phoenix Prioress's health."

Meaning I'm supposed to spy on her? At least that explains why Vivaine put me there. Does the Dragon Priory not have enough influence on the Phoenix Priory to get anyone else to inform on Narine?

Gwen remained unruffled. "We're all very worried about *Prioress* Narine's health." She emphasized the title. "High Prioress Vivaine is glad to see you've started attending to the mail. That is a task the Phoenix Prioress should not be burdened with."

Sable looked sharply at Vivaine. Sitting at the table, she spoke with the other two prioresses, giving every appearance of gentle innocence.

She was watching me?

Gwen let out a little snort of derision. "The Holy Mother led me to believe you were clever. I thought you'd understand that the High Prioress knows everything."

Sable looked at the Mira incredulously. *She had nothing better to do today than watch me read Narine's mail?* The folded letter in her sleeve felt suddenly horribly obvious.

Gwen glanced down at Sable's arm. "You aren't forbidden from contacting people outside of the priory," she said. "Or from attempting to blindly help groups of people you don't even know. But don't forget that the High Prioress is Amah's vessel. The goddess shows the Holy

Mother things she needs to know to keep the people safe, and so Prioress Vivaine is always aware of things that are important."

Sable felt the warmth of Gwen's words but shook her head. *That is not remotely close to the truth.*

Gwen shot her a frown and squeezed Sable's arm. "It is true, and I know you felt it."

You believed what you said, Sable corrected her. *But believing something doesn't make it true. How long have you worked for Vivaine?*

Gwen's frown deepened, and she ignored the question. "So you can only feel whether someone believes what they're saying?"

Of course. I can feel whether you are being truthful or purposefully deceptive. But what you happen to believe in your head may have nothing at all to do with reality. This nonsense with Vivaine is an excellent example.

Gwen's mouth tightened into a thin line. "You will refer to the Holy Mother by her appropriate title."

That's unlikely. There had been a time when Sable had been shocked to hear Atticus call High Prioress "Vivaine," but while they'd practiced the play, Sable had grown comfortable with it. *Vivaine doesn't deserve respectful titles, and I'm definitely not going to use them when I'm thinking in my own head.* She glanced at Gwen. *If you've worked for her for any amount of time, I doubt you really believe she learns everything from Amah.*

"The Holy Mother doesn't get all her information from the goddess. She also has faithful followers who share with her what they see happening in the world."

Sable let out a short laugh. *Normal people call those "spies."*

Gwen rolled her eyes. "I don't expect someone like you to understand the dedication other people have to the goddess."

I understand dedication to the goddess. What I don't understand is dedication to Vivaine.

"And yet here you are, working for her."

That is not out of loyalty, I assure you. Sable's gaze wandered across the veiled abbesses lining the walls of the room. It was a small comfort that servants here didn't wear veils, so at least Sable wasn't relegated to the ranks of faceless abbesses.

Position is crucial, Atticus had told her once. *If you want to strip a character of their voice, move them to the periphery until they become part of the backdrop.*

The old traitor had been right about that at least.

It hardly mattered that Sable's face was visible when her voice had been stripped away. She was shoved into the background and muzzled. If this room was a stage, then the table was the focal point. Everyone around the outskirts existed merely to set the mood.

Sable's gaze fell on Vivaine. All those weeks trying to understand the prioress, all that energy trying to imagine what Vivaine must really be like, and Sable had landed so far from the mark.

"You hardly know her well enough to decide that," Gwen pointed out.

Sable snapped her attention back to the Mira. *How can you read my mind? Half the time I have enough scattered thoughts in my head I can barely make sense of them.*

"It is a noisy, unpleasant place," Gwen agreed.

And you hear everything in it?

"I hear most clearly what you're focused on."

Sable paused. *So, if I were to focus on reciting lines from plays and ignoring whether or not people in this room are speaking the truth, you'd merely hear the plays?*

"I could still tell what you felt about the truth, but it would take more work. So when the Kalesh get here, focus on the meeting."

Sable turned to face the Mira. For the first time today, she felt a tiny sliver of control. *You need my cooperation.*

"No. I don't."

Really? You can sort out small, minor fluctuations in the warmth of the room that I'm not paying attention to? While I'm loudly and passionately reciting the poem Epophus composes for his love? How much are you picking up about the prioresses right now? Because even from this distance, if I focused, I could confirm that Eugessa is almost constantly lying, but I've been ignoring them.

Gwen tightened her grip on Sable's arm. "You promised the High Prioress you would help."

No, I promised her I would support her in public and attend meetings where you'd read my mind to find out if people were telling the truth. I never promised to help you do your job.

Gwen let out an irritated breath. "What do you want, Issable?"

Sable thought back to Atticus's words. *Even a silent actor can demand attention*, he'd said, *if you just keep them near a central character. Before long the audience will be dying to know who they are and what they're going to do. And how they reached their position of influence.*

Sable glanced at the council table. *I want to stand behind Narine's chair. The closer I am to people, the more clearly I can feel them.*

Gwen gave her a flat look. "And, as Atticus says, you'll demand people's attention, even if you're silent."

Sable shrugged. *If I'm going to help you, I should get something out of it. It's up to you, of course, but I should warn you that from back here I will feel less of people's words, making it harder for you to detect. And I remember the lines to a lot of plays.*

Gwen glared at her, but before she could answer, footsteps rang out in the hall, and three Kalesh men strode into the room. Two were soldiers, wearing their black uniforms with red and gold accents, leaving the third man to be the new ambassador.

Sable cleared her throat and looked up at the ceiling. *How does that poem start? Oh, yes. Demonda, my love! Time slogs along and I am dying. I cannot breathe, I cannot move until you are near me—*

Gwen clenched her fingers. "Fine. But I will be speaking to the Holy Mother about this."

Excellent. Sable started forward, and Gwen came along with her, still holding her arm until they stood behind Narine's tall chair.

Vivaine frowned, but Gwen made a series of hand signals, and Vivaine, with a small scowl, refocused on the Kalesh.

Unlike the last ambassador, this one was old. Easily as old as Atticus. And, unlike Ambassador Tehl, there was no pretense that this man wasn't part of the military. His hair was a stormy grey, and his face was weathered with the look of a career soldier. A puckered scar ran from his temple down to his jaw, leaving a bare path through his grey beard. He didn't wear a uniform, but his black robe with the blood red dragon snaking down the center managed to look crisp enough to be one.

His expression was one of detached, military sternness, and Sable smiled. *Do you think Vivaine will charm this one into marrying her?*

"Focus, whiner," Gwen whispered.

The ambassador hadn't reached the table before Eugessa rushed toward him, her white robe billowing about her.

"Ambassador Bastian! We are appalled and sickened by the events of last night!" Eugessa set one hand on the ambassador's arm, her rings glittering. "To have such a great man as Ambassador Tehl murdered, right here in the Sanctuary! How can we possibly make amends?"

"Please come in, Ambassador." Vivaine's composed voice carried over Eugessa's babble. The High Prioress motioned to the tall chair next to her own at the head of the table.

The ambassador extricated his arm with a polite nod to Eugessa and moved to stand next to Vivaine.

"We are greatly distressed over Ambassador Tehl's death," Vivaine said, the truth of her words wrapping warmly through the room.

"I know you had grown close to him," Ambassador Bastian said gravely. "My sympathies to you as well."

Vivaine inclined her head and gave him a mournful smile. She turned toward Narine's chair. "Have you met Prioress Narine?"

The ambassador bowed his head at the elderly woman. "It is an honor to meet you, Prioress."

The man's words were unusual. They were true, that was certain. There was a warmth to them, but it was a very simple warmth. He almost spoke with the sort of truth a child did. Plain and simple.

An odd quality for a diplomat.

Next to her, Sable caught a flash of motion from Gwen's hand as the Mira straightened her fingers. They were standing so close behind Narine's chair, no one besides Vivaine would see the movement. The High Prioress's eyes flickered over, but she gave no reaction.

"I am sorry for your loss," Narine told the ambassador. "It is always tragic to lose a life to violence."

The ambassador nodded in acknowledgment.

"Of course, we all support the High Prioress's act of mercy in releasing the prisoner this morning," Eugessa said, and Sable felt the cold of the lie from across the table.

Gwen closed her fingers into a fist, and Vivaine's only sign of noticing was her jaw tightening ever so slightly in irritation.

"But," Eugessa continued, "it does leave an ache to have some justice brought to bear." At the warm truth in those words, Gwen opened her hand again.

Sable shifted. It was unnerving how easily Gwen read her mind.

"Mercy should always come before judgment," Narine said. "Drawing others to renounce the darkness and come to the light is the greatest work we can do."

"Well said," Vivaine agreed. "Let us hope all involved in this tragic act are drawn toward the light." She gestured to the chair behind the ambassador. "Although this tragedy is very fresh in our hearts and minds, we believe the most important work we can now do is to complete the treaty Ambassador Tehl was so close to signing."

The ambassador started to sit and let his gaze travel around the edges of the room, taking in the guards and the veiled abbesses.

His gaze caught on Sable, and he shoved himself back to his feet.

His military reserve cracked, and he flung a finger at her. "You! *Zabat*!"

Sable flinched back from the fury in his voice, which cut across the table like a blazing whip.

One of the Kalesh soldiers rushed around the table and grabbed Sable's arms, yanking her away from Gwen and twisting her arms up behind her back with an iron grip.

CHAPTER FOUR

SABLE TRIED to twist out of the Kalesh soldier's grasp, but every motion caused pain to shoot up into her shoulders.

Narine turned in her chair, her eyes wide. "This is unnecessary!"

"Issable is not a rebel," Vivaine said. "She has pledged herself to the priories."

Sable couldn't pull her eyes away from the ambassador's face. His gaze dug into her, filled with anger and something deeper. Something challenging and deadly. His jaw clenched as he visibly tried to regain control of himself. "After her role in last night's murder, you dare to bring her here?"

Vivaine set her hand on the ambassador's arm. "She had no part in the assassination."

The ambassador studied Sable's face with a ferocious intensity. "That woman is dangerous." This time the truth in his words wasn't simple—it was deep and rich and rolled out like heat from an oven.

"Ambassador Bastian," Vivaine said firmly, "Sister Issable has joined the priories and placed herself under our authority. And under our protection," she emphasized the last word.

The ambassador didn't relax.

"I personally guarantee," Vivaine continued, "that if she does

34

anything to endanger anyone, the consequences will be immediate and severe." The prioress brightened with a golden light, warmer than the cool stone of the walls. "She is no threat."

Ambassador Bastian drew in an angry breath. His gaze raked over Sable again before he gave his soldier a quick nod. The pressure on Sable's arms released so quickly that she stumbled forward.

Gwen shot out a hand to catch her as the soldier strode back over to the ambassador.

"Still want that attention?" Gwen whispered.

The ambassador ordered his expression almost back into his original sternness. "You will regret this choice, High Prioress." His words were warm and filled with deeply held belief.

Sable rolled her shoulders to soothe the ache. *He's speaking the truth,* she pointed out to Gwen.

Next to her the Mira opened her hand and gave Sable an irritated look.

Vivaine ignored them both. The ambassador sat stiffly, fixing his focus back on the table. Vivaine sat as well, as calm as if nothing untoward had happened.

The Dragon Prioress motioned for one of her abbesses to bring the scroll. Vivaine spread it out, angling it so the ambassador could see. "Here is the treaty Ambassador Tehl and I were working on. As you can see, we had agreed that the Kalesh will have the opportunity to purchase unclaimed land in the mountains for mining. He and I were finalizing the location of the housing for the Empire's diplomatic delegation. His request was that it be immediately outside the Sanctuary Walls, while I had offered a house near the seaward edge of the city." She fixed him with a sad smile. "I didn't have a chance to tell him yesterday that I had changed my mind. We are happy to grant the Empire a spacious home immediately outside the Veil Gate."

The last part was cold with lies. *She just decided that right now, didn't she?* Sable asked. *To placate the ambassador?*

Gwen ignored her. If the ambassador was impressed with this offering, he didn't show it.

"In return," she continued, "the Empire had agreed to leave any military force out of Immusmala and not interfere politically with the city itself."

Ambassador Bastian barely glanced at the scroll. "The Empire has been generous and patient up to this point. But if you continue to insult the Dragon Emperor with assassinations and traitors and schemes of alliances and marriage—"

Vivaine stiffened at the word.

"—or any attempt to limit our autonomy, your fate will be swift." The ambassador's words were calm but firm. He waved his hand toward the treaty. "That agreement died with Ambassador Tehl. The Empire has the same demands as before. Full access to the mountains and the mines we have provided the funding to create and housing for a garrison of Kalesh soldiers here in the city to protect our interests."

Vivaine opened her mouth to object, but the ambassador continued. "When word of Ambassador Tehl's assassination reaches the emperor, I assure you the terms of any treaty will sour considerably. It will please His Eminence if he also receives news that you have finally agreed to our small requests after so many months of delay."

As with everything the ambassador had said, these words were true, and Gwen opened her fingers. Vivaine's gaze rested on Gwen's hand for just a moment before she looked back at the scroll.

Sable leaned forward and set her hands on the back of Narine's chair. The High Prioress couldn't agree to this. A garrison of soldiers embedded in the city?

Eugessa leaned forward. "There is nothing unreasonable about that request. Of course you should be able to protect yourselves and your interests here. Last night proved that necessity."

Vivaine's jaw clenched, and she turned to Narine. "What is the opinion of the Phoenix Priory?"

Narine shook her head. "It is not the priories' place to have any opinion on the activities of foreign states. It is only our place to shepherd the hearts of the people."

Vivaine gave Narine a regretful look. "If only there were someone else to take on the burden of negotiating with our foreign friends." She turned back to the ambassador and clasped her hands on the useless treaty. Her knuckles grew white, but her voice remained calm.

"Housing for fifty Kalesh soldiers in the city," she agreed. "We'll have something ready by month's end."

Sable opened her mouth to object, but Gwen clenched her arm in warning.

"A hundred soldiers. In a fortnight." Ambassador Bastian's tone was unyielding. "We must keep our interests safe."

Vivaine frowned. "We don't have room in the city for a hundred soldiers to—"

"Yes, we do," Eugessa interrupted. She snapped her fingers at an abbess close to the door. The woman hurried into the hallway and came back with a short, sickeningly familiar man in a rich brocade vest of gold and black. His walnut hair curled around his narrow face in barely tamed waves.

Sable gripped the back of Narine's chair.

"This is Kiva." Eugessa simpered at the Kalesh ambassador. "He is a respected member of the Merchant Guild."

Sable let out an incredulous breath, but Gwen's grip tightened so sharply it turned to a grunt of pain. Kiva glanced across the table, and when his gaze fell on Sable, his eyebrows rose in surprise.

"Kiva has offered housing for the Kalesh from his own property," Eugessa continued.

Of course Kiva knew this was going on. Sable squeezed the back of Narine's chair until the edges of the wood dug into her palms. Kiva's jays—the network of spies he'd roped Talia into—probably knew everything the Kalesh had been doing all summer.

She shook her head at the man. It was only a month ago that he'd been introduced to Eugessa. He certainly didn't waste time slithering his way up the power structure.

Kiva bowed to the ambassador. "I have two large, unused buildings inside the wall dividing Dockside from the rest of Immusmala. They lie only a short distance from the docks and have easy access to the rest of the city."

Sable stared at him. That area had been abandoned for years. The large buildings that had housed dock workers had fallen into disrepair and were now used for Kiva's smuggling operations.

"They need some work, but I could have them ready for your men in a fortnight." Kiva glanced at Vivaine. "If I were given some financial help from the city in return."

Vivaine gave him a flat look.

"How many men will they hold?" the ambassador asked.

"Well over one hundred," Kiva answered.

"Agreed." The ambassador turned to Vivaine. "Assuming the Dragon Prioress has no further objections?"

Vivaine hesitated only a moment before nodding curtly.

The ambassador rose. "I will be moving into the quarters Ambassador Tehl used here in the Dragon Priory this afternoon. Send the agreement to me when it is drafted, and I will sign it." Without another word, he started toward the door.

Eugessa rose and fell in next to him, setting her ringed hand on his arm. "It's so nice to have a decisive man to work with," she said as the two stepped into the hall, followed by the other Kalesh and a string of abbesses. Ryah gave Sable a quick glance before ducking out with the others.

When Sable turned back to the table, she found Kiva watching her with an amused expression, his gaze lingering on the white robe she wore. She glared back at him.

"An honor, as always, Holy Mother." He gave Vivaine a bow. She acknowledged him with a cold nod, and he left the room.

Gwen dropped her hand from Sable's arm and stepped away.

Sable took a step toward the High Prioress.

"How could you?" Sable demanded. "How could you possibly give them that?"

"Issable!" Narine said sternly.

But Vivaine shoved herself up from the table, her eyes blazing, her finger stabbing toward Sable. "This is your fault. Make no mistake." She started for the door but paused to give Sable a withering look. "When this city falls, know that it was you who brought down the first stone."

PART II

The expected Kalesh army did not sweep through Immusmala that year. There was no burning or ravaging, no ash or ravens.

Instead, the Empire came like termites, gnawing into the flesh of the city, burrowing into its very core.

-from *The First Queen* by Flibbet the Peddler

CHAPTER FIVE

Eleven months later

Moving quietly in the still dark room, Sable stoked the coals and fed them some wood, coaxing the fire back to full strength. It was still early summer, and the mornings had warmed enough that Sable wore only her thin socks, but Narine still wanted her couch pulled close to the hearth while she slept burrowed under a heavy, wool blanket.

Next to the mantel, Innov glowed like soft embers, her flame-red head tucked alongside her wing. The fire brightened until it outshone her feathers, and Sable felt a ripple of uneasiness at how faded the phoenix and the prioress both looked.

Changing out of her sleeping shift, Sable pulled on her plain servant's dress, letting the simple fabric drape almost to the floor. Countless times Narine had offered Sable the fitted robes of an abbess, made from fine, soft linen, but it felt more independent to look like a servant than to blend in with all the abbesses surrounding her, even if the logic of that didn't hold up. Besides, even with a robe that wasn't strongly connected to the priories, Sable still felt a pang of distaste when she put it on, as though each morning it renewed her pledge to serve Vivaine.

A quiet knock brought Sable to the door. She pulled it open, and Pixy stepped in with her oversized basket of mail.

The veiled abbess set down the basket on the edge of the wide desk and leaned close. "Amah's blessings in paper form," she whispered dramatically, "brought to you today, thanks to my dedication and obedience." She smiled, the side of her mouth twisting against a puckered scar from a childhood burn that snaked up her cheek and into her hairline. "Many blessings be upon my head."

She held out a pile of letters, and Sable took it quickly. Purn should have returned yesterday from her latest trip out of the city. Sable held the letters near the candle and flipped through the pile, finding the letter addressed in Leonis's quick, messy hand. For the last six months, ever since the task of answering Narine's correspondence had been relegated to Sable with no oversight at all, Purn had taken to merely dropping Leonis's letters into the mail wagon when it rolled into the Sanctuary.

Sable was about to put down the rest of the letters when she saw another bright white letter addressed to *Issy* in an elegant, artistic script that she hadn't seen in weeks. She flipped it over to see Talia's yellow seal, stamped with a stylized flower.

"Thank you, Pixy!" she whispered.

Behind her gauzy veil, the abbess raised an eyebrow. "Certain letters make you happy enough I'm beginning to suspect people send you gold."

"What would I do with gold?"

Pixy shrugged. "Give it to me? I'd leave the priory, settle down as an eccentric wealthy woman who was always veiled and rarely left her house." She paused. "I'd name myself Lady Veil, and there'd be constant speculation as to who I was. The local children would dare each other to peek in my windows, where they'd find nothing but terrifying monster masks looking back at them, just to keep things deliciously strange."

"I would love to see that happen." Sable set down the rest of the mail. "You are wasted delivering mail here, Pixy."

"True." The abbess frowned at the discarded pile. "Um," she continued quietly, "as ordered, correspondence from the Dragon herself was placed on top so that you could not possibly miss the hallowed word of our great High Prioress, may Amah bless her with itchy boils on her backside."

Sable laughed. Pixy was the only person Sable had met in the priories whose dislike of Vivaine mirrored Sable's own. Pixy was also the only other person Sable had met in the priory who didn't want to be called "Sister" or really want to be there at all. Her scar disfigured the right side of her face so severely, she'd joined the priories when she was young merely for the chance to wear a veil every day.

"I acknowledge that you did your duty. Consider the Dragon's invitation duly noted and cast aside with great boredom," Sable said.

The abbess grinned and picked up her basket. "Enjoy your mail. I have other people who will be much less enthused than you to get their own piles, and it wouldn't do to keep them waiting." She turned toward the door. "Do let me know if that gold shows up," she whispered over her shoulder.

Sable sat down, pulling out the white letter addressed to *Issy*, smiling at the name Talia had decided was safer than either Issable or Sable.

She opened the letter.

Issy,

I'd apologize for being lax in my correspondence, but seeing as you are far worse, and when your rare letters come, they hold no interesting gossip at all, I refuse to feel any sense of wrongdoing.

I overheard several conversations that might interest you. L.T. has been hosting more Kalesh captains lately, so there are often soldiers in the house.

Sable scowled at the paper. Lord Trelles was entirely too supportive of the Kalesh.

I'm sure you don't like the idea, but the men are polite, and Lady Ingred and I have both enjoyed their company.

. . .

"I don't like that idea at all," Sable said quietly.

What you will like, though, is that there's some discontent among the common soldiers. They're convinced that Immusmala is too far from the Empire, and they're not receiving the support they should. The generals speak of more troops coming, but the common soldiers don't believe them.

I know you mentioned in one of your short, business-like letters that friends of yours believe the Empire overextended itself and is weakening at the edges. For what it's worth (and I'm not sure it's worth much), the uninformed, often uneducated soldiers seem to agree.

Sable straightened. Jae's and Serene's studies in the Dragon Priory library over the last year had led them to just that conclusion. That the fabled might of the Empire was waning. Although Serene was always quick to point out that idea was based mostly on conjecture and extrapolation.

You probably won't agree with this, but from talking to the soldiers, I think we should be grateful for how the last year has gone. Most places the Kalesh take an interest in are taken over militarily. The fact that things have stayed amicable so far seems like a very good thing.

The trade they're bringing is helping the city, too. K. has opened two new textile mills in Dockside, and now fifty people have jobs who didn't before.

"Then the Kalesh are helping Kiva," Sable muttered at the letter. "Not the city."

I know you'll think that means they're only helping K.,

. . .

Despite herself, Sable let out an amused breath.

but they're not. I've convinced him to let me organize the distribution of extra supplies. I have a network of people delivering food and clothing to the poorest in Dockside. In the last month, I've been able to feed dozens of families who would normally go hungry. I don't think even you can find fault in that.

Sable reread the paragraph, unexpectedly impressed Talia had organized so much, and more impressed she'd convinced Kiva to let her.

You remember my friend Callie? I've found work for her outside of Dockside with a seamstress. The demand for Kalesh designs in clothing is so high they work nearly nonstop. Despite all the hard things around me, I'm finally able to protect the things I care about.

There are rumors of trouble brewing in the north, although I doubt I need to tell you about that. You've been rather coy about all that.

Sable paused. Coy about what?

The juiciest bit of news I've heard lately is that Mardella, the daughter of Lord Carlinton, ran off and wed a butcher's boy without telling anyone! An abbess near the river wed them in secret, and the butcher boy gave Mardella a ring of carved ivory from the tusk of a wild boar he killed himself. Which is either artless and romantic or a bit barbaric—I can't decide which.

Lest you feel any undue pressure to write me back—if I attended every political meeting with the Kalesh, I'd have enough interesting things to share that I'd have to write you a book—let me relieve you by saying that I'll be at the Dragon Priory's dinner during the festival. Hopefully we can find some time to talk then, when you'll undoubtedly share all the exciting things I miss by living outside the Sanctuary. Or you'll be you and warn me of the dangers of the Kalesh.

In all seriousness, I hope Narine is well enough to attend. Both for her sake and because I would love to see you.

-T

Sable smiled at the paper. Talia would be sorely disappointed if she knew how boring meetings in the Dragon Priory were. The Kalesh were continually trying to expand the number of soldiers they housed in the city, Kiva continually offered them new buildings, Eugessa continually simpered over anything the Kalesh said, and Vivaine deftly delayed every official decision that had political ramifications.

Narine, on the other hand, refused to participate. If she attended the meetings, it was usually to share some message of condolence or congratulation. More often than not, though, Narine sent Sable to not participate in her place.

Sable glanced back at the curious line about being coy. If Kiva somehow knew Purnicious was taking letters north to the rebels, his spy ring was considerably better than she'd thought.

Setting aside the puzzle, she picked up Leonis's letter.

His letters were always purposefully unsatisfying. For the past year, she'd sent whatever information she could find about the Kalesh to him, but she'd made him swear not to send her anything but vague reports of the rebels back. Sable never could shake the feeling that Vivaine was watching or that the mail was somehow monitored, even if Sable could never see signs of it being tampered with.

She examined the wax with the tree stamp that Leonis used, but the seal looked unbroken.

The tree itself wasn't exactly like the small, glowing tree he always traveled with, but it was close enough to give her a pang of homesickness. Or whatever the equivalent word was if you missed traveling instead of staying home.

She broke open the letter.

Dear Sneaks,

We're currently guests of Lord Loren. Of the five squabbling Northern

Lords, his territory is the smallest, his capital city, Marshwell, is small enough that 'city' is a stretch, and Loren himself is a smallish sort of man.

The most valuable thing about Little Loren, though, is that your favorite rebels are currently camping nearby, which makes forwarding your correspondence a simple task. They found your map of the Kalesh trade routes very interesting.

The latest unsettling rumors here are that the Kalesh are mining farther and farther north in the Tremmen Hills. Of course, this is a double-edged sword. No one wants the Kalesh too interested in this land, but what if there is gold in the Scale Mountains? This question has driven normally sensible northmen mad. They're abandoning their homes and heading to the hills with shovels.

Why humans are so taken with that gaudy, glittery metal is beyond me. Most of humanity's problems stem from them being too much like dwarves.

It is the greatest pain of my life that you insist I don't tell you details about your rebels. Because there are things you would like to know. Like—

There was a jagged end to the word, and the writing changed to Thulan's thick hand.

This is why Leonis cannot be trusted with sending you letters. The man is incapable of keeping a secret. He's like an overgrown child who gets all giddy when he has something fun to share.

I don't get giddy.

Of course, I also don't feel compelled to keep things secret. But since Leonis is shouting unrepeatable things at me right now, I will merely end with this:

Up until this time, no one's heard much from your rebels. All their actions have been small and localized.

But all that is about to change.

Get ready. Things will start getting fun soon.

CHAPTER SIX

SABLE REFOLDED THE LETTER QUICKLY. Thulan's words weren't enough to cause the rebels any problems, but Sable still glanced up at the window, her heart beating faster.

Aside from the occasional complaint by the Kalesh of irritating bandits attacking their supply lines or an especially well-orchestrated theft of something valuable, she'd heard nothing about the rebels. For the past several months, she'd continued sending Leonis information more out of a desperate need to do something than out of any real hope that it was making a difference.

But if the rebels were gaining enough strength to be heard of, even down here in the city...

Narine was still sleeping, so Sable took the letters to the fireplace and tossed them into the flames, watching until they blackened and turned to ashes.

The rest of the mail, surely full of mundane priory business, sat on the desk waiting, but Thulan's words left her feeling antsy. Outside, the world had an orangish hue, and Sable crossed the wide, stone floor to the window. The Sanctuary Wall blocked her view of the horizon, but above it, the sunrise splashed in bright swatches of pink and orange across the high, thin clouds. It tinted the stones of the Dragon

Priory and the white rock of the Sanctuary Wall until everything glowed.

She lingered, leaning against the cool stone wall, wrapped in the longing sunrises brought. The longing to be on a hill with no walls to be seen. She could almost feel the solidity of Reese beside her, the familiarity of the acting troupe sleeping nearby. The pure freedom of being where she wanted, with the people she wanted.

Today the longing was almost palpable. The Red Shield Festival was in full swing, and tonight red lanterns would fill the sky over the Sanctuary, just as they had a year ago as she waited to escape Immusmala with the troupe.

On the other side of the room, Narine stirred, and Sable turned away from the window.

"Don't stop watching the sunrise on my account." Narine's voice was papery soft.

Too soft.

Sable crossed back to the couch. "How are you feeling? Are you cold?"

Narine looked at Sable gently. "You miss them." Her words sank into Sable, warm and true as they so often did.

"They're just sunrises. New ones happen every day."

"You know I didn't mean the sunrise." Narine pulled the blanket up to her neck, and Sable made sure it was tucked around her feet. "Don't worry—if I were your age, I'd rather spend a sunrise with a handsome young man than with a dying old woman."

Sable's hands faltered at the last three words. "If you're dying," she said, trying to keep her voice light, "you're doing it slower than anyone I've ever seen."

The prioress gave a shadow of a smile, but her lips were pale, barely darker than her skin.

"And besides," Sable said, standing, "I never said Reese was handsome."

"Is he?"

Sable shrugged, but a smile crept across her lips. "He had a certain charm."

The prioress turned her face toward the fire. "Can you remember his face?" Her voice was low. "People I haven't seen in a long time... sometimes I can't remember their faces."

Sable glanced out the window, thinking of the way Reese always watched the world more closely than she did. The way his hair brushed his shoulders and his beard had those strands of red interlacing with the brown. The way his expression, so often serious, would crack into a smile when she caught him off guard.

But, as thoughts of Reese always did, the image shifted to him, standing on the gallows, fixing her with a look of fury as she pledged herself to Vivaine. Sable refocused on the blanket, smoothing it with quick, brusque strokes. "I remember."

Narine looked up at Sable. "Why don't you like to talk about them?"

Sable studied the prioress. She was remarkably direct this morning, and something about it felt troubling. "There's nothing to say."

"It's better to speak the truth or nothing at all," the prioress said. "What are you afraid of, Issable?"

Sable turned to kneel by the fire, letting Narine's question worm into her. It was the question the old prioress always headed for. Whenever Sable tried to keep the conversation light or avoid saying what was really on her mind, Narine would ask the question she'd asked people a thousand times. *What are you afraid of?* Always asked gently, always asked using the person's name.

And no matter the answer, the fears were never discounted.

Sable absently added wood to the flames.

It had taken months of Narine asking before Sable had answered truthfully. Months more before she realized that the seemingly disconnected question always made sense. Whether she was frustrated or angry or troubled, at the root of it all, she was usually afraid of something.

"I miss the people I used to travel with." That wasn't the answer, but it was easiest to approach fears from the side. She never could quite figure out what she was afraid of when she tried to see it head on. "But it's not only the people. There was a freedom to those days."

Sable watched the flames flicker. They didn't dance as wildly as campfire flames did under an open sky.

"A freedom you don't have here."

Sable paused at the woman's bluntness. Usually the prioress phrased things as a gentle question, regardless of whether she knew the truth. It was only when she was very tired and alone with Sable that she dropped the pretense of not knowing.

The heat flared up, and Sable backed away, watching the flames explore the edges of the new wood. "A freedom I've almost never had and always wanted."

And there it was.

The fear, sitting right in front of her.

"I'm afraid," Sable said quietly, "I will never have it again."

Narine made a hum of acknowledgment. "You've always had true freedom, though," she pointed out. "You still do. The freedom to do good."

Sable snorted. "Very true, Holiest of all Holy Mothers. But that's not the sort of freedom I'm missing. The time I spent with the troupe seems like a different life."

Narine looked pensively into the fire. "I've been in the priory nearly all my life. If I ever had a different life, I barely remember it. Anyone who comes here stays forever, so there are very few people I've had the luxury of missing. Except my sweet sisters who've gone before me to the Golden Land to meet Amah."

The note of melancholy in Narine's voice made Sable's glance at her. There'd been more and more of that lately. "What about the crotchety sisters? The ones too mean for Amah to take? Or do you not miss those?"

Narine laughed. "Sister Mellidred *was* very crotchety."

"I've heard stories." Sable stood and brushed off her hands.

Narine made a noise that might have been a laugh, but it was too weak and quiet to tell. She lay with her eyes closed again, having barely moved since she'd woken.

Sable went to the cabinet for the tea leaves, then grabbed another glass jar as well. She pulled the cork out with a quiet pop and dropped a pinch of the buttery rich, yellow powder into a waiting cup.

"Don't waste the tintis root," Narine said.

"At least I know your hearing isn't fading," Sable answered, leaving the expensive powder in the cup. Narine liked to save it for special occasions, but the number of special occasions Narine made it to were dwindling.

Sable pulled out three large leaves from the tea bowl and began to break off the ridge along their outer edge, breathing in the mild minty smell that always lurked in Narine's room.

"Just drop the leaves in the cup," Narine said. "You don't need to do the extra work."

"Serene says the leaves are more effective without their outer edges."

"She does not."

Sable grinned and faced the prioress. "True, but does the tea taste better when I break off the ridge, Holy Mother?"

Narine narrowed her eyes.

Sable held up a finger. "It is best to speak the truth or say nothing at all."

Narine blew out an irritated breath. "Yes. It tastes better."

"Then I'm breaking them off." Sable turned back to the tea.

"I never should have told you about the leaves."

"But then you would have missed out on so much happiness. I'm choosing the freedom to do good. You should be pleased." Sable dropped the tea leaves into the cup and covered them with hot water.

"Is tonight Prioress Vivaine's dinner?" Narine's voice was a bit stronger.

"Yes." Sable sat on the end of the couch. "I can send your regrets to the Dragon Priory."

"Nonsense." Narine shifted and pushed herself up into a sitting position. "Of course I'll be attending."

Sable raised an eyebrow. "Sitting up on your own doesn't mean you're strong enough to go to dinner. Even one of Vivaine's dull state dinners."

"*Prioress* Vivaine," Narine corrected her.

"I can make sure someone sends you a whole plate of Eugessa's cinnamon bread if that's the draw."

"*Prioress* Eugessa," Narine said. "And it's not the dinner, although the cinnamon bread is delicious. The real draw is the lanterns."

"The lanterns are a good reason to go," Sable admitted.

"I'm giving you some warning so you have time to wiggle out of it and find someone else to accompany me," Narine said with a smile.

"Normally, I'd start wiggling this very moment, but Talia will be there."

"Oh, good. It's been too long since you've seen her." Narine considered Sable. "It's been too long since you've seen anyone but me. You should leave the priory more often."

Narine's hands were folded carefully in her lap, as they always were when she didn't want it to be obvious that she didn't have the strength to move them.

Sable sat down next to her. "I leave nearly every other day for exciting meetings at the Dragon Priory."

"You know that's not what I mean," Narine said with a note of reproach.

Sable reached over and set her hand on Narine's. "Your hands are still freezing. I don't know why I'm surprised you don't tell me these things."

"My hands have been cold for as long as you have been alive. There's no reason to bring it up."

"True. It's not like there's anyone in the room who could get you an extra blanket or stoke the fire or get a cup of tea for you to hold." She stood and went to check Narine's tea. A dish of wrinkled, red berries caught her eye. "The kitchen sent up the last of the dried scarletberries. Would you like them?"

"That would be lovely. And some extra for Innov."

Sable gave the prioress a dish with a pile of the berries, and Innov flew to the arm of the couch. Narine held up a dried berry, and the phoenix nipped it quickly from her fingers.

"You *should* leave the priory more often." The prioress's voice was surprisingly firm.

Sable set the teacup on the table next to Narine and crossed her arms. "Putting aside the fact that leaving would make dear Vivaine incredibly angry—"

"Prioress Vivaine," Narine corrected her gently.

"—I don't have anywhere to go," Sable continued. "And as far as

Lady Ingred is concerned, Talia doesn't have a sister in the priories. Getting a visit from me could cause her a great deal of trouble. Ryah is nearly always stuck at Eugessa's side—"

"Prioress Eugessa," Narine corrected her again.

"And dear *Prioress* Eugessa is not fond of me. So I doubt it would be good for Ryah to spend time with me, either. Jae and Serene are eternally buried in the library of the Dragon Priory, and every other friend I have has been banned from the city."

"None of that means you can't leave the priory for something enjoyable."

Sable let out an annoyed breath. "I'll make you a deal, Holy Mother. You start telling me when your hands are cold, or when you want *anything*, and I will plan a trip out of the priory for something enjoyable."

Narine gave a little laugh. "You have a deal."

Sable paused at the unexpected answer.

The prioress offered Innov the last of the scarletberries. "But I have the trip planned already. Between the Red Shield Festival and the Midsommer Festival, I like to travel north and visit the abbeys under the protection of the Phoenix Priory."

Sable stared at her. "You're not planning to do that this year."

"Why not?"

"Because you've barely got off your couch in two days!"

"I can lie in a wagon just as well as I can lie on the couch."

"No, you can't. Wagons are incredibly uncomfortable."

"I've ridden in a wagon before, Issable," Narine said mildly. "We will be gone for well over a fortnight. We leave after the festival."

"Holy Mother," Sable said, stepping forward, "you are not strong enough for a long journey."

"And so I should do what, Issable?" the prioress asked, her voice weary. She lifted one hand and ran her finger down Innov's glowing chest. "Sit in this room until I die in my sleep?" She looked at Sable with clear eyes. "I want to leave the priory, too. I want to see the Tremmen Hills and breathe air that hasn't stagnated in a stone room all day."

The words stirred the longing in Sable again. Yes, the Tremmen Hills and the wild, free air of the countryside.

"I want to see the people who write letters to me all year long," Narine continued. "Letters I don't even have the energy to read anymore." She smiled at Sable. "So, my dear Issable, what I want is for you to accompany me."

"Holy Mother—"

Narine held up a hand. "The deal was I tell you what I want, and you leave the priory."

Sable grimaced at how mercilessly the wagons would jounce Narine's frail bones, but the woman's face was set. Sable nodded. "Fine, but I get to pack things for you. And organize your wagon. And plan your food. And you will always tell me when your hands are cold."

Narine smiled widely. "I agree to your terms." Innov nudged Narine's hand. "Sorry, my flame. That's the end of the berries."

Innov chirped and nudged Narine's hand with her beak.

"For the record," Sable said, "I think this is a terrible idea."

"Everyone does, I'm sure." Narine gave her a conspiratorial look. "But it will be a bit of an adventure, don't you think?"

"I'm not sure bumping along in a slow wagon and visiting rural abbeys qualifies as an adventure," Sable began, but the brightness in Narine's eyes, which had been weary for so long, chased away any other objections.

The idea of a journey caught hold of something inside Sable, and a long-suppressed eagerness sprang to life.

The prioress gave Sable a knowing look and leaned forward. "I know you want to go," she whispered.

The words were warm with truth, and Sable couldn't stop the smile that spread across her face. She leaned toward the older woman and let her own truth add to the warmth. "I do," she whispered. "I really do."

CHAPTER SEVEN

THE HOT EVENING sun heated the side of Sable's face as she stood two steps above the end of the long line of feasting tables laid out before the Phoenix Priory. The festival crowd filled the Sanctuary Plaza in a sea of bright colors and lively motion. The boisterous clamor of count-less conversations echoed off the stoic walls of the priories as the sharp scent of spiced bread drew more and more people to the feast.

The prioress herself stood at the center of the long row of tables, Innov perched on her arm. Narine handed loaf after loaf across the table, talking and laughing. When she reached across the table to set her hand on a forehead, giving a blessing from Amah, the woman's hand didn't tremble. She stood tall, and, while she didn't walk through the crowd as she'd done in years past, she was more animated than Sable had seen her in weeks.

An abbess came down the steps, carrying a basket of waxed cheese rounds just brought up from the cellars. She joined the dozen other white-veiled women moving through the people.

Sable stretched to see over the crowd. Eugessa's tables looked to be empty of the rich pastries she always served, and Vivaine's tables were running low of meats and fruits. But even though the crowds had been just as thick at Narine's priory all day, she'd prepared so much bread that the tables and even the stairs behind them were still mounded with baskets.

Three Kalesh approached from the Dragon Priory, and Sable picked out Ambassador Bastian among them. He caught sight of her and turned to approach, stopping at the base of the stairs.

"Festive day, Issable," he said politely. His accent always drew out the beginning of her name in a long "ah" sound.

"Festive day, Ambassador," she answered. Except for their very first meeting, where the man had denounced Sable as a dangerous rebel, he'd never been anything but polite to her or anyone else. And unlike the other diplomats she'd met, he almost always spoke truthfully.

His appearance was neat and controlled. The only thing about him that hinted that he hadn't always been a diplomat was his scar.

Today he used the same unassuming, pleasant tone he always used, and despite the fact he was Kalesh, she found him too amiable to properly dislike.

"I saw the good Prioress Narine is out," he said, "and came to offer my congratulations on her good health. We've missed her in so many councils of late."

"She'll be pleased to see you." Sable motioned him to come behind the table. "I hope you're ready to receive a blessing from Amah, though, because she hands out more of those than loaves on days like this."

"It seems unwise to not accept blessings when they're offered, especially from the Phoenix Prioress." He gestured for the two soldiers with him to wait, then glanced back at Sable. "What do *you* hand out on festival days, Sable?"

"Invitations to ambassadors to step behind tables where usually only those dedicated to the priories are allowed."

"Indeed." He smiled, but the look in his eyes stayed gauging. "You're behind the table. Are you dedicated to the priories?"

Sable considered the question. "I'm dedicated to the Phoenix Prioress, which counts for a great deal around here."

"Ah. Well, I'll move along and greet the prioress in case any other ambassadors show up looking for their turn."

He walked along the table and spoke to Narine for a few minutes. When he returned, he held up two fingers. "She blessed me twice."

Sable raised an eyebrow. "She's probably trying to wash away the blights and wrongs of your foreign, heathen soul."

He gave a short laugh, but it had a self-mocking edge. "If I'd known her blessings washed away wrongs, I'd have asked for a hundred more." He gave Sable a nod. "Festive day, Issable."

"Festive day, Ambassador," she said, watching the curious man head into the crowd.

She soon lost sight of him, but her attention was caught on a young boy standing on a tall planter, one arm wrapped around the tree as he scanned the festival. After a moment he made a series of hand signals, and Sable followed his gaze. In the crowd of people pressed up to the food, it was impossible to find the mark he'd just called out to his partners, but someone was about to lose something valuable.

It felt odd that those things still went on. The gangs still roamed the streets, gang bosses still controlled them, festival goers still lost the valuables they were foolish enough to dangle out in the open.

"Festive day, Sable," a slow voice drawled from close behind her.

She stiffened but forced herself to glance back at Kiva calmly. He leaned against the column on the step above her, and she felt a jab of annoyance that she hadn't noticed him approaching. "No one from outside the priory is supposed to be behind the table," she pointed out.

"The ambassador was."

"By invitation."

"So," he said, "you invite a Kalesh ambassador back here, but not your old friend from Dockside?" Kiva wore a brocade vest, colored a dark, shimmering emerald that reminded Sable uncomfortably of his poisonous green snake. He had trimmed his curls shorter, and while they were less unruly, they also hid less of the thin ruthlessness of his face.

"Of all the things I've called you, Kiva, and all the things I've wanted to call you, 'old friend' isn't even close."

He grinned at her, then nodded his chin back toward the boy on the planter. "You miss it, don't you?"

"Working for you?" she asked. "Not the tiniest bit."

"You should. At least my priorities align with yours." He looked at Narine. "I'm not focused on baking bread and purposefully avoiding responsibility when we need to be focused on the Kalesh."

Sable crossed her arms. "On providing them housing in Dockside? How many buildings is it now? Is it your goal to be their nursemaid and make sure their stay here is so comfortable they move in for good?"

He gave her an amused look. "I control where they live. I have eyes on them at all times. They're paying me a lot to contain them in my one small corner of the city."

"Until they stop paying you. And decide to just take whatever they want."

Kiva shrugged. "When they change tactics, so will I."

"That is a talent of yours," she said dryly, "finding new ways to keep people trapped."

"I'm rather proud of that skill. It's served me well over the years. Not with you, of course, but with most people." He smirked. "I've tried to make up for my failure with you by working extra hard on Talia."

She gave him an unamused look, which he returned with a calculating one.

"You're an odd case, Sable. Without being pushy or showy, you became one of my most competent thieves. Then you successfully escaped me. I won't pretend that didn't make me angry, but I'll admit, I was also a little impressed.

"Not as impressed as when you came back, though, because you didn't come back quietly. You came back on a stage, drawing the attention of the entire city." He let out a laugh. "I have never been so enamored of a play as I was that night in the Grand Stadia. I was ready to swear my loyalty to Vivaine that moment. And yet…"

He gave her white servant's robe a derisive look. "You live with prioresses and chat with ambassadors, yet somehow Vivaine has muzzled you. You had a voice once, very briefly. You were a force to be reckoned with. Now you're…mute."

"Is there a point to all this, Kiva?"

"I'm pleased Narine does nothing that matters. Her voice would shift the balance we've worked so hard to achieve. But you're wasted here, focusing on that old woman. Whatever it is that you did on stage last year, you should be using that now. You could walk down these steps right now, and you and I could work together."

Sable turned to face him. "People don't work with you, Kiva, they work for you. And if you think I'll ever do that again, you're more of a fool than I've ever suspected."

The oily smile she'd grown to hate over the years spread across his face. "You will, Sable. Because neither you nor I want the Kalesh running this city, and at some point, you'll realize we are stronger together."

"I cannot imagine any scenario where that would happen."

"Then you should expand your imagination." He looked back at the boy on the planter who was signaling another target in the crowd. "Until then, keep in mind the one thing festival days always teach us: that people who dumbly focus on the wrong things are very easy to take advantage of." He pushed himself off the column and started down the steps. "Festive day, Sable. You know where to find me when you change your mind."

Sable stared after him as he disappeared into the crowd, shifting her shoulders to slough off the sour feeling he always left her with.

*...at some point, you'll realize
we are stronger together, Sable.
-Kiva*

She turned her attention back to Narine and saw that the prioress had grown a bit pale and was resting against the table.

Sable crossed over to her. "Would you like help inside, Holy Mother? It's near time to prepare for the rest of the evening."

Narine looked regretfully at the piles of bread still left. "It's a bit early for that still, but thank you for not pointing out that I look exhausted." She took Sable's offered arm. "Standing didn't used to be so tiring."

Sable helped the prioress up the stairs, moving slowly. They reached the top, and Narine paused to look over the Sanctuary. "In a better world, every day would be a feasting day, Issable."

Sable almost agreed, but the young boy was still on the planter. "In a better world," she said instead, "a feasting day would be everything you think it should, and humans wouldn't be quite so much like themselves."

Narine patted Sable's hand. "Then we'd have nothing left to work toward."

"Let's work toward getting you to your couch for a rest." Sable started forward again. "Or you'll doze off into your soup at Vivaine's fancy dinner."

When Narine didn't correct her with "Prioress Vivaine," Sable cast a worried look at the frail woman and slowed her steps. The dozing off at dinner might be unavoidable.

"The abbesses will be here soon," Sister Hetty whispered, searching through a line of veils hung in Narine's large but scarcely filled closet. "You let her sleep too long, Issable."

"I tried to wake her three times," Sable whispered back, taking the prioress's formal robe from its thick, carved hook in the center of the closet's wall. This fabric was pristine, shimmering silk, with pearls embroidered along the bottom, climbing up in tendrils of flame.

Hetty pulled out a long, sheer veil with a similar pattern of tiny pearls. "Where are the taller white boots?"

Sable pointed to the corner.

Hetty hurried over to them. "The abbesses will be here long before we can get the prioress in all this."

"Then the abbesses can wait," Sable said firmly.

"The Choosing ceremony won't," Hetty pointed out. "Which necklace?"

Sable scanned the pegs on the wall, each holding a necklace of silver with diamonds or pearls. "Bring the middle three, and she can choose."

"You're going to find something reasonable to wear tonight, right?"

Hetty looked critically at Sable's plain robe. "You can't go to the dinner in that."

"I'm just there as her caregiver," Sable said. "I hardly need to dress elegantly."

Hetty made an exasperated noise but followed Sable out to find Narine leaning back on her couch, her eyes closed.

"Time to get dressed, Holy Mother." Hetty's voice was torn between respectful and anxious.

It took longer than usual, and three pauses to rest, to get Narine dressed in the robe and the veil and the tall boots. But when the abbesses arrived to escort her to the ceremony, Narine was selecting her necklace.

"The prioress has had an exhausting day," Sable said as she let the abbesses into Narine's room. "She'll need to lean on someone's arm for the walk to the Grand Stadia, and don't make her stand long before you go to your seats."

"Stop mothering me, Issable," Narine said from where she sat on the couch, letting Hetty adjust her necklace. "These sisters are capable of conveying me safely to and from the building next door."

Sable came over to her. "Let me at least walk you over, and I can wait by the door until you're done."

Narine shook her head. "Take the time for yourself, Issable." She glanced at Sable's plain robe that had a smudge of dirt on the side from when they'd been out at the feast. "We do have a formal dinner to attend tonight. Go enjoy a long bath. I know you won't wear anything as nice as an abbess's robe, but see if you can find something fancier than what you're wearing."

Hetty nodded emphatically next to her.

"The High Prioress has put a lot of planning into this night," Narine said. "The least we can do is show our appreciation by dressing nicely."

"Well, I certainly don't want to disappoint the High Prioress." Sable managed to keep her tone almost sincere.

The abbesses around her nodded and murmured in agreement.

Narine gave Sable an amused look. "These sisters can escort me straight to dinner after the ceremony, and you can resume your worried care of me in the banquet hall."

"I reserve the right to continue worrying about you while you're gone," Sable said, helping the prioress stand, "but I will meet you at dinner, and I hope you have a lovely time at the Choosing."

Narine patted Sable's hand before taking the offered arm of an abbess and leaving the room. The rest of the holy sisters trailed behind them, and Hetty followed.

Sable gladly pushed the door closed behind them and leaned against it, the room beautifully empty and quiet. A bath did sound good.

Sable headed to the long room at the far end of the priory. The baths were gloriously deserted while all the abbesses were busy with festival tasks, and Sable climbed slowly into the hottest pool, letting the heat seep into her and wash away thoughts of everything else.

She stayed in the quiet baths, washing her hair twice for good measure and soaking as long as she dared before heading back to her own nook off Narine's room.

When she entered, a white dress lay across her bed. It wasn't in the style of an abbess's robe, but it had long, draping sleeves and a high waistline embroidered with white thread.

I found something reasonable, a note in Hetty's hand read. *Adding a necklace would not go amiss.*

Sable laughed and changed into the new dress. The fabric was soft and smooth, and the dress fit well enough that she felt almost refined. The idea of wearing one of Narine's necklaces felt inappropriate, though, so she merely brushed out her hair and headed to Vivaine's bound-to-be-dull state dinner.

The vegetable garden between the two priories was empty and quiet except for the muffled sounds of the festival floating over the wall from the Sanctuary Plaza. But when Sable pulled open the side door of the Dragon Priory, the faint sound of shouting echoed from somewhere down the long hall. She started toward it, and the closer she drew to the banquet hall, the louder the voices became, accompanied by the thuds of someone pounding on a table.

Sable reached the vaulted entrance hall just as Kiva shoved his way through the front door, his face savage, almost frenzied.

He caught sight of Sable and jabbed a finger at her. "This'll change things!" he shot at her. "Mark my words, this is the tipping point!"

She stopped, more at the rich warmth of his words than his biting tone. Kiva never spoke the truth that clearly.

He strode up to her, close enough that she could see the flecks of yellow in his eyes, and leaned forward. A cruel smile twisted his lips. "This is when you're going to want that voice back that you gave up when you let Vivaine own you."

CHAPTER EIGHT

KIVA SPUN AWAY from Sable and strode toward the growing shouts and clamor. She followed him through the open doors of the banquet hall to find the room in chaos.

Narine was already seated in her chair, looking alarmed. Vivaine stood at the head of the enormous table, her face pale. Eugessa was frozen in her seat, her eyes wide. In the middle of the room, the Kalesh delegation faced off against two Northern Lords across the table.

A Kalesh general pounded on the table and shouted over the rest of the room. "The north attacked our mine! Killed our men! We demand retribution and recompense! You have declared war on the Empire!"

Sable moved toward Narine's chair. The Kalesh generals she'd met over the months in the priories fell into two categories: soldier or diplomat. This man was soldier through and through. His hair was grey but still cut in the close, unforgiving style of the ranks. He was burly, but unlike most of the older officers, nothing about this man had softened with age. Fury colored his face a dark red.

Next to the general stood Ambassador Bastian, along with four more soldiers who each had enough bands on their sleeves to be nearly generals themselves.

"The Merchant Guild has been hit too," Kiva broke in, striding to the table and slamming down the handful of papers he held. "Two different supply lines attacked! Gold, tools, and food stolen!"

With a burst of noise from the hall, two more merchants stormed into the room, shouting about destruction of property.

"We have attacked nothing!" the larger of Northern Lords declared.

"Your cowardly attacks have been going on for weeks!" the general shouted back. "But this is too much! Mine workers murdered!"

Sable reached Narine's chair and took her usual place behind it while Gwen stepped up close. The silver edges of the Mira's robe glittering subtly, as she set her hand on Sable's arm.

What happened? Sable asked.

Gwen ignored the question. "Are they lying?"

Sable concentrated. The room was filled with so much shouting and chaos, it was nearly impossible to pick out the warmth from any particular person's words, but the general, at least, believed what he said.

Gwen gave Vivaine a discreet series of hand signals.

"General Goll." Vivaine's voice swept through the room, reasonable and calm. "You have every right to be upset, but our northern friends are as shocked by this news as we are. Surely you can see they were not responsible."

No one paid the High Prioress any heed. Across the hall, Serene moved through the crowd with a grim face, coming to stand next to Sable.

"What's going on?" Sable asked her quietly.

"The Kalesh received a raven today claiming one of their mines was attacked last night."

"It's not the Northern Lords," Kiva said. "That rebel group that's been causing problems along the Black Hills are not under any particular lord. They are led by a man named Tanis, and he's been harassing people for months, but this attack far outstrips his others. Something has emboldened him."

Unlike in the hall, these words were back to Kiva's usual twisted mix of truth and lies that Sable had no hope of sorting out. Gwen left her hand half open for Vivaine to see.

Several people shouted about the rebels, and Sable forced her face to stay impassive.

She certainly hadn't needed to wait long to find out what Thulan had meant.

Tanis...She tested out the name. It was a good name for a rebel leader, and while she hadn't had any part in helping them find the mine, if the rebels had also attacked the caravans carrying gold, clearly Tanis had put the map she'd sent of Kalesh trade routes to good use.

"Don't you think it's foolish to be helping a group you know so little about?" Gwen said in hushed tones.

"The rebels are actually fighting the Kalesh," Serene whispered around Sable. "That's worth supporting."

"And the less I know about them," Sable said quietly to Gwen, "the less you know about them."

"How does that make your actions any less misguided?" Gwen asked.

"Atticus, Leonis, and Thulan know more, and they support them," Serene pointed out.

"Well, if the *acting troupe* supports the rebels," Gwen said dryly, "they must be a trustworthy group."

"I'm still waiting for Vivaine to demand I stop sending them information," Sable said.

"The High Prioress likes to let you feel like you're accomplishing something." Gwen looked pointedly across the table. "The burly man across the table is Lord Perric," she whispered. "He rules the largest territory in the north. Is he telling the truth about not being involved?"

General Goll had begun another tirade, and the two Northern Lords were talking over him in such a cacophony of noise, Sable couldn't possibly sort out who, if anyone, was lying. Every Kalesh, including the normally reserved Ambassador Bastian, was standing and shouting.

There're too many of them talking to sort out. Sable focused on the chaotic swirl of warmth. *As far as I can tell, everyone believes what they're saying.*

The table was set with the priory's best dishes, bottles of wine were waiting to be poured, but no one except Narine sat in their seats.

Wide-eyed abbesses pressed back against the wall, more serving trays in their hands, unused to such behavior in the priory.

On the far side, the two Northern Lords were dressed in dark military uniforms. Lord Perric dwarfed a smaller man whom Sable had seen before. Lord Runess, the man whose army Andreese had served in. The two faced the Kalesh side by side in an unusual show of unity.

At the far end of the table, Lady Ingred stood surrounded by her father, Lord Trelles, and a handful of merchants.

"Someone owes us a lot of gold," the barrel-chested Trelles yelled.

At Ingred's shoulder, Talia looked around the room nervously. She wore an expensive-looking green dress with an embroidered dragon visible around the waistline. The Kalesh general pounded the table again, and she flinched.

General Goll shouted over the other voices. "I demand that you find this Tanis and bring him to face us. Or we will take Kalesh troops into your countryside to do it ourselves!"

There was a moment of shocked silence. The words were warm, and Gwen's hand opened, but Vivaine didn't bother to look over. Everyone in the room knew that threat was true.

"That," Vivaine said, an icy bite to her voice, "would be considered an invasion. I'm sure your diplomatic presence here has no intention of taking any military action on our land."

"The general spoke out of turn." Ambassador Bastian gave Goll a fierce look. "The Empire has no intention of using their military in this situation."

The red-faced general shut his mouth but continued to glower across the table.

The High Prioress stood glowing with a soft whiteness as she raised her hand for silence. "We have also heard of this Tanis," Vivaine said, "and agree that something must be done. Even before this attack, I had personally sent scouts to discover the location of these rebels. If he is responsible for this, we will bring him to the city to face justice for his violence."

Her words were warm, as they almost always were, but Sable frowned at the High Prioress. The woman's extensive network of spies and informants made Kiva's jays look like a child's attempt at gathering information.

"If she knows Tanis exists," Serene said under her breath, "she surely knows where he is."

Sable nodded. "How long ago did she send those scouts?" she whispered to Gwen. "Weeks ago?"

Gwen didn't answer.

General Goll leaned on the table. "While we wait however long that will take, who is going to repair the damage we've suffered?" he demanded. "Our new mine is destroyed, and the road to it blocked! There is no other way to it through those blasted, rock-strewn mountains!"

"Rock-strewn?" Lord Runess's voice cut across the table.

General Goll stopped short.

"How far north are you mining?" Lord Perric asked. "Because the mountains west of Immusmala are not rock-strewn. They're quite green."

The general shifted. "They're only green down here by the sea, where you call them the Tremmen Hills. A mere two days north of here, where they turn into the Scale Mountains, they become rocky."

"They don't become rocky," Lord Perric said, a dangerous edge to his words, "until you reach lands controlled by the north."

An uncomfortable silence fell in the room, and the sense of unity among the Northern Lords solidified into something almost tangible.

Sable glanced at Serene to see if the claim was true, and woman gave a small nod.

"The Kalesh Empire has no treaty with the north," Lord Perric continued, "so there would be no way they would be mining in our hills, would they?"

The ambassador cleared his throat. "We inquired as to where the northern lands began and were told they began north of the Black Hills."

Vivaine's gaze flickered to Sable and Gwen. But the ambassador's words, as always, were warm and true. Gwen signaled as much, and a slight crease appeared in Vivaine's brow.

Lord Perric's face twisted in outrage. "North of the Black Hills?

Lord Loren controls the entirety of the Black Hills along the base of the Scales. By the time the mountains have become rocky, you are in our territory."

Ambassador Bastian shot an indecipherable look at General Goll. "We were told otherwise."

"We were," the general agreed.

Goll's words twisted across the table with the cold sharpness of a lie, and Sable straightened.

At Gwen's signal, Vivaine's face grew grim.

"Just because Lord Loren is the weakest of the Northern Lords," Lord Runess said, "do not make the mistake of thinking he is unsupported."

"I assure you," the ambassador said, his words still warm, "that we had no intention of mining in the northern lands."

"Regardless of where we were," the general interrupted, "our property was destroyed, and our men were attacked and killed. Not just soldiers, but hard-working men, merely doing their job. We demand someone bring those responsible to justice!"

But the dynamic in the room had shifted. The general's threats were not met with shocked outrage by the north but with a steely, cold anger of their own.

"My lords," Vivaine said, "and Mr. Ambassador. Clearly there has been some sort of confusion. Let us sit and discuss how we can sort out exact borders so that no one is impinging on each other. Then together we can investigate this attack. We must find out who is responsible."

Vivaine's final words were cold.

"She already knows who did it," Sable said quietly to Serene.

Despite Vivaine's request for everyone to sit, the delegations remained standing.

"My lords," Vivaine said, leaning forward, her voice an anchor of calm in the tumultuous room, "these sorts of situations are exactly the reason I have called us all together. None of us desire the violence that comes from simple mistakes. We have the opportunity to create bonds between each other that will promote peace in all our lands and keep our people safe and prosperous. Let us not throw away the chance on misunderstandings."

"Indeed," a placid voice drawled from the end of the table.

Sable stiffened and leaned forward. Through the Kalesh she caught a glimpse of Kiva's unruly curls.

"The Holy Mother speaks the truth," Kiva said. "In fact, even the High Prioress of the Dragon Priory is not immune to mistakes."

Vivaine fixed Kiva with a look of vague interest, but the knuckles of her hands whitened.

"My network of merchants," Kiva continued, "was able to bring me some news of this attack just before I came tonight."

"Merchants" was a generous name for the people Kiva employed. "Spies" was more accurate. Sable glanced at Talia, but her sister showed no sign of discomfort. Over the last year, Talia had settled more comfortably into the role of Lady Ingred's secretary, and if the calm disinterest in her face now was any indication, she was getting much better at wielding her role as Kiva's spy.

"Unfortunately," Kiva said, "the information I have received paints an unsettling picture. The attack was definitely carried out by the band of rebels who have been harassing our Kalesh friends for weeks."

Vivaine gave him a nod. "That is a reasonable conclusion. Those rebels have proven themselves repeatedly to be enemies of the Kalesh."

"And not merely any enemies," Kiva agreed, "but *known* enemies."

This time Vivaine's eyes narrowed, and Kiva gave Vivaine the same smile Sable had seen a thousand times. The one that always reminded her of his horrible, little green snake. The predatory smile of a gang boss who knows he has the upper hand.

"I'm afraid, Holy Mother," Kiva said, "that we are all familiar not only with Tanis, the leader, but also with his second-in-command."

Sable tensed and glanced at Vivaine in time to see a muscle in her neck twitch. A hint of disquiet rolled through Sable at the High Prioress's reaction.

"And this isn't the first time he's attacked the Kalesh." Kiva's eyes flicked to Sable. "A year ago, his attack was more direct. A knife thrown from the shadows of a stage."

Sable stiffened, and next to her, Serene drew in a breath.

Kiva leaned forward, fixing Vivaine with a hard look. "The same young man responsible for assassinating Kalesh ambassador Tehl. The young man *you* pardoned—even after his confession, even when you had him in your hands and had the chance to carry out justice."

Sable stared at him, her disquiet turning to cold fear.

Kiva gave a humorless smile. "Our rebels are led by none other than Andreese of Ravenwick."

CHAPTER NINE

THE HARD EDGES of Narine's chair bit into the edges of Sable's palms as she turned to look at Vivaine.

Reese? Reese was second-in-command of the rebels?

The emotion that crossed Vivaine's face first, so quickly Sable almost missed it, was one of anger, before it was replaced with less genuine-looking shock.

Sable stared at her. This was not news to the High Prioress.

"Your weakness, High Prioress," Kiva said bluntly, "has put our Kalesh friends at risk."

The power structure of the room shifted.

How long has she known that? Sable demanded of Gwen.

The Mira didn't answer but kept her eyes on the table, gauging people's reactions.

The Kalesh delegation swung its attention back to Vivaine with dark, threatening looks. Lord Runess dropped his gaze to the table, a slight crease between his brows as he considered the information about the man who used to fight for him.

A murmur of angry muttering rippled through the merchants.

Eugessa fixed Vivaine with a blatantly accusing look.

Sable glanced down the table at Kiva, shocked that he'd actually publicly attacked Vivaine. He caught Sable's eye and raised an eyebrow, as though daring her to speak.

Not far from him, Talia's eyes were locked on Sable as well, her expression apologetic.

For the first time in any meeting Sable had attended, the Dragon Prioress stood vulnerable, and she had the decency to look appalled.

Vivaine kept her eyes fixed on Kiva. If Sable hadn't caught that initial reaction, she wouldn't have guessed Vivaine already knew all of this.

"The young man from last summer?" Vivaine said faintly.

"Indeed." Kiva sat down in his chair, his smile verging on smug. "As you can see, we've all made our own mistakes in this situation."

Vivaine sank into her chair. "I'm so sorry," she said, her voice low. "I thought he would learn his lesson. I thought he would forsake the violence."

Her tone was contrite, but the coldness of the words bit into Sable.

That is the boldest lie I've heard tonight, Sable thought, purely for Gwen's benefit.

The Mira, her hand tense on Sable's arm, made no response.

Vivaine looked down at her own hands, clasped on the table. Her hair hung down, hiding her face. If Sable forgot everything she knew about the woman, she could almost believe Vivaine was crushed with shame.

"This is another example of the weak leadership of this city." General Goll thrust a finger at Vivaine. "When you allow weak-willed women who lack the strength to carry out justice to control your halls of power—"

"You will hold your tongue, General." Ambassador Bastian's voice cracked with authority. Goll snapped his mouth shut but left his finger pointed at Vivaine for another breath before crossing his arms.

Vivaine didn't raise her face to look at him, but her knuckles were white. Through the High Prioress's hair, Sable caught sight of a vicious look on Vivaine's face.

The expression quickly faded, though, and when Vivaine looked up, she merely tossed a dismissive glance at the general, as though he wasn't worth answering. Having been the recipient of that look often,

Sable bit her lip to keep from smiling at the indignant flush on the general's face.

The High Prioress addressed the table in a calm but restrained voice. "This makes everything I have to say to you even more timely. Tonight, I had planned to invite you all to a summit on neutral ground."

A faint look of surprise crossed Eugessa's face. She glanced at Kiva, who met her look with a slight frown.

Serene straightened, looking sharply at the High Prioress.

"Enough conflict has been stirring," Vivaine continued, "that we need to sit together and forge a way ahead to make peace." She gave the lords at the side of the table a slight nod.

Her voice was filled with the calm authority she brought to every situation, and the light that surrounded her had shifted so that her entire end of the room was slightly brighter than the rest.

"The north has expressed a desire to formalize trading of lumber with both the Kalesh and the south," Vivaine continued, as though Kiva's accusation and the general's insult had never happened. "And with the increased interests in mining, having agreements in place that allocate resources and land will minimize any future miscommunications."

She paused, and her voice grew heavy. "In light of the news that I am partially responsible for the violence that is occurring right now, it is more important than ever that our interactions be held somewhere outside of the authority of any of us." Vivaine's gaze swept the room. "The monks on Tutella Island have agreed to host a summit."

"Tutella is in the north," Kiva objected.

"Yes," Eugessa agreed, her voice irritated. "That's hardly neutral."

But somehow, Vivaine had pulled the balance of power back to herself, and everyone else considered the proposal with curiosity. Vivaine didn't deign to react to Eugessa's complaint.

It was Lord Perric who answered. "The island may sit in the north, but the monks serve Isah, not any particular lord."

"Where is Tutella Island?" Ambassador Bastian asked.

"In the Black River," Vivaine answered. "It is settled by monks who have dedicated their lives to peace and helping the poor. They understand the rising tensions and were glad to offer the settlement on the island for peace talks. No weapons, just leaders and their immediate staff."

Serene leaned closer to Sable. "Tutella is a good choice," she whispered.

"You've been there?" Sable asked.

Serene shook her head. "Always wanted to."

"How are a handful of monks going to ensure our safety?" General Goll asked, his arms crossed.

Vivaine gave the man a condescending smile. "While these monks are dedicated to keeping peace, they believe that sometimes that requires fighting those who would take it away. They are known for both their expansive gardens and orchards where they grow food to share with the needy and their extensive military training. Many of the monks were soldiers earlier in life and have chosen to put their skills toward a more peace-promoting path."

General Goll raised an eyebrow. "Peaceful warrior monks?"

"With their own island," Lord Trelles agreed. "And they are known everywhere for their disinterest in political connections."

"I would have to speak to the Merchant Guild," Kiva said, not totally masking his annoyance.

"There's no need." Lord Trelles waved him off. "The Guild would be amenable to having a summit on Tutella Island."

Kiva's mouth tightened at the dismissive tone, but he didn't argue.

"Tutella is a good choice," Lord Perric agreed.

"I will attend," Lord Runess said, his arms still crossed. "When does it start? We need to collect maps of Lord Loren's territory so we can settle who owns this new mine."

Ambassador Bastian nodded to Lord Runess. "We would be happy to see any maps of the area. If we mined on land we were not permitted to, we shall find a way to make restitution."

General Goll bit back whatever response he had. He pulled out his chair and sat stiffly.

"Yes," Vivaine said. "Please have a seat."

The room was filled with shifts and mutters as people moved to find their seats.

Serene moved away around the table until she reached an empty chair next to Jae near the far end.

When the room had settled, Vivaine continued. "We will get to the bottom of this attack on the mine and discover who is responsible. If it is these rebels, then we will find a way to deal with them, which shouldn't be terribly difficult. The single-minded reliance on violence to further a cause is the sign of weak leadership." She didn't look at General Goll, but the man's face reddened even further. "No matter whose land the mine is on, attacking and killing the workers is not the answer. If Andreese of Ravenwick is involved, then he will be found and made to answer for his actions."

This speech by Vivaine was such swirling mix of warmth and cold, biting lies, Sable didn't bother to decipher it.

"Unless there are objections," the High Prioress continued with a tone that expected none, "the summit will begin in ten days. There will be houses for delegations from each northern territory and from the Kalesh. There is room for three representatives from the Merchant Guild and each of the three priories." She looked around the room. "The monks insist that no weapons come onto the island, and any who would join the summit must pledge to keep peace while they are there. The monks take on themselves the security of all of us. And anyone who knows them knows they can be trusted.

"There will be designated areas on either shore of the river where your retinues may camp." Vivaine paused, meeting the gaze of many around the table. "The goal of this summit will be to create a lasting, mutually beneficial treaty between the south, the north, and the Empire, spelling out clearly the scope and limitations of each group's interests." She gave a slight smile, encompassing the entire table. "I have no doubt we can come to an arrangement that is beneficial to all."

"As we've come to trust," Lord Trelles said, his own smile calculating, "the Dragon Priory has stepped up to lead us toward peace. Prioress Vivaine, you are appropriately famed for such peacemaking efforts."

Vivaine gave him a gracious nod in acknowledgment. "Here at the priory, we are driven to protect as many as we can, and that is only possible when the world is at peace."

She motioned to the abbesses standing along the back wall. "Let us begin this evening anew. Tonight, Prioress Eugessa has provided us with a selection of breads and pastries fit for a king." She gave Eugessa the benevolent look Sable had come to hate. "Because we all know the Priory of the Horn is appropriately famed for bringing delicious delicacies."

A ripple of amusement went through the room, and Eugessa gave a smile that didn't reach her eyes.

"Our friends from the Merchant Guild," Vivaine continued, "have brought some rare black fish from the deep waters of the Southern Sea, and Lord Perric has brought us legendary northern venison. Our Kalesh neighbors have provided a traditional Kalesh dish of hot grains and apples, flavored with spices brought from the heart of the Empire itself." With everyone seated, abbesses quickly filled the table with dozens of dishes. "Let us set aside what troubles us and enjoy the tastes of each other's worlds."

The room fell into a quiet buzz of conversation, only vaguely hinting at the tension underlying it all. Prioress Eugessa snapped her fingers toward two abbesses, and they began to pour wine.

Narine politely took samples of each dish, including a small piece of Eugessa's cinnamon bread. Before the plate could pass, Sable reached forward and put two more large pieces on Narine's plate.

"Issable!" Narine whispered.

"If you'd taken the right amount," Sable whispered back, "I wouldn't have had to do that."

Narine muttered something Sable couldn't understand, but the prioress picked up a piece of cinnamon bread and took a bite. Gwen moved away to stand closer to Vivaine, and Sable stood behind Narine's chair during the long, dull period of time while everyone ate.

Narine sat next to a Kalesh soldier who gave short, emotionless answers to any question she directed at him. On her other side, Vivaine presided over the end of the table, having a light conversation with Eugessa and Lord Perric. It took an eternity for everyone to eat, but when they had finally finished, Vivaine rose and invited them to the next room, where they could relax until the red lanterns were lit.

Sable glanced out the stained-glass window at the end of the room. It was dark, but it must be an hour or two until midnight.

Everyone rose from the table and began to work their way out of the room. Narine stayed sitting in her chair, leaning her head back, and the room emptied.

"I'm so glad you came tonight, dear." Vivaine came over next to Narine. "We've all been concerned about you."

"Thank you," Narine said, reaching out to take Vivaine's hand. "It was lovely to leave my room for a bit. And I couldn't stay away from the lanterns."

Vivaine's brow creased, and she took Narine's hand with both of her own. "Are you cold, dear?"

"My hands decided long ago," Narine said, "that they had no need for warmth anymore."

Sable looked at an abbess who was standing attentively behind Vivaine. "Could you get Prioress Narine some mint tea?"

"Yes," Vivaine said. "Warm tea. Quickly." She fixed Narine with a fond smile that looked more genuine than any expression Sable had seen on her face during the entire evening. "I've spoken with the monks on Tutella Island. We'll be housed in the town of Aedis, and we have a house specifically for you. It has a large fireplace. We will do everything we can to make you as comfortable as possible."

Narine patted Vivaine's hand. "You are too kind to think of me, but all that is unnecessary."

Vivaine shook her head. "I insist that you have a comfortable place to stay. The merchants and Northern Lords can fit in the smaller, drafty houses. You know it won't bother them anyway. These young people are never cold in the summer."

"No, dear," Narine said. "I won't be at the summit."

Sable's hands tensed on the back of the chair.

Vivaine's eyebrows rose in surprise. "But we need you there."

"You know how I feel about these sorts of things. I am leaving to go north in a few days, but it is not to organize political alliances. I want to see my abbeys again, one last time. There are dear friends who live away from the city, and I haven't seen them in ages. I'm sure this will be my last chance, and I have no desire to waste it on politics.

There are individual hearts to reunite with and dear souls under the Phoenix Priory whose needs I want to see to."

Vivaine looked like she might argue, but instead, she nodded. "You are an inspiration to us all, dear." She turned to an abbess waiting dutifully near the wall. "Please take the Holy Mother in to one of the chairs near the fire, and find her a blanket."

Vivaine made a quick gesture toward Gwen, and the Mira stepped closer to Sable. "You stay," she whispered.

Narine left the room, leaning on the arm of the abbess, and Vivaine dismissed the other abbesses who were lingering.

The sounds from the hall faded, and Vivaine glanced at Gwen. "Let Argyros in, then leave us and close the door."

Gwen opened a thin, unremarkable door on the far side of the room, and the silver dragon moved smoothly in. It was eerie how often that dragon was just out of sight around Vivaine. His scales caught the light from the window, and icy glitters danced along his back and over the edge of his folded wings. He moved up next to Vivaine, his head at the height of the table and his tail reaching almost back to the door.

Sable shifted until the chair was between herself and the dragon.

Vivaine set her hand on his head, taking a deep breath. Where Narine's phoenix was all firelight and warmth, Vivaine's dragon shimmered like moonlight and frost.

Gwen gave the High Prioress a bow and stepped into the hall, swinging the heavy council room door closed with a solid thump.

Vivaine turned cold, grey eyes on Sable. "Before we begin our conversation, and you argue with me about how much you cannot do what I need, I want you to understand exactly what is at stake."

Sable looked warily between Vivaine and her dragon.

"Your little rebel Andreese has made some dangerous enemies for himself. Enemies who would be very, very interested in finding out where he is. In fact, a person who knows where he is might be able to use that knowledge to barter for almost anything right now."

Sable's stomach sank. "And you know where he is."

Vivaine gave a grim smile. "And I know where he is."

CHAPTER TEN

"YOU HAVE a spy in the rebel camp?" Sable asked, shaking her head. "Of course you do."

"You need to get Narine to that summit," Vivaine said with a note of command in her voice.

"Me?" Sable asked.

"The priories must present a united front. Narine isn't obsessed with power and wealth like Eugessa. If she comes to the summit, she'll vote against the Kalesh taking over more land or gaining more power." Vivaine leaned forward. "Find a way to get Narine to the summit."

"It won't do any good." Sable pulled out Narine's chair and sat in it. "She doesn't want to have anything to do with political decisions. Even if she went to the summit, you know she won't take part in any political decisions."

Vivaine looked down at Argyros, dragging her fingers gently over the scales on his head. When she looked up at Sable, the change in the prioress was so stark that Sable pulled back.

"I've had enough of your defiance." Vivaine's words were quiet but cut through the room like a whip.

"I'm not defying you," Sable objected.

"I know you can feel it," Vivaine continued slowly, as though trying to keep control of herself. "Things are shifting. I have delayed as long as I can, but our time is running out. I need Narine to participate."

"What am I supposed to do?"

Vivaine's eyes narrowed with irritation, but when she spoke, her voice was measured. "I don't think you understand the full situation here." She leaned forward. "I could tell the Kalesh, and Andreese's entire band of rebels would be dead in a matter of days." Vivaine sat down in her own chair, her back straight. She left her hand on Argyros's head, and the dragon kept his reptilian eyes fixed on Sable. "I wouldn't mourn them at all. His continual, escalating violence is destabilizing the entire situation and disrupting all attempts at peace."

"Attempts at peace?" Sable demanded. "You are the only one who thinks that's still possible. For all your councils over the past year, can you name one time the Kalesh haven't gotten exactly what they wanted?"

"My city is safe." Vivaine's words lashed out like a whip. "What is gold compared to the lives of the people here? I have kept peace here in the midst of a Kalesh invasion, and if you think it has been anything less, you are more foolish than I thought."

"The Kalesh presence grows by the day. You have kept nothing safe! How can you give up our freedom so easily?"

Vivaine's face curled into a look of contempt. "What freedom do you think I'm giving up?"

"The ability to…" Sable gestured to the priory, to the city. "To be who we are. To do what we, as a people, want to do."

The High Prioress stared at her. "I had no idea you were still so naive."

Sable bristled at the words, but Vivaine continued, "Unanchored freedom is a child's dream. No one finds meaning there. It's a temporary escape from real life. Meaning and value come through finding something worth fighting for and sacrificing yourself for it. Even your sister knows this."

"What does Ryah have to do with this?"

"Not that sister. Ryah is a sheep, going wherever she's led. Talia is the only one of you three with any mettle. Despite all the hard things around her, she's thrown herself into protecting what she cares about. Clawing out something powerful for herself and her friends. You've done nothing but chase fame and power. You don't know the first thing about sacrifice."

Despite all the hard things around her, she's thrown herself into protecting what she cares about. The words, almost a direct quote from Talia's letter, sounded horrible and twisted from Vivaine's mouth. Sable gave a disgusted laugh. "So you *are* reading my mail."

The High Prioress gave her a condescending look. "You're sending information to a dangerous rebel group. Yes, your mail is monitored. It's been interesting to see what you thought worth sending them and what Talia thought worth sending to you. For a girl who loves rumors and secrets, she's certainly sitting on a few. Can you imagine the gossip if someone let it be known that Talia isn't even a merchant's daughter, but only a spy for Kiva in Trelles' household?"

Sable leaned closer to the woman. "Leave my sisters out of this."

"They can't be left out of it." The High Prioress waved her fingers at the walls around them. "We never can escape these things we love. They always pull on us, keep us from moving ahead unencumbered."

Vivaine sank back in her chair, rubbing her hands across her face. The motion was shockingly defeated. The light that constantly surrounded her dimmed until the room itself darkened and Vivaine was just another woman in a white robe.

When she lowered her hands, there were shadows of exhaustion under her eyes. "True freedom only comes when you realize that those anchors are what we fight for," Vivaine continued, as though she were talking to a difficult child. "There are four people who will decide the city's vote at the summit. Each priory has one voice, and the Merchant Guild has the other. Kiva and Eugessa will want to support the Kalesh at the summit, but if Narine votes with me, the votes will be a tie, and a tie is decided by the High Prioress."

"You are always looking for ways to play people off each other," Sable said. "You have so much influence--use it to bring us together!

You could convince Eugessa and everyone else to vote on your side because our unity might drive the Kalesh out, and it would be far more powerful than if you gain their votes because of maneuvering."

Vivaine shook her head. "The Kalesh are here in a diplomatic capacity, and we need to keep it that way. We're walking a delicate line here. If we unite and try to force them out, they'll bring their army, and we are too weak to face that. I know you've seen the death and destruction they rain down. How can you suggest anything that would bring more of that?"

Sable's retort died at the memory of Ebenmoor and her own parents.

Vivaine pointed at the door.

Sable turned, and the dark, carved wood shifted, stretching to the side until a crack she hadn't noticed at the edge widened. Sable grabbed the arm of the chair, but everything aside from the door was still.

Vivaine stretched her fingers toward the crack, and Sable's view of it widened further until she could see into the hall. The shifting image made her dizzy, and she gripped the chair until the wood dug into her hands. It had been nearly a year since Vivaine had bent the light to show Sable a scene from far below the priory where her friends had been imprisoned. She'd forgotten how disorienting it was.

This current view shifted until it raced through the priory, sailing past abbesses and through a door into a room filled with milling people. Vivaine's hand started to shake, and the view slowed, coming to focus on the elderly Phoenix Prioress, sitting in a chair by the fire.

Vivaine looked at the scene with an unreadable expression. "Am I to believe you can't convince one dying woman of the need to protect the people she loves?"

Sable shook her head, her eyes fixed on Narine. "She won't do it. She believes with the core of her being that it's not her place to rule. There's no way I can change—"

"Last year," Vivaine cut Sable off, "you stood on the stage of the Grand Stadia and gave a speech that convinced a thousand people the Kalesh were attacking. People who had unquestioningly accepted the

Kalesh up to that point. Until Ambassador Tehl spoke, you had every single person swayed to your way of thinking."

"Exactly! I may be able to make people believe my words for a moment, but I can't change their minds completely. Otherwise my speech last year would have worked, the Kalesh would be gone, and I'd still be an actress."

Vivaine raised an incredulous eyebrow. "You mean to tell me you can't convince Narine that this is important? She is a frail old woman."

"She is a woman who knows her own mind. I can't change her feelings on participating any more than I could change yours."

Vivaine gave a derisive snort. "Yet you try to change mine every time we talk."

"That's just more proof that I truly can't!" Sable snapped.

At her sharp tone, Argyros shifted his head. Light shimmered across his snout, but his grey eyes were flat, the slitted pupils boring into her, emotionless and predatory.

Sable pressed back into the chair.

Vivaine closed her fingers, and the image disappeared, jarring Sable's view back to the closed wooden door. The High Prioress shook out her hand, her breathing a little heavier than normal. "Narine is dying. There are three potential successors, but the process of selecting one, and then instating the new prioress, takes at least three months. If a treaty isn't finished before we lose Narine, the city's fate will be in the hands of the merchants and the Priory of the Horn. Then you *will* see the Kalesh getting everything they want."

Sable stared at her, open-mouthed. "Even Narine's death is only a political tool for you to use."

The words caused a flicker of disquiet to cross the High Prioress's face, but she continued as though Sable hadn't spoken. "Use whatever skill you have to change her mind." She stood and met Sable's gaze with perfectly cold eyes. "Because if you are incapable of getting Narine to vote, then I have no incentive not to use Andreese's location as a bargaining tool."

She pushed off the table and strode to the door. Argyros followed, his scales sliding over the stone floor with a dry hiss. With a swish of Vivaine's hand, the light from the nearest candles wrapped around her, making her white robe glow faintly again and catching in silver strands of her hair. The light smoothed her face, erasing the signs of exhaustion. It slid along the dragon as well, turning his cold scales into a shimmering surface of silver.

Vivaine cast one last blistering look at Sable. "You have ten days." Without waiting for an answer, she opened the door and left.

CHAPTER ELEVEN

SABLE LEANED her head back in Narine's chair, drinking in the quiet of the empty banquet hall. The revelations of the night jostled each other for attention.

Reese was with the rebels.

No wonder Leonis had been anxious to give her details.

And they had actually destroyed a Kalesh gold mine and attacked merchant shipments.

"Well, Thulan," she said, pushing herself out of the chair. "You were right. I heard about the rebels. But I'm not sure I'd say this is 'getting fun.'"

Sable followed the noise of the dinner guests to a large room near the front of the priory. A trio of abbesses sang in one corner, filling the room with quiet, soft music. Little tables lined the walls, heaped with fruits and desserts. Vivaine's guests milled somewhat cautiously around each other.

Sable crossed to where Narine and an abbess were seated by the fire. The Prioress held her tea in one hand and set her other on the abbess's head in blessing.

"Thank you, Holy Mother," the abbess said gratefully, blinking back tears and standing.

When the younger woman left, Narine looked up at Sable's face and sighed. "The High Prioress put you in the middle of all this, didn't she?" she asked.

Sable moved a small table closer to Narine's chair. "That's what she does."

Narine set down the teacup. "She should know better than to think I'd go to her summit, though."

Sable sat in the chair the abbess had vacated. "Vivaine is remarkably stubborn when it comes to controlling people."

"Issable," Narine reproached her.

"She's nearly as stubborn as this Phoenix Prioress," Sable continued, "who, after finding sitting in a chair at dinner to be thoroughly exhausting, is still planning a month-long trip."

Narine smiled tiredly. "The Phoenix Prioress prefers the word fiery to stubborn. It's more in keeping with the symbol of her priory."

"Well, Your Fieriness, would you like to go somewhere quiet to rest for a bit? We could sit together and plan our trip." She looked around the room at the milling people. "If you stay here, you're bound to be roped into hours of conversation."

"The trip is planned," Narine said. "I've made it dozens of times. Let's stay and see if we can encourage any peace between the groups that are here tonight."

"Be careful, Holy Mother. That almost sounded political."

"I have no interest in trying to direct their lands." Narine leaned back in her chair. "But it would be worthwhile to soften their individual hearts toward each other. That's the real battle, you know. Keeping the heart soft. Especially to those who have wronged you. If we could all accomplish that, there'd be no need for peace summits or treaties."

Sable let out a tired laugh. "I doubt you've ever had a hard heart toward anyone in your entire life."

"'Tis a struggle every day," Narine said softly. "Perhaps the real reason I'm so tired is that I have to work harder at it than most."

Sable opened her mouth to answer, but an abbess approached Narine, looking hopeful. Sable stood, offering the woman her chair. "I'll see if there are any good desserts, Holy Mother."

Leaving the two to talk, Sable started for the nearest dessert table until she caught sight of Talia standing alone near one at the end of the room.

Taking a slow, meandering route, Sable moved over until she stood next to her sister.

"Good evening, Holy Sister," Talia said with a grin.

"Good evening, heathen merchant's daughter," Sable retorted. "You look lovely."

"You look—" Talia paused, and her fingers tapped on the table. "If I could use some of my powders on your eyes, and we could do something with your hair, the robe itself isn't terrible. It's less servant-ish than usual, at least."

Sable raised an eyebrow. "So the robe is fine—it's my head that's the problem."

Talia pressed her lips closed to hide her laugh. "They keep everyone at the priories looking so plain. It could be so much better."

"There are a lot of things that could be better." Sable turned back to the table, picking up a small plate. Several of the desserts were things that Narine might eat.

Talia glanced over her shoulder. "I can't believe Reese is responsible for the mine! And some of the attacks on the merchants! But more than that, I can't believe you never told me about him being with the rebels!" she whispered. "I know you don't tell me much, but I had to learn about it from Kiva!"

"I learned it from Kiva, too," Sable answered, dropping a tiny, sugar-crusted pastry onto her plate harder than she'd meant to. "Just tonight."

Her sister stared at her, shocked. "Reese didn't tell you?"

"I haven't talked to him since..." Sable gestured around the priory. "All this started."

Talia blinked at her. "Amah's shiny bum, Sable! Why not?"

Sable laughed. "Is Amah's bum shiny? Vivaine's is sort of shiny, but it's a fake shininess."

Her sister smiled. "Don't change the subject. Why haven't you talked to him?"

"We didn't really part on good terms."

"When you…saved his life? I can see why that would cause a rift," she said dryly.

"He hates the priories," Sable said, "and I joined them."

Talia looked expectantly at her. "To save his life."

"Talia," Sable said, exasperated, "we haven't talked. That's it. I had no idea where he was until tonight."

"Well, find a way to talk to him," Talia said, growing serious. "He needs to be careful. The merchants are getting angry. They're banding together and hiring more guards."

"He probably knows that already," Sable pointed out. Before Talia could respond, she changed the subject. "I got your letter. You've certainly managed to turn this situation into something good."

"I've tried." The note of pride in Talia's voice was unmistakable.

Sable glanced at her little sister. "I admit, I'm impressed."

Talia motioned across the room. "Callie made a suggestion about a new scarf to Lady Ingred while delivering her dress this morning, and Ingred liked it so much she decided Callie needed to come tonight to keep charge of all her accessories."

Talia's old friend, so clean and nicely dressed Sable barely recognized her, stood against the far wall, clutching a box and looking overwhelmed. Two other women stood next to her carrying their own small, ornate chests.

"Ingred brought extra accessories tonight?"

"She wanted to bring a second wardrobe so she could change before the lantern ceremony, but the priory informed her it couldn't spare a room for her, so she's left with merely changing her jewelry, shoes, and scarf."

"How will she ever bear it?"

"Not graciously, if her initial reaction to the priory's decision is any indication."

Callie's blonde hair was pinned into braids, her dress plain but high quality, and her face still held the slightly vacant expression Sable remembered from the days in Dockside.

"Kiva isn't using Callie to spy too, is he?" Sable asked. "She isn't savvy enough to pull off being a jay. She's barely holding it together standing against the wall at a dinner party."

"She's not a jay," Talia whispered, "she has a legitimate job working for a seamstress. She lives above the shop, eats with the seamstress's family, and has clean, well-made clothes. She's never been in such a good position—" Talia stiffened. "Ingred is coming."

Sable focused on the table, picking out two tiny sweet rolls.

"Talia," Lady Ingred said from directly behind Sable, "where's your father?"

Sable twitched at the question. She turned slowly to look at Talia, who had gone very still.

Lady Ingred gave Sable a disinterested nod before refocusing on Talia. "My father has been looking for him, and the man has disappeared."

Sable raised an eyebrow. "Your *father* is here?"

Ingred shot Sable an indignant look, as though appalled Sable had dared to speak.

"Lady Ingred," Talia said quickly, "this is Issable. She is the caretaker of Prioress Narine."

"I hope the prioress is in good health," Ingred said with an air of indifference. "Your father?" she said impatiently to Talia.

"Of course," Talia said, not meeting Sable's eyes. "I saw him near the windows."

Lady Ingred waved her words away. "Ah, here he is."

Sable followed Ingred's gaze.

Stepping out of a knot of people, Kiva strolled up to the dessert table, giving all three ladies a wide smile.

"Lady Ingred," he greeted her with a bow. "And dear," he said, resting his hand comfortably on Talia's shoulder, "what desserts are there that your old man might like to eat?"

CHAPTER TWELVE

SABLE STARED AT KIVA, then looked back at Talia. "*This* is your father?"

Talia stood stiffly next to the table, only meeting Sable's glance for a moment before looking away.

"Good evening, Holy Sister," Kiva said with a wide grin. "Are you acquainted with my daughter?"

"I thought I was," Sable said slowly.

"Kiva," Ingred said, shifting until her back was to Sable. "My father's been looking for you."

Kiva gave her a bow. "I am at Lord Trelles's disposal."

Ingred turned and started toward her father, but Kiva lingered.

He gave Talia a self-satisfied smile. "You look lovely tonight, dear. Keep up the good work, and make time to speak with me later." He turned an amused look on Sable. "And you look...a bit lost, to be honest. Even after a year, the white of the priories still doesn't suit you. Washes you out. Makes you...unmemorable. Just another faceless, useless woman trapped in these buildings."

"Kiva," Talia said reproachfully.

The man shrugged. "The good Prioress Narine does look frail tonight. Our conversation earlier may be more timely than I thought.

When your old prioress dies, and you're done wasting all your potential, come find me."

"Kiva," Talia said more firmly.

"What?" he asked. "Sable and I are working toward the same goals." He paused. "Well, maybe there's one goal we don't share. Andreese of Ravenwick has become an irritatingly sharp pebble in my shoe."

Kiva gave her a lazy smile. "I realize you have feelings for the man. I was a little fond of him myself after his assassination scheme created such upheaval last year. The opportunities that sprang from that one night earned him my goodwill for nearly a year. But attacking the mine was foolish."

"I didn't realize you were so protective of the Kalesh," Sable said.

"I am protective of my own interests." Kiva put his arm around Talia's shoulders in a fatherly gesture. Talia tensed but didn't move. "And I know that you are protective of some of my interests as well."

Sable glared at Kiva's arm as though she could shove it off her sister with pure fury.

"If Andreese causes the Empire to drastically increase their military presence here, that is going to disrupt my plans. And at that point, I may need to do something about him." His smile widened. "A few drops of vayakadyn venom in Andreese's drink, and it would be over. By the time the stomach pains hit, it would be too late for an antidote. The next day, his tongue would turn black, and any problems he could cause me would be over."

Sable crossed her arms to hide the chill the description gave her. Venom from Kiva's little snake was his favorite weapon. An uncomfortable number of Kiva's enemies ended up dead, their tongues black with the telltale sign of vayakadyn venom. "What do you expect me to do? I have no say over Andreese."

Kiva gave a little laugh. "No one believes that. You've proven yourself time and time again to be a resourceful woman. Especially when it comes to protecting those you care about." His smile fell off his face. "If you care anything for the rebel, Sable, rein him in."

He glanced across the room toward Lord Trelles. "Have a lovely time together, ladies." He gave Talia's shoulders one last squeeze with his arm. "I'll speak with you later, my dearest daughter." Without waiting for them to answer, he left.

"Sweet Amah!" Sable growled, turning to stare at Talia. "What have you done?"

Talia opened her mouth, but no words came out.

"Your *father*?"

"Be quiet!" Talia held out one hand. "It happened last winter. Lady Ingred started asking questions about my family, and so Kiva and I decided we would say he is my father."

"You decided this last winter?" Sable hissed at her. "And you're just telling me now?" She slammed her dish down on the table before she hurled it at Kiva's disappearing head. "How could you?"

"It was the obvious thing to do." Talia's expression changed from embarrassed to angry. "I needed a way to see Kiva easily. Before last year, none of the merchants really knew who he was. This way, Lady Ingred just thinks she happened to get the daughter of the newest up-and-coming merchant as her secretary. And I have access to Kiva whenever I want. All the things he and I had already told Ingred about my family worked with Kiva as my father—"

"Of course they did! This is what he'd always planned!"

"Don't you think I know that?" Talia demanded, her voice low and angry, "But you are not the only one with plans and the need to use the things around you to accomplish them. I have done more in the past six months than I ever imagined I could do. And I can't do it without Kiva." She held up a hand to stop Sable's next words. "Yes, I know he is using my position for his own purposes. But I am also using him. A year ago I was a girl who worked in a bakery. Now I have access to information from the wealthiest, most powerful merchants in the city, and I have control of where large amounts of food and supplies are distributed." She glared at Sable. "For all your planning and conniving, what are you doing? You've done nothing but trap yourself under Vivaine's thumb."

"You think I had a choice?"

"I have no idea. It's been years since I knew what you were doing or why. But I did have a choice. And I took it. And I'm happy about the things that I'm doing."

"But…" Sable stared at her. "Your father?"

"This is exactly why I didn't tell you. Because even though you, of all people, should understand the need to compromise what you really want to get the little you can, you never allow me the same right."

The words struck deep, and Sable shifted. But everything inside her rebelled against the idea of Talia working so overtly with Kiva.

Something from Talia's letter came into focus. "You said you get to distribute extra supplies," Sable said slowly. "But Kiva isn't usually in possession of so much stolen merchandise that he needs help distributing it."

Talia's indignation faltered.

Sable took a step closer to her. "And you asked if Reese was responsible for *some* of the attacks on the Kalesh."

Talia dropped her gaze to the plate in her hand.

"Kiva's doing it!" Sable whispered, staring at her sister in shock. "He's responsible for the attacks on merchants, isn't he?" Sable looked across the room to where the man talked amiably with Lord Trelles and Lady Ingrid. "He's attacking merchants close to Immusmala and blaming it on the rebels." Sable turned back to Talia. "Did he attack the mine?" she demanded.

"No!" Talia said vehemently. "I was talking to him when he got that news. He was shocked. He's angry because it's upsetting the balance between the Kalesh and the rest of us. Says it makes things too unstable."

Sable shook her head. "I can't believe he's targeting his own associates. Let me guess, the merchants who have been hit are Kiva's rivals."

Talia lifted her chin. "The merchants who've been attacked near Immusmala are corrupt, dangerous men who are getting in the way of things the Merchant Guild is attempting to accomplish."

Sable's mouth dropped open. "The Merchant Guild is sanctioning this? Attacks on their own people?"

Talia shifted the plate in her hand. "Kiva decided that it was better if the guild didn't know the details. So they couldn't be held responsible."

"So in other words, Kiva is doing everything purely for his own gain."

She expected Talia to object, but her sister shrugged. "I'm sure he is. But I'm not. Regardless of what you think of Kiva, the men he's stealing from are horrible people. If their valuable supplies reach families who actually need them, I'm not going to complain."

Sable searched her sister's face. The last year had changed Talia. The carefree naivety that had worried Sable so much before had faded, replaced by a new stubbornness that might be even more worrisome.

Talia glanced across the room to where Lady Ingrid was talking with Lord Trelles and Kiva. "I want to hear what they're talking about." She gave Sable an apologetic look. "I know that somehow you are still trying to protect me from all this. Maybe you're right and everything I'm doing is foolish, but it's the only thing I know how to do. And from where I am, it feels like I'm doing something good."

"I know." Sable blew out a short breath. "And I shouldn't be surprised that you found a way to put hope into a situation as miserable as Kiva's. You managed to take a stick of charcoal and make our dingy, nasty little room in Dockside into a work of art." She picked her plate back up so she wouldn't reach out to her sister. "Just be careful."

"I will." Talia gave her a grin as she picked up her plate of cookies. "It was good to see you."

Sable nodded and watched her cross the room. Talia's back was straight, her head held high, and Sable felt almost like she was watching a stranger.

A stranger who'd become taller, more elegant, and probably more practically useful to the world than Sable herself.

CHAPTER THIRTEEN

On the far side of the room near the fire, a handful of people surrounded Narine, so Sable took the plate of desserts and moved to the nearest corner where a cluster of comfortable-looking chairs sat unoccupied. She sank into one, slumping back into the soft cushions. She couldn't see Talia or Narine from here, and she stared unseeing at the crowd until it became nothing but a shifting, droning mass.

Sable took an uninterested bite of the pastry, but it tasted like honey and creamy goat cheese, and out of the entire night, it was by far the best thing. It was almost good enough to make her stand up and find another.

Before she could take such a drastic measure, Serene stepped out of the crowd and crossed to a chair next to Sable. She was dressed in her customary dark robe. Over the past year she'd moved from a dark grey to almost black, and while it wasn't as out of place as normal tonight, that bit of darkness among the unrelenting white of the priories always felt like a bit of sunshine. The thought made Sable smile and wonder if anyone had ever compared the serious woman to sunshine before.

"In all the state dinners I've attended here," Serene said, dropping into a chair next to Sable, "that was definitely the most interesting."

Sable nodded. "Interesting is one word for it."

Jae came toward them pushing Merrick in a wheeled chair. Sable gave Jae a smile as he settled the old man's chair and sat in one himself.

"Hello, Merrick," Sable greeted the man who'd mentored Jae and Serene for years. He'd come to the priory last year when Vivaine had taken all his books from Stonehaven. He'd never fully recovered from the illness he'd fallen prey to on that trip, and Jae and Serene had cared for him here at the priory ever since.

"Good evening, Sable," Merrick said warmly. "You look a bit unsettled by the evening. I gather you didn't know either that your friend Andreese was involved with the rebels?"

Sable laughed. "I did not. And the worst part is that argument over dinner was the least unsettling thing I've heard tonight."

The rest of the room thrummed with conversations, but their corner was separated a bit from the crowd, and at questioning looks from the three around her, Sable filled them in on Vivaine's threats and Talia's ill-conceived relationship with Kiva.

"You've had a rough night," Jae said, shaking his head.

"I have something that will make it better." Serene pulled something out of one of the many pockets in her robe. "It seemed like a good gift before, but compared to the rest of your night, it's a spectacular gift." With a flourish, she held up a small book. "I found it."

"Another book about the Kalesh?"

"No," Serene said. "This is the book I've been looking for about how someone like you learned to sense the *vitalle* around them."

Sable straightened. Several times over the past year, Serene had tried to get Sable to sense any sort of heat aside from the truth in people's words, but they'd had no luck.

"The idiots here had shelved it with biographies instead of magic. Not even autobiographies, which would almost make sense, but with the artist biographies." Serene let out an exasperated sigh and waved the small, leather-bound book titled *The Butterfly Song by Pedreck of Thrushton*. "But the fact that it was misshelved might have saved it. More and more of the books on magic are missing. The abbesses tell us they're being read, but whole shelves are empty."

Serene had been complaining about books missing for months. "There are too many rooms here I can't search. Did you know they've even closed off the rooms with the holy writings? No one can see the writings on Amah without Vivaine's explicit, written approval—"

"Serene," Jae interrupted. "The book?"

"Does it talk about feeling the truth?" Sable asked.

Serene paused. "Close enough. Pedreck claims the first time he felt his powers was when someone sang passionately. They weren't singing the truth exactly, but they meant what they sang, and he felt a warmth."

Sable leaned forward to see the book better. "Pedreck learned how to use magic?" she whispered, the words almost too much to hope for. "He learned to do more than feel it?"

Serene nodded. "Yes, a lot more." She handed Sable the small volume.

Sable ran her hands over the soft, brown, leather cover.

"The first thing Pedreck did was learn to sense it," Serene continued. "When Jae or Merrick or I cast out, we send out a pulse looking for *vitalle* around us. But Pedreck's method was different. He used the music to echo off living things around him. Once he could sense them, he could begin to access the *vitalle* he found."

She looked around the room. "All around us are bright people—"

"*Bright* might be the wrong word for Sable," Merrick pointed out. "She feels the truth, so it's likely she'll sense *vitalle* as a feeling, not a sight."

Serene nodded. "That's a good point. I'm going to say something truthful, Sable, and instead of feeling just my words, see if you can feel the people around you."

At Sable's nod, Serene said, "I wish we were all at Stonehaven."

Sable felt a tendril of warmth at the truth in the words. She closed her eyes and tried to feel where it came from.

"I hate how they organize books here," Serene added, her voice annoyed.

These words were even stronger, and Sable focused, trying to sense anything around her that felt alive. But there was nothing. She shook her head and opened her eyes. "All I feel is the words themselves."

"I didn't expect you to get it on the first try," Serene said. "We're going about all this backwards. Most people move *vitalle* the first time because there's some sort of emergency. It's done out of a panic, not sitting calmly in a crowded room."

Sable glanced at a merchant who'd stopped by a nearby table to pick out some pastries, but he moved away again, and she leaned closer to Serene. "How did you first move it?"

Serene turned her palms up. A thick scar ran around the outer edges of each, and thin lines of white and red puckered tissue criss-crossed the center. "When I was fourteen, I was shopping with my mother, and a man rushed out at us, shoved me into the bushes, and held a knife to her throat, demanding money." Serene rubbed the scars. "All I remember is wanting to destroy the knife. I reached for it and..." She shrugged. "It melted."

Sable stared at her. "You melted a knife?"

"It didn't melt completely, but the edge dulled and the point drooped. At the time I had no idea what was happening. My hands felt like they'd caught fire."

Sable glanced at Jae and Merrick. "How did you find these two to train you?"

"It was the scars," Jae said.

"Not too long after the knife incident, Jae came to my town." Serene smiled at her husband. "I sat for hours in the square listening to him talk. My scars were still new and itchy." She paused. "Jae notices everything going on in his audiences."

"Not everything," Jae objected.

"Pretty much everything," Merrick said.

Serene nodded. "So he noticed me scratching my palms, and afterwards he came up to me, showed me his own palms, and said, 'The itching stops eventually.'"

Sable looked between the two of them. "That seems...fortuitous."

Jae nodded. "People with our skills are drawn to each other."

Serene shook her head. "Not all of us believe that."

"But many of us do," Merrick said.

"For instance," Jae said, "whatever skill you have, Sable, is somehow similar to Atticus's, and you two were drawn together."

"I just loved his plays," Sable said.

"A lot of people love his plays, but they don't end up traveling with him," Jae pointed out.

Serene sighed. "This is going to support Jae's theory, I'm sure, but when was the first time you saw Atticus?"

"It was years ago," Sable said, "not long after I'd come to the city with my sisters. I was in Dockside and in need of a good hiding place. So I hid inside an old warehouse and found Atticus and his troupe practicing. I lay in the shadows watching for hours. I'd never heard such amazing stories."

Serene pointed at Jae. "Don't be smug."

Her husband grinned at her. "Even you can't explain away that level of coincidence, dear."

"Anyway," Serene said, gesturing to the book. "Read Pedreck's words. Maybe it will give you ideas about your own skills."

Sable opened it to see wide, smooth handwriting filling each page. There were pages that looked like songs and pages with sketches. She paused on a page that showed a circle of people with a single person standing in the middle. Long, flowing lines wrapped toward the central figure from the ones around it. They swirled a bit like eddies in the water. There was something right about the drawing. Something that reminded Sable of the truth.

"Thank you," she said fervently.

Merrick's head sank back against his chair.

"I think Merrick and I have had enough fun for the night." Jae stood. "Goodnight, Sable."

"Reese and the rebels have been hiding from their enemies for months," Merrick said, giving Sable a reassuring smile. "I'm sure they'll continue to do so."

Sable didn't feel particularly convinced, but she nodded and watched Jae wheel Merrick's chair away.

Serene stayed sitting, looking after them pensively.

"How is Merrick?" Sable asked.

Serene sighed. "Not well."

"Why is it that people like Merrick and Narine are weak, and people like Vivaine and Eugessa are hale and hearty?"

Serene watched Merrick's chair disappear. "I don't know."

They were quiet for a few minutes.

Sable held up the book toward Serene. "How soon do you need this back?"

"That book is not going back to the library. If you finish with it, I'll smuggle it out with the others."

"You're stealing books?"

"Rescuing books," Serene corrected her.

"How many have you rescued?"

A conspiratorial smile curled up the side of Serene's mouth. "About a hundred."

Sable's mouth dropped open. "Where are you putting them?"

"They've been passed along to a merchant who takes them out of the city to Atticus." Her smile widened. "I don't even pay the man. He says getting to read the books is payment enough." Serene sobered. "Of course, Vivaine stole thousands of books from Stonehaven, so I've barely started to get them back, and a good number of them I can't find."

They sat quietly, watching the crowd mingle in the room.

"What am I going to do about Narine?" Sable asked. "She is adamantly against going to the summit." Sable rubbed her hands across her face. "I don't want to force a dying woman to go somewhere she doesn't want, but Vivaine will make Reese and the rebels pay dearly if I don't."

Serene sighed. "She will. And the truth is, Narine would be a good addition to the summit. We could use her patience and calm."

"I know. As much as I hate to agree with Vivaine, if I could convince Narine to participate, I would."

"Well, you'll be traveling with her for days. Maybe you'll find the chance." Serene stood. "I'm going to go check on Jae and Merrick." She gestured to the book. "Read how Pedreck did things. I have high hopes that it will give us something to work with."

Sable ran her thumb over the letters stamped into the cover. Maybe the voice she was missing had nothing to do with speaking her opinion in council rooms. Maybe there was a way to use a different sort of voice—one that had felt so out of her reach, she hadn't even dared hope for it before.

A door cracked open somewhere inside her.

Despite all the troubles that had filled the night, here was something that held the hint of light.

She nodded. "Me too."

CHAPTER FOURTEEN

TORCHES WRAPPED in Sailor's Hope, a seaweed that burned red, bathed the Sanctuary in a ruddy glow. Narine settled into the chair that had been set for her in front of the Dragon Priory, and Sable positioned herself behind it. Along the edges of the Sanctuary Plaza, carts and stages lined the wall. She looked along them, unconsciously searching for the green light of Leonis's fairy tree.

But of course, Atticus and the troupe weren't here.

In the dull red of the torchlight, Sable caught glimpses of monstrous masks. Near the front, a tall figure loomed, draped in black. His face was hidden by a red veil, and his robe seemed more like a sliver of shadow than a costume. Another stood farther back to the other side, and another at the edge of the crowd. There were definitely more baledin than normal. It seemed the city had not forgotten Atticus's play.

A bit of brightness caught Sable's eye from near the Phoenix Priory. Innov soared out an open window and winged over the crowd. Faces turned up, and murmurs rippled through the Sanctuary. Against the darkness of the sky, she looked like a blaze of fire, trailing a glowing, arcing path. The phoenix flew over the baledin, and in the glow of light from her feathers, the shadow robe transformed into mere cloth.

Narine held out her arm, and Innov settled on the prioress's sleeve with a burst of embers.

"Hello, my flame," Narine said, unfolding a cloth and revealing several bits of venison. Narine offered a piece, and the phoenix snatched it up.

Eugessa strode out from the Dragon Priory, her hand resting on the black neck of her unicorn. Innov leaned her head forward for the last piece of meat, but her sharp eyes followed the creature. The unicorn moved like a dark shadow, except where the torchlight traced the muscles of his flank and neck or glittered in the spiral of ridges that wound up his horn.

Eugessa and the unicorn moved to the far side of the portico just as a shimmer of light came from inside the Dragon Priory. Vivaine stepped outside, her robes glowing softly like moonlight, and Argyros slid after her, his silver scales matching Vivaine.

Innov shifted on Narine's arm.

"Peace, my flame," Narine said softly, running the back of her fingers down Innov's chest. "Peace." But Narine's mouth pulled into a disapproving line as she watched the dragon crawl next to Vivaine.

The High Prioress stepped to the front of the portico, a pure white figure against the red of the Sanctuary. The crowd quieted as she held up her arms. "This world is filled with darkness. It crowds around us. It fills the gaps in the light."

"Left to ourselves," Vivaine continued, "we would be lost. The monsters that rule the night would take us all. But we are not alone. Isah has taken pity on us. He stands before us with his great shield, holding back the darkness." She raised her hand toward a huge stack of wood piled near the bottom of the priory steps. A Mira standing next to it touched a piece of wood. The pile stayed dark for a heartbeat, then flared to life, flinging bright, warm flames into the night.

Sable waited for the sense of awe and power to wash over her as it always did. But tonight there was nothing. The flames merely burned a pile of old wood.

"Tonight, let the monsters burn," Vivaine called out.

The crowd let out a roar of approval. The monstrous masks that had been worn during the festival were flung onto the flames. The baledin let his black cloak fall off, revealing a normal man underneath. Someone grabbed the cloak and hurled it toward the fire, where it joined the rest, fueling the growing pillar of light.

Around the Sanctuary, other bonfires flared. Each growing brighter as costumes and masks were thrown onto them. The Sanctuary brightened from brooding red to warm, glowing gold.

Vivaine let the celebration continue for several minutes. When the masks and costumes were burned, she stepped again to the front of the portico and raised a red lantern. A Mira stepped up next to her.

"Great Isah," Vivaine called out. "Spread your protection over our land. Hold back the darkness. Let us rest easy beneath your shield."

A tiny flame appeared in the lantern, then grew to a bright tongue of fire.

Slowly, the lantern lifted out of the Mira's hands and floated into the sky.

In the crowd, hundreds of dark lanterns were lifted above people's heads. Sable caught sight of several Mira walking through the crowd, touching lantern after lantern, starting pinpricks of light.

One by one, the lanterns brightened and rose into the air. "May the Red Shield of Isah protect us." Vivaine's voice spread through the plaza.

Sable waited to feel the stirring inside her at the familiar words. But there was too much Vivaine in them.

Against the night, the lanterns forming the red shield rose, passing the roofs of the priories and rising until they were higher than the spires, free of the Sanctuary, removed from Vivaine and her maneuverings. A net of light standing against the black sky.

The breeze off the ocean caught them, and they started to drift north. Sable's hands tightened on Narine's chair.

"May you draw us after you," Vivaine called. "At the end of our days, may we find our resting place in the Golden Land."

"Soon," Narine said, quietly enough that Sable almost didn't hear. Her face was turned up toward the lanterns. The light from the bonfires glistened on her wet cheeks. "We will follow you soon."

"Soon," Sable agreed. She let the floating lights pull at her, longing to see the hills again. The forests, the great Black River. The wicks on the lanterns would only last a few minutes. They would barely pass the edges of the city before they would burn out and fall. But when she and Narine left... "Soon we will go even farther than them."

Narine kept her eyes on the lanterns but shook her head slowly. "Impossible. There is nothing farther than the Golden Land."

───

Two Sanctus guards helped Narine out of the small litter they'd carried her home in, and Sable pulled her blanket out of the way so she could lie down on her couch.

"Thank you," the prioress said to the guards, and they left.

Sable tucked the wool blanket around Narine's feet.

"Thank you, Issable," Narine said softly without opening her eyes. She lifted her hand and set her cold fingers gently on Sable's forehead. "You are a dear blessing, straight from Amah."

If she heard Sable's snort of laughter, she didn't show it. Her hand fell back down onto the couch, and in moments the prioress was sleeping.

Sable sank down on the far end of the couch, trying to relax, but the events of the night were too loud in her mind. She pushed herself up and stoked the fire, then went to the cabinet and pulled out the bowl of tea leaves, bringing the minty scent into the room.

Innov perched next to the fire as usual, the phoenix's eyes fixed on the sleeping prioress.

"Isn't there anything you can do for her?" Sable asked the bird. Innov, as always, ignored her. "You're magical, right? Although besides the fact that you seem to be constantly burning, I'm not sure I've ever seen you do anything particularly magical." Sable's fingers itched to touch the bird's feathers. Narine ran her fingers over the fiery bird so easily, but Innov never let anyone else near.

Sable had tried to touch the phoenix only once. The bird had fixed her with the most vicious look Sable could imagine from a bird. Sable hadn't tried again.

"When you're close to Narine," Sable said to her, "she is stronger. I don't know if you're doing something, or if she just loves you enough that it makes a difference." The phoenix kept her eyes fixed on Narine. Sable got herself a cup and dropped some mint tea leaves in. She glanced at Innov. "What are you going to do when Narine is gone?"

Innov twitched, almost like she was shifting away from the question.

Sable paused with a leaf in her hand. "You can understand me, can't you?"

The bird didn't acknowledge her.

"Too late." Sable added the last leaf to her cup. "You gave yourself away." She watched the phoenix carefully but couldn't tell if the creature was listening. "What am *I* going to do when Narine is gone?"

The question hung in the air for a long moment. The priories would choose one of the highest-ranking abbesses to be the next Phoenix Prioress, but whoever it was would have no need of a caregiver. "I have a sneaking suspicion Vivaine will make me come to the Dragon Priory. But that sounds miserable." She turned to face the couch, standing next to Innov. "Actually, just having Narine gone sounds miserable."

The phoenix shifted and made a slight cooing noise.

"Before knowing her, I wouldn't have believed anyone could be so genuinely kind." Sable could feel the warmth of her own words. Whether Innov understood her or not, it'd been a long time since Sable had said anything that felt so true. Like she had so long ago on the stage, she could imagine her words filling the little space between the mantel and the couch. Wrapping around the prioress. Maybe doing the impossible and warming her.

Sable looked at the phoenix. "Want to know the truth? There's been something utterly safe about living in this room for the past year. I haven't known anything like it since I was a child. And it's not just the walls, or the fact that there's plenty of food, or that I can take a bath every day if I want to. It's Narine. She is utterly safe. And I'm afraid, once she's gone, I will never find that again."

As she spoke, Sable felt a flare of heat from Innov. She waited for the cascade of sparks, but the phoenix stayed unusually dim.

A new worm of worry threaded through Sable. "Are you all right?"

She stepped closer, and Innov shifted away on her perch. The motion sent down a shower of embers, and Sable felt a wave of heat.

That was the normal heat that Innov always gave off—but it wasn't the same sort of warmth Sable had felt a moment ago.

Sable stared at the bird. What she'd felt a moment ago was more like the heat of someone telling the truth.

She moved the slightest bit closer to the bird, trying not to spook it.

Sable closed her eyes, regathering her thoughts about Narine. "Being near Narine makes me feel safe," she repeated, pouring the truth into her words, letting them flow into the room around her. "I never worry she'll judge me for saying the wrong thing or doing the wrong thing."

Sable opened her eyes, but Innov stood perfectly still on her perch, her orange eyes fixed on Sable. Not a feather twitched, not a single gleam of coal-red light shone on her. Not a single spark fell.

And yet Sable felt her, like a torch blazing in the warmth of her words.

"But there's more than that." Sable stared at the bird, her heart pounding as she put words to a truth some deep part of her had known for a long time. "With Narine I never worry that I'm afraid of the wrong thing. She never belittles fears or brushes them off. She just acknowledges them, and they lose some of their strength."

Her skin tingled with the intensity of the heat. The phoenix was her own fire. Distinct from the warmth of Sable's own words, but somehow similar to it, brighter and warmer by a thousandfold.

Sable's fingers stretched out toward the phoenix. "What if, after she is gone, there is no one to help my fears feel…less?"

Innov kept her eyes on Sable, and for once, she didn't move away as Sable's fingers drew closer.

The heat of Sable's words began to fade. She became aware of the cold stone beneath her feet and the mundane heat of the fire behind her. The glowing warmth she felt from Innov faded too.

Sable's hand paused, and the phoenix shifted her wings. Glowing lines appeared between her feathers. But the bird didn't move away. Sable reached forward until her finger brushed down Innov's chest.

The feathers weren't as hot as Sable had expected, but they were warm. Like bread just out of the oven.

Sable's heart quickened. "I felt you," she whispered.

Sable ran her fingers down the feathers on Innov's chest. With each stroke, a shower of sparks fell, cascading down like tiny shooting stars.

"You felt it too, didn't you?" Sable whispered.

The phoenix gave no response, but she didn't move away from Sable's touch.

"I never thought I'd feel anything like that." This time, aside from the truth in her words, she immediately felt the heat of the phoenix.

Sable closed her eyes. In addition to Innov, she could sense heat from herself. Not as blazingly hot as a phoenix, but like a bed of coals.

She turned to look at Narine. The prioress was fast asleep.

Sable sat on the couch and set her hand gently on the blanket over Narine's feet. "I'm terribly worried about you," she whispered. It didn't take any effort to put truth into those words.

But compared to the fiery phoenix, Narine was barely a candle flame. The prioress was dim and cold, her body feeling almost hollow.

Sable took a shuddering breath. "Oh, Innov, what are we going to do?" She sank back into the couch and glanced over at Narine and the watchful phoenix.

I can feel them.

Worry and exhaustion from the night swirled around in her, but she stood again, finding Pedreck's book and returning to read it by Narine's feet.

Narine's condition settled in her stomach like a cold rock, and yet around it, for the first time in longer than she could remember, something that felt like hope flickered to life.

CHAPTER FIFTEEN

SABLE OPENED her eyes to find Narine's room bright with sunlight. She groaned and stretched from where she was curled at the foot of Narine's couch. Pedreck's book lay next to her where she must have dropped it when she finally fell asleep.

Narine was curled up on the other end of the couch, her eyes closed.

Sable rubbed her eyes and sat up. It was hours past dawn. The pile of today's mail was sitting on the desk, and the faint scent of bread came from a tray set just inside Narine's door. Sable was rising to get it when she noticed how pale Narine's face was.

She set her hand on the prioress's shoulder, but the woman didn't stir. Narine's forehead felt cold and damp, her cheeks dry. Her breathing was shallow and slow.

Sable shook Narine's shoulder, but the prioress just groaned and kept her eyes shut. Sable glanced over to find Innov curled up on the floor under her perch, her head tucked tight against her wings and her feathers duller than the dying coals.

A cold fear wound through Sable, and she ran to the door. A passing abbess looked at her in surprise.

Sable grabbed the woman's arm. "Get Sister Orna from the Dragon Priory!"

The abbess looked at her in alarm, and Sable propelled her down the hall. "Hurry!"

Sister Orna was the Prime Healer from the Dragon Priory. In addition to the lesser healers from the Phoenix Priory who checked on Narine daily, Orna visited once a week. And as much as Sable hated to give credit to the Dragon Priory for anything, their reputation for healing was well deserved. Narine was always noticeably stronger in the days after Orna's visits.

The healer wasn't due for two more days, and Sable stood at the door, watching the abbess hurry away and hoping Orna was somewhere easy to find.

Leaving the door open, Sable brought the bread to a table near Narine and rubbed the prioress's shoulder. Narine's brow creased, but she didn't wake.

Sable eyes felt gritty with exhaustion, and she sank to her knees on the hard floor. She'd stayed up for hours reading Pedreck's book, studying how he'd used music to sense and ultimately use magic.

Sable hesitantly set her hand on the prioress's shoulder. "I want you to wake up," she whispered, the truth of it instantly warm around her.

Narine, though, was even dimmer than she'd been last night. There was a warmth in her chest like old, dying coals, but most of her body was dark.

The door shoved open and Orna strode in, carrying her hefty chest of herbs.

"She's not waking up—" Sable started.

"Give me space." Orna waved her out of the way.

Sable stepped back, watching as the thin healer leaned over Narine, feeling her forehead and listening to her breathing. She felt along the sides of Narine's neck, and the prioress's head moved limply with the motion. Orna stretched one of Narine's eyelids open, none too gently, and the prioress still didn't wake.

Sable stood back, torn between stark fear for Narine and irritation at Orna's brusque treatment of Narine. The healer went to her medicines, clucking and muttering as she shifted bottles around.

"Can you tell what's wrong?" Sable asked.

Sister Orna merely gave her usual noncommittal grunt. She pulled out a vial of bright red liquid and ran her thumb over the smooth glass. With a dissatisfied sounding huff, Orna dripped a tiny bit into the prioress's mouth.

She stuffed the cork back into the vial and tucked it away before wiping her hands on her apron and hefting up her heavy box of herbs.

"That's all I can do," she said. "Get the door, please."

Sable walked to the door and stopped in front of it, crossing her arms. "Well, is there anything *I* can do?"

"Pray for her," Orna responded. She dropped her gaze to Sable's servant's robe. "Or have an abbess pray for her. The goddess controls her fate. She may wake. She may not." The healer looked pointedly at the door.

Sable yanked the heavy door open and crossed her arms again to keep herself from hitting the woman with it on her way out.

Sister Orna marched out and walked straight into a young abbess carrying a tray of bread. The chest of medicines crashed to the ground, and round loaves bounced down the hall.

The girl gasped and apologized, scrambling to clean up.

"Watch where you're going!" Orna snapped, kneeling to gather up the spilled bottles and jars.

Sable picked up a loaf that had rolled into Narine's room.

Past the healer, Pixy hurried down the hall, setting her basket of mail down and picking up several bottles of medicine. "That wasn't Sister Jenna's fault."

Orna held up a broken bottle dripping a thick, milky fluid and shook it at Jenna, sending little drops flying across the hall. "If anyone gets the wet cough next winter, girl, you'll be to blame if they die."

Jenna paled, and Sable opened her mouth to object to such a ridiculous statement, but Pixy spoke first.

"She isn't to blame now," Pixy said calmly, scooping up some scattered leaves, "and she certainly won't be to blame next winter. Pine root glaze is easy enough to find. You'll be restocked in a fortnight."

"Excuse me, *courier.*" Orna snatched a pouch out of Pixy's hand. "You study healing for five years, then care for the sick and dying for another twenty, and *then* you can tell me whether or not I should be upset about the destruction of my medicines."

"It's not the knowledge of medicine that's in question here." Pixy sat back on her heels. "It's the fact that Amah calls us to care more for each other's souls than for our own personal desires and plans."

"How dare you lecture me?" Orna slammed shut her case and stood. "The Holy Mother will hear of your impudence." The healer heaved up her chest of herbs and strode down the hall.

Pixy handed Jenna the last loaf of bread with a smile. "May Amah keep your steps from any more overhasty healers."

Sister Jenna gave her a weak smile back and hurried away down the hall, clutching her tray of bread.

Pixy picked up her basket and glanced down the hall after Orna. "That woman is dour enough to make a healthy person sick."

"I agree." Sable paused at the sight of the mail. "Could I have a word with you?"

Pixy nodded, and Sable ushered the courier inside, then closed the door behind her. She gestured to Narine asleep on the couch and kept her voice low. "Your words of wisdom are wasted on Orna. She's probably yelled at at least two more people by now."

"Softening Sister Orna's crusty old heart isn't my job," Pixy whispered, setting the mail basket down on the desk. "But Amah can hardly expect me to right all the wrongs in the world. I only feel compelled to address the ones that happen within my reach."

Sable considered the abbess. "That's the most genuinely religious thing I've ever heard you say. I wasn't sure you believed Amah is real."

"Of course Amah is real. But maybe not much like what the world thinks of her. The holy writings are almost never concerned with the things people attribute to them."

"You've read the holy writings? Aren't they locked up somewhere secret in the Dragon Priory?"

A small, gauzy smile was visible through Pixy's veil. "No one questions where the mail courier goes. When I carry a bundle of letters, I can walk into any room I want."

Sable nodded. "I always did like the freedom of a courier. What do the writings say?"

"Very little about wearing white robes or having hierarchies of novices and abbesses and prioresses, even less about locking the writings up where no one can see them. But an awful lot about keeping your heart soft and doing good to those within your reach."

"That's the sort of goddess I could respect."

"And god. Isah is there too. Amah and Isah are so connected, they're almost one being. It's only the priories that leave Isah out of most things." Pixy leaned easily against the desk. "It's a twisting of the truth done to solidify their own power."

Sable raised an eyebrow. "That's a strong accusation."

Pixy gave her a half smile. "Who are you going to tell? Most abbesses don't fully trust you, you hate the Dragon, and if you told the Phoenix Prioress, I imagine she'd be proud of me."

Sable laughed. "All very true." She glanced at the couch, but Narine hadn't moved. Sable lowered her voice anyway. "Pixy, aside from you, who touches the mail between when it enters the priory and when it comes to me?"

Pixy crossed her arms. "Pella did something, didn't she?"

"Who's Pella?"

"The abbess who sorts the mail. She's shifty. Like a snake in seaweed."

"Why do you say that?"

Pixy hesitated. "I know it sounds crazy, but I swear I once saw her unseal a letter and read it. But when I found the letter in the pile to be delivered later, it looked perfectly sealed."

Sable sighed. "That doesn't sound crazy at all."

"Pella also loves the Dragon," Pixy continued. "To the point where I wouldn't be surprised to find scales growing on her. She told me once that Narine should learn from Vivaine how to be a real prioress."

"No one finds that odd? That someone shifty and loyal to Vivaine is in charge of the mail in the Phoenix Priory?"

"No one but you thinks loyalty to the Dragon is a bad thing, and I doubt anyone notices her shiftiness besides me. I'm the only one who works directly with her. Pella keeps her head down and does her job efficiently, which is really all anyone asks of a mail courier. No one cares what they act like," Pixy pointed to her own face, "or what they look like, as long as they get their mail in a timely manner."

Sable considered Pixy. "Are there other abbesses in the Phoenix Priory you think love Vivaine more than Narine?"

"A few."

Narine stirred and groaned, and Pixy picked up her basket.

"Don't leave yet." Sable hurried over to the couch. "How do you feel, Holy Mother?"

"Like I went to a party last night," Narine said weakly, "and stayed out too late."

Sable sank down on the end of Narine's couch. "You've just missed Sister Orna."

Narine frowned. "It's not her day to come."

"True, but when I couldn't wake you up this morning, I got nervous."

The prioress stretched and sat up. "I think I may have overexerted myself last night."

"Yes," Sable said. "Which brings up a very legitimate question. If sitting in a chair for a few hours in the priory next door exhausts you like this, should you really leave for a trip tomorrow?"

"We're going on the trip," Narine said firmly. "And we're done discussing it. What I would love right now is some tea. And maybe some breakfast."

"I can find you some breakfast," Pixy offered.

"Thank you, dear," Narine said.

"I'd like Pixy to come north with us," Sable said.

Pixy stopped in the act of picking up her basket, and Narine raised an eyebrow.

"Then she should come along," the prioress said, giving Sable a curious look. "Assuming she'd like to, of course."

Pixy took a step toward them. "I'd love to!"

Narine smiled at her. "It's settled, then. You're coming on our adventure."

Sable stood and crossed the room to Pixy. "Our slow-moving, rather dull adventure," she said, walking to do the door with the abbess. "But we do get to leave the city."

"I haven't left the city in ten years." Pixy's voice quivered with excitement.

"I feel like I haven't left it in a hundred," Sable said.

"Are we going to the summit?"

Sable paused. "That's still undecided. We'll be mostly visiting Narine's abbeys. We leave tomorrow, and we'll be gone for several weeks. While we're traveling, I want you to tell me if you see anything shifty among the other abbesses. Or any undue love for the Dragon."

Pixy grinned at her. "I get to travel *and* keep my eye on untrustworthy people? I've never been more thrilled."

Narine was sitting on the couch, talking quietly to Innov, who had roused herself enough to perch on the prioress's arm. The phoenix's feathers glowed slightly brighter than before.

"Could you get a message to Serene for me in the Dragon Priory?" Sable asked. "To meet me in the garden after lunch?"

"You're taking me on a trip out of the Sanctuary," Pixy said. "I'll get a message to the moon if you want it."

CHAPTER SIXTEEN

"I'm an idiot!" Serene paced on the garden path. Her face was lit with more enthusiasm than Sable had seen in months. "Why was I having you try to feel people? Why didn't I think of Innov? She's brimming with *vitalle*. Like Vivaine's dragon or Eugessa's unicorn. It never occurred to me that you see the phoenix all the time!"

Sable sat on one of the covered benches tucked along the Sanctuary Wall. This one was overhung with ivy to the point where it felt almost like a secret nook.

The sun was high and hot, but in the midst of Serene's impassioned words, Sable could also make out the heat emanating from Serene herself, like a bright, healthy campfire. Sable closed her eyes, trying to feel out past Serene, but the abbesses working in the garden were too far away.

Serene rubbed her hands together. "I have so many more books to share with you now." She paused, a frown creasing her brow. "If I can find them. It's getting worse. There are books I know I shelved recently that aren't there anymore."

"It's the Kalesh, isn't it?" Sable glanced toward the priory. "Vivaine wouldn't be hiding books. Would she?"

Serene shook her head. "Vivaine has no fear of magic. The more people she can control who have magical skills, the stronger she grows." Serene look sharply at Sable. "Speaking of that, don't let her know that your skills are growing."

Sable glanced at the Dragon Priory. "Thankfully, even if Vivaine's watching, she can't hear us, and I think I can avoid Gwen and her mind-reading until Narine and I leave tomorrow. You are the only person who knows. And Innov, I suppose, but I get the feeling that phoenix doesn't like the Dragon Prioress. The few times Narine has brought Innov to the Dragon Priory, the bird glares at Vivaine the entire time."

Serene looked thoughtfully up at the grey clouds. "It makes sense that Innov wouldn't like Argyros, at least. Vivaine's dragon is an intrinsically opposite sort of creature from the phoenix."

"Like Narine is an intrinsically opposite sort of creature from Vivaine." Sable sank back on the bench. "The wrong prioress is growing weak."

"Merrick is worsening too." Serene sat next to her. "It feels like the best of us are fading."

Sable glanced over at her. "Will he travel north for the summit?"

"He wants to, but he's not strong enough." Serene sighed. "I don't want to believe he's dying, but it's getting harder to ignore." She looked across the garden, her eyes unfocused. "He wants me to run Stonehaven when he's gone."

"You're the obvious choice."

Serene shook her head. "Stonehaven should be run by someone kind and gentle and patient. Not someone who gets furious when a book is misshelved."

"Then you and Jae should run it together. You can keep the books in order, and he can take care of the kind and patient part."

The garden was quiet. The only sound some soft murmurs of conversation from the abbesses.

The trip north with Narine would start tomorrow, and despite all the worries Sable had about the trip, the idea of leaving the priories and traveling shone like a beacon of light.

Sable sat forward. "I'm leaving the priories!" She glanced at the garden, but none of the abbesses were paying them any attention. "Purnicious?" she said quietly.

In a moment, the kobold appeared in the corner of the nook, tucked behind the ivy, hidden from the garden. "Hello, mistress!" She beamed at Sable.

"Purn! Narine and I are leaving the city tomorrow. Will you come with us?"

Purnicious gave a little yip and clapped her hands. "Finally! I hate you being inside these priories where I can't get to you!"

"I'll be with Narine most of the time," Sable said, "so you'll have to stay invisible, but it will make me very happy to know you're there."

"Anything's better than this place! Where are we going?"

"Narine is visiting her abbeys, but we also need to get to a summit Vivaine has called for."

"I heard Lord Trelles talking about that. Even Lady Ingred and Talia are planning to go." Purn's look turned worried. "The merchants are all very mad at the rebels, though. Very, very mad." She glanced around, then leaned forward, "And they say the wastrel is one of them!"

"I just learned that myself," Sable said. "In fact, Reese is the reason I need to get Narine to the summit. If I don't, Vivaine is threatening to tell everyone where he and the rebels are."

Purnicious's long ears drooped down in worry. "Lord Trelles has been yelling about shipments that the rebels took."

"That isn't all Reese," Sable said. "Kiva's been attacking merchant wagons down here near the city and blaming the rebels."

Purnicious gave a growl and crossed her thin arms. "That man is as vile as his slithery green snake. Did you know sometimes he walks around with it in his vest pocket?"

Sable stared at her, thinking of Kiva at the feasting tables with his snake-green vest on. She shuddered. "I hope something spooks it sometime and it bites him."

"Maybe I'll spook it," Purnicious muttered.

"The rebels should be warned about all this," Serene said thoughtfully. "They might not be prepared for how many enemies they're amassing."

Sable nodded. "When we get out of the city, I'll write to Leonis. No, we'll need to work faster than having Leonis wait for his rebel contact to come pick up the letter." She paused. "Do you think you could find the rebel camp, Purn?"

Purnicious tapped her chin thoughtfully, "There is a creation of kobolds northwest of Polbrook. They'd know where a camp of humans was."

"A creation?" Sable asked.

"A group of kobolds living together away from humans. It's tricky business. We have to hide, lest greedy humans come and put us in danger merely so they can save us. Then kobolds end up bound to wicked families. But when we get together, we want to build things." She gave a guilty smile. "Sometimes elaborate things, so hiding can be tricky. Creations tend to move around often."

"But you could find them?"

"If I came close, they would find me. They wouldn't give away the location of their creation to a bound kobold. I'd be too likely to come back and tell you where it is." Purn's face brightened. "I need to go make myself traveling clothes!"

With a pop, she disappeared.

"I'll hopefully see you at the summit," Serene said, standing. "I'm going to go tell Jae about your breakthrough with Innov. And look for more books for you."

Serene strode away through the garden, and Sable stretched her feet out, relaxing onto the bench. The wall of the Sanctuary stood tall and solid around the garden, but tomorrow she'd leave it and head north. Until this moment, the leaving had been the important part of that idea. But now…the rebels were in the north. Reese was in the north. Leonis and Thulan and all the people who were actually fighting against the Kalesh were in the north.

The desire to go find them all surged up in her, but the thought of Narine made her pause. She couldn't leave the prioress, not when Narine was so weak.

In a much more confining way, the constant threats against Ryah or Talia that Vivaine had held over Sable for the last year wrapped around her like a net.

But the strands had grown thin. Both Talia and Ryah were firmly established in their new lives. The biggest risk to them, really, was that Sable's presence would cause them trouble.

Sable shook her head, and the net sloughed off like frayed threads.

Once Narine was gone, there'd be nothing to keep Sable here.

She looked north. The wall of the Dragon Priory, and the Sanctuary Wall beyond that, blocked the view, but somehow the northern lands felt almost attainable. Once Narine was gone, Sable wasn't going to wait around for Vivaine to find a new use for her. Once Narine was gone, Sable would leave and go north and finally join people who were making a difference.

A pop sounded next to her.

Purnicious appeared next to the bench, her eyes wide and frightened.

The front of her shirt was covered with blood.

CHAPTER SEVENTEEN

"PURN!" Sable grabbed her shoulders. The kobold's blue hands were covered with blood, and there were streaks of red down the front of her tunic. "Where are you hurt?"

"It's not me! Lord Trelles was attacked! When I got home, there was a bad, bad smell in the storehouse. I found three workers dead and Lord Trelles stabbed in the leg, lying unconscious!" Purn's eyes were wide with fear. "There was so much blood."

Sable gripped Purn's shoulders. "Talia?"

"She's fine. I blinked over to check on her right away, and before I could get back to Lord Trelles, another worker had discovered him. They said one of the storehouse doors had been broken into and things had been stolen. They're all blaming the rebels!"

"Inside the city?" Sable shook her head. "No. It's Kiva, but no one's going to believe that. I hardly believe it. Why attack Trelles?" The scene at Vivaine's dinner came back to her, Lord Trelles accepting the invitation to the summit on behalf of the Merchant Guild, blithely overstepping Kiva's role of spokesperson for the Guild. "Never mind."

Purnicious grabbed Sable's leg. "When I left, Lord Trelles was yelling for messengers to go to all the other merchants, telling them to bring extra men north! He wants to gather a force to destroy the rebels!"

Sable sank back on the bench. If the merchants banded together, they could raise a force of several hundred people. From the hints Sable had gotten from Leonis, the rebels were a fraction of that size.

The weight of Vivaine's threats settled over Sable again, and she rubbed her hands across her face. "I think we'd better get a message to Reese sooner rather than later. If I write one, could you leave today?"

Purnicious nodded, and Sable stood. "Thank you, Purn. Would you mind keeping an eye on Talia until I write it? Just in case?"

"I'll keep two eyes on her," the kobold said, "and I'll be ready when you call me." She disappeared with a pop.

Sable pushed the paperwork that still needed to be done to the side of the desk and pulled out a clean sheet of paper.

She paused, glancing up at the window through which Vivaine had spied on Narine. It had been a constant question over the last year: Was Vivaine watching?

But Sable reached the same conclusion as always. It didn't matter. Unless Sable managed to find a closet or a room that was utterly dark, Vivaine could find some way to bend the light and watch her. Sable had toyed with that idea when she first began writing Leonis but quickly realized that even if she could make it impossible for Vivaine to watch her, she still couldn't hide things from Gwen. It was impossible to not think of the thing she wanted hidden from Gwen when the woman touched her. At some point early on, Sable had stopped trying.

And since Vivaine already knew everything that would be in this letter, there was no point in trying to hide it.

Sable tapped the quill against the inkwell and turned her attention back to her more pressing problem: the defiantly blank page in front of her.

How was she supposed to start? There were too many conflicting things to say.

She couldn't picture Reese anywhere but on the gallows, stupidly sacrificing himself and glaring at her as she tried to stop it. With effort, she pushed that image aside and searched for a different one. There was the first time she'd held a sword. He'd been so appalled at her grip. At that memory, others surfaced. How long he'd worked with her on the different movements. How he'd been so steady next to her as they drew close to Immusmala. He'd taken his self-appointed task of being her bodyguard so seriously that it made her smile.

Just start, Narine would say. *Sometimes words need to move before they find their way to the real, deep truths.*

Sable wasn't able to remember every word she heard people say, but the ones with a memorable cadence, like in a play or a speech, she could. And nearly every word spoken by Narine. The old prioress spoke simply and honestly, but there was a richness to her words that cemented them in Sable's mind.

Sable put the quill to the paper.

Are you still angry? Because when I think about the last time I saw you, I'm still furious. How could you put us all in danger? They had Ryah—

No. That wasn't right. True, she wondered if he was angry. And true, she was still furious that his actions had put them all in danger. But if she were being honest, the one thing she wanted to tell him was how desperately she missed last summer. How simple everything had been. How much freedom they'd had. How much she missed sitting with him and watching the sunrise.

Sable crumpled up the paper and pulled out a new one.

Sunrises weren't the point right now. The point was that he was in a great deal of danger. She almost touched the quill to the paper to say Vivaine knew where he was, but she paused again. If Purnicious was caught carrying this letter, it would be best if it didn't contain any names.

. . .

The woman who undoubtedly holds a sword more naturally than I do knows where you are. She has a spy in your camp.

There is a summit on Tutella Island between the north, the south, and the Kalesh. You've made a lot of enemies among them all, and there's talk of gathering a force to come find you.

Beyond that, what was there to say? Certainly nothing that felt suitable for a letter meant to warn him of danger.

Please be careful.
  -Your former sword student

There was so much blank space left on the page.

The things she wanted to say crowded in her head, but none of them would fit. Not here.

She blew the ink dry and folded the paper. Reaching for the wax, she paused, glancing toward Narine's couch.

"I know," she muttered toward the sleeping woman. "Speak the truth or nothing at all." Sable unfolded the paper. "So far, I've managed the nothing at all part quite well." She tapped the quill on the paper. But what was the truth?

She heard Narine's gentle voice in her mind. *What are you afraid of, Issable?*

I am afraid, she admitted silently, *that what I did last summer, pledging myself to Vivaine, broke...whatever it was he and I had. And that it's too late now to fix it.*

She dipped the quill into the ink and moved to the bottom of the page.

What are the sunrises like up north? Up where there is freedom to see them from anywhere you want? This place is too walled in and missing rooftops flat enough to sit on.

. . .

She paused.

It's also missing people to share them with.

She read the words again. It wasn't everything she wanted to say, but it was part of it. She blew it dry, folded the paper, and sealed it with wax before she could overthink it further. She couldn't risk stamping it with Narine's seal, but she wiped off the end of the quill and carved the rough shape of a sword into the soft wax.

With Narine still asleep, Sable went out to the garden, moving away from the priory door to a shadowed space beneath an apple tree.

"Purnicious?"

The kobold popped into view, and Sable handed her the letter. "Find us on the road when you're done."

Purn nodded. "It'll take at least three days to get to him, but I'll hurry."

Sable knelt to hug the kobold. "Please be careful."

Purnicious patted her hand. "You too, mistress." With a pop, she disappeared.

Sable glanced out from under the apple tree, looking north where Purnicious was heading. "Tomorrow," she said to the tall wall in her way. "Tomorrow you won't block everything I want to see."

Early morning light trickled over the Sanctuary Wall. Sable spared it a glance as she carried a last pile of blankets to a waiting wagon.

"You had to block one last sunrise, didn't you?" she muttered at the wall.

Pixy walked past with a basket full of bread, and Sister Hetty directed a handful of abbesses and Sanctus guards as they finished loading the other two wagons.

Sable stepped back into the cool, dim entry hall. A glitter of light caught her attention. Gwen leaned against one of the stone columns, her hands folded and tucked inside her shimmering silver sleeves.

Sable let out an annoyed breath. They'd almost made it out of the Sanctuary without having to deal with the Dragon Priory again. She considered walking past the Mira, but the hall was reasonably busy with abbesses and guards, and she might as well deal with this in a public place instead of having Gwen follow her to Narine's room.

Sable crossed the hall and stopped several paces from the Mira.

"The High Prioress would like your assurance you'll be at the summit," Gwen said bluntly.

Sable folded her arms. "I would like her assurance she won't tell people where the rebels are. After the attack on Trelles, the merchants are out for blood."

The Mira's look turned exasperated. "It's not that simple."

"Actually, it is. The attacks on the merchants weren't the rebels, and if I know that, surely Vivaine knows it too."

"True. But revealing it to be Kiva would serve no purpose."

Sable shook her head slowly. "So she knows the truth but will hide it."

Gwen shrugged. "There has been nothing as polarizing as these rebels. When people feel divided, they get angry and possessive, and it spurs them to look to their own safety. Which is the exact mindset they should have right now."

"So they're easy to manipulate?"

Gwen sighed. "You know how the game is played, Sable. Even you can see this is a strong opportunity for the High Prioress."

The coldness that twisted in Sable felt surprisingly like betrayal. She turned away from Gwen and stared out the from door of the priory at the activity near the wagons. She let out a laugh that sounded more bitter than angry. "I actually thought she'd keep her end of the deal."

But the truth was, Vivaine would never give up an opportunity like this. She was the person with the information everyone wanted.

"The High Prioress expects you at the summit." The threat in Gwen's words was palpable.

Sable turned back to the Mira, crossing her arms. "Well, the High Prioress can learn to be as disappointed in me as I continually am in her."

"You cannot just walk away from this," Gwen hissed. "Narine is essential, and we all know her time is limited."

"It is," Sable agreed, "and you've helped me to see that I don't want her spending her last days acquiescing to Vivaine's demands."

Gwen took a step closer, her jaw clenched in fury. "Get Narine to the summit. Stop being idealistic and stupid. Stop risking the safety of the people you love, and do what you promised Vivaine you'd do."

A passing guard looked over curiously at the two of them.

Sable pressed her lips shut. She reached out and grabbed Gwen's arm. *The High Prioress is a selfish, corrupt coward.*

Gwen's face turned livid.

Sable gripped the Mira's arm tighter. *I am tired of bending to her threats. If she harms my sisters, or Andreese, or anyone else, that is on her head, not mine. I am done with her. And so is Narine.*

Sable shoved Gwen's arm away and strode toward Narine's room, not bothering to look back.

CHAPTER EIGHTEEN

SABLE'S HANDS still shook with anger—and something that felt uncomfortably like terror—by the time she reached Narine's room, but she found the prioress sitting on her couch, her hands folded in her lap.

"Are we ready?" Narine's eyes were bright.

Sable forced herself to smile at the prioress. "Just one last thing to pack." She called for the two Sanctus guards in the hall.

"Let's get you out of their way." Sable helped Narine stand as the prioress looked at her quizzically.

The guards grabbed each end of the couch and carried it out of the room.

Narine stared after them with an open mouth.

"You said I was in charge of packing," Sable said, "so I'm making sure that you are as comfortable as anyone can possibly be in a wagon."

Narine let out a laugh, setting one hand on Sable's arm. "You're bringing my couch?"

"As long as I've known you, you've never gone a day without lying on it."

Narine held out her other arm, and Innov flew over from her perch, the trail of sparks falling across the now empty stretch of floor.

The prioress started after her couch. She hesitated at the door, murmuring something Sable couldn't quite hear. There was a deep warmth to the words, though. In them Sable felt the glowing fire of Innov and Narine's own duller heat, her cold hand almost feeling warm on Sable's arm. Then the prioress straightened her shoulders and stepped into the hall.

They reached the front doors just as the guards lifted the couch into the back of a wagon. Aside from a few trunks of clothes, a pile of blankets, and a small, sturdy table, the wagon was empty. They set the couch along one side.

The wagon itself was a stunning yellow, with tall, wooden walls and a curved, wooden roof. Green window shutters were flung open on each side, and the entire back hinged open in two wide doors. The other two wagons waiting beside it were simple, covered only with white canvas and filled with practical supplies for the distant abbeys. Next to the vibrant yellow caravan, the other two looked like dutiful, reserved abbesses.

Sable pulled out a folding step from the back of the yellow wagon.

The prioress took in the step, then the couch, then the wagon. "Where did you find this?"

"When you want something for the Phoenix Prioress, people are always glad to help. I actually had the choice of three walled wagons. But I liked the color of this one the best."

Narine shook her head. "This is all unnecessary."

"It's quite necessary," Sable assured her, helping her step up into the wagon.

Narine stood in the middle of it, turning slowly to take it all in, then sank down onto her couch. Sable pulled a blanket off the pile and spread it out over Narine. Innov flapped off Narine's arm and perched on an iron bar that stuck out from the front of the wagon. The wall near it and the floor beneath it were covered with thin sheets of metal, which caught the shower of sparks. Narine looked quizzically at the setup.

"When I commissioned the perch to be added, the smith was worried about a phoenix in a wooden wagon." Sable set a pillow along one end of the couch. "I assured him that Innov would never set anything on fire near you, but he insisted that there be added precautions."

Sister Caryn came up to the open door of the wagon. The round, greying abbess was the healer who most often cared for Narine, and she stood now holding a cup with a tight lid.

Sister Caryn offered Narine the cup. "Here is your morning tea, Holy Mother. Do you need anything else?"

Narine shook her head and took the cup with a bemused smile. "What else could anyone possibly need?" She looked at Sable. "I should've had you with me every time I traveled."

Sable sat next to her, the familiar scent of mint making the wagon feel almost homey. "Are you comfortable?"

Narine reached over and set her chilled hand on Sable's. "It's perfect."

"Is everyone ready?" Sable asked Sister Caryn.

The abbess glanced around the side of the wagon. "Sister Fray just arrived."

"We're bringing two healers?" Narine asked.

"But Sister Orna hasn't arrived yet," Caryn finished.

Sable frowned at her. "Sister Orna?"

Caryn nodded. "I got a note from Prioress Vivaine this morning that Sister Orna would be joining us."

"No," Sable said flatly.

"A healer from the Dragon Priory?" Narine said. "That is not necessary."

Sable glared at the spires of the Dragon Priory through the window of the wagon. "The Phoenix Prioress is ready to leave, and we don't need to take Prioress Vivaine's healer from her." She glanced at the older woman next to her. "With your permission, Holy Mother, we'll be off."

Narine nodded, a bright, wide smile spreading across her face. Sister Caryn left the doors at the back open and disappeared toward the driver's bench.

The Phoenix Prioress gazed out the window across from her, her eyes looking past the Sanctuary Wall that blocked their view, toward something Sable couldn't see. "Yes. It's long past time," Narine said softly, almost to herself. "Let's be off on our last great adventure."

The wagon jolted to a start and bumped over the cobblestones. In mere moments, they slipped out of the confines of the Sanctuary.

They rolled into a market square, and people looked curiously at the bright wagon.

"The prioress and the phoenix!" someone called.

More faces peered into the wagon as they went past, voices calling out greetings to Narine.

She raised her hand, murmuring a prayer until the wagon turned into a quieter street.

They left the back doors open, and Narine watched it all with childlike enthusiasm. The silver of her hair caught the morning light. Her cheeks had a slight rosiness, and even though she sat heavily back on the couch, she looked happier than Sable had seen her in weeks.

As they left the Sanctuary farther behind, something changed about the prioress. Her shoulders relaxed, and Sable felt a jab of worry that the woman was fading with exhaustion. But that wasn't it. Narine's face was relieved and...peaceful. As though she'd just set aside something heavy.

The shift was profound. Foundational. Wiping away a fierce determination that had been part of Narine every hour of every day, which Sable hadn't even noticed until it drained away.

Sable realized that the things the prioress had spoken of seeing— the Tremmen Hill, the forests—these were all at the beginning of her trip. She'd never once mentioned traveling the Black Hills or crossing the wide, grassy Eastern Reaches.

The prioress's murmured words when she'd left her room suddenly made sense. She had said goodbye.

Narine was not planning to return.

Sable looked away from the prioress before Narine could see the tears that pricked her eyes.

Narine squeezed Sable's hand gently. "Thank you," she whispered.

Sable couldn't bring herself to answer.

They wound through the city and down hills until the wagon passed under the city gate. Despite the ache deep inside her for

Narine, something loosened inside of Sable. She rolled her shoulders and took a deep breath of the fresh air. She caught a hint of the scent of trees, and she shifted to see out the windows.

Sable kept her eye out for the first sign of the Tremmen Hills. But for all Narine's talk of longing to see them, the prioress was asleep long before the mounds of green slid into view.

Late afternoon sun streamed down in long, slanted rays, warming Sable's dark hair and making the tiny, white wildflowers under her feet give off a mild, fresh scent.

While the horses rested, Sable stood with Narine on the well-traveled road. A forest crowded close, the old, thick trunks growing up into a tangled canopy of light-dappled leaves. The ground beneath Sable's feet felt solid and stable after the bumping of the wagon.

The prioress turned her face toward the sun and closed her eyes. "Can you hear that?"

The quiet drone of bees was interrupted only by the quiet conversations farther up the line of wagons. "Hear what?"

"The trees." The prioress looked so enthralled that Sable closed her eyes to listen.

The leaves nearest them made light, papery sounds against each other. While farther away through the trees, the rustle was a bit deeper, growing and cresting in waves tumbling over the treetops.

Birds chirped to each other deep in the branches, and a squirrel let out a burst of chatter that drowned out the other sounds.

Sable turned to the prioress and opened her mouth, but the careworn look Narine had carried for so long was fading, and her face was set in such a blissful expression, that Sable merely said, "I can hear it."

Without opening her eyes, Narine reached out and took Sable's hand, squeezing it with her thin, cold fingers. "Thank you for coming with me." Her words swam warmly around Sable.

Sable's hand tightened on Narine's. She watched the prioress, too many emotions warring with each other to find anything to say.

The prioress breathed in. "This is where I should be, here at the end."

A deep ache tore through Sable, hopelessly entangled with the raw goodness of seeing Narine so happy.

"This is where I should be," Narine repeated. The prioress's words felt warmer than even the heat of the sun on Sable's cheeks.

In that warmth, Sable herself burned bright and hot, but Narine stood like a tall, thin pillar of ash-coated coals.

There were no words to put to this moment, so Sable closed her eyes and listened to the trees.

CHAPTER NINETEEN

CANDLELIGHT FLICKERED over the rough wood walls and the long list of supplies spread out in front of Sable on the table. She adjusted numbers, recording which crates the Sanctus guards stacked next in the corner of the kitchen.

Narine and Abbess Nell, the cheerful, middle-aged woman who ran this abbey, sat close to the stove on Narine's couch. Narine had protested loudly when the two guards had brought it straight into the kitchen, but Sable had told Abbess Nell how cold the prioress always was, and that had settled the matter.

Sable was close enough to hear the conversation between the prioress and the abbess. Despite the fact that Sable knew Narine was exhausted from the day, she sat patiently and listened while Nell gave an official-sounding report about the abbey. It didn't take long until the conversation turned deeper. Sable hid a smile when she heard Narine ask, "What are you afraid of, Nell?"

Pixy moved into the kitchen, setting a basket of tools on top of the crates. "That's the last of it," she said, sitting beside Sable.

Sable nodded and marked them off her list, putting down the quill and leaning back in her chair.

Pixy pulled the map over closer to her. "How far north are we going?" she asked, keeping her voice low.

Sable pointed along the Black Hills near the river. "We'll cross the river at a ferry near the hills."

"So we aren't going past the hills."

Sable glanced over at her. "Are you relieved or disappointed about that?"

"Both, maybe. I've never been north of the Black Hills. I've heard there are elves and dwarves and monsters up there."

"You don't have to go north of the hills for that." Sable studied the map, then pointed at the Nidel Woods, sitting at the foot of the Marsham Cliffs. "There are elves in these woods, and dwarves live in the cliffs." She paused. "Or they used to."

Pixy stared at her. "You've seen elves and dwarves?"

"There's a dwarf in Atticus's acting troupe, Thulan. She took us to meet other dwarves when we were looking for a safe place to spend the night, but the entrance to the dwarven caves was destroyed for some reason. I did meet some elves, though."

Pixy stared at her. "What are they like?"

"Surprisingly like humans," Sable said. "The one who was in charge was fairly unpleasant, but we talked to another named Cintis whom I liked very much." She ran her fingers over the trees marking the Nidel Woods. "As far as monsters go, though, the only ones I met were Kalesh."

Pixy was quiet for a moment. "You've had a much more interesting life than I have."

Sable shook her head. "I had an interesting month traveling with the theater troupe. Aside from that, I lived in Dockside, and the only interesting things that happened there tended to be dangerous and illegal."

"Were you born there?"

"No," Sable said slowly. "I was born in a small town named Pelrock." She pointed to a blank space on the Eastern Reaches, not far from the sea. "I lived there with my parents and my two sisters until..."

"The Kalesh came," Pixy said. "And destroyed the town."

Sable looked up sharply at her.

The abbess gave a small shrug. "I was at the Grand Stadia last year when you did your play and gave your speech about the Kalesh." She picked up the quill. "Where did you say it was?"

Sable pointed to the place where Pelrock was labeled on the map back on Narine's desk.

"Does anyone live there now?"

Sable nodded. "I saw it mentioned in a letter to Narine once."

The abbess looked over the map, then drew a dot for Pelrock, matching the dots for other small towns. She wrote its name in neat letters. "The Kalesh don't get to erase our towns."

Sable stared at the little dot, her chest tight.

"Is it hilly or flat near Pelrock?"

"Hills covered in grass."

Pixy nodded and drew some hill shapes around the town. "What were your parents like? Were they actors like you?"

"No. My parents were..." Sable paused. "I was only fifteen when they were killed, and I didn't realize it at the time, but they didn't do much of anything. Our house was just like all the others in town, but they must have had money, somehow, because they didn't have to work.

"Most of the men in the town were fishermen. Twice a year they'd take all the boats and go out to the far shoals and use enormous nets between the boats to catch blackfish. The entire village would spend the next two days preparing and smoking the catch to live off of for the next several months. My father, Stephan, would always help with the blackfish catches, but beyond that, he never fished. He did some scribe work for the town, since no one there could read or write, but the people rarely paid him.

"My mother's name was Amelia. She taught us how to read and spent a lot of time in her garden. When I was old enough to watch my sisters, my parents would go on hunting trips together. My mother could shoot better than anyone in the village, but my father insisted she never go out hunting alone."

Sable paused. "No, not insisted—he never told her what to do. He just asked her not to go alone, and so she waited for him. She had this elvish bow…"

The memory of that bow falling from her mother's lifeless hand stopped Sable's words. Her parents had held weapons that night as though they were fighters, not a scribe and a gardener. They'd understood the Kalesh words…

"Amelia and Stephan," Pixy said slowly, drawing ripples along the shoreline of the Southern Sea. "Those are good names."

"Where were you raised?" Sable asked, pushing away thoughts of that horrible night.

"Not far from Folhaven. My father is a cobbler, and my mother is a seamstress." Pixy told of her younger brothers, and Sable focused on the words until the memories of Pelrock and the Kalesh attack faded into the background of her mind.

Eventually Pixy left to go to bed, and Abbess Nell said goodnight to Narine. The prioress placed her hand on Nell's head in blessing, then pressed a kiss to her forehead.

Sister Caryn came and fussed around Narine, but the prioress insisted she felt fine, so Sable helped her settle on the couch. Despite her protestations, the prioress barely had time to thank Sable before her eyes closed.

Sable added some wood to the stove. Innov perched on the back of a chair, her eyes fixed on the prioress.

"I haven't seen Narine this exhausted before," Sable said quietly, putting truth into the words and stretching out her senses toward the bird.

The phoenix flared into a blaze of warmth. Sable studied the bird. "You can feel when I…Serene calls it casting out. I don't think the term fits, exactly, but it's close." The bird didn't move, but Sable concentrated, and instead of a blaze, the warmth began to focus, coalescing into the shape of the phoenix.

Sable smiled at her. "It's getting easier to do. At least, it's easier to feel you." She turned back toward the prioress, and her smile faded. From Narine, only a few steps away, Sable could feel nothing.

"I haven't seen Narine this exhausted before," she repeated, searching for some sign of heat from Narine. It was there, but very, very weak. "And this is only the first day."

The phoenix made a small noise, something like a coo. She tossed her head and rustled her wings, causing every feather to glow like coals, and bits of light showered off her.

"I know." Sable watched the sparks trickle through the air. "I haven't seen her this happy, either. I suppose we'll just have to help her get whatever rest she can."

Sable's shoulders and hips pressed against the hard floor through the thin cushion that made up her bed. This was the third abbey they'd stayed in and by far the smallest.

When the ache in her hips grew unbearable, Sable rose and went to the couch. Narine slept, but her brow was wrinkled in discomfort. Sable adjusted her blankets. Despite the fact that Sable had expected Narine to be exhausted from all the travel, the prioress greeted each new abbess with enthusiasm, sitting and talking late into the night, sharing their fears, touching the abbesses' foreheads in blessing before they left.

There was a lively glint to the old prioress's eyes that Sable had never seen before. But during the day, as the wagon trundled down the roads, Narine barely left the couch, dozing fitfully amidst the motion.

Sable found an extra blanket and lay it out on top of her own thin cushion. It didn't make it comfortable exactly, but it helped.

Wind gusted through the night, and the small abbey creaked and groaned. Sable's worries crowded into the gaps between the loud rushing of the wind.

It had only been three days since they'd left the city, and Purnicious probably hadn't even found Reese yet, but the thought of how many people wanted him dead gnawed at Sable as she dozed.

"Issable!" Narine's whisper cut across the room. "Issable!"

Sable was up and crawling toward the prioress before she was fully awake.

The prioress grabbed Sable's hand with ice cold, shaking fingers. "You're here," Narine said, her voice full of relief, her grip tight on Sable's hand.

"Of course I'm here. Are you in pain?"

Narine clasped Sable's hand with both of her own. "I thought I was alone in the dark," she whispered.

In the dim orange firelight, Narine's eyes were wide. Sable set her free hand on Narine's forehead. The prioress's whole body was shaking.

"I'm here," Sable repeated, feeling powerless to say anything more useful. "I'm always here."

Narine pressed her eyes closed and took a shuddering breath.

"What's wrong?" Sable asked.

Outside, the wind plunged through the forest, rushing past the abbey like a wild river, shoving against the walls and through cracks around the windows.

Narine shook her head. "It's nothing." Her words were so quiet, Sable barely heard them.

The prioress's face was drawn in an expression Sable hadn't seen before. The thought of the prioress being in pain was chased away by something more unsettling.

Narine was afraid.

Sable clasped both of the woman's hands in her own but hesitated before asking the next question. There was an audacity in daring to ask Narine such a thing.

Except, Sable realized, in the past year, she hadn't heard a single soul have that audacity.

"What are you afraid of, Narine?" she asked gently.

Narine's eyes opened, but instead of the sharp look Sable had expected, Narine's expression was almost desperate.

"I'm afraid of dying, Issable," she said softly. "Isn't that so unspiritual? Like everyone else, I'm terrified of dying. Not of being dead. I'm ready to go to the Golden Land with Amah, but the dying..." She gripped Sable's hand tighter. "What if it hurts?"

Sable bit back the words that jumped to her mind to downplay the fear. Narine never did that. She acknowledged fears, stood in solidarity against them.

Sable settled against the front of the couch, imagining herself in Narine's place. "The thought is terrifying."

Narine curled her legs in closer. "I'm afraid it will hurt more than I can bear."

The wind battered at the abbey, and Sable gipped Narine's hand. "I'm afraid of the same thing for you. I'll stay with you until the end, I promise."

Narine closed her eyes, but her grip didn't relax. "Thank you."

Any answer Sable had caught in her throat, so she just tightened her grip.

It took longer than usual, but eventually the prioress's hand relaxed, her brow smoothed, and her breathing fell into the long, regular sounds of sleep.

CHAPTER TWENTY

TWO NIGHTS LATER, Sable sat in another abbey, watching Narine closely. The prioress had barely spoken with this current abbess before falling asleep, and everyone had left to let her rest.

Narine slept now, but something about how she lay bothered Sable. Her shoulder stuck up jaggedly against the blanket, bony and thin. Her face was wan, and dark smudges shadowed her eyes.

So far, the wagons had kept the schedule of all the other trips Narine had taken over the years, but…

Sable found Sister Hetty and the other abbesses from Immusmala getting ready to sleep. "The prioress needs more rest. We'll stay here another day."

"She agreed to that?" Hetty asked.

Sable paused. "I'm not going to ask her. She can't keep up this pace."

Hetty turned to Sister Caryn with a questioning look. The healer paused, then nodded. "Rest would do her good."

"Then we'll rest here tomorrow," Sable said.

Sister Hetty glanced into the room where Narine slept, a crease of uncertainty in her brow. "She won't like this."

"Then she can be angry with me," Sable said firmly.

Hetty and Caryn exchanged looks. Finally, the healer gave a grudging nod.

Sister Hetty sighed. "I'll arrange it."

───────────

The extra day's rest helped. Or Sable imagined that the dark lines under Narine's eyes faded a little. But when they finally set out again, the prioress could barely walk to the wagon. The bright enthusiasm that had lit her face during the first days had faded, and she did nothing more than lie on her couch and stare dully out the window at the passing world.

When she finally fell asleep, she slept heavily for the rest of the day.

The village they rolled into that evening was small and cozy, but when the wagons stopped, Narine didn't stir.

Sable set her hand on Narine's shoulder to wake her and tensed.

The prioress felt warm. Sinking down next to her, Sable felt Narine's forehead and hands. Every part of the prioress was feverishly hot.

"Sister Caryn!" she cried out.

The healer came running, and Sable backed out of the wagon as more people crowded in. Caryn called for the guards to carry Narine into the abbey.

They lifted the couch out, and Sable almost missed Innov, perched in the far corner. The phoenix was so dim she barely glowed in the shadows.

Sable scrambled back up into the wagon. Innov shrank back, but Sable moved closer anyway. The bird's feathers were dull, and her tail hung limp. Sable reached out to touch her, and Innov shifted away, but only a single spark fell from her tail, and only her chest and the front of her wings glowed with the motion.

"Oh, Innov," Sable breathed. She reached out a finger tentatively. The phoenix didn't move, and Sable touched her gently. The feathers felt warm on the back of her fingers, but not hot. "Not you, too."

The phoenix pressed her chest against Sable's hand and, with a flap of her wings, hopped heavily onto Sable's outstretched arm.

Sable drew a sharp breath as the talons wrapped around her white sleeve, but the bird's grip was gentle. Innov leaned toward the wagon door and Narine.

"Yes, she'll need you close. And maybe you need her close, too." The truth of her own words filled the wagon, and Innov grew warmer.

Innov let out an irritated-sounding caw and flapped her wings, pulling Sable's arm forward.

Sable ducked away from the hot feathers. "Sorry."

Inside the abbey there was a flurry of activity around the prioress. Sable wove her way through the crowd of abbesses and pulled a thin, wooden-backed chair up next to Narine's couch. Innov hopped onto the back.

The bustle had a frightening urgency to it, and Sable backed away, but the room was tight and there was nowhere to stand that was out of the others' way. She went outside and sank down on the back of the yellow wagon.

A few minutes later, an abbess Sable didn't recognize hurried out of the abbey and ran down the road toward the main square of the village.

Sable sat in the yard of the abbey, watching the occasional villager pass along the road, hearing the other abbesses and guards bringing supplies in from the wagons, and wondering whether this small corner of the world would be where Narine's grand adventure would draw to a close. It was a heavy, numbing sort of thought, and Sable just sat with it while the afternoon grew later.

Eventually Sister Caryn came out and sat on the back of the wagon next to Sable. The healer's normally cheery face sagged with something Sable didn't want to name. "We've lowered the fever a bit. But there's not much we can do for her. She was too weak for the usual herbs to make much of a difference. I had to give her some blood thistle, which helped a little."

Sable straightened at the words. "I remember blood thistle from the play about Vivaine and the baledin. It strengthened people dying from the white death. It makes her heart beat stronger, doesn't it?"

Caryn nodded but frowned toward the abbey. "It took more than I expected, though. A lot more." She sighed. "The prioress's condition is quickly moving beyond my skill."

The abbess who'd run into the village earlier came back down the street, waving her arms. "I found a healer!" she called.

Next to her, a thin woman strode down the street.

"Sister Orna!" Caryn said sounding more relieved than shocked.

Sable stared at the dour healer, stunned.

Caryn climbed down and hurried to meet her. "How did you get here?"

"I've been following you for days." Orna pushed past Caryn and dropped a medicinal-smelling satchel on the back of the wagon. "Tell me Narine's symptoms and everything you've done."

Caryn shifted at the hostility in Orna's voice, but she explained Narine's fever and what they had tried. "The only thing I had left to give her was blood thistle."

The color drained from Orna's face. "You didn't!"

"I…" Caryn took a half step back. "There was nothing else we could think of. Her heartbeat was weak and slow. I know it's a last resort but—"

"Are you *trying* to kill her?" Orna demanded, grabbing her satchel and rushing into the abbey.

Caryn followed her while Sister Orna called out curt commands. Sable stood in the doorway, her arms folded tightly, watching the frantic activity. Through it all, Narine lay still and silent, her forehead creased with pain.

Sable watched Narine's face, hoping desperately to see the anguish fade from it, but even though the prioress stayed mostly senseless, she shifted restlessly, as though trying to escape something.

Finally, Orna ordered all the abbesses and guards who had been helping out of the room, telling only Sister Caryn and Sister Hetty to stay.

Sable slipped inside and moved over to sit next to Narine. The prioress had a cool, wet cloth on her forehead and a poultice sitting on her chest that gave out a pungent smell. Narine let out a whimper and shifted.

"Is she in pain?" Sable whispered.

"It certainly looks like it," Orna retorted.

"Will she make it?" Caryn asked, her voice small.

"If she stays here?" Orna crossed her arms. "No. The care you've given her up to this point has been incompetent and inadequate!"

"She wasn't sick before tonight," Caryn objected.

Orna ignored her and swung her attention to Sable, fixing her with a cold, vicious look. "The High Prioress knows you are the one who told Prioress Narine to leave without me."

Hetty frowned at the accusation and took a step closer to Sable. "The Phoenix Prioress felt we didn't need any more healers."

Sable glanced at the abbess, surprised the woman had defended her. "Thank you, Hetty, but Orna is right. It was me. Because Narine wanted a peaceful trip on her own terms, not one pestered and manipulated by the Dragon Priory."

Both Caryn's and Hetty's mouths dropped open at Sable's tone, but Orna just let out a dismissive sniff. "The High Prioress was right about you. You're insolent and irreverent. And it's criminal that you've duped the Phoenix Prioress into trusting you." Her expression turned to a sneer. "Your decision to leave without me may cost the good prioress her life. I hope you're proud of yourself."

Orna turned to the two abbesses. "If the prioress stays on this journey, she will die in one of these backwoods, ill-equipped, ignorant abbeys. But Amah has blessed her by bringing her so far north. We are only a long day of travel from Tutella Island, where the High Prioress has more healers and there is a fully stocked supply of medicines. We leave at dawn."

Sable stood. "No."

Orna gave her an incredulous look. "This is not your decision."

"It's not yours either." Sable stepped around the couch. "The Dragon Priory has no authority here at all. What happens to the Phoenix Prioress is her own decision, and she does not want to go to the summit."

"We don't know what the prioress wants," Orna said condescendingly, "because you let her fall so ill she is now senseless."

Sable stepped closer to the healer. "Narine came on this trip so she could die in one of the these 'backwoods, ill-equipped, ignorant abbeys!'"

Next to her, Hetty gasped.

"You will address the prioress with respect!" Orna commanded her.

"I respect the prioress more than you could imagine," Sable said, "and I respect that her only other wish was to stay away from the political maneuvering and manipulations Vivaine is using that summit for."

"Issable!" Hetty whispered in a scandalized voice.

"The Phoenix Prioress did not intend to die in some rustic abbey of a curable fever," Orna said. "When the cure was only a day away."

Sable crossed her arms. "We're not going to the summit. We are from the Phoenix Priory, and only the Phoenix Priory will decide what happens with our own prioress."

Sister Orna stepped forward until she was close enough that Sable could feel her breath. "You're right, but you're nothing more than a servant in the Phoenix Priory, and none of this is up to you."

She turned to Caryn and Hetty. "If we leave at dawn, we can actually help the Holy Mother by dusk tomorrow night. If we don't, she'll be dead not long after."

The two abbesses glanced at Sable.

Sable shook her head. "She does *not* want to go to the summit."

"We're not taking her to the summit," Caryn said, "we're taking her to the medicine."

"If they can cure the fever," Hetty added, "we can't keep her from that."

Orna's gaze moved between the two abbesses and Sable. She shook her head slowly. "I don't know how you managed to wheedle your way into control of this situation, Issable, but know this: If the prioress is kept from the help she needs, or even if she's delayed to the point where I can no longer help her, I will make sure the entire world knows it was *you* who refused to save her. That it was you who sentenced the Holy Mother to death in an obscure corner of the land when help was within your grasp." Orna's gaze raked over Sable. "Everyone will know that you were the one who killed her."

Orna's words oozed out of her warm with truth, and Sable's resolve cracked.

She searched the healer's face. "You can help her on the island? You can actually cure the fever?"

"If I get her there fast enough."

The words were true, and both Caryn and Hetty gave Sable pleading, earnest looks.

From the couch, Narine gave another whimper. The sound was frightened and small, almost like it belonged to a child, and the last of Sable's resolve crumbled.

Sable let out a ragged breath. "We'll leave as soon as it's light."

CHAPTER TWENTY-ONE

THE ROOM at the back of the abbey smelled faintly of vanilla and sawdust.

"Welcome to the sorts of rooms the rest of us have been staying in." Pixy stepped past Sable. "Guaranteed to make you realize what a blessing your bed in Immusmala is."

A workbench filled one side with neatly stacked cuts of wood piled on one end and tidy tools hanging on the wall above it. Newly made crates were stacked high against the walls to make room for two bedrolls on the floor. Sable looked inside the nearest crate, and the scent of vanilla wafted out from lines of white candles.

"We are in Norreny, aren't we?" Pixy asked. "My mother loves these candles! She buys six of them every year at the spring market and saves them for special occasions. They burn slow, and the whole house smells like vanilla."

The light outside was fading, and Sable sank down onto one of the beds. Whatever padding it had was thin, and she could feel the hard floor beneath her, but she lay down anyway.

"The prioress hasn't improved at all, has she?" Pixy asked.

Sable shook her head. Each time Orna had spoken of getting to the summit, there'd been truth in her words that she could help the prioress, but Narine was so weak…

Pixy stood quietly for a moment, then said, "They said there would be tea. I'll go get us some." The door closed softly, and her footsteps faded down the hall.

Sable closed her eyes and lay, feeling oddly numb, until she heard a soft pop next to her.

Her eyes snapped open, and she saw Purnicious's little face above her, peering down at her sympathetically.

Sable pushed herself up to sit by the kobold and wrapped her arms around her. "Purn! I'm so glad you're back!"

Purnicious's bony arms wrapped gently around Sable's shoulders. "I saw the good prioress," she said quietly.

Tears rose to Sable's eyes for the first time today. "I don't suppose kobolds have healing powers?"

Purnicious took a step back, her ears drooping down at the end, and shook her head. "Many have tried, but we can never manage to bellish inside a person."

"I don't think anyone can bellish as much as Narine needs right now." Sable lifted Purn's chin and looked into the little blue face. "It heals something inside of me to see you."

Purn smiled shyly and leaned closer. "I found the wastrel!" She pulled a tightly folded letter out of the bright purple cloak she was wearing and held it out proudly to Sable. "It took me longer than I expected. But I found a kobold who took me to the rebel camp."

Sable took the letter, gripping it so tightly that the edge crumpled in her hand. "And Reese is all right?"

"As troublesome and willful as ever," Purnicious said, but her tone was unusually kind for speaking of Andreese.

"Was he…" Sable paused, glancing down at the letter. "Angry?"

Purnicious let out a peal of laughter that filled the room. "Angry? I thought he was going to pick me up and shake me because I couldn't get him the letter fast enough." She spread the purple cloak out so Sable could see it. "And he gave me this. Isn't it beautiful?"

Sable raised an eyebrow. "It is. It came from Andreese?"

Purnicious grinned. "He said he'd never been so happy to see a rotten blue creature like me, gave me more food than three kobolds could eat, and made me tell him everything I knew about you from the last year. Then gave me this cloak, and look at how pretty it is! It needs barely any bellishing at all, although I might add some white trim…" The kobold gave Sable a wry smile. "I'm pretty sure I'm not the one he wanted to give a gift to, but seeing as this cloak would barely cover your shoulders, I'm going to keep it."

"You deserve it." Sable glanced at the letter. "Where was their camp?"

"In a beautiful valley near the foot of the Scale Mountains," Purn answered. "They're a small group, but well hidden." She glanced at the thin bedrolls on the floor and made a disapproving noise. Kneeling, she set her hand on the fabric, and Sable felt it thicken beneath her.

"If it's not too hard," Sable said, "could you thicken Pixy's bed as well?"

Purn nodded and turned to the other bedroll. "I should go before she comes back. But I'll be close. Do you need anything else, mistress?"

"No." Sable held up the letter. "Thank you for this."

There was a pop, and the kobold disappeared. "Anything for you, mistress," Purn said from the empty space.

Reese's letter was folded into a square, sealed with a blob of wax that had a funny, crooked looking sword pressed into it.

Sable was starting to break the seal when the door swung open to reveal Pixy holding two cups of tea.

"Who were you talking to?" the abbess asked in a whisper, looking around the empty room. "And where did you get a letter? I'm the one who's supposed to deliver those."

Sable paused, trying to think of an excuse, until she realized that Pixy had never given a reason not to trust her. "I was talking to Purnicious, and she's a kobold."

"You have a kobold?" Pixy looked around the room with wide eyes. "Is she still here? What is she like? Can she really make anything you want?"

"Purn," Sable called quietly, "come out and meet Pixy."

With a pop, Purnicious appeared next to the workbench, studying the abbess.

The abbess gasped. "You're so beautiful! And blue! I have never met a kobold! This is the best day of my life!"

Purnicious's expression softened. "If you're a friend of my mistress, then I'm pleased to meet you."

Pixy shifted on her bedroll. "Did you make this more comfortable? Because it's gloriously thick compared to what I was expecting."

"Purn makes the world around her a better place," Sable said sincerely.

"Well, thank you! This is the most comfortable bed I've had since we left the city!" Pixy glanced at Sable's letter. "A secret kobold bringing secret letters! This is a delightful thing to have walked into!" She looked closer at the wax seal with the crooked sword. "That's not one I've seen before."

"It's from Andreese of Ravenwick," Purn said conspiratorially.

Pixy's eyes widened. "The assassin?"

"He's not that bad all the time," Purn said, and Sable gave the kobold a surprised look. Purnicious shrugged. "I like this new cloak."

Pixy was staring at the letter. "Isn't he with that rebel group? Working for that man, Tanis? That's what the rumors say." She gave Sable a probing look. "What does a famous assassin who's working with a small rebellion write to you about?"

"Probably that he misses her," Purnicious said smugly.

Pixy's eyebrows rose. "Oh, it's *that* sort of letter!"

"Will you two stop?" Sable broke the seal and unfolded the paper. She held it up toward the window to catch the evening light.

To the once famous actress,

Thank you for your warning. We have suspected a spy for several months, but we have enough enemies that we weren't sure whose spy it was. This helps us narrow down the suspects. We move regularly, but we will continue to take precautions.

We hadn't realized the merchants were after us as well, but Purn explained everything. It was good to finally get proof that you have been our ears in the Sanctuary. I had suspected, but Leonis and Thulan never would admit to anything. I admit I had hoped it was you, and not some merchant or abbess who might be untrustworthy.

I think you would like our fearless leader. He has been effectively disrupting the enemy's supply lines, and, as you know, has recently found some more interesting opportunities.

We aim to convince the Kalesh that their presence here is too costly to be worthwhile. If we can begin to drive them off, we hope the rest of the north will join with us in pushing them out. The world has been abuzz with news of the coming summit you mentioned, and it seems possible that all five Northern Lords will attend. That is nearly miraculous, and hopefully signals a new feeling of unification that the north has been sadly lacking.

You imagine more freedom to see sunrises than I have. I suppose I exchanged the "freedom to see them from anywhere" for the chance to take a stand in something this important. As much as I love a good sunrise, it was an easy choice.

The choice was possibly made easier by the fact that the sunrises here are merely serviceable. They manage to get the sun up into the sky each morning, but they're lacking some essential thing.

If you ever happen to extricate yourself from your current prison, come north. Perhaps we can watch one together and figure out what's been missing.

Tell Purn not to preen too much about her new cloak.

-R

Sable went back to the top of the letter and began rereading it until Pixy cleared her throat.

"You're smiling," Pixy said. "Please tell me he wrote juicy things. I have never gotten a love letter!"

"It's not a love letter," Sable said. "It just a thank-you for my warning."

"A loving sort of thank-you?" Pixy asked.

"No." Sable folded the letter back up.

"Then can I read it?"

"No." Sable held out her hand for the tea Pixy was still holding.

The abbess held the cup out of Sable's reach. "No tea unless you promise to tell me everything there is to know about you and the infamous Andreese."

"There's nothing to tell," Sable said.

"I'll tell you everything," Purn said, coming to sit next to Sable on her mattress.

"Agreed." Pixy handed Sable the tea and sat on her own bedroll, looking eagerly at the kobold.

"I've known the wastrel longer than my mistress, actually," Purnicious began. "In fact, the way we met her was through the tragic attack and destruction of Ebenmoor, where both Andreese and I lived. We were the only two survivors, and the Kalesh who had attacked us had almost tracked me down to kill me, too, when my mistress saved my life." Purn gave Sable a devoted look.

"I was hiding under a bush, scared to death," Sable said, "and I motioned for her to join me."

Purnicious raised a finger. "No talking! This is my story." She turned back to Pixy. "Now, Sable and the others had already found Andreese, wounded and unconscious near the smoking ruins…"

Sable rubbed her eyes. She'd stayed up late into the night talking with Purnicious and Pixy about the adventures the theater troupe had encountered the year before, and they'd laughed until Sable's cheeks felt sore.

But in the dimness of the predawn abbey, the worries for Narine crowded back in. Sable thanked the local abbess for her hospitality and headed out to the yellow wagon as Narine was lifted onto it on her couch.

"There's no need for you to be in here," Orna informed Sable, pushing past her and motioning for Sister Caryn to get into the wagon. "The prioress needs to be cared for by competent people."

Caryn gave Sable an apologetic look but climbed up after Orna.

Sister Orna ordered the yellow wagon to take the lead, and they set out at a quick pace as soon as the road was bright enough to see well. Sable walked alongside it, wishing she could hear the quiet conversation between Orna and Caryn. Pixy walked with her for much of the morning, but even she was subdued.

They reached the Black River near midday and turned north without stopping. There were other travelers on this road. Ahead of them, a line of merchant wagons moved slowly, surrounded by a surprising number of guards. Behind them in the distance, another set of wagons could be seen making its slow way north.

Clouds of dirt rose from the wheels, and Sable moved to the grass off to the side. The wide waters flowed by next to her, moving slowly south.

The hills crowding up against the river grew steeper as they moved north, and the road grew more shadowed until, by the time the sun had sunk low, they were traveling on a narrow strip of ground between a tall cliff and the water.

They rounded a turn, and the towering rock face swept back, revealing a wide, cliff-edged valley. The sun brushed the tops of the hilltops, casting a golden glow over clusters of tents set up near the road. The river stretched across the mouth of the valley, and a long, wooded island sat a little way offshore.

The first tents they rolled past were lined up in a perfect square with Kalesh soldiers moving among them. The Sanctus guard driving Narine's wagon called out a question.

"Prioresses on island," one of the soldiers called back, his accent thick as he motioned farther up the road. "Bridge ahead."

Sable met the gaze of the Kalesh soldier as she passed them, bracing herself for the stiffness she had encountered in the soldiers at Vivaine's meetings. These men, however, merely watched them curiously. One of them motioned to the bright yellow wagon and said something that made the others laugh.

Dozens of Kalesh tents lined the road, but none of the other soldiers paid them any heed.

Sable fell back to walk where she could see Narine. Orna dozed in a corner of the wagon on a pile of blankets, and Caryn sat on the edge of Narine's couch, her face lined with worry.

Not far down the road, the tents changed to a cluster of white pavilions surrounded by wagons. Abbesses and Sanctus guards moved among them.

There was a commotion ahead, and the wagon rolled to a stop. Sable stepped around the side to see a cart with a broken wheel clogging the road in front of them.

Narine's Sanctus guards moved forward to help heave the broken cart out of the way, and Sable tapped her fingers impatiently on the yellow wall.

A rough laugh came from next to her. "Could that be Issable of Shadowfall?"

Sable turned at the stage name Atticus had always used for her.

"Could it be her? Right here before my eyes? And looking so holy?" A dwarf leaned on the side of a small handcart at the side of the road, grinning at her through a short-trimmed, russet beard.

Sable stared at her, barely believing her eyes. "Thulan!"

CHAPTER TWENTY-TWO

SABLE THREW her arms around the dwarf, smelling the familiar scent of leather.

"That's enough, girl," Thulan sputtered, patting her on the back awkwardly. "You're gonna choke me with your flowing white robes." She pushed Sable back to arm's length. "And what are you wearing? I thought you were supposed to be part of the priories now. But this isn't an abbess's robe. This is almost as bad as that horrible thing Ryah wore when she insisted on saving that funeral in Folhaven last year."

"It's not quite that bad."

Thulan looked the same as always: short, stocky, still wearing her well-worn leather vest. Sable's eyes lingered on the bracers on Thulan's arms. "Waiting for a fight?"

Thulan gave an annoyed grunt. "Hasn't been a single fight yet. But I have hope. Sticking the Kalesh, the north, and the merchants this close together, there's bound to be some fun eventually."

"I'd be stunned if there weren't." Sable glanced into Thulan's handcart, which was filled with potatoes, bread, and smoked fish. "What are you doing here?"

"You don't think Atticus would have missed this spectacle, do you?"

"I suppose not. I got your last letter just before everyone found out the rebels had attacked that mine." Sable shook her head. "I can't believe you kept the fact that Reese was part of the rebels a secret."

"Leonis wouldn't have if left to his own devices. But Reese has a few too many enemies after last year's knifing incident to be spreading his whereabouts around."

"Have you seen him?" Sable asked.

"A couple times, if we were close enough to the rebels when it was time for their messenger to come get your latest letter."

"I can't believe you stayed with Atticus all this time. When you left Immusmala last year, I thought you were going to go look for the dwarves."

"I was, but then…" Thulan shrugged. "I kept finding other things to do."

There was a brusque tone to her words, and Sable didn't press the issue. "How did Atticus manage to get himself invited to the summit?"

"He didn't. He hasn't been invited anywhere important since the debacle with the Kalesh ambassador. But you only need an invitation if you're going onto Tutella Island." Thulan gestured around them at the spread of tents. "The rest of this circus is just here to keep tensions high and make the peace talks more complicated." She grinned at Sable. "Wanna smuggle us onto the island with you?"

"I'll bring you and Leonis, but Atticus can stay out here and rot."

Thulan raised an eyebrow. "He thought you might be angry."

"Angry? He sold me out to Vivaine! Told her everything I could do. I've been trapped working under her for a year!"

The dwarf raised her hands. "I'm not here to defend the old man. But you should let him explain."

"The man said he'd never use my secrets against me, and he lied." Sable shook her head. "I'm not interested in talking to Atticus."

Thulan studied her for a moment, then shrugged. She glanced at the yellow wagon next to them. "Do you have the Phoenix Prioress stored in that awful, gaudy wagon? Because it really feels like her wagon should be red."

Sable nodded. "She's…not well."

"I'm sorry. I always liked her the best of the gaggle of useless prioresses holed up in that Sanctuary."

Ahead of them, the guards dragged the broken cart the rest of the way off the road.

"The monks will let you onto the island with the prioress. But if you get a chance, come see Leonis and me. Atticus wastes all sorts of time away, gabbing with whoever he can find. We're set up between the Northern Lords and the Dragon Priory tents." She gave a smirk. "Of course, Leonis is going to hate that I talked to you and he didn't, so if you can't come out, his irritation will be satisfying enough for me."

Narine's yellow wagon started forward, and Sable reached out and put her hand on Thulan's shoulder. "I can't tell you how good it is to see you."

Thulan glanced back down the road. "Is Ryah coming?"

"I would imagine so. Eugessa is fond of her—at least fond by Eugessa's standards, so she usually keeps Ryah close. I'll tell her you're here." The wagon moved past, and Sable gave Thulan one last smile. "It is so good to see you."

"So you keep saying," Thulan grunted, but there was a warmth in her eyes.

Sable hurried after the wagon, which was turning onto a smaller road toward the river. She glanced back once and saw Thulan wheeling the handcart down the road. The mass of tents and pavilions and people camped along the road felt less foreign knowing Thulan and Leonis were among them. Even knowing Atticus was there made things feel more familiar, she admitted.

Narine's wagon stopped again when it reached three men, who could only be Tutella Monks, blocking their way onto a narrow, wooden bridge. Each wore thick leather armor strapped over dark tunics and pants. Swords hung at their waists, and a dozen paces behind them, another warrior stood with a curved bow in his hand.

Across the bridge, the island stretched out in both directions. Downriver, Sable could see nothing but trees, but upriver, flickers of light were visible through the dusky forest.

"We bring the Prioress Narine of the Phoenix Priory," the driver told them.

One of the monks stepped forward. "The prioress herself must ask permission to cross onto the island," he said sternly.

"The prioress is ill," Sable said, walking toward him. "We are in a great hurry."

"I'm sorry to hear that." His voice was sincere. "But I'm afraid I still need to see the prioress with my own eyes before the wagons are allowed to continue."

"This way," Sable said. "Although you have nothing but our word that she is the Phoenix Prioress."

"I've had the pleasure of meeting Prioress Narine twice." He followed Sable around the corner of the wagon to the open door. He peered into the wagon.

Innov perched on the end of the couch, but she was terribly dim. Her feathers were a dull brick red and hung limply. She let out a low, unhappy sound,

When the monk saw Narine, he closed his eyes. "Holy Isah, send your strength."

"May we pass?" Sable asked.

He nodded. "I'll lead you in to Aedis." He started toward the front of the wagon, and Sable followed. "The Sanctus guards may drive her in, but they'll need to leave their weapons here. After the prioress is settled, only five attendants may stay with her on the island. The rest may return to the camping area designated for the priories."

While the supply wagons turned around and the Sanctus guards driving Narine's wagon handed over their weapons, the monk gave Sable a sorrowful look. "Whatever medicine or skill we have is at your disposal. Many of our monks are elderly, and we have helped many through their last days."

"Thank you," Sable said quietly.

He started across the bridge. "I'm Sam."

"Sable," she said. "Or Issable, I suppose."

He raised an eyebrow and looked at her closely. "Ah, the prioress's caregiver." At her surprised look, he smiled. "I've been put in charge of hosting this summit and made an effort to learn the names of most of the people who would be coming. The Prioress Narine has few attendants, and I was already familiar with you, actually, because I was in Immusmala for the Midsommer Festival last year and saw your play."

"Ah," Sable said. "My former life."

"Former lives tend to pile up the longer you're alive," he said easily. "Do you prefer Sable or Issable?"

"I'm not sure it matters which I'd prefer. Here, with these people, I'm Issable."

Sable glanced down into the water below them. Even in the dusky light, she could see deep into the clear water. Stones in blues and greys and light purples covered the bottom of the river, shifting and blinking beneath the rippling surface.

"That's one of my favorite parts of the river," Sam said. "If you enjoy fishing, the darker pools along the shoreline there are excellent choices."

"I've never fished in my life," Sable said. At Sam's vaguely surprised look, she said, "I lived in Immusmala near the docks. I've smelled enough fish to make the idea of fishing rather unappealing."

"Ah."

He turned onto a smooth road leading farther up the island. Ahead of them, torches made a path of firelight winding through the trees, and Sable caught a glimpse of the lights ahead.

"How many monks live on the island?"

"Around forty. Once we had as many as sixty, but we've shrunk some in the last decade."

"Did you all used to be soldiers?"

"Most of us," Sam answered. "There are a few who come from more peaceful pasts, but most of us are here because we fought too many battles and spilled too much blood. In my former life, I became a soldier to protect the people I loved, but that's never what I did. The fights I was ordered into were merely helping Lord Perric expand his holdings."

Sable's feet crunched over old pine needles on the road, the wagon creaking along behind them. The sun had set, and while the sky was still bright, there were deep shadows under the trees, except where the torchlight traced out a winding path.

"Some men can reconcile themselves to that life," Sam continued, "and keep their humanity. But it ate away at me until everything that had been good about me had been hollowed out. I started to fight recklessly, just wanting it to be over. I went into every battle as though it were my last, but time after time I survived.

"Worse, I was promoted. The captain admired my spirit and put me in charge of more and more men until I commanded half our battalion."

He shook his head. "The last battle I fought in was for control of a small village. Troops from Lord Darien were faced off against us across a wide field of crops. When dawn came, two Tutella Monks walked into the center of the field—with nothing but their leather armor and swords—and faced down both armies. They demanded we take our battle elsewhere and leave the villagers' crops alone."

Sam shook his head. "I had never seen bravery like that. Two men facing down two entire battalions of soldiers, just to save the crops of some village we didn't even know the name of.

"At that moment I knew those monks were the men I had always wanted to be. I was nothing compared to them, but they were about to die protecting people who could not protect themselves, and if that day was going to be my last, I wasn't going to die fighting on the wrong side."

Sable looked over at him. His eyes were distant, his hand gripping the hilt of his sword.

"What did you do?" she asked.

He blinked and gave her a grim smile. "I told my men to stand down, and then I walked out into the middle of the field and stood with the monks."

CHAPTER TWENTY-THREE

SABLE STARED AT HIM. "Did the battalions attack?"

"No," Sam said. "My own men, aside from being very confused, refused to fight me. My captain tried to order the other unit in our battalion across the field, but knowing they'd be outnumbered all by themselves, they refused as well. Lord Darien's troops were confused enough by the chaos in our lines that they waited to see what was happening, and my captain took the opportunity to retreat so he wouldn't be soundly beaten.

"After some awkward milling about, Lord Darien's troops left too." He was quiet for a long moment. "I hadn't done anything as heroic as the villagers thought. I'd merely shifted which side I was going to die on, but for the first time in years, I was proud of the choice I'd made. The monks invited me back to the island, and I went in the hopes of finding a way to repay the world for all the pain I'd caused."

They rounded a bend in the road and found themselves in an open, grassy stretch leading up to a stone wall. The top was lined with torches illuminating the leather-clad archers who stood watch.

"Welcome to Aedis, Issable." Sam waved to the man above the

arched gate, and he nodded back. "It's not a particularly glamorous town, but it's been my home for nearly a decade."

Sable looked at Sam. "Has it worked? Has living here helped you repay the world?"

"No." He let out a sigh. "It turns out I can't undo the wrongs I've done. Isah knows this, though. None of us are given the chance to go back and change our choices. Instead, we are given new choices each day. We have the chance to continue to do wrong, or to fight the harder battle and choose to do right. The weight of that responsibility is heavy, but it also gives me hope. Because if I can choose to do better, so can you, and so can the leaders who will be at this summit. As dark and hard as this world is, the truth is that we all have the power to make it better. And that is a hope that helps me get up every morning. Because if a brutal, heartless killer like myself can stop killing and try to change, then anyone can."

They walked through the arch under the thick stone wall. The road ahead wound uphill between small, timber-framed buildings. Dark tiles covered the roofs, and many of the windows were lit with firelight. Sable peered through the wavy glass at the warm light as they passed.

"I don't have much hope that the Kalesh Empire is going to change," she said.

Sam nodded slowly. "Nor do I. But Isah calls us to have hope in hopeless situations."

They reached a cobblestone square lined with timber-framed houses. Lanterns hanging on the front of each building splashed arcs of golden light on the ground. Ahead of them sat the largest building Sable had seen on the island, a tall, long structure with three thick chimneys and a broad front door.

"And so here we are," Sam said, "at a summit of people who do not seem able to find peace between themselves, at the point where hope feels more like a dream than a real possibility. But we're here, nonetheless." He motioned to several of the houses lining the square where wagons and carts were being unloaded. "And not just us. The priories and the merchants and the Kalesh all began arriving today as well."

"But maybe not out of hope," Sable pointed out. "It's more likely they're here in an effort to expand their own power."

"True. But I showed up at that field to fight Lord Darien's men to the death," Sam said simply, "and ended up at a very different place. Isah does not always let us accomplish our goals."

Sable gave a little laugh, "If Isah is in charge of goal accomplishments, he's been busy keeping me from mine."

Sam grinned at her. "It feels that way more often than I'd like to admit."

At least a dozen abbesses moved through the courtyard.

"Is the Dragon Prioress here?" Sable asked Sam. "We're in need of her healers and medicine."

"She arrived not long ago. I believe you'll find her in the gathering hall." He motioned to the large building. He looked around the square fondly, then nodded up to the wall that wrapped behind the buildings. "Despite your worries for the prioress, I hope you are able to make yourself at home here, Issable. If you're looking for a nice view of town or the river, the wall is an excellent choice. I have friends who spend much of their time up there."

He paused, and the slightest smile crossed his lips. "It was *very* nice to meet you, Issable." With a bow, he turned and motioned the Sanctus guard driving Narine's wagon toward a medium-sized house at the side of the square.

Sable looked after him, considering the interesting man until she caught sight of Narine's couch in the back of the wagon. The need to talk to Vivaine made Sable turn toward the gathering hall. The High Prioress would be thrilled that Narine was here, but as soon as she saw the Phoenix Prioress's condition, Vivaine would realize the futility of expecting anything from Narine.

Sable stepped through the front doors of the gathering hall into a wide, open hall scattered with tables and chairs. The center of the floor held a huge, rectangular fire pit where three fires burned, each cooking a spit of lamb. Only a few of the torches around the room had been lit, and the edges of the large hall were full of shadows.

Several doors stood open off the room, but voices and light came from only one. Sable crossed to the door and saw Vivaine's back.

Gwen stood at the prioress's shoulder, the glittering hem of the Mira's robe matching the silver scales of the dragon along the floor near Vivaine's feet.

Sable paused at the doorway as Vivaine faced an elderly monk in the large study. The man stood in front of a heavy desk, and the walls held dark bookshelves packed with books and scrolls. More monks stood along the walls, their worn leather armor looking warm and brown next to Vivaine's subtle white glow. Sable caught a glimpse of a handful of other men standing along the wall next to the door, wearing common woodsmen's clothes.

"Do you agree to promote peace with your words, striving toward understanding and unity and working only for the furthering of a treaty?" the monk asked the High Prioress.

"I do," she answered.

"Do you agree to promote peace with your actions and to pledge the members of your delegation will do likewise?"

"I do," she answered.

"Do you agree that all points of view are welcome at this summit, whether or not they are in agreement with your own, and do you agree to hear their perspectives with an open mind and a willingness to consider them as valuable as your own?"

Vivaine paused but nodded. "I do."

"Excellent." The monk smiled warmly at her. "Then welcome to the summit, High Prioress. We are honored that you chose our island for such a historic event."

"We are pleased to have found such neutral ground," she answered graciously. "I have been assured the merchants will be arriving this evening, and the Kalesh ambassador is already here. I will make sure everyone knows to visit you to pledge their vows. Several of the Northern Lords are not expected until tomorrow, so I planned on beginning our talks in earnest two days hence."

"That was our expectation as well."

Vivaine gave him a nod. "Then, if there is nothing else?"

The monk held up his hand. "There is one more delegation you should be aware of."

Vivaine paused. "What delegation?"

"I remind you of the vows you just made." The monk motioned toward the men standing along the wall behind Vivaine. "And remind them of the same."

Sable leaned into the room and saw a man of average height step toward Vivaine. Sable could only see the side of him, but the temple of his dark hair and a good portion of his beard were filled with grey. The scabbard at his waist was simple and well used, but empty.

"High Prioress," the monk said, "may I introduce Tanis of Stormfeld."

Vivaine took in the man with a shocked expression.

"Tanis," the monk continued, "represents a group of northerners from several territories who have differing opinions on the Kalesh presence here than their lords."

"I'm aware of Tanis's rebel group," Vivaine said slowly.

"It is an honor to meet you, High Prioress," Tanis said with a bow.

Vivaine did not offer even a nod in return but studied the man closely. "It was a bold move to come here, Tanis."

"I heard there was a peace summit to discuss the Kalesh presence, and since that is a topic of great importance to us, it seemed logical to come."

"This summit was announced less than a fortnight ago," she said. "You're well informed for a man who hides in the woods."

Tanis smiled easily at her. "Not as well informed as you, Holy Mother, but I try."

Vivaine considered him. "Perhaps it was not all that bold of you to come after all, secretly appearing at a summit once your enemies have pledged not to harm you."

"You're certainly not our enemy, are you?" Tanis asked. "Because I don't recall having any interaction with the priories of the south before this moment."

"I am the enemy of anyone who disrupts peace in my land," Vivaine answered. "And you have certainly done that with your most recent attacks."

"Any violence that has occurred lately has been instigated by the Kalesh," Tanis said simply, his words warm.

"The slaughter at the mine?" Vivaine said coldly. "Am I to believe the mine workers attacked you?"

"I will be happy to tell the entirety of those events to the full summit." Tanis was still unruffled.

Vivaine turned back to the older monk. "The rebels' presence will lead to violence. Many coming here have been attacked by Tanis's men or had their possessions stolen."

"The purpose of this summit is to address such issues without violence," the monk reminded her. "Tanis and his people were not expected, and we have no housing for them on the island, but upon their vow of peace, we invited them to join the summit meetings during the day."

Vivaine turned calculating eyes back to Tanis. "We'll have a discussion about the mine when the Kalesh are present, then. We will discuss who is responsible and who is required to pay restitution."

"And you'll listen impartially?" another man asked from along the wall.

A shock of familiarity ran through Sable at his voice.

"Because we all know the Kalesh will lie and claim their innocence," he continued, sharply enough that Argyros turned his head to look at the man. "But you have far too many spies, *Holy Mother*"—there was a decided air of contempt in the title—"to believe their story. You have too many spies to not already know the truth of what happened, and yet you stand here and feign ignorance."

Sable stepped forward, her heart beating uncomfortably fast, until she could see his familiar, bearded face.

Standing along the wall, his arms crossed and his face dark, stood Andreese.

CHAPTER TWENTY-FOUR

REESE'S IRRITATION with Vivaine was so obvious and so familiar, Sable had to stifle a grin.

"This man is a known assassin," Vivaine objected to the monk she'd given her vows to.

"Who has agreed, along with everyone else, to remain peaceful here," the monk answered. "We are happy to extend people the opportunity to pursue peace, no matter their past."

"The whole world knows you're trying to gain favor with the Kalesh," Reese continued as though the High Prioress hadn't spoken. Tanis gave him a warning look, but Reese ignored him. "You would serve the entire land better if you got off your fancy, white pedestal and started to find a way to really protect us."

"Andreese," Tanis said with a warning in his voice.

But Reese stepped toward Vivaine. "It's absurd how much power you wield, and yet you do nothing useful with it. Every person in the south would follow you if you called them to stand against the Kalesh." He flung his hand out, encompassing everything around them. As he did, his gaze flicked over toward the door. "All you have to do is actually take a stand—" He froze, his eyes fixed on Sable.

Vivaine, whose face had been growing more exasperated as he spoke, followed his glance.

"Issable!" The High Prioress took a half step toward her.

At the name, Tanis looked over at Sable curiously, then turned back to Reese with a raised eyebrow.

"Issable," Vivaine repeated, a surprising amount of relief in her voice. "Where's Narine?"

Sable pulled her eyes away from Reese and walked into the room. "They're moving her into one of the nearby homes."

The high priestess nodded, regaining her composure. "She's resting well?"

"No," Sable said. "Narine came down with a fever yesterday. Sister Orna didn't have the herbs she needed, so we brought her here. But..." Sable couldn't bring herself to finish. The word hung in the quiet room. "The prioress needs your healers," she said to Vivaine, "and your medicine," she told the monks.

Vivaine closed her eyes. When she opened them, they held something Sable couldn't read.

"Will you all excuse us?" she said.

"Of course." Tanis gave Vivaine another bow and turned to Sable. "Please convey our hopes for swift recovery to the prioress."

Sable nodded. Reese was still watching her, his expression conflicted enough that she couldn't untangle it. She tried to give him a small smile, but amidst the talk of Narine, she couldn't quite manage it. He took in the white dress she was wearing and frowned slightly.

Tanis left the room, and his men followed. Reese hesitated for another breath and opened his mouth. But with another glance at Sable's white robe, he turned and left.

"What a touching reunion," Vivaine murmured.

"I'm sure you have much to discuss, High Prioress." The monk motioned for the other monks in the room to file out. "Please use the study as long as you need, and our healers and herbs are at your disposal for whatever the Phoenix Prioress needs."

Vivaine nodded and waited until the monks had left the room before turning to Sable. "Tell me what happened."

Gwen started toward Sable, and Sable shot her an irritated look. "I'm not going to lie about Narine."

The Mira paused, and Vivaine waved her off with a tired gesture.

"Her fever isn't responding well to the herbs," Sable said.

"Which herbs?" Vivaine asked.

"More than I can name," Sable answered. "None of which helped. Right before Sister Orna caught up with us, Sister Caryn gave Narine blood thistle to strengthen her heart. I honestly don't know what Orna gave her after that, but Narine hasn't improved since last night, and Orna was convinced if we got her here, you'd have what she needed to help."

"Blood thistle?" Vivaine's face had paled, and she reached out her hand to steady herself on the mantel. "You could have killed her!"

Sable drew back at the hostility in Vivaine's voice. "She'd be dead by now if Caryn hadn't given it to her."

Vivaine's face grew furious. "Sister Orna should have been traveling with you!"

Sable paused at the woman's unexpected anger. "Wait—blood thistle is a dark red liquid, isn't it."

Vivaine's hand tightened.

"Sister Orna's been giving Narine a dark red liquid for months, every time she visited!" Sable stood speechless for a moment. "You've been dosing Narine with blood thistle? For months?"

"It's strengthening properties are well documented when given in the proper dosages," Vivaine snapped.

"Every time Orna came, Narine grew stronger." Sable shook her head. "You've been poisoning her with blood thistle?"

"I've been giving her strength."

"Why?" Sable demanded. "So you could keep her healthy enough to vote with you?" A wave of disgust rose at Vivaine's callousness. "Is this why she's been in pain? Because she's missed doses of blood thistle?"

A pang of something almost like guilt crossed Vivaine's face, but when she spoke, her words were still cold. "Her pain is because she overexerted herself to a dangerous extent."

"Narine is dying!" The words tore out of Sable with a rawness she hadn't expected. "And all you care about is your politics."

Vivaine drew herself up. "I have known Prioress Narine for forty years," she said coldly. "I have been mourning that we are losing her for longer than you can imagine. The fact that you hastened this by not caring for her properly just compounds all the problems you've caused. And yes, I care about the summit. Because I care about the people we need to keep safe."

Sable stared at her. "You always focus on the wrong thing. You always choose the wrong side."

"There are no choices! We are doing the only thing we can. Stop being childish. There is work to do, and with Narine so gravely ill, we have very little time." She paced in front of the desk. "I will send Orna what she needs. Keep your useless healers away from Narine before they kill her. We'll do what we can, but at this point, you've guaranteed that Narine's time will be very short." She pointed a finger at Sable. "You convince her to vote." Her voice curled through the room, sharp and scathing. "Convince her by *any* means necessary. We are out of time. Do not test me, Issable. The consequences of your defiance in this will be swift and dire."

Vivaine stepped closer, drawing herself up until Sable had to look up at the tall woman. "*Nothing* is more important to me than getting this treaty settled. And I need Narine. I don't care if she stays in bed and we send witnesses to take her vote from there. But you will convince her to participate."

Sable curled her hands into fists. "No, Vivaine. I am done doing what you want. Narine is dying, and I will do everything I can to make her comfortable." Her own words filled with truth, pouring out of her like a wave of warmth, slipping in between them all. Gwen's eyes narrowed, and she glanced around the room, but Sable ignored her. Instead, she took a step toward the High Prioress. "You will not trouble Narine with the politics of your summit. She will not vote for you. Nothing will come into her house that will cause her any discomfort or grief."

Vivaine let out a low laugh. "You don't decide any of those things.

Your situation has not changed. If anything, the people you've been protecting are in more danger now than ever.

"Andreese has walked into this lion's den on his own," the High Prioress continued. "Atticus and his troop of misfits are actually camped within my priory's reach. Your sister Ryah is on her way here with Eugessa, and your other sister is traveling toward us with the merchants and her *father*." Vivaine's lips curled around the last words. "Nothing has changed for you, except that your position is more precarious than ever." She gave Sable a condescending look. "Issable, when will you learn that you should not make me your enemy?"

The worry about Narine that had gnawed at Sable for so long curdled into fury, and she glared at the High Prioress. The light wrapping around Vivaine was too white. Too bitter cold.

Once, so long ago that it felt like a different life, Sable had thought the High Prioress was a candle flame, glowing with goodness. But Vivaine was nothing but ice, chilling the flesh of everything she touched, freezing down to the very marrow.

"A year ago," Sable said, "I admired you. I didn't know who you are or what you're capable of. I didn't know that you can take something as pure as light and twist it into a lie. I didn't realize how you use your position and your words and your spies to manipulate everything around you." The truth in Sable's words poured out, warming the air around her.

Gwen straightened, staring at Sable as the energy filled the air. Vivaine gave no indication that she could feel anything.

Sable stepped closer. "But now I do." The air heated until Gwen shifted back.

Sable kept her eyes fixed on Vivaine's cold, livid face. "Now I know who you really are. When we left Immusmala, I told Gwen that I am done with you and your plans, and I stand by that."

The warm air pressed around them all, but Vivaine didn't flinch.

The corner of the High Prioress's mouth curled. "Regardless of what you think, Issable, you and I are terribly alike. And we are not done." She leaned closer until Sable could see dark flecks in her silver eyes. The light from Vivaine's robe was harsh and jagged. "You and I may never be done with each other."

Sable shook her head. "All this time, I've done what you want because of the secrets you know about me. But I know your secrets, too, Vivaine."

The prioress's eyes narrowed.

Sable let the threat hang in the air as she turned to leave. She paused at the door, looking back. Vivaine stood straight, her eyes cutting with an icy rage.

"I will do everything I can to see that Narine is left in peace." Sable funneled all her fury at Vivaine, and all her love for Narine, into the words. "Everything I can," she repeated, letting the truth build up like a solid thing, like a wall that Vivaine couldn't cross. "It's time you learned, Vivaine, that you shouldn't have made me your enemy."

She didn't wait for an answer before turning and striding out of the room.

PART III

History is made of up threads.

Sometimes you can almost see them, almost trace the path of one, almost see how it weaves in with the others. Sometimes you can almost see the back of the tapestry. Those are the times you know that everything is hopelessly tangled into knots.

But still, you can't quite help trying to follow the threads.

-Flibbet the Peddler

CHAPTER TWENTY-FIVE

OUTSIDE, the world had dropped to a deep blue, and a handful of stars twinkled in the eastern sky. An abbess hurried into Narine's house. Through the door, Sable could see a tumult of activity, and she turned away from it, ducking down a thin alley between Narine's house and the larger one next to it, coming out behind them onto a thin, grassy swath beneath the wall.

A chorus of frogs croaked away merrily, hidden in the shadows, and the scent of flowers wafted from some unknown direction. She drank it all in until she noticed a thin ladder clinging to the wall.

Crossing the grass quickly, she climbed up.

A walkway ran along the top of the wall with a parapet along the outer edge, reaching to Sable's shoulders. Monks were stationed along the wall, more than half of them facing into Aedis. Which was probably wise since the rebels had come. She wasn't quite high enough to see over the roof of Narine's house, but glimpses of the square were visible past it.

Sable peered into the square, looking for any sign of Reese, but there was nothing to see but merchants, abbesses, and Kalesh. She turned away and crossed her arms on top of the parapet wall. Aedis sat at the tip of the island, and the river split around the wall below her, nearly touching it. Upstream, the trees on either side of the water covered the ground with a rough mantle of shadows, but the river was a wide, glossy path, reflecting the rich blue of the sky.

Sable kept her eyes on it, wishing it would flow through her and smooth the edges of her worry and frustration.

A rustle sounded near the top of the ladder, and she turned toward it, backing against the wall.

"I don't know if I'm happy to see you," Reese's voice rolled quietly through the dusk, "or if I'm still furious that you aligned yourself with Vivaine."

Sable opened her mouth to answer, but his tone had been indecipherable, and with the torchlight of the square behind him, it was impossible to see his expression. He finished climbing onto the wall and turned toward her, stopping a few steps away.

Torchlight lit his side, and his face was so familiar that she wanted to rush forward and make sure he was real. But the last year stretched out between them, and Sable shifted. Her arms hung awkwardly, as though they were too long or not quite her own.

She crossed them, but they didn't fit quite right. "I could say the same to you."

He leaned an elbow on the parapet, looking far more comfortable than she felt. He raised an eyebrow. "You're angry that I aligned myself with Vivaine?"

There were changes in him. His beard was longer, his hair too. His face was more drawn, his eyes more serious. The torchlight caught on a thin scar on his temple, and she thought of him slouched in the corner of the cell under the Dragon Priory, that cut bleeding down his cheek and into his beard.

A bit of torchlight lit his frown, and her stomach sank at the expression. It reminded her a bit of how he looked at Kiva.

"No," she answered. "I'm not sure if I'm happy to see you, or still furious."

"You have no reason to be furious at me."

Her disappointment and awkwardness drained away in a flare of irritation. "Are you serious?"

"Yes." His scowl deepened. "You're the one who threw away the chance at freedom that I handed to you."

"Chance at freedom? The entire troupe was arrested because of your knife!"

"Why do you think I let them catch me? With me to blame, the rest of you would have been released."

"And you would've been hanged!"

"That was the price I was willing to pay for doing what had to be done!"

Sable's arms tightened around her chest. This conversation was going all wrong. The tone in his letter had given her a slight hope, but if, after nearly a year, all this anger was still between them…

She felt a pang of regret for the number of things that had broken that night in the Grand Stadia.

"It wasn't a price I was willing to pay," she said.

His eyes bored into her, filled with a fierce intensity. "You were supposed to be free," he whispered. His gaze dropped to her white dress. "Not enslaved to Vivaine."

Her anger flared again. "You think I'd stand by and let them hang you?"

"You weren't even supposed to be there." He shook his head, sinking back against the parapet. "You were supposed to have escaped the Sanctuary and made it somewhere safe." His look turned defeated. "Why were you still there?"

"I was going to escape…but then I realized the chaos was a perfect cover."

"For what?"

"Getting into the Priory of the Horn and stealing Eugessa's butterfly ring."

He blinked at her. "You didn't."

Sable gave him a small smile. "I managed to get into Eugessa's washroom while she was taking a bath."

"She let you in? While she bathed?"

"It turns out those abbess veils can be useful. I just went in with the dozen abbesses there to give her soap or towels or whatever else she wanted. She took off the ring, and I stole it. But the door to the plaza was guarded, so I had to go through the Dragon Priory to find a way out." Sable paused. "That's when Vivaine found me."

His eyebrows rose. "Vivaine caught you inside her own priory?"

Sable's smile widened. "Standing in her private chapel."

Reese stared at her, then a quiet laugh rolled out of him. "No."

"I was getting ready to break a huge, stained-glass window, in what would have been a fruitless attempt to escape, when Vivaine walked in."

He shook his head. "That is terrible luck."

"Not luck." Sable's smile faded. "She used Purnicious to find me."

Reese sobered. "So she had Purnicious, the troupe was arrested, and I was set to be hanged." He studied her, his face taking on a resigned look. "Let me guess. Vivaine held all that over you."

Sable plucked at the front of her white robe. "I certainly didn't pick this role myself."

He frowned. "But what did she want with you?"

She shot a glare across the river toward the torchlight from the camps. "Atticus told her that I can feel the truth."

His mouth dropped open. "He what?"

She nodded. "After all that time assuring me he'd never share my secret, he poured it out to Vivaine one of those times he snuck off to see her." All the anger from the past year came back. "So yes, I have plenty of reasons to be furious. With Atticus, for selling me out." She pointed at Reese. "And with you for working with him and starting this whole mess by throwing that knife."

Reese took a half step forward, and his voice took on an almost desperate edge. "I had to do it. You know your speech hadn't worked. We had tried and failed." His expression held a complicated mix of emotions, and the air between them grew warm with the truth of it all. "I had to do it." A tendril of something wound through the warmth. Not coldness, not a lie, but something.

Sable's real question pushed to the surface. "Why didn't you tell me?" The words pulled up the root of the anger that had festered over the past year. "You planned it all with Atticus, but you never told me."

"I couldn't have you part of something so...ugly." His final word blazed with truth. "I needed you to be safe."

She didn't want to believe him, but the warmth of the words wrapped around them both. In it, she caught the sense of him, standing there like a bonfire of life and heat.

She let out a long, annoyed breath. "Well, I needed you to be safe, too."

He crossed his arms. "Well, here we are. Both safe."

She waved her hand at the town. "If you consider being on an island with people who hate each other safe."

He turned toward Aedis, sinking back against the parapet. "I don't, actually."

Sable leaned against the wall a few steps away from him. A bit of breeze blew down the river, pushing her hair into her face, and she swept it back. Her irritation had banished some of her awkwardness, but there was still a distance between them.

She hadn't expected things to be like they were last year, not really. But whatever this was felt disappointing.

She shoved away all the old frustrations and glanced at him. "That was a good speech you were giving Vivaine earlier about her spying."

He almost smiled. "Until you barged in and interrupted it."

She shrugged. "I can give you lessons on how to ignore distractions if you'd like. I once was a famous actress, you know."

The hint of a smile disappeared, and he gave her a probing look. "Are you still acting?" He glanced down at her white robe. "Because I'm not sure what to think of you dressed like that if you're not."

"If I'm acting, I've done it poorly. I've never been able to make this thing feel comfortable, and I doubt I've convinced many people at the priory that I belong there. Atticus would be sorely disappointed." The mention of Atticus's name stopped her, and she changed the subject. "Aren't you only allowed on the island during the day?"

Reese glanced up at the dark blue sky. "Officially, yes."

"Then what are you doing skulking around in the darkness?"

"Turns out that's what uninvited, mostly unwanted guests do. They skulk, trying to figure out where their enemies are."

"Are you saying I'm your enemy?"

He let out a laugh that caught her off guard. "I hope not. I skulked around waiting for you to finish talking to Vivaine earlier, too, and heard your speech to her." Sable winced, but Reese just laughed again. "*That* was a good speech. I almost cheered from outside the window."

Sable shook her head. "It was all empty threats. There's nothing I can do against Vivaine, really." The wind blew her hair into her face again, and she pushed it back with more hostility than it deserved.

"Why not?"

"The latest reason? You."

Reese straightened. "Me?"

"She's been holding it over me that she has a spy in your camp. She knows exactly where you are, all the time. And she's willing to tell the Kalesh."

Reese stared at her. "I'm back to being furious at you."

"Because I was trying to keep you safe?" she demanded.

He crossed his arms. "I don't need to be kept safe."

"Really? Because a lot of people want to kill you. The kind of people who kill people."

"People have been trying to kill us for the last year," Reese said in exasperation. "That's nothing new."

There was a pop next to Sable on the wall, and the tiny, blue form of Purnicious appeared.

The kobold smiled widely up at Sable. "Good evening, mistress! I just found out Talia is here—" She paused, glancing between Reese's scowl and Sable's frown. "Good evening, wastrel. Are you angering my mistress?"

Andreese crossed his arms. "No more than she's angering me."

Purn sniffed. "I'm sure you deserve it."

"I thought my gift of that pretty purple cloak had changed your feelings about me," Reese said.

"It is a very nice cloak," Purn admitted. "But you still need to treat Lady Sable with the respect she deserves. Or..." She reached up and touched Reese's shirt.

The fabric began to shrink, tightening across his chest and around his arms.

"Purnicious!" he hissed, pulling at the collar that was tightening around his neck.

"Leave his shirt alone, Purn," Sable said, watching in amusement as Reese strained against the fabric.

The kobold sighed but dropped her hand.

"Put it back to how it was before," Reese demanded.

"I would," Purn said. "But shrinking is much easier than expanding." She looked at his shirt critically. "It was too loose before, anyway. Now it's better. Now my mistress can see your arm muscles. There's not much redeeming about you, wastrel, but you do have nice arms."

"Purnicious!" Sable said, exasperated. "Put his shirt back to normal."

"Do I have to? It will take a lot of time and energy, and I really think I improved it."

"Purn," Sable said with a little smile. "Fix the shirt."

The kobold sighed again but stepped up to Reese and set her fingers on the cloth. She closed her eyes, and slowly the shirt loosened. When she finished, it wasn't quite the same as it had been. It was more tailored across his shoulders and down his sides.

"This is still not back to how it was." Reese tugged at the shirt.

"No. It's better," Purn said smugly. "You're welcome."

Reese started to object.

"It does look better," Sable agreed.

He stopped, narrowing his eyes at Sable as though trying to tell if she was serious.

"Now," Sable said, turning back to Purn, "how is Talia? And is Ryah here?"

"Ryah is busy in Prioress Eugessa's house, and Talia is very busy in Lord Trelles's house." She sent an exasperated look across the square. "Lady Ingred brought an entire wagon full of dresses, so Talia will be busy for the whole night unpacking them and hanging them up."

"Why would she bring a wagon load of dresses?" Sable asked.

"*I need options,*" Purn said in a nasal, reasonably accurate imitation of Ingred's voice. "*You can never know what the right dress is until the day arrives.*" She rolled her large, purple eyes. "She's had nearly every dress she owns altered so she can have the option to wear them up here in what she calls the wilds."

Reese glanced down at the snug square. "Wilds?"

"Every hem had to be raised so it wouldn't drag on the filthy ground." Purn gave an irritated huff. "You know how much I enjoy clothes, mistress, but Ingred wearies even me." She held out the skirt of a light yellow dress she was wearing. "Although I am able to get some beautiful scraps to use for myself." The kobold glanced at Sable's plain, white robe. "Can I make anything for you?"

"I think I'm stuck with plain white for a bit longer." Sable set her hand on Purn's shoulder and stood.

Purnicious glanced back down toward the square. "Unless you need me, mistress, I'm going to help Talia. Only she and Callie know about me, and in such a small house, I may have to stay invisible all the time, but I'd like to try to help."

Sable frowned. "Why does Callie know about you?"

"Who is Callie?" Reese added.

"A friend of Talia's from when we lived in Dockside. She's..." Sable paused. "She's cheerful, and a little dense."

"She and Talia are inseparable," Purnicious said. "Talia's been so much less lonely since Callie started to visit Lady Ingred. I tried to stay hidden, but Callie walked in as Talia and I were talking one day." The kobold looked worried. "Talia said she can be trusted to keep our secret. I hope it's all right with you that she knows."

Sable looked skeptically at the kobold.

"Talia should know whether her friend is trustworthy, shouldn't she?" Reese asked.

"You would think," Sable said. At Reese's raised eyebrow, she added. "Maybe I don't give Callie enough credit."

"She seems trustworthy so far." Purnicious glanced back toward the square. "If you don't need anything, mistress, I'll go see if I can help with all the dresses."

"If Talia can get away from Ingred, let me know," Sable said. "Maybe she and I can meet somewhere. At this point my only plan is to try to make Narine comfortable and try to avoid Vivaine."

Purnicious wrinkled her long, blue nose at the High Prioress's name. "I wonder if I could bellish the fabric of her robe so she can't make it glow anymore," she muttered.

"I would love that," Sable said.

"Good night, mistress!" Purnicious gave her a quick smile, which turned faintly disapproving when she looked at Reese. "Good night, wastrel." She popped out of view.

"Vivaine makes her robe glow?" Reese asked.

Sable nodded. "Vivaine can…move light. Or twist it, or something. She can draw light from a window and wrap it around herself. It's how she always appears to be glowing."

Reese stared at her. "Which she uses to make everyone think she has Amah's blessing?"

"Yes. And she can see things that are far away. Last year in her chapel, she showed me all of you in the cells under the priory without either of us moving. She uses it to spy on people."

Reese frowned. "How far can she see?"

"She said seeing through the priory was exhausting to her, so not too far."

He glanced over at the gathering hall. "But she could be watching us right now?"

"For the past year, that's been my constant question: Is Vivaine watching?" She turned to glare at the hall, hoping Vivaine was paying attention. "Except I can't bring myself to care if she's watching me anymore." She considered Reese. "Although she might be keeping an eye on you."

"Tanis has promised to obey the truce."

Sable raised an eyebrow. "Have you?"

CHAPTER TWENTY-SIX

REESE SMILED. "I've made the same vows everyone else has. I can't imagine I'll get to the point of exchanging friendly greetings with the Kalesh, but if we can drive them out with diplomacy instead of fighting, I'll be happy. That's not how the Kalesh work, though. We need a show of strength, and that is something this land doesn't have. We're all too divided."

He turned to look at the buildings around the square. "That's the real reason we're here. We've been trying to unite the Northern Lords, but after generations of petty squabbling and border disputes, it's nearly impossible. I'm astonished all five are coming to the summit. Since we've never had the chance to speak to all of them at once, Tanis decided we should risk coming even without an invitation."

"What do the northern lords think of him?" Sable asked. "From the council meetings in the south, it seemed like they were all familiar with him."

"Tanis grew up in Lord Perric's army. Which is the largest northern army by a significant amount. He rose to captain before he began to object to the way the lords fought amongst themselves. There was a falling out between him and Perric, and while Perric wanted to discharge Tanis for insubordination, the troops were so loyal to him, Lord Perric thought some of the men would revolt.

"Tanis left on his own, though," Reese continued, "after promoting another popular man to captain. Said if any other men wanted to leave, they should do so of their own accord, not just to follow him."

"What did Lord Perric do?"

"Nothing. As far as he was concerned, it worked out perfectly. Over the years, Tanis has traveled the north, mostly helping to rebuild areas that have been damaged in skirmishes but sometimes stepping in to try to facilitate more peaceful solutions. He's not loyal to any of the lords, despite several of them offering him land to buy that loyalty, so he's usually an impartial voice in negotiations. The lords seem to respect him, even though they're annoyed he won't serve any of them."

"Has Tanis made any progress uniting them now?"

"Every time we think we have, something happens to destabilize it again. Some stupid border dispute or a skirmish in a remote area. Last week there was a problem between Lord Darien and Lord Runess over a herd of pigs. They were found along the border between the lands, and a farmer from each side claimed them." He let out an annoyed breath. "Turned into a pitched battle between two villages, which resulted in six deaths, and then someone slaughtered half the pigs." He glanced at her. "How are we supposed to unite them when they can't even sort out pigs peacefully?"

"None of them want unity?"

"The three lords on the western side of the Black River are open to discussions, but they're the smallest territories. Even united they're not as strong as Lord Perric. They'd be slightly bigger than Lord Runess, though. The biggest problem is Perric and Runess both have vast forests and are deep in discussions with the Kalesh about lumber trade. They want to be able to negotiate on their own without having to take the other territories into account, so they stall any attempt to unite with the western territories."

"If they are more concerned about lumber than unity," Sable said, "they can't be convinced the Kalesh are actually a threat."

He nodded. "The farther they are from Kalesh activity, the less they see them as a threat. Lord Loren owns the land the Kalesh were mining, so he's convinced they're a threat, but his territory is the weakest. It's mostly sparsely populated farmland."

Sable glanced at him. "The Kalesh claim you and Tanis attacked that mine in the night and killed all those miners."

He faced her, looking faintly betrayed. "And you believed them?"

"No. What really happened?"

He looked over the wall. Across the river, the tents of those not invited onto the island glowed with firelight. Past them, a wide valley snaked away into the Black Hills, lined with dark forests. Past it all was the jagged, black outline of the Scale Mountains.

"We were headed to destroy the mine. Tanis had been gathering information for several weeks, and we planned everything for late evening so that none of the mine workers would be underground. Our plan was to collapse as much of it as we could then get away before they caught us—except they knew we were coming.

"We were ambushed just outside the mine. Kalesh soldiers attacked, but we outnumbered them, so they used the miners for their front line. The poor men were armed with pickaxes and shovels. One miner tried to get out of the fight, but the soldier behind him cut him down. After that, the miners fought in earnest, and we had to fight back."

He was quiet for a moment. "Every miner died, and most of the Kalesh soldiers. The others retreated. We didn't even collapse the mine. Just damaged the entrance." He shook his head. "We still don't know who told them we were coming."

"Maybe you have more than just Vivaine's spy in your camp."

"Tanis thinks we have three. One that works for Vivaine, one giving information to the Kalesh, and another feeding information to the Northern Lords, who seem to know more about us than they should."

"You should keep closer tabs on your people."

"I've suggested that. But Tanis says the point of what we're doing is to allow people to be free. And if we start demanding proof of their loyalty, then we're no better than the Kalesh."

"Tanis and Narine would get along well. She's adamant that people be free from any kind of tyranny."

Reese looked over at her. "I can't imagine Vivaine agrees with a mindset like that."

"She doesn't. But Vivaine, much to her consternation, does not control Narine. So Narine refuses to vote in Vivaine's councils, claiming it isn't the priories' place to rule. Which, on one hand, makes me happy. But on the other," she sighed, "Narine's voice could sway things."

"Her presence here might disrupt the summit."

"I doubt it. Even if she's well enough, she won't vote. She won't take part in any of it. If we're lucky, no one will pay her any attention."

"Right," Reese said dryly. "Because the Phoenix Prioress isn't important."

"It's hard to remember that she is," Sable admitted. "She's so… unassuming. But she's also universally respected. I think if she spoke at these meetings, her words would carry weight. She's always on the side of peace, and she never wants power for herself."

Reese studied her while she spoke. "You sound like you respect her, too."

"I do. I've never met anyone quite like her."

"If she doesn't want power, what does she want?"

Sable smiled faintly. "She wants people to be free from their fears."

Reese considered her words. "But she's not interested in freeing them from real, living tyrants?" His question was more curious than accusatory.

"I've asked her that countless times. She always says our fears are tyrants. Usually worse than the living ones."

A monk approached along the wall, the torchlight catching along the edges of his leather armor.

He drew closer, and Sable recognized Sam. She glanced up at the sky that was definitely not a daytime color, and then at Reese, who should have been long gone.

But Sam merely gave her a friendly smile. "Good evening, Issable," he said. "I see you found her, Reese."

Reese looked at him in surprise. "You two have already met?"

"This is my island." Sam gave Reese a friendly slap on the shoulder. "I meet everyone. Have a nice evening, you two." He grinned and continued down the walkway.

"You know him?" Sable asked. "And he doesn't care that you're still here after dark?"

"I know most of the monks." Reese watched Sam disappear down the wall, which was now nearly pitch black in the gaps between the torches. "Tanis has worked with them for years. We help deliver food and supplies to some of the more remote towns. Sam and I have traveled together a few times. He's a good man."

Reese leaned against the wall, looking up into the darkening sky, his expression serious again. Something about his face reminded her of how unsatisfied he'd always been at how she held a sword, and it made her smile.

He glanced down at her. "Something funny?"

"Just remembering how impossible you were to please as a sword teacher."

A smile cracked through his gravity. "You were terrible at it." He held her gaze, studying her as though looking for the answer to some question, then reached into the collar of his shirt and drew out a small pendant. He pulled the leather cord over his head and held the necklace out to her.

She took the pendant and lifted it up to catch a bit of torchlight. It was a roughly carved wooden sword, not much larger than her thumbnail. "What is this?"

"The afternoon before your performance in the Grand Stadia, a boy was selling necklaces on the street." His smile widened. "It's the worst sword I've ever seen."

The blade bent in the middle so the tip pointed off to one side, and it didn't even line up with the hilt, which was skewed a bit itself.

Sable let out a laugh. "It looks like it was carved by someone who's never seen a sword."

He nodded. "But if you hold *that* sword the awful way you always did when you started movement two..." He looked at her expectantly.

"Movement two?" It had been a year since she'd thought about the sword exercises he'd given her, and it took her a moment to remember it. She shifted her feet, moved her elbow out slightly, and raised the sword pendant in front of her chest.

He let out a chuckle. "See? If you hold it all wrong, as you always do, the tip of this sword actually points up, as a sword should to start movement two."

She grinned at the tiny blade. "They should make a real sword exactly like this, just for movement two." She held the necklace back out to him, but he shook his head.

"I bought it for you. Only, when I got back to the Stadia, your hair was all"—he wiggled his fingers toward his head—"elaborate, and you were dressed so…" He shook his head. "You were too elegant for a sword that looked like it had been carved by a drunk man."

Sable looked at the necklace, then back at Reese. "You kept it? All this time?"

He shifted. "Well, no one else would want such an ugly thing."

The tiny sword spun slowly from the cord, the torchlight catching on all the crooked angles. Sable pulled it over her head. "I like it." She settled the pendant on the front of her robe. "How does it look?"

His smile faded as his gaze lingered on the white, formless serving robe she wore. "Anything's an improvement over priory white." He shifted to face the town of Aedis.

Sable rolled the little sword between her fingers, watching his face turn serious again. "This last year," she began, then paused, unsure of what she wanted to say. "Has it been hard?"

"In some ways." He glanced at her. "Has yours?"

She almost laughed. He'd spent the year as a rebel soldier, and she had stayed safely enclosed in a comfortable priory. She started to shake her head, but she could almost hear Narine's words. *It's best to speak the truth or nothing at all.*

She looked down at Narine's house. "Yes, although probably in different ways than yours." She felt him watching her and glanced over.

A smile played at the edges of his lips. "You write terrible letters," he said. "You had a whole year's worth of news, and you told me nothing but that the priories don't have flat roofs. Which I already knew."

"It wasn't just friendly correspondence," Sable protested. "And yours was no better."

He shrugged, and his smile widened. For the first time all night, she caught a glimpse of a familiar, old expression. "I thought you liked your letters short and terse and impersonal."

He glanced over Sable's shoulder, and the smile fell off his face. He pushed himself off the wall. "Kalesh," he said, his voice harsh.

Sable turned to see two men walking along the wall. Even in the dimness, the Kalesh robes of the first man were visible.

Regardless of what Reese had said about following the truce, he moved to stand beside her, his hand going to where his sword hilt must usually sit. Finding nothing there, he crossed his arms.

"I'll keep them here," Reese said quietly. "You can take the ladder and get into Narine's house. They won't bother you there."

"There's a truce," she reminded him. "They won't bother me anywhere."

He gave her a quick, disbelieving look. "This peace is held together by a thread. These are not our friends."

The Kalesh man in the front came closer, and Sable recognized the ambassador. The torchlight caught off the long scar on his cheek.

"Issable?" he called to her in a friendly voice. "What an unexpected pleasure!"

Reese turned slowly to look at her. "At least, they're not my friends."

CHAPTER TWENTY-SEVEN

"Good evening, Ambassador," Sable said, ignoring Reese's shock.

General Goll stopped just behind the ambassador, his face far less friendly.

"It is a pleasant surprise to have Prioress Narine attend the summit," Ambassador Bastian said. "I hope she is in good health."

"I'm afraid she is not," Sable answered. "She did not intend to come here. We were traveling to visit some of the abbeys she oversees when she fell gravely ill. We brought her here in the hopes that someone could help."

The ambassador's face grew grim. "I'm sorry to hear that. If our healers can be of any use, they are at your disposal."

Sable gave him a grateful smile. "Thank you."

Behind Ambassador Bastian, General Goll was studying Reese.

The ambassador turned an amiable smile toward Reese. "I don't believe I know your companion."

Sable glanced at Reese. "I believe you do, by reputation. Ambassador Bastian, may I introduce you to Andreese of Ravenwick."

General Goll's expression turned bleak, and he reached for his sword, which wasn't on his hip either. He started forward, but the ambassador, whose expression had also darkened, held up his hand. The general bristled but stopped.

Reese took a step forward, but Sable set her hand on his arm. "I was under the impression that the summit was established under the flag of truce," she said quickly, moving up to stand in between Reese and the Kalesh. "If I'm not mistaken, the point of all this is to meet without violence."

"This man was not invited." General Goll fixed Reese with a look of pure hatred.

"Tanis and Andreese have already spoken to the monks and the Dragon Prioress," Sable said. "And have been invited to the summit. You have all sworn the same vow of peace." None of the three men around her relaxed. Underneath her hand, Reese's arm was hard. "Andreese, may I introduce you to Ambassador Bastian? And this is General Goll."

At the general's name, Andreese drew in a breath. *"Masar ze Marabi!"*

The ambassador straightened at the Kalesh words, and the general gave Andreese a wolflike smile.

"What does that mean?" Sable asked.

"The Butcher of Marabi," Reese answered.

"An unfortunate nickname," the ambassador said. "General Goll led a military encounter near the town of Marabi years ago." As always, the ambassador's words were true.

"A successful military encounter," Goll added.

Ambassador Bastian shifted. "Yes." The ambassador's tone remained confident, but for the first time in her acquaintance with him, Sable felt the cold trace of a lie in the word.

"It wasn't successful for the people of Marabi." Reese's voice was low. "He killed them all, Sable. Every last one of them."

"People who are weak should not rebel," the general said. "Quelling a violent rebellion is always a success."

"The people around Marabi were farmers." Reese took a step forward. "Your men butchered them and their families."

"Those farmers were hiding a violent, insidious faction of rebels who were planning an assassination on the emperor himself," Goll said coldly.

"An assassination?" Reese gave a derisive snort. "The only things those rebels had ever done was to burn down the silk factories along the northern ridge. They were murdered because they cost the Empire too much money."

The general leaned forward. "That is something you might want to keep in mind."

"Issable is right," the ambassador said firmly. "The point of this summit is to settle these differences peacefully. The Kalesh intend to abide by the truce." He gave the general a pointed look. "Including not threatening the people we've come to treat with."

The general's expression didn't change, nor did Reese's.

"Issable," the ambassador said with a slight bow of his head, "always a pleasure to see you. And, Andreese, I am hopeful we can come to terms that lead to peace."

"Peace is what we are after," Reese answered, keeping his eyes fixed on the general.

"Until tomorrow, then," the ambassador said, turning and setting his hand on General Goll's shoulder.

The general held Reese's gaze for another breath, then spun on his heel and headed back down the wall. The ambassador followed.

Reese turned to face Sable. "I had no idea you were on such friendly terms with the Kalesh ambassador and the Butcher of Marabi."

"I am *not* on good terms with the general. But Ambassador Bastian has always been a proponent of peace between the Kalesh and us."

He stared at her. "You can't believe that."

"Yes. Actually I can." Sable crossed her arms. "I know when he's telling the truth, remember? You know the one thing he lied about just now? That the fight at Marabi was a success."

Reese scowled at her. "You expect me to believe that the ambassador for the Kalesh Empire isn't impressed with General Goll's most famous victory?"

"I expect you to believe that he was lying about it being a success,"

Sable said bluntly. "I have been in meetings with Ambassador Bastian for nearly a year, and I can tell you the man wants peace."

"At what cost?"

"He's Kalesh," Sable said. "He wants the same thing all the Kalesh do. Control of our gold mines. But he and the general are very different men."

Reese shook his head slowly. "Bastian would not have been appointed ambassador unless he is utterly loyal to the Empire." His brow creased. "There was a Bastian. He was a pellot—a military leader. Like a captain. He put down a rebellion in the northwest corner of the Empire, in an area called the White Wood." Reese looked along the dark wall in the direction the two Kalesh men had disappeared. "I remember it because it was led by a woman—a woman Pellot Bastian defeated."

"It might not be the same man," Sable said.

"The last ambassador was a retired general. Everyone high in the Kalesh government is a retired general. If this isn't Bastian of the White Wood, then I promise you he has an equally violent past."

The idea of Ambassador Bastian as a ruthless general didn't sit right.

When she didn't answer, Reese said, "No matter how nice he is to you, Sable, we can't trust the Empire."

Trust is given to individual people, not entire nations, Sable heard Narine's voice say.

"Then what's the point of trying to create a treaty?"

"I'm not sure there is one," Reese said. "What we should be focusing on is providing a stronger, more united front against the Empire. As far as I'm concerned, the value of everyone being here is the chance to unify the north, not to come up with a way to diplomatically control the Kalesh."

A low bird call sounded from across the buildings, and Reese glanced toward it. "I need to go." He moved to the top of the ladder.

She felt a flash of disappointment and took a step after him. "Reese."

He stopped, but his face still had the hard, distant look, and she couldn't decide what she wanted to say.

"Be careful here," he said. "There are too many powerful people in one place."

"You be careful too," she answered, "with all your skulking."

She thought he'd smile, but his look stayed solemn.

"You do make me a little furious," he said, "but I am happy to see you, Sable."

The warmth of his words wrapped around her so strongly that she leaned into them, closing her eyes at the sheer comfort of them.

She opened her eyes to answer him, but he was halfway down the ladder. She watched until he reached the bottom, but he didn't look back up before heading off along the base of the wall, disappearing into the darkness.

She leaned back against the parapet and ran her fingers over the little sword pendant. The night sky had darkened almost to black, and dozens of stars twinkled down at her. There was a vast, blanketing peace about it, hovering just too high for her to reach.

CHAPTER TWENTY-EIGHT

THE NEXT MORNING, Sable woke to the hushed tones of four abbesses busily working around Narine. She'd lain awake for hours the night before, her brain churning through thoughts of Vivaine and Narine and Reese and the Kalesh until her head had ached with exhaustion. This morning, her eyes felt like someone had poured sand into them.

Judging from the light trickling in the windows and the number of candles lit around Narine, it was barely dawn. Sable settled back into the cot someone had nestled against the wall for her.

The house they'd given Narine was snug and tidy. The timber framing was visible from the inside, too. Thick beams of rich, textured browns crisscrossed on the stucco walls. The ceilings were low, and the front room held a wood stove, a small table, and several chairs. Most of which had been pushed out of the way so that Narine's couch could be situated near the stove. A tiny table sat near each end of the couch, filled with herbs and medicines.

A short, skinny hallway at the back led to a washroom and the back door, and a stairway climbed to a room upstairs where the other abbesses had slept.

Sable sat up. "How is she?" she asked Sister Caryn, who was puttering near the stove.

Caryn paused. "She's more comfortable than she was yesterday."

On her couch, Narine lay still and pale. Sable worked her way between the abbesses and sat by Narine's curled up legs, reaching out to take the prioress's hand in her own. Narine's fingers were ice cold and limp.

"Is there anything I can do?" Sable asked.

Caryn sighed. "I don't think there's anything anyone can do."

The front door opened, and a white figure stepped inside.

"Holy Mother!" Caryn dropped into a curtsey.

Vivaine smiled benevolently and moved into the room, bringing a bit of the dawn's grey light with her.

Dozens of flashes of light scattered across the walls as Vivaine's dragon slid through the door behind her, his silver scales shimmering like stars.

The whole room hushed at the sight.

"Sister Orna told me everything up through midnight," Vivaine said, stepping toward Narine. "Tell me what's been done this morning to treat the prioress."

Sister Caryn pulled her eyes away from Argyros and started her report while the other abbesses backed out of the way.

Vivaine came over to the couch and gave Sable an expectant look, as though waiting for her to move.

Sable gave her a cold smile back but stayed sitting near Narine's feet. "Good morning, Holy Mother. How kind of you to come visit us."

Vivaine met her glance unapologetically. "I couldn't bear not to come."

Those words were at least true.

"It's so hard to remember you were once a healer," Sable said. "Long...long ago."

Vivaine smiled at her faintly. "It has been a long time."

An abbess brought over a stool, and Vivaine sat down, setting her hand gently on Narine's forehead. She began to ask the abbesses a series of questions while Argyros slid closer.

"We've tried everything we can think of." Caryn clasped her hands with worry. "The Kalesh sent over a healer last night, as did the monks, but none of their remedies worked any better than our own."

As the warmth of Caryn's words wrapped around Sable, she began to feel something else. First, beyond Vivaine, a hot, molten heat emanated from the dragon. Vivaine herself simmered like a bed of coals. Caryn too, and the abbesses farther away were like smoldering fires.

But from Narine, there was almost nothing. Sable gripped her hand, but there was barely more warmth from the prioress than from the couch itself.

Over next to the mantel, sitting on her perch, Innov was equally cool, her feathers so dim that in the shadowy edge of the room, the bird was barely visible.

Vivaine kept one hand on Narine's forehead and set her other hand on Argyros's scaled head.

Innov let out a squawk and shifted on her perch. No sparks fell from her feathers.

Vivaine began to pray quietly, just loud enough that the abbesses could hear what she was doing.

Slowly the High Prioress grew warmer, drawing heat from Argyros. As she did, Sable sensed a faint pulse of warmth in Narine. It had nothing to do with Vivaine's words—the High Prioress's prayers felt empty—but somehow Sable could feel every person in the room.

Sable leaned forward, but Vivaine didn't stop. The High Prioress now glowed with a warmth second only to Argyros.

The windows of the room were brightening gradually, and Vivaine herself seemed to be as well. Argyros's scales glittered with the reflected light.

Narine drew in a deeper breath, and her feet shifted beneath the blanket, pressing against Sable's leg. Vivaine continued her quiet prayer, and the blazing heat from Argyros continued to flow through the High Prioress into Narine. Between Sable's hands, Narine's fingers warmed.

The Phoenix Prioress's eyes fluttered open.

Sister Caryn let out a gasp and stepped forward. "Praise Amah!" she breathed.

Vivaine pulled her hand off Narine's forehead and off the dragon. The heat of the High Prioress faded slowly back to what she'd been before as Vivaine fixed Narine with a dazzling smile. "Dear Sister, we were afraid we'd lost you."

Narine blinked up at Vivaine, then she took in the room, and she was silent for a long moment until her gaze landed on Sable. "You brought me to the summit." Her voice was whisper-quiet, but the accusation in her words hit Sable like a punch.

"Of course they did," Vivaine said warmly. "It's where you should have been the whole time, my dear."

Narine flexed her fingers. She looked at Vivaine, then her gaze dropped to Argyros, who waited next to the High Prioress. "What did you do?" she whispered.

"She prayed for you!" Sister Caryn crowded up close to the couch. "And Amah healed you!"

Narine kept her eyes on the dragon. Innov squawked again from her perch, the noise sounding almost threatening.

"Even Innov is excited!" Sister Caryn said. "She's been terribly low the past few days. Almost no fire in her at all." The abbess turned toward Vivaine. "We are forever in your debt, Holy Mother."

The High Prioress stood, still glowing slightly. "Thank Amah, not me. I did nothing."

Sable flinched at the frigid bite of the lie.

Vivaine gave Narine a gentle smile. "I'll leave you to rest, dear. It does my heart good to see you awake." She waited a moment, as though waiting for Narine to thank her. When the Phoenix Prioress stayed quiet, Vivaine patted her gently on the shoulder. "I wish I could stay longer, but the summit begins tomorrow, and the rest of the delegations will begin arriving today."

"I won't be voting," Narine said.

"No one expects you to, dear."

The lie in that line was so sharp that Sable was astounded no one else could feel it.

"Just get some rest." Vivaine turned and left the room, Argyros following after her. When the door closed behind her, the room darkened.

Innov let out an irritated squawk and flapped her wings. With an effort, she flew over to the end of the couch. Narine pulled her hand out of Sable's grip and ran it gently down the bird's feathers. The prioress's face was drawn with something Sable had rarely seen —anger.

"The prioress needs rest," Sable told Caryn. The abbess nodded and motioned for the others to leave. They filed upstairs.

Sable waited for Narine to speak, but the prioress kept her focus on Innov.

"Would you…like some tea?" Sable asked softly.

The prioress's finger paused on the phoenix's dim chest. "You brought me to the summit." Narine's voice was so papery thin Sable barely heard her, but the words smoldered with her displeasure.

Sable leaned toward her. "I didn't know what else to do. We were in the forest, and there was nothing else around. There was nowhere to take you."

The prioress let out a tired breath and turned, her expression so raw that it clawed into Sable. "Why do you think I took myself to the forest?"

Sable shifted against the warm truth of Narine's words. "I couldn't just let you die."

The edge of betrayal that seeped into Narine's eyes cut into Sable.

"I thought you, of all people, would understand the freedom I was after."

The blazing force of those words wrapped around Sable, and she couldn't breathe.

Narine's brow creased in something that looked like pain, and she turned back to Innov. "You've merely given me more days of waiting." The phoenix's feathers were dull, and not a single spark fell from the bird as Narine ran the back of her fingers down the bird's chest. She let her hand fall. "I can't hear the trees," she whispered.

The warmth of Narine's words seared through the cozy house until the room was stifling, the walls too close. Sable closed her eyes. There was no sound of trees, no sound of…anything. They might as well have been in Narine's room back in the priory. Sable slid off the couch and dropped to her knees, taking Narine's hand, the realization of what she'd done rising to choke her.

"I'm so sorry." The words barely made it out. She looked helplessly at the prioress. "I couldn't let you die." The words sounded small and hollow.

Narine sighed. "And you think you stopped that?"

Sable dropped her gaze to the prioress's thin hand. No, none of this would change anything.

Unless Vivaine *had* somehow healed her.

There was more color in Narine's cheeks than normal, and her fingers weren't ice cold. "What did Vivaine do to you? Do you feel better?"

Narine's lips tightened into a thin line. "Don't let her do that again."

Sable opened her mouth to ask more, but Narine just gave her a flat look.

"Do *not* let her do it again."

Sable drew back at the ferocity in the words but nodded.

Narine closed her eyes. "Yes, I would like some tea," she said, her voice tired.

Sable hesitated, guilt and worry and frustration warring inside her. But Narine coughed, a dry, raspy sound, and Sable turned to heat some water.

CHAPTER TWENTY-NINE

THE MORNING SUN poured into the front windows of the little house, bringing in warmth and enough light that Sable could see that Narine's cheeks held their slight color, even while a string of abbesses and monks stopped by to wish her well. Whatever Vivaine had done, Narine was stronger than she'd been in months. She sat on the couch, attentively listening to each person who came, not once laying her head back in exhaustion.

When an abbess brought Narine's lunch, Sable followed the most recent guest to the door, ready to shut out the world and give Narine some quiet while she ate.

Until she saw a slim figure walking up to the door, carrying a plate of cinnamon bread.

"Ryah!"

Her youngest sister beamed at her. "We heard that Prioress Narine was here and had to come see how she was."

Behind Ryah, Prioress Eugessa strode across the square. She wore her white gown, but her neck and wrists glittered with necklaces and bracelets. Her hands were crusted with rings, and her hair, which was currently dyed a rich purplish brown, had little sparkling gems nestled in it.

"Narine will love the bread," Sable murmured, "but did you need to bring the prioress?"

"Prioress Eugessa is very excited to see Prioress Narine," Ryah said quietly but earnestly. "I don't believe she expected to see her again."

"Well," Sable whispered as Eugessa drew closer, "I doubt I can keep her out." She raised her voice. "So do come in. The prioress will be very excited about the bread."

Sable held the door open for Ryah, who crossed the room to where Narine sat on the couch. Eugessa reached the door and paused, fixing Sable with an irritated look. "I did not expect to have the pleasure of seeing you, Narine," Eugessa said loudly into the room. She lowered her voice and glared at Sable. "Nor did I think Vivaine controlled you so completely that you'd drag Narine somewhere she didn't want to be."

Without waiting for Sable to answer, Eugessa brushed past her and headed toward the couch. Sable followed, moving Narine's lunch to make room for the cinnamon bread.

Narine smiled up at Eugessa and Ryah. "How kind of you to think of me. How on earth did you make cinnamon bread here?"

"The monks were more than happy to hand over the use of their kitchen to my staff." Eugessa's words were cold enough that Sable could imagine how eager the monks had actually been. "They were going to feed us nothing but vegetables and lamb for the whole summit," she said with a laugh. "We'd all be as scrawny as you by the end."

Sable shot Eugessa a scowl, and Ryah's smile turned uncomfortable, but the Prioress of the Horn merely flounced down on the couch and took Narine's frail hand in her own jewel-encrusted fingers.

"My dear," Eugessa began in a motherly voice, "now that you're somewhere civilized, you must do nothing but rest. Do not let Vivaine drag you into all these silly summit meetings. I've instructed the kitchen to make you cinnamon bread every day, and I insist that you stay on this couch and rest."

Sable walked away from the couch to the counter along the wall, reaching for the pitcher of water to fill the kettle.

Ryah joined her. "I think Eugessa means well," she whispered.

Sable gave her sister a doubtful look. "She just wants what she always wants, which is for Narine to stay out of the council meetings. But since I want Narine to rest as well, I'm hardly going to object."

"Prioress Eugessa was sad after she said goodbye to Prioress Narine in Immusmala." Ryah glanced back at the two women on the couch. "When she returned to her room, she dismissed everyone, and I'm positive I heard her crying."

Sable tried to keep a skeptical look off her face. "She can't be sad to lose the threat of Narine changing the balance of things."

"I'm sure she's not. But I do think she genuinely cares for the prioress. She doesn't have cinnamon bread made for anyone else."

Sable turned to watch the two women. Narine should have been dwarfed by the size and the noise and the glittery colors of Eugessa, but the Phoenix Prioress somehow managed to fill her own space on the couch. Narine set her thin hand on Eugessa's head in blessing and said something quietly. Whatever it was, Eugessa closed her eyes, and for just a moment she looked like all the abbesses who came to Narine for comfort.

But then Eugessa straightened, and when Narine lowered her hand, Eugessa patted it with a placating gesture. "Promise me you will rest," she demanded loudly. "I will not stand for you being up and about. All of the conflict between the Kalesh and the rebels and the merchants will do nothing but trouble you. Promise me you will stay here and enjoy the peace of this lovely home." The slightly patronizing glance she shot around the small house disappeared when she turned back to Narine and smiled again.

Sable turned back to the kettle and started to fill it.

"I really am pleased to see you," Eugessa finished, and a bit of warmth pressed against Sable.

She glanced toward the prioress in surprise, and some water splashed down the side of the kettle.

"See?" Ryah whispered.

Sable gave her a reluctant nod and put the kettle on top of the wood stove. Ryah found a towel and cleaned up the spilled water.

"I ran into Thulan on the west bank of the river," Sable said.

Ryah's face lit up. "How was she?"

"She seemed good. She, Leonis, and Atticus are camped near the priories and the merchants on the riverbank."

Ryah gave a wide smile. "Maybe I can find a way to get over there and see them."

"You look tired, dear," Eugessa said loudly, rising from the couch. "We'll leave you to rest." She came across the room to stand next to Ryah. "I hope you've had a nice chat." She gave them a sugary smile, then focused on Sable.

"Whatever Prioress Vivaine says," Eugessa said in a quiet tone, "everyone knows you have a great deal of sway over the Phoenix Prioress. I expect you to do your job and take good care of her. The woman needs rest. The High Prioress may be determined to have dear Narine at these councils, but that is not acceptable." She lifted a hand to toy with the necklaces hanging around her neck. The ring on her smallest finger glittered with cloudy blue gems. Sable glared at the butterfly ring before refocusing on Eugessa's face.

"I know," Eugessa continued, her voice lower and sickeningly sympathetic, "that at times Prioress Vivaine has"—she paused, as though looking for a delicate word—"*reminded* you that dear Ryah is under the supervision of the priories. Perhaps that fact has led you to feel beholden to the High Prioress, but I want to remind you of the real truth." Eugessa set her other hand firmly on Ryah's shoulder. Ryah shifted slightly under the weight. "Ryah is not under the supervision of Prioress Vivaine. She is under mine." Her fingers tightened, and Ryah winced. Eugessa kept her eyes fixed on Sable. "You shouldn't be worried about what you think the High Prioress holds over you. There are other things to worry about."

Eugessa's lips spread in a humorless smile when she dropped her hand from Ryah's shoulder. She glanced back at Narine. "Get some rest, my dear," she called sweetly, "and enjoy the bread."

The Prioress of the Horn started toward the door. "Sister Ryah," she snapped, without looking back.

Ryah rubbed her shoulder and handed Sable the towel. She gave Sable a troubled look before following the prioress.

Sable gripped the towel tightly as she watched Ryah's small, white form hurry out the door.

"Come sit." Narine patted the couch next to her. "Have some bread while it's warm."

Sable walked over and sank down, picking up a piece of bread. Her fingers sank into a sticky swirl of cinnamon. She took a bite, and the warm, sweet taste was surprisingly comforting.

"See?" Narine said. "Cinnamon bread makes everything better."

Sable let out a huff of amusement. "It does nothing of the sort. But it is delicious."

Narine smiled. "It is."

They ate in silence, and before long, Narine rested her head back. Sable helped her lie down and pulled a blanket over her.

For the next couple of hours, Sable turned away any visitors who came to the door. Whichever monk normally lived in this house had a handful of books on a shelf. The largest of the set was titled *Noteworthy Battles*, and Sable pulled it down and flipped through it. The book described six different battles, complete with maps and diagrams of troop movements. There were discussions on defensive positions and how they were attacked, the decisions made by the opposing sides, and the merits of each.

The work was surprisingly engaging, and Sable sat at the table under the window, learning more than she'd ever expected to about the ways battles were won.

Four of the six battles had been won by a vastly inferior force, mostly by pitting their own strengths against their larger enemies' weaknesses, and the correlation to the current situation with the Kalesh was undeniable.

She was on the fourth battle, completely absorbed in how a small band of men was weakening a strategic section of a huge city wall, when there was a quiet knock on the door, tapped out in a cheery little rhythm.

Sable glanced out the window and saw a merchant's handcart. Colorful wares spilled out from under the wooden lid. She opened the door and found a man who smiled at her through his curly, blond beard. "Hello, I was wondering if the good prioress is well enough for a visit from an old friend."

Something about the man struck Sable as familiar. His curly beard was matched with blond eyebrows that were a bit on the bushy side. He was short and wiry, dressed in flowing pants colored a deep red, a white shirt bright enough to fit in with the abbesses, and a jaunty suede hat flaunting a long, blue feather.

"I'm afraid she's sleeping," Sable said.

But Narine's voice came faintly from inside. "Who's at the door, Issable?"

"A very old friend," the man called out with a mischievous sort of smile.

The man looked too young to be a very old anything, but Sable heard a rustle, and Narine peered over the back of the couch. "Flibbet?"

The man's smile widened.

"Come in! Come in!" Narine called. "How long has it been?"

Sable raised an eyebrow but moved out of the way, and Flibbet gave her an elaborate, flourishing bow before he came into the room and strode to the couch.

"It's been entirely too long," he said, taking a chair from the table Sable had sat at and setting it in front of Narine's couch. "I'm in Immusmala several times a year, but they never let peddlers into the Sanctuary unless there's a festival, and your stuffy Sanctus guards never let me into your priory to say hello. They seem to think I'm not serious about knowing you."

Narine glanced at his hat. "It's hard to understand why anyone wouldn't take you seriously."

"I know," he said, grinning.

The man's quick smile struck Sable again as familiar, but she couldn't quite place where she'd seen him.

"Issable," Narine said, "come sit with us. This is my very old friend, Flibbet. And Flibbet, this is Issable, who's been my companion for the past year."

Sable pulled her own chair over and sat.

Flibbet gave Sable a polite nod. "When you have a celebrated actress for a caregiver, Narine, she doesn't really need an introduction."

"I was only an actress very briefly," Sable said.

"But very famously," he answered. "I actually saw you perform three times. I'm well acquainted with Atticus and try to never miss a show of his if I'm nearby. I saw your portrayal of Vivaine the first night of the Midsommer Festival, and I was also in the Grand Stadia during the...dramatic performance there." He shook his head. "Up until the moment the ambassador was killed, it was possibly the best performance I've ever seen." He paused. "I haven't always been a great fan of the High Prioress, but that night, I almost became one."

"Well, I hope that's worn off by now," Sable said grimly.

Flibbet's smile turned wry. "It has."

Sable frowned at him. "When was the third time?"

"I saw you act in Folhaven as well."

"The night before the festival? You watched the play about Vivaine three times?"

"No, I saw you act in Folhaven weeks earlier. You played the role of Lady Argent in the story of Terrelus."

Sable winced. "I'm so sorry you had to see that. That was the first show I ever performed with Atticus, and...it was rough."

Flibbet laughed a long, rolling sound. The freeness of it caught at Sable, and she found herself smiling too.

"The beginning was painfully awkward," he agreed, "but by the end I was astounded that Terrelus could ignore your pleas and keep on his foolish, tragic path."

Narine leaned forward, her eyes bright. "You never told me this story, Issable."

"Well," Flibbet said, settling back in his chair, "it's one you should hear. The play began splendidly, as Atticus's plays always do, until a very small, very timid Lady Argent stepped out on stage."

Sable grimaced as Flibbet recounted how disastrous the scene had been. But his telling was so lively and light, Narine began to chuckle.

When Flibbet stood and acted out the wooden way Sable had talked, and how stiffly she'd held her arms, Sable smiled at the accuracy of it all.

"At the end of the scene," he said, "Argent's final words—that glorious plea to the stars for hope—fell to the stage like a rock. And she just stood there, looking utterly lost."

Sable's smile was half grimace. "I was supposed to finish speaking back near the curtain, but I'd forgotten and was up at the front of the stage."

Flibbet's eyes gleamed with mirth. "So she just said the line again, no better than the first time, and practically ran off stage."

Narine let out a laugh that rang through the room like the priory bells, and Sable grinned at the sound. She hadn't heard Narine laugh in months.

"That was an excellent story, Flibbet." The prioress wiped her eyes. "I had no idea you began so awfully, Issable! The only time I saw you act, it was so masterful. I thought you'd always been that perfect."

"She was a very quick learner," Flibbet continued. "By the end of the play, Lady Argent received the loudest cheers."

Sable shook her head wryly. "That night was awful."

"Awful nights make the best stories," he said. "Most of my favorite stories weren't funny until long after they happened."

Sable straightened at the sentiment. "That's where I know you from!"

CHAPTER THIRTY

"You were at the Red Shield Festival last year!" Sable said to Flibbet. "You were near Atticus's stage, and you sold me leeswine in exchange for two cheap copper hairpins."

"Plus the story behind them," he added. "I already recognized you, but I didn't think you'd remember a single peddler among all the bustle."

"That wine was my introduction to Atticus's troupe," Sable said. "It was a very important bottle. You also told me that my night didn't seem funny then, but it might in the future."

Flibbet's smile widened. "And does it?"

Sable paused. She'd stolen those hairpins from some wealthy woman to pay for the wine, and she'd been working so hard to get Talia out from under Kiva's grip. But that was also the night she'd convinced Leonis to help her pretend to be arrested...it was like thinking of a different life, the distance lessening the fears and making her feel rather fondly about Leonis and his constable costume. She nodded. "A bit."

Sable looked between Flibbet and Narine. "How do you two know each other?"

"Flibbet and I grew up in the same town," Narine looked critically at Flibbet's curly, blond beard. "Although you don't look like you're old enough to have known me back then."

Sable nodded in agreement.

"Even if you can't see the years," he answered, "I assure you I can feel them." He turned to Sable. "I've known Narine since she was sixteen years old. Back when she had the sharpest tongue in Brecklen."

"Narine?" Sable said in disbelief.

He nodded. "One day, she found me 'loitering' in front of the abbey. She gave me such a dressing down that an audience gathered! Said I was making the abbey look 'shabby and disreputable.' I remember clearly because shabby rhymed with abbey, but when I pointed that out to her, she was not amused."

Narine smiled fondly. "He was covered in dirt. Absolutely covered. At first, I didn't even know who he was."

"And we all know," Flibbet said, "being dirty because you've been working hard all day is a terrible thing."

"I can't believe she yelled at you!" Sable said. "I've never heard her yell at anyone."

He leaned toward Sable and said, in a conspiratorial whisper, "Everyone in Brecklen called her Mean Narine."

Sable let out a burst of laughter. "No!"

"It's true." Narine smiled ruefully.

Flibbet nodded. "She could lash anyone with that tongue."

"How often did she yell at you?"

"Daily."

Narine objected, but Flibbet nodded sagely. "At least until I started peddling. One of Narine's jobs as a young abbess was to visit two outlying abbeys each month to bring them supplies, and the abbey enlisted me and my cart to help her. It took a few trips, but she eventually became less bossy." He let out another laugh that almost brightened the room. "Do you remember the time that one abbess berated you for taking those papers?"

"It was only three pages," Narine said to Sable. "I'd taken them to give to the children who lived in a tiny little cottage behind the abbey, but Sister Protty was furious. She kept records of all of the supplies in the abbey. Spent hours a day recording things. And if you took anything without telling her…" Narine shook her head.

"Not long after," Flibbet said with a grin, "the Phoenix Prioress came from Immusmala to visit, and Narine decided to get even."

"There was no reason for all the records," Narine explained. "The prioress wasn't going to look at them or care about them. She just needed a general sense of how the abbey was doing."

"So," Flibbet said, "Narine slipped into Protty's office the night before the prioress was to arrive and rearranged everything. She took piles of papers and mixed them into other piles, and she rearranged all the books on her bookshelf. She even pulled out the stitches in Protty's record book, mixed up the pages, and sewed it back together!"

Sable stared at Narine. "You did?"

Narine nodded, her wide smile almost girlish. "It took the entire night."

Sable sat back, trying to imagine Narine so young and petty. "Flibbet, I am so happy you came by tonight. I had no idea Narine wasn't always perfectly gracious and kind to everyone."

Narine looked fondly at the peddler. "It was Flibbet who helped me change, actually. Something he said once."

He frowned at her. "I don't remember you ever listening to a word I said."

"I usually didn't, but I had yelled at a younger abbess for having a dirty gown, and you told me that I shouldn't lash out at people just because I was afraid."

Flibbet's brow creased. "I don't remember saying that."

"Well, you did. We were in that small town with the huge tree in the square."

"Telton," Flibbet said.

"Yes, that was it." Narine paused. "I yelled at you for such an outlandish suggestion, but the words plagued me." She smiled self-consciously. "For a while they just made me angry with you, but eventually, I realized you were right. I had yelled at that abbess because I was afraid to be like her. Afraid that if I wasn't perfect—perfectly dressed, perfectly dutiful, perfectly perfect—that everyone would know the truth. That I was lost and unsure. All day, every day."

She glanced at Sable. "That changed everything for me. It didn't take too long to realize that everyone around me was suffering from the same thing. Not the exact same fear, of course. Everyone had their own version. But it wasn't lords or prioresses who controlled me or the people around me, it was the fear inside us. Fear we fed and nurtured, even as it wrapped chains around us."

Narine looked down at her hands. "Once you see everyone around you as terrified creatures, trapped in their own fears, it's easy to have compassion on them."

"You did ask me once what I was afraid of," Flibbet said slowly, "and I couldn't answer you."

Narine grimaced. "I wasn't very good at talking about it back then. No one talks about the things they're afraid of, you know. They try not to think about them at all unless they're awake and alone at night when the thoughts are nearly impossible to avoid. So it's a hard subject to broach, and I wasn't particularly good at connecting with people yet."

Flibbet grinned at her. "No, you were still mostly insulting. But the question stuck with me nevertheless, and the answer, when I found it, changed everything for me as well. I had bought my peddler's cart from an old man who wanted to spend the rest of his days in front of a hearth instead of sitting on a hard wagon seat, but I was afraid to leave the few towns I knew. I was afraid that if I went somewhere new, I'd be so insignificant that no one would even notice me." He glanced at Sable. "And while it's true that a peddler needs to be noticed, a human being does, too."

"That's what convinced you to finally leave?" Narine asked. "You'd talked about it for so long."

He nodded. "The fear wasn't unfounded, but when I realized it was the thing keeping me from actually setting out to see the world, it felt less..."

"Powerful," Narine offered.

Flibbet nodded. "And so, Narine, I have always felt indebted to you for that question." He paused. "Of course, if I'd known how pivotal my words had been in your life, I would have considered us even."

"Do you ever go back to Brecklen?" Narine asked. "The abbey isn't there any longer, so I have no reason to visit."

Flibbet nodded and began to tell her what had changed in the town over the years. Sable sat back and watched Narine's face as he talked. She smiled and laughed, was surprised at who had gotten married, and grew quiet when he told how many of their old friends had passed away.

"But the years have been good to you?" Narine asked him. "And you still enjoy wandering around as a homeless peddler?"

"I do." He smiled. "It's an interesting life, trying to always have the thing the next person you meet will need, or at least want." His smile faded, and he studied her. "I've gotten good at it, over the years. I almost always have something fitting. Except today."

Narine looked at him questioningly.

"I almost didn't come," he continued, "because I know for certain that I have nothing in my cart that will interest you." He leaned closer. "What is it you want, Narine? Now. Here. In this place, what do you need?"

She rested her head back on the couch, her face smoothed of its normal lines of exhaustion and discomfort. "You've already given it to me. I'm so tired, Flibbet, that I'd nearly forgotten how long and rich this life has been." She looked down at her hands. "These last weeks have been hard. I've been thinking only of the present moment, surrounded by this last, looming fear. It's drawing closer, and I can't see its shape."

Her words were low, and the warmth of them wrapped around Sable, growing like some sort of inevitable pressure. The conversation felt suddenly intimate, and Sable stilled.

"I've been so wrapped up in *now*," Narine continued, looking back up at him, "that I've forgotten all the goodness of the past." She smiled warmly at him. "I'm so very glad you decided to come."

He reached forward and patted her hand. "As am I, Narine."

The gesture was so gentle that Sable stood and walked to the stove to give them more privacy. "Would you two like some tea?"

"Of course," Narine answered happily, and Sable set the kettle on the stove.

Flibbet glanced out the window where the light was fading toward dusk. "I'm afraid I don't have time. I visit the island several times a year, so I convinced the good monks to let me on to see you today, but they made me promise to be off by sunset."

He stood, still holding Narine's hand in his own. "It has done my heart good to see you again."

She looked up at him with a lively smile, and Sable caught a glimpse of the young abbess Flibbet had known.

"Mine too," the prioress answered.

He set his other hand gently on Narine's head and leaned close. "Take heart, old friend. The struggle left will be short, and you are strong enough to face it. Take heart in the knowledge that you've done well, through all these long years. Your well-deserved rest is near at hand."

Narine's lips pressed together. The tears in her eyes caught the firelight from the stove and glowed with warmth. "Thank you," she whispered.

The little peddler leaned forward and pressed a kiss to her forehead, then, with a final squeeze, he set her hand gently down on her lap.

Narine closed her eyes, and Flibbet quietly left.

CHAPTER THIRTY-ONE

SABLE FOLLOWED FLIBBET OUT, giving Narine some peace. She found the peddler at his cart.

He studied Sable. "It's...*interesting* running into you again, Issable." His words were musing, almost more to himself than her, but in a breath, he flashed her his wide grin. "Until we meet again!" He lifted the handles of his small cart, heaving it into motion and whistling a jolly, lilting tune. Before he reached the edge of the square, though, it grew more melancholy.

The sun was setting behind Narine's house, trailing fingers of fire through the high, wispy clouds.

Sable sank down on the front step, leaning back onto the recessed door. The cobblestone square was picturesque. The entire walled town was perfectly snug, in fact.

With the exception of the large gathering hall, the buildings were all small and simple, their faces crossed with dark timbers, their roofs dark with rounded tiles. Small windows tucked into the walls were paned with wavy glass, the firelight inside making them look like rippled honey.

There was plenty of activity, although none of it paid attention to her. Eugessa had settled into the largest house on the far side of the gathering hall, and her abbesses had been emptying carts into the building for hours. Merchant wagons sat in front of the next three houses. Sable watched the activity for a few minutes, but it was impossible to tell which house Talia must be in. The rest of the houses were busy with Kalesh or Northern Lords.

The only quiet spots on the square were Narine's house and the large one between it and the gathering hall, which must be where Vivaine and her people were already settled.

Two monks came into the square, lighting lanterns that hung near the house doors. The square started to feel like an island of light in the growing dark.

Sable looked away from the people moving around and focused on the buildings. Even though they marked out the square, it wasn't a neat one. Each house was turned a bit from its neighbor, some set back a bit, some pushing forward. Some were connected to each other with little, slanting walkways. Between others were oddly sized nooks and alleys.

Aside from the tension of the summit, this was a peaceful place.

One of the monks drew near Sable.

"Good evening," Sam said. He came closer and lit the lantern hanging next to Narine's door, then turned to look across the square. "I see you've discovered the draw of Red's stoop."

Sable glanced at the unpresuming, recessed doorway, which had nothing red about it. "I have?"

Sam nodded. "When I first came here, Red lived in this house. I don't know his real name. He was just Red. He was old when I came to the island, but when he was younger, he used to watch the sunset from the wall. When his knees grew stiff, he took to sitting here, on his own stoop. Every single night, regardless of the weather."

Sable glanced up. "But we're facing east. We can't actually see the sunset from here."

"I pointed out that exact thing to him once, offered to let him sit on my stoop." He pointed across the square at a west-facing house in the corner that was currently crowded with Kalesh soldiers. "He said he'd spent his life watching sunsets, always wishing he were somewhere more like them, somewhere bright and beautiful and free. And he'd finally found it, right here. So he sat on his stoop and watched while the lanterns were lit, and the windows brightened, and claimed the best thing about sunsets was that it made home look even more like home."

Sable took in the square. The buildings seemed to cluster together around the lantern light, banding together against the approaching night. "It's been a very long time since I lived somewhere I loved that much."

Sam leaned against the wall and looked at the town with a contented expression. "It took me nearly forty years to find mine."

"I hope the turmoil of the summit doesn't ruin your peace."

"We work under the belief that peace is stronger than turmoil, even if it doesn't always look that way. I hope the peace of Tutella Island quenches the turmoil of the summit."

Sable glanced at Kiva's home and the buildings housing the Kalesh. "I think that will take more than pretty sunsets."

Sam shrugged. "Perhaps, but good lighting is always the first step." He pushed himself off the wall. "Best get back to the lanterns before it gets too dark." He turned to face her and raised one hand, as though offering a blessing. "May you find your home as Red did, and may it bring brightness and beauty and freedom."

He said the words effortlessly, as though offering such a thing was the most natural thing in the world, but the idea dug into a longing buried so deeply inside Sable that for a moment she couldn't breathe.

Sam was already heading toward the next unlit lantern, and she sank farther back into the doorway. She could see what Red had loved about this place, but sitting here, in the midst of it, something felt off. As though even the town knew she didn't really belong here.

The clouds had faded to a faint blue against the darker sky, and it was past time to check on Narine.

She started to stand, but something caught her eye across the square. A movement in one of the alleys. She looked into the shadows but couldn't see anything. Someone was there, though. She was sure of it. And from their position, they had to be watching either Narine's house or Vivaine's next door.

Sable ran over the day in her head. Of all the visitors she'd had, only Eugessa had been threatening. Vivaine wanted Narine safe and well. The string of abbesses who had come to talk to her had been nothing but relieved to see her awake. Sable glanced over at Eugessa's house. The prioress wouldn't actually harm Narine, would she?

Eugessa's house was abuzz with activity.

Sable looked back at the alley. It was still dark between the buildings, but if Sable had any money to bet, she'd wager that the person was gone. She looked around the rest of the square, but nothing seemed out of place.

Kicking herself for looking away, she stood. If nothing else, she should lock the back door into Narine's house.

"Issable," a voice called out.

She turned to see Ambassador Bastian coming out of one of the Kalesh houses. He strode across the square, holding up a package. "I heard that Prioress Narine was feeling better today and brought her some red petal tea." He handed her a small box.

Sable took it and caught the scent of cinnamon and spices.

"Back in the Empire, this tea is a favorite of those who are feeling weary. They say the red flower of the juka plant strengthens the soul." He smiled widely. "I think that's ridiculous, but the tea is delicious."

Sable glanced past him at the alley. "Thank you. I will get it to the prioress."

Instead of leaving, the ambassador turned to face the square. "It's a remarkable little town the monks have built, isn't it? Reminds me a bit of a village I visited a very long time ago." His eyes unfocused. "That one was tucked in a thin mountain valley. The buildings were similar, though, and it had the same warm feel, like sitting at a hearth."

Unlike his normal formality, he spoke casually, as though they were merely two neighbors exchanging pleasantries on the front stoop. Maybe it was because the man was so relaxed, but his accent was stronger than usual. It caught on the rough edges of words and hardened them to a point.

Sable studied him, waiting for him to get to the point of what he really wanted from Narine, as everyone else had done. But he seemed content to watch the activity in the square. In the torchlight, the scar running from his temple down to his jaw was a dark line through his grey beard.

"Is there something I can help you with, ambassador?"

He turned and studied her. The torchlight etched the wrinkles on his face, and she was surprised at how many there were.

"I had not expected to see you with Andreese of Ravenwick."

Sable straightened, but there wasn't any hostility in his voice, just a thoughtfulness, as though he were mulling over some new idea.

"I realize I shouldn't be surprised," he continued. "After all, the young man was a companion of yours before Ambassador Tehl was killed."

She didn't have a response for that, but it was hardly a secret that Reese had traveled with the troupe. "Yes," she answered. "He was."

The ambassador gave her an approving look. "I've always liked that about you. There's no maneuvering in your words. Just blunt honesty. You don't find that often in my line of work."

She almost pointed out that he hadn't heard her speak enough to possibly know that, but instead she asked, "Is there something you want to ask me?"

He gave a wry smile. "Do you know where Andreese is?"

Sable raised an eyebrow. "If I did, it's unlikely I would tell the Kalesh."

He grinned and nodded. "Which is why I wasn't going to ask you. But you wanted to know." He turned back to the square. "The official answer is that the rebels are nearby, but not housed on the island. They are only allowed on the island during the day. Their presence here is...complicated."

"It seems to me that the point of this summit is to work things out between the Kalesh and"—Sable paused, waving her hand around the square—"everyone else."

"True. Which was complicated enough without the addition of another hostile faction. Thus the complication."

"There's a very simple solution," she answered. "The Empire could leave."

He gave her an amused look. "I've been in this part of the world for nearly a year and a half, and not a single person has said that to me. Even though everyone is thinking it."

"That's because they all waste time not saying what they should. If you get a chance to speak with Andreese, I'm sure he'll tell you to leave."

"Ahh," the ambassador said, sobering. The word seemed to encompass some sort of conclusion. He was silent, watching people move through the square. "How is it that Andreese speaks Kalesh?"

Sable brought the box of tea to her nose and breathed in the smell. "You should ask him that."

"If I get the chance, I will." The ambassador paused again.

"If you're here to get information about Andreese," Sable said, "I'll tell you the same thing I told him when he asked about you. Andreese wants peace. And he would rather see it obtained without violence." She looked up at the ambassador. "Under very different circumstances, you and he might've gotten along well."

Ambassador Bastian searched her face, frowning as though he'd found something amiss. "Under different circumstances, we might be living in an entirely different world." He blinked, and the frown smoothed. "Andreese called you Sable, I believe?"

She nodded. "A name from another life."

He studied her a moment longer, then gave a friendly smile. "I have several of those myself. Lovely as always to talk to you, Issable." His accent drew out the first syllable, rounding it almost to an "ah" sound. He inclined his head toward her. "Please pass on the Kalesh delegation's best wishes to Prioress Narine for renewed strength and the hope that we will see her soon."

"If you see her soon, it will be at the summit," Sable pointed out. "Are you sure you don't want me to pass on some message to her encouraging her to vote along with your views? That seems to be everyone else's goal."

The ambassador shrugged. "I have no doubt her votes would be cast in opposition to mine. But the prioress is not a threat to the Kalesh." He looked across the square at the activity from Eugessa and the merchants. "The ruling classes are never the ones who give the Kalesh trouble. They know how to compromise. It's the rebels, driven by their own battle cry, who can't be negotiated with."

"I'm sure that's true," Sable agreed. "But there's something admirable in their courage and conviction, don't you think?"

He paused, and his expression grew troubled. "Admirable, yes. But often fatal." He sighed. "Regardless, I believe the good prioress's voice is one that would promote peace in the negotiations, and that would be a good thing."

Sable raised an eyebrow. "Do you speak for all the Kalesh?"

He gave a tired sigh. "I'm sure I do not. But please tell Prioress Narine that I wish her well anyway." He took several steps before pausing. "Do be careful, Issable. Make sure you don't underestimate your enemies."

The words swirled warmly past her. "Who exactly do you think my enemies are, Ambassador?"

He shot her an amused smile. "I'll let you decide that." He gave her a slight bow and turned away.

Bastian took several steps before pausing. "Do be careful, Issable. Make sure you don't underestimate your enemies."

Sable watched him cross the square back toward the Kalesh housing, wondering what the point of that conversation had been. The questions about Andreese had felt secondary. Yet she couldn't quite pinpoint what the ambassador had been after. She sighed. The politics of the summit were already exhausting, and it hadn't even started yet.

A shuffling noise at the side of the house made her spin toward the darkness between Narine's house and the next.

"That was a fascinating conversation," Reese said quietly from the shadows.

CHAPTER THIRTY-TWO

SABLE GLARED at the shadowy form of Andreese. "Why are you lurking in the dark, eavesdropping on my conversations?" she whispered.

"It was a conversation in a public square. If, while waiting my turn to speak with the very popular Issable, I happened to overhear it, that's hardly eavesdropping."

She crossed her arms. "It was you in the alley across the square before, wasn't it?"

"I thought you saw me." He stood in shadows, and she couldn't see his face, but his voice sounded pleased.

"Why are you creeping around like a criminal?"

"Because Tanis agreed that we dangerous rebels would be off the island by sunset."

Sable pointed up at the dark sky. "You do know what sunset is, don't you?" She stepped out of the doorway, joining him in the alley.

"There were too many interesting things going on to leave so early," he said. Now that she was closer, she could see him studying her. "Like meetings between you and the Kalesh ambassador."

"That was more weird than interesting." She glanced back at the people still moving around the square. "We should move farther back. If I noticed you lurking, someone else could too." She moved away from the square until she reached the back corner of Narine's house. Between her and the wall surrounding the town was nothing but deep shadows. Reese stopped behind her.

"Say something true," she whispered to him.

There was a pause. "I find it *very* interesting how close you are to the Kalesh ambassador."

Sable scowled at the words, but the truth of them was like a breath of warmth, filling the air around them. She concentrated, but beyond herself and the blazing tower of heat that was Reese, standing very close behind her, she felt no one nearby.

She turned and had to tilt her head up to look up into his face. "I am not close to the ambassador."

Reese continued to peer along the wall.

"There's no one nearby," she told him.

He glanced at her with the stubborn set to his brow that said he was going to check for himself.

She set her hand on his arm. "Serene taught me a new...skill. Just trust me, there's no one nearby."

He raised an eyebrow. "Really?"

"Really. Now, why were you lurking next to Narine's house?"

"I saw you sitting there and thought I'd come over and say hello, but the ambassador got to you first." He paused. "Why didn't you tell him where I learned to speak Kalesh?"

"Besides the fact that it's not my job to introduce you to the world, I didn't know why he was asking." She pulled her hand off his arm and frowned down at the box of tea. "I actually don't know what the point of the entire conversation was. Except I think he learned whatever he wanted to know."

"Then he wasn't after information about me, because you didn't tell him anything." He tilted his head and considered her. "And he didn't ask much about Narine."

"I know. I thought he'd be trying to pin down whether she will vote. Like Vivaine did, and Eugessa. I'm half expecting a visit from Kiva to do the same."

"The fact that she's so sick isn't deterring any of them?"

"Oh, they're not bothering Narine with it. Except Eugessa, but no one expects her to have any tact. Instead, they talk to me and remind me how much they all hold over me." Sable leaned back against the wall. "You'd be amazed at how many things there are." She could see Reese more clearly now. He'd lost his new, guarded look and watched her with an old, familiar expression.

"It was simpler last year," she said.

"I don't remember simple. I remember Ebenmoor burning, and fights with Kalesh in the woods, and a lot of worry about the Empire and Talia and Vivaine."

Sable sighed. "No, I suppose none of that was simple."

"And I remember a lot of people holding things over you then, too, all trying to make you do what they wanted."

"I wish they'd stop doing that."

He laughed quietly and leaned back against the opposite house. "One thing was easier. I didn't have to sneak around quite as much to have a conversation with you."

Sable raised an eyebrow. "All this lurking was to talk to me?"

He grinned, and the easiness of it made her smile back. "No. My real reason for staying later tonight was to see which merchants were here." His grin soured. "I saw scabby little Kiva. How did he wriggle his way into all this?"

"He's been in league with Eugessa for ages. My favorite part about his schemes is that he set himself up as Talia's father."

Reese's eyebrows shot up. "And Talia let him?"

"She thinks it's a grand idea. She's convinced Kiva to give her the things he steals so she can redistribute them to the poor."

"Really?" Reese glanced toward the square. "That's impressive."

Sable scowled at him. "Don't be positive about the fact that she's so entangled with Kiva that I will never get her out."

"Maybe she doesn't want you to get her out."

She pushed herself off the wall. "Do you think I'm going to leave my sister working for that monster?"

"No. I expect you'll come up with some way to rescue her."

"Yes, I will. And you might want to help, because Kiva's taking advantage of the fact you've been attacking merchant wagons to launch some attacks of his own as far south as Immusmala and blame you."

He let out a snort. "If we had enough people to be both here and down near Immusmala, we'd be doing a lot more than harassing merchant carts."

"He even attacked Lord Trelles's house."

Reese raised an eyebrow. "That's a bold move. No one would suspect that he attacked his own daughter's house."

Sable turned to glare toward the square. "Except, since he obviously didn't carry out the attack himself, he trusted Talia's safety to some of his thugs."

Reese let out a laugh, and Sable spun toward him. "What's funny about that?" she demanded.

"You haven't changed a bit."

"What's that supposed to mean?"

He began counting on his fingers. "Vivaine, Eugessa, and Kiva find you important and dangerous enough to personally threaten you if you don't do what they want. And somehow, you've taken all that in stride. But someone does something that threatens one of your sisters, and you're ready to go on a rampage."

"Well," Sable said, her anger fading a little, "people should stop threatening my sisters."

"I certainly will never threaten them." He paused and looked at her thoughtfully. "I think I can add the Kalesh ambassador to the list of people who find you important."

"He's barely ever spoken to me. Last night on the wall and tonight are by far the most words we've ever exchanged."

Reese shook his head. "I don't think he came to find out about me or Narine. I think he came to find something out about you."

Sable started to object but stopped. "If so, I don't know what it was."

His eyes were fixed on her with an expression that was part worry, part...something else. The distant look was gone, and he pushed himself off the wall, taking a step toward her.

"Come with me," he said, his voice low.

Sable tensed at the fierceness in his voice. "Where?"

"Away from here. I have a way off the island. Just leave with me. Get away from all of this mess."

The idea caught at her.

"You can't want to be here," he continued. When she didn't answer, he added. "You can join Tanis and help us fight! Or not," he added quickly. "You can find a cottage in some town somewhere. Or in the woods."

He took another step closer. "Don't you want the freedom to just…" He gestured past the wall surrounding Aedis.

The longing dug into her and pulled so strongly she almost took a step toward him. No more Vivaine. No more politics or Kalesh or Kiva.

"The freedom to listen to the trees," she said.

Reese let out a breath that sounded like a laugh. "Well, this time of night you'll mostly hear frogs and owls. And there's a yellow beetle that makes a loud clicking noise when it jumps." He grinned. "But if you can ignore all that, yes, you can listen to the trees."

The idea was so tempting, it ached.

Freedom.

"I know you want that," he said quietly.

Sable pulled her eyes away from him and looked at the dark window of Narine's house. "I do," she whispered. "More than almost anything."

Reese grew quiet, and when she turned back to him, his expression was unreadable. "That 'almost' is going to keep you here, isn't it?"

The ache to leave warred with something deeper. "I can't leave Narine." The words came out in a whisper.

Reese opened his mouth as though he might argue but only sighed. "You wouldn't be you if you could, I suppose."

"Come meet her tomorrow," Sable said.

"I doubt the prioress wants to meet an assassin."

"You're not an assassin," she objected.

He raised an eyebrow at her.

"Fine, if we're being particular, you did assassinate someone, but Narine's ridiculously kind. And she's nice to soldiers and guards all the time who have killed people in battles, which is essentially what you did."

Reese shook his head, and the look was back in his face, the hard edge she couldn't decipher. "That's not how people see it. And Narine doesn't need the added complication of being seen with me."

"Come meet her," Sable repeated. "I want you to."

A low whistle, almost like a bird call, sounded through the night, and Reese glanced out of the alley. "I need to go."

A different whistle sounded, and Reese paused, listening. The first call repeated, and he shifted toward the back of the alley.

"Your ride off the island?" Sable guessed.

He gave a small smile. "Something like that."

Sable reached out and set her hand on his arm. He stopped, his arm tense below her hand. "Will you come meet her tomorrow?"

He looked down at her hand, then set his warm, rough fingers on top of hers. "Yes."

"Thank you," she said quietly.

His hand tightened on hers. "Good night, Sable."

The sound of her name—her real name—was so familiar in his voice, her answer got stuck in her throat.

He ducked around the corner and out of sight.

"Good night, Reese," she whispered after him.

The night was so still and peaceful, she didn't go in the back door but walked slowly back to the square. Warm firelight glowed through many of the windows, but the town had quieted.

A bright square of firelight lit the ground in front of Narine's house as well, and Sable glanced up to see the front window blazing with light. She frowned at it. Some abbesses must have come back and lit the lights. Which better not have disturbed Narine if she'd been sleeping.

Sable pushed the door open and ran into the out-flung arm of a Sanctus guard she didn't recognize, holding her back.

The room was crowded with people. Two of Narine's abbesses stood against one wall, three more whom Sable didn't recognize near the stove. Another Sanctus guard was stationed near the hall to the back door.

Gwen stood near the end of the couch with her hand on Narine's head, the silver-edged cuff of her sleeve resting on the prioress's hair.

Worse, Vivaine knelt on the floor, leaning close to the Phoenix Prioress.

The silver tail of the dragon snaked out around the end of the couch.

Sable pressed against the arm of the Sanctus guard, but he shifted to block her way. "Get away from her," Sable hissed at Vivaine.

The High Prioress gave no response beyond murmuring something quiet to Narine. Gwen's brow was furrowed in concentration.

"Gwen," Sable called. "What are you doing?"

The Mira kept her attention on Narine. There was a rustle of activity at the couch, and then Vivaine rose holding a piece of paper.

"Ah, Issable," High Prioress said pleasantly. She nodded to the Sanctus guard, and he let Sable pass. "We were just discussing you."

Sable hurried toward the couch as Gwen backed away. Argyros, whose head had been hovering near Narine's feet, shifted back, fixing Sable with his slitted, grey eyes. Sable dropped down on her knees next to Narine. The old prioress's eyes were closed, but her forehead was creased into a frown.

"What did you do?" Sable demanded.

"We were merely discussing with Narine the fact that you will be her voice in the summit tomorrow. We all agree she shouldn't be troubled by such things."

Sable glanced around the room. The two Sanctus guards stood impassively by their doors. All the abbesses nodded sympathetically. Gwen met Sable's gaze for just a moment before looking away.

Innov, so dim Sable barely noticed her, slept on her perch.

"The Phoenix Prioress wants nothing to do with your summit." Sable took Narine's hand in her own. It wasn't warm, exactly. But it wasn't cold.

"She doesn't want to attend herself," Vivaine agreed, "but she just signed permission for you to speak for her. She's very concerned about the freedom of her people."

Sable set her hand on Narine's forehead. There was no sign of the fever, but Narine's skin felt damp. "Yes, she is," Sable said without looking at Vivaine. "But she doesn't think your summit is the solution. And she would never sign that paper willingly."

"There are plenty of witnesses in the room who saw her do it," Vivaine said mildly. She held out the paper. "We spoke about the importance of the day tomorrow, and Narine acknowledged that it was time she voiced her opinions."

There was a wretched warmth to Vivaine's words, and Sable looked at the paper in disbelief.

Beneath the words giving Sable permission to vote in her stead, Narine's thin, shaky signature was drawn. Sable's stomach dropped, and she looked from the dragon to Vivaine to Gwen. The Mira met her gaze, but her normal stubborn expression was troubled around the edges.

"Narine's abbesses agree," Vivaine continued, "that you are the one who knows her best and can be trusted to vote in the right way." The words were said with the perfect touch of earnestness, but Sable felt the familiar threat wrap around her. The cunning mix of truthfulness and lies flared the fury in Sable to a new level.

"What did you do?" Sable repeated, standing and taking a step toward the High Prioress.

Vivaine patted her on the shoulder in a motherly sort of way. Sable yanked her shoulder away from the woman's touch.

"The summit starts midmorning tomorrow." Vivaine rolled up the slip of paper. "I'm leaving several of my healers here to help care for Narine. Our dear sister is, I'm afraid, a bit past your ability to care for." Vivaine gave Sable a benevolent smile. "We all appreciate how well you've cared for her for the past year. You can, of course, continue to sleep here as well."

Vivaine paused at the end of the couch to set her hand gently on Narine's head. Sable clenched her hands into fists at her side to keep herself from slapping the woman's hand away.

Vivaine whispered something that sounded like a prayer but felt like tepid emptiness, then with a small sigh, moved toward the door.

Sable spun toward the Mira still standing near the couch. "Gwen!" Sable said. "What did she do?"

Gwen glanced toward Narine, then back to Sable. She opened her mouth to say something, but Vivaine called to her from the door, and she pressed her lips closed.

Sable stared at the Mira, who'd grown at least familiar over the past year, if not friendly, and a terrible fear took root.

Gwen could read minds, much the same way Sable could read truth.

What if Gwen could also push her thoughts on someone else, the way Sable could infuse her words with truth?

Sable's mouth dropped open. "What did *you* do?"

The hard look on the Mira's face cracked slightly with the question, but she just shook her head and, without a word, followed Vivaine out of the house. The Sanctus guards left, closing the door, and the abbesses in the room fell into murmurs of conversation, heating up the fire and bustling around.

Sable sank down on the floor by the couch, picking up Narine's hand. The prioress's normal peaceful expression was marred by something that looked almost like pain. Sable gripped Narine's fingers in her own.

An older, broad-shouldered abbess from the Dragon Priory strode up beside Sable. "Out of the way, dear," she said briskly. "Let us near the Holy Mother."

"Work around me," Sable said between clenched teeth. "I am not leaving Narine's side."

The abbess scowled at the words but shrugged.

Sable ignored the abbesses, watching Narine's breaths continue, slow and shallow.

"What did they do to you?" she whispered.

CHAPTER THIRTY-THREE

SABLE WOKE to a shooting pain in her neck. She still leaned against the side of the couch, her head resting awkwardly on the cushion. She sat up and groaned, trying to straighten her shoulders and her neck.

The sky outside was bright, and an abbess puttered near the stove, which, judging from the warmth of the room, must have been kept burning all night. The table was cluttered with bottles of herbs, giving off an acrid scent that scraped Sable's throat.

Sable leaned closer to Narine but found her no different from the night before. Her breathing was shallow and slow, her skin clammy, and the crease of a frown still sat between her brows.

A wave of anger rolled over Sable, mixed with the worry that had kept her up most of the night. She dropped her face into her hands, pressing her fingertips into her skull.

"I'm sorry," she whispered.

Narine gave no sign of hearing her.

The broad-shouldered abbess strode into the room with a brusque greeting. Her eyes slid over Sable's appearance with a disapproving look. "There's warm water in the washroom."

Sable glanced down at the wrinkled night shift she'd changed into last night. Perhaps it was time for a bit of cleaning.

In the washroom, Sable splashed her face, trying to rinse off the heaviness of the morning. The water washed away the sharpest edges of her exhaustion, but everything else was too jagged for the water to smooth.

Leaning over the bowl, she stared at the thin, wavy reflection of her own face, turning her situation over in her mind. The fury she'd felt last night was still there, simmering at the idea that Vivaine had manipulated Narine.

But a new thought wormed its way through her anger.

The High Prioress had handed Sable the power to vote.

Deep inside Sable, a crack of light broke into the dark cell where she'd been held silent for the past year, where her voice had been chained by Vivaine's threats.

This new brightness fell across the floor, demanding attention, pulling her notice to the open cell door.

She shifted.

Vivaine had come last night with more threats and more chains, but this time, the High Prioress had left the door open.

Sable's hands tightened on the side of the basin of water, sending ripples across its surface. A year ago, Vivaine's threats had been solid and heavy. Unbreakable. But today they felt old and brittle.

Sable pulled against them, and they cracked.

Vivaine had handed Sable the power to vote.

She gripped the basin, her knuckles white, the bright truth sitting in front of her.

Vivaine would insist Sable side with the Dragon Priory, and Narine wouldn't want her to vote at all. But today, neither of those women got to choose.

Today, finally, Sable could speak for herself.

She felt a twinge of uneasiness at the way Narine would disapprove, but as much as Sable respected the woman, Narine had missed an opportunity to do good in these meetings. And the heart-wrenching truth was that this was the only chance Sable would have to attend a summit in Narine's place.

Deep in the cell, she flexed against her bonds. The chains tightened, but she took a deep breath and shoved herself up.

The chains splintered, scattering across the cell like shards of ice.

Sable stood in the washroom and rolled her shoulders, buffeted by burning hope and swirling fear. Vivaine would be furious. Eugessa, Kiva, and the ambassador would all be furious. Narine would be disappointed.

But for the first time since she had stood on the stage for her last performance, she had a voice.

She strode back to the main room and opened the small closet holding her clothes.

Her servant's dress had been replaced with a single, pristine, white robe. A proper abbess's robe.

Vivaine must have switched it.

She glared at the robe, toying with the idea of going to the summit in her wrinkled, thin sleeping shift instead. The thought of Vivaine's outrage if she did made her smile.

Sable reached out and ran her fingers down the sleeve. The abbess robe was made of smooth, soft fabric, nicer than anything she'd worn in ages. But it was just another attempt of Vivaine's to control her. To show the world something that wasn't quite true.

The thought stopped Sable's hand.

Vivaine was putting on a play, trying to convince the summit that Sable was Narine's real voice. And here was Sable's costume.

The whole idea of the summit shifted. Instead of a room full of leaders, Sable saw it how Vivaine must. An audience who, if the prioress could control the story well enough, would respond according to her plans.

Sable let out a short laugh and pulled the robe off the hook.

Vivaine intended it to trap Sable in the role of a faithful abbess, living to serve the priories, a faceless, mindless follower. Sable thought of all the places she'd gotten into years ago in Dockside by dressing as a faceless, nondescript courier. Being dismissed as such led to all sorts of interesting opportunities.

But costumes held more nuance than that. An abbess robe connected Sable to the priories, which meant her voice would carry the authority of the priory.

"All right, Vivaine," she said. "I'll play in your little show. Let's see who's better at their role."

CHAPTER THIRTY-FOUR

SABLE STOOD at the window in the abbess's robe, watching through the wavy glass as the Kalesh, the merchants, and even Tanis and Reese entered the summit hall. Her earlier anger and determination had waned, tempered by nervousness and a gnawing worry for Narine.

Sable went over and knelt close to Narine. "I don't know what you think of this," Sable whispered. "But you wanted me free from tyranny, and maybe today I can find a little of that freedom."

Sable waited for some response, but the prioress didn't stir. With a sigh, Sable stood and brushed off her robe.

Outside, the midmorning sun poured down, landing warm on Sable's cheek. The buildings of Aedis stood comfortably around the square, watching the proceedings with a steadfast air. Sable breathed in some of its peacefulness, trying to quell the tumultuous emotions inside her.

She stepped into the cool entry of the gathering hall. The huge room just inside the front doors was mostly empty. A few abbesses and assorted servants clumped together here and there. But in the light from the windows, Sable could see the entire back wall, which had been shadowed the first night.

The wall was covered with bookshelves. She stopped, staring at them. There must be hundreds of books. Thousands even.

Tables were set in front of the shelves, and a handful of them held monks bending over a book or scratching out words on parchment.

A monk and a dark figure moved near one end, and Sable hurried across the room toward them. "Serene!"

Serene turned to face Sable, and a wide smile spread across her face. "Sable! Can you believe this place? I had heard the monks had a library, but I never imagined it to be this huge."

The monk gave her a smile, and Sable realized it was Sam.

"Sam is helping me," Serene said. "You would not believe how many interesting books there are here. I may stay for a while once the summit is over." She stopped, actually focusing on Sable and taking in the abbess robe she wore. "What are you doing here?"

"You and I need to talk," she said to Serene.

Sam handed the book he was holding to Serene. "I'll give you some privacy. You can find more books on the healing arts over near the corner." He paused and dropped his voice. "And anything we have on foreign cultures will be on the far wall. Second bookshelf."

Serene thanked him, and he left. Across the hall, a rolling murmur of voices floated out of one of the rooms, and Serene glanced at it. "You're going to the summit?" she asked Sable in disbelief.

Sable explained about Narine's illness and the paper Vivaine had convinced her to sign.

"The High Prioress is growing bolder." There was nothing complimentary in Serene's tone. "She was bolder back in the city too. She's being less diplomatic about things. I asked about some missing books, and she told me if I continue to complain, I won't be welcome in the priory any longer."

Sable frowned. "Does that mean she knows the Kalesh are taking books? Or is she?"

Serene shrugged. "Whatever it is, she's less and less an ally of ours." She glared toward the summit room. "She demanded I come here and record the summit for her, but now, I'm not allowed in the room."

"She just wanted you out of the priory?"

"That's what I'm guessing. She says she'll give me an update each day that I can put into an official report."

"Well, I can give you what I remember too," Sable offered.

Serene nodded. "That will help." She glanced around. "Jae stayed in Immusmala," she said. "Vivaine wasn't happy, but he was sick before we left. Not terribly, but he played it up as worse than it was. Most of the Kalesh are here, so he stayed to try to get a handle on the parts of the library we are usually kept away from."

"Maybe he'll find the missing books." Sable glanced toward the summit door.

"If not, this library might have copies of what we are missing. Or things close to it. Their collection is amazing." Serene flipped open the book she was holding. "I found two of the books on *vitalle* that I'd been missing. And Sam just told me they have dozens of books about the Kalesh."

"Does everyone know Sam the Monk?" Sable asked.

"Probably," Serene answered. "He's in charge of distributing the food the monks grow to outlying communities. He's come as far as Merrick's before."

Voices grew louder from the summit room, and Sable glanced toward it. "Will you check on Narine today?"

Serene tucked her book back into its spot on the shelf. "I'll go right now."

"I'm afraid Vivaine did something harmful to her."

Serene's mouth pressed into an angry, thin line. "I'll see what I can do."

"Thank you." Sable faced the summit room. "Wish me luck."

"You need more than luck."

Sable sighed. "I know."

Serene headed outside, and Sable walked over toward the door of the summit. Seeing Serene had shifted something. Her anger toward Vivaine was lower, more of a brooding bed of coals, and the sense of loneliness that had been hanging on her all morning had lifted. Straightening her shoulders, Sable stepped up to the door.

The room was crowded with people.

At the head of the table, her white robe glowing with its usual faint light, Vivaine stood with her back to Sable, speaking with the Kalesh ambassador. The High Prioress twitched her head slightly toward the door but didn't turn. Her shoulders relaxed, though, before she continued her conversation.

Sable glared at the woman in the hopes that Vivaine was using her skills to watch the door.

The long table with three chairs at the head filled the room. Vivaine stood behind the center chair, her hand resting on its back. Eugessa was seated past her, carrying on an animated conversation with Kiva and Lord Trelles, who sat along the far side. Two other merchants and three Northern Lords filled out that side of the table. The end across from the prioresses held the Kalesh delegation, and along the near side, Sable could see the backs of two more Northern Lords, along with Tanis and Reese.

Scattered around the walls were abbesses and servants and soldiers, looking oddly bare without their weapons.

Gwen caught Sable's eye from behind Vivaine and motioned Sable to the spot behind the remaining chair on the prioresses' end.

A fresh wave of anger rose in Sable at the sight of Vivaine and Gwen, but she walked up to her usual position behind Narine's chair. Gwen stepped closer, and Sable fixed the Mira with a withering look.

"If you try to touch me," Sable said, low enough that only Gwen could hear, "I will tell this entire room what you can do and how Vivaine uses you."

Gwen's eyes tightened at the words, but she paused.

Sable stepped closer, fixing the Mira with a look of pure loathing. "You shouldn't have touched Narine."

Gwen flinched at the words, and Vivaine paused her conversation with the ambassador to glance at Sable.

"Issable." Vivaine's voice was calm, but there was an edge of irritation in her eyes. "I was afraid you weren't coming."

Ambassador Bastian looked surprised to see her but greeted Sable with a friendly nod.

Sable set her hand on the back of Narine's chair. The abbess robe felt longer and heavier than the simple dress she'd worn for the past year. Too tight on her upper arms, too flowy near the wrists. Sable shifted, settling into it as merely the newest in a long line of costumes, and glanced at the stage around her.

Vivaine had set the props out perfectly. Narine's chair was pulled up tight to the table, waiting for Sable to dutifully take her place behind it.

Sable gave Vivaine an easy smile. "I'm sorry it took me so long." She pulled out the chair. "I should have gotten to this place a long time ago."

Turning away from Vivaine, Sable took Narine's seat.

CHAPTER THIRTY-FIVE

Out of the corner of her eye, she saw the High Prioress's hand clench, and Sable resisted the urge to smile. Instead, she focused on looking at ease, as though she had every right to take Narine's place.

Vivaine wasn't the only one who noticed the act of defiance. Around the table, conversations quieted as more and more eyes around the room fixed on Sable.

"What are you doing?" Eugessa demanded.

Lord Trelles fixed Sable with a scornful look. "You're sitting in the prioress's chair, woman."

Sable's hands clenched in her lap, and she opened her mouth, but Vivaine spoke first.

"Yes," the High Prioress said, turning to face the table. "As I was just telling the ambassador, I was able to speak very briefly with Prioress Narine yesterday. I'm afraid she's terribly weak, but she was concerned about the summit. She decided Sister Issable would come in her place." She held up the slip of paper from yesterday. "She requested that I write down her desires so there would be no question."

The end of that was a lie, but Eugessa took the paper from

Vivaine's hand and unrolled it. She studied it, then nodded. "It is Narine's signature."

"There were seven witnesses in the room," Vivaine said, smiling gently, "if anyone here doubts my word."

A few people in the room exchanged glances, but no one objected.

The expressions around the table varied from amusement on Kiva's part to anger in the face of General Goll to narrow-eyed calculation on the part of Eugessa.

Sable finally glanced over to where Reese and Tanis sat. Tanis nodded to her, his own face a mix of curiosity and thoughtfulness. But Reese was staring at her with raised eyebrows. A smile twisted up the corner of his mouth, and he shook his head in disbelief.

With all the eyes of the table on her, Sable kept herself from smiling back.

Past Reese, Sable recognized the plain figure of Lord Loren, somewhat dwarfed by the barrel-chested Lord Perric.

"Unless anyone objects," Vivaine said briskly, "let us begin."

There was a general shuffling in the room as people settled in their seats.

Vivaine gestured toward two men who stood along the back wall holding large scrolls. "First, we have two different cartographers here to discuss the border of Lord Loren's land in relation to the newest mine that the Kalesh had begun—"

"Before our men were slaughtered," General Goll shot at Tanis.

"Before your soldiers attacked us, using the mine workers as shields," Tanis answered calmly.

The room erupted into chaos. The shouts of the different people in the room swirled around like some sort of storm. Each voice believed what they shouted, and the room filled with the warmth of it all. Sable sank back in her chair.

"Our cartographers," one of the Northern Lords shouted over the din, holding up his own map, "prove that you were digging on our lands!"

"—waylaid merchant caravans in the south!" one of the merchants yelled at Tanis.

"—attacked our soldiers unprovoked!" General Goll pounded on the table.

A thread of cold wound its way through all the noise. Sable sat straighter, looking around the room. Someone had just said a blatant lie.

She scanned the table. Kiva was quiet, watching the chaos with sharp eyes. Two of the merchants were shouting near him. Sable focused on them, but there was only warmth from their side of the table. They were furious about the attacks, and they legitimately believed Tanis was to blame.

Tanis shook his head, denying the accusations loudly, his own words spreading across the table warmly.

But more and more of the table turned their shouts against the rebels.

"We were assured the mine was not on Lord Loren's land!" Ambassador Bastian interjected from the far end.

Sable leaned forward, trying to isolate the ambassador from the rest of the table. He continued to protest that they had done nothing wrong, and Sable thought she could sense warmth from him.

"We were attacked without provocation," General Goll shouted.

Sable was so focused on that end of the table that she felt a sharp slash of cold.

She twitched, and Vivaine glanced over.

"We were mining on approved land," General Goll continued, pointing at Tanis, "when these barbarians came out of the woods to slaughter us!"

There was still so much shouting in the room that Sable wasn't positive, but the feel of that end of the table was definitely chilly. She leaned forward, as though moving a few inches would help cut through all the other noise.

Next to her, Vivaine looked between Sable and the general. Beneath the edge of the table, Vivaine stretched out her fingertips. The room twisted slightly, and the general flew closer. Sable grabbed the edge of the table as it contracted until the man was almost within Sable's reach. She pressed back in her chair, but nothing else had moved. The sides of the table still stretched away like normal—it was only the general's seat that had drawn closer.

Sable turned to Vivaine, and the High Prioress looked pointedly at the general. Sable refocused on the man.

He was still yelling, and while his voice came from across the room, it was simple now to focus on his words.

"Our research showed that the land was in the southern territories," he shouted.

The words sliced past her with a blast so icy cold that Sable shivered. Vivaine's eyes narrowed at the general.

At his pounding, the room quieted some. "We have been attacked without provocation!" he thundered, the words frigid. "Those men"—he jabbed a finger toward Tanis and Reese—"set upon us like monsters, murdering our men and destroying our rightful property!"

The rest of the room quieted, and Vivaine relaxed her fingers. The general receded back across the room.

Sable glanced at Vivaine. The High Prioress still watched the general closely but didn't interrupt the shouting.

"These rebels must pay!" a merchant shouted.

"With their lives!" The general stabbed a finger toward Andreese. "That man should have hanged a year ago! The fact that he sits at this table is an insult to the Empire! We demand justice!"

The fury in the room was almost palpable. As it focused on Tanis and Reese, it solidified into something dangerous. Tanis looked wary, and Reese sat tense in his chair, his expression guarded.

Sable looked down the table at the furious general. "Do you have these maps?" she called out.

Her voice was lost in the din, so she stood and leaned forward onto her hands. "General Goll," she said more loudly, "do you have these maps?"

There was a pause in the shouting.

The general fixed her with an insulted look. "Of course we have the maps," he said with warm words.

Ambassador Bastian turned to Sable, studying her.

"Could you show them to us?" Sable asked.

"Sit down!" Eugessa said in a scathing voice. "You're here to vote in Prioress Narine's place, not question the general."

"It's a valid question," Tanis said. "If the Empire was given a map that shows they were in the right, let us see it."

General Goll snapped his fingers, and one of the Kalesh soldiers along the wall behind him stepped up, holding out a roll of parchment. The general took it and tossed it onto the middle of the table.

Lord Loren unfurled the map and studied it, his brow creasing in a frown. "Who made this? The entire southern border of my land is wrong."

The general shrugged. "We purchased maps of this entire land over a year ago."

His words were still cold with lies, but even as the rest of the table peppered him with questions, his confident, condescending tone was unflustered.

The guard who had handed General Goll the map returned to his place to stand stiffly along the back wall. All the soldiers along the wall stood straight-backed, with their usual military bearing, but for this particular one, there was an added level of discomfort.

Sable stayed standing, watching General Goll shout again about the attack. The tide around the table refocused on the rebels. Tanis continued to refute the idea that his people had attacked at all, but no one was listening.

Ambassador Bastian stood at the end of the table and raised his hands for silence. The room quieted, but the air was filled with tension. "We have used the set of maps we purchased last year in every one of our mining endeavors." Unlike the general, the ambassador's voice was calm and warm. "If the map is inaccurate, then we will gladly purchase a better one, and we will gladly enter into discussions with Lord Loren about what to do with the area we disturbed." He gave a slight bow to Loren.

Vivaine relaxed the slightest bit in her chair. Sable kept her eyes on the general, who gave no acknowledgment of the ambassador's words.

The soldier behind him, however, visibly relaxed.

"Soldier," Sable said, "did you help the general obtain the map?"

The eyes of the room snapped back in her direction, and Eugessa gave an exasperated huff.

"Is this abbess going to run the entire summit?" General Goll demanded.

Sable ignored him. "You, sir, the soldier who gave him the map. Were you involved in buying it?"

The soldier tensed and glanced at the general.

"Prioress Vivaine," the general snapped, "control your people!"

"It's a simple question," the prioress answered calmly. "Unless you have a reason we shouldn't ask your soldiers about events that they may have been involved in?"

"I have already answered your questions," the general retorted. "And I'm happy to answer any more you have. But this is a summit between the leaders of the land, not the servants. Why should we listen to this woman?"

Eugessa nodded in agreement and opened her mouth.

But Sable leaned forward and poured the truth of her next statement into her words. "Because *this woman* thinks you're lying."

CHAPTER THIRTY-SIX

WARMTH FLOWED OUT FROM SABLE, spreading across the table like a rolling mist. Prioress Eugessa shifted against it in irritation, and the merchants frowned. The Northern Lords, though, turned slowly to face the general. The whole table, in fact, turned to look at General Goll, except for Andreese, who kept his eyes fixed on Sable with a questioning look. She gave him the slightest nod before noticing that Ambassador Bastian was watching also.

The ambassador looked between Sable and Andreese, his face unreadable.

"I can't imagine anyone cares what you think," the general said derisively. He dismissed her with a wave of his hand and turned to Vivaine. "But if the priories cannot control their abbesses enough to keep them from interrupting an important discussion, how can we trust them to have any sort of authority in the south? Perhaps we're wasting our time negotiating with prioresses who are losing control of their people."

Sable kept her eyes fixed on the general, her irritation at his arrogance growing. The different sides of the table shifted, glancing between the Kalesh and the priories. Vivaine sat stiffly in the chair next to Sable, her face schooled into a look of thoughtfulness, but her hands clenched in her lap beneath the table.

"Prioress Narine cares what I think," Sable said. That statement was perfectly true, and she poured her own warmth again into her words. "I've been assigned the duty of taking her place here, giving me as much right to speak as anyone else at the table. And I think you're lying." The air hummed with the blistering heat of her words, and all down the table, she could see people responding. The slight tilt of a head, a crease of consideration in a brow.

Sable waited for some sort of support from Vivaine, but the High Prioress was silent.

It was the Kalesh ambassador who spoke first. He turned to consider General Goll, then addressed the soldier behind him. "Did you help obtain the map?"

"Bastian!" General Goll protested, outraged.

The ambassador held up a finger to stop the general and continued to look at the soldier expectantly.

"I..." The soldier's eyes shifted between the general and the ambassador.

"Look at me when I'm speaking to you, soldier," the ambassador said sharply.

The man's eyes snapped to the ambassador's, and he drew himself up straighter.

"It is a simple question," Bastian said. "Did you help obtain the map?"

The soldier swallowed. "I did, sir."

"And they were from a reputable source?"

The soldier nodded quickly. "We purchased maps of the land from a cartographer in Immusmala last summer. He was said to be the best."

The man's words were true, but he was choosing his words too carefully.

The ambassador nodded and turned back to the table. The soldier shifted back against the wall.

"This was obviously an honest mistake," Eugessa said. "The Kalesh have already offered to work with Lord Loren on—"

"And this particular map?" Sable interrupted, addressing the soldier again. "Did you buy *this* map last summer from the reputable cartographer in Immusmala?"

The soldier stiffened again. Ambassador Bastian's brow creased in a frown, and he turned back to the soldier. The man opened his mouth then closed it again.

"Soldier," Ambassador Bastian commanded, "you've been asked a direct question."

The soldier's eyes flickered once to General Goll, then he looked back at the ambassador. "No, sir," he said finally.

The general's jaw clenched, but Ambassador Bastian fixed the soldier with a dangerous look. "Explain."

The soldier kept his eyes averted from General Goll. "That particular map was drawn last week."

The ambassador's eyebrows shot up. "By whom?"

General Goll stared at the soldier with a livid expression, but the soldier kept his gaze studiously trained on the ambassador.

"By one of the camp scribes."

Ambassador Bastian crossed his arms and turned slowly back to the general. "What do you know about this?"

"It was drawn last week off the original map," Goll said.

The ambassador raised an eyebrow and looked back at the soldier. "Is that what you saw?"

The soldier shifted. "I never saw another map like that."

Sable sank back down in her chair. Vivaine glanced at her and gave a quick, approving nod.

Ambassador Bastian, his face angrier than Sable had ever seen it, turned back to Goll. "Explain yourself, General."

"There's nothing to explain," Goll said. "We had a map showing the border. I wanted a copy to bring with us here, so I had a scribe make a copy."

The words were frigid with lies, but judging from the expressions around the table, Sable didn't need to point that out.

The ambassador leveled a furious look at the general, then turned back to face the table. "I assure you all, a full investigation will be made into this matter." His hands curled into fists at his side. "If I find

that our people knowingly mined beyond the borders of our agreements, I assure you full restitution will be made."

"We've already agreed to that," Goll snapped. "Why exactly are we
avoiding the actual issue here?" He pointed a finger at Sable. "Why
are we allowing her to distract us from the fact that these rebels"—he
swung his finger over to point at Tanis—"attacked and murdered our
people without provocation?"

But the general's words didn't carry the weight they had earlier,
and quite a few faces around the table watched the general with the
new level of distrust.

"If Ambassador Bastian says he will look into the matter of the
map," Vivaine said smoothly, "we will set that aside for a moment."

The ambassador nodded in acknowledgment and took his seat, his
back stiff.

The Northern Lords didn't object, but they muttered to each other
and glared at the Kalesh.

Vivaine glanced around the table, and despite her calm demeanor,
Sable could see her weighing the attitudes of the room. "To the matter
of the attacks at the mine," she said, "we have heard General Goll's
accusations, but I have heard a different story from Tanis." She
gestured to the man.

The leader of the rebels stood and explained how his men had set
out to destroy the mine, since it had been unlawfully built, but had
been ambushed by the Kalesh. Unlike earlier, the rest of the table
listened to the story, casting occasional glances toward the Kalesh
general, who limited himself to glaring at Tanis but saying nothing.

Sable sank back in her chair. The story coming from Tanis was
warm and true, his answers to any questions the same. When Lord
Trelles demanded to know why the rebels had been attacking
merchants in and around Immusmala, Tanis's denial of the acts was
met with at least some measure of consideration.

Sable caught Kiva's eye, toying with the idea of exposing his role in
the attacks, but she had no proof.

Vivaine moved the discussion along, sidestepping any further
mentions of the issue of the mine and laying out a proposal for trade
routes between Immusmala and the north.

Sable stayed quiet, growing slowly more irritated at the casual indifference everyone felt toward the Empire expanding their trade routes. The Northern Lords were obviously divided in their support for the Kalesh. Lord Perric, whose holdings were by far the largest of the northern territories and had the best lumber forests, agreed strongly and often with the Kalesh ambassador. Lord Loren, whose holdings were the smallest and weakest in the north, showed much less enthusiasm.

Tanis didn't speak much but watched the discussion closely, and Sable got the feeling he saw more in the interactions than she did.

Lunch was brought in by monks, and the conversations continued. Twice, Sable caught the Kalesh ambassador studying her, not bothering to look away when she noticed.

It was nearly dinner when Ambassador Bastian rose. "There is one more thing that would greatly increase the efficiency of trade between our lands."

"What is that?" Vivaine asked.

"Increased trade means increased ships from the Empire," Ambassador Bastian said. "In an effort to not crowd Immusmala's already busy docks, we propose that you allow us to purchase land on which we will build our own port." He paused. "At the mouth of the Black River."

The room fell into stunned silence.

"You wish to own the mouth of the only river that leads inland?" Vivaine asked slowly.

For once, Sable agreed wholeheartedly with the tone of Vivaine's voice.

CHAPTER THIRTY-SEVEN

"Only a small area at the mouth of the river," the ambassador assured Vivaine. "The river delta is deep enough for our seafaring boats to enter and dock. We would be able to ship supplies to our mines easily, without disrupting the commerce of your city. And the lumber trade from the north could come straight down the river to our docks."

The ambassador looked calmly around the table, as though this were a rational request. "We could build our own housing for the soldiers who will help safeguard our supplies and won't need to impose any longer on our friends in Dockside for living quarters."

Kiva studied the ambassador with narrowed eyes, his outrage barely concealed. It seemed his jays hadn't gathered this piece of information for him. Had the Kalesh request not been so audacious, Sable would have been amused. The rent Kiva charged the Kalesh in Dockside must have made him a fortune. The idea of the Kalesh moving out of the city looked as though it was causing him physical pain.

The only person from Immusmala nodding was Eugessa. "I think it's a wonderful idea," she said. "The docks in Immusmala are overcrowded with the addition of the Kalesh ships." She glanced at Kiva, who nodded in somewhat reluctant agreement. "And the traffic in the streets has increased as well. The Empire could load their ships near Folhaven and not interrupt the daily lives of the people of Immusmala." She glanced at Vivaine. "I know some people have been uncomfortable with the number of Kalesh in the city. This feels like an excellent solution for all sides."

"Excellent solution?" Sable objected. "Giving a foreign empire a foothold at the mouth of the one river that connects the north and the south?"

Eugessa turned a contemptuous look at Sable. "What exactly, in your illustrious experience as an actress or a caregiver to an elderly woman, gives you such insight into these matters?"

Sable opened her mouth to retort, but Tanis spoke first.

"She raises the obvious objection."

"What land do you control, exactly?" Eugessa asked him. "I'm still not certain why your opinion matters in this summit. Or why your presence is allowed. This is a conversation between the south, the Kalesh, and the Northern Lords. It doesn't involve brigands who terrorize honest men just going about their daily jobs."

"I think it's worrisome," Lord Loren said from Tanis's side. "And I do own land. The river is the main source of trade between my farmers and the cities to the south. I'm not comfortable with a foreign empire having the ability to interrupt that."

"We have no desire to interrupt trade," Ambassador Bastian said. "We merely want a place to load our boats that is more convenient and less disruptive than the docks in Immusmala."

"And we're supposed to just trust that you'll never use it to your advantage?" Sable asked. "Because the Empire has such a reputation for keeping to themselves?"

Eugessa let out an annoyed huff, and Lord Perric frowned at Sable.

But Ambassador Bastian just gave a wry laugh. "The Empire has a reputation for doing what is profitable for itself. And being able to transport goods easily between this land and the Empire is profitable."

"And what about when it becomes more profitable to just take us over and absorb us into the Empire?" Sable asked. "Can you honestly say that having control of the main river won't be strategic in accomplishing that?"

Bastian smiled at her, but his gaze had a sharpness to it. "I won't say that, merely because I wouldn't want you to accuse *me* of lying in front of the whole summit."

There was a ripple of amusement around the table.

The ambassador kept his face pleasant. "But I would wager that the Empire has more might and more reach than any of you currently understand. If we want to take over your land, we don't need to own the mouth of the river."

There was an uncomfortable silence around the table.

As always, the words from the ambassador were warm. There were no threads of coldness, no hints of deceit. Just plain, simple truth.

"But," the ambassador continued in a relaxed voice, "what we want is merely an efficient trade route. Letting our boats dock at the mouth of the river will assist in our transport of materials and supplies to and from the mines, and it will make trading with the north simpler as well."

More truth.

"It would make things easier," Lord Perric agreed. "The larger merchant caravans have a hard time moving through Immusmala, but if we were to trade with the Kalesh at the Black River, we could increase the lumber shipments to at least twice the size we currently have."

"That's an advantage I hadn't even considered," Ambassador Bastian said, turning his attention away from Sable.

The conversation continued, but with less outrage than Sable had expected.

The smaller of the Northern Lords spoke out against it, but Lord Perric and Lord Runess treated the idea with cautious interest. Tanis vehemently opposed it, pointing out how the Kalesh continued to spread, and this would only increase that.

Sable watched the reactions closely, weighing responses, but the longer the discussion continued, the less sure she was that enough people would vote against it to stop the Kalesh from getting, once again, exactly what they wanted.

"The longer you let this go before voting," Sable said quietly to Vivaine, "the more support you're losing."

"There's always tomorrow," Vivaine murmured. "You never know whose minds will change overnight."

Sable let out a snort. "The way Narine's mind was changed?"

Vivaine gave Sable a scathing look, but the smell of roasting meat wafted into the room, and the High Prioress let out a breath of relief.

She stood, raising her hand for silence. "This is a proposal that certainly warrants more discussion, so I propose we hold off on voting until tomorrow. For now, our hosts have provided dinner, and I invite you all to adjourn to the gathering hall."

Sable started to rise with the rest of the table.

"Stay a moment longer," Vivaine said quietly to her.

Sable started to shake her head.

"Please," the High Prioress added.

The word was so out of character that Sable sank back against the tall chair back, watching the room empty. Reese gave her a quick, unreadable glance as he left with Tanis, the two of them talking quietly with Lord Loren.

Kiva waited until everyone but the prioresses had left before walking behind Sable's chair. Pausing on the side away from Vivaine, he leaned close to her ear and said quietly, "The more I see you work, the more I realize I did not fully utilize your skills when you worked with me."

Sable turned to face him. His face was so close she could see flecks of yellow in the muddy brown of his eyes.

His teeth flashed in a cold smile. "It makes me wonder...what skills does Talia have that I'm not aware of?" With a grin, he strode out of the room. She dug her gaze into him, as though it could bore through his expensive red vest and stab him in the back.

"You," Eugessa's voice snapped. The Prioress of the Horn stood, leaning on the table, digging her own gaze into Sable. "I don't know how you manipulated Narine into giving you this, but it's not going to work. You've been a brash, power-hungry, conniving snake this whole time, but you do not have the right to be here."

Eugessa's voice was venomous, and Sable glanced at Vivaine, but the High Prioress merely watched, offering Sable no support.

"Narine," Eugessa continued, "trusts you, for reasons I cannot fathom. And now, as she is weakening, you come here and betray everything she stands for."

Sable opened her mouth to object, but the words hit too close for her to refute them.

"If you're going to claim you represent Narine, you could at least attempt to do something she would approve of. Which means standing respectfully *behind* her chair and keeping your mouth shut." Eugessa gave her a look of pure loathing. "You are a disgrace to that seat."

Eugessa strode out of the room, and Sable watched her go with a mix of fury and guilt.

"Well," Vivaine said with a tired voice. "If your goal was to make enemies, I believe you succeeded."

"My goal was to vote against the Kalesh. If I'd known you didn't even intend to have any votes today, I would have stayed with Narine." Sable spared a part of her glare for Gwen, who still stood behind Vivaine. "She was not well when I left this morning."

Gwen had the decency to look away, but Vivaine didn't blink.

"Tomorrow, I want to vote," Vivaine said, "and if we're going to get the outcome we both want, you're going to have to control yourself and stop accusing people of lying and trying to take over our country."

"The general was lying," Sable answered. "And the Kalesh do want to take over our country."

"Was the ambassador lying too, then?" Vivaine asked.

Sable paused. "No, he wasn't. But you don't honestly believe that they don't want the military advantages of controlling the river."

"Of course they do." Vivaine leaned her head back in her chair. "Which is why we need to handle this carefully." She let out a tired sigh. "I don't want to work with you, Issable, any more than you want to work with me. But for the love of Amah, Narine, and everything we both cherish, just support me tomorrow. I'll see to it that the right number of votes swing our way. But you need to stop derailing the conversation."

"Derailing?"

"This is a diplomatic summit," Vivaine said. "Everyone knows half the things said are lies. The trick is to outmaneuver them despite that."

"Well," Sable said dryly, "I see how you ended up in charge of it all, then. Working your way around lies and half-truths is one of your strengths."

Vivaine pushed herself up. "If you actually care about this land, be helpful tomorrow," she said wearily. "For a single day, try to not make my life harder."

CHAPTER THIRTY-EIGHT

VIVAINE STRETCHED her fingers toward the window, brightening just to the point that she was the brightest thing in the room, then closed her eyes and schooled her face into a calm expression.

Outside the door, the gathering hall was filled with voices. Vivaine started toward it. "There is still a lot to do tonight," she said, keeping her eyes on the door. "Don't do anything stupid."

When Vivaine reached the door, she glanced back at Gwen, who hadn't moved. "Gwen," she said impatiently, "come." Without waiting, she walked out.

Gwen stood, staring after her with an expression Sable couldn't decipher. But she merely folded her hands together at her stomach, tucking them inside the silver-edged cuffs of her long sleeves. Without a word, she followed Vivaine.

Sable leaned back in the chair, feeling utterly exhausted. The gathering hall was filled with people and noise, and she lingered in the quiet room until the rich scent of roasting meat swirled in again, and her stomach pointed out that lunch had been many long, irritating hours ago.

She pushed herself up and went out into the hall, which was filled not only with the leaders from the summit but also the soldiers, abbesses, servants, and merchants who supported each delegation. The long fire pit that ran down the center of the room held three different fires, adding more warmth to the room than it needed. Sable paused outside the summit door.

Along the back of the room, toward the bookshelves, she caught a glimpse of a wide table heaped with food, and she skirted around the edge of the room toward it.

Somewhere, stringed instruments played a jaunty tune, the cheerfulness of the melody jarring against the tension that had filled the day.

She caught a glimpse of Reese near the other side of the room, but he was standing among a handful of people she couldn't see clearly. She spent a moment looking for Talia or Ryah, but the cluster of merchants along the far side of the room was too much to see through, and there were too many white-robed abbesses to pick out a single one.

The only person easy to find was Vivaine, bright white against the golden firelight that filled the rest of the room.

Sable piled a plate with some lamb, cheese, and enough honey rolls to stuff Narine, if she happened to be awake, and wove her way through the room.

"Sable!" a voice called as she neared the door. She turned to see Talia moving through the crowd, dressed in a bright dress, her hair twisted up elaborately on her head.

"I heard Narine had come." Talia reached her, her face worried. "Is she as ill as people say?"

Sable gripped the plate and nodded.

Talia's brow creased with sympathy, and she set her hand on Sable's arm, just for a breath. "I'm sorry."

Callie, smiling brightly, stepped up next to Talia. "Isn't this place so quaint? It's like a toy village, and the monks are like toy soldiers. I could just squeeze them!"

Sable stared at her. "The warrior monks? You want to squeeze the well-trained, dangerous monks?"

"There *is* something picturesque about the whole thing," Talia said, giving Sable an annoyed look.

"If I ever pull a Rabbit," Callie continued blithely, "I'm escaping to a place like this."

"Pull a Rabbit?" Sable asked.

"Get out of the city," Callie explained. "Do something amazing enough to earn complete freedom from Kiva, like Rabbit did, and just...leave." Her smile brightened. "Maybe they should change the phrase to 'pull a Sable!'"

"I hardly just left," Sable objected.

"You're out of Dockside," Callie pointed out. "And Kiva doesn't hold anything over you anymore."

Sable glanced at Talia. "If only that were true." She shook her head. "The more I learn about Kiva, the less I think Rabbit is real. He's probably a story Kiva made up to give everyone hope. If you ever bring something amazingly valuable to Kiva, he'll just demand something more."

Callie looked undeterred. "Rabbit is real."

"He is," Talia said. "I've met him."

"You've met the man who earned his way out of Dockside?" Sable said, not bothering to hide her skepticism.

Talia nodded. "He comes to visit Kiva occasionally. Sometimes offers him information for a fee. I've started seeing him more often lately."

Sable let out a snort. "So the legendary Rabbit is real, but he still works for Kiva."

"I don't think he works for Kiva." Talia frowned. "Kiva talks to Rabbit differently than to other people. More like an equal. He never demands anything, just pays him if the information is good, and then Rabbit goes on his way."

"Still, that's a little depressing," Sable said. "I've always thought of Rabbit as this mythical figure who strode out of the city and made some amazing life for himself. But mythical figures shouldn't still hang around with Kiva once they have the chance to escape."

"I don't think Kiva's that bad," Callie said. "He's taken good care of Talia and me."

"Don't try to convince Sable of that," Talia said. "She's convinced he's a monster who lives to manipulate and use us all."

"Because he is," Sable said.

"That's harsh," Kiva's voice drawled from behind Sable. "I would have expected your time with the good Prioress Narine to have sweetened you a bit, Sable."

She turned to find him standing close behind her. He was barely taller than her, and his face was uncomfortably close. She resisted the urge to step back but shifted her plate until it sat between them, giving her at least a little space . "Narine is a big supporter of always speaking the truth."

Kiva smirked at her, but his eyes turned calculating. "Must be why you and she are so close. Your drive to find the truth in the summit today was…eye-opening."

Sable studied him, trying to figure out what he meant by that, but he merely continued to look at her with his smug, predatory smile.

"I was surprised to see your old friend here." Kiva motioned toward the corner of the room where Reese and Tanis had been talking. "Seems his brush with death last summer didn't deter him from fighting the Kalesh."

"What do you want, Kiva?" Sable asked him.

"Just to say hello to my daughter." He leaned around Sable and gave Talia a complacent smile. "Did you have a pleasant trip, dear?"

"I need to bring the Phoenix Prioress her dinner," Sable said flatly. She glanced at Talia and Callie. "Be careful of the company you two keep tonight. There are some unsavory folk about."

Talia gave an amused laugh. "Goodnight, Sable."

"Unsavory?" Callie asked Talia, glancing around the room.

Sable shook her head and worked her way through the people toward the door, trying not to bump her plate.

She'd only taken a few steps when Kiva grabbed her arm and stopped her.

"Be careful, Sable," he said, his voice holding a dangerous edge. "Starting fights in the summit is a good way to get the attention of powerful people. Not the sort of attention you want."

Sable twisted her arm away from him, almost spilling her dinner. "Luckily, you've given me years of practice at dealing with that. You should be careful yourself, Kiva. When you picked Eugessa, you picked the losing side."

"We'll see." He grinned. "Never a dull moment with you, Sable. Looking forward to the performance you have in store for us tomorrow."

She leaned closer to him. "Maybe I'll share who's really responsible for the attacks on the merchant wagons."

He shrugged. "No one would believe you."

She glared at him. "Your attack on Trelles could have put Talia in danger. If anything happens to her—anything at all—I'm holding you responsible."

Kiva gave her a dismissive look. "Talia is under my protection. No one will harm her."

"Because you care for her so deeply?" Sable asked dryly.

He let out a short laugh. "No. Although I am fond of her, just like I'm fond of you." He leaned closer. "But she'll be safe because there are two ways to control people, Sable. The first is to crush them. To hurt them in ways they can barely survive, to quench any fire they ever had. Now, every once in a while, someone comes through that with some life left in them, but usually they're only good for doing menial work and taking simple orders.

"If you need someone to be able to think clearly and make quick, intelligent decisions, you don't crush them, you give them the choice to serve you. I need Talia to be beautiful and charming and clever. She can't do that if she's hurt, and so she will be safe." He took in Sable with a look that made her skin crawl. "You're a beautiful woman, Sable. Why do you think no one ever bothered you in Dockside?"

She drew back from his wolfish expression.

"You were far too clever and creative to damage. So I kept you safe." He motioned toward the other side of the room. "The High Prioress understands this. It's why she lets you remain such an obnoxious, interfering irritation. She needs you engaged and clear thinking. So she's kept you safe."

Sable's hands shook with outrage at the words and at how true they felt.

"You don't realize how powerless you truly are here," he continued. "If I wanted someone gone from this summit, it's only a matter of how. A quick knife in the back? Or do I have the time to use something more elegant?"

"Vayakadyn venom isn't elegant," Sable said, disgusted.

"Of course it is. A bit of poison in their food tonight, and by the time the stomach pains hit tomorrow, there's no real way for them to know who did it."

"The black tongue once they're dead would point directly to you."

"It might point you to me, but most people don't know much about vaya venom. I guarantee none of the northern lords know about our little coastal snake. Does Andreese even know about it? I would wager he doesn't. Shall I introduce him to it?"

Sable drew back and glanced at the pocket of his vest. "You did not bring that horrible creature here with you."

"Of course I did. I couldn't leave her at home to get lonely. She might wander out and bite someone I liked."

"How is it that the rest of the summit doesn't see what a foul little scab you are?" Sable hissed at him.

"Because people see what they want to see." He patted her shoulder. "Have a good evening, Sable."

She jerked away from him, and he laughed before turning back to the room.

Sable turned and hurried out into the square, breathing in the cool evening air and gripping the plate tightly. Without pausing, she crossed to Narine's house, stepping inside and shutting the door firmly behind her.

The room was quiet and empty, with the exception of an elderly abbess doing some needlework at the table near the front window. The stove burned with a cheery fire, and Narine still lay curled up on the couch, and Sable leaned her back against the door.

"Good evening," the abbess said pleasantly.

"Not so far," Sable muttered. She pushed herself off the door and started toward Narine. "Has she woken yet?"

"No," the abbess answered, turning a sorrowful look at Narine. "No change since this morning. She doesn't seem uncomfortable, though, so we haven't given her any herbs."

Sable caught the abbess looking out the window toward the light of the gathering hall.

"Why don't you go get dinner?" Sable told her. "I'll sit with the prioress for a while."

The abbess gave her a quick smile and tucked her needles away before hurrying out the door.

Sable carried the plate to the table by the couch, pushing aside bottles of herbs and medicines to make room for it. Innov slept on a perch near the stove, and Sable ran her finger over the phoenix's feathers, which were barely brighter than the dusky room around them. Turning to Narine, Sable set her hand on the prioress's forehead.

Narine wasn't cold. Her forehead was sweaty and warm. The elderly prioress still had a slight wrinkle in her brow, the echo of the frown she'd had this morning.

Sable picked up a piece of cheese and sat on the couch near Narine's feet, sinking into the soft, russet cushions. She closed her eyes and leaned back as the room spun slowly around her.

The squeak of the door roused her, and she turned, catching a glitter of silver on a white sleeve.

CHAPTER THIRTY-NINE

"How is the prioress?" Gwen asked quietly, closing the door behind her.

Sable shoved herself off the couch, pointing her still uneaten cheese at the Mira. "Get out of this house!"

Gwen raised her hands in front of her. "I just need to know she's all right." Rich warmth flowed into the room at the words.

"All right?" Sable stormed toward the Mira. "How could she possibly be all right when you—" The words caught in Sable's throat. "She hasn't woken up since last night!"

Gwen's brow creased in uncharacteristic guilt. "Not once?"

"What did you do to her?"

"I didn't—" Gwen stopped. "May I go to her?"

Sable glared at her. "Why?"

The Mira gave a small, uncertain shrug. "To see if I can help." The words were warm and true, and Gwen held Sable's furious gaze. For once, there was nothing confident in the Mira's look.

Sable shook her head. "Tell me what you did."

Gwen swallowed and looked back toward Narine's couch. "Sometimes I can...suggest thoughts to people." She shifted and clasped her hands together inside her silver cuffs. "It's never very strong. I could convince a child they wanted a honey roll instead of cake, maybe. But most adult's opinions are too strong to sway." She paused.

"And?"

"And Vivaine asked me to come with her when she visited Narine last night, because she wanted to see if I could plant the idea in Narine's head that the voting was a good thing." Her look turned pleading. "Which I know you agree with."

"I'm not interested in agreeing with you on anything right now." Sable crossed her arms. "You said your little trick wouldn't work on an adult."

"Which I told Vivaine," Gwen said quickly. She glanced behind her at the door. "But she insisted I try to help Narine see the importance of the vote."

All of Gwen's words were true. Which only increased Sable's annoyance. "Narine is a grown woman. She understands exactly what's going on. She just disagrees with Vivaine on what to do about it."

"You've wanted her to vote for the last year!" Gwen said.

"Not like this!"

Gwen rubbed her hand over her mouth. "I know. I didn't want to do it either, but sometimes Vivaine is...hard to resist. Especially if Argyros is near."

Sable almost retorted that it was simple to argue with Vivaine, but Gwen's words were deeply, fervently true. "You did this because you're scared of Vivaine's dragon?"

"Not scared of him," Gwen shook her head. "Or maybe I am scared of him, but that's not why I did what she wanted. There are times when...I *have* to. I can't explain it, but even though I didn't want to help her, I was compelled to." She looked back at Sable. "And I didn't have a strong reason to say no, because I didn't think it would work anyway."

Sable let out a frustrated breath. "What happened?"

"I sat touching Narine's feet while Vivaine talked. I tried to impress on Narine the importance of voting, but her mind fought back, the way adult minds always do. She recognized the thought as not her own, and she got angry. But before I could stop, Vivaine grabbed my shoulder and I felt…" Gwen shuddered. "Something move through me, into Narine. Something hot."

Gwen stared toward the couch, her eyes unfocused. "I couldn't stop," she said. "I couldn't let go of Narine. I couldn't do anything."

The Mira pressed her eyes shut and hugged her arms in tightly. "I felt it," she whispered. "I felt Narine's mind…break."

A stab of horror shot through Sable. "Break?"

Gwen nodded, her own expression horrified. "All her resistance just crumbled." She rubbed her forehead, scrubbing it with her palm, as though she could erase the memory.

Slowly, fury started to push Sable's horror back. "Did Vivaine feel it?" she demanded.

Gwen nodded, the action quick and jerky. "She knew. She knelt next to Narine and asked her whether it wouldn't be better if you voted in her stead. Talked to her like she was a small child. And Narine just…agreed."

Sable's hands clenched into fists, smashing the cheese between her fingers.

"Vivaine plans to come tonight to check on her," Gwen said, "but I thought if I came first, maybe I could help or…something. Or at least tell Vivaine how Narine is, and maybe she won't come." She glanced toward Narine with a worried expression. "I don't want Vivaine to come again," she finished in a whisper.

Sable stepped back from the warmth of the Mira's words. She took a deep breath. "Can you help Narine?"

Gwen hesitated. "I don't know. But I would like to try."

"Do you intend to harm her?"

"No," Gwen said vehemently.

"Are you here because Vivaine sent you?"

"No." Gwen gave a humorless laugh. "She wants me chatting with your Andreese tonight to see what the rebels are planning."

Sable frowned. "Then she should have you snoop around Tanis's brain, not Andreese's."

"Except she also wants to know if you and Andreese have something planned."

"You could have just asked me that."

Gwen gave an exasperated sigh. "You won't let me touch you, remember?

"I hardly expected that to stop either of you. And isn't she going to be angry that you're not invading Reese's mind right now?"

"I already talked to him." Gwen gave Sable a thoughtful look. "I see why you like him. He's very...honest."

"What is that supposed to mean?"

"People's heads are noisy, conflicted places," she answered. "Most of them aren't thinking of any one thing in particular. They're focused on what they're doing, but their minds are also worrying about things at home, or money, or what the people around them are thinking of them. They are distracted by everything, and most thoughts are just fragments and reactions."

Gwen shook her head. "During a conversation, it's even worse. Because they're thinking of what they're going to say, and why they're saying it, and how much of it is true, and what the real truth is. All at the same time. It's like four people talking at once."

"So?"

"So, he isn't like that. He thinks something, and then says it. Or doesn't say it. It's refreshing."

Sable felt unexpectedly annoyed. "I'm surprised he talked to you. He's not fond of the priories, or Vivaine."

"No, he is not. But he was too polite to walk away." Gwen looked back toward Narine. "May I?"

Despite Gwen's honesty, Sable studied the Mira for a moment, then nodded.

Gwen moved over to the couch and knelt. She set her hand on Narine's thin shoulder and closed her eyes.

On her perch, Innov stirred.

Gwen sat quietly for a few minutes, her brow creased in concentration. Finally, she sat back on her heels and opened her eyes. She shook her head slowly. "Her thoughts are very quiet, and very simple. She's tired and..." She glanced up at Sable. "Afraid."

Sable's eyes narrowed, but Gwen put her hand on Narine's shoulder again. In a breath, Narine's brow smoothed back into its normal calm expression.

"What did you do?" Sable demanded.

"I told her Vivaine and Argyros are gone." Gwen sank back. "And that you are here."

"Oh…" She looked at Narine's still form. "Thank you. Is she going to wake up?"

"Maybe. She was hiding, but now that she feels safer, she might wake."

For the first time since the fever hit, Narine looked like she was just sleeping peacefully. The way she had napped every day that Sable had known her. She was too thin, and too pale, and this wasn't just a nap to regain her strength, but it was a small relief.

"Thank you," Sable said again.

Gwen rose. "I'll tell Vivaine that Narine is still unconscious and that there's been no change since last night. It's what she'll want to hear anyway, and hopefully it'll keep her from coming tonight." She paused. "I wish I could do more. I wish…" She trailed off, looking at Narine. "If the prioress wakes," she said finally, "please tell her I'm sorry."

Sable nodded, and Gwen let herself out of the house. Sable sat on the couch, watching Narine.

"I wish you'd wake up," she whispered. "Although I understand if you don't want to. Not here." She glanced around the snug house. "Actually, the town itself is lovely. Dozens of little buildings all built with timber frame and tiled roofs. It looks like something out of a story."

Narine didn't move.

"I know that it's pure selfishness to want you awake," Sable continued. "But I can't help it. I miss talking to you, and I'm not ready for you to…not wake up." She rose and found a pile of soft towels folded on a shelf. Taking one, she gently wiped the last of the clamminess off Narine's forehead. "Your hands are turning cold again. And I'm actually a little relieved. If I make you tea, will you wake enough to hold it? I'll add extra tintis powder, and you can complain that it's unnecessary. Or I can tell you all the horrible things Vivaine has done recently. This time you might not even remind me to be respectful."

A small groan came from Narine, and Sable grabbed the prioress's hands. Narine's eyes fluttered open, and she tensed when she saw the room.

Sable shifted in front of her. "Narine!"

The prioress's eyes focused on Sable, and she let out a shallow sigh of relief.

"How do you feel?" Sable asked. "Are you cold? Do you want more blankets? Tea? Honey rolls?"

Narine let out a laugh that was barely more than a breath. "I had the most horrible dream." She closed her eyes for a long moment, and the crease in her brow returned. "Was it a dream?"

Sable paused and gripped Narine's hand tighter. "No."

Narine opened her eyes and met Sable's gaze. "What did I agree to do?"

"You didn't agree to do anything," Sable began, but Narine's patient expression made her close her mouth. "Vivaine made you sign a paper saying I was to vote for you."

Narine showed no surprise. "And did you?"

Sable shifted. "There was no vote today."

Narine considered her. "If there had been?"

Sable looked down at Narine's hands. "If there had been a vote about the Kalesh getting anything more than they have already, I would have voted against it."

Narine didn't answer, and when Sable looked back up, the prioress was looking sadly at Innov.

"I know you don't want me to," Sable said, "but Vivaine convinced everyone I was supposed to, and…I think it's important."

Narine kept her eyes on the sleeping phoenix. "I'm tired of being a prioress," she said softly. "I'm tired of people wanting me to choose things for them and make decisions that I can't see the repercussions of. I'm tired of Vivaine wanting to control me. I'm tired of Eugessa doing selfish, ugly things in Amah's name."

Sable stared at Narine, shocked.

"It's a relief to have handed off that responsibility." She looked at Sable. "Although I feel bad pressing it on you."

"You didn't press anything on me," Sable objected. "Now that you're awake, we can tell everyone what Vivaine did."

Narine shook her head. "I'm not proud enough to think that I always know best. Maybe I should have been voting all this time, like you've been begging me to. Maybe I've chosen silence because it was easier."

"You chose it because you didn't want to play Vivaine's game," Sable said.

"Well, the one thing I know about you, my dear, is that you aren't interested in playing Vivaine's game either. I've given you my permission to vote, and regardless of the circumstances, I will let it stand." Narine gave Sable a sad smile. "I'm so terribly tired. My arms feel so heavy, and I just want to curl up by the fire and sleep. Unless their vote comes very quickly, you may not have a Phoenix Prioress to vote in place of."

Sable drew in a breath. "I don't want you to go," she whispered.

Narine's smile turned gentle. "When I'm gone, promise me you'll leave. Don't let Vivaine keep you here."

Sable opened her mouth, but a quiet knock on the door interrupted her. Sable flinched at the noise.

"If it's Vivaine," Narine said grimly, "don't let her in."

Sable shot a glare at the door. "If it's Vivaine, I'm going to punch her in her glowing white face."

Sable looked out the front window. The world outside had fallen into darkness, and the figure on the front step was definitely not glowing white.

Sable opened the door to Reese holding a bowl of scarletberries.

CHAPTER FORTY

REESE HELD OUT THE BOWL. "The monks grow their berry bushes in a half-buried building with windows for a roof," he said.

Sable stared at him. "What?"

He looked down at the heap of red berries as though that answered her question. "That's why they're ripe. It's over a month early."

Sable laughed. "I don't know when scarletberries ripen."

"After the pineberries flower, but before the apples turn yellow." He held up the bowl as though she should be impressed. "Easily a month from now."

"If the young man has scarletberries," Narine's voice came weakly from inside, "let him in."

Reese's eyes widened. "Gwen said she was sleeping," he whispered.

Sable frowned. "You should *not* talk to Gwen." The words came out more hostile than Sable had intended.

He looked at her in surprise. "Why not?" A little smile curled up the side of his mouth. "Are you jealous?"

"No, I'm not jealous," Sable snapped. "She can read your mind."

His smile froze. "What?"

"She can read your mind. Vivaine sent her to see what you know about the rebels' plans. And—" Sable paused.

"And what?" Reese asked, his voice outraged.

"And whether you and I have anything planned."

He paused. "What would we have planned?"

"I have no idea!"

Reese shot a glare toward the gathering hall. "She can read my mind?" He shifted his shoulders, as though trying to shake off an unpleasant weight. "That's so...invasive."

"Tell me about it," Sable muttered.

"Didn't someone mention scarletberries?" Narine called.

Sable motioned Reese in and shut the door behind him. The room had grown dim, and Narine was lit mostly by the orange light of the wood stove.

"Narine," she said, bringing Reese over in front of the couch. "This is Andreese. Andreese, the Phoenix Prioress."

Reese gave her a polite nod of his head, but instead of her usual welcoming smile, Narine studied him with a thoughtful expression. "The assassin," she said finally.

Sable stared at her, speechless.

Reese's eyebrows rose. "Among other things."

"Why did you do it?" Narine asked.

There was nothing accusatory in the words, they were more probing, as though Narine were trying to sort out a puzzle. Sable opened her mouth to object to the question, but Narine's eyes stopped her. For the first time in weeks, they were clear and focused.

Reese didn't look away from the prioress's gaze. "Because he was the leader of the Kalesh forces that were taking over Immusmala and had destroyed my home and killed people I loved. A fact no one believed. And because, even though no one had officially said it, the Empire had declared war on us."

"So it was a military action."

Reese nodded. "As far as the Kalesh are concerned, we've been at war with them for well over a year. We just never put up enough of a fight for them to warrant the expense of sending many actual troops. They're winning easily without any bloodshed."

Narine considered his answer. "Then you're a soldier?" She glanced at the common, undyed shirt he wore. "Who disguises himself as a woodsman?"

Reese let out a short laugh. "Among other things."

Narine still didn't smile at him.

Sable felt a tickle of irritation at the woman. "I should have introduced Reese to you yesterday, Holy Mother, when you were still kind to strangers."

The prioress shook her head. "This man is hardly a stranger. I have heard many, many things about him."

Reese glanced at Sable, still looking amused. "Do you talk about me a lot?"

"No," Sable retorted.

"In all fairness," Narine said, "it hasn't all been from Issable. Although the most interesting parts have been." She studied Reese again, looking troubled. "And I don't have time to waste talking to you about unimportant things."

"I prefer straight questions anyway." Reese held out the bowl. "Before you continue, would you like some scarletberries?"

"I would like all the scarletberries," Narine said, eyeing the bowl. "But that feels greedy, so I will settle for some."

Sable shook her head. "If I'd had any indication the prioress was feeling so…plucky tonight, I would have warned you off, Reese." She went to a cupboard along the wall and pulled out three bowls.

The room was growing dark, and she lit three oil lamps. When she turned to set one near the couch, Reese was helping Narine sit up. His arm looked enormous wrapped around the prioress's thin shoulders.

From her perch by the stove, Innov squawked, and Reese glanced over. He paused, looking at the bird.

"She's beautiful, isn't she?" Sable asked, setting down the lamp.

Reese nodded, watching the barely visible glitter of light trail off Innov.

"You should see her when she's bright." Sable turned back to the bowls and divided up the berries.

Reese pulled two chairs up near the couch. Sable handed out the bowls and sat in a chair.

Reese sat in the other. "What is it that you're trying to figure out about me, Holy Mother?"

"Yes," Sable asked, picking out one of the bright red berries. "What are you grilling him about?" She popped the berry into her mouth. It was perfectly ripe, bursting with sweetness but still keeping the sharp tartness at the edge.

Narine smiled at Reese for the first time. "I'm trying to balance what I know of you from the many and varied rumors I've heard with the fact that Issable is so fond of you."

Reese glanced at Sable with a little smile. "She is?"

"She is," Narine said before Sable could object. "And I wouldn't expect her to be fond of a violent man." She paused. "Are you a violent man?"

Reese considered the question. "There's been more violence in my life than I wish there'd been. But sometimes there are battles that need to be fought."

Narine popped a scarletberry into her mouth and chewed it thoughtfully. "Did you attack those mine workers? Was that a battle that needed to be fought?"

Reese shook his head. "We did not attack them. Tanis and I had planned to collapse the mine during the night while no one was in it. But the Kalesh attacked us first."

Narine nodded. "And if the Kalesh send an army, will you fight them?"

"Yes," Reese said without hesitation. "But if the Kalesh send an army, this land will fall. We're too divided and too weak to stand against them."

"So you agree with Issable that I should have been voting against the Kalesh expansion for the past year?"

"Yes," Reese answered, with a glance at Sable. "But I don't think we can stop them diplomatically. We need to unite the north and the south. We still might not have the strength to stop an invasion, but we'd be more prepared." He shook his head. "But we can't even get the Northern Lords to agree on anything, never mind get Immusmala and the southern towns to come together. It's our disunity that the Kalesh are capitalizing on. They know they can continue to mine and move through the land unhindered because we're too busy bickering with each other to stop them."

"Even if the north unites," Sable said, "I can't imagine Vivaine agreeing to anything that lessens her hold on the south."

Narine chewed another berry and looked between Sable and Reese. "What do you two intend to do about that?"

Sable let out a laugh. "We don't intend to do anything."

Narine raised an eyebrow. "Really?"

"I'll vote tomorrow against the Kalesh getting land at the mouth of the river," Sable said, "But that's as far as my powers go."

"I'd love to do…something," Reese said. "But at this point, I don't know what would unify everyone. Aside from an invasion, and if we wait that long, it'll be too late."

"So you're not here to assassinate this ambassador?" Narine asked him.

Reese shook his head. "No."

"Why not? What has changed?"

"A lot of things," he answered. "First, I'm not working alone anymore. Also, it's no longer a secret that the Kalesh are trying to expand their power here. Last year no one knew what the Kalesh were doing, and had Vivaine signed the treaty with Ambassador Tehl, the south would have been lost." He glanced over at Sable. "And I can't kill this ambassador because I've discovered he's Sable's very special friend."

"He is not my friend," Sable said, annoyed. "I regret letting you in here, Reese. I should have taken the berries and closed the door."

Narine was watching Reese thoughtfully again. "Why are you here?"

"He's at the peace summit with everyone else," Sable answered, "because he's part of this whole mess."

"Oh, I know why he's at the summit," Narine said. "I want to know why he came to my house tonight."

Reese paused with a berry halfway to his mouth. "I came to talk to Sable."

"About what?" Narine asked. "To plan something against the

Kalesh during the vote tomorrow?" There was an odd edge of amusement in her voice, but she kept her face serious.

"No," Reese said slowly, dropping his hand. "I just wanted to talk to her."

"About?" Narine pressed.

Sable's fingers stopped, stuck in her bowl of berries.

Reese's gaze glanced toward Sable but returned to the prioress. "I don't know. I just wanted to see her."

A small, triumphant smile curled just the corner of Narine's mouth. "Because you've missed her."

"Narine!" Sable objected.

Reese looked down at the red berry and rolled it slowly between his fingers. A rueful smile spread across his face. "Yes, because I've missed her."

Sable's fingers tightened, and a scarletberry smashed between her fingers. Reese glanced over at the crushed fruit, and his smile grew.

Narine sank back, smiling widely. "Issable has been afraid that you didn't miss her."

"I wasn't afraid," Sable objected.

"Of course you were," Narine said, her voice calm and gentle. "And when we have the chance to see if our fears are real, we should always take it. Because now you don't have to worry anymore." She turned back to him. "From the relieved expression on your face, you were afraid of the same thing. So, now that you can set that very immediate fear aside, what else are you afraid of, Andreese?"

Reese looked at her uncertainly for a breath, then glanced at Sable.

"Narine," Sable broke in, "I assured Reese that you were kind and understanding. Not some kind of inquisitor. People don't just have their deepest fears sitting on the tip of their tongues. That's the real reason no one talks about them." She paused. "Except you. And you never rush into it like this."

Narine fixed Sable with an impatient look. "How much time, exactly, do you think I have to get to know him?" Without waiting for an answer, she turned back to Reese. "When you're awake at night, and there is nothing but yourself and the darkness, what are you afraid of, Andreese?"

Sable let out an exasperated breath, but Reese considered her words.

"I'm afraid that when it comes down to it, we cannot beat the Kalesh." He shifted. "I'm afraid that any future I want to build will be tainted because they'll be here and there will be fighting, or they will just do what they always do, and come in and wipe out anything that's ours, and just absorb us into the Empire." He paused, nodding slowly. "I'm afraid we can't stop the Empire."

Narine gave a hum of acknowledgment. "I am familiar with that fear myself."

Sable glanced at her. "You are?"

The prioress looked pensively down at her remaining scarletberries. "I'm also afraid that the fight against them will change us."

Reese's hand tightened on his bowl.

"I have been afraid," Narine continued, "that my fear of the Kalesh will cause me to compromise the things I hold dear."

Sable felt a worm of guilt stir inside of her.

"And what if we already have?" Reese asked.

Narine raised her face, her expression heavy. "Then, from this point on, we decide we are done compromising."

The knuckles on Reese's hand were white, gripping his bowl. His jaw twitched under his beard. "And if it led us to the point where we assassinated someone?" he asked, his voice barely above a whisper.

Sable sat very still. The tension in Reese's body was visible, and Narine met his gaze with her usual gentle attention, all traces of her earlier hounding gone. Sable's hands tightened on her own bowl. She had never thought about whether the assassination had been hard on Reese. The only thing she'd ever felt had been anger that he and Atticus hadn't told her first.

"A heavy weight to carry," Narine said quietly. "But as much as we'd like to change things from yesterday, all we can do is decide to live in a way today that we will not regret tomorrow."

Reese let out a long breath. "That's not easy."

"No," Narine agreed. "The right choices rarely are. More often than not, the wrong choice is the easier of the two."

The prioress's hand slipped off the side of her bowl and fell heavily on her lap. She was already leaning back against the couch, but her head lolled to the side. Reese leaned forward, his face worried.

"Oh, Narine," Sable stood and handed her bowl to Reese. "We've exhausted you." She wrapped her arm around Narine's shoulders and helped her lie on her side while Reese cleared the chairs away. Narine gave a grateful hum and closed her eyes.

Sable pulled the blanket up over her, but it was thin, and even though the room was comfortable, Narine's hands were terribly cold. "Reese, could you add some wood to the stove?"

He hesitated only a moment at the odd request on the warm evening before heading for the stove.

Sable went to the short hallway leading to the back of the house and found a thick quilt in the closet.

She was stepping back into the room when the window past Narine shattered.

A streak of fire arced into the room, and a bottle smashed into the floor. Burning liquid sprayed out, and an explosion of flames spread across the floor and sprayed up onto the couch.

The blanket lying over Narine burst into flames.

CHAPTER FORTY-ONE

"NARINE!" Sable shouted, rushing toward her.

Fire flared up from the burning liquid. Heat rolled off the waist-high flames in a scorching wave, searing Sable's cheeks and driving her back.

Narine cried out and scrambled to the far end of the couch, trying to get out from under the blazing blanket.

"Narine!" Sable held the thick quilt up to block the heat and flames as she tried to get closer.

Reese raced around the far edge of the fire to Narine and threw off the burning blanket. Narine's robe was scorched and blackened, and Sable caught a glimpse of raw, burned flesh through the fabric.

He scooped Narine up, and she clung to him as he carried her away from the fire. He set her down against the far wall, and Innov, dim and weak, flew heavily over and landed on the floor by the prioress.

Flames blazed up from the couch cushions with loud hisses and cracks as exposed wood from the couch frame caught fire. Flames filled the floor in front of the couch, so Sable stood at the foot of it and beat at the flames with the quilt. Black smoke billowed up, hit the low ceiling, and rolled out in all directions.

"Sable?" Reese shouted, running toward her.

"The floor!" Sable yelled, pointing to the wide circle of flames blackening the slats of wood.

Reese ripped a curtain down from next to the shattered window and beat at the edges of the fire, putting out small sections at a time.

But the couch cushions were covered with the burning liquid. Every time Sable put out one section, flames near it would set it ablaze again. Acrid smoke swirled around her, burning her throat.

Sable swore and shook out the quilt, tossing it over the couch like a mantle.

For a moment, there was no sign of the fire.

Then a charred circle bloomed on the fabric.

She swatted at the hot spot with her hand, smothering the flames that tried to burn though, until the heat singed her palm and she yanked away.

Reese worked his way closer on the floor, putting out the fire and leaving a wide, blackened stretch of wood.

A new circle of blackness grew on the quilt. Sable swore and slammed her hands down on it, snuffing it out. Another appeared further down the couch, and two more near the edge. Tiny bits of flames stretched out of the darkest ones.

"Stop!" she said through gritted teeth. Sweat dripped down Sable's face and neck as she climbed up onto the quilt, slamming her hands down again and again, smothering the flames trying to burn through. Each time her hands hit the hot blanket, pain shot through them.

Waves of heat filled the room, scorching hot, swirling around Sable, almost more smothering than the smoke.

A wide, charred circle exploded out of the quilt, and a finger of flame reached out of it. With a yell, Sable slammed her hands down on it. "Enough!"

The word rushed out of her, hot and furious.

Pain ripped through her hands, as though they were on fire themselves.

Smoke filled the air above her, billowing lower.

She pressed down as hard as she could on the quilt. "Enough!" she snarled at the fire through clenched teeth. Her hands screamed in pain, but she kept them pressed down, her arms shaking.

Slowly, she realized that there were no more flames.

She stood and backed away. Trails of smoke rose from the edges of the blackened quilt.

"Reese?" she called, her breaths coming heavy and raw.

He beat out the last of the flames on the floor. "I'm fine." He coughed. "Are you hurt?"

Sable held her hands gingerly in front of her. Her palms were red and blistered. Bits of charred fabric stuck to her skin, and she curled her fingers, cradling them to her chest. "Not much."

She turned to look for Narine. The prioress was huddled against the wall, her legs pulled up in front of her, the skin on them blackened and burned. Her body shook violently.

"Reese," she whispered, the word rough with smoke and terror for Narine. "Find who did this!"

Reese hesitated only a moment before nodding. He ran to the window, crunching over the broken glass. Wrapping some of the singed drape around his hand, he knocked out the last of the window-pane. He peered into the dark alley, then grabbed an oil lamp and climbed outside.

Sable bent down to stay below the worst of the smoke and ran to Narine.

The prioress's breath came in gasps, cut through with ragged coughs. Through the scorched holes in her robe, Sable could see patches of the woman's skin on her stomach and the front of her legs, blistered and burned. Innov had climbed up, and Narine held her pressed against her chest.

Sable looked wildly around the room. How could no one have seen the chaos and come to help? But the front door was still closed, and the windows were shut against any chill that the summer evening would have brought to Narine. The only open window was the broken one, leading into the narrow side alley.

A closed window was just above them, and Sable reached up, trying to keep her head under the smoke. Her fingers fumbled against the latch, and pain stabbed into her hand. She tried again, but her burned fingers refused to press hard enough to unstick the latch.

Narine coughed and wheezed, and Sable sank back down next to her. She needed to get Narine out of the smoke. The front door was closer than the back, but Narine could never walk that far.

She took a breath to call for help, but the smoke caught in her throat, and she doubled over, coughing.

"Purnicious!" Sable gasped.

In a heartbeat, there was a little pop next to her.

"Mistress—" Purn's cheerful greeting cut short in a gasp.

"Open the windows! And the doors!"

Purn clambered up onto the table and flipped the latch, swinging the window above them open. Cool night air rushed in, pouring down over Sable and Narine as smoke snaked out the top of the window.

With a pop, the kobold appeared across the room, opening the doors and windows. The smoke lifted, and Sable gulped in deep breaths of the clean air. Purnicious disappeared, and Sable heard her upstairs, opening more windows.

Narine's head sank back against the wall.

"Narine!" Sable crawled closer to her.

The prioress opened her eyes. Innov was still nestled against her chest, but Narine lifted one hand slowly and grabbed Sable's shoulder. "Leave here," she whispered.

The severity of Narine's burns wrung at Sable's chest. "The healers have to come soon!" Her words bubbled out sounding desperate. "They'll help you!"

"No." The word was quiet, but it pulled Sable's attention back to Narine's face. The prioress looked haggard. The phoenix leaned against her, dull and exhausted. Narine's white robe was scuffed with grime from the floor and streaks of soot, but her eyes were perfectly clear. "Leave this place, Issable. Go where you can have a life that is free from…all of this."

Sable shook her head. "I'm not leaving you."

"I like Andreese," Narine continued, ignoring the words.

Sable let out a short laugh. "You could have fooled me."

Narine gave her a weary smile. "I had to know what kind of man he is. There was no time for politeness." She patted Sable's shoulder. "I like him. He doesn't shy away from his weaknesses, but he wants to do good."

A round of coughing wracked Narine's body, and she tried to cover her mouth, but her arm was too weak.

"Purnicious," Sable called. "Can you find Narine a drink?"

The kobold appeared in the room and rushed to the table next to the couch where Narine's old tea sat. Bringing it quickly to the prioress, Purn held the cup out.

Narine looked at the little creature in amazement. "A kobold!"

"Narine," Sable said, "this is Purnicious."

"It's nice to meet you, Holy Mother," Purn said with a curtsey. "My mistress speaks very highly of you."

"Mistress?" Narine glanced at Sable in surprise.

"I accidentally saved her life," Sable said.

"She bravely rescued me from a Kalesh warrior who was going to kill me," Purnicious corrected her.

"Purn," Sable said, "go find Talia or Ryah so they can send help!"

The kobold disappeared.

"She can't come into the priories," Sable said. "So she's spent the last year near Talia."

Narine made a tired hum of understanding. "I'd almost forgotten that magical creatures are kept out of the priory." She looked down at Innov. "Except for our own," she said fondly. She rested her hand on the phoenix's side, moving her thumb slowly across the bird's feathers. Curled up against the prioress, Innov glowed slightly.

"Issable," Narine said so softly that Sable had to lean closer. "I'm tired. All I want to do is curl up and sleep." The prioress's voice was so weak and weary. Her breath short and labored.

"You can sleep soon," Sable assured her, watching the door. The room had cleared of most of the smoke, but pain throbbed in both her hands, and her throat was raw.

"No, Issable," Narine said.

Sable paused, looking back at the prioress.

Narine's face had an oddly vulnerable expression. "I want to *sleep*."

The words sent a shiver of uneasiness through Sable.

"But it's hard to truly go to sleep," Narine said quietly, "when I know you're here, waiting for me to wake again." Her expression took on a pleading edge. "Promise me you'll leave."

Sable reached for Narine's hand, but an arc of pain lanced across her palm when she opened her fingers, and she stopped. "I don't want to leave you," Sable whispered.

"I don't want to leave you either, my dear," Narine said with a gentle smile. "But my days are too short now to pretend it's our choice." She took a breath and coughed weakly. "Andreese seems like a resourceful young man. I'm sure if you ask him, he'll get you off this island and away from here. Promise me you'll go find a life away from the priories."

Sable cast around for a reason to object. "But the vote tomorrow," she said weakly.

Narine let out a tired sigh. "After the vote, then. Promise me you'll leave."

Sable swallowed, starting to shake her head.

"Please." Narine's skin was grey, and her lips were almost colorless.

Sable kept her eyes on Narine's face, trying not to look at the horrible burns on her stomach.

Reluctantly, Sable nodded.

"Thank you." Narine was quiet for a long moment, then the very edge of her mouth turned up in a smile. "I love you, Issable. Like you were my own daughter."

The prioress reached out a hand and pulled gently on Sable's shoulder. Sable leaned forward, and Narine stretched up and pressed a kiss to Sable's forehead. The prioress's lips felt cold, but Sable closed her eyes, and despite the light touch of the kiss, she felt a warmth trickle down into her body, loosening the tears that had been afraid to fall, tightening her throat, and filling her chest with a fierce pressure.

Sable leaned her head into the blessing. "I love you too, Narine."

"May you receive as many blessings in this life as you've given to me," Narine whispered before leaning back against the wall. The prioress's eyes slid shut.

Sable pressed the back of her hand against her mouth, tears streaking down her soot-covered cheeks.

Footsteps pounded up to the front door, and voices called out. Several abbesses rushed into the house, covering their mouths at the last of the smoke.

"The prioress needs a healer!" Sable choked out.

One ran back out the door, shouting for help, while the others crowded around Narine, and Sable backed away to give them room. The room still smelled strongly of smoke, but Sable could see the ceiling clearly again. Two healers ran in and knelt over Narine. The prioress let out a whimper, and Sable flinched at the noise.

Who would try to kill a dying woman?

A white wall of abbesses surrounded Narine, and Sable hesitated. But there was nothing for her to do here. She turned and ducked down the short hallway toward the back door.

The air outside was like a wave of cool water rushing over her. She took a deep breath of the freshness, coughing again as she ran to the alley along Narine's house. A pall of smoke still filled the gap between the houses, but the alley was quiet and shockingly calm after the chaos of the fire.

Sable blinked away the tears that filled her eyes and looked around her. To her right, the town wall wound away toward the gathering hall. The din of voices floated through the night, and the window she could see at the end of the hall was bright with light. Vivaine's dinner must still be going on. To her left, everything was dark and quiet. The torchlight from the square and the bright moon shining high in the eastern sky sent slanting paths of gold or silver light out between the buildings, breaking up the shadows.

She glanced up on the wall and saw a single monk looking in her direction. He pointed left, and she turned and jogged in that direction.

She passed the last two houses along this edge of the square, where the wall continued along the river but a small, moonlit alley between the buildings branched off into the town toward a brightly lit street. Reese was hurrying toward her.

"Sable!" He broke into a run. "Are you all right?"

Sable nodded, meeting him between two long, low houses. "Did you find him?"

Reese's gaze locked on her hands, which she held gingerly in front of her. "You're hurt!"

"I'm fine," she said, irritated. "Did you find him?"

He didn't look away from her hands. "One of the monks saw someone running away from the house after they heard the glass break, and they gave chase but lost him in the forest outside the gate. There are more looking for him now."

Sable glared into the darkness.

"They know this island perfectly," he said. "They'll find him."

He reached for her hands, and she flinched back. He raised an eyebrow and gave her a little smile. "Do you think I'm going to poke your burns?"

She smiled self-consciously, letting him take her hands gently and turn her palms toward the moonlight.

Both of her hands were burned, a row of blisters outlining her palms. The skin across them was tight and dark in the silver light. She tried to straighten her fingers, but the moment the skin pulled, pain shot across it.

His frown deepened. "Are you hurt?" He rubbed his thumb across the back of her hand. "More than this?"

Sable looked down at their hands and shook her head. "I'm fine. It's just…Narine."

She expected him to press the issue, but he just stood quietly, his hands holding hers up, his presence solid and calm.

She'd forgotten that about him. How he could just be near. Present, but somehow not demanding anything. Something deep inside her loosened.

"Narine is dying." She glanced up at him, half expecting a wry comment about how obvious that fact was. But he just looked down at her and tightened his hands ever so slightly. "I know everyone knows that, but she…wants to. She says she's too tired, and she wants me to leave so she can go to sleep without feeling like she needs to wake up."

He was silent for another long moment. "I'm sorry."

She took a step toward him, and he pulled one hand off hers, giving her room to turn and lean her shoulder against his chest. He wrapped his arm around her shoulders, and she sank against him, pressing her forehead into the crook of his neck. He smelled of leather and smoke, and she buried her face in his shirt, where it was warm and dark and sheltered. Tears filled her eyes, and she squeezed them shut.

She stood in the shallow edge of the grief she'd lived with for months, but the swelling, inevitable wave of loss she'd tried so hard not to look at drew close. It rolled toward her, and the ache rose, swirling, soaking, drowning every bit of space she'd tried to surround herself with. Lifting her almost off her feet with a relentless, latent power that dwarfed her.

The tears spilled out of her eyes and into the warmth of Reese's shirt. He stood solid and still, his arm tight around her. He didn't loosen his grip when her shoulders started to shake. Instead, he leaned his head down, his cheek and his breath warm against her hair.

The swell of grief rolled over her, past her, leaving her drenched in the truth that she was finally, inevitably losing Narine.

She sagged against Reese, hearing his heart beat low and loud. And faster than she'd have expected.

He tightened his hand on her shoulder. "I like Narine."

Sable let out a short, unsteady laugh and wiped her cheek on the back of her hand before glancing up at him. "She likes you, too."

He raised an eyebrow. "She could have fooled me."

Sable smiled weakly. "That's what I told her."

Reese's gaze snapped up over Sable's head, back the way she'd come. Sable turned to see two figures, one in white and one as dark as the shadows, hurrying toward them.

"Gwen?" Sable asked. "Serene?"

"Sable!" Serene called out, her voice low.

Gwen ran close, glancing back the way they'd come. "You need to get off this island! Now!"

CHAPTER FORTY-TWO

"BOTH OF YOU NEED TO LEAVE," Serene said, breathing heavily.

Sable stared at them, trying to fathom why the women who'd never had two civil words to exchange were standing here together. "What are you talking about, and what are you two doing with each other?"

"I needed Serene to help me find you," Gwen answered.

"Why?"

Gwen grimaced. "Because Vivaine is blaming you for the fire."

Serene nodded. "Both of you."

"She announced that Amah had just shown her a vision," Gwen shot a dark look in the direction of the gathering hall, "of you, Andreese, plotting to kill Narine, and Sable helping you. That you tried to make it look like an accident by burning down the house."

"It wasn't us!" Reese gestured back toward the woods. "The monks saw the man who did it run away before I came out."

"Of course we didn't do it," Sable said. "She doesn't get visions from Amah. Either she was watching us and knows exactly what happened, or, more likely, she's just taking advantage of an opportunity. But why would anyone believe I want to kill Narine? And why would Reese? Narine's voice in the summit would support the rebels."

"Vivaine says it was only you who supported the rebels, Sable," Serene answered, "because you were working with Reese. But Narine was going to make you vote with the Kalesh."

"That still makes no sense," Sable said. "With Narine gone, I couldn't vote at all."

Gwen raised her hands. "I'm not saying it makes sense, I'm just saying that Vivaine has declared it true, said that Amah showed her the whole thing. Everyone believes her. She's calling for your arrest."

"She's rallying all the Sanctus guards to search for you," Serene added, "and the merchants, and most of the Northern Lords. The Kalesh are angry because they think you were trying to weaken their support in the summit. Really, everyone is furious, and you two need to get off this island. Now."

"I'm not leaving," Sable said.

"I saw the person who started the fire," a voice said from the shadows.

Sable spun to see Pixy standing at the edge of the nearest house. "Where did you come from?" Sable asked.

"I followed you from the house." Pixy looked at Reese. "I wasn't sure who he was, though, so I was waiting to talk to you." She gave him a wry smile through her veil. "I assume you're Andreese, the rebel who does not write love letters?"

"Pixy," Sable said, "you saw who started the fire?"

The abbess nodded. "I was on the wall, trying to get away from all the noise of the dinner when I heard the glass break. I saw someone run away—someone short and stocky, with a beard—I think it was a dwarf."

Sable frowned. "A dwarf?"

Reese nodded slowly. "The one footprint I saw in the alley was really wide."

"Then Pixy and the monks both saw the real culprit escape," Sable said. "I'm not leaving until they find whoever it was and we find out why anyone would try to kill a woman who was already dying!"

Gwen shook her head. "Everyone knows Andreese is friends with the monks and Pixy is a friend of yours. Vivaine will say they're lying to protect you both."

Serene stepped forward and grabbed one of Sable's hands, pulling it into the moonlight. "What happened?"

"She burned her hands while putting *out* the fire that tried to kill Narine," Reese said, his voice angry.

"And I'm going back to Narine now," Sable said. "She's been badly hurt, and I'm not leaving her alone with Vivaine's lies. I am done letting that woman twist the truth." She started forward.

Gwen grabbed her arm, searching Sable's face. "Sweet Amah! You don't know?" She glanced at Serene. "Narine's gone."

"Where?" Sable demanded. "Did Vivaine take her?"

"No, Sable," Serene said gently. "She's gone. The healers did what they could, but…"

Sable stared at them both, her mind refusing to accept the words.

"She'd breathed in too much smoke," Serene continued softly, "and she was badly burned. It was just too much."

"No." Sable shook her head, the motion feeling unsteady. "I just talked to her…"

Gwen turned at Reese. "Can you get off the island without being seen?"

He nodded.

"Then you need to go. Quickly," Serene said. "And take Sable with you."

Reese glanced at Sable. "If she wants me to."

Sable kept shaking her head. "No, I'm not leaving her! She was alive. The healers were there…"

"Narine is gone," Gwen said, her voice gentler than Sable had ever heard it. "You have no reason left to stay. You can't vote, and there is no one in power who will believe your story."

Sable drew in a breath. Narine was gone. The fact was too big, too gaping to comprehend. "What are they going to do with her?"

Gwen paused at the question. "She'll be entombed in the crypt below the Phoenix Priory." She reached out to touch Sable's arm, but Sable flinched back away from her touch. Gwen stopped and pulled back her hand. "They'll never let you near her body, Sable. Vivaine is livid. With Narine gone, her chance at controlling the vote is gone as well. This took her last chance to control the summit. Regardless of whether you are responsible, she's funneling all that anger toward you." Her brow creased. "I've never seen her this angry."

Reese turned toward Sable. "Will you come with me?"

She looked for a reason to refuse, but there was none. With Narine gone, there was nothing here to hold on to. Talia was deeply tangled in Lady Ingred's world, and Kiva's. Ryah was equally unattainable in Eugessa's grip.

Sable nodded numbly.

"Will you take me too?" Gwen asked, her voice tight.

The unexpected question broke through the haze in Sable's mind.

"Why?" demanded Reese. "So you can spy on us for Vivaine?"

"No," Gwen said flatly. She turned to look at Sable. "Because I'm also tired of doing what she wants." The warmth of her words spread through the cool alley. "For years I've explained away her actions, justifying the questionable things she's done because she wanted the best for her people. But now..." She shook her head. "She knows you didn't do this, and yet she wants to see you both hanged. I won't be a part of it any longer."

The air around Sable hummed warmly with Gwen's words. "She's telling the truth."

Reese let out a disapproving growl. "I don't trust her."

"Understandably." Sable ignored Gwen's insulted look and faced Reese. "But do you trust me?"

He blew out a breath. "Yes."

"Then hurry," Serene said, glancing back over her shoulder, "and be careful."

Reese gave Gwen's white robe an annoyed look. "Getting off this island requires sneaking through dark places. Sable's dress is so smudged with smoke it's basically grey. But you...Can you take off your glowing robe with the sparkly edges?"

Gwen crossed her arms. "My undergarments are white as well."

"Here," Serene said, exasperated. She pulled open the front of her dark grey robe and reached into a pocket, pulling out some folded paper and a small quill. She handed them to Reese and reached in another pocket. A tiny ink bottle, a stick of wax, two more folded bits of paper, a stub of a candle, and a small tinderbox were piled in Reese's hands before she was done.

"How many pockets do you have in there?" Reese asked.

"Nine." Serene pulled off the robe and handed it to Gwen. She looked strange in only a thin tunic and pants. "Take care of this. I like it. And if anyone asks, I'm telling them you stole it from me when you left."

Gwen pulled her arms through the robe and fastened the clasps down the front. Her expression was as serious and confident as ever, but her skin looked pale. Sable couldn't tell if it was the dark color of the robe, the moonlight, or if Gwen was actually afraid.

Reese handed all Serene's things back to her. "Let's go." He started toward the wall. "Stay close."

Gwen, after one last glance toward the square, straightened her shoulders and followed.

"Sable," Serene said quietly. "Be careful. And stay away from here. Vivaine is…" Her hand tightened. "I've never seen her like this."

Serene glanced down at Sable's hands, and a smile crept across her face. She turned up her own palms, and Sable could see the outline of round scars on each.

Sable stared at their hands, taking in all four matching marks.

"Stay with Reese," Serene said, "and I'll find you. We have a lot to talk about."

CHAPTER FORTY-THREE

REESE AND GWEN waited at the end of the alley until Sable caught up before Reese led them along the wall, keeping to the shadowed side of the houses, moving quickly through the patches of moonlight. Behind them, back toward the square, voices rose, and Reese broke into a jog.

A low whistle sounded through the night, and he paused. He whistled back, two quick notes, then stepped into a deep corner of shadows.

"We wait here," he whispered.

Shouted commands came from toward the square, and Sable strained to see in that direction.

"We need to move," Gwen said sharply.

"We need to wait," Reese answered. "Be quiet so I can hear."

The noises from the square drew slowly closer, though, and Sable was about to tell Reese she agreed with Gwen when a very low whistle came from close by.

Reese whistled back.

A monk stepped out of the shadows of the next building and hurried over to them. Sable caught a glimpse of Sam's face.

"The door at the corner is unlocked," he said. "And the bridge is ready. You don't have much time."

"Did you find the man who started the fire?" Reese asked.

Sam shook his head. "He had a boat waiting on the far side." His voice took on a hard edge. "We will catch him on the river."

Reese grasped the man's forearm. "Thank you."

Sam nodded, returning the grip. "Tylar is waiting at the bridge. Get off the island quickly, and put some distance behind you before you stop." He turned to Sable. "You were right about the island not being enough to keep the summit peaceful. I'm ashamed that we couldn't keep Narine safe. We *will* find the man who did this."

Sable swallowed against the emotion Narine's name elicited and nodded. "A friend of mine thought he looked like a dwarf."

Sam frowned. "That fits with what others described."

His gaze caught on Sable's hands, which she still held gingerly. He took a step toward her, his expression darkening. "You were injured too."

"It's nothing," Sable answered, turning her palms away from him.

"She burned them putting out the fire," Reese said.

Sam's hands clenched into fists. "I swear Narine will have the best care possible."

Sable opened her mouth but couldn't find the words.

"Sam," Reese said, "Narine is dead."

Sam stared at Reese, then turned to look back up into the village. When he turned back, his face was thunderous. "We do not take our vows lightly."

He dropped to a knee in front of her, and Sable took a step back, glancing at Reese and Gwen.

"Narine had no family, but Flibbet told me today how close she was to you. So the debt we should owe her family, I swear, this night, to you," Sam said. "The Tutella Monks will find the man who killed the good prioress. And from this moment, Sable, we are bound to you. You have a home on our island if ever you want it. And if you ever need any help that we are able to provide, it is yours."

"That's not necessary." Sable reached forward to pull him up, but the moment she moved her fingers, pain shot across her palm.

Sam reached out and, with gentle fingers, turned her hand and pressed his lips to the back of it. His wavy beard brushed against her fingers, and his lips pressed firmly against her skin. "It *is* necessary. The vow is given, and every monk is bound by it."

Sable glanced at Reese, but he was watching Sam with approval.

"Tonight," Sam said, letting go of her hand and rising, "we will protect your escape." He turned to Reese. "Go quickly. Get her off the island and remove all signs of the bridge." He reached out and clasped Reese's hand. "Get word to us when you can."

Reese nodded. "This way," he said to Sable, starting toward the next building.

Voices called out from somewhere nearby, and Sam glanced in their direction. "Be safe, Sable," he said. "And move quickly." Without another word, he turned and strode down a narrow alley leading deeper into the town.

"The priory is Narine's family," Gwen whispered in an irritated voice. "Not you."

Sable glared at her. "If you say one more thing about Narine, I will leave you here with Vivaine." She started after Reese.

Gwen didn't answer, but she fell in behind Sable. Reese led them along thin alleys to the edge of the town. The wall, which had been following the riverbank to this point, turned sharply inland. In the very corner, a narrow door was set into the stone. Reese moved quietly to it and pushed it open, motioning for Sable and Gwen to follow him into a short passage under the wall. Reese closed the door behind them, plunging them into darkness before he squeezed past them to crack open the door on the outer edge of the wall. The moonlight slanted brightly across the grass outside. Reese waited at the cracked door before pushing it open and stepping out. He motioned for them to follow.

The forest surrounding the wall had been cleared for several hundred feet, and there was nothing but moonlit grass between them and the shadows of the trees.

Reese fiddled with the door, then pushed it closed. A muffled clunk sounded from inside, and he pulled on the door. It didn't move, and he gave a grunt of approval before stepping up close to Sable.

"Does the trick Serene taught you work well enough to tell if anyone is up on the wall or lurking in the trees?" he asked quietly.

Sable glanced around. The distance to the top of the wall was close enough, but the trees were possibly too far away. "Maybe. Say something true. The truer, the better."

He paused, then leaned up close to her ear. "I'm sorry that Narine is gone." His words were warm, and immediately she felt the heat of him and Gwen near her. "But I can't deny the fact that I am very, very, very glad you're coming away with me." His hand brushed the back of hers, and she twitched at the touch. The deep, warm, vibrant truth in his words caught at her, and for a moment she forgot about looking for people. She closed her eyes and leaned her shoulder against him. Suddenly, pinpricks of heat glowed from the blades of grass at her feet, spreading across the ground toward the trees. Behind them, the wall was cold and empty.

Sable concentrated on the grass, but she couldn't quite feel it all the way to the trees.

"More," she whispered, leaning harder into him.

He gave a short huff of amusement. "I didn't realize you were so desperate to hear how much I've missed you."

"Reese!" She shoved her shoulder into him. "This isn't easy. Say more things that are true." She turned to glance into his face, which was very close. "And try not to be so distracting."

He raised an eyebrow. "I can't help it if you're distracted by me."

"I thought we were in a hurry," Gwen said from where she leaned against the wall.

Reese ignored her. "All right, more truth, less distractions." He thought for a moment. "I'm not surprised that you've managed to get the monks bound to you."

The grass lit up again near her feet. Sable closed her eyes.

"Absolutely everywhere you've ever been, you seem to gain the notice of the people in control. And not just the notice of them—they focus on you. It's like you're some sort of light that they're all drawn to."

His words wrapped around them and spread through the air. The grass warmed again, and after a breath, Sable felt the tall, steady heat of the nearest tree trunk. Then the next one, and the next. Each tree was just warm enough to feel, but so tall they stood out distinctly against the night around them.

"Atticus told me once that he had a feeling you were bound for greatness," Reese continued.

Sable frowned at the mention of the old playwright but kept her focus on the trees. She could sense faint trunk after trunk, deep into the woods. But there were no flaming pillars that would indicate a person.

"And the more I get to know you, the more inclined I am to believe him," Reese finished.

"She's not bound for greatness," Gwen grumbled. "She's just good at inserting herself into the existing power structure and milking it for her own power."

Sable turned to stare at the woman. "You, of all people, know that I in no way inserted myself into the priories." She turned away. "I already regret letting you come."

"We can still leave her behind," Reese said hopefully.

"I'm not a fan of yours, Issable," Gwen said, and her words were perfectly true as well. "But you don't deserve whatever Vivaine will do to you. And I'm done with her." The ferocity of those words sent a ripple across the grass, lighting each blade and flowing into the trees, showing Sable the trunks for at least fifty paces into the forest.

Sable glared at the Mira. "Fine. But from here on, stop talking." She turned to Reese. "There's no one near us."

Reese spared a scowl for Gwen before leading the way toward the forest.

They walked through the woods, heading for the far end of the island. The trees weren't thick, and shafts of moonlight bleached patches of the forest floor to greys and milky whites between the shadows. They reached the main road onto the island, but after checking to make sure no one was near, Reese led them across it and back into the forest.

The trail narrowed, and Sable's robe snagged on the brush between the tree trunks. Her hands hurt too much to reach down and free the fabric, so she just strode forward, tugging her dress through the brambles with long strides. Gwen kept up a near constant flow of muttered curses.

"Amah's wrinkly bum!" the Mira snapped, tangling in a long branch that cracked loudly in the darkness. "Can no one make a proper path around here?"

"Keep it down, Holy Sister," Reese said in a low voice.

Far behind them, a voice called out, and another answered. A glimpse of torchlight flickered far back through the trees. Gwen snapped her mouth shut.

Reese kept a quick pace. The sound of the river grew louder, and the trees grew farther apart from each other, making the path less constricting. Suddenly, Reese paused and held his hand up for them to stop. A quiet whistle came from up ahead, and his shoulders relaxed. He whistled back, and a broad-chested man stepped out of the shadow of a wide tree and came toward them.

"Tylar," Reese greeted him quietly.

Tylar clapped Reese on the shoulder. "I hear you're leaving in a hurry." He glanced behind Reese, and his eyebrows rose. "Sable!"

"How many of these rebels do you know?" Gwen muttered to her.

"I met Tylar last year in Immusmala before the Midsommer Festival. He and Reese used to fight together under Reese's uncle." Sable looked curiously at Tylar. "But you were fighting for Lord Runess. How did you get here?"

"Reese has been recruiting fighters from all over the north." Tylar grinned and glanced around the woods. "I left my comfortable barracks and three hot meals a day because he promised me a glorious death fighting an all-powerful enemy. Instead, I'm manning a post at the end of an island, all alone in the woods."

Tylar was tall and broad, with the same easy smile she remembered from last summer. After the horrors of the night, the man's easy humor was like something from a different life, and Sable smiled despite herself.

"Talk while we walk, Ty," Reese said. "Is the bridge secure?"

"I'm insulted that you'd even ask," Tylar answered.

Reese started forward again.

Tylar paused and looked at Gwen. "I don't believe we've met, but any friend of Reese's is a friend of mine."

"I am not his friend," Gwen said, crossing her arms.

"No, she's not," Reese said over his shoulder.

"All right, then," Tylar said slowly. "I don't know Sable well, but Reese did talk my ear off about her a few times, so any friend of hers is—"

"I'm not friends with either of them," Gwen said.

"I did not talk your ear off," Reese called over his shoulder.

Sable started after him, and Tylar fell in next to her.

"I'm just going to talk to you," he said. "Everyone else in your group is cranky." He gave her an appraising look. "I didn't think I'd run into you. Reese told me you were here, but you were trapped with the white witches."

"The who?"

"Those women who dress in all white."

Gwen gave an irritated huff.

"The abbesses are not witches," the Mira said from behind them.

Sable leaned closer to Tylar. "You can't listen to her. She's one of them."

He glanced back at Gwen. "But she's wearing black."

"It's a disguise." Reese said. "Don't let her touch you."

Tylar laughed.

"No, honestly," Sable said. "You don't want her to touch you."

His smile faded, and he looked warily at Gwen. "Frightening. And a bit intriguing."

"Frightening and unpleasant." Reese looked over his shoulder. "Let's hurry."

They walked for a few minutes in silence until Sable caught Tylar looking at her. When she glanced at him, he motioned to her crooked sword necklace. "I see you and Reese found time to catch up."

Sable touched the necklace with the unburned tip of her finger. "It doesn't really feel like we've caught up."

He looked ahead at Reese's back, then continued in a low voice, "Well, he's been giddy ever since he saw you."

"I can't imagine Reese giddy."

Tylar grinned. "He's good at acting unruffled, but I've known Reese since he was sixteen. What others might call 'mildly pleased,' I can see for what it really is. He's giddy."

They reached the edge of a wide patch of grass drenched in moonlight, and Reese stopped. Sable and Tylar came up next to him, and Gwen crowded close behind. The clearing was flat and clear until it ended abruptly at a sharp drop to the river.

Reese looked questioningly at Tylar.

"If anyone got past me," Tylar said, "they move like a ghost."

Reese nodded, then started across the clearing. Gwen followed him, but Tylar set a hand on Sable's arm to stop her.

"I don't know what you and Reese have—or don't have—going on right now," he said in a low voice, "but I haven't heard him talk about a woman like he talks about you in…well, ever. So whatever happens, just treat him nicely. He's had a rougher year than he lets on."

Sable opened her mouth but didn't have a response to that.

Tylar glanced behind them into the woods. "We'd better get you off this island quickly."

Behind them, flickers of torchlight showed through the trees.

They hurried over to a stand of trees at the edge of the water where Reese and Gwen stood.

Below them, the river raced by, a frothing, churning mass of water. The moonlight skittered on the white surface as it swirled over rocks and sprayed mist into the air.

Sable stared at the rapids, wondering where the bridge was. There were only three long, thin lines, glowing silver in the moonlight, hanging like threads strung across the river.

A narrow rope bridge.

Bits of twine lashed the ropes together, giving the entire thing the look of a torn spider web. Beneath the flimsy bridge, the water surged and crashed over half-submerged rocks.

"No," Gwen said resolutely. "I am not crossing that."

"Then you can stay and explain to Vivaine how you managed to be all the way down here," Reese said. "It won't bother me if you do."

"We don't have long until the white witch's henchmen get here," Tylar said, "so decide quickly."

Sable leaned forward. The river raced past, a chaotic thundering, living thing, its single-minded purpose to hurl itself heedlessly into the unmoving rocks. The ground under her feet tilted to the left, and she pulled back, blinking to banish the dizziness. "Have you crossed this before?"

"Several times," Reese assured her. "It's bouncy, but if you focus on the far shore and hold the hand ropes at the side for balance—"

The thought of the rough rope sliding against Sable's blistered palms made her cringe, and she pulled her hands up next to her chest.

Reese frowned. "That's going to be a problem. You need to be able to hold the ropes."

Through the trees, more torches flickered.

"We'll cross together," he said. "You use me for balance, and I'll hold the ropes."

Tylar frowned. "One at a time, boss. I don't know if it'll hold both of you."

"Well, I don't have a better option, and we're running out of time."

Tylar looked disapproving but didn't argue.

"See you across the river, Ty," Reese glanced at Gwen. "You're on your own. If you can, follow us. If that's too much for you, then enjoy staying with Vivaine."

Tylar nodded. "I'll tell you every embarrassing story about Reese I can remember, Sable, on the way back to camp."

Sable smiled at him. "That sounds entertaining."

"Oh, it will be." Tylar grinned.

"I've just decided you'll need to scout far ahead of us tonight to make sure our path is safe," Reese told him as he moved out onto the bridge. "Ready, Sable?"

She stepped out behind him, setting one foot on the bottom rope. It was considerably thinner than her shoe. She leaned forward and slid her arms around Reese, squeezing his ribs and staying far enough back that she could lean her forehead against him and look down the narrow space between them at the thin rope. He moved forward a step, and she set her other foot carefully in front of the first. He started walking slowly, and she followed.

The first few steps weren't terrible. The rope quivered under their feet, but Reese was stable enough.

She tilted her face up, anxious to hear anything besides the raging river. "How'd you get Tylar to join you?"

Reese turned his head, and she strained to hear him. "Tanis and I visited Lord Runess several times, trying to get him to support us. My uncle was not impressed with me, and Runess didn't give us much attention, but when I found Tylar, he said he'd been learning things about the Kalesh ever since he saw our show in Immusmala, and he was convinced they were a threat."

"Lord Runess just let him leave?"

"No. Runess declared anyone who went with us would be considered a deserter and be arrested on sight if they ever returned."

"And Tylar still came?"

"His parents are gone, and he has no siblings. Said he'd been looking for an excuse to get out of the squabbles of the north." Reese glanced over his shoulder. "The man's a good fighter, and a good friend. If I had a hundred just like him, we could make a difference against the Kalesh."

The farther they moved from the shore, the more unstable the bridge became, swinging and bouncing with each step. Reese gripped the hand ropes, but occasionally they listed to one side or the other. Sable pressed her face against his back, looking down just enough to see where to put her feet and trying to ignore the wild chaos of the water below her. It surged past them, swirling downstream, making her feel like they were fighting the current, even up above the water.

"Sable," Reese said over his shoulder, "stop leaning."

She focused on his back and realized she'd been leaning upstream. She was straightening, about to apologize, when her foot slipped off the rope.

She let out a shriek, and her arms clenched around him. He let go with one hand and grabbed her arm, pinning it to his chest. Her foot scrambled for purchase. When she felt it beneath her shoe, she clung to Reese for another minute while the bridge bounced and swayed beneath them.

His hand gripped her arm tightly. "Please don't fall," he said over his shoulder.

Sable took a deep breath, trying to calm her racing heart.

"It's not far now," he said. "Ready?"

She nodded against his back, and he started forward again, slowly.

A gust of wind shoved at them, knocking them to the side, and Reese leaned heavily on the downstream rope. A snap vibrated down the bridge, and the hand rope twisted.

Reese swore and froze.

"What was that?" Sable asked, her arms clutched around him.

"I think the rope is unraveling."

"What?"

He stayed still for another moment while the bridge jounced and swayed beneath them. "Maybe there shouldn't be two people on this bridge."

CHAPTER FORTY-FOUR

THE LEFT HAND rope sagged a little, but Reese kept his hand on it, moving forward again, taking faster steps.

Sable's legs felt unsteady, and her arms ached, but she stared at the rope in front of her toes and kept moving.

They finally reached the far bank, and Reese took several steps onto the grass before Sable let go, dropping to her knees on the solid ground.

He went to where the bridge was tied to a tree. "This hand rope frayed at the knot. Gwen shouldn't cross." He waved his hands toward the far side, making a series of broad gestures. "Tylar and Sam can get her off the island another way—" He swore, and Sable looked up to see Gwen starting out onto the bridge.

He signaled again, and Tylar leaned out after her, calling something to Gwen, but she waved him off with an irritated motion and kept moving slowly away from the island, her motions tense.

Sable came up next to him. The moonlight outlined the knot that held the hand rope to the tree. One of the three cords that twisted together to make the rope had snapped and unraveled. It dangled down, leaving only two cords still snaking into the knot.

"Hurry up," Reese hissed at Gwen.

Over the rush of the river, there was no way she could hear him, and she continued at a snail's pace, shuffling her feet forward. When she was almost halfway, she faltered, leaning heavily on the frayed hand rope.

A twang rang out, the sound thrumming down the bridge like someone had plucked a lute string. The second cord spun free, unraveling a handsbreadth, leaving only a single thin cord holding up the hand rope.

Reese reached out and grabbed the rope where it was still whole. "There's no way I'll be able to hold her up if this breaks!" He wrapped his other arm around the tree anyway.

Sable stretched out her hand, as though she could stop Gwen from plummeting into the water.

The Mira righted herself but stood frozen, looking down to the churning water.

Upstream on the edge of the island, a torch came into view at the edge of the trees.

"If they look hard, they're going to see her," Reese said. "The moon's too bright not to." He waved to Tylar and motioned for him to head back into the trees, but the man just shook his head and stayed at the other end of the bridge. Reese swore. "He should just leave."

"Keep moving, Gwen!" Sable called urgently.

But the Mira stood completely still, staring down into the water.

"We have to help her!" Sable said.

Reese shook his head. "I can't go out there. I'm surprised it's holding her weight." He looked at Sable. "You go. Keep moving away from the river, up that wide valley into the hills. Keep going uphill toward the northwest slopes and find a place to hide. I'll wait as long as I can for her, then I'll find you."

"I'm not leaving." Sable grabbed the side rope that was still taut. "Gwen!" She kept her voice low but pushed her need for the Mira to hear her into the word. "Gwen!"

The foaming rapids were loud enough to drown out her voice, but Sable felt her words move out over it with...not warmth. She paused. Maybe they held a warmth, but not in the usual way.

In the middle of the bridge, the Mira finally looked up.

Sable waved her hands, gesturing broadly for her to come, pushing the words toward her again. "You have to move! Vivaine's people are coming!"

Gwen hesitated, then took a step forward. Her face looked like a sliver of pale moonlight compared to her dark robe and dark hair. She moved another tiny step forward. Every line in her body was rigid with terror, and Sable felt a twinge of pity. The Mira's face dropped down to stare at the water again.

"Gwen," Sable called, fueling the words with her desire for the Mira to hear her, waving her arms to get Gwen's attention. "Don't look down, look at me. The water can't touch you once you get to us."

Gwen's face turned up toward Sable again, her eyes wide with fear.

"Yes, just walk to me." Sable gestured with exaggerated motions for her to come. There was a definite feel to her words now. They didn't move in a wide, warm swirl like the truth did. These words were focused. All the normal warmth narrowed into a razor-thin trail of heat that wove through the jumbled air currents above the water and tethered to Gwen.

The Mira took another step, her eyes fixed on Sable.

"Almost done," Sable said, sending out more threads of heat. "Just a bit farther. The river is nothing, just look at me. Almost done." She waved the woman closer.

The torches upstream were also getting closer, and Gwen moved a little faster. Whenever Sable stopped talking, she felt the fiery threads break apart, and so she continued pushing her words toward Gwen. It was impossible that the Mira could hear them over the constant rushing of the water, but Sable could almost imagine the strands drawing the woman closer.

"Hurry, hurry, hurry," Reese chanted under his breath, watching the torchlights.

When Gwen neared the end, Sable leaned out over the edge of the water. She held out her hand, cupping her fingers to protect her palm. Gwen grabbed her wrist and pulled herself onto the bank. She grabbed Sable's other arm too, her whole body trembling.

"No more high places," she whispered, clenching Sable's arm, pushing her back away from the bank. The Mira's body curled forward, her dark hair hiding her face.

"We need to move." Reese raised a hand to Tylar.

On the far shore, Tylar slashed at the ends of the bridge, and the ropes fell into the river, churning on the surface for an instant before they were sucked under. With a wave, Tylar ran toward the trees.

"Gwen!" Reese called. "Get moving, or stay here and wait for Vivaine. But either way, let go of Sable."

Gwen dropped her hands and straightened. Her face was tight, but she swiped her hands down Serene's dark robe and straightened her shoulders. "I'm coming with you."

"Wonderful." Reese headed into the trees. "Let's go."

"Are you all right?" Sable asked her.

"Fine," Gwen said brusquely, starting after Reese.

"You're welcome," Sable muttered under her breath.

The uneven ground caught at Sable's foot again. Roots and rocks seemed to reach out specifically to trip her. The paths Reese led them on wound through the dark shadows of the forest, past the outskirts of the camps along the river, and into the wide valley to the west. They moved at a brisk pace until Reese stopped them in a glen.

"We need to decide what we're doing," he said, keeping his voice low. "I don't think we're being followed, yet. It'll take them some time to backtrack to the real bridge and cross." He looked at Gwen. "Sable and I are leaving. Where are you going now?"

Gwen stared at him. "With you."

Reese raised an eyebrow. "I'm not bringing Vivaine's personal henchwoman into our secret, hidden camp."

"Gwen left Vivaine," Sable said.

"So she says." Reese crossed his arms. "Even if I trusted her enough to bring her, the rest of them would lynch me for it."

"We can't just leave her here," Sable said. "She's spent her life in the priories. I doubt she knows how to survive on her own in the forest."

"She cannot come to camp."

Gwen looked between Sable and Reese, her face pale again. "I can help you." Her voice had a tinge of desperation. "I can tell you everything Vivaine and the Kalesh have talked about. I've been in every council meeting and diplomatic session she's participated in for the past three years. I know details of what she's planning with all the different groups."

"Or you could spy on us then run back to Vivaine and tell her everything you've learned," Reese pointed out.

"She's left Vivaine," Sable repeated.

Reese shook his head, unconvinced.

"Trust me," Sable said. "Vivaine forced her to use her skills to…"

Gwen's lips were set in a furious line.

"Just trust me," Sable said to Reese. "She's done with Vivaine."

"That doesn't mean we can trust her," he pointed out.

"That's true." Sable paused, then turned to Gwen. "Do you intend to betray the rebels by telling the priories, or anyone else, what you learn if Reese brings you to their camp?"

Gwen shook her head.

Sable sighed in exasperation. "You have to answer with words."

"Right," Gwen said. "No, I don't intend to betray the rebels by telling the priories or anyone else what I learn." Her tone was annoyed, but her words were warm, and Sable nodded to Reese.

"As odd as it sounds," the Mira said, shifting uncomfortably, "I would like to offer you my help. I have some skills you might find useful. And lately I've been thinking more and more that your people have the right of it. The Kalesh are slowly taking over, and no one in Immusmala or the north are serious about stopping them."

Reese glanced at Sable questioningly. All Gwen's words had been true, and Sable nodded.

"Tell me about your skills," he said.

Gwen swallowed. "I can hear someone's thoughts if I'm touching them." She gave Reese an apologetic smile. "Which is why Vivaine wanted me to talk to you. She knew I could learn what Tanis was thinking if I could get close enough to you."

Reese nodded. "Sable told me that."

"And?" Sable prompted Gwen.

Gwen's look grew a little guilty before she added, "And, in limited circumstances, I can influence a person's thoughts."

Reese glanced at Sable, understanding dawning. "That's how Narine was convinced to let Sable vote for her."

"I didn't want to do it," Gwen said quickly, and she looked at them desperately. "Vivaine did...something. A bolt of power went through me, and I couldn't stop." She turned to Sable with pleading eyes. "I wanted to stop."

Her words were still warm, but Sable crossed her arms. "You shouldn't have even tried a nudge."

"I wanted to show Vivaine that it wouldn't work," Gwen said, "so she would give up the idea."

"She's telling the truth," Sable said reluctantly to Reese.

Reese considered Gwen for a long moment. "Those are useful skills." He paused. "I'll bring you to the camp on the condition that you come blindfolded. You can present your request to Tanis, and if he approves, you can stay."

Gwen nodded quickly. "Agreed."

Reese scowled at her for another moment. "I hope I don't regret this."

Sticks and brambles tore at the skirt of Sable's abbess robe as she followed Reese along the valley floor for hours. He found one narrow game trail after another through the woods, moving steadily uphill.

Sable's exhausted legs protested, but Gwen grumbled so loudly behind her that Sable bit back her own complaints and followed.

The moon hung high in the western sky when they came out of the forest to find themselves at the base of the northern side of the valley. Sheer rock walls made up most of the valley wall, but a steep, grassy path wound up between two cliffs.

Sable couldn't quite hold in a groan when Reese started for it.

He glanced back. "Just up above those rocks," he said. "Then we'll rest."

"I knew you hated me," Gwen muttered, "but I didn't know you'd torture Sable like this."

Reese ignored her and struck out up the steep slope.

The burns on Sable's hands still stung, but she held the front of her torn, filthy abbess's robe up out of the way with her fingertips and followed him up the slope.

Their path led higher than the cliffs to where the ground leveled out to nothing more than a gentle uphill. The forest began again a little higher than where they stood, but Reese led them instead to a jumble of large boulders. When he reached them, he slipped through a gap in the rocks.

Sable followed and found him standing in a grassy nook between the larger rocks. The rocks at the lower edge were short enough to see over, and Sable joined him, looking back over the valley. She leaned gratefully on a rock, crossing her arms on top of it and resting her chin on them.

The moonlight bleached the color out of the world. The long, sloping floor of the valley looked like a shaggy carpet of trees that stretched all the way back to the snaking line of the grey river. Pinpricks of light clustered together at the distant camps along the shore, and Aedis was a snug clump of lantern light at the tip of the island.

A few strings of torches wandered between where they sat and the island, but none were close.

"We'll stay here until dawn." Reese turned and sat with his back to a rock.

"Dawn?" Gwen protested. "We can't sit here all night."

Reese glanced up. Only a handful of clouds, misty white in the moonlight, blocked any of the sky. "Why not? It's a beautiful night."

"Is it too far to your camp to go now?" Sable asked.

"It's not far at all. Maybe an hour of walking. But it's not a path you want to take in the dark. We'll go at dawn."

Sable sat, and Gwen, after a last grumble, dropped down against a rock across from them.

The rock behind Sable was hard and a little cold, but she felt her body sinking down against it. A wave of exhaustion rolled over her.

She set her hands on her lap, leaving her palms up. The burns on her palms were agonizing, and a slicing pain crossed her palms every time she stretched her fingers. She closed her eyes, thinking of the snug, little house on the island, the way Narine had slumped on the floor of the smoky room. Sable felt the prioress's kiss on her forehead.

Narine was gone.

The truth of it sat, huge and unmoving. The last year stretched out behind her in a string of days and nights pulled up near the fire. The relentless battle to keep Narine's hands warm. Countless cups of tea.

Sable could almost smell the leaves, feel the crisp crunch when she broke off the bitter edges, see the swirl of the steam from the hot water.

Her mind replayed the events of the night—the glass breaking, the fire spraying across the floor. Narine had been so thin and frail, leaning against the wall, her skin burned, her face and robe tainted with smoke.

Who would want to kill a dying prioress?

The flames had been so destructive and fierce, licking out from the edges of the quilt. Sable looked down at her palms, burned just like Serene's.

Had she really done magic? Had she put the flames out with more than the quilt? She had told it to go out, that much she remembered, and her palms had burned as she did. Or was it merely the fire that had burned her?

She looked up at the stars. The moonlight washed out all but the brightest, and her eyes followed the vast tracts of black emptiness.

The space left by Narine was like that. Huge and empty. Like something Sable had been standing on, something foundational and steadfast, and it had just disappeared.

She leaned back against the boulder. Yes, Narine had been like the huge rock. Like the hill itself. She had been so quiet, but so very steady.

Sable rested her head back and closed her eyes, her mind shying away from the truth of what had happened. Instead, it fluttered between memories. Mundane moments, mostly. Fire and tea and the couch. Narine always patient, always calm, always listening. Always good. The opposite, in almost every way, of Vivaine.

Prioress Vivaine, Narine would have corrected her.

Except that voice was gone.

Sable squeezed her eyes shut, and tears rolled down her cheeks.

What are you afraid of, Issable?

She let out a jagged breath and looked back up at the dark sky. If there was an answer, it was too vast and too painful to put into words.

CHAPTER FORTY-FIVE

A HAND on Sable's shoulder woke her from a grey, drifting dream. She opened her eyes to find the sky a similar color, an empty greyish blue, devoid of stars. Reese's face was above her. Sometime during the night, she must have lain down next to the rock, and her shoulders and neck protested as she tried to straighten them.

"Not too long until sunrise," Reese whispered. He was hard to see in the dimness, but the guarded look was still there. He gave her a bit of a smile, but it didn't quite look real. "If you actually are interested in how sunrises look here in the north."

Her eyes felt gritty from the short night of sleep and swollen from all her tears, but she nodded. She went to push herself up, but her palm touched the ground, and pain shot into it. She curled it to her chest with a groan.

He reached out and helped her sit, frowning at her hands. "When it's light, we'll find something to wrap those in. There are healers in camp that can help," he whispered.

She rubbed her face with the back of her hand, trying to rub away some of the exhaustion. Reese was so serious again.

His hair had regained a little of the wildness she remembered from traveling with him before. It was long enough to brush his shoulders, and the waves that had been neatly combed at the summit were tousled a bit. There was something comforting about Reese in this more familiar form.

Except for that new, unfamiliar look he often had. It wasn't fear, but something more like watchfulness.

He's had a rougher year than he lets on, Tylar had said.

It wasn't watchfulness in his face, Sable realized. He was unsure. She frowned at him. Even when they had stood in a meeting with two gang bosses, desperately outnumbered by their thugs, he hadn't looked unsure.

At her look, he shifted. "If you just want to sleep more," he said quietly. "I understand."

"As tempting as it sounds to lie back down on the hard ground, it turns out I've waited a very long time to see a good sunrise." She stood and glanced down the valley to the horizon, which was lightening to a colorless grey. "And this looks like a perfect place."

Reese glanced at Gwen, who was curled up on her side nearby, and motioned for Sable to follow him. He led her back out of the boulders and downhill to the edge of the cliff. A wide, flat rock jutted out over the edge like the front stoop of some enormous house.

Sable stepped out onto the rock, turning to take in the vastness of the view. Layers of hills rolled away to the horizon. The Black River was a sweeping line of light grey wandering past the end of the valley, like a tiny thread of the sky had fallen and gotten caught in the trees. A breeze blew down the valley, and she wrapped her arms around herself, careful to not touch her palms to anything. "This *is* perfect."

She turned to find him watching her, his face once again unreadable.

"I don't have a blanket this time."

She raised an eyebrow. "Really, you didn't think to grab one when we were running for our lives?"

He almost smiled at that. When he didn't say anything else, Sable looked around the flat rock. "You're the sunrise expert—where should we sit?"

He glanced toward the edge of the rock hanging out above the steep drop-off. "That depends on how much you trust me."

The question felt heavier than it should. More serious.

She gave him a rueful smile. "You were my own personal body-guard. I trusted you with my life."

His jaw tightened at the words, and he did not smile back.

"And," she continued, gesturing back toward the island, hoping it hid her disappointment, "no matter what has changed between us, I did just run off into the night with you, over a horrible rope bridge, and through the forest for hours. I think it's safe to say I still trust you."

The words seemed to answer a question for him, and he let out a breath that was either relieved or resigned.

"Then the best seat is at the edge." He turned and walked to the end of the rock. He was so close to the drop-off that Sable's heart lurched, but he sat down easily, hanging his feet over the lip.

She followed, slowing as she drew closer to the edge. The hillside below them plunged away, and the world seemed to shift beneath her. She stopped a few steps back. "Reese," she said, her voice unsteady.

He gave her the ghost of a smile. "If you weren't wearing that ridiculous abbess's robe, I'd tell you to sit back there, and scoot forward. But I'm pretty sure scooting is out of the question in that. Unless you want to show a lot more leg than modest abbesses are supposed to show."

"I'm hardly an abbess," she answered, her eyes locked on the distant bottom of the valley.

When she still didn't move closer, he held out his hand. "I promise I won't let you fall."

His smile was gone, but his words were warm. She dropped to her knees and moved forward slowly. He took hold of her arm with a steadying grip. She moved up until she was almost next to him, then sat, only her feet sticking out over the edge. Her heart was pounding, but she scooted forward until her knees reached the edge and her feet hung freely. The hem of her robe swirled in the slight breeze, and she set her hands in her lap, hoping the robe wouldn't decide to fly up.

When she was settled, he let go of her arm. The emptiness under her feet was terrifying and invigorating. He was close, and she almost leaned into him, but he just folded his hands in his lap and looked out into the valley. She stared down at the dizzying depths below her. The world felt alarmingly airy, and she shrank tighter into herself, fighting off the hint of panic that was threatening.

"Don't look down," he said. "Look up at the view."

She pulled her eyes away from the valley and focused on the horizon.

The world was flung out in front of her, boundless and wild. Wisps of light crept into the valley from the approaching sun. Hills rippled away into the distance, the nearest a rich charcoal blue, each layer toward the horizon growing more pale and less substantial. The river, still looking like a sliver of misplaced sky, wound through it like a stream of light. And the sky itself…The sky spread over it all, not only above her in a pale, creamy yellow but beneath her, filling the valley, rising up the hillsides, swirling around the rock and running its fingers through her hair.

She breathed it in.

Freedom.

Finally.

No Sanctuary Wall. No Vivaine. No city politics. No Kiva. No Eugessa. No Ambassador Bastian with his strange questions. She could stand up at this moment and go…anywhere.

Far down the valley, Tutella Island sat like a treed lump in the middle of the river. Talia and Ryah were still there, but the thought felt less terrifying than it had in the past. With both Sable and Narine out of the picture, Eugessa had gained a huge boost. Ryah would no longer be a piece to leverage against Sable. And Reese had been right about Talia—she didn't want Sable to rescue her.

Ryah had managed the unthinkable—Eugessa actually liked her—and Talia had outplayed Kiva to accomplish her own goals. Sable felt a fierce pride in her two sisters.

No, neither of them needed protection anymore.

A swirl of early morning breeze rolled past, and the last vestiges of the cage that had surrounded Sable disintegrated at its touch.

She was free.

She and Reese sat like tiny dots in a world wider than she could take in, and instead of feeling dwarfed by it, she felt…reassured. She was small, but so were the Kalesh, and the priories, and Kiva. All her worries and fears were small, fleeting things in the grand scheme of the world.

Beside her, Reese looked out over the world as well, silent and steady. As steady as the hills themselves.

Maybe some of the reassurance was because of him.

"How do you do that?" she asked him.

He glanced at her. "Do what?"

"You sit there and do nothing, and yet you make me feel…calm."

His look turned disbelieving. Almost insulted. "Calm?"

She nodded. "Everyone else in my life always wants something. Kiva, Vivaine, even Atticus wanted me to perform just right. Narine didn't, I suppose, but every moment with her was laced with worry. But you're different. You have this ability to just be here. It's incredibly calming. Last year, when we sat on that roof together—" Reese tensed again, and she stopped, kicking herself for bringing up something from so long ago.

He was still staring at her, and she couldn't quite make out his expression. It certainly wasn't the pleased look she had expected. She pulled her arms tighter against herself, trying not to notice how it let more empty air surround her.

"Anyway," she finished lamely, "I know things are different now. But being close to you is still calming. That's all."

He let out a laugh that felt almost harsh.

She frowned at him. "I gather I don't have the same effect on you."

He turned back toward the sunrise, shaking his head slowly. In the past she'd always felt like he was watching their surroundings, absorbing details she wasn't even noticing, but now he gazed into the distance with an unfocused look. The hard edge was back in his expression.

"Last year…" he said, sitting stiffly as though he were forcing himself to speak, "before I threw that knife. I thought you and I…"

Her stomach sank at his rigid tone. "Reese," she began, not wanting to hear what he had to say.

But he continued anyway. "That knife changed things." He

dropped his gaze to his own hands. "Most mornings, when I wake up, my first thought is a wish that I hadn't thrown it."

She stilled at the unexpected words.

"And the few times I'm convinced it had to happen, I wish it had been someone else's job." His gaze flickered toward her, but then went back to his own hands. "I have fought in battles for my uncle. I fought men during the past year with Tanis. Men have died because of me." His voice was so low that Sable leaned closer, trying to hear, but trying not to touch him. "But those were during battles, and whether it makes sense or not, that's different from the ambassador."

He turned his face toward her, just a little, but didn't look up. The hard edge of his expression had sharpened into self-loathing. "He was sitting in a theater, enjoying a show." His words pushed out, as though they'd been pent up for too long. "Unarmed. Surrounded by women and families." He looked up into Sable's face, his look so raw and torn. "He was unarmed, and I hid in the shadows and killed him."

He had stood in the dark fringe of the stage. The knife had flown out of that darkness and—she shut her eyes against the violence of the memory.

"I killed an unarmed man in cold blood." The words wrung out of him, tinged with desperation.

She opened her mouth to object, to assure him it had been necessary, that he'd done nothing wrong, but she stopped. It was more complicated than that. She could hear Narine warning her not to belittle another's pain and guilt. He had killed an unarmed man in cold blood, and the weight of that must be terrible.

"It has never occurred to me," she said, "how heavy that must feel for you."

He focused on her hands, lying palms up on her lap, but didn't answer.

Sable searched for something to say. Discarding all the platitudes and easy answers that came to mind. The new somberness in him, the new flinty look in his eyes suddenly became clear. It was regret. Guilt.

What would Narine say to him?

She almost laughed at how obvious the answer was.

But she couldn't ask that. She wasn't a prioress he'd come to for wisdom and absolution. Once, maybe she'd have dared to ask something so personal, but it had been too long.

Except Narine was right. There was freedom in the simple act of naming fears.

Sable glanced up at him again, and the wretched edge to his expression made the decision. He might resent the question, and resent her, but maybe it would give him relief, and that chance seemed worth it.

She reached her still-aching hand over tentatively, setting the back of it against his folded hands.

He tensed but didn't move away.

Trying to infuse each word with the emotions she felt, in all their complexity, she asked quietly, "What are you afraid of, Reese?"

The words tumbled out into the valley, and instantly she regretted them. They were too intimate. He didn't owe her an answer. He didn't owe her anything at all. She'd overstepped, as though they weren't almost strangers.

She opened her mouth to tell him as much, but he spoke first.

"I'm afraid that it changed me," he whispered. He didn't unfold his hands, but he pushed them against the back of hers. "I'm afraid that it broke something so deep inside me that I can't ever fix it. That it was a moment I cannot undo, and it's unraveling me."

The ache in his voice seeped into her, and she turned her hand to grip his.

"Sable!" He pulled his hands away, but not before her palm brushed against his thumb and pain stabbed across the blisters.

She let out a gasp and yanked her hand away.

He stared at her. "That was..."

"Stupid," she managed, pressing her eyes shut.

He let out a short laugh. "Yes." She felt his fingers touch the back of her hand as he gently turned it over, showing the angry blisters covering her palm. The skin on his hands was rougher than she remembered, but his touch was light. She opened her eyes to see him focused on her palm. His thumb ran slowly over the back of her fingers. "I'm afraid," he said, his voice barely over a whisper, "that throwing that knife changed what you think of me. That it also broke whatever it is you and I had."

Every fiber of her focused on the slow motion of his thumb.

"I know it's been a long time," he continued, "and that you've had plenty of time to change what you think of me, but every morning I regret that I threw that knife and wish that somehow we could go back. Let the bloody Kalesh take over the whole land, I don't care." He raised his eyes to hers, his look so fierce she couldn't breathe. He clenched his jaw, but the next words spilled out. "I've missed you, more than I knew it was possible to miss someone. But I understand," he said fervently, "if you don't feel the same way. I honestly do."

His eyes searched her face, then he lifted her hand, turning it and pressing the back against his chest. She could feel his heart beating, pounding, almost as fast as hers.

He leaned closer, his normally steady expression ragged, his gaze boring into her. "So, no, when I sit close to you, I don't feel calm."

She looked down at her hand, feeling his heartbeat thrum against it, mirroring her own. "When I joined Vivaine, I thought you'd hate me for working with the enemy. I was furious at you for ages, but as Narine was so right in pointing out to me, it was mostly because I was afraid you'd never want to be close to me again."

He was quiet, and she looked up to find him watching her, a slow, genuine smile spreading across his face. He let go of her hand and wrapped his arm behind her, setting his hand on her hip. "Just how close, exactly, did you want to be?"

He pulled on her, scooting her closer. Her legs shifted against nothing but air, and she let out a little shriek, suddenly reminded that she sat at the edge of a drop-off. Every muscle in her body tensed. Her calves squeezed back against the edge of the rock, and she leaned into his side.

Reese was perfectly still. As solid as the rock itself.

"Is this close enough?" His voice was right against her ear.

She turned to see a hint of his roguish smile, the one she hadn't seen since they'd hidden in that alley in Dockside, hoping to avoid being seen. The terror of the drop beneath her shifted into something else. Still terrifying, but also hopeful. Painfully, terribly hopeful. The feeling climbed up her throat, and she found it suddenly hard to speak.

"Almost," she managed.

He reached up and set his hand on the side of her neck, just under her ear, sliding his fingers back into her hair. He paused, his gaze dropping to her neck. He pulled his palm forward until it rested against her neck, against her pounding pulse. His mouth twitched in a wider smile. "So, I make you feel calm?"

Her heartbeat hammered against the warmth of his hand. "On one level." Her voice came out unsteady. "On other levels, though, it's a bit more...volatile."

"Volatile?"

Sable swallowed. "I'd say happy, but it's more terrifying than the word happy encompasses."

He leaned closer, his gaze holding hers. "You make me happy."

For a moment there was nothing in the world but him. The rock and the valley fell away.

A burst of brightness flashed in the east, and his eyes flicked toward it.

The sunrise.

A tiny part of Sable's mind noted the perfect timing of the event.

Until Reese paused, his eyes narrowing at the brightness.

With a flicker of annoyance she'd never expected to feel at a sunrise, Sable turned.

The light was not the sun.

The eastern sky had brightened, but the land itself still lay in shadowy blues.

Except one dazzling bit of light, one blazing torch rising above the island.

Reese's hand tensed on her neck. "What is that?"

The fire rose higher, like a burning lantern from the Red Shield festival, except this light didn't waft, it surged up, drawing out a spiraling, glittering trail of light as it rose.

"Innov," Sable breathed. The sparks behind the phoenix were brighter than she'd ever seen. Innov blazed like a bonfire against the dark landscape, so bright that the trees below her cast spinning shadows as she rose.

"The phoenix?" Reese asked. "But she was so…dim."

Innov turned in a wide arc, and the hope Sable had always felt from the phoenix burned with a new, fierce, unfettered fire.

"She's been reborn." Sable watched the phoenix surge up the valley, a cascade of light pouring out behind her. "She's beautiful."

Reese's arm tightened around Sable's back. "She's getting closer," he warned.

Innov *was* getting closer. She soared up the valley with strong, sure wing strokes.

They scrambled to their feet and backed away from the edge of the rock as Innov shot up above them. Stretching her wings, she wheeled overhead, spiraling lower until Sable could see her fiery feathers, outlined with the red of burning coals, fingers of flames rippling along her wings. Innov's eyes fixed on Sable.

It took until Innov was almost on top of them to be able to see that the phoenix herself was tiny. In the midst of the shining light, her body was barely bigger than Sable's hand.

"Sable…" Reese stepped back.

The phoenix swirled closer, her eyes fixed on them, and Sable held out her arm. Innov tucked her wings and dropped, flaring them at the last moment as she landed, her claws wrapping gently around Sable's sleeve.

Sable stared into the wide, orange eyes of the newborn phoenix.

CHAPTER FORTY-SIX

SABLE HELD her arm out awkwardly, expecting Innov to feel heavy, but she was as light as a candle. She peered into Sable's face and let out a sharp caw.

The phoenix was astonishingly small and young. Her head was tiny and almost round, supported by a slim neck. Her eyes, huge orbs in her small head, were still orange, but they glittered with other colors. Not just yellows and reds, but flecks of rich blue, and glints of purple. Her body was thinner, too, more streamlined, her feathers shorter and sleeker.

More than all that, the bird was a towering pillar of heat, hotter than she'd ever been before. Reese took a step back, leaning away from her.

Except, while Sable could recognize that Innov was blazing hot, she felt nothing but warmth from the phoenix. It seeped into her arm, pressing up through her chest, spreading into the dark, tumultuous depths inside her. It swirled around the cold grief of Narine's death until it warmed, thawing emotions Sable didn't wanted to face.

A cascade of sorrow spilled out, but that cold, damp sadness warmed as well, turning bittersweet. It didn't disappear—in fact, it expanded, washing up against everything else, taking up more space than Sable wanted it to. But it was different now. Still sad, but less…hollow.

"Do you think Narine is happy?" Sable whispered to Innov. "Wherever she is?"

The phoenix didn't answer. She merely looked at Sable, pouring warmth into her.

With every breath Innov took, sparks showered off her, landing on the rock and glowing briefly before fading. But not a single spark landed on Sable's arm.

"Innov," Sable said. "Why are you here?"

The phoenix blinked, then tilted her head, looking around the rock.

"We need to move." Reese started back toward where they had slept.

Sable nodded absently at him. She reached out a tentative hand and ran the back of her fingers down the bird's glowing chest. Sparkles of light burst out from between her feathers, the deepest ones a vivid blue among the other fiery sparks.

"Sable," Reese said with more urgency. "Your shiny bird just rose into the air, circled a few times to make sure she had the attention of every single person looking for us, then flew directly to you."

Sable glanced down in the valley, realizing that Innov must be visible even from the island in the pre-dawn light.

She shook her arm. "Go on, Innov. Go back to the priory. There'll be a new prioress soon who'll need you."

Innov let out an annoyed squawk and tightened her grip on Sable's arm.

"Until that sun rises, she's a beacon for anyone to find us." He frowned back at the bird. "Hopefully she's not so bright that she'll still be visible after that."

The sun was nearly up, and the world was growing brighter by the moment, but the phoenix blazed like a bonfire.

"Innov," Sable said, "if you're staying, could you dim down a bit? Just for a little while?"

The phoenix blinked her round, orange eyes, then looked away, as though bored.

"I guess that's a no," Sable said.

"Perfect." Reese said. "Nothing like trying to pass unseen accompanied by a blazing bird." He started back toward where they'd slept. "Gwen!" he called out. "If you're coming with us, it's time to go."

Sable followed him, her arm still held out away from her. Innov lit the ground ahead of them like a bright torch. When they stepped between the rocks, Gwen was sitting up, groaning and stretching her back. The Mira froze when she saw them. "Sweet Amah! Why do you have Innov?"

"You're the one who spent your life in the priories," Sable said, "you tell me. Why did she come here?"

Gwen stared at Sable as though she'd done something criminal. "What did you do? When a Phoenix Prioress dies, Innov flies away. No one knows where. She always returns when a new prioress is selected."

"Which takes weeks," Sable said. "Or months."

"We have the bird for weeks or months?" Reese asked. "Where are we going to stash a flaming bright phoenix?"

"I have no idea," Sable said.

"Innov doesn't like *anyone* but the Phoenix Prioress," Gwen said stubbornly.

"You two can figure out why we have the glowing beacon while we walk." He turned and scanned the hillsides behind them. "We'll have to head away from camp for a bit to throw off the audience we now have. Let's hope once we reach the trees, her light is hidden enough that we can double back."

He set out along the top of the cliffs, keeping below the tree line as they moved farther away from Tutella Island. Innov was perched next to Sable's wrist, shining like a tiny sun, undoubtedly visible from nearly every point in the valley.

The phoenix blinked slowly and shuffled closer until her feathered side pressed against Sable's upper arm. Sable shifted to cradle the bird, and Innov burrowed down, curling her head around by her wings and snuggling up to Sable's chest, like a small, fiery bundle.

"Why," Gwen said, exasperated, "in the name of sweet Amah, is Innov with *you*?"

Sable scowled at her. "Maybe because I've been in the same room with her for a year now while we both cared for Narine."

"Doesn't matter. Innov only likes the Phoenix Prioress."

Reese glanced back to see the bird nestled in Sable's arm. "Seems like you might not know what you're talking about, Oh Holiest of Sisters."

Gwen ignored him. "You," she pointed at Sable, "are *not* the Phoenix Prioress."

Sable stopped and stared at her. "Of course I'm not! You think I wanted Innov to come here?"

Gwen crossed her arms. "You've always wanted more power than you have."

"Only because those of you in power never did the right thing!" She took a step toward Gwen.

"If you two can't talk and walk fast," Reese called back to them, "then discuss this later. We have a ways to go still."

Gwen groaned, and Sable lengthened her strides to get away from the Mira. Innov's body was like holding a warm cup of tea. Except softer. The heat from her body seeped into Sable, starting on her arm, spreading through her chest, loosening a tightness in her throat that had been there since she'd promised Narine she'd leave, kneeling in the smoky, scorched room.

Reese kept up a fast pace until they passed the end of the long rock faces. Below them, the valley wall smoothed to a steep but navigable slope, and he angled up into the trees, still moving away from the island. They continued into the forest until the trunks behind them blocked out any view of the valley.

Innov's warmth flowed deep into her, loosening everything a little. Sable drew in a deep breath. Her lungs stretched with it as she breathed fully for the first time in what felt like weeks.

Her legs, which had been burning from the climb, felt stronger. The tight tangle of emotions from last night and this morning slackened a bit, and Sable looked down at the glowing bundle. "I can see why Narine felt stronger when she touched you," she whispered. She ran her thumb along Innov's feathers, watching the sparks of color shower off the bird. "I'm going to assume you're not going to start a forest fire—"

Sable's hand froze with her thumb extended. She stretched her thumb back farther, then opened all of her fingers.

The pain in her palm was nearly gone.

The surface that had been blistered was still an ugly, deep red, but the puffy, shiny blisters now looked more like an old scar. She opened her other palm and felt a shooting pain. Gingerly, she shifted Innov until that palm pressed against Innov's back. Now that she was focusing on it, there was a different sort of warmth on her burned skin than everywhere else. A numbing, probing heat.

Sable held her palms against the bird until, when she stretched her fingers, she had nothing but a dull ache and a new tightness across the skin.

"Thank you," Sable whispered to the sleeping phoenix.

Reese found a game trail winding back down the valley toward the island. "Hopefully no one can see Innov from here." He took in Sable, holding the sleeping bird. "And hopefully she doesn't fly up and announce that we're backtracking."

"That's a lot resting on hope," Gwen pointed out.

"I'm sorry. I don't have more experience hiding a newborn phoenix, your holiness," he answered, starting down the trail.

The path stayed deep in the woods, still moving gently uphill along the wall of the valley, back in the direction they'd come.

"Are we ever not going to go uphill?" Gwen said from the back, her breath coming fast. "Is your camp at the top of a mountain?"

"Everything is uphill from a river," Reese pointed out.

They trudged on in silence for a long time. Gwen breathed heavily, stumbling occasionally and muttering curses under her breath. Even the renewed strength Sable felt from Innov began to wane, and her legs started to burn with the exertion.

"Not to sound too much like Gwen," Sable said, "but do we have a lot more uphill? And if so, could we take a break?"

Reese glanced around the forest. "We can rest here. Before our holy sister goes much farther, she'll need to be blindfolded, anyway."

"I do not need to be blindfolded!" Gwen objected. "Besides, you already have spies in your camp—I doubt the location is a secret from Vivaine."

"Whether it is or not, we've gone to some effort to keep the entrance to the camp hidden, and I'm not just walking you through it. I still don't trust you," he said bluntly.

Gwen looked blankly around the forest. "I could never, in a million years, lead anyone even to where we are right now, never mind onto some hidden trail."

Reese turned and crossed his arms. "No blindfold, no camp."

Gwen glared at him. "Where are you going to find a blindfold?"

He gave her a humorless smile. "From your white robe. If you're not part of the priory any longer, that shouldn't be a problem, right?"

The Mira pinched her lips together, but she reached down and grabbed her hem. With a sharp jerk, she tore off a strip of the silver-edged hem. "Happy?"

"I'm not sure yet." He held out his hand, and she handed him the fabric. Reese held it up across his eyes, then nodded. "This works. Turn around."

Gwen scowled but turned, and Reese tied the blindfold tightly across her eyes.

"I'm going to trip," Gwen protested.

"Probably," Reese said, stepping up to her. "Time to forget which direction we're going." He took her shoulders and spun her in place.

"This is ridiculous," she said, but he continued to spin her. When he stopped, she stood unsteadily.

"Now we can go." Reese took Gwen by the arm, leading her forward. He gave Sable a smile, gesturing toward the path.

"Sweet Amah," Gwen grumbled. "You realize I can read your thoughts, and you're thinking about our path."

Reese let go of her arm like it was a snake. "That's a flaw I didn't think about."

"I'll guide her," Sable said, shifting Innov to one arm. The phoenix let out a little snort but didn't wake. Sable set her other arm against Gwen's hand. "I'll just look down in front of our feet, and she'll get no good sense of where we are."

"I already have no sense of where we are," Gwen said. "This is stupid. If I wanted to know the path, I wouldn't have pointed out that I could read your mind, Andreese."

Sable exchanged looks with Reese. That was a good point.

"It *is* a good point," Gwen agreed.

Reese frowned at the Mira. "What do you think?" he asked Sable, taking in the phoenix nestled on one arm and the Mira on the other, and an amused smile spread across his lips. "I'd like her blindfolded until we get into the canyon, but you look a little encumbered."

The distant edge that had plagued his expression for the past days had faded, and he looked at her with an old familiarity. She smiled back. "If you can't take the Mira, do you want the shiny bird?"

Reese looked at the curled-up phoenix. "I think she'd like to stay with you."

"How long does Gwen need to be blindfolded?" Sable asked.

He peered up at the bits of hilltop visible through the trees. "Not too long. Once we're in the canyon, there aren't any landmarks visible, and she can take it off. A quarter of an hour, maybe."

Standing in the forest, he looked utterly comfortable in a way he hadn't at the summit. He still wore the shirt Purnicious had bellished, and for all his complaining the other night, it did fit him well.

"I can be encumbered for a quarter of an hour," Sable said.

He flashed her a smile. "Then the blindfold stays on."

"Could we start, then?" Gwen asked. "Or do I have to stand here and listen to Sable think about how good you look in that shirt?"

Reese raised an eyebrow.

Sable jabbed her elbow into Gwen's side. "I will walk you into a tree."

"I'd know you were planning to," the Mira answered.

"Let's hurry," Sable said to Reese. "I don't want her touching me any longer than she has to."

Reese gave Sable that roguish smile again and headed up the path. Sable closed her eyes, wishing fiercely that Innov had waited a bit longer to make her grand appearance this morning.

"For the love of Amah," Gwen muttered, "please think about something else."

"Come on." Sable pulled her forward. "Let's get this over with."

Sable followed Reese, keeping her eyes fixed on the ground in front of her, attempting to focus her thoughts merely on the obstacles of the path. The trail wasn't particularly wide, and Sable was tempted to make Gwen walk along the rough edges of it. Instead, she walked along the side herself, letting the Mira have the smoother ground.

Ahead of them, Reese turned onto a thin game trail. He moved confidently, and Sable wondered how much of these hills he was familiar with.

"You're thinking about him again," Gwen said, an edge of complaint in her voice.

"You know," Sable snapped, "for someone who needs our help, you're not being particularly pleasant."

Gwen pinched her mouth shut, and they walked in silence for a few minutes. The Mira took cautious steps, holding her free hand out in front. She didn't stumble often, though. In fact, most of the time she stepped over obstacles in the path.

"Can you see?" Sable demanded.

"No," Gwen said, exasperated. "You can. And I can see your thoughts. If you're focusing on the path, I get a reasonably good idea of it."

Sable frowned at her, and Gwen's feet hesitated.

"I cannot see the path when you're looking at me, though," the Mira pointed out.

Sable looked back down, and they started again. "How does it work? Can you see whatever I can?"

"No. Not with you. With some people I can. Some people think in vivid images. But you are easier to hear than to see. You talk in your mind, and I hear it. Visually, things are foggy. I get an impression of the shape of the path, but it's enough to avoid rocks." She turned her head toward Sable, as though she could see her. "On the rope bridge, how did you do that?"

"Do what?"

"You called to me, and it made me feel...brave."

"I'm surprised you could hear us over the river. I could barely hear Reese calling you, and he was right next to me."

The crease in her brow deepened. "I couldn't hear anyone but you."

Sable stopped, making Gwen stumble to a halt. "You could hear my words?"

The Mira nodded. "You said the river was nothing."

"I was talking quietly." Sable paused. "Can you read my mind if we're not touching?"

"I've never read anyone's mind without touching them. Thankfully." Gwen shuddered. "It's exhausting enough hearing people if I touch them." She shook her head. "No, on the bridge, I looked up because I thought you had come back out on the bridge with me."

Sable stared at her. "It worked?"

Gwen snorted. "Your voice was as clear as it is now."

CHAPTER FORTY-SEVEN

SABLE STOOD PERFECTLY STILL, continuing to stare at Gwen. It had actually worked? She'd managed to move her voice past all the noise and reach the Mira?

"Is there a problem?" Reese called from up the path.

Sable started walking again, and Gwen fell in next to her. Innov stirred, and a shower of sparks fell off her, fading before they hit the ground.

Sable looked up ahead at the trees, her eyes unfocused, her heart quickening.

It had worked.

Gwen's foot caught on a rock, and she let out a yelp of pain, yanking on Sable's arm to stop herself from falling. Innov woke and squawked at the jolt.

"Could you refocus on the path, please, instead of contemplating your newfound skill?" Gwen complained. "Or can I take this useless blindfold off yet?" she called up to Reese.

"This is the price you pay for serving Vivaine so loyally," he called back.

Gwen's face hardened at the words, but she didn't say anything else.

JA ANDREWS

Innov wiggled her head back down by her wing.

Sable started forward again, watching the path in front of her this time. "What exactly ended that loyalty you had for Vivaine?"

Gwen didn't answer right away, and Sable went back to focusing on the roots and obstacles in their path.

"I've been working for Vivaine since I was eighteen," Gwen said finally. "I was ecstatic when she chose me to serve in the Dragon Priory. I never imagined I'd work with her daily. My family was far away, but Vivaine let me into her life. I celebrated festivals with her and the highest abbesses. She always had time for my questions and allowed me into nearly every meeting. She's the closest thing I've had to family since I joined the Mira at fourteen."

Gwen was quiet for a moment. "But over the past year, she's grown increasingly...cold. She's always done what was needed to make sure she was working for the good of the people, sacrificing whatever was needed for their safety. But since Ambassador Tehl was killed, she's been different."

"Was she in love with him?" Sable asked.

"No, I don't think she had any particular feelings for him, but she did believe their marriage would keep the city safe from the Empire. When he was killed, everything she'd done for months came crashing down. Ambassador Bastian is a different sort of man, and she's been off-kilter for the past year." Gwen let out a breath. "She's been growing more...hostile."

Sable nodded. "That, I've noticed."

"I've helped her for years by reading the minds of those she was treating with," Gwen continued, "always with the goal of keeping the people safe. I would do it to learn what people really wanted so we could negotiate more effectively. But for months now, it's felt more like spying on people than trying to accomplish a goal. And the situation with Narine..."

Gwen's voice caught on the prioress's name, and she swallowed. "That night with Narine, Vivaine was...cruel."

The Mira's whole body was tense, her hand tight on Sable's arm. "I thought Vivaine would calm down and regret what she'd done. But she didn't." She shook her head. "I couldn't stay with her after that."

Ahead of them, the trail wound along a thicket at the base of a tall rock outcropping. But instead of following the trail, Reese paused and let out a series of short whistles.

A response came back, and he ducked into the bushes.

"Will you ever go back?" Sable asked. "Or are you leaving the priories forever?"

"I don't know how I could go back, not after this." Gwen waved her hand vaguely at the forest around them.

They reached the point where Reese had disappeared and found a branch of the path winding away through a narrow gap in the thicket.

"You'll have to walk behind me," she told Gwen, stepping in. The Mira put her hand on Sable's shoulder and followed close behind, muttering curses every time a branch scratched her.

The path wrapped around the outcropping of rock, and the thicket ended. Sable lurched to a stop, standing on a ledge at the end of a long, narrow valley. The ground dropped sharply down in front of her, and the path wound away to the left, scratched into the steep, rocky slope. Below them, the valley was forested with dark pines and light, shimmery aspens.

Gwen gasped, and her hand tightened on Sable's shoulder.

"You can take off the blindfold now," Reese told Gwen with a smile, "although with how you felt about the rope bridge, you may not want to."

Sable shifted her shoulder away from Gwen, and the Mira took off the blindfold with a look of terror. She stared at the tiny path along the rock face. "You can't be serious."

"There is only one path into the valley from this end," he said.

Innov stirred, lifting her head to blink at the view. Then, with a rippling trill, she launched herself off Sable's arm.

"Innov! No!" Sable called after her, but the phoenix didn't soar up above them—she spread her wings and glided out over the valley like a brazen beacon through the air.

"That bird has a flair for the dramatic," Reese said.

"If I could fly," Sable said, "I'd follow her. This valley is stunning."

He smiled. "Tanis also has a flair for the dramatic. He picked this place."

"I can't go on that," Gwen choked out from behind him. Her eyes were still fixed on the thin path.

"You can walk between Sable and me," Reese said. "You've come this far, Holiest of Sisters. There's no turning back."

Gwen shook her head, but when he started toward the trail, she hurried after him, grabbing a fistful of the back of his shirt.

"Sure," he said dryly, "you can hold on."

He stepped onto the thin path, and, with a whimper, Gwen followed him.

Sable trailed after, captivated by the view.

There was no sign of a camp. Not a single sign of morning cook fire smoke. Which was odd, since despite the shadows in the deep valley, it must be long past time for people to be waking.

Sable paused. On Tutella Island, the summit would be getting underway.

"Reese!" she called up to him. "They think you started the fire! If Tanis goes to the summit today, they'll blame him!"

"I doubt he went," Reese said over his shoulder. "He'll have heard what happened. In more detail than we know, probably. We have scouts that ferry information to camp. I'm sure he knew about the fire and the search for us long before midnight."

"Between your spies, and everyone else's spies in your camp," Sable said, "it's astonishing we need a summit. Seems like everyone knows everyone else's plans anyway."

Reese snorted. "True. Maybe it's all the spies who wield the real power in this mess." The words made him frown, and he glanced back at Sable. "They are essential though."

His tone was odd. Almost like he was trying to convince himself, but he continued down the path without saying more.

Their path wound steadily down the rocky slope, widening as it plunged into the cool air of the forest. Gwen released her death grip on Reese's shirt, and Sable moved up next to him.

"What's it like living here?" The trees around her made a shushing noise in some breeze she couldn't feel, and everything was almost too perfect to believe. "I can't imagine living somewhere like this."

He glanced at her. "You might be less enamored when you see how rustic it all is."

She shook her head. "There's nothing stifling here. No priories or Kiva or Kalesh. It's like some hidden refuge from everything."

Reese's brow creased. "I don't know if there are refuges like that. It all creeps in, even here. Everything we do is focused on where the Kalesh are and what they're doing. We have to get information about the merchants and the Northern Lords. We're a little removed from the politics, but it still wiggles its way into everything we do."

He sighed. "Tanis tries to stay apart from most of it, but it's impossible. Sometimes he has to make concessions he doesn't want to, or ally himself with someone he doesn't completely trust, just to move our cause forward." He glanced at Sable. "You may not like all of Tanis's methods."

"Are you trying to drive me away?" Sable asked.

He smiled. "No, just give you a sense of what it's really like. For all its flaws, it's still better than any other cause I've ever been a part of." He paused. "Except maybe our time with Atticus."

"How did you end up here?" Sable asked. "And reach a point where Tylar called you boss?"

"I've known Tanis for years. He served as a captain under my uncle in Lord Runess's forces back when I first joined the troops. He wasn't the highest-ranking officer, but even then, his opinions carried weight. He comes from a huge family that settled along the Black River, so he has cousins in nearly every Northern Lord's army. And somehow he managed to stay on good terms with most of them. He has a knack for gathering information and allies, and eventually he became a fixture in summits whenever the lords would attempt to write treaties. When I left Immusmala last year—"

"When you were banished for assassinating a diplomat in a theater," Gwen pointed out from behind them.

Reese's jaw clenched. "When I left last year," he continued, ignoring her, "I came north with no real plan. My uncle was furious at me even before I killed the ambassador, so there was no way he would have welcomed me. But then I heard rumors that Tanis had left Lord Runess and was forming a group set on fighting off the Kalesh.

Seemed like the sort of place that might not hate me, so I tracked them down."

"And obviously it went well, if you're now second-in-command?" Sable asked.

Reese shrugged. "I supported everything Tanis was doing, and I had a lot of knowledge about the Kalesh from all the things we'd learned with Atticus, so we started working closely together."

Sable looked ahead through the trees. A whole group of people actually working to curtail the spread of the Kalesh. Not negotiate with them, not try to eke out profit from the Empire. Just trying to drive them out.

It was like a breath of fresh air.

"Where do all your people come from?"

"Most have been displaced because the Kalesh destroyed their homes. We have a good number of people from the eastern reaches who came west to escape the attacks but didn't want to go to Immusmala once they heard how many Kalesh were there. Many of our newest people are from Lord Loren's lands. Farmers and cattlemen whose lands and farms have been damaged or taken by Kalesh soldiers who are supposedly only there to guard the merchants but make it their habit to ransack homesteads that they find.

"Everyone in camp has a reason to hate the Kalesh, and no one is under any illusions that the Empire's presence here will result in anything but the destruction of our land."

"Sounds refreshing," Sable said, "after a year of trying desperately to convince anyone that that Kalesh are even a threat."

The path swung alongside a river bubbling with clear water, turning to head upstream. Sable caught the scent of something cooking. Something earthy and sweet.

Through the trees she caught glimpses of the cliffs around them, rising up like a wall. Not like the Sanctuary Wall, though. These cliffs weren't holding them in—they were holding out the rest of the world. Sable gazed up at them, basking in the openness, the otherness of it all. This was no clump of priories holding to a frustratingly rigid hierarchy or slums controlled by a corrupt gang boss.

The scent of breakfast grew stronger, and her stomach grumbled.

Sable's pace quickened as they crested a shallow rise and found the camp.

The trees were spaced more broadly here, the ground beneath them cleared of brush. Several dozen green canvas tents nestled between the trunks, and people moved around talking quietly to each other.

At the first tent they came to, a man with disheveled brown curls gave Reese a nod and looked curiously at Gwen. But when his eyes landed on Sable's white abbess's robe, he scowled.

Near the center of the cluster of tents, a burly man crouched by a wide, flat rock that emanated heat. Lumpy hotcakes sizzled on top, giving off the sweet smell of baked apples. With a knife, the man lifted the edge of one cake, then wiggled the knife in farther and flipped the lumpy cake over.

The rock appeared to be sitting directly on the ground, and there was no sign of a fire under it or near it. Sable glanced up at the man to ask him about it but found him frowning at her clothing.

"Is Tanis here?" Reese asked him.

The man's scowl lingered on Sable. "Command tent. He ain't gonna be happy you brought one of those, though. Word is the priories have declared us their enemy."

"So it would seem," Reese said dryly. "Thanks, Terrane." Turning, Reese continued through the camp.

Sable hurried up next to Reese. "Was that man cooking on a rock?"

Reese nodded. "Smoke from a dozen campfires would broadcast our location." He reached a tent that was significantly larger than the rest and ducked inside. Sable and Gwen followed.

Inside, the tent was mostly empty. The floor was covered with reed mats. An assortment of clothes and weapons were stacked along the back wall near a bedroll.

The majority of the center was cordoned off with four large logs, and inside them, papers filled the floor. Maps were spread out, their corners weighed down by rocks, and tightly rolled messages were stacked in neat piles.

Sitting on the log on the far side, Tanis held a charred stick like a quill, leaning over a map near his feet and talking quietly with an older man with a keen, narrow face.

Reese stopped and stiffened at the sight of the man, and Gwen bumped into his back. She let out an irritated huff.

A flash of relief crossed Tanis's face at the sight of Reese. "I was about to send out a search party. Trouble getting here?"

"Not trouble, exactly." Reese stepped away from Sable so Tanis could see Gwen. "But we had a new friend in tow."

Tanis's eyes narrowed at Gwen, and he stood. Sable expected the narrow-faced man to give her the same look of disdain the others had, but instead he studied them with rapt attention.

"And there was a phoenix." Reese glanced back out the door. "Who's here somewhere. I hope. Anyway, there were delays." His words were short, irritated.

"A phoenix?" Tanis asked, glancing between Gwen and Sable. "*The* phoenix?"

"Do you know of another one?" Reese grumbled.

Sable raised an eyebrow at his irritated tone but turned to the rebel leader. "The bird came with me, and if I knew why, I would tell you. Or how to make it leave. Or what it wants. Or what I'm supposed to do with it."

Tanis considered her. "Hello again, Sable. Reese has warned me that things get interesting around you."

The other man's attention shifted purely to Sable, and he studied her so intently that she shifted.

Tanis gave her a faint smile. "Nice to see he finally convinced you to visit us. He's assured me you would be a great asset to our cause, so you're welcome to stay." He gave a small shrug. "Assuming you want to."

"She might have," Reese muttered, "until now."

Sable glanced at him, wondering what he was talking about, but Tanis spoke again, more soberly this time.

"I'm sorry to hear about Prioress Narine, though. I met her once, years ago, and she was a kind soul."

Sable nodded. "She was."

"The valley might be compromised," Reese said to Tanis. "The entire world saw the phoenix fly up to where Sable was this morning. I tried to leave a false trail, but depending on how many people Vivaine sends after us, they might find the thicket."

Tanis frowned. "Do we need to close it off?"

Reese shook his head. "I don't know. Is Tylar back yet?"

"No. And one of the scouts from last night still hasn't reported." Tanis looked down at a map on the ground. "I'll send someone up to see how many people are looking for you. But tell Terrane we may need to trigger that rockslide he's been dying to cause."

Tanis turned to the man next to him. "We'll pick this up later." Seeing the man still focused on Sable, he added, "Ah, I forgot you might already know Sable."

Sable straightened, and Reese let out a defeated sigh.

The man smiled at her, but the probing look didn't leave his eyes. "Only by reputation. I left Dockside by the time she began to make a name for herself."

Sable stared at him. "Dockside?"

"Well, then," Tanis said, "let me introduce you to a man with a history surprisingly like your own. Sable." He motioned to the man with a flourish. "This is Rabbit."

CHAPTER FORTY-EIGHT

SABLE STARED at the narrow-faced man, who was watching her with an amused grin.

Rabbit? The Rabbit whom she'd heard stories of for years?

His presence was like a dark, angry blot on the valley.

"That man," Sable stabbed her finger at Rabbit, "works for Kiva."

"What?" Gwen fixed the man with an appalled look.

"I sell Kiva information sometimes," Rabbit said easily. "I do not work for him."

"Like information about the rebels?" Sable asked. She turned to Tanis. "Here's one of your spies. My sister has seen Rabbit selling information to Kiva in the last few months."

"Talia's a sweet girl," Rabbit answered. "Naive, but sweet."

"Yes, Rabbit brokers deals between us and Kiva when we have information the other needs," Tanis said. "But Rabbit has his own network of people from Folhaven all the way up to the Northern Lords. He has more information about the world than anyone else I know of. Add in Kiva's network of spies in Immusmala, which is second only to Vivaine's, and the information we get from them is essential to our success."

"You're..." Sable pulled her eyes off Rabbit to look at Tanis. "You're working with Kiva?"

"Impossible," Gwen said flatly.

Tanis shrugged. "It's hardly a secret. The other merchants are paying Kiva for information, and Eugessa is as well, I'm sure. I would wager some of the Northern Lords use our friend Rabbit here to keep tabs on the south."

Rabbit gave a little smirk.

The tent was suddenly too close, and Sable whirled to face Reese, who met her gaze with a grimace. She took a step back from him. "You're working with Kiva," she accused him.

Reese took a step closer to her. "Not willingly," he assured.

"That's true," Tanis said. "Reese has been against my relationship with Rabbit from the beginning. But he cannot deny that it's contributed to our success."

Reese shook his head slowly. "Not today it hasn't."

"I am not staying with a group who's under Kiva's control." Gwen crossed her arms. "This whole rebellion is a farce. Andreese, take me out of here. You can blindfold me for the whole day, just get me out of here."

"We are not under Kiva's control," Reese answered, exasperated.

"This may be the first time Gwen and I are in complete agreement." Sable glared at Reese. "What is it you said? I may not like all of Tanis's methods? When exactly were you going to tell me about this?"

Reese didn't look away. "I was hoping you'd learn enough about us before you met Rabbit that you'd understand the necessity of him."

Sable stared at him. "You..." Her fingers clenched into fists, and the ache from the still healing burns felt good compared to the gaping betrayal blossoming in her chest. "You..." The sheer number of words she wanted to hurl at him was paralyzing. "You lied to me," she said through clenched teeth.

"Sable," Reese said, holding out his hands. "It's not like you think."

"For once," Gwen said, "Sable is thinking exactly the right thing. Your rebel group," she continued, her voice dripping with contempt, "is no different from the merchants or the Northern Lords."

"Or the priories," Sable added. She looked back at Tanis and Rabbit, shaking her head. "I was stupid to think otherwise."

Gwen turned and walked out of the tent.

Reese stepped forward, one hand outstretched as though he would stop Sable from following, but she glared at him, funneling all her fury into the look, and he stopped.

She strode outside. Around her, the camp went about its morning routines. Sable's white abbess robe garnered her some curious looks, but she ignored them.

The cool morning air did nothing to take the edge off her anger. Rabbit. Here.

She ground her teeth together. Kiva's conniving fingers were everywhere. She glanced around the valley, its beauty marred by the thought.

"That went well." Rabbit's voice came smugly from the tent behind her.

"Reese," Tanis said, a note of command in his voice.

"I know," Reese answered with a sigh. "Thanks *so much* for being here this morning, Rabbit."

At Reese's voice, Sable started after Gwen, who was heading the wrong way.

"Sable!" He called from behind her.

She didn't slow. Gwen was stalking past the hot rock, heading deeper into camp instead of toward the river. Cooked hotcakes were set along one side, and people from the camp took a few as they passed. The burly man scooped more blobs of lumpy batter onto the rock, and they sizzled.

Sable toyed with the idea of heading straight for the path out and letting Gwen wander.

"Sable!" Reese repeated from close behind her, and she heard his footsteps running toward her.

She whirled to face him. "Get away from me."

"Let me explain."

She shook her head, the motion jerky. "There's nothing for you to explain. I thought this place might be different. I thought *you* were different. But it doesn't matter. Everywhere I go it's the same.

Everyone compromises, everyone is under the thumb of the most corrupt, powerful people." She glared around the camp. A cold thread wound its way through her, eating away at the refreshing, wholesome feeling the camp had had earlier. "I cannot believe I was stupid enough to think this would be different."

People around the camp stopped to watch, and Gwen had paused.

"You're going to complain about people compromising?" he asked her. "You? Who worked for Vivaine for the past year?"

"You're right," she said, "I was part of it too. But I thought I was getting out. I thought that somewhere, I might find a place that was different." She shook her head. "I'm done, Reese. I'm done caring. There is no way to fight the Kalesh, because, honestly, we're no better than they are. We're just comfortable here with the familiar level of corruption and control the powerful wield over us. Gwen!" she called. "I'm leaving. If you want to come, stop walking the wrong way."

Sable turned toward the path along the riverbank, not caring whether Gwen followed. She heard Reese give an exasperated sigh, but she didn't turn. She strode through the camp, ignoring the glowers she caused. The coldness in her spread, and she recognized it for what it was. Or rather, for what it wasn't. The hope that had filled her this morning was crumbling, and in its place there was nothing but hollowness.

When she passed the tent closest to the path, the man with the disheveled brown curls gave her dress the same disapproving look he had last time.

She fixed him with a glare of her own. "You cannot possibly hate this robe more than I do."

She stalked past him until the path wound into the trees and out of everyone's view. She scowled down at the dress.

"Purnicious?" she called quietly. "I'm far from the island, but I need you. Come when you can. I'm ready for those new clothes you've been wanting to make me. Something easy to travel in. Any color but white."

There was a little pop, and Purnicious appeared a few steps ahead, beaming up at her.

Sable stumbled to a stop in surprise. "Purn! How did you...?" She knelt down by the kobold. "It took hours to get here from the island!"

"I know!" Purnicious grinned. "I followed you! After the fire, when you and Reese ran off, I was going to let you know I was there"—her face turned distasteful—"but that horrible Mira was with you. So I've stayed hidden the whole time."

Sable wrapped her arms around the kobold's bony shoulders. "I'm so glad you did." She pulled back. The light yellow dress Purn had been wearing at the summit had transformed into a pair of yellow pants and a flowy tunic embroidered with a latticework of violet threads, clearly bellished from the fabric of the purple cloak the kobold wore.

But the most surprising thing was that Purn's wild, curly black hair was pulled back into an intricate braid. Strands of hair wove between each other, creating a wide plait with a rippling pattern. "Your hair!"

Sable tried to trace a single strand, but it was impossible. With her hair pulled back, Purn's face looked narrower than ever, and her normally covered pointy, blue ears were enormous.

Purn gave her a shy look, her ears dipping down bashfully. "Talia taught me how to do it. I can do yours too, if you'd like. Your hair is long and straight, like Talia's, which makes it so much easier."

Sable smiled at her. "Maybe later."

"I don't have clothes for you," Purn said with a frown. "But I can start working on something."

"Did you follow me into Tanis's tent?" Sable asked.

Footsteps sounded behind them on the path, and Purn glared over Sable's shoulder, her ears drawing back.

"Sable!" Reese called.

The kobold pushed past Sable and strode up to him, pointing her long, bony, blue finger up at him. "You are so, so much worse than a wastrel!" Her little voice was furious. "You get away from my mistress, and stay away!"

Reese ignored the kobold and stepped past her with barely a glance. "Sable, you can't go."

Sable stood. "Yes. I can, and I'm going to."

"You do not tell my mistress what to do!" Purnicious said from behind him.

Sable nodded. "Exactly, Purn."

"You can't just walk out of here," Reese repeated. "You'll just—" His eyes widened, and his fingers went to his collar, which had started to press against his neck. "Purn!" he bellowed, turning to face the little creature. He knocked her hand away from his shirt and stretched his neck, scrabbling to get his fingers under the fabric. "Loosen it!" His voice sounded hoarse.

Purnicious darted closer and grabbed the hem of his shirt again, and the rest of it shrank, the fabric pulling tight around his arms. In a breath, he could barely lift them. He swatted her hand away again, stepping back.

"You do *not* tell my mistress what to do," Purn repeated, her voice furious. "You apologize for your lies. Right now!"

Sable glanced down at the glowering kobold. "So you were in Tanis's tent."

"I heard every horrible word." Purn glared up at Reese.

His face was turning a dark, purplish red while he tried to pull his collar away. "Sable!"

Sable crossed her arms. "You should apologize before you run out of air."

He managed to slide one finger into his collar and yank. The fabric ripped like thin gauze, and he drew in a deep, gasping breath, stepping forward to tower over Purnicious. "If you touch me again, I will break your skinny little arm! I was not telling your mistress what to do, you crazy blue monster!"

"Leave Purn alone," Sable said firmly.

"Leave her alone?" he yelled. "She just tried to kill me!"

"It's Purnicious," Sable said dismissively. "She wouldn't have killed you."

"The fabric would have ripped before it strangled you." Purn came to stand next to Sable, crossing her own arms and glaring up at him. "To shrink the shirt, I have to shrink each thread, so by this point there's hardly anything to it."

The kobold reached up and yanked on the hem of his shirt. The fabric tore halfway up his stomach, not quite aligned with the tear coming down from his neck, and the front of the shirt twisted and bunched with his every breath.

His face had lost the purple hue, but it was now crimson with fury. He pointed a finger at Purn, then shifted it to Sable. "You two are like a tiny little force of destruction. All those people who think you have something worth controlling, Sable? They don't know the half of it." He shifted his finger back to Purnicious. "You are unhinged. I am dreading the day the two of you decide to take on someone powerful."

The kobold looked up at him smugly. "I have warned you a thousand times to treat my mistress well."

"I do treat your mistress well!" he roared at her. "I have done everything in my power, since the day I met her, to keep her safe, regardless of the fact she keeps throwing herself into danger!"

The shirt was still skintight around his arms and stretched so thin along the top of his shoulders it looked like it would rip with every breath. The torn front flapped and wrinkled, making the whole thing hang so awkwardly that Sable had to bite back a smile.

"The day you met me, you hated me," Sable pointed out. "For the first few days, really. You were terrible."

"And I *still* tried to keep you safe from the Kalesh who attacked the wagons. Even though you decided to take on a huge soldier with only a pointy stick!"

"I made that pointy for her," Purn said proudly.

"I know!" he yelled. "You always help her! And she's reckless enough without you!"

Sable grinned down at Purnicious. "All I want from her today is some new clothes."

The kobold grinned back, the smile so wide it lifted even her ears.

"Could I get new clothes too?" Gwen's voice called from the path.

Purn's eyes narrowed as she watched the Mira approach. "No. I don't like you."

"No one does, it seems," Gwen said grimly. "I was wondering when your little kobold would show up, Sable."

"You," Purn said, pulling out her bony finger again and pointing it at the Mira, "should not be trusted. I know what you did to Narine."

Gwen met the kobold's glare. "So no new clothes, then?" She took in Reese's shirt. "Actually, if this is your handiwork, I'll find something to wear through more conventional methods."

"Funny," Reese said dryly. He turned back to Sable. "You can't leave the valley—"

Purnicious raised a warning hand toward him. "That's not your decision, chesty man."

He glared at Purn before turning back to Sable. "If you leave this camp, you will walk into a dozen search parties looking for you. There is no way you'll get out of that valley without being caught, even if your phoenix friend doesn't find you and announce where you are to the world." He looked at Sable, a note of imploring intertwining with his anger. "Just stay a few days. We'll keep track of the search parties, and when they stop looking, if you still want to leave, I will take you anywhere in the world you want to go. I promise." He lifted his arm to run his fingers though his hair, but the tight sleeve stopped him. "Purnicious! Will you fix the blasted shirt so I can move?"

"If you ask nicely," the kobold said.

"Please," he growled.

Purn smiled up at him and set one finger on the ripped edge of his shirt. The fabric grew transparent, then disintegrated, bits of thread tumbling to the ground, leaving him shirtless.

Reese's jaw dropped open, and he stared at her, shocked.

"I'm sorry," Purn said sweetly, "was that not what you meant? It's not constricting you anymore."

"It's definitely an improvement," Gwen said.

"I only had two shirts, Purn!" Reese said.

Sable caught a glimpse of a long, thick scar wrapping around the side of his stomach, new enough to still be dark red, the skin around it puckered.

Reese turned to Sable, his face annoyed enough that she had to bite back another smile. "Will you please stay a few days?" he managed through clenched teeth.

She glanced at Gwen. Reese was right—it was stupid to walk back out into that valley. Even if Innov didn't reappear and show everyone where she was, there was no way Sable would get through all those search parties, especially with Gwen along.

Sable nodded.

Reese let out a relieved breath and did run his hands through his hair this time. "Good. Come back to camp, and we'll get you someplace to stay."

"Don't tell her what to do," Purn warned.

Reese glared at her. "*Please* come back."

"Lead the way," Sable said.

Reese turned and stormed back up the trail.

As he passed Gwen, she smirked at him. Purn, with a little giggle, popped out of view.

He led them back to the burly man cooking hotcakes. "Terrane, this is Gwen and Sable. Do we have a tent that they could use for a few days?"

Terrane glanced up. "Sable? Your Sable?"

"What?" Sable demanded.

"She is not *my* Sable," Reese snapped. "Do we have a tent?"

The man frowned. "I suppose. I figured if you ever managed to get her here, she'd share your tent."

"Absolutely not!" Sable said.

"Well," Terrane said, "he ran off into the woods after you, and now he's back without his shirt."

"The tent, Terrane," Reese growled.

Terrane gave Sable a grin. "Trip and Shady are gone for at least a fortnight. We can put them there."

"Great," Reese said. "Get them situated."

"Yes, sir, boss," Terrane said, still grinning.

Reese muttered something and turned back toward Tanis's tent.

Gwen's eyes lingered on Reese. "I like Purnicious more than I thought I would."

"I'm pretty sure he'll find another shirt," Sable pointed out.

"A shame," Gwen said.

Sable felt a flicker of irritation. "I didn't realize you were so interested in him."

"Oh, I'm not. But that doesn't mean he doesn't have some admirable qualities. Even if he's a bit too woodsy and uncivilized."

The tent Terrane led them to was small, only roomy enough for a bedroll along each side and space along the back wall for a few supplies. Whoever Trip and Shady were, they didn't have many belongings. There were two chests that held bundles of well-worn clothes, a lantern with a nub of candle in it, and an assortment of rough tools.

Gwen gave a sigh of relief and dropped down onto one of the bedrolls. "Who'd have known that a few blankets could be so comfortable?"

"Anyone who's ever slept on the ground," Sable answered, sitting on the other bed.

"I'm certainly not upset that I made it this far in life before having to do that," Gwen said sleepily. "Last night was horrible."

Sable didn't answer. Last night had been fairly horrible, and this morning had been…She sighed. This morning had been so perfect, she should have known it was too good to be true.

Gwen's breathing grew regular, and Sable lay back on her own roll, staring at the bland sand-colored tent wall above her, trying not to think about any of it.

A bright light glowed outside the tent, starting in the far corner above Gwen's head and moving quickly along the side, like someone running past with a lantern. The light curled around to the front of the tent, and Innov banked her little wings, soaring in through the open tent flap and landing next to Sable.

Sable smiled at the tiny bird. "I thought you'd left."

Innov hopped closer, then jumped up onto Sable's chest, curling herself into a ball and tucking her head down near the front of her wing. Sable set her hand on the phoenix's back. "I'm glad you didn't," she said. "And thank you for healing my hands. I didn't even know you could do that." She paused, contemplating the bird. "You're the reason Narine lived as long as she did, aren't you? When she touched you, you were able to heal her." Sable frowned. "That and Vivaine giving her blood thistle every week." She sighed. "You're probably the reason Narine survived that, aren't you?"

Innov shifted into a tighter ball.

"I'm glad you did," Sable said to her. "She needed you."

The phoenix gave no sign of hearing, and in a moment, her breathing was deep and regular too. From the spot where she lay, a soothing warmth flowed into Sable's chest, moving slowly out to fill her body. The hollow feeling that had been growing in her since Tanis's tent lost its cold bite. It didn't leave completely, but the bits of hope that still survived at the edges gained a little strength.

She stroked her finger along Innov's back, sending a spray of sparks into the air. "Maybe I need you too."

PART IV

Queen Issable had a great fondness for scarletberries, which do not thrive as far north as Queenstown.

Every year, after the pineberries flowered, but before the apples turned yellow, her husband would disappear for a week and return with an enormous basket of perfectly ripe scarletberries.

-from Flibbet the Peddler's *Fairly Useless Facts About Fairly Interesting People*

CHAPTER FORTY-NINE

THE SOUNDS of the morning drifted into the tent, and Sable stared out at the triangle of camp she could see through the open flap. Despite the calming warmth of Innov, Sable's head spun with thoughts she couldn't sort.

Rabbit was here. The thought churned something old and deep inside her. Even here she wasn't free of Kiva.

She closed her eyes. Not that she'd ever really be free from him, not as long as Talia…

An uncomfortable parallel occurred to her, and she opened her eyes.

Talia was hardly Rabbit, but Sable *had* been using her for months to get information from Kiva, or from Lord Trelles. She rubbed her hands over her face. She was just as guilty as the rest of them. It felt different, though, getting information for an important cause, instead of just for her own advancement.

Even as she had the thought, she felt the hypocrisy of it. If she'd had access to the sort of knowledge Rabbit had, she'd have done whatever she could to use it well.

Tanis would be a fool to ignore such a chance. The only real question was whether Talia was right that Rabbit worked on his own instead of exclusively for Kiva.

A little pop sounded, and Purnicious appeared at her feet, holding a bundle of fabric. "I have clothes for you!" she said cheerfully.

The light yellow tunic the kobold was wearing now had a bright orange ruffle around the hem, which clashed gleefully with the purple embroidery. Sable winced. "And I see you found something for yourself. I should have been more specific about mine than 'not white.' You didn't bring me anything gaudy, did you?"

She sat up, gently setting Innov down on the bedroll.

Purn wrinkled her nose. "I resisted. If we're sneaking through the woods, I thought you should wear something boring." She held up a pair of light brown pants with large pockets on the sides, a rust red tunic, and a pair of leather boots.

Sable took the shirt. "Purn, they're so...reserved. How did you make these so fast?"

"I didn't—I followed the wastrel to his own tent, where he went to find himself a new shirt," she said with a smirk. "He seemed nervous when I appeared. But I informed him you needed something else to wear so that people would stop glaring at you. He got dressed in his new, boring, poorly fitting tunic and found me these from a pile in a different tent."

Sable stood and dropped the tent flap before pulling off the abbess's robe. She almost tossed it on the bedroll but paused. The fact that it was from Vivaine made her want to toss it in a fire, but there was something final about taking off the white. One of the threads connecting her to Narine stretched thin, then faded away. Sable sighed and dropped the white dress.

The new tunic was loose, and a flash of color caught her eye as she pulled it over her head. Sable frowned and pulled it away, trying to see into it. The inside of the collar was lined with the same bright orange fabric as Purn's frill.

Sable glanced at the kobold.

Purn grinned. "I wasn't going to leave it completely boring."

Sable drew the crooked sword pendant out of the shirt, running her fingers over it.

"I could fix that," Purn offered. "Make it prettier, at least. Make it less…wastrel-ish."

Sable dropped the necklace and let it lie on the tunic. "Maybe someday." She pulled on the pants, and Purn looked at her critically.

"They don't quite fit. Stand still." The kobold set her hands on Sable's legs, and the fabric shortened a bit and slimmed to fit her waist. Purn motioned for Sable to bend down, then dragged her finger along the shoulders. They tightened until they fit perfectly. A thin line gathered along Sable's ribs, taking the flowing shirt and forming it into something almost pretty. Purn stepped back. "That's better. I'll keep working on it."

Sable looked down. There was not a speck of white anywhere on her. "Purn. I love you."

Purnicious beamed up at her.

A familiar voice called out in the camp, and Sable pushed open the tent flap. A knot of people stood around a cart.

"Flibbet!" Sable said. "How did he get here?"

"The old peddler is here? Oh, I like him," Purn said decidedly.

"When did you meet him?"

"I heard part of the conversation he had with Narine," she said.

Sable glanced down at the kobold. "I forget that you can hear what's going on around me, now that I'm not in the priory." She considered the little creature.

The idea of Purn knowing what was going on around her felt surprisingly…not invasive. It was almost comforting.

Purn nodded. "It was such a relief when you left the priory and I could feel you again and hear what was going on around you and make sure you were safe."

She set her hand on the kobold's shoulder. "I'm glad you're here."

Flibbet called out a greeting to someone, and Sable stepped out of the tent. Behind her, she heard Purn pop out of view. Sable crossed over to his wagon. The little handcart had transformed. What had been the cover now stood upright, a handful of colorful, random objects hanging from pegs. The inside of his cart was laid out with trinkets and folded clothes. A blanket and a lantern. Far fewer wares than he'd had when he'd stopped by Narine's house at the summit.

The peddler haggled cheerily with Terrane over the value of a thin, metal tool.

"It will save your fingers," Flibbet pointed out, looking up at the larger man. "Slide right under those hotcakes, and you won't get burned."

Terrane looked at the tool and nodded. "I'll give you sixteen buttons for it."

Flibbet raised one bushy blond eyebrow. "Buttons? Don't insult me. How about that trinket." He pointed to a white rock hanging from a leather thong at Terrane's neck.

"No," the big man said flatly. "Three piping hot apple hotcakes."

Flibbet narrowed his eyes. "Four."

Terrane nodded and took the tool. "More hotcakes," he called out to the camp at large. "There'll be more cakes 'til the apples run out!"

The peddler held up a wooden broom and glanced around the group. "Someone here must have a use for this beauty—" His gaze caught on Sable, and he paused, blinking at her in surprise. "Issable? You're...here?"

The rebels standing around looked at Sable curiously. She heard the words phoenix and abbess muttered. She shifted, feeling a bit like she'd stepped on stage.

Sable gave Flibbet a tight smile. "I was going to say the same to you."

He stood with the broom still raised, staring at her with a perplexed expression. "Yes, you could," he said almost to himself. His gaze caught on her traveling clothes, and he blinked. He lowered the broom. "If you're here, then Narine is..."

Sable swallowed the tightness that rose in her throat and nodded. "Last night."

Flibbet let out a long sigh. He set the broom back in his cart and closed the lid. "This is heavy news. If you'll excuse me, folks, I need a few moments. My cart will be near Terrane's rock in a bit."

The gathered rebels looked at Sable with varying levels of curiosity and irritation, but they dispersed.

Flibbet leaned against his cart. "Did she go peacefully?"

Sable closed her eyes against the image of Narine curled up against the wall. "No," she said. "There was a fire."

Flibbet's eyes widened, and he turned, his gaze growing distant as though he could see the island through the hills between them. "The Phoenix Prioress dies in a fire," he said quietly, the words heavy, almost angry. "That is…" His hand clenched into a fist, and Sable couldn't decipher the emotions on his face. "Did she suffer?"

Sable's answer caught in her throat. "Not for long," she managed.

He closed his eyes and stood perfectly still. "Poor, dear Narine," he murmured.

When he turned back, something in his expression had grown old and weary. His hair was still blond, but it wasn't hard to believe now that he had known Narine when she was young. He shook his head slowly. "Poor, dear Narine."

She took a deep breath and nodded. Poor, dear Narine.

His eyes came back into focus and settled on Sable. His brow wrinkled. "You are here," he said, puzzled. "Before I even arrived."

She raised an eyebrow at the odd little man. "Did you expect me here later?"

"I didn't expect you here at all. How did you—" He snapped his fingers. "The young man who works with Tanis is the fellow who ended your show in the Grand Stadia with so much…flourish. I hadn't realized he…" The man stopped, stroking the end of his beard and looking off into the trees again. "It makes sense, though," he mused. "In a way." He looked back at Sable. "What is his name again?"

"Andreese." She studied the peddler. The aged look had stayed in his eyes, and she wondered how she had ever thought he didn't look old. "You are a very strange man."

A grin split his face, and he let out a chuckle. "I'm sorry, my dear. I usually try to hide it more. You've caught me off guard this morning." He patted his cart. "I meet a lot of people in a lot of places. But I don't often run into someone twice on a seeming coincidence." He gestured to her. "And it's incredibly rare to meet a third time. These sorts of things get me thinking about how we're all connected and the threads that run under the surface of everything. Makes me wonder if I could step back far enough, could I sort it all out? Maybe all the ways our lives intersect makes some vast, glorious tapestry."

Sable let out an amused breath. "Was that explanation supposed to make me think you're less odd?"

He scratched under his beard, his smile turning rueful. "I suppose not."

She frowned at his cart. It rolled on two large wheels, far too widely spaced to have fit down the path into the valley. "How did you get that down here?"

"When I visit Tanis's camp, I come from the west." He motioned toward the far end of the valley. "It takes an extra day, but the eastern entrance..." He gave a shiver. "No, thank you. The western road is still steep, but much wider."

He studied her. "Why are you here? With Tanis? Are you staying? Is this where...?" He glanced around the camp. "It feels too small," he said to himself, "but..." He turned back to Sable and focused on her with an unnerving intensity. "Are you part of *this* now?"

Sable paused. "I don't know. I thought I wanted to be."

"But?"

"I thought Tanis was different," she said slowly. "I thought I agreed with everything they were doing, but then I found out they were connected with someone I disagree with. Strongly. On everything. And now I don't know what to believe or who to trust."

Flibbet tapped his chin. "Let me guess. It has to do with Rabbit."

"How'd you know that?"

He shrugged, "I think he's the only one at camp from as far south as you are. And if rumors about Rabbit are true, he worked for a gang boss in Immusmala once. Kiva, unless I'm mistaken. Which means you have had run-ins with Kiva as well."

"You could say that," Sable said. "You know a lot for a random peddler."

"It's all in the threads, you see. After a while, they're easier to pick out. They're always being plucked, but some plucks send vibrations moving through interesting tangles." He nodded slowly, then blinked and looked back at her. "What drew you to Tanis in the first place?"

"He's actually trying to drive out the Kalesh," Sable said.

"Everyone else is just letting the Empire grow stronger and stronger. Reese said the rebels were trying to unify the north, and that is exactly what has to happen." She leaned against his cart too, looking out across the camp. "Actually, what needs to happen is for the north and the south to unite. But that feels impossible."

"But now you think Tanis is working with a corrupt man in Immusmala, so maybe he's corrupt himself," Flibbet said slowly. "You trusted Andreese, and Andreese trusted Tanis, but maybe whatever this place is, it's all a lie."

Sable nodded. "And I can't even fault Tanis, because he'd be foolish to give up the sort of information Rabbit has. But I don't know if I can join a group that's working with Kiva."

"You could leave. You wouldn't be the first person to wash your hands of all the madness and go live by yourself somewhere peaceful."

"That sounds very, very appealing."

"I know." He patted his cart. "I have yet to find a place to settle into."

Freedom. Actual freedom from all the angling and scheming. The sounds of the camp swirled around them on the morning breeze, but she felt utterly separated from all of it. There was a huge distance between herself and these people. Maybe leaving would be for the best. She could go north. As far north as she could, as far from the Kalesh as she could, and let the rest of the world run itself into the ground.

"Or," Flibbet said, "you could take the world as you find it, broken and jagged and weak, and you could step right into the midst of it. Take what it is and spend yourself making it what it should be."

Her thoughts of freedom grew gauzy and thin in the face of those words.

Unanchored freedom is a child's dream, Vivaine had told her the night of the state dinner. *Meaning and value come through finding something worth fighting for and sacrificing yourself for it.*

Even though they had been Vivaine's, the words rang uncomfortably true. Just like Flibbet's.

Take the world as you find it, and make it what it should be.

The idea resonated inside her.

She closed her eyes. Trying to make the world what it should be, even one tiny piece of it, sounded exhausting, but…possible. Rich.

The idea of freedom dissolved, shredding and fluttering away like the last lingering bits of dream in the light of morning.

She opened her eyes to see Flibbet looking at her sympathetically. "Choosing freedom would be easier," he said quietly.

"It would." She looked down and caught sight of the sword necklace. The bent, off-center blade felt uncomfortably appropriate. If she were a sword, she undoubtedly would look like this one. Never quite pointed in the right direction, not lined up the way she was expected to be. But maybe, if she held herself the right way, if she did the movements she was meant for, maybe she could do *something*. "And yet…"

Flibbet sighed. "And yet."

CHAPTER FIFTY

SABLE STOOD SILENTLY NEXT the peddler for a few moments, watching people wander over to Terrane and get hotcakes. Until the peddler stirred.

"It occurs to me," Flibbet said, "that I offered you nothing last time we met." He lifted the lid of his cart, showing the broom and the blanket and the other assorted, equally uninteresting items. "What is it that you need, Issable?"

"Just Sable," she said, "and the only thing I'd really like is a way to beat the Kalesh once and for all and end this mess."

He let out a chuckle and moved the broom to the side, rummaging through the items underneath. "A big thing to fit in a small cart."

"And most likely an impossible thing," she answered. "I doubt there's anything more powerful than the Empire."

"Love," Flibbet said, offhanded.

She stared at him. "I ask for a way to defeat the Empire, and you offer 'love.'"

He grinned and nodded.

"Because love is gonna come down like a giant broom and sweep the Kalesh back to their own lands?"

He let out a rolling laugh. "That would be something to see. But love rarely does things on her own. It's people who love who do the astonishing things."

"Like defeat Empires," Sable said dryly.

"Exactly." He looked up at the treetops around them, his gaze lingering on a nearby aspen whose pale green leaves fluttered and shimmered in the breeze. "It's hard to stop someone motivated by love. They're transformed into something more than themselves."

He refocused on her, cocking his head to the side. "I don't have a way you can beat the Empire, but I have the way others have." He shifted a blanket out of his way, revealing several small holes in the wood underneath it. He stuck his fingers through them and pulled, lifting the center of the cart top away. Setting the wood to the side, he peered inside.

Sable leaned closer and let out a gasp. The entire bottom of the cart was filled with books.

"I happen to have a book that you might be interested in." He reached in, feeling blindly off to the side in the shadows. He pulled out a brown volume. "It details some of the rebellions—" He stopped, staring at the book in his hand. "This isn't right." He tossed the book down on the blanket and peered into the shadowy edges of his cart.

Sable picked up the book. The words *Dangerous 'Shrooms* were written across the cover, along with a detailed drawing of a tall, skinny mushroom.

Flibbet reached back in, frowning, and pulled out two more. *Edible Birds Eggs* and an incredibly thin book titled *Mrs. Poosley's Mushroom Clover Bread.*

He stared at them. "This is wrong," he muttered. "All wrong." He pulled out three more books, glaring at them in turn. "No. No. No." He tossed them aside, stepping back to look at his cart as though he'd never seen it before.

"How did all these get moved— Serene!" he hissed.

"You know Serene?" Sable asked.

"That woman!" Flibbet growled, reaching into the bottom of his cart and pulling out handfuls of books. "I have told her a thousand times to not touch my books! And yet—Wrong!" He flung this pile of books on top of the others. "Wrong! Wrong! Wrong! This is going to take hours to fix! HOURS! How am I supposed to find anything in this mess?"

The books that he threw out followed a pattern. First food-related books, then two on medicinal herbs, then one on farm animal ailments. Sable pressed her lips together to hide her smile. "Serene does think books should be filed by subject."

Sable looked from the books to Flibbet, the answer to a mystery coming suddenly clear. "You're Serene's merchant! You've been taking books out of Immusmala for her!"

Flibbet leaned into his cart, sticking his entire arm in and pulling a pile of books out of the dark corners. "Not after this!" His voice came muffled from the cart. "She broke my cart!"

He froze, then slowly stood back up. "She broke my cart," he repeated, turning to Sable with a lost expression. "I didn't think anyone could break it, but Serene could...she's...What if I can't fix it?"

Sable blinked at him. "Can't you just put the books back the way you had them?"

"I don't know how they were organized," he said faintly, sinking against the cart. "How could I? How could I possibly know which I will need next?" He gave Sable a desperate look. "How could I ever know that?"

Sable shifted. "Flibbet, every moment I talk to you, I'm more convinced that you are the strangest person I've ever met." She glanced at the cart, which was now strewn with jumbled piles of books.

Flibbet didn't answer, but instead turned and leaned his elbows on his cart, dropping his head into his hands, muttering something despondent.

Even though Flibbet couldn't see her, Sable pointed toward the rock where Terrane cooked. "I'm going to get some hotcakes." She glanced at the cart. "Good luck sorting all that out."

She was starting past him when Flibbet straightened, still staring down at his cart.

"Issable..." he said.

"Just Sable, please."

He picked up a very small, tawny-colored book. "Yes, Sable," he said absently. He held up the book. "This is not what I was looking for," he said slowly.

Sable just stared at him, out of responses for his strange behavior.

"But," he said, his old grin spreading across his face, "it may be exactly what you need." He held out the book triumphantly.

The title *Ghost of the White Wood* was inked large and neat across the front.

Sable took it and flipped it open. The bottom of the first page held a row of sketched pine trees with flames dancing across their tops. Written above it, the words *Ghost of the White Wood* were surrounded with swirls of smoke.

She frowned. Where had she heard of the White Wood?

Before she could recall the words, Flibbet burst into laughter so gleeful it was almost a cackle. "The story of another rebel."

"This is the story of a rebellion against the Empire?" Sable asked.

"Of a pivotal player in a rebellious area." He nodded in a self-satisfied way. "A woman who caused the Empire a great deal of trouble."

Sable flipped through the short book. Each page was filled with neat writing. A handful of maps and diagrams were peppered through. She paused at a drawing. The background was a loosely sketched camp of tents. In front of it, drawn with thick, flowing strokes, stood a woman with long hair. Her dress streamed behind her in the wind, and there was the impression of a bow in her hand. Every line of her body spoke of fierce determination.

Flibbet peered at the page. "I think you're going to like this tale."

"I can't pay you. I literally have nothing but these clothes."

He glanced at her new tunic and pants. "What happened to that white robe you were wearing before?"

"I do have that," Sable agreed. "It's ripped and stained with smoke and soot, but it's in my tent. Assuming Purn hasn't already used it for something else."

"Who's Purn?"

"A friend who dearly loves fabric." She held up the book and looked at him skeptically. "You'll take an old, dirty, white dress in exchange for this?"

"Of course."

Sable shrugged. "Then I'll go get it." She glanced at the piles of disorganized books. "Good luck fixing your cart."

"Oh," he said easily, picking up random books and tucking them back inside without bothering to look at their titles. "It's fine."

Sable shook her head at the strange man and headed off to find the dress.

She set the book down next to the still-sleeping Innov and grabbed the abbess's robe. When she returned, Flibbet had set up his cart near Terrane's cooking rock and was surrounded by people from the camp. He took her dress with a quick nod, then went back to haggling with a stern woman over a dented cook pot.

Terrane crouched by his rock stove, lifting hotcakes gently off the stone with the new tool from Flibbet. He offered one to her.

She took a bite and found a lump of warm apple cooked into the cake. It was surprisingly good, whether from the sweet fruit or the fact that her last meal seemed like a month ago, she wasn't sure. She took another big bite.

"Tasty, isn't it?" Terrane rolled back on his heels, looking pleased with himself. "I make the best hotcakes this side of the Black River."

Sable swallowed. "Is there fierce hotcake competition among the tiny towns and farms this side of the river?"

"Fine. I make the best hotcakes north of Immusmala."

"That sounds more impressive. They are tasty, although they're the first hotcakes I've had north of Immusmala, so I can't say for sure I couldn't find better."

"You can't." He shrugged. "Because these are the best."

Heat poured off the rock, warming Sable's legs. She bent down to find where the fire was situated, but the rock sat directly on the ground.

"How is this hot?" she asked Terrane.

The burly man wiggled his fingers at her. "Magic," he whispered.

She paused. Along with the heat of the stone, she could feel the other sort of warmth in his words. She raised an eyebrow. "Show me."

He let out a rolling laugh. "The little lady wants a demonstration! Doubts Terrane's magnificent skills," he called out loudly.

A few of the people around Flibbet turned their attention to Terrane, nudging each other and moving closer expectantly.

"Flibbet!" Terrane called. "Do you have any paper?"

"Not that I'd give you," Flibbet answered.

Terrane leaned toward Sable. "Stingy man," he said. "Doesn't appreciate a good show." The burly man glanced around and pulled up a tuft of tall grass. "Doesn't think that fire itself is amazing. That being burned is the greatest end a piece of paper could hope for." He spread the grass out in his hand like a fan and dragged his finger across the tips of the blades.

There was a rush of *vitalle,* and Sable expected a huge fire, but one by one, the pieces of grass burst into tiny flames until the entire edge of the fan was burning. The line of fire curled the ends of the grass and slid lower.

He moved his fingers along the fan, almost like plucking the strings of an instrument, and the flames danced. Single blades burst suddenly bright or dimmed and smoked. With a series of quick flicks, he made a pattern of sparks shoot off.

The spectators gave a cheer, and he drew his hand back, slowing the fire until the flames seemed to burn impossibly slow. Instead of flickering, they swayed, slow and steady.

Sable took a step forward. The warmth she felt from the grass had nothing to do with the fire. Each time Terrane wiggled a finger, she felt a sudden, intense flash of heat.

"Terrane!" Reese strode up from behind Sable. "No fire!"

Terrane's fingers snapped shut into a fist, and the flames snuffed out. "Sorry, boss. Just showing this young lady that I wasn't lying about using magic," he said easily, dropping the grass to the ground.

"I doubt she's as impressed by that as you're expecting." Reese picked up a hotcake. Beside him, Tanis turned his gaze to Sable with a probing look.

She ignored them both. The way Terrane moved *vitalle* felt wild and unfocused. "That was...interesting."

"Interesting?" Terrane looked slightly insulted.

Sable glanced at Tanis and Reese. "Why do you call Reese boss? I thought Tanis was the boss."

"Tanis is the chief," Terrane corrected her. "And we don't call Reese boss because he's *the* boss. We call him that because he's bossy."

"Shut up, Terrane," Reese said around a mouthful of cake.

"See?" Terrane said with a grin.

Sable nodded. "He taught me some sword work once. He was very bossy."

Reese opened his mouth to object, but before he could answer, there was a commotion on the path leading out of camp.

A man came sprinting off the trail, angling toward them.

"They're coming!" he called to Tanis, his breath coming fast. "The priories called for a manhunt, saying Reese killed a prioress and stole her phoenix. The camps along the river are emptying, and everyone is headed this way, calling for blood!"

CHAPTER FIFTY-ONE

ALL ACTIVITY in the center of camp stopped as people turned to the scout.

"How close are they?" Tanis asked.

"An hour, maybe two." The man breathed heavily. "They saw the phoenix fly toward this end of the valley and are following it. They don't know exactly where our trail is, but with the amount of people coming, they'll find it."

The attention of the rebels shifted to Sable, and she swallowed down the hotcake in her mouth. Reese grimaced and tossed his own half-eaten cake back down onto the rock.

Tanis rubbed his hand over his face, then gave a sharp nod.

"Strike camp." he said. "Windswept. No fires, no noise. Everyone out the western road in under a half hour. We're heading north to Steepdale. Go!"

The camp burst into activity, with everyone scattering toward tents.

"Sorry, Tanis," Reese said heavily. "I should have taken them somewhere else."

Tanis shrugged and looked around the valley, an edge of regret in his expression. "I think our time at the summit was done, and we were getting a bit too comfortable here."

"I'll take Terrane and block the eastern trail," Reese said.

Tanis nodded and turned toward the command tent, where people were already carrying out bundles of papers, packing them into a waiting wagon, which was being hitched to a horse.

"How are you going to block it?" Sable asked.

"We'll collapse some rocks above the trail. It'll seal off the narrowest part of the entrance," Reese said.

"And tell the entire valley where you are," Sable pointed out.

"The entire valley already knows where we are," he answered.

"Not exactly, but you start rolling rocks around and they'll hear it from the island."

"We have to block the entrance, or anyone who finds it will be right behind us. The wagons move too slow for us to get away."

"So block the entrance with something quieter," Sable said. "Purn can grow the bushes. She could close up that thicket. If you can clear away any tracks leading to it, that should keep people from finding the trail."

Tanis had paused to listen to the conversation. "What are you talking about? No one can grow bushes fast enough to help."

Sable hesitated, waiting to see if Reese would explain, but he merely waited for her to. "Purnicious is a kobold."

Tanis raised an eyebrow. "A phoenix and a kobold? And here all this time I've thought Reese was exaggerating when he talked about you." He shook his head and patted Reese on the shoulder. "I think you actually undersold her. Go deal with the eastern trail. However you can." He started toward the command tent. "See you in Steepdale."

"Where's Innov?" Reese asked.

Sable paused. "Sleeping. I hope."

"Get her and Purn, and meet me back here."

Sable raised an eyebrow. "You are bossy."

Terrane grinned, and Reese scowled at both of them.

"Terrane," Reese said, "you're coming too, just in case the thicket thing doesn't work. Bring your sticks." He turned and strode off toward a line of tents.

Sable hurried back to her own tent to find two rebels calling for Gwen to get out so they could pack it. Sable ducked inside and scooped up Innov, who was still curled in a fiery ball. The little book from Flibbet lay on the bed, and Sable fit it into one of the pockets in her pants.

"What's happening?" Gwen asked blearily.

"Vivaine saw Innov," Sable answered, tucking Innov into the crook of her elbow. "And she's sent everyone this way after us."

Gwen sat up, her eyes widening. "Where will we go?"

"The rebels are escaping," Sable ducked back out of the tent. "Just go with the wagons."

"Wait!" Gwen called. "Where are you going?"

"To have Purnicious block the eastern entrance. Help them strike camp."

"I'm not staying here with a bunch of strangers," Gwen said, stumbling out of the tent.

Sable whirled on her. "These strangers let you stay here when probably they shouldn't have. And I'm going back up the path that runs along the cliff." Innov stirred, and Sable set a hand on her back.

Gwen's eyes flickered toward the rocky face at the eastern end of the valley, and she paled.

"Stay here and be helpful," Sable said. "Reese and I will catch up later." She strode back through camp, toward Terrane's rock. Reese was already there, buckling on a belt. From one side hung a sheathed sword, and along the front three short knives were tucked into their own sheaths.

Terrane slung a long bag over his shoulder. Thin pieces of wood poked out the top. He stopped, his eyes fixed on Innov. "Is that—?"

Reese shook his head. "No, Sable. We are trying to be stealthy."

"What else am I supposed to do with her?" Sable asked. "Besides, if she's with us, she can't inadvertently lead anyone to the camp."

He let out an annoyed growl. "Just keep track of her." He turned and started toward the path at a jog.

When they were deep in the trees, he stopped and turned to Sable. "Purn can do this, right?"

"Purnicious," Sable called quietly, and there was a little pop next to her.

Purnicious appeared, looking suspiciously back at Terrane. "Of course I can, wastrel," she said to Reese. "Those thickets are terribly overgrown. A baby kobold could close them up." She turned to Sable. "I'll go ahead and do it. I can get there faster on my own. You can all go back with the camp."

"Wait," Reese said, "I need to get through and make sure all signs of the trail are gone before you close it."

Purn nodded. "I'll get started and leave a little opening for you."

"Be careful," Sable said, and Purnicious popped out of view.

Terrane looked at Sable curiously. "How did you get a kobold?"

"By accident," Sable answered.

"Let's go—" Reese stopped, frowning down the trail behind them. "Someone's coming."

Gwen hurried around the last bend. "I'm coming with you," she announced, her voice breathless.

"No," he said flatly.

"I'm not going somewhere with a whole camp of people I don't know," she said firmly.

"You will do nothing but slow us down," Reese said. "I don't have time to coddle you on the steep path."

She glared at him. "I don't need coddling. And I could be useful to you."

"How?"

"There are search parties out there, right?" she asked. "Well, if we run across any, I can tell you everything they know with just a touch."

"With any luck, we'll be done before the search parties get near us," Reese said.

"Because you've had such good luck up to this point?" Gwen asked.

Reese scowled at her. "You can come, but only because I don't have time to make sure you go back to camp. Keep up. No one is helping you on the cliff, and if you fall behind, it's your own problem."

Gwen nodded, and the four of them started off. Reese kept a quick pace until the land started to rise and he settled into a steady walk. Sable's legs burned as the path got steeper, and her breath came faster. Behind her, Terrane seemed to be having no trouble for such a large man.

They climbed out of the forest and back onto the thin path that clung to the rock face. Gwen's breath became ragged, and Sable glanced back once to see the Mira staring resolutely up the path, her face pale and her hands held out to the side for balance.

When they reached the top, the gap in the thicket was so thin it was hard to find.

Purnicious stepped out of it and frowned. "It took you long enough," she said to Reese. "I tried to hide the trail a bit on the other side already."

He nodded and turned sideways to fit through the hole.

Long thorns Sable hadn't noticed the first time they'd come through the bushes caught at his sleeve, and he stopped to untangle it.

"Did you add the thorns?" Sable asked Purn.

The kobold smiled up at her. "The ones that grew here were too small. I just helped them be a bit longer. And pointier."

A hiss of pain came from inside the thicket, and Purn grinned. "Looks like it worked." She gestured to the hole. "You can fit through without getting poked, mistress. I sized the hole for you."

Sable heard Reese curse again and bit back a smile. "We do need him to make it through. And we are in a hurry."

Purn sighed and touched the nearest branch. With a whispery sound, the gap in the thicket widened.

Terrane peered into the small hole. "I'll just stay here."

Sable ducked inside. The branches rose from the ground in a tangle, making a rough wall on either side and intertwining above her head in a lattice. The outer edges of the thicket were covered with olive green leaves like a canopy, tinting all the bare branches in the interior the color of old grass. Sable turned sideways, avoiding the thorns and shuffling toward the other side. In her arms, Innov cast a circle of warm golden light on the nearest branches.

When Sable reached the other side, she found Reese gathering fallen branches and positioning them across the thin trail leading into the thicket. He rolled a rock over where the path branched off, tucking some moss around it and sprinkling the area with a handful of pine needles.

"Purn did a good job," he said, surveying the forest floor.

"You sound surprised," Purnicious said from the edge of the thicket.

He stood back and surveyed the thicket. "It looks good. Let's head back through, and, Purnicious, you can finish closing it—" He stopped and held up his hand for silence, cocking his head.

Down the hill there was a crack of a stick. Reese turned, scanning through the trees.

Sable stepped up next to him. "Say something true."

He glanced over at her. "You make my life complicated," he whispered.

The warmth of his words flowed around them, and Sable shot him a glare. Beside her, he radiated as much warmth as a bright campfire, and in her arms, Innov flared hotter. Sable ignored them both and focused down the hillside. The tree trunks rose around them in columns of gentle warmth, but just out of view, a towering pillar of heat was moving directly toward them.

"One person," she whispered, pointing toward the warmth. "Coming this way."

He eased one of the knives out of his belt. "But I admit you have some very useful skills." The warmth around them grew, and Sable tensed. There were more people moving up the hill behind the first. Dimmer, and farther away, but still headed in their direction.

"And more," she whispered, backing toward the thicket. "Following the first. Five or six more."

Reese hesitated just a breath before tucking the knife back in his belt. "Let's go," he breathed. "Purn, close it up behind us."

They backed toward the thicket just as another crack sounded from below them. The first person was getting steadily closer. Sable focused down the hill, trying to feel them, but without any words, she could feel nothing.

A pulse of…something rolled up the hill, making each tree glow with warmth. It swept over them, and Reese flared with warmth next to her, Purnicious turned into a tiny blaze of heat, and in her arm, Innov fairly exploded with heat.

Sable jerked to a stop, focusing down the hill. The pulse rolled past them, making the thicket warm briefly before disappearing all together. That had been different from when Reese's words had warmed things up. That had been sharper, more focused. More...serious.

Reese put his hand on her arm and pulled her toward the thicket. "Time to go," he whispered, and the truth of his words spread out again.

The figure below them was closer, and something struck her as familiar. Sable pulled her arm away from him. He swore quietly and drew a knife from his belt. "Sable, we need to go."

Each time he spoke, it was easier for her to sense the people down the slope. She heard a shout, and the figures started running forward. Six of them closed in on the first.

The lone person whirled to face them.

"It's a woman," Sable whispered. "They're closing in on her." Sable stared into the woods as though she could see through the trunks. Someone shouted something.

"*Hulpac uznet*," the woman called out.

Reese straightened. "That's Kalesh!"

At the woman's voice, Sable realized why she'd seemed familiar. "It's Serene!"

Reese took a step forward. "Are you sure?"

Sable nodded, gripping his arm. "What did she say?"

"*Stupid decision*," Reese answered.

"Sounds like Serene," Sable said.

"*Morduv'a*," one of the Kalesh shouted.

"They're going to kill her!" Reese launched himself down the hill. "Purn! Get Terrane!"

Purnicious popped out of sight. Sable hesitated, clutching Innov to her chest. Six Kalesh soldiers, and she had nothing. No weapon. Nothing.

Another shout from Serene jolted her into motion, and she broke out into a run after Reese.

Behind her she heard Terrane shoving his way through the thicket. Sable pounded down the hill, her feet skidding and shifting on loose sticks and small rocks. Innov woke and gave an irritated squawk, shifting to get free.

"No," Sable snapped, tucking the bird tightly under her arm. "You stay."

Innov squawked again and pecked at her arm with her sharp beak, leaving a long scratch.

"Innov!" Sable hissed, funneling all her frustration into her words. "Stop it!"

The bird fixed her with a sullen glare but stilled.

Sable caught a glimpse of a clearing through the trees. Six Kalesh soldiers approached Serene, four spreading out to surround her while two held back. She stood defiant in a new robe, this one pitch black, her hands held out to the side, her fingers bent into claws.

"Don't be stupid," Serene's voice snapped through the trees. "I work for the priories. I know Ambassador Bastian."

"*Zabat*," the tallest soldier hissed.

Serene let out a low laugh. "Not up until now, but being attacked by soldiers is the sort of thing that turns someone into a *zabat*."

"Take her," the soldier in the back commanded. "She's unarmed."

Sable stumbled to a stop at a break in the trees, leaning on the nearest tree, her heart pounding. Her fingers dug into the bark as the men drew closer to Serene.

A cold smile spread across Serene's face, and she flexed her fingers.

A tall soldier sheathed his sword and lunged for her, wrapping his arms around her waist and lifting her off the ground. Serene clamped her hands around his neck and leaned close to his face. "Never assume a woman is unarmed," she hissed.

His eyes bulged, and he shifted his weight, a confused look coming over his face. The other soldiers shifted closer, looking amused at the fight Serene was putting up. But the man who held her wavered unsteadily for a breath, then crashed down onto his knees.

The other soldiers started for her just as Reese raced into the clearing.

"Serene!" He yelled. "Lean back!"

Serene shoved at the soldier's neck, straightening her arms and arching her back away from him. He blinked blearily at her, and his arms loosened.

Reese flung a knife, and it sank into the man's chest, just under Serene's arms. The soldier's eyes flew open, and he dropped Serene to grab at the knife. She fell back hard on the ground, scrambling back to her feet while the man toppled over, lifeless.

Sable slipped closer to the glade, Innov gripped in her arm. The phoenix's attention was fixed on the clearing.

"Morning, Serene," Reese said lightly, moving to the side. He held his sword low, and two of the soldiers turned to face him.

"Andreese," Serene said, facing the other men. Her breath came fast, but she stood steadily, her hands held out in front of her again, fingers curling. Strands of hair hung down around her face, loosened from her braid. "Thank you for the help, but it was unnecessary."

"I know," he said easily, "but you can't expect me to pass up a chance like this."

The Kalesh soldiers exchanged looks. One of the men hanging back had a red band of an officer across his shoulder, and he looked at Reese shrewdly. "Andreese?" He drew his own sword and stepped forward.

The soldier next to him caught sight of Sable and pointed, rattling off something in Kalesh. She distinctly heard the word "Issable."

The officer smiled. *"Prej naj pellot."*

The soldier turned and sprinted downhill.

"No," Reese said flatly. He pulled out another knife and threw it in one smooth motion. It slammed into the soldier's back, and he fell to the ground, dead. "No reporting to the captain."

The officer stepped up next to his four remaining soldiers and barked off commands in Kalesh. They shifted, one facing Serene, one turning toward Sable, and the officer and the last, tall soldier squaring off with Reese.

The one who turned to face Sable was young and short, but his narrow face was hard. He stepped closer, holding his sword low, fixing Sable with a contemptuous glare.

Innov stretched her neck out toward him and let out a vicious caw.

The officer moved to the side to flank Reese. "Put down your weapons, and we will not hurt the women."

Reese stepped backwards to keep both the officer and the other man in his view. "If you think I'm the one you have to worry about here, you're even more dense than you look."

"And the murderess in the trees?" the commander asked. "Is she a match for a Kalesh soldier?"

Reese glanced over at Sable. "You'd think not, but I recommend your man approach with caution."

"There are dozens more Kalesh in these woods," the officer said. "Close enough that you will not escape."

Reese glanced questioningly at Serene.

She nodded. "Maybe hundreds. That's why I was coming to find you."

The officer gave Reese a level look. "You are outnumbered and outmatched. We have a saying in the Empire. *Vede ak z'nic'u.* Know when you have lost."

"We're not good at losing." Terrane's voice came from the edge of the woods. He held one of the long sticks of wood from his bag between his fingers. A flame danced on the end of it.

The officer shrugged. "Then you will lose poorly." He motioned to the tall soldier beside him, and the man started to back up toward the tree line, watching Reese's knives closely.

"Terrane," Reese said. "No one leaves."

Terrane grinned and knelt down, setting his hand on the ground and touching the flaming end of the stick to the grass by his fingertips. Fire snaked out from him, slithering across the grass, wrapping around the soldiers, corralling them together. The tall man who was backing away stopped, looking warily at the flames.

"Go!" the commander barked, and the man started again, but the flames in front of him flared up, and he pulled back, his eyes drawn up to the puff of smoke rising above his head.

"No smoke!" Reese ordered.

Terrane's grin faltered. "Fire makes smoke, boss."

"No smoke!" Reese repeated.

Terrane narrowed his eyes, his smile turning to a grimace. The line of flames grew vibrantly white and sharp. Blades of grass blazed up while those next to them stayed green. Terrane gritted his teeth, and the line of fire grew brighter. The trees past them rippled in the heat, but no smoke came out of the top.

Sable backed away from the flames, even though they were far away. Unlike the smooth flow of energy from Serene, the *vitalle* moving in the fire was savage. It held its form, but only barely.

Serene's eyes widened, and she looked at the wall of fire in alarm. "What are you doing?"

"Stopping him," Terrane answered through gritted teeth.

"You're going to burn down the mountain!" Serene snapped.

The officer shouted something, and the short soldier facing Sable started toward Terrane, moving warily.

"We should hurry," Serene called to Reese, "before your fire friend lights the entire forest."

Reese lunged forward at the officer, and the ring of steel on steel filled the clearing.

"And we should try to *not* draw attention!" Serene yelled again.

Reese fell back, moving to the side, his eyes fixed on the officer and the taller soldier.

Serene stretched her fingers toward the soldier nearest her. He grabbed her wrist, raising his sword to her neck.

"No hands on my neck, *zabat*," the man said with a thick accent.

Serene lifted her chin and gave him a wicked grin. Sable felt a rush of warmth pour out of the man and into the ground. His mouth dropped open, and he blinked at Serene. The fingers on his hand turned white where he gripped Serene's wrist. He tried to pull away, but his hand was locked onto her.

Sable could almost see the *vitalle* draining out of him, filling the ground beneath him with a pool of heat. Her palms tingled at the memory of putting out the fire at Narine's, the feel of the energy of the flames draining away.

The man dropped his sword and tried to pry his hand off Serene's wrist. His fingers still didn't move. He fell to his knees, and she leaned down until her face was almost touching his. "Who needs your neck?" she whispered.

The kneeling man's *vitalle* still poured down into the ground. His face was pale, and his fingers scrabbling against his other hand were weaker. He swayed on his knees.

Around them, the white-hot fire still blazed. Terrane's hand was planted on the ground, his fire keeping the soldiers from escaping and creating a wall between himself and the one soldier trying to reach him.

In Sable's arms, Innov was blazing hot. The bird strained her neck toward the soldiers, her pupils angry slits in her orange eyes.

Despite Serene's fierce expression, her arm shook where the man gripped her.

The tall soldier ran toward her.

"Go ahead." Serene fixed him with a cold smile. "Touch me."

He paused.

"Kill her!" the officer ordered, still grappling with Andreese.

The tall soldier raised his sword high over Serene.

CHAPTER FIFTY-TWO

SABLE CLUTCHED Innov to her side and lunged at the soldier attacking Serene, slamming her free hand onto his back.

He lost his balance and twisted, his sword crashing into the ground inches from Serene.

"Stop!" Sable hissed, pouring all her fury and terror into the word. Pain erupted across her palm, but she shoved it harder against him. There was so much *vitalle* in the man, Sable was momentarily stunned. He was a towering inferno of heat and energy.

He spun toward her, but she slammed herself into him, knocking him off balance. Innov burst out of her arms like an explosion of sparks and fire and flung herself at his face. The soldier stumbled backwards, and Sable shoved him down, climbing on top of him and slamming her hands down onto his chest.

"No more," she hissed. Pain arced across her palms again, but she focused on where the man touched the ground, focused on pushing his molten *vitalle* into the ground.

The man gasped and shoved at Sable, pushing one of her hands off. But Innov hurled herself at his face again, scratching at his cheeks with her claws, and he grabbed for the bird.

"No more!" Sable growled at him, closing her eyes and blocking out everything but the flow of energy. She ignored the pain in her hands, focusing instead on how the man's feet grew dark and cold, how his hands were growing sluggish.

Beneath her, he dimmed from a body full of blazing fire to a pile of coals centered in his chest.

His hands went limp and fell to the ground, and Innov hopped back, sparks cascading off her, her feathers flaring with tongues of fire.

Sable rolled off him. Her palms screamed in pain, and she cradled them to her chest. Her breath came in rough gasps.

The soldier lay still and bone white.

Serene's attacker lay senseless on the ground as well, and the officer and the remaining soldier watched them all warily.

"You know the rest of your saying, right?" Reese asked the officer. "*Vede ak z'nic'u,* know when you have lost, *ta bujju spoju,* then fight on."

The officer glared at him.

Sable stared at the man lying next to her on the ground. He was so terribly still. Her legs began to shake, and she reached tentatively forward to touch him. She tried to think of anything true to say, anything that would let her see if there was any life in him at all. But no words came. He was too pale.

"Do we kill the rest?" Terrane asked.

Reese shook his head. "I'd rather not. But we can't have them following us." The truth in those words was enough for Sable to catch a glimpse of energy burning low in the man's chest and winding up into his head.

She drew her hand back and pulled her gaze away from the motionless man.

Serene walked up to the short soldier who had been trying to get closer to Terrane. The Kalesh man's eyes widened with terror as Serene approached, and he tried to raise his sword, but Serene didn't pause. She pushed his sword away and slapped her head onto the man's forehead. "*Dormio.*"

The soldier's eyes slid closed, and he crumpled to the ground.

Terrane lifted his hand off the grass, and the fire around them died. He gave Serene an approving look. "Not bad."

"You!" Serene stepped over the sleeping soldier and strode up to Terrane. She looked slim and small in front of his big form, but she fixed him with a glare and pointed a finger up at him. "You are a reckless danger to everyone here! What do you call that uncontrolled disaster of a fire? The one you left untethered—in the middle of a forest!"

He raised an eyebrow. "I call it hot." He smirked at Reese. "And smokeless."

"You almost killed us all!"

"But I didn't," he said. "I saved us. You're welcome."

Serene spun to Reese. "Where did you pick up this fool?"

Reese still stood facing the officer. The Kalesh man glanced around the glade, then dropped his sword.

Serene started toward the man but caught Sable's gaze and stopped. She came and knelt next to her, looking from Sable's face to her red palms. Sable tried to look at the man lying in front of her, but her gaze refused to rest on him. His face was so young, and his expression was so terrified. "Is he dying?" she whispered.

Serene set her hand on the man, and one eyebrow rose slightly. "Almost." She closed her eyes, and Sable could feel heat move out of the ground and up into the man, like a rush of air breathing life back into the coals. The man stirred, and Serene put her hand on his forehead. "*Dormio.*" At the word, the man stilled again. "He'll sleep for a long time. But I don't think he'll die." Serene glanced at Sable's face, then down at her hands. "He would have killed any of us without a thought."

Sable nodded, looking away. "I know."

"How did you get to this part of the valley?" Reese asked the officer.

The man looked stonily back but didn't answer.

Sable stood and stretched her fingers. Her palms weren't blistered, but they were an angry red, and the skin feel taut and thin. Innov flapped up from the ground, and Sable caught her, tucking her back into the crook of her arm. The phoenix still blazed with fire, but where the feathers touched Sable, a soothing warmth poured into her. She pressed her palms against the bird's sides, and the tingling warmth seeped into them.

Innov nestled down, tucking her head back against her wing.

"How many more Kalesh are coming this way?" Reese asked the officer.

The Kalesh man crossed his arms and clenched his jaw.

Sable felt the pulse move through the forest again, this time obviously originating from Serene.

"That was you!" Sable said. "That's what you call casting out?"

Serene gave her a half nod, focusing on the mountainside around them. The people near Sable blazed up warmly. The trees of the forest were vague columns of heat, and farther down the hillside, dozens of bright dots filled the trees.

"There are a lot," Serene said. "Quite a few are moving in this direction. I don't think our skirmish was very quiet."

Sable spun back up hill toward the entrance to the camp. "There are more moving along the path near the thicket."

Reese swore. "Have Purn close it! Now!"

"Purnicious!" Sable whispered. "Close the thicket!"

She heard a small pop uphill. Gwen stood a dozen paces away, half hidden behind a wide trunk, looking down at where Purnicious must have just been. She looked up and met Sable's eyes with an alarmed look. "What about us?"

"We'll take a different route to Steepdale," Reese said.

"Then let's move," Gwen said, hurrying down to the clearing and looking warily through the trees. "Because it sounds like we're being surrounded."

"In a minute." Reese motioned to the men lying on the ground. "Can you be sure the ones still alive won't wake soon?" he asked Serene.

She nodded and knelt next to the soldier who'd attacked her.

Reese turned to the officer. "What were you supposed to do if you caught Sable and me?"

The men held Reese's gaze but didn't speak.

"This is taking too long," Gwen said, irritated, stepping out of the trees. She strode over to the officer, who leaned away from her in surprise. Grabbing his arm, she peered into his face. "He followed Serene up here, suspicious she was a *zabat* and hoping she'd lead him to more. Which she did. A fact he's surprisingly smug about, given the condition of his men." Gwen cocked her head. "If he caught you and Sable, he was supposed to bring you back to the island alive. Not necessarily unharmed though. For a public trial." She frowned. "Any of your companions were assumed to be *zabat* and should be killed."

The officer stared at Gwen, his mouth dropping open.

Sable walked over to stand next to Reese. "What's a *zabat*? A rebel?"

Reese nodded. "Literally it's a fire starter."

Sable frowned. "That's what Ambassador Bastian called me the first time he saw me."

"You had just been involved in the assassination of his predecessor," Serene pointed out.

Sable nodded slowly. "He was very angry."

"So you two didn't start out as fast friends?" Reese asked dryly.

The officer tried to pull his arm away from Gwen, but Reese raised his sword point toward the man's chest. "Stay still."

"Andreese." Gwen looked up at him, her face troubled. "They have a prisoner already. Someone connected with the fire."

"Who?" Sable asked. "The person who started the fire?"

Gwen shrugged. "He doesn't know. Vivaine is holding whoever it is for the trial." She glanced at the officer, who was pulling away from her, looking appalled. "This man assumes he'll be executed along with you two."

Sable's hand curled into a fist. "I knew Vivaine knew who did it."

"When is this trial?" Reese demanded.

Gwen closed her eyes. "These men were to search for you all day but be back to the camps outside the island before sunset."

Reese swore. The sun was already high in the sky. "Anything else interesting in his head?"

Gwen paused. "He's shocked and frightened by the people in this group. Especially Serene, although he's not fond of me. He's never met people like us." She laughed. "Except you, Andreese. He thinks you're surprisingly bland, with the tiresome heroics of the common soldier."

Reese gave the man a flat look. "I was going to have Serene put you to sleep gently."

He slammed the pommel into the side of the officer's head. Gwen gave a little shriek and yanked her hand away. The man crumpled to the ground.

Serene stopped next to the officer and touched his head. "He'll be out for a while." She stood and dusted off her hands.

Reese glanced up the hill. "Terrane, you take everyone up through that narrow valley with the waterfalls." He walked to the first soldier who'd attacked Serene and knelt, pulling his knife out of the man's chest. He hesitated a breath before carefully wiping the blade off on the edge of the man's shirt. "When you reach the top of the pass," he continued, pushing himself up and heading toward the soldier who'd tried to run, "take the right trail. It'll lead you eventually down to the road Tanis has the others on. You should catch up with them tomorrow if you keep a good pace."

Sable couldn't see his face when he knelt by the other soldier, but Reese's motions were slow as he retrieved his knife from the man's back. Almost heavy.

"Where are you going?" Sable asked.

He tucked the last knife into his belt and stood. "To see who Vivaine has."

"Then I'm coming with you."

He looked at her with a tired expression. "I'll move faster and quieter without you."

"The man killed Narine," Sable said flatly. "I'm coming."

"Which way is the narrow valley?" Serene asked.

Reese pointed west.

Serene cast out again toward the west, and the forest lit up with the heat of at least a dozen search parties. She shook her head. "We won't make it that way."

Turning east, she cast out again. Far down the hill there were countless specks of heat, but nothing higher on the slope. "There are only people down low in that direction."

"That's because there are cliffs keeping them from moving higher." Reese nodded to Sable. "The cliff we were at this morning begins not far from here."

He kept his face neutral, but Sable felt a pang of something like regret at his words.

"Anyone following us," Reese continued, "would have to come this far west or find the very well-hidden ravine that cuts through the cliffs that we used last night."

Innov shifted in Sable's arms, and a shower of sparks fell.

He scowled at the bird. "We can follow the slope above the cliff. It'll bring us very close to the island. Even without our own personal fire beacon, I can't imagine a group this large will sneak past unnoticed, but they'll have no direct route to where we are."

Purnicious popped into view at Sable's hip, her shoulders sagging. "The thicket is closed."

"Good." Reese said.

"Are you all right?" Sable asked the kobold.

"It was just a lot of branches," Purn answered tiredly.

Reese glanced at the forest, then at the bodies strewn around the clearing. "Is anyone particularly close to us?" he asked Serene.

She cast out yet again. "The group that was near your thicket moved off to the west. We have a few minutes."

"Then let's make these men less obvious." Reese grabbed the officer's hands and started to drag him toward some low bushes along the tree line. "And check them for food. It will be a while before we meet up with Tanis on the route we're taking."

Sable set Innov down gently at the base of a tree, and the phoenix didn't even stir.

"Is she going to burn down the forest?" Terrane asked, eyeing the fiery ball of feathers nestled against the trunk.

"She never sets anything on fire." Sable reached down and grabbed the wrists of the man she'd attacked. It was heavy just lifting his limp arms. Her palms ached, but she gritted her teeth and pulled. It was like tugging a sack of wet sand across the ground. His head sagged toward the grass, and he caught on lumps in the ground she could barely see.

She stared at his face, which was slack. Without the scowl, he looked even younger, and a tangle of contradictory emotions rose in her.

His uniform caught on something, and she staggered to a stop, having to jerk him into motion again. Her legs burned with the effort, and her back ached before she'd even reached the bushes.

She finally heaved him next to the others. Gwen pulled a tightly wrapped bundle from a pack on one of the soldier's backs and found a short stack of flatbread. They rummaged through the others' packs and found more on everyone but the officer.

When they were done, Purn gritted her teeth and touched the branches, extending them over the soldiers. One of the men groaned, and Serene smacked her hand onto his forehead, holding it there until he stilled. When she pulled her hand back, her palm was red.

Reese and Terrane lifted the two men killed by Reese's knives and pushed them underneath their own bush. Reese's face was stony, and Terrane, for once, was quiet.

When they were done, the clearing looked a bit disheveled, with the long grasses matted down in places. Reese turned away from it and, without a word, started through the trees.

Terrane and Gwen followed.

Sable and Purnicious fell in next to Serene, bringing up the rear. "How did you find us?"

Serene stretched her hands and looked critically at her palms. "It's Innov. She's so bright I could sense her, even from the island. I saw her fly out this morning, and when she stayed nearby, I thought she might have found you. And even if she didn't, it was long past time to leave the priories. I sent word to Jae to take Merrick and get out of the city. I don't think Vivaine is going to tolerate us after all this."

"Why on earth would you think Innov had come to me?" Sable frowned down at the sleeping bird. "I never expected her to."

"I couldn't think of anyone else she'd go to, and she was so easy to sense." Serene studied Sable. "Although now I'm wondering if I could also sense you a little. How much *vitalle* have you been moving?"

"None, I don't think, until that soldier back there." Sable motioned back to the clearing. "An attacking soldier is motivational. If I hadn't seen you do it first, I don't know what I would have done."

Serene frowned at Sable's hands. "How are your palms healed so fast? They were blistered last night."

Sable glanced down at Innov. "Put your palm on her side."

Reaching out warily, Serene set her palm on Innov's feathers. With a grunt, she yanked her hand back, causing a shower of sparks to shoot out. "She's so hot!"

Sable stared down at the bird. The phoenix looked like a fiery ball of feathers, but all Sable could feel was warmth. "She doesn't feel hot to me. And touching her healed my hands."

Serene's brow creased, and she looked ahead. "Innov never burned Narine, either," she mused.

Sable nodded. "I'm sure she healed Narine just a little every time they touched." She looked down at the bird. "Narine was always stronger with Innov close, but until now I thought it was just because they loved each other."

"And now she heals you…" Serene said slowly. "I had thought that Innov came to you because you were familiar. But maybe there's more."

"If you say she thinks I'm the new prioress," Sable said, "I will jab you in your sore hands. It is just that I'm familiar. Since you taught me to sense *vitalle*, she's taken more of an interest in me, that's all." The bird was still sleeping heavily. "I think she just needed someone to carry her around until she grows a bit, and she figured I was sentimental enough to do it."

Serene gave an unconvinced hum. "Now I want access to the priories' books again. I never studied much about the phoenix. I wasn't even sure it was the same one who came to each new prioress."

"The books! You can't leave all the books!"

Serene glared in the general direction of the island. "I've saved the ones I could. There are so many more, but I'll have to find a different way to get them back."

Sable shifted Innov to pull out the small book from her pocket. "I met Flibbet in the rebel camp."

"You did?" Serene took the book with interest. "He's an odd man, isn't he?"

"Yes. And he's very angry with you for reorganizing his books."

"They were completely unorganized." Serene opened the tawny cover and brought the book close to her face. "I gave him this one. I haven't read it, though. Just saw from the map that it might be from the Empire and smuggled it out."

Reese led them at a brisk pace through the trees moving slowly uphill until off to their right they caught glimpses of the valley. The hillside they were on tumbled down past the edge of the trees until it simply ended at the top of a sheer cliff. The floor of the valley was visible hazy and far below.

Serene glanced up from the book and cast out regularly, but the search parties stayed behind them and far below the cliffs.

The sun began to sink into the west, and the path moved downhill. The cliffs grew closer together and shorter. The trees grew sparser as well, until they were walking across a grassy slope above one cliff and below another.

The cliffs below them were impassably steep, but the valley floor and the island grew clearly visible below them. The Black River wound past, clear and blue. Individual people could be seen moving around the camps along the riverbank. There was a bustle of activity near the bridge to Tutella Island.

Reese kept them back away from the edge of the cliff, staying low and trying to keep out of view of anyone from the camps who happened to look up at the rock face. Sable pulled the edge of her tunic up and wrapped it around Innov, hiding her light.

The cliffs lined the side of the valley almost all the way to the river, turning north with just enough room for the River Road to continue north along the water's edge. Sable focused on the turn in the rocks ahead, anxious to get around the corner and headed upriver instead of walking within view of the entire summit camp.

Before they could make the turn, though, Reese's eyes caught on the activity at the bridge, and he stopped. "Take the others on," he said to Terrane. "There's a shallow cave not too far up the river. Wait for me there."

JA ANDREWS

Terrane nodded and motioned for the others to follow him. Gwen stayed close to him, and Serene, with an absent nod, kept her nose in the book and followed.

Reese crouched lower and headed for the edge of the cliff. Purn, after a moment's hesitation, popped out of view, but Sable was reasonably sure she hadn't moved away. Sable moved up beside Reese.

"Go with Terrane," he said quietly to her.

"You realize you're not my boss," Sable said back to him, wrapping Innov a little tighter in her tunic.

"I feel sorry for anyone who ever is," he muttered. "It's not like you'll listen to them any more than you listen to me."

He moved forward, staying low, until he crouched behind a large boulder. Kneeling, he peered over it toward the camps.

Sable scooted up next to him, stretching her neck to see over the rock. The commotion at the bridge settled, and a platform became visible. Reese frowned at it, then scanned the rest of the camp. Most of the people were gathering near the platform.

"What's that for?" she asked.

"I would assume it's for our impending public trial," he answered.

"It's going to be a dull trial without us," Sable pointed out.

The sun sat low over the western hills, and a stream of search parties trickled down the valley, joining the others near the platform. Sable unwrapped Innov from her shirt and gently put the sleeping bird down in a crook between some rocks until she was well hidden from the valley.

Motion across the bridge caught Sable's eye, and a group of people moved into view, led by a tall woman in an unearthly bright white robe. Beside her, the glittering scales on Argyros caught the setting sun. Flickers of light sparkled on the trees and people around him.

Sable let out a growl at the sight of the two of them. Reese spared the prioress a glance, then went back to watching the crowd.

The people quieted as Vivaine crossed the bridge and climbed up onto the platform. Argyros followed, moved fluidly up the stairs, staying next to his mistress. A Mira followed them as well, her white robe glittering with silver along the edges. She stopped a respectful

398

distance behind Vivaine. Sable recognized her but didn't know her name.

The Dragon Prioress herself walked to the front of the platform with Argyros, the end of his tail lashing from side to side. The dragon was always fierce, but now he moved like a predator, his body low, his reptilian gaze fixed on the front of the crowd.

A ripple went through the crowd closest to him as people pulled back.

The Mira's hands flashed with motion, and Vivaine began to speak.

"Dear friends," she said in a somber voice, "tonight is a sorrowful gathering."

Sable flinched, and Reese tensed. Vivaine was far enough away they couldn't see her expression clearly, but her voice sounded as though she stood right in front of them.

"As you all know, our beloved Phoenix Prioress was murdered last night, the victim of a cowardly attack," Vivaine said, her voice magnified by the Mira's magic.

In addition to being able to hear the words clearly, Sable could feel that they were rich with warm truth.

"Her attackers," Vivaine said, her voice heavy with grief, "were none other than the same man who killed the Kalesh ambassador last year and the prioress's trusted handmaiden."

Angry mutters rolled through the crowd, and Sable wished they could feel how cold Vivaine's lie was.

"She knows that's not true." Sable glared at her. "I hate that woman."

Argyros lashed his tail again and leaned against Vivaine. She set her hand on his silver-scaled head.

"Issable and Andreese have escaped, for now," Vivaine continued, her voice growing angry, "but we have many people searching for them, and I assure you they will be found and brought to justice. But we do have another person who was involved."

Reese leaned forward, his gaze locked on a spot in the crowd where three Sanctus guards moved in a tight knot, pushing a man toward the platform. Through the guards, it was hard to make out anything about the man.

"Who is…?" Sable asked.

The guards dragged him up on to the stage, spreading out a bit and letting everyone see the thin man with bright red hair.

Reese swore and gripped the rock, his knuckles turning white. "That's Tylar!"

CHAPTER FIFTY-THREE

"EVEN THOUGH WE do not have Issable and Andreese, we do have one of their fellow conspirators." Vivaine motioned for Tylar to be brought to the center of the stage.

He struggled against the ropes binding his arms behind his back, but the guards pushed him forward.

"You chose your companions poorly," Vivaine said to him. "You helped them escape the island, and they repaid you by leaving you behind."

"I stayed behind by choice," Tylar said, his voice just as easy to hear as hers. "And they didn't start that fire."

Argyros shifted, turning to face the man, pushing against Vivaine enough that she swayed to the side.

"They lied to you," she said sternly, "and used you to save themselves." He started to object again, but she spoke over him, her unnaturally loud voice drowning his out. "Do you deny that you are part of a band of rebels, committed to attacking the Kalesh and derailing any attempts at peaceful negotiations with them?"

"No," Tylar said.

"Do you deny," Vivaine continued, her voice snapping with anger, "that you helped Andreese and Issable escape from the island under the cover of night?"

"I helped them leave the island—"

She interrupted, her voice taking on a terrible coldness. "You helped them even though they had just murdered our beloved Phoenix Prioress?"

Argyros dropped his head lower, his eyes fixed on Tylar like a cat stalking its prey.

Tylar drew back from the creature. "They didn't kill her."

The sun dropped behind the mountains, saturating the clouds with a vibrant orange, diffusing a soft, warm light down on the crowd. Vivaine took a step toward the man, her robe brightening until she looked like a pillar of white light.

"The two of them were in her house before the fire broke out." Vivaine's voice rolled out with a savage edge. "And then left her there like cowards!"

Tylar shook his head and opened his mouth to object, but Argyros shifted again, pressing up against Vivaine's thigh. Tylar's mouth stayed open, his eyes locked on the dragon.

Vivaine bowed her head, touching her fingertips to her forehead in prayer.

Sable leaned forward against the rock, her heart beating quickly, not only at Vivaine's obvious, unsettling fury, but at Argyros, who grew more agitated by the moment. Sable had never seen the dragon anything but coldly composed.

Vivaine raised her face back toward the crowd. "Amah tells us to always err on the side of mercy," she continued, regaining a little of her composure, "and last summer we did. Issable was forgiven for her role in Ambassador Tehl's death and accepted into the priories in the hope that Amah's light would cleanse her soul. And Andreese was pardoned at the moment of his execution, spared and given the chance to change his life for the better. To set aside his violent ways and seek after peace.

"But neither of them repented." Vivaine dropped her hand onto Argyros's head, her body rigid with fury. "Prioress Narine trusted Issable completely, drawing the young woman under her wing, sleeping in the same room as her, even letting Issable have control over the prioress's daily activities. And in return, Issable used the prioress to steal into council meetings like a snake, pushing the prioress relentlessly until poor Narine granted her even the power to vote on the priory's behalf."

Sable glared down the cliff at the woman. The mixture of truth and lies in the words swirled around Sable with icy and fiery blasts.

"And then," Vivaine continued, her voice dropping low and growing terribly cold, even has her robe brightened, "when the prioress finally realized who Issable truly was, the snake enlisted the help of her vicious, violent partner, Andreese, and together they murdered a dying old woman! Burning her alive!"

The crowd roared out in shock, and the silver dragon shifted from side to side, his head swiveling back and forth between Tylar and the roiling crowd.

"She's lying," Sable hissed. "She knows we did nothing. This is all for show."

"And you!" Vivaine spun toward Tylar, stabbing her finger toward him, her voice full of vicious, coiling heat. "You are as guilty as they are!"

Sable reeled back at the ferocious truth in her words, and Reese scrambled to his feet.

"So you will pay as they will!" Vivaine shouted. "With your life!"

She whirled back to the crowd, her robe swirling around her like frothing, rabid moonlight. "Amah has found this man guilty!"

The crowd roared to life again, and Sable shoved herself to her feet.

"Liar," she hissed, shoving the words all the way down to the prioress, sending them out as she had to reach Gwen on the bridge. "You know that's not true!"

From down below on the platform, Vivaine's head snapped up, searching the rocks where Sable and Reese stood.

"You vile, manipulative liar!" Instead of sending her furious words out as threads, Sable poured them down the cliff and across the gathered crowd to reach Vivaine where she stood on her platform. "That man is innocent, and you know it!"

Vivaine's attention snapped to the cliff, and her eyes locked on Sable.

The whole world shifted. The valley floor surged up. The cliff shrank until it was no taller than a step.

Reese swore and grabbed the rock for balance.

The crowd split and bent to the side as Vivaine twisted the light and the platform appeared to draw so close Sable could see the flecks of light on the wood, reflecting off Argyros's scales. She kept her eyes fixed on Vivaine as the world around them distorted, contracting until they seemed to stand face-to-face.

Next to Sable, Reese gripped the rock, his gaze shifting from the normal world to the deformed shaft of light that brought only the image of Vivaine and her dragon terrifyingly close. The rest of the stage, including Tylar, still appeared distant.

The Dragon Prioress glared at Sable, but there was a wariness to her posture.

Sable gave the woman a cold smile. "Your Mira isn't the only one who can cast a voice far away."

Reese straightened, coming to stand next to Sable. He set his hand on his sword hilt, as though Vivaine were actually within reach. The crowd pointed up toward the cliff, clearly seeing Reese and Sable still far away.

"Issable and Andreese," Vivaine said slowly, dropping her hand down to rest on Argyros again. "I didn't think you had the courage to show."

The truth of Vivaine's words swirled across the apparently small distance between them, just as they would if she were really standing a few paces away.

In that truth, Sable felt something else. Argyros burned with a ferocious heat. Beneath his cold, silver scales, he seethed with a blazing, feral fire.

And that heat flowed effortlessly up Vivaine's arm, filling her with her own flames.

"You are lying," Sable repeated loudly, pushing her words toward Vivaine, willing them to spread past the platform and into the crowd. "You know Reese and I didn't hurt Narine, and you know Tylar is innocent."

A ripple ran across the chaos of faces and bodies in the crowd, and Sable gave Vivaine a grim smile. "It's time the world found out how manipulative and deceitful you are. I bet you know who really started that fire. But the true story doesn't fit your purposes, does it? And so you twist the truth until it suits you."

Vivaine shook her head slowly, her face taking on a long-suffering look. "Ever the actress, aren't you, Issable?" The High Prioress stood straight on the stage, the picture of stoic conviction. "Always playing to the crowd, spinning your tales, trying to twist the hearts of the good people around you."

"Never quite as well as you." Sable pushed her words down toward the crowd again. "Let Tylar go."

Argyros let out a low growl, and even knowing the dragon was actually far away, Sable had to force herself not to pull back from his vicious, slitted eyes. Vivaine's fingers tensed on his head, and Sable felt again the rush of heat moving from the dragon to the prioress.

From the distorted faces of the crowd that Sable could still see, most of the people were looking up at the cliff.

"Come take his place," Vivaine said, "and I will release him." Her eyes flicked to Reese. "Come accept the justice you should have tasted a year ago."

Reese started to nod, but Sable set her hand on his arm.

"You know who started the fire," Sable said, "don't you?"

Vivaine met Sable's gaze. "Yes," she answered, the words true and warm. "You."

The last word was an outright lie, and Sable let out a humorless laugh. "We both know that's not true." She took in the prioress's overly white robe, exhausted by the constant falseness the woman exuded. "It is over, Vivaine. Narine is gone, and your attempts to control her, and me, are gone as well. If you ever loved Narine, let this man go and find the monster who set a dying woman on fire. But stop whatever game you're playing here."

Vivaine's eyes widened in outrage. "How dare you speak the prioress's name?" Her voice cut through the air. "How dare you mention that great soul? You are nothing but a festering rot, devouring all that is good around you."

Sable paused at the fury in her voice. This wasn't Vivaine's normal anger, this was something far deeper. More animal.

Argyros's claws flexed, gouging into the wood of the platform. The scales on his sides rippled as his breath came faster. He leaned against his mistress's leg, blazing brighter and hotter, filling her with his vicious heat.

"I have suffered your insolence for too long." Vivaine's voice seethed with anger. "I had hoped the Phoenix Prioress's gentle presence would soften your heart. But you are corrupt and deceitful, through and through." Her voice held a savage bite, and a wild, brutal look filled her eyes. "You will face justice." She flung her hand at Tylar, and the man flinched. "As will all who align themselves with you."

Vivaine kept her gaze locked on Sable, but Argyros slid behind his mistress, turning to face Tylar. He moved slowly, smoothly, not drawing attention away from his mistress.

The dragon grew hotter, until Sable could feel waves of heat pouring off him, and at Sable's feet, Innov uncurled herself.

The warped faces of the crowd looked up the mountain, muttering and frowning.

Behind Vivaine, Argyros slithered closer to Tylar. His silver jaw opened, and a shimmer of white light glittered along his flank as he drew in a breath.

"Vivaine..." Sable breathed, her eyes locked on the dragon.

The prioress's eyes widened, and she spun, thrusting her hand toward the dragon.

Innov screeched and flung herself into the air.

Argyros breathed, and with a roar like a raging wind, a stream of flames blasted out, enveloping Tylar in a wall of flame.

The guards dove away from the blaze.

For an instant, Tylar's face twisted in shock and pain, until the flames brightened to a blinding white, swirling and spiraling up into the sky.

The inferno raged for a breath, but when the dragon cut off the flames, there was nothing left but ash.

CHAPTER FIFTY-FOUR

"No!" The word tore out of Reese's throat, and he lurched forward, reaching over the rock as though he could span the distance between them and the smoldering remains of his friend.

"Vivaine!" Sable hurled the word out, her voice trembling with fury and horror.

The Dragon Prioress stood frozen, her back to Sable. Her hand still stretched toward Argyros, but her fingers trembled.

The crowd stood in shocked silence.

Innov shot up toward the blue sky, letting out a cry that echoed through the valley.

Sable's breath came in a ragged gasp. "What have you done?" she whispered to Vivaine.

Vivaine's head twitched slightly to the side, and Sable caught a glimpse of her wide, horrified eyes.

"Vivaine!" Reese thundered, the sound loud enough to reach the valley on its own. "You will pay for this!"

At his words, Vivaine's hand closed into a fist, and she turned.

Whatever horror Sable had seen in Vivaine's expression was gone, replaced by a dreadful calm. She let the silence fill the valley again for a breath. Argyros slid up beside her, and after the slightest hesitation, Vivaine set her hand on his head. She didn't even need to speak for Sable to feel the dragon's heat pour into her.

The prioress faced Sable and Reese, her chin raised, her eyes stormy. "You have brought Amah's judgment down on this man." Vivaine's voice throbbed with fury and pain.

The lie was so sharp it cut into Sable like a knife, and she flinched. "That was not from Amah," Sable said.

Vivaine's jaw tightened at the words.

High in the darkening sky, Innov let out another shriek. Her feathers erupted with fire until she blazed like a tiny sun. She dove toward Sable, tearing through the dusky sky, leaving a wide, glittering trail of sparks behind her.

The outcropping grew brighter as the phoenix plunged closer. Sable held out her arm, and Innov flung out her wings, the tips of her feathers brushing across the side of Sable's face, leaving a tingling trail. The bird landed, gripping Sable's outstretched arm with sharp talons.

The phoenix shifted, agitated, her eyes locked on the dragon.

Vivaine shook her head slowly, her shoulders rising and falling with deep, furious breaths. "The audacity of poisoning the newly reborn phoenix against the priory!" She turned to the crowd and pointed up the cliff, her finger jabbing at Sable and Reese. "You can see their guilt and their cowardice! Who will bring them back to face justice?"

The people shifted, looking between Sable and Vivaine.

"Amah requires justice," Vivaine cried, fixing Sable with a withering look. "For the death of Prioress Narine and the theft of the phoenix."

A grumble rippled through the crowd. The prioress held Sable's gaze for a moment longer, the tiniest hint of satisfaction curling up the corner of her mouth.

Then Vivaine waved her fingers, and the image of her vanished. In front of Sable was nothing but the rocky top of the cliff, the crowd visible far below. The white form of Vivaine stood tall in the center of the empty platform, her hand resting on Argyros's glittering head.

"Good people!" Vivaine's voice rolling through the valley. "We will pay gold for the capture of the murderers!"

The crowd shifted. The edges of the audience frayed, tight groups of people starting for the cliff.

"One pouch of gold for each of them." Vivaine pointed up at Sable and Reese. Her white robe lit the entire stage, turning Argyros into a shimmering creature of light. "Dead or alive."

The crowd splintered as people spread through the small alleyways of the camp toward the cliff.

Sable stepped back from the rock. Innov lit the entire outcropping like it was midday, and Sable looked around for somewhere to hide.

Andreese stared at the dark smudge on the stage where Tylar had stood, his face bleak and furious.

"Reese," she said, setting her hand on his arm. Beneath her fingers, his muscles were taut and his arm shook. "We need to move."

"I'm going to kill her," he breathed.

"Not if a feral crowd kills us first." Sable pulled him back away from the edge.

He resisted for a moment, but torches flared to life near the edge of the camp. "You need to cover your fire bird," he said without turning to look at her. "Feral things are drawn to fire."

Sable knelt behind the rock, turning to face Innov. "I need to cover you up."

The phoenix wobbled unsteadily on Sable's arm.

Shifting so that Innov was tucked more into the crook of her arm, Sable ran her finger down the orange-feathered chest. The phoenix leaned against her finger. "You were magnificent. And someday, when you're bigger, we will make Argyros pay for what he did."

Innov shoved her beak against Sable's hand.

"I don't have any food." Sable pulled up the edge of her tunic, wrapping it around the bright bird. "Go to sleep, Innov," she said softly, stroking the side of the phoenix's neck until her orange eyes started to close. "Good girl."

With a final, soft caw, Innov tucked her head down near her wing, and Sable wrapped the tunic all the way over her.

Sable looked up to see Reese standing back several steps, watching her with a guarded expression.

"Can you see her?" she asked.

His gaze dropped to the bundle of tunic, and he shook his head. Sable stood, and his eyes stayed fixed on her. "I take back what I said on the island." He searched her face. "You have changed a great deal from last year."

Distant shouts echoed up from the valley floor.

"I think I may still need a bodyguard though," she said with a small smile.

His brow creased. "I don't think you do."

"Could we have this discussion while we walk? I'm not interested in falling into Vivaine's clutches tonight. Not when I just got out of them."

He looked back at the now dark platform and closed his eyes, letting out a long, slow breath, stifling an angry growl. With effort, he turned away. "Stay close." He started in the direction the others had gone, moving along the top of the cliff as it turned north to follow the river. "The path gets precarious up ahead."

Sable fell in behind him. "That's not particularly surprising at this point."

The sky above them turned a deep, rich blue, and Sable's feet stumbled against rocks she couldn't see in the shadows of the cliff. Reese walked in front of her, silent and tense. Behind them, the valley fell out of view, and the sound of the crowd dimmed.

They hadn't gone far before Reese let out a low whistle. An answer came back from deep in the shadows, and the blocky shape of Terrane stepped onto the path ahead of them.

Without stopping, Reese moved past him and continued down the dark path. Serene and Gwen stepped out of the shadows as well, the little form of Purnicious next to their legs.

"Purn told us what happened," Serene said, her voice grim.

Gwen shook her head. "You couldn't have seen what you think you saw. Vivaine would never let Argyros do something like that!"

"The corrupt prioress who secretly wants to rule the world?" Terrane asked. "Of course she would. I'm surprised she hasn't done it sooner."

410

Gwen gave him a scathing look. "You have no idea what you're talking about, you ignorant hill creature. The Holy Mother wouldn't execute someone like that."

Sable held out her hand to Gwen, and the Mira, after a moment's hesitation, took it. Sable let the memory of Vivaine and Argyros play, letting Gwen feel all the truth and lies that Vivaine had told. Sable flinched at the memory of the burst of fire.

Gwen yanked her hand back, staring at Sable.

Sable nodded. "It's been a long time since I thought well of Vivaine, but…"

Gwen turned slowly back in the direction of the island, her expression betrayed. "I never would have thought she'd do that," she whispered.

Sable set her hand on Gwen's shoulder. *Me neither.*

Reese led them at a relentless place for hours as the trail snaked through the rocky outcroppings. The nearly full moon slipped above the eastern horizon, casting lines of slanted light and pitch-black shadows across their narrow path.

"My feet are killing me," Gwen said from behind Sable.

Sable's toe caught on a rock she couldn't see, and she stumbled forward, grabbing onto Terrane for balance. He was breathing heavily and paused.

"Is Reese going to make us walk all night?" Gwen asked.

Sable glanced behind them. Past the dark silhouettes of Serene and Purnicious, there was no sign of pursuit along the dark hills. "I doubt anyone could possibly find this trail in the dark." She glanced at Terrane. "Do you have any idea where we're headed?"

Terrane shook his head.

"Well, call up to Reese," Sable said, "Ask if we can take a break."

Terrane turned and stopped. "Um…"

"What's um?" Gwen leaned around Sable's shoulder.

"Reese is gone," Terrane said.

411

He leaned to the side, and the moonlight showed the path winding through the rocks ahead of them with no sign of Andreese.

"Where'd he go?" Sable asked.

"I have no idea," Terrane said, holding up his hands. "I'm just the cook. I don't usually hike around these hills like the rest of the rangers."

"Do you think he knows we're not rangers?" Gwen grumbled.

"If my rangers made half the noise you're making," Reese's voice came from a deep shadow just past Terrane, "we'd have never accomplished anything." He stepped out from behind a tall rock. "This way."

He disappeared into the shadow again and reappeared past it up the hill. They followed him to the mouth of a small cave.

"We'll rest here for a few hours," he said as everyone filed in.

Gwen went as far in as she could and dropped to the hard, cold stone with a sigh of relief, and Terrane sat heavily across from her. The space was barely wide enough for them to stretch out their legs.

"I hate sleeping in the wild," Terrane grumbled, shifting his back against the hard rock. "There's never a cot. Or a blanket."

"Or a pillow," Gwen added.

"At least we have food." Terrane pulled out one of the packets of flatbread from his bag. "Bland food, but at least it's food."

Sable moved to the side, pulling her tunic off Innov enough to let out a little light. The phoenix was still nestled into a ball, sleeping heavily. She glowed like a bed of coals, casting a deep, red light though the cave. There was a nook at the bottom of the wall, and Sable unwrapped the small bird and squatted down to tuck her into it. Even sleeping, the bird shone with a surprising amount of light into the cave, and Sable lay in front of Innov, blocking most of it, in case it could be seen from the outside.

The ground was hard against Sable's shoulder and hip, but her body sank down against it anyway. Innov's warmth radiated against Sable's back, and she scooted closer to the bird until she touched the phoenix. Terrane leaned over and handed Sable a piece of flatbread that was so dry it crumbled in her fingers. She took a bite and closed her eyes, and the cave began to spin around her.

A little hand touched her shoulder, and Sable felt the fabric of her tunic thicken ever so slightly under her shoulder.

"Thank you, Purn."

"There's not much I can do with it," the kobold apologized. "I need something fluffier, like wool."

"It's perfect." Sable patted Purn's hand. The kobold's fingers were cold, and Sable turned to look at her. "Are you cold?"

Purn gave her a weary smile. "Just tired. There was a lot of bell-ishing today."

"Come lie next to Innov." Sable scooted forward. "She'll warm you up, and she might even give you a little strength."

Purnicious peered over Sable's back at the phoenix, her purple eyes wide with wonder. "Of course she will," she whispered almost reverently. "She's a phoenix."

"If you have any advice on how to care for her, I'd love to hear it. I've never taken care of a baby anything, never mind a baby bird that's always on fire."

Purn nodded eagerly and moved slowly around Sable. With a bit of shifting, she settled down next to the phoenix, and Sable glanced over her shoulder. Innov's red glow turned Purnicious's skin to a deep magenta.

"If you touch her," Sable whispered, "is she hot?"

Purn reached out a single knobby finger and brushed it gently over Innov's feathers. "Not hot, just...full."

"That's a good word for her." Sable turned forward again with the two little bodies tucked up behind her. "Good night, Purn. Thank you for all your help today."

"Good night, mistress. I'm sorry about Narine, but I am glad you're away from the priories."

Sable closed her eyes, letting the cave spin again, not even caring that the ground was still hard. "So am I."

Footsteps scuffed toward the opening. "I'll keep watch," Reese said.

Sable cracked an eye open, astonished that he was still standing.

Serene stepped up next to him. "How long has it been since you slept?"

He crossed his arms. "A while."

She pointed to the cave floor. "Get some sleep. You have to lead us to safety tomorrow. It would be nice if you had your wits about you."

"I can't sleep." Moonlight lit the side of his face. "Not after what happened."

Serene set her hand on Reese's shoulder. "I can tell if anyone's coming," she said. "At least lie down and rest."

He rubbed his hands over his face. "Fine." He sank down against the wall near the door, leaning his head back and closing his eyes, the muscles in his jaw tight.

Serene watched him for a few moments. "Do you want help sleeping?"

He cracked an eye open. "I don't want to be knocked unconscious. Thanks anyway."

She gave him a flat look. "I can help you fall asleep. Just normal sleep."

"No. We need to be up and moving before dawn. We need to be off the cliff and into the trees before its bright enough for everyone to see us."

"I'll wake you up," she said.

He gave her a long look.

When she spoke again, it was so quiet Sable almost couldn't hear her. "It'll stop the memory of Tylar from repeating in your head. At least for a while."

Reese looked hard at Serene, then nodded. She reached forward and brushed her fingers across his shoulder. She whispered something, and his shoulders relaxed. He blinked at her slowly before his eyes slid shut and his breathing deepened. His jaw loosened, and his head lolled to the side.

Serene watched him, her expression sympathetic. Then she turned and sat near the opening. Sable felt her cast out, sending a pulse down the mountainside. There was no warmth, aside from the thin carpet of grass, and Sable let her own eyes slide closed again. The image of Tylar and Vivaine sprang to her mind, but she leaned back against Innov and Purn, focusing on the warmth from the phoenix and the comforting feel of the kobold until everything else faded away.

CHAPTER FIFTY-FIVE

THE CAVE WAS STILL DARK when Serene set her hand on Sable, trickling a little warmth into her shoulder. Sable took a deep breath, the sleep slipping away, replaced by a bit of unexpected energy. She shifted, and her stiff back ached in protest. With a groan, she rolled over.

"I agree," Serene said. "But Reese is making us move again. Something about search parties and life or death."

Innov stirred, and the tiny fingers of flame that licked along the edge of her feathers cast a reddish glow across the cave. Purnicious sat up and yawned.

Serene moved on to where Gwen lay. When she set her hand on the Mira's shoulder, the woman twitched and her eyes flew open. She blinked up at Serene, but the woman was already moving on to Terrane.

Reese stood at the entrance, shifting his attention between the sky outside and the slowly rising group. His face was drawn, and when he met Sable's gaze, she saw the same cold edge from the early days, when he'd just survived Ebenmoor's destruction. "We need to move," he said in a quiet, emotionless voice before looking back outside.

"Where are we going?" Gwen asked.

"We need a plan," Serene agreed, her voice tired and short. "I don't want to wander these cliffs forever."

"We need to get off this mountain and into the forest before the sun comes up," Reese said. "We can stop and make more plans when we're safe in the trees."

"Well," Serene said, irritated. "What are we waiting for?"

Reese raised an eyebrow at her tone.

"She's worried about her husband." Gwen pushed herself up from the floor.

Serene spun to glare at the Mira.

Gwen shrugged. "You are. You think he may end up trapped down in the city with Vivaine if he doesn't get your letter in time, and since you left with Issable, Jae may be in a lot of danger."

Serene took a step toward the Mira, her face furious. "Do *not* read my mind."

Gwen held up her hands. "You touched me this morning to wake me up. It's not my fault you were thinking so loudly."

"It won't happen again," Serene said flatly.

"That is fine with me," Gwen said. "Your thoughts are depressing."

Serene stalked out of the cave.

Sable picked up Innov to tuck the bird back into her tunic. The phoenix woke and nipped at Sable's hand.

"Knock it off." Sable pulled the shirt tighter around the bird. "You're too bright to carry into the night. If you could turn yourself off, we wouldn't have to do this."

The phoenix let out an annoyed trill, trying to spread her wings, but Sable kept her tucked close.

"Once the sun rises and we're in the trees, you can let her out," Reese said.

The phoenix shifted and squawked, and Sable began to feel some heat radiating into her stomach. "Don't you dare singe this shirt," she snapped at the bird. "If you're visible, Vivaine will find us. And Argyros will kill me, just like he killed Tylar."

Innov twitched but relaxed slightly.

"Ready?" Reese asked. "Because that's a fate I would like to avoid."

Sable nodded and headed out of the cave after Serene.

The thin trail stayed along the top of the cliff until the entire mountainside turned away from the river. The lowest curve of the moon brushed a ridge to the west, but the stars were already fading in the east, and Sable looked down on a wide flatland filled with dark smudges of forest that stretched endlessly north. The Black River snaked its way north as well, through hills and patches of cleared farmland.

The world was still robed in dark blues when their path turned steeply downhill, and they passed into the shadows of the trees as the moon finally slipped behind the hills. Reese stopped them next to a stream before they'd gone far.

Purnicious hollowed a little bowl out of a piece of wood, and the group took turns drinking.

Sable sat down against a tree and unwrapped Innov. The phoenix lay curled so tightly into a ball that Sable could have cupped her in both hands. A low level of worry simmered in Sable at the sight. There was something off about the bird. She seemed to be weakening.

Serene sat next to her, leaning against the trunk wearily.

"Did you sleep at all?" Sable asked.

A gnarled tree root twisted out of the ground between them, and Serene set her hand on it. "I don't know that I could have slept much anyway with Jae still in the Sanctuary." In the warmth of her words, Sable could feel a trail of heat moving up from the root into Serene's hand. "If he doesn't get my message and get out of the city before Vivaine gets back…"

"He's smart," Sable said. "I'm sure he'll move quickly once he gets your message."

"Except Merrick can't move quickly," Serene said.

Terrane came over with more of the soldier's flatbread. "This is the end of the bland soldier rations. Make sure you savor it."

The bread was even drier than it had been the night before, and the hollowness in Sable's stomach was the only reason she swallowed it.

"So," Gwen said, leaning against another tree, "what is our plan?"

"Tanis went to Steepdale," Reese said. "That's the only place I know of where we have allies, so it's where I'm headed. From there, you all are welcome to head wherever you want. Actually, you're welcome to do that right now, but if I were you, I'd avoid going south for a bit."

"You don't really want to go to the rebels," Gwen said to Sable. "Do you?"

Sable ran her fingers along Innov's back. "Actually, I do."

Reese looked at her with an unreadable expression. "Even with Rabbit there?"

Sable met his gaze. "Kiva has a ridiculous amount of information about what's happening in the world," she admitted. "Having access to that is smart."

Reese studied her but didn't say more.

Purnicious popped into view so close to Reese that he flinched. "That is a bad idea, mistress."

"Where do you go all the time?" Reese asked, scowling at the kobold. "Do you just lurk around us invisible, eavesdropping?"

"Hardly. Why would I walk all day with you when I can blink ahead of you, then relax in a patch of sunlight until you reach me?" Purn turned back to Sable. "We don't need to stay with the wastrel."

"I know, Purn," Sable answered. "But it's foolish to write off the rebels when I barely know them."

"Rangers," Reese said. "Only the priories and the Kalesh call us rebels. Tanis calls us rangers."

"Lord Loren calls you rebels," Sable said. "Leonis told me as much in a letter."

"Fine, the world calls us rebels. But we're not. We're against the Kalesh taking over. We couldn't be rebels unless they'd already taken over and we were trying to overthrow them."

"That is a good point," Serene said. "Calling them rebels actually gives the Kalesh more significance than they have."

"What are we going to do in Steepdale with the rebel rangers?" Gwen asked.

"We need to find a way to unite the north," Sable answered.

Terrane let out a short laugh. "Good luck with that. The lords can barely be civil to each other. They're not going to unite."

"They were unified when they discovered the Kalesh were mining on their land without permission," Sable pointed out.

"Maybe," Reese said, "but none of the Northern Lords will give up their position and bow to another. They've spent too many generations fighting each other."

"Then the Kalesh will destroy us all." Sable laid her head back against the tree. "The north needs to unite, then convince Vivaine to join with them too."

Gwen snorted, "What about Vivaine makes you think she'll deign to become a part of some grand conglomeration of leaders?"

"She might if she gets to lead it," Serene said with a wry smile.

Reese laughed. "The day the Northern Lords submit themselves to a southern woman is the day I'll let Purn dress me."

Purnicious perked up. "I've never wanted Vivaine to gain control of the world more!"

"Your priorities are all out of whack, Purnicious." He looked ahead of them, down the thin path that wove away under the thick canopy of leaves. "We'll follow this trail for a few hours, and we'll reach the River Road. I doubt we'll run into many people in the woods. There are a few trails that head off to smaller villages, but most of what's west of here is uninhabited forest."

"Elven forest," Purnicious agreed.

Reese frowned. "The woodfolk say there are elves, but most people think that's just old wives' tales."

"Oh, there are elves." Purnicious peered into the woods. "Or there were once. Far from here though. Over near the roots of the mountains."

"We aren't heading toward the mountains." Reese turned to Serene. "Once we reach the river, there may be more traffic, and I'm not sure what the general public around here thinks of Sable and me. So if you could keep track of when people are near us, that would be handy."

Sable felt a pulse roll past her, and the group around her flared into bundles of heat huddled together beneath the taller tree trunks that stood like towers of old coals. Above their heads, the limbs glowed with muted heat, and each leaf shifted for just a breath into smoldering embers.

"There's no one near us now," Serene said.

Reese leaned back on the tree. "We'll rest a few more minutes, then."

Sable grabbed Serene's arm as the leaves shifted back to snips of green rustling gently against each other in the breeze. "I felt the leaves! Yesterday, when you cast out, I only felt the people and a little bit of the trunks."

Serene raised an eyebrow. "You're progressing fast."

The early morning sunlight slanted through the forest, sifting through the tree trunks. It fell on bits of fern, brightening their fronds to a dazzling green against the shadows. A patch of golden light lit a tree near Sable, catching in the beads of sap that bubbled up from a scar in the bark.

"It feels odd," Sable said. "As though I've always known it was there, just didn't quite feel it."

Serene nodded and pulled her hand off the tree root. She looked a bit more awake. "Trees have a tremendous amount of *vitalle* in them. You can syphon off enough to give yourself or someone else energy, and if it's a full-grown tree, it won't even notice. The *vitalle* will burn your hands long before you'll deplete the tree to a level that will damage it."

Sable peered through the trunks that stretched endlessly into the distance. "They don't seem that…full."

"Their *vitalle* moves in tiny pinpricks that start in the leaves when the sunlight hits them." Serene cast out again, the wave directed up above them, and the leaves of the thick tree they leaned against glowed as though someone had blown across a bed of coals. "The sun isn't on them yet, so you can't tell, but each one will collect specks of light and move it ever so slowly into the tree. It'll spread along tiny paths, filling nearly every bit of the tree." The leaves above them settled back to green as her wave rolled past and disappeared. "It's not bright the way a moving creature is bright, but it's tremendously powerful."

"It's nothing compared to fire," Terrane said.

Sable pulled her gaze out of the treetops to see Terrane, Reese, and Gwen all watching them.

"Fire has a use," Serene said, frowning at the man, "but it's short-lived and difficult to keep steady."

"Who wants steady?" Terrane picked up a twig and touched the end. A flame burst into life.

"Your fire in the woods yesterday was barely controlled," Serene said. "We're lucky you didn't light one of the dead trees near the edge of the clearing. With the heat you'd created, you could have set the whole hillside ablaze."

"The boss is the one who insisted on no smoke," Terrane said, "and to have no smoke, you need to burn it hot. It wouldn't have reached the trees. I had it on a shorter leash than that."

Serene gave him a disapproving look. "Any leash you had was thin and precarious."

Terrane shrugged. "It worked. Fire isn't like a tree, where you pull out a tiny bit of power to do a tiny job. Fire is strong and wild. The trick is to give it some freedom, to let it consume the way it wants to. And then rein it in at the edges."

"I hope I'm not around the day you realize how easily fire burns up reins," Serene said.

Reese stood. "You two can bicker about fire magic while we walk."

"You have a better way to control fire than a leash?" Terrane asked skeptically as he stood also.

"You keep it small," Serene said. "The value of a fire is its ability to create massive amounts of *vitalle* from a small amount of fuel. The fire isn't the weapon—you use its power to do other things."

The two of them followed Reese and Gwen, their disagreement continuing until Sable grew tired of listening to it and turned her attention to the forest around them.

The day was mild, and the dew-wet earth muffled their steps, releasing the rich, old scents of leaves slowly disintegrating into the earth. The horror of the execution felt like it belonged in a different world, and Sable walked along the soft trail, letting the quiet of the forest seep into her as they wound north.

Every few minutes, a pulse from Serene washed over her, momentarily blazing her companions and the trees into pillars of heat, making Innov flare up like a flame, and showing that no one else was nearby.

As they moved farther from the cliffs, the land flattened and a few other trails joined them from other corners of the forest.

When they intersected a road wide enough for a small wagon, Reese paused. "This should lead us down to the River Road." He turned to Serene. "I doubt this one will be too busy. How far can you sense?"

"Along the open path, I should be able to feel reasonably far." She faced downhill and cast out.

Instead of pulsing out a circle around them, Sable felt only the trees down the road grow warm. The wave went farther than Sable expected, and at the very edge of it, much farther down the meandering path than was visible, something hot flared up.

"There's a small group ahead of us," Serene said.

"How many?" Reese asked.

"Two or three."

"Moving this way?"

Serene shook her head. "They're too far away to tell."

Reese started down the rough, wagon-rutted road. "Let me know if they get closer."

They walked for a few minutes before Serene cast out again. This time the heat was closer.

"There are three," Serene said. "Coming this way."

Reese paused, considering her words.

"There are five of us," Terrane pointed out, "plus a kobold. Those are probably just local woodsmen."

Reese looked them over. "If Sable hides Innov, I suppose we're not terribly identifiable."

Purnicious popped into view, a long swath of dark purple fabric in her hand. She held it out to Sable. "To carry Innov."

The fabric was shaped into a sling and made from the same purple as the cloak Purnicious wore—the cloak which was markedly shorter than it had been. Sable pulled it over her head, and the fabric formed a pouch at her stomach. She tucked Innov in.

Purnicious leaned forward and dragged her finger along the edge of the sling, tightening several spots until it held the phoenix snugly. "I thought the purple was dark enough to hide her light well."

Sable shifted the fabric until Innov was covered. "It's perfect, Purn!"

They started down the road again, and Sable fell in next to Serene, who cast out several more times. Finally, Sable could distinguish them enough to sense that two were tall and one was short. "A family?" she asked Serene.

But Serene's brow had contracted, and she frowned down the road. "Not a family…"

Reese stopped while Serene cast out again.

Sable felt the three distinct people not terribly far around the next curve. The two taller ones were brighter than she'd expect from this distance, and the shorter one was too thick to be a child. Something about them struck Sable as familiar.

One of the taller forms flared suddenly into a hot blaze, and a thin, weak pulse rolled back up the road at them.

Sable straightened. "What was—"

Serene let out a squeal so exuberant that Sable spun to stare at her. The woman took off running down the road, her black robe billowing out behind her.

Recognition of the three shapes clicked into place in Sable's mind. "Oh!" She started jogging after Serene. Behind her, Reese swore and followed. When they reached the bend, he pulled ahead of her, a knife in his hand.

"You don't need that," Sable said with a grin. "There's only one person Serene gets that excited about."

They cleared the turn to see Serene run full speed into the arms of Jae, nearly knocking him over. Behind him, Leonis beamed at the two of them, while Thulan scowled.

"Sneaks!" Leonis called, stepping around Jae and Serene. "We've been looking for you!"

"How'd you—" Reese started.

"Talk later!" Thulan strode up the road toward them. "Serene, stop strangling Jae. We've got to move." She pointed at Reese and Sable. "You two do not want to keep going toward the river."

CHAPTER FIFTY-SIX

THULAN AND LEONIS strode up to Reese and Sable.

Leonis was dressed in light-colored traveling clothes, a pack and his bow slung across his back. Thulan looked the same as always, dressed in rough wool and leather. Her hammer was tucked into her belt, and leather bracers were tied up her forearms.

"You two look like you're ready for a fight," Sable said.

"There's a decent number of bounty hunters back along the River Road looking for you two," Leonis said cheerfully. "Most of them seem a bit dense, but they're highly motivated. Some are certainly headed this way. It took longer to find you than we expected, so we don't really want to dally."

"Unless you fancy fighting off farmers and honest folk who are blinded by the ridiculous reward Vivaine has put on your heads," Thulan agreed.

"How did you find us?" Reese asked.

"Jae has some uncanny ability to track Serene," Leonis answered. "Something about feeling her cast out even if she's really far away."

Serene's face was still buried in her husband's neck, and Jae smiled at them over Serene's shoulder, giving them a small wave.

"We've decided it's creepy." Thulan frowned back at the two of them. "Serene! Enough! When did you become so sappy?"

Sable glanced at the others, who were all watching with raised eyebrows.

Serene pulled away from Jae. "I was afraid...Vivaine was so angry, I was worried you wouldn't get out of the city fast enough." She paused. "How *did* you get here so fast?"

"I left the city days ago." Jae paused. "Merrick died."

Serene closed her eyes, and her shoulders dropped.

"Have this depressing conversation while we walk." Thulan glanced around the woods. "Serene, your husband is useless at your trick, but can you tell if anyone is following us?"

Serene opened her eyes and faced down the road. She cast out again in a long, thin wedge that encompassed the general direction the road headed in the trees. At the edge of her wave, Sable felt a clump of warm shapes.

"Yes," Serene answered in a low voice. "At least a dozen."

"If the general state of the River Road is any indication, there will be a lot more than that soon," Thulan said. "They're searching up every one of these little roads they can find. Where did you all come from?"

"A tiny path not too far back, but I have a general idea where this road heads," Reese answered.

"Then let's put some distance between us and your hunters," the dwarf said.

"Who are these people?" Terrane asked Gwen from where they stood near the bend in the road.

Reese made quick introductions. "I know of another path north that doesn't go close to the river." He looked back up the road. "I guess we'll see if this connects to it."

Purnicious popped into view by Sable's side. "We don't want to go deep in these woods," she whispered.

"Why not?" Sable asked.

The little, blue kobold looked warily down the path. "These woods are wild."

"Most forests are wild." Reese started back up the road away from the river.

Purn shook her head. "Not like this." She turned to Leonis. "You know they're wild."

The half-elf looked ahead of them down the road. "We can turn north long before we reach that part, Purn."

"I hate traveling with you people," Gwen said. "You never go anywhere comfortable or safe."

"You're free to leave at any time," Reese called out over his shoulder.

She ignored him. "What's ahead of us in the forest?"

"Elves," Leonis said.

"And monsters," Purn added.

Gwen's face paled. "What kind of monsters?"

Purnicious grabbed Sable's hand. "Can't you feel it? There are monsters."

"You're feeling the elves," Leonis said. "The elves of the Green-wood are old. Older than my people. And their trees are so old they're brimming with power and almost sentient. But the trees can't hurt us, and the elves won't bother us as long as we don't do anything to make them mad."

"Like what?" Gwen asked.

"Like chop down trees or light a fire."

"We'll turn north long before we reach the Greenwood." Reese continued up the road.

Purn gave Sable a worried look. "I'll scout ahead." With a pop, she disappeared.

No one, aside from Gwen, looked particularly bothered by Purn's worries, and Sable fell back to walk with Thulan, Leonis, Serene, and Jae.

"Merrick went in his sleep," Jae told Serene, "two nights after you left to come north. Without him there, the priory felt so empty, and I realized that it had been months since we'd accomplished anything worthwhile there. I decided that I'd come find you and see if I could convince you not to go back."

Serene smiled at him. "Let's never, ever go back."

"I did grab a few more books on the way out."

"That's why I love you." Serene hooked her arm in his.

He looked at her quizzically. "Are you all right?"

"Now that you're here, I am," she answered.

Jae gave her a bemused smile. "Well, you'll love me even more when you find out I have three books with me right now, just in case I ran into you. Three versions of the same event, actually. The assassination of Lord Dorring."

Serene's eyes lit up, and she peered over his shoulder at his pack. "I do love you more!"

"I ran into Atticus when I reached the island," Jae continued, "and discovered Vivaine was getting ready to make some sort of announcement." His face darkened. "I didn't expect an execution."

"Where is Atticus?" Sable asked.

"He took the wagons north," Leonis said. "Some of the lords are gathering near Steepdale. We figured you might not know how much momentum the search had gained, so we thought we'd head you off if you got too close to the river. Jae could feel Serene doing her magic searchy wave thing this morning, so he had a sense of where you were."

"What was happening at the summit when you left?" Sable asked.

"It was falling apart," Thulan said. "Northern Lords storming off north raging at Vivaine for executing a northerner, Eugessa running away screaming that someone was murdering prioresses, the Kalesh pouting because no one had handed them the land yet."

"It wasn't quite that blatant," Leonis said, "but it was close. Things were not particularly peaceful at the peace summit last night. The different camps were in an upheaval of packing and arguing. Atticus decided that being known associates of you and Reese might not be a positive thing, and we'd best be moving along quickly. We started north well before dawn today."

"If Atticus is driving one wagon," Sable said, "who's driving the other?"

"Some lucky farmer he's overpaying to get the wagons up to Steepdale."

"The north is furious with the south," Leonis said. "If we can get far enough north in the woods, we should escape all the southerners who are hunting you two. They won't come too far into the north."

"Thulan," Sable said thoughtfully, "were there any other dwarves around the summit?"

Thulan raised an eyebrow. "Not that I saw. Why?"

"Because a friend of mine saw the person who set Narine's house on fire, and thinks it was a dwarf."

Leonis edged away from Thulan. "I always knew you'd snap someday..."

Thulan rolled her eyes. "I was helping you take all that money from those terrible card players that night from sundown to when we saw the smoke from the island," she said. "Besides, if I'd gotten onto that island, the only place I would have burned down was Prioress Eugessa's house so I could spring Ryah free and bring her back to the world of decent humans."

"Let's backtrack and do that right now," Sable said.

Thulan grinned. "How sure was your friend that it was a dwarf?"

"Someone short and stocky with a beard." Sable shrugged. "Might not really have been a dwarf."

"If there was one near the summit, I didn't see them."

They wound deeper and deeper into the woods, moving more westward than north. Reese considered a few smaller paths that led north, but they were ill-used enough that they were unlikely to lead anywhere useful. Serene cast out regularly, and the people she could sense fell farther behind. They occasionally passed villages and home-steads, but the farther they went, the fewer people they encountered.

Sable's feet ached, but Leonis and Thulan provided distractions with their constant stream of tales about the past year and the horrible actresses they'd worked with. Jae chimed in with a story he'd heard about a haunted fishpond, and Serene had gathered herself enough to mock his dramatic pauses.

The familiar voices filled the woods around them with a lightness that Sable hadn't felt in ages. The sun dropped lower in the west, and the forest took on a vivid green. The slanting rays worked their way through the branches and lit the forest floor with patches of brightness, dappled with wildflowers. The trees themselves were taller here, older and wilder.

The deeper they went, the quieter Leonis grew, and Sable caught him looking uncomfortably up into the treetops.

"You can feel it, can't you?" Purnicious said, popping into view between him and Sable.

Leonis nodded.

"Feel what?" Sable asked.

"Elves." Leonis studied one particular spot in the canopy, then shook his head. "I can't see any, but they're here."

Ahead of them, Reese stopped. "Is that going to be a problem? Because I haven't seen any other roads we can take, and at this point, backtracking sounds...irritating."

"They don't seem angry," Purnicious said. "It just feels like the trees are watching."

"They probably are," Leonis said. "But no, it doesn't feel hostile. You'd know if they didn't want us here." He glanced around. "It would be unwise to build a fire, though."

Gwen sighed. "So no hot meal, then."

"We don't need a fire for heat," Terrane said with a grin.

The shadows in the forest were growing longer before the road turned sharply north at the edge of a clearing. The wide, grassy glade was surrounded on three sides by a steep rock wall.

"We'll stop here," Reese said. "No one seems to be following us, but at least this is more defensible than anywhere else we've passed."

"Unless more people come than we can fight off," Thulan said, "and we're trapped against the rocks."

"If someone's following us with a bigger force than this group can handle, it won't matter if we're by a cliff or not," Reese pointed out.

The clearing was long enough that the tips of the Scale Mountains could be seen over the rocks. Reese frowned at them. "We came farther west than I wanted to. It's going to take all day tomorrow to get back to Steepdale, if this road takes us there. If we have to find our way through the forest on our own, it's going to take longer."

Sable crossed the wide clearing and sat down with her back to the cliff, stretching out her aching feet. The forest around had definitely begun to take on an odd, watchful feel, but not in an alarming way. It felt old and steady. The trees along the edge of the clearing were tall pines and thick-trunked, leafy trees. Strands of wispy, pale green moss hung from all the branches.

Leonis wandered over to a particularly huge oak growing where the forest met the rocks. The gnarled trunk, which was three times broader than the half-elf, rose so close to the cliff that every branch bent away from it.

Leonis set his hand on the tree and looked up into the branches. "This is old. Older than the others."

"Are there elves nearby?" Sable asked him.

He held his hand on the tree for a moment longer, then pulled it off with a sigh. "Impossible for me to tell. The trees never talk to me. The elves certainly know we're here, but if they bother to come close, we won't know it."

"So..." Gwen looked around at the others. "Didn't someone say something about a hot meal?"

Reese walked over to a line of low bushes along the edge of the trees. He carefully reached between the dark green leaves and pulled out a bundle of small berries. He tossed it to Gwen. "Tonight, the forest is your kitchen. There's plenty of food within a hundred paces."

The Mira peered down at the tiny, red berries. "I may be hungrier than this."

Reese waved at the bushes. "Then find more. Those are snowberries, and the red ones are ripe. The whiter ones taste terrible. And be careful of the thorns."

"In addition to the delicious berries," Terrane said to Reese, "if you hunt us up something yummy, I'll make it hot."

Thulan grunted in agreement. "Knowing we'd find you and your hunting skills was one of the draws to coming out here."

"Because our lives being in danger wasn't enough?" he asked.

"That played a role," the dwarf said.

Reese sighed and pushed himself away from the tree. "Gather some berries, and I'll see what I can find. And don't start any fires, Terrane." With that, he headed into the forest.

"He really is incredibly bossy," Gwen said, popping a berry into her mouth.

"You don't know the half of it." Terrane pushed himself off the stump and went to the bushes. "Tanis put him in charge of weapons training not long after he showed up. What had been nice, leisurely archery sessions turned into day-long, grueling drills on not only archery, but also sword fighting and knife throwing. And no one ever graduates because he's impossible to please."

"I believe it." Sable moved over to the bushes near him. Little clumps of red berries were nestled between the leaves and short but sharp-looking thorns.

"Although," Terrane said more seriously, "I'll admit the boss does know how to throw a knife. Never seen anyone as accurate as him."

"That, we did know," Gwen said somberly.

Terrane stopped and glanced around the group, as though suddenly remembering whom he was talking to. "You were all there," he said slowly, "when he killed the ambassador. Did he really kill him from twenty paces? Straight through the heart?"

Sable blinked away the image of the ambassador toppling back, the knife sunk deep in his chest.

"At least twenty paces," Gwen answered.

The big man let out a low whistle. "And, Sable, you really accused the Kalesh of attacking the Eastern Reaches? Right there on stage in front of everyone?" He grinned at her. "You're a bit of a legend around here."

Sable opened her mouth to explain that the whole troupe had been involved in that, but Terrane continued, "Partly for the guts it took to stand up to the Kalesh, but more for managing to make the boss sweet on you."

Sable's mouth stayed open, but anything she had to say evaporated from her mind.

"And Terrane," Reese said, striding out from beneath the huge oak, "is known for exaggerating and flapping his mouth about things he doesn't understand." He tossed three fat rabbits to Terrane. "When his only job is to cook."

Terrane left the grin on his face. "Didn't expect you back quite so quick, boss. Thought the bunnies might be farther away."

Reese gave him a flat look.

"But the forest is our kitchen," Terrane added quickly. "Three delicious rabbits coming up." He pulled out a knife and began skinning the hares.

Gwen, after a disgusted look, stood and walked away from him.

"You won't be disgusted once you smell them cooking," he called after her.

Terrane pulled off the skin with a yank and moved over to a wide, flat rock, partially buried in the middle of the clearing. He brushed off dirt and pine needles, then set his hand on it. Sable felt a rush of *vitalle* pour out of him and into the stone. It was a noisy sort of rush. More chaotic than anything Serene ever did.

Serene narrowed her eyes at him. "Your path is undefined. You're going to catch the grass on fire."

Terrane shrugged. "It's grass. If it lights, you stamp it out."

Serene gave an irritated huff. "Who taught you? You're wasting so much energy. Just focus the path. You don't have to cover the whole rock—the heat will spread."

Terrane shot her a scowl. "No one taught me. I've been cooking on rocks every day for a twelvemonth. I know what I'm doing."

"The grass is on fire over here," Gwen said, pointing to the side of the rock away from Terrane.

"Well, stamp it out," he snapped, dropping the rabbits onto the stone with a sizzle. "Anyone else who criticizes my cooking gets no food. And if you want those berries to taste better, set them on the edge of the rock. They're delicious warm."

Gwen took a handful of berries and dropped them onto the rock. "The rabbit does smell good," she admitted.

"Of course it smells good," Terrane muttered. "Unless you all want to be hungry later, you should pick more berries."

"I saw a path up the rock," Reese said. "I'm going to see if I can figure out where we are. Don't eat all the rabbit." He walked toward the oak tree, his shoulders tense.

He'd looked like that since the execution yesterday, Sable realized. She felt a little pang of guilt that the afternoon had pushed thoughts of Tylar from her mind. After a moment's hesitation, she dropped the rest of her berries into her pocket and followed him.

She stepped over a massive root of the old oak, and a twig cracked loudly under her foot. Reese glanced over his shoulder and paused. When she reached him, he was looking up the cliff face. She opened her mouth, but everything that came to her mind to say was too trite.

"Someday," he said quietly. "I'm going to find Vivaine, and I'm going to kill her."

CHAPTER FIFTY-SEVEN

THE TRUTH in Reese's words swirled warmly around him. His eyes held a challenge, as though daring Sable to object.

"I won't stop you," she said, "but her dragon might have something to say about it."

"Good. Because I'm going to kill it, too."

"Someone should." Sable sighed. "I should have stayed and faced her. Then she wouldn't have searched for us and found Tylar."

He shook his head. "She'd have killed you. After she lost Narine..." He was quiet for a moment. "There would have been no way to reason with her. She needed someone to crush in a show of power." He glanced down at her. "And from the way she looked at you when we were on that cliff, I think you were her first choice."

"Tylar didn't deserve that," Sable said quietly.

Reese started forward. "No one deserves that." They moved along the base of the cliff, winding through thick, old tree trunks until they reached a portion of the rock that rose more gradually. Reese found a game trail and started up it. Reaching the top of the cliff, Sable looked out over the edge of a wide, rocky plateau, scattered with rocks and green ferns. The sun was sitting just above the blue outline of the Scale Mountains.

Reese climbed up on a pile of boulders and sat on a wide ledge, facing east across the forest and leaning back against the rock.

Sable clambered up next to him, taking in the view. To the south, the cliffs they'd been on yesterday shot up from the flatlands like a squat wall. Everything else was forest, flowing over hills and moving gradually lower like a rough, green sea until it was lost in the hazy distance.

They sat in silence for a few minutes before Reese spoke, keeping his gaze fixed on the forest. "Vivaine had every reason to execute me last year, and she let me go. But Tylar had done nothing, and she knew it."

"She's grown more..." Sable paused. "Unhinged, I suppose, and more attached to Argyros. He's never far from her these days. I don't think she kept him that close a year ago. Something passes between them when she touches him." She glanced down at Innov sleeping in the sling.

"Innov does it too. When I touch her, the warmth I feel isn't only physical. She trickles energy into me." Sable turned her hands over on her lap, showing her palms. They were red still, but it was the dark color of an old burn, nearly scarred over. Her right hand looked slightly worse where she'd touched the soldier in the clearing, but that was healing quickly too.

Reese leaned forward to see her hands better, but unlike the other morning when they'd sat together on the cliff, he didn't reach out to touch them.

"When I first saw you on the island," Reese said, still looking at her hands, "I thought you hadn't changed at all. But now you've adopted a baby phoenix, nearly killed a man by touching him, carried on a conversation with Vivaine from a ridiculous distance, and you talk about magical creatures oozing special powers into people like it's a normal thing." He looked into her face, studying her. His words were warm and truthful. He opened his mouth to say more but closed it again and looked back over the valley.

"Those are all very recent changes," Sable said. "It was only a couple weeks ago that I first even felt the *vitalle* in Innov. But that unlocked something." She stretched her fingers. Since they'd left the island, things had been so chaotic and terrifying and exhausting, she hadn't really thought through what she'd done.

The fingers of her right hand curled closed as she thought of the soldier in the clearing, how fast the *vitalle* had drained out of him at her touch.

Speaking to Vivaine across the valley had been simple, though. Now that she thought about it, the ability to push her words through the air felt more like something she'd always known was possible. Something her voice had been waiting to do.

Except the first time she'd talked to Gwen on the rope bridge, it hadn't felt easy. It had taken effort and concentration.

Sable frowned across the valley. "Actually, the things I did yesterday are a significant step up from anything I was capable of before. Serene says that most people move *vitalle* at first because there's some sort of danger. Maybe being chased by Vivaine was what I needed."

He let out a short laugh. "In the weeks I traveled with you, you were in mortal danger at least four other times from Kalesh soldiers or Kiva. And none of that ever triggered anything like this."

"You're right. In fact, yesterday I had you and Terrane and Serene around me. I didn't even have to fight. I could have hidden."

"You never hide."

"Neither do you," she pointed out.

Innov stirred and stretched her head up out of the sling, blinking sleepily.

"Hello, sleepy head." Sable dug a couple of berries out of her pocket. The phoenix snatched them up greedily. Sable fed her several more before Reese spoke again.

"I'm sorry I didn't tell you about Rabbit."

Sable's hand stopped with a berry halfway to Innov.

"I should have," Reese continued, watching her. "I knew how you'd feel about him, even if he wasn't directly working for Kiva anymore."

She forced herself to meet his gaze.

His eyes were troubled, and there was a shadow of defeat in them. "I wanted you to love camp the way I do, or at least like it, and get to know Tanis, and…" He trailed off, sinking back onto the rock behind them. "But I should have told you."

"Aside from Rabbit, I did love camp."

"I meant what I said before. Once I get everyone else somewhere safe, I will take you anywhere you want to go."

Sable looked out over the forest. "I want to stay with you."

He tensed.

"With the rebels," she clarified quickly. "I mean the rangers. I was being unreasonable before. The truth is, I used Talia the exact way Tanis is using Rabbit, and for the exact same reasons. I can hardly fault him for it. I was so relieved to be away from Vivaine and Kiva that running into Rabbit was like a punch in the gut."

Reese considered her words. "I'm sure it was."

"This evening is too beautiful for a depressing topic like Kiva." She glanced over at Reese. "Let's talk about something else. Like how people in your camp know who I am."

Reese grimaced. "When I joined the rangers, there were already a few people who'd come north from Immusmala with the story of what had happened. They knew who I was, and who Atticus was, and who you were." He glanced at her, rubbing his hand over the back of his neck. "The rumors about how attached you and I are were…exaggerated."

"I noticed."

"I've tried to set them straight, but…" He gave her a smile that looked more like a wince. "You know how rumors are."

Innov let out an annoyed squawk as she strained to reach the berry Sable was still holding. Sable brought it closer, and Innov took it eagerly.

Reese leaned over to look at the fiery bird, his shoulder brushing against Sable's.

"She sleeps a lot." Reese looked curiously at the bird. "And I rarely see her eat."

"She's never eaten much." Sable offered another berry. "Narine fed her bits of fruit or meat, but I never got the feeling Innov needed it. Until now." Sable frowned at the bird. "The little she has pestered me for food is more than she ever pestered Narine."

"She needs to get energy from somewhere. It can't be easy to produce fire all day."

Sable straightened. "Fire! I kept one going constantly for Narine, but Innov perched close to it all the time."

"And you haven't had her near any fires at all."

"Oh, Innov." Sable leaned closer. "I'm sorry. Smoke is sort of a problem for us right now." She offered another berry, but the phoenix took it with less enthusiasm. She tried, half-heartedly, to spread her wings in the sling but gave up quickly, and her eyes slid closed. Sable felt a jab of worry. "Poor thing, no wonder she's tired, making fire all day and occasionally bursting into dramatic flights. Not to mention all the energy she's spent healing my hands." She considered the sleeping bird, a new thought occurring to her. "But not just healing...I think she's giving me power."

"Power?"

"It wasn't being chased by Vivaine that's changed things for me." Sable turned her hands over, showing her healing palms. "I've been able to do more magic since Innov came to me."

Reese reached out tentatively toward Sable's hand and touched the edge of the burned skin on her palm.

"All of this is a bit unnerving." He trailed his finger across her palm.

The scar muffled the sensation to only an indistinct pressure. "Agreed."

His finger lifted off her skin. "You could suck the life out of me, couldn't you?"

She gave him a flat look. "Not as quickly as you could stab me with your knife."

He paused. "I see your point."

"If anything," Sable said, "this makes us a little more even."

"No," he said with a small laugh. "That's not what it does." His smile faded, and he pulled his hand away. "It does, though, make it clear that you aren't in need of a bodyguard."

Sable reached out tentatively and set her hand on his. His fingers tensed. "What if I want one?"

He didn't move for a moment, then he shifted his hand, intertwining their fingers. "You shouldn't. It's a useless position. Even last year, before you discovered all your new skills, I wasn't under the illusion that you needed my protection. I chased you around while you threw yourself into ridiculous situations, but I rarely did anything actually protective."

"I don't throw myself into ridiculous situations," she objected.

He looked at her with a raised eyebrow. "How long has it been since you picked a fight with the High Prioress—arguably the most powerful woman this side of the Empire? Not even counting the very public argument you had with her last night in front of the entire world?"

A smile crept across her face. "It hasn't been particularly long." She nudged his shoulder with her own. "Maybe you *should* wash your hands of me."

He looked back across the forest, his gaze following the rise and fall of the treetops. His thumb rubbed slowly along hers. "I tried to last year. I thought I had."

The heat from his words pressed against them, filling the gaps of air between her and Reese and the rocks. His tone hadn't changed, but he grew ever so slightly brighter. Reddish strands peeked out from the brown in his beard.

"But the instant Purn showed up with that letter from you…" He shook his head and met her gaze. His words were blazing hot, and he brightened until she could see honey-colored flecks in the brown of his eyes. He focused on her like he was desperately searching for something he needed. "And here I am."

The red strands in his beards looked soft, and she untangled her hand from his, daring to lift it to his face. The wiry hairs tickled her fingers, and her fingertips slid in, finding his warm skin. "Here we both are."

A smile started somewhere near his eyes, slowly spreading to the corner of his mouth. He lifted his hand to her cheek, and she leaned into his touch. Something grew so painfully taut in her chest that she could barely breathe.

Innov shifted and gave a muffled squawk, and Reese's hand twitched.

Sable closed her eyes. "Innov," she said through gritted teeth, "if you interrupt this a second time, I will sell you to the next merchant I meet."

The phoenix stilled, and Sable opened her eyes.

Reese raised an eyebrow, amused. "Selling her feels extreme."

"It isn't."

He smiled and leaned closer. "I don't want to wash my hands of you."

The truth of those words blazed up, swirling around them like a firestorm.

"Please don't." She pushed as much of the fierce ache in her chest into the words as she could.

His lips touched hers, hesitantly at first, then stronger.

The firestorm of heat coalesced around them, and she drew it in like a drowning woman gasping for air.

She pulled the warmth closer, desperate to cross the space that had been between them.

His fingers tightened in her hair, then clenched painfully. His body stiffened, and he wrenched himself back, pushing her away. She let out a gasp as air filled the gap between them, cool and empty after the heat.

He drew in a ragged breath, scrambling backwards, his face pale, his lips bone white. He fell heavily against the stone, his hands shaking.

Sable stared at him, realization turning to horror.

The warmth—it hadn't been drawn from the words around them. She'd drawn it straight out of him.

"Reese!" She reached toward him, and he flinched back.

He opened his mouth, but no sound came out. Instead, his eyes slid shut, and he slumped back against the rock.

CHAPTER FIFTY-EIGHT

"Reese!" Sable scrambled closer to him.

His skin was deathly pale, his body limp and still.

She slammed her hand onto his chest, "I'm sorry!" Under the warmth of her words, she could feel the *vitalle* in his body, muted and dim.

"No, no, no!" She pressed her hand into him, closing her eyes and willing some of her own warmth into him. A slow tingle moved through her hand.

Innov, trapped between them in the sling, squirmed and screeched.

"Innov! Help me!" Sable yanked the fabric apart and dumped the phoenix out onto Reese's chest. "Help him!"

Innov scrabbled up to her feet with a squawk. Reese's chest rose in a shallow, slow breath. Sable shoved her palms back onto Reese, forcing warmth into him. It moved, but too slowly. Her palms started to burn.

"Please!" Sable pleaded with the phoenix. "I can't put it back fast enough!"

Innov flapped her wings, and flames licked along her feathers. Spreading her wings, she lay down on Reese's chest. The phoenix's warmth washed over Sable's hands, sinking into Reese like water into parched ground.

Sable closed her eyes, willing more and more heat to flow into Reese. His heartbeat thudded slow and weak.

"Please," she whispered. "Please!"

Reese's chest rose with a shuddering breath, and he rolled onto his side, coughing, sending Innov tumbling.

The phoenix scrambled upright, and Sable grabbed her before she could spread her wings and fly.

Reese looked up at Sable, his eyes wide. "What...?" He raised a shaking hand to rub his face.

"I'm so sorry!" She reached toward him, but he flinched away, and she stopped.

He was still so pale.

"I'm sorry," she repeated, her voice shaking. "I didn't realize I was doing anything."

His mouth dropped open. "You didn't realize...?"

"I just...I just wanted you closer," she whispered.

He gave her an incredulous look. "Most women would use their hands to solve that problem."

Sable bit down on her lip to fight off the sudden urge to laugh. "I didn't think of using my hands."

He stared at her, speechless.

She offered him a small smile. "I guess I'm not most women."

He let out a little huff of laughter that ended in a cough and closed his eyes. "No. You're not." He groaned and touched his chest where Innov had sat. He opened his eyes to peer down at the scorch mark on his chest. "Did you burn me?"

Innov chirped, and Sable rubbed her finger over the phoenix's neck. "Innov helped me...fill you back up."

His brow creased. "With what? Fire?"

Sable shifted. "With the *vitalle* that I accidentally pulled out of you."

His head sank back as though the act of looking down had exhausted him. "Sable," he said slowly. "This was my last shirt."

A bubble of laughter rose up in her, partly from relief, partly from the fact that there was a wide, phoenix-shaped scorch mark crossing the front of his shirt. She tried to hold it in. "I'll have Purn fix it."

"Absolutely not."

The laugh escaped, and she rubbed her mouth to keep away more. "I promise she'll fix it right. Put it back to exactly what it was."

His eyes slipped closed. "If she disintegrates this one, I'm going to dip her bony, blue fingers in sap and wrap them in so much fabric she won't be able to touch anything ever again."

Sable grinned. "How do you feel?"

"Like I've just run for three days straight."

"I can give you more energy."

His eyes flew open, and he shifted away nervously. "No, I'll just rest a little, I think."

"I know what I did." She grimaced. "I swear it won't happen next time."

He let out a weak laugh. "You're assuming that I'm going to kiss you again." He rubbed his hand against his lips, which were still nearly white. "I don't think kissing you is worth it."

She paused, and then she felt the thread of cold in his words. "I know that wasn't entirely true."

He met her gaze, his face exhausted. "I'm at least going to wait until I can feel my lips again before deciding." He poked at his lips. "If I ever feel them again."

"I am sorry," she said again. "I told you all these skills are a bit new." She offered him a tentative smile. "If it helps you feel any better, it was a very nice kiss."

"It started off decent." He closed his eyes. "Do you have any of those berries left?"

"I gave them all to Innov." Sable glanced down the hill. "Terrane is probably done coking the rabbit by now."

"Let's go see." He crawled toward the side of the rock.

"Maybe you should rest a little more." Sable tucked Innov back into the sling. The bird had fallen asleep again looking dim, and Sable wished they could build a fire tonight.

"I'm hungry." Reese slid off the edge of the rocks and stood, one hand leaning on the boulders.

Sable scrambled down next to him. His face had regained a bit of color, but he swayed as he stood. She ducked under his arm to help steady him.

He looked suspiciously down at her. "You're not going to suck the life out of me again, are you?"

"Probably not." She started forward, and he came with her, leaning on her shoulders. "I forgot how heavy you are."

"Good thing you took all my strength," he said dryly. "Should make you extra strong."

She glanced up at him. "I wish. I think it turned into heat, warmed me up a little, then disappeared."

"Nice to know it went to good use."

Sable set her sore palm gingerly against his side. She focused on where her hands touched him and slowly, trying to keep it from becoming hot, trickled some *vitalle* into him.

By the time they reached the clearing, he was standing a bit taller and his lips were almost back to their normal color.

Serene looked up from reading. Her brow creased when she saw Reese. "What happened to you?"

Sable helped him reach the huge oak. He slid down to sit with a sigh of relief. Serene looked questioningly at the two of them, and Sable felt her cheeks flush.

Serene's look shifted to amusement. "Ah. I should have warned you about that."

Sable stared at her. "You knew this would happen?"

"Strong feelings do tend to trigger people's...skills."

"Whatever you did, I applaud you, Sable," Terrane said. "I haven't seen the boss that weak...ever."

Sable glared at him. "Shut up, Terrane."

From next to Serene, Jae gave Reese a sympathetic wince that ended in a chuckle. "Serene nearly killed me the first time I kissed her."

"This is what happens when someone kisses Serene or Sable?" Thulan asked with a grin.

"Terrifying!" Leonis said. "If I'd had a role where I kissed Sneaks, I could have died, right there on the stage."

"You'd have been fine, Leonis," Serene said. "We need to be kissing someone we're attracted to."

Leonis leaned toward Thulan. "I'd be dead," he whispered loudly.

"If this is what they do to men they like," Gwen mused, "what do they do to men they hate?"

"I shudder to think," Terrane said.

"Keep talking," Serene said, "and you'll find out. Someone be useful and get Reese some rabbit."

She came over to the oak and held out the book she'd been reading. "You're going to find that very interesting reading, Sable."

Sable took it. It was the small brown volume, *Ghost of the White Wood*, Flibbet had given her back at the rebel camp.

Serene knelt down next to Reese and studied his face, not quite hiding her amusement. "You're in better shape than Jae was."

"He looked worse before," Sable said. "Innov helped me with him. I thought I'd killed him."

Serene laughed again and set one hand on the tree and the other on Reese's shoulder. Sable felt the shifting of *vitalle* flowing out of the tree, warming Serene, then slipping into Reese. It was much more orderly and controlled than Sable had managed, and Reese lay his head back against the trunk with a sigh of relief.

After a few minutes, Serene stood and stretched out her hands. "You'll feel better in the morning."

Terrane brought over two sticks with pieces of cooked rabbit skewered on the ends, offering one to Reese and one to Sable. The meat was a little tough, but tasty.

"Purn?" Sable glanced around the clearing.

The kobold popped into view next to her, her eyes bright with amusement. "Hello, mistress."

"Could you please fix Reese's shirt? Innov scorched it a bit."

"Ah, the bird," Terrane said to Gwen. "I thought Sable had set him on fire."

Sable ignored them. "Can you put it back to how it was before?"

Purnicious nodded and stepped up next to Reese.

He gave the kobold a warning look. "Don't do anything..." He wiggled his fingers at her. "Purnish. Just put it back to how it was."

The kobold examined the fabric, then wiped her hand slowly across Reese's chest, lightening the charred marks. "Only the front of the threads is scorched. I can clean that off easily, and there's enough unharmed fabric that it'll be easy to fix." She focused on his shirt, running her bony, blue fingers across it in different directions, leaving cleaner and cleaner swaths in her wake.

She glanced over her shoulder at Sable with a toothy grin. "At least this should keep the wastrel treating you respectfully from now on."

Reese glared at her. "I was being respectful, you little, blue monster."

Purn shrugged. "Regardless, it's a good warning." She looked critically at his shirt. "You know, a collar and a short split right here at the neck would help the fabric lie better—"

"Put it back to how it was, Purnicious," Reese growled.

"I promised him you would," Sable added.

Purn let out a sigh. "Boring. Boring. Boring," she muttered, swiping her hand across his shirt with each word.

The group settled down, and Sable leaned against the tree next to Reese.

She pulled out the book from Flibbet. The thin, leather cover was smooth and worn a bit at the edges, the fawn coloring fading to grey near the top corner. The clearing was growing darker, but on the first page, she could still clearly make out the sketch of pine trees underlining the title, *Ghost of the White Wood*.

Where had she heard of the White Wood? Not from one of Atticus's plays. It had been much more recent than that. She ran her fingers over the words and tried to remember. It certainly hadn't been something like a play or a speech. Words with a cadence that strong would have stuck in her memory. This had been in passing conversation.

On the back side of the title page was a note.

This story is compiled from firsthand accounts of the Ghost of the White Wood in the 184th year of the Empire, gathered from M and B themselves. While it is not the story that is circulated by the Empire, it is, to the best of my knowledge, the more faithful account of those days. - Soren, bard of the Taken Lands.

She turned the page to find the heading *Melia* written neatly in a bold hand. Below it, instead of a historical account, she found the opening of a story. A woman named Melia preparing an ambush of a Kalesh carriage with her elven friend, Evay.

Melia herself, known as the Ghost of the White Wood, led a group of local townsmen in the successful ambush, only to discover it had been bait to discover her location.

The next morning, the town was overrun with Kalesh soldiers, and the people were threatened with their lives if they didn't reveal the Ghost's whereabouts.

The story was well-written, and Sable followed along fascinated as Melia snuck into the town square, listening to the Kalesh captain threaten to murder every woman in the town until the Ghost came forward.

Sable turned the page and froze.

The young Kalesh captain's name was Bastian.

CHAPTER FIFTY-NINE

SABLE STOPPED short at the name.

That was where she'd heard of the White Wood.

When Reese had stood on the wall of Aedis and accused Ambassador Bastian of putting down a rebellion and defeating the woman who'd led it. Reese had called him Bastian of the White Wood.

Next to her, Reese was sleeping, slumped back against the tree.

Sable rose and walked across the clearing to Serene. "Bastian? Ambassador Bastian?"

Serene sat by the trees with Purnicious's purple cloak spread out before her, the three books Jae had brought open next to each other. "It would seem so. That Bastian gets a wound from his temple to his cheek."

It was growing harder to see the words in the dying light, but Sable read how Melia had surrendered herself to Bastian to save the town, and he'd taken her to the ruthless Prince Turrn, son of the Kalesh emperor himself.

From a nearby tree, something flickered, and Jae held up a glowing, green ball.

He handed it to Serene, then added three more balls of plain-looking moss. Serene pushed a tiny bit of warm *vitalle* into those, setting them aglow too with an eerie luminescence. She lined them up on the purple cloak along the top of her open books.

"Can I have a spooky green light?" Sable asked, setting her book down on the edge of the cloak.

"It's Elfshair," Leonis explained from where he lay sprawled out under a tree. "It glows when it's warmed."

Jae tossed Sable a ball of moss. "You can make your own. Just push a little *vitalle* into it."

His words were casual and simple, but Sable hesitated. The ball of moss was nothing more than loosely rolled, wiry strands, tangled together in a roughly spherical shape.

"It's not alive," Sable said. "How can I add *vitalle* to it?"

"It is alive," Jae said. "It's just not very energetic on its own."

Sable focused on pressing *vitalle* into it, but the strands that touched her hand were so thin and wispy, she couldn't quite force the energy into the right places.

"I need some light," she whispered to it. The warmth of her words wrapped around the moss, and tiny streams of *vitalle* flowed out of her palm into it. The fibers touching her skin started to glow, and lines of green snaked deeper into the tangle until the whole ball glowed.

Sable rolled the ball slowly between her palms, inordinately pleased by the strange light she'd just created.

"Nicely done," Jae said, tossing another ball to Serene.

Gwen came over, nudging one of the glowing orbs with the toe of her shoe. "Are they hot?"

"No," Jae said. "Care to try one? I would bet you can do it too."

The Mira frowned at him. "I don't move *vitalle* the way you people do. I don't move anything. I just know your thoughts if I touch you. No pushing, no adding."

"Yes," Jae said, pausing. "We've discussed your skill. It's unusual. But somehow you are creating a connection between your mind and someone else's, so you must be moving *vitalle* somehow."

Gwen's frown deepened. "You've discussed me?"

"You're an interesting case," he answered easily, holding out a ball of moss. "Just take the life that is in you, the energy that fills your hands and your arms and your chest, and press it into the moss."

Gwen looked at him skeptically. "I'd like to keep the life that is in me, in me."

"This only takes a tiny amount. The pain would stop you long before you'd reach the point where you'd give up too much *vitalle*." He held up his hand, showing the ugly, rough scar across his palm.

Gwen took the moss and furrowed her brow, but the tangled ball stayed dark. Terrane walked up beside her and touched the ball with one finger.

Sable felt a rush of heat, and the moss began to smolder.

"Control it," Serene said sharply. "You're not setting it on fire, you're just giving it some *vitalle*."

"Fire would be brighter," he grumbled, but he touched the moss again. This time Sable could barely feel the warmth, and the moss started to glow.

"How did you do that?" Gwen demanded.

Terrane shrugged. "I woke it up. Or rather, I nudged it without waking it, because waking it would have set it on fire, and Serene would get crabby."

Gwen put the ball on the ground with the others. "That makes no sense at all."

"It just takes some practice," Jae said. "A word can help with focus. Try *elucida*. It means 'to light.'"

Gwen strode over to the nearest tree, where the strands of Elfshair hung down from the lowest branch in long, wispy clumps. "Show me again."

He joined her and touched the moss, setting it aglow. The two of them moved around the edge of the clearing, but only Jae's efforts left a trail of green dangling from the branches.

Sable turned back to her book. The moss wasn't as bright as a candle, but she could make out the words and drawings on the page.

Melia was a fascinating character, along with her elvish friend, Evay. Sable read of how Melia had become the most wanted rebel after assassinating a cousin of the prince.

Bastian, however, was loyal to the Empire. Sable's blood chilled as she read his opinion that the massacre of a rebellious town was justified if it ensured peace in the region.

"I don't like young Bastian," Sable said.

"No," Serene answered, glancing up from her books. "He's unsettlingly Kalesh, isn't he?"

Half the trees now held gauzy trails of glowing moss. The evening breeze dragged fingers through it, making the feathery strands sway gently. The near side of the glade was bathed in viridescent light. The tree trunks and branches looked as though they'd been infused with emerald light that slid between the darker knurls of bark.

"Well, this is getting festive." Leonis pushed himself up from where he lay and walked over to the large oak. "Terrane, can you get that rock of yours hot again? Because barbed acorns are delicious when they're roasted, and that is a barbed oak."

"Do you see any foamy ale trees?" Thulan asked, lying on her back with her arms behind her head. "Because foamy ale is delicious even if it's not roasted."

"Foamy ale sounds delicious," Terrane said, walking over to the oak. "But it's the wrong time of year for acorns."

"Not from the barbed oak." Leonis picked up a fat acorn. "These fall in autumn but won't sprout until late summer. If they're broken or have holes, they'll have weevils. The good ones will have solid shells."

"This time," Serene said to Terrane, "when you warm the rock, try to put the *vitalle* in slowly."

Terrane scowled at her. "If you put it in slowly, it heats the rock slowly. The faster you do it, the better."

"You're making it so much harder than it needs to be," Serene said. "What if someday you need to conserve your energy for something? You can't waste it all on one unorganized, inefficient surge."

"Once you've cooked on a rock for an entire camp for months on end, you can have your own process, but this is how I do it." He slammed his palm down on the center of the stone, and *vitalle* smashed into it. Some rushed into the stone, but spears of heat shot out in different directions, like churning, wild horses stampeding into the forest.

Sable took a step back from the storm of *vitalle*.

Jae ducked and spun toward the rock. "What was that?" he demanded.

Serene stared at Terrane. "That was the clumsiest, most incompetent, most inept use of energy I have ever seen!"

"The rock is hot." Terrane dropped a handful of acorns on it. "That's all that matters."

"Leave Serene and Terrane to bicker," Leonis called to Thulan, "and come help me gather acorns."

"Why me?" Thulan asked, not bothering to get up. "Get someone else."

"Because you're short, so you're closer to the ground." Leonis threw an acorn, and it bounced off her forehead. "And I'm going to continue to throw them at you until you get up."

Thulan caught the next acorn that flew toward her and whipped it back at Leonis. "Nuts feel depressing after talking about ale," she said, but she pushed herself up and picked up the acorn Leonis had thrown.

Sable was watching the two of them toss acorns and snide remarks at each other when she saw movement at the base of the trunk where Reese slept. Purn crossed her arms and looked at him critically. She shook her head and muttered, then knelt down and set her hands on a patch of something dark growing next to him.

What looked like thick, spongy moss grew and spread away from the tree until Purn's hands were covered up to the wrists. She stood and untied a sash from her waist, folding it and setting it neatly on top of the moss. Then, moving more gently than Sable would have expected, Purn took hold of Reese's shoulders and pulled him over, setting his head down on the thick pillow she'd made.

"That was awfully nice, Purn," Sable said quietly. Across the clearing, the kobold glanced over. "Someone might think you're starting to like him."

Purnicious blinked out of view, and Sable felt the slightest hint of a breeze near her shoulder.

"He's growing on me." Purn's little voice came from the empty space beside Sable. "Like a mold, or an especially bad case of warts, but growing nonetheless."

The ground was hard, and the air grew cooler as night fell. Sable's feet ached, and the day had held much less food than was comfortable, but she looked around the clearing feeling more at home than she had in ages.

Next to her, Serene was watching Jae and Gwen with a troubled expression. "I don't know how he has so much patience," Serene said. "I'm terrible at teaching things."

"You were patient with me for the past year," Sable said, "when I couldn't do anything you were trying to teach me."

"That's different," Serene answered almost absently. "I like you."

Sable laughed. "Maybe Jae isn't more patient—maybe he just likes more people than you do."

Instead of laughing, Serene turned a stricken expression on Sable. "I don't like people," she said, as though this were a new, horrible idea. "How can I help people when I don't even like them?"

"You've never liked people. Why is it bothering you tonight?"

Serene looked down at the three books, her gaze unfocused. "Merrick's gone. If Stonehaven disappears, there will be no place for people like us to come together." She looked up at Sable with a hint of desperation in her eyes. "But I can't do what Merrick did. I don't like people!"

Sable let out a laugh, but Serene sank back against the tree.

"Not that it matters anyway," Serene said. "With everything we've taken back from Vivaine, we still only have about a hundred books. I don't even know how to begin to build back up the library."

"Maybe whatever happens next will be different from what Merrick had." Sable looked around the clearing at Terrane heating the rock and Gwen attempting to make moss glow. "Maybe instead of leading people, you can gather together anyone you know who has skills and see what they want. You don't even have to be friendly to them," she said, waving her hand to where Gwen and Jae were drawing back near them. "Let Jae do that. Just bring them together and see what happens."

Serene frowned at the idea but didn't object. The strong scent of roasted acorns wafted across the clearing, rich and almost buttery. The voices of the others rose and fell, Terrane's loud laugh ringing out as Leonis acted out some ridiculous thing.

Thulan came by, offering handfuls of hot, nutty acorns.

Sable turned back to her book.

Melia escaped her bonds and stood behind Bastian with a knife, offering him his life if he would spare the town that was about to be massacred.

Then Melia and Evay, each with their elvish bows, ambushed Prince Turrn, killing him and his corrupt colonel.

After Melia successfully escaped, Bastian and another man lied, twisting the truth to make Bastian look like the hero, bringing him fame and power.

Sable sat back, closing the book. "I still don't really like young Bastian," she said.

Serene nodded. "For a moment in the middle of that story, I thought he was going to listen to Melia and do something non-Kalesh. But, alas."

Sable nodded, feeling oddly depressed by the tale. "I suppose I shouldn't have thought better of him."

"Melia, though," Serene added, "is a woman I would like to know."

Sable grinned. "If she were here now, I'd sic her on Bastian again."

At the other end of the trees, Jae was lighting strand after strand of moss hanging from the oak tree. Gwen tried repeatedly, but it was always Jae who got them to light. There was so much moss dangling from the wide-spread branches that the entire underside of the tree glowed brightly.

"I told you," Gwen said, irritated, "I cannot move *vitalle* the way—"

A loud, threatening rumble rolled through the trees.

The clearing fell silent.

The rumbling continued, and the ground under Sable quivered.

"Did we make the elves angry?" Gwen asked, stepping back.

The thundering grew. The sharp crack of wood echoed through the night.

"That is not elves," Leonis said, backing slowly away from the trees.

Serene cast out, and the wave spread, setting the trees themselves aglow briefly before it traveled deeper into the forest. More and more trunks flared into warm columns until the wave swept over two shapes that burst into massive, blazing towers.

"What are those?" Sable scrabbled to her feet, staring into the forest as the wave dissipated and the crashing, massive forms faded.

The ground shook, stronger this time, and Reese woke, shoving himself up, a knife in his hand. Another crack cut through the din, much louder than a breaking branch. Serene and Sable moved toward the center of the clearing where Leonis was picking up and nocking his bow and Thulan was pulling her hammer from her belt. Reese and Jae drew closer also, with Gwen hiding behind them.

"Serene," Reese said, "what is that?"

Serene cast out again, catching the two shapes so terrifyingly close, they were almost visible through the trees near the oak.

This time they were outlined perfectly. Huge, almost human forms with legs wider than trees, bodies the size of huge boulders, and wide, thick heads that reached high into the branches.

"Trolls," Jae said faintly. "Those are trolls."

CHAPTER SIXTY

"Trolls aren't real." Gwen's voice came weakly from where she stood behind Reese and Jae.

"Oh, well, then," Serene said. "We're fine. No chance of being trampled. Or eaten."

Gwen's face grew paler.

The group strung out in a jagged line, looking warily in the direction of the noise. Serene stood next to Sable on one end, stretching her fingers and focusing deep into the woods. On Sable's other side, Thulan took a step forward, swinging her hammer.

"Anyone know how to fight a troll?" the dwarf asked.

"Be another troll?" Leonis offered.

"I heard they don't like fire," Terrane said from the far end.

Leonis nocked an arrow. "No fire!"

A huge pine near the oak bent to the side with a deafening crack, and a huge, misshapen face glowed eerily in the mosslight. Its lumpy, thick hide was caked with clods of dirt and patches of sod. The tree crashed to the side, and a second troll appeared, shorter than the first.

"A mother and son," Thulan said. "This just keeps getting better."

"Why are they here?" Gwen asked.

"Trolls like food," Jae said, "and bright, shiny things."

"Like roasting acorns and glowing moss?" Gwen asked. "Can you put out the moss?"

Jae shook his head. "Elfshair glows for hours."

"They're also drawn to magic," Serene said. "Like huge bursts of *vitalle* someone might use to heat up a rock."

Terrane glanced down the line at her. "Oops."

The trolls stood at the edge of the clearing, blinking at the green light.

The *vitalle* of the creatures was palpable. Serene hadn't cast out again, but Sable could feel an oppressive, simmering heat roll off them.

"We need to split up," Reese said in a low voice from the far side of the group. "They're not bright. Let's move out of the way before they realize there are other things to eat here than acorns. Jae, Gwen, and Terrane, follow me toward the oak tree. The rest of you move toward the trees on the other side. Once we reach the forest, we'll let them enjoy the bright clearing and the yummy acorns, and we'll get away."

"I like that plan," Gwen said.

"Slow and steady." Reese stepped sideways toward the oak.

Serene started the other way, and Sable stayed close to her, keeping her eyes on the trolls. Thulan and Leonis followed.

The mother troll took a step into the clearing.

Sable felt heat roll across the clearing. "They have a lot of *vitalle*," she said softly.

"They're sustained by magic," Serene answered. "They can sleep for years without eating."

"What do they eat when they're awake?" Sable asked.

"Anything they want," Serene answered.

The sling at Sable's stomach shifted, and Innov's head slid out of the fabric. She turned inquisitively toward the trolls. In the dim green clearing, the phoenix was a bright orange light.

Sable shoved the phoenix down, but Innov flailed until one flaming wing shot out the top of the sling, shoving the fabric so far to the side that her body tumbled out. Sable caught her, but Innov clawed and flapped, shooting out sparks and flares of light, her orange eyes fixed on the trolls. She wasn't strong enough to fly, but she beat her wings awkwardly.

The young troll took a step toward Sable, closing half the distance between them in a single stride. Serene broke for the trees, and Sable ran after her. Leonis's bow twanged, and Sable looked back to see Thulan hurl her hammer. The arrow hit the troll just below the eye and skittered off to the side as though it had hit a rock.

Thulan's hammer bounced off the huge forehead with a dull clang and spun toward Sable. She pulled up short as the hammer flew a few steps in front of her. The troll stopped too and swiped his hand across his head, letting out a roar.

"This is not good," Thulan said.

Innov flapped again, and the troll refocused on Sable, lunging forward again. Sable started to run, but the troll's thick fingers wrapped around her, squeezing her ribs until she could barely breathe.

The ground fell away in a dizzying yank as the troll snatched Sable up. She held Innov up away from the enormous fingers.

The troll's skin was a greyish green, dotted with wide, rough warts. He fixed his beady eyes on the fiery form of Innov. Sable twisted against his hand, but his fingers were rough like ancient, thick leather, hardened with age. He drew her close and let out a deafening roar, blowing wet, musty breath into her face, like air from an old, dank cave.

He shook Sable until her head snapped from side to side. Pain shot down her back, and she tucked her head down against his fingers. The shaking lit the phoenix's feathers with a blaze of light.

The troll leaned closer.

Far below, Serene raced up and slammed her hand onto his leg. Sable felt massive amounts of *vitalle* drain out of the troll into the ground.

But there was so much blazing heat in the creature, he merely scowled and swung his other hand down. It slammed into Serene, sending her flying, smashing into the cliff and falling to the ground.

"Serene!" Jae yelled, racing out from the trees behind the trolls, darting across to where she lay.

The young troll took a step after him.

Sable thrust Innov in the troll's face. "Look at the light!" she shouted. "Leave them alone and look at the pretty, bright bird!"

The troll paused, transfixed by Innov again.

"Sable!" Reese yelled from the edge of the trees behind the trolls.

Sable tried to shift in the troll's grip, but all she could do was kick her feet, which dangled alarmingly high above the ground. "I can't move!"

Reese stepped cautiously into the clearing, moving up behind the younger troll. He held a knife in his hand that looked ludicrously small.

"Mistress!" Purn's little voice squeaked.

"Purn!" Sable leaned over to see the blue face below her, the kobold's eyes wide with fear. "Can you shrink him or something?"

"I could barely shrink one of his toes!"

"Then do that!" Sable called.

There was a moment's silence.

"He has no toes!" Purnicious shouted. "How can he have no toes?"

Purn set her hand on the stumpy end of the troll's leg. The edge of it begin to disappear.

The troll shifted and shook his foot, nearly sending Purn flying, but she blinked out of sight and reappeared next to the other leg, which she immediately began to shrink. "He's too big!" the kobold called up.

Sable could still feel the warmth from the phoenix flowing up her arms. She drew it in, trying to think of something that would harm such a huge creature.

No, not harm it…

Sable fixed the troll with as firm of a look as she could manage. "Put us down!" she commanded him, forcing as much *vitalle* as she could into the words.

The troll blinked at her, then his fingers loosened, and Sable started to slip through his grip.

"No!" she yelled. "Hold us and put us down! But do it gently!"

The troll squeezed her again and shook his head, letting out a low growl. He opened his mouth and pulled her toward his jagged, broken teeth.

Sable shoved back against his hand. Innov squawked and bit his finger, but her beak scraped across the thick skin like it was a rock.

"He's stupid, Sable!" Serene called in a pained voice from where Jae was helping her up. "Use simple directions!"

The troll pulled her toward his rough, black tongue, his wet, hot breath making her gag.

Forcing down her growing panic, Sable focused on the strength from Innov again, and she called the next word out with as much force as she could. "Stop!"

The troll's hand stopped, his teeth poised above and below her.

"Set us down on the ground," she said clearly.

For a moment, the troll didn't move, but the warmth of her words spread out, filling the gaping hole of his mouth, then moving out to gather in a cloud in front of his face.

Slowly, his hand pulled back and lowered until he jammed Sable's feet down onto the ground. She felt the impact up her spine, and a grunt of pain escaped her. He held her there, peering at her with a puzzled bleariness.

"Let go," Sable commanded.

He paused, then let go.

She stumbled backwards, and Innov rolled free, tumbling across the ground in a swirl of light.

The troll's eyes followed the phoenix.

Reese skidded up next to Sable and moved between her and the troll, a knife in his hand. "Are you hurt?"

Sable pushed herself up with a groan. "Not permanently."

The mother troll stomped toward the stone where a handful of acorns still roasted. Thulan and Leonis, trapped between her and her son, stood side by side.

"I can push her back with fire!" Terrane called, setting his hand on the grass.

"No fire!" Leonis yelled.

The mother troll reached for the acorns, thrusting her hand onto the hot rock. There was a sizzling noise, and she reared back, howling. Thulan and Leonis took the chance to dart along the cliff toward the oak, but she bellowed and lunged toward them, cornering them against the cliff.

"Fire!" Thulan called. "Terrane! Use the fire!"

A line of flame shot out from Terrane's hand, racing across the grass and snaking through the thin gap between the troll and the cliff, flaring up into a wall of fire.

The mother troll stumbled back.

"Not at us!" Leonis pressed himself against the rock, squirming away from the flames. "At her!"

Terrane dropped his other hand to the ground, and the fire moved away from the cliff, driving back the mother troll.

The younger troll was momentarily distracted by the wall of fire near his mother, and Sable crawled forward to pick up Innov. The troll snapped his attention back and grabbed for Sable again.

A knife flipped through the air and sank into his eye.

The troll let out a shriek that made the ground shake. His mother spun toward them, and Reese grabbed Sable's arm, pulling her back.

The wall of fire lengthened, shooting across the grass between them and the troll, corralling both huge creatures back toward the woods.

The younger troll knocked the knife from his eye, howling in pain.

Innov burst out of Sable's arms and flung herself into the flames. The phoenix landed, her body dark red among the flames. Flames licked along the edges of her feathers. She stretched her neck and let out a fierce, wild cry that echoed off the cliffs.

"Too hot!" Serene called from where she still sat on the ground. "It's too hot, Terrane! Control it!"

The flames licked higher, moving slowly across the clearing, scorching the ground and driving back the trolls.

"Stop!" Leonis shouted, running over to Terrane. "Don't burn the trees!"

The line of fire stopped moving—but so did the trolls.

Innov soared up into the sky, leaving a trail of fire behind her as she arched through the night, spinning and diving back into the flames, where she skimmed across the ground.

"How long can you hold those flames?" Gwen shouted.

"Not long!" Sweat rolled down Terrane's face. "We need to drive them off!"

"With what?" Thulan yelled.

Innov flew past Sable, weaving through fire, dazzlingly bright.

"Innov!" Sable ran toward the fire. "I need you!"

"Sable!" Reese called after her, a note of exasperation in his voice.

The phoenix burst out of the fire, whirling around Sable, surrounding her in a blinding fountain of sparks. Sable held out her arm, and Innov landed on it, bright as a rising sun.

Heat poured into Sable's arm, flowing up to her chest, filling her with a blazing, burning power. She stood across the fire from the trolls and poured every bit of Innov's strength into her words.

"Go!" The words rang out in the clearing rich and full and strong. Innov's power thrummed through her, and she funneled it into her voice. "Go home!"

The trolls stumbled back but paused.

"GO!" Sable shouted, filling the clearing and the woods beyond with the word.

The trolls turned and crashed away through the woods.

The *vitalle* from Sable's words faded away, and for a breath there was nothing but the sound of the flames crackling and hissing.

Innov let out a joyous shriek and dove back into the flames. The heat from the phoenix cooled, and Sable sank to her knees, suddenly hollow.

"Sable!" Reese called, his voice far away.

The fire wavered before her as Innov pelted through the flames.

"Terrane!" Leonis shouted. "The oak!"

Sable blinked toward the huge tree and saw flames licking up the canopy.

Reese's footsteps pounded up next to her, and he dropped down beside her. "Are you all right?"

"I..." She stopped, not at the concern in his eyes, but at the surging fire she felt beneath his skin.

The clearing swayed, and a fog crept across her vision. His arm wrapped around her, and she could feel the heat of him across her shoulders.

"Put it out!" Leonis yelled.

The line of flames winding across the clearing flickered out, leaving only smoldering grass.

Innov shot from the new darkness like an arrow, racing up into the black sky.

Across the clearing, the oak tree blazed.

"Terrane!" Leonis roared.

"I can't put out the tree!" Terrane yelled. "I was keeping the other fire lit! That's burning on its own!"

The flames on the tree were hot in the normal sense, but beneath them, Sable could see the branches and trunk shining with *vitalle*. Slower, more ponderous, but unimaginably deep.

"Serene!" Leonis shouted, running toward the oak. "Purnicious!"

Jae, Serene, and Purnicious all raced toward the oak, each one a blazing figure of barely controlled fire. Sable had the vague sense that there was heat being drawn away from the tree, but the fire was already huge, and they were pulling away such a tiny amount. Up in the burning branches, the flames broke open the edges of the *vitalle*, and the life of the tree raced out to join the thrashing flames, billowing up into the night in a cloud of smoke.

As she watched, a line of flames leapt over to the branch of the nearest pine.

Reese frowned at her. "Are you all right?"

She nodded slowly. "I can see...everything."

His brow furrowed. "What does that mean?"

Flickers of light in the woods caught her eye.

A dozen shimmering, radiant creatures raced toward them under the darkness of the trees. She tried to focus on them, but they looked as if they were made of glittering fire. As though the sparks from Innov's feathers had coalesced into tall, thin figures. She grabbed Reese's leg where he knelt next to her. "What are those?"

He shifted and swore.

There was a rustle of air, and Purnicious's voice came from the empty space beside Sable. "The elves," Purn whispered.

The green moss still glowed from branches along the edge of the clearing, and the fire from the oak cast an orange glow against the cliffs, but the elves ran into the clearing like a row of tiny suns.

Every one of Sable's companions stopped and faced the elves.

463

All but one of the elves ran for the burning trees. Serene, Leonis, and Jae backed away.

The brightest elf stayed at the edge of the clearing, his gaze sweeping over the group with fury. Past the glittering fire that seemed to fill him, Sable could make out a thin face framed by long, white hair.

"You!" His voice hit Sable with the force of a shove, and she flinched. Reese's arm tensed around her shoulders.

"You have destroyed the oak," he continued, his words squeezing around her. "She who has given us her voice and sustained us for eight hundred years."

Sable curled away from the pressure.

"What's wrong?" Reese whispered.

"His voice..."

Reese pulled his arm off her shoulder, shifting in front of her.

"We will not look away this time." The elf's voice rolled out again, and Sable pressed against Reese's back as the pressure returned.

"This time?" Reese's voice felt gloriously normal.

"This time you have come too far and caused too much pain!" The elf's voice slammed through the clearing.

Invisible ropes tightened around Sable's chest, binding her arms to her sides.

"We have never been here—" Reese gasped as his body was yanked forward, his arms pinned to his sides.

Sable struggled against her unseen bonds, but they were as unmoving as the troll's stone fingers.

Around her, every companion stiffened, their arms bound to their sides. Even Purnicious slowly came into view next to Sable, grunting and twisting against the restraints.

The elf waved his hand at them, leaving a streak of golden light across Sable's vision, and the clearing around her dimmed. She tilted to the side, shadows rushing in from the edges of her vision until the only thing she could see was the elf, glowing like a piercing light. She started to topple, but before she hit the ground, even the elf was swallowed by the darkness.

CHAPTER SIXTY-ONE

DAYLIGHT STREAMED through a tangle of thorny branches only inches in front of Sable's face. She lay on her side on the ground, blinking at the brightness. She looked up to find the brambles rising overhead, arching in a wide, unbroken dome. Next to her, Thulan lay asleep. Past the dwarf, the rest of her companions were all lying inside the strange prison cell.

Sable sat up and nudged Thulan. Through the wall of branches, the morning light angled sharply through tall, wide-trunked trees. The forest was open enough that bright green grass and wildflowers carpeted the ground. Outside the enclosure, nothing moved.

Thulan opened her eyes, then scrambled to sit. Leonis slept at her feet, and she prodded him with her boot. "Wake up, you mangy half-elf. We're trapped in some stupid, elven prison."

Leonis and the others stirred.

Thulan reached for her belt, but there was no hammer. "I bet those useless elves left it in the clearing! I've had that hammer for thirty years!" She pushed herself up and moved to the thorns. "This wall is ridiculous. If they imprison people for things as minor as accidentally hurting a tree, they must lock up a lot of people, and you'd think they'd have learned to make stronger cells."

She grabbed a long, smooth section of branch to break it but yanked her hands off with a gasp.

Three new thorns jutted out from the wood, their tips wet and red. Thulan swore and held out her palms, where three punctures welled up with blood.

Purnicious frowned at the wall. "I can't blink through it."

"Can you make a door?" Sable asked.

Purn touched one finger gingerly between the thorns.

Nothing happened. Purnicious frowned at the wall. "I can't grab hold of the—" She let out a little yelp and pulled her finger off a sharp thorn.

"Touching it seems to make it unfriendly," Gwen said. "I vote we stop touching it."

"I could try fire," Terrane offered.

"No!" Sable's answer rang out with a chorus of others.

Serene knelt next to the wall and set her hand on the ground. "Maybe I can draw the *vitalle* out and at least make it brittle." She sat for a moment, but nothing changed. "I think we can rule out magic."

"Of course magic won't work," Leonis said dully. "We're in an elvish prison. If it's made to hold elves and their magic, it can easily handle all of you."

Gwen shoved her tangled hair out of her face. "What are they going to do to us?" she asked Leonis. "What's the penalty for burning down a tree?"

"Depends on the tree. That oak was old."

Reese peered through the tangles. "Where are we?"

"Far from the clearing," Leonis said. "We're near the elves' homes —you can feel it in the trees."

Reese looked up into the treetops. "*You* can feel it in the trees," he corrected Leonis. "The rest of us only feel like we're trapped inside a ball of thorns."

"I can feel it," Purnicious said.

"So can I," Serene agreed.

Beside her, Jae nodded. "Me too."

"These trees are..." Terrane paused. "Different."

Reese glanced at Sable with an irritated look. "I suppose you can feel them too?"

She started to shake her head, but Serene cast out, and the trees past the enclosure flared up like pillars of blazing fire.

"Ooooh," Sable breathed, turning to take in the towering trees while Serene's wave faded.

Gwen straightened, looking up into the trees. "I do feel....something."

"I feel like you're all weird," Thulan muttered.

Reese nodded. "They are."

"Can you sense Innov anywhere?" Sable asked Serene.

"No, but the trees are so bright, it's hard to see much else."

Reese walked over to Sable. "Do you think she's...gone?"

"Maybe." The sling hung empty at her stomach, and to pull her mind away from the fact that Innov might not be coming back, she turned her attention to Reese. His face had regained its normal color. "You look better this morning."

"It's been a while since you tried to kill me," he agreed with a small smile. "Which I appreciate."

"Who was the elf last night?" Sable asked. "His words were more powerful than any elf I've ever heard."

Leonis nodded. "He spoke with more authority than the captain of the guard among my father's people. Any of you humans can speak with authority, but for an elf, that quality comes from actually having the power to command."

"How many things outrank captain of the guard?" Thulan asked.

Leonis turned back to face the woods. "Not many."

"I don't like him," Purnicious said in a small voice. "I do not like his voice."

"Neither do I," Sable said. "What's going to happen to us?"

"If we were in my home," Leonis answered, "there'd be a hearing before all the elves, and the king would pass judgment. But here, I have no idea."

"You will be tried."

The words slammed into Sable's side, and she nearly fell into Reese. Leonis recoiled from the voice.

A line of elves ringed the enclosure. Closer than the others stood the elf who had spoken last night. His long, white hair framed an ancient face set in an impassive expression.

"Where did they come from?" Thulan asked under her breath.

"My nightmares," Gwen muttered.

This morning, the elves didn't shimmer with power. Their skin varied across different shades of brown, some as light as birch bark, some as dark as damp earth. Their faces were thinner than humans, and smoother. Their hair was long and colored like fall leaves, some bright red and coppers, some gold, some rich brown. Some fading to grey and white.

"I am Andolin, ruler of the Greenwood," the white-haired elf said, and Sable drew back from the force of the declaration. "And I accuse you of trespassing in our land and destroying an elder oak."

Leonis flinched. "An elder tree," he whispered. "That's not good."

The elves circling them were uniformly severe and uniformly ancient, except a female elf standing to the left of the king. She seemed much younger than Andolin in a way Sable couldn't quite pinpoint, and instead of hostility, her gaze ran over the group with curiosity. Her hair was bright and golden, glowing when it caught bits of the morning sunlight, and the simple dress she wore was very pale green and only reached to her knees.

"You will stand before our people and be judged." King Andolin drew himself taller. "And then you will be condemned."

The younger elf's brow creased.

"What's the point of the trial if you already know we'll be condemned?" Thulan asked.

Leonis motioned for her to be quiet, but the dwarf ignored him and stepped forward.

"We didn't try to kill your tree," Thulan said. "We were attacked by trolls. We did our best not to use fire, but it came down to a question of life or death."

"And you chose death," the king said flatly.

Thulan crossed her arms. "*Our* life or death, not your tree's. *I* would be dead if Terrane hadn't lit the fire—"

"Don't tell them it was me!" Terrane whispered.

"And so would Leonis, who's half-elven, which should mean something to you heartless—"

Leonis grabbed her and yanked her backwards. "Stop talking," he said through clenched teeth.

"They have other trees!" Thulan waved her hand around at the forest. "And we didn't mean to burn that one down. We tried to put it out! It is stupid to care this much about a tree!" She turned back to the king. "Plant an acorn! Another will grow!"

"Shut up, Thulan!" Leonis hissed.

The king's face had grown darker and harder the more Thulan spoke.

"Your own words have condemned you," the king declared.

The words slammed into Sable, and she gasped. Reese shifted himself between her and the king. Sable leaned against him to block out the smothering force, and then she realized the king's words weren't completely warm. A thin, chilly thread ran through them.

"By fire you destroyed the elder tree," Andolin declared, "and so by fire you shall be destroyed." The trace of untruth still wove through the force of his words.

"I thought you didn't like fire," Terrane said.

"Terrane!" Leonis snapped.

Terrane scowled. "Well, it's a double standard."

Sable pushed herself away from Reese and stepped forward to face the king. "You don't really believe we're guilty."

The king shifted his gaze to her, his face contemptuous, but Leonis's gaze snapped to Sable, and he straightened. Next to the king, the younger elf gave Sable a curious, searching look.

Leonis stepped in front of the others, his shoulders straight, his hands clasped behind his back, where Sable could see his knuckles were white.

"King Andolin," he began, offering the king a low bow, "we are deeply grieved over the loss of the elder oak. We came to your woods in peace and sheltered beneath your trees as weary strangers. The oak offered us acorns, and we ate them."

Sable recognized his tone from plays when he portrayed an especially grave character.

"One of us was wounded," Leonis said, gesturing at Reese, "and he rested beneath the tree's boughs and was restored."

"Boring them with our life story isn't going to help," Thulan muttered.

"Shut up, Thulan," Jae muttered. "That is not what he's doing."

Leonis ignored them both. "The Elfshair moss welcomed us, Your Majesty, and after a dangerous journey, we sheltered in the hospitality of the forest. We were spending the night in peace until the trolls broke into the clearing by snapping the pines guarding it, attempting to steal the sustenance the forest had provided us and threatening our persons."

"What *is* he doing?" Sable whispered.

Jae gave her a tight smile. "Reframing the story."

"But it was not only us they threatened," Leonis continued. "Their wild hunger snapped limbs from the tall pines and uprooted the very trees that had been protecting us." He paused. "We did start a fire to drive them back, to stop their rampage. We tried to keep the flames only on the grass, which renews in the turning of the season, but the great oak, whose limbs had sheltered us, was not unharmed."

The king looked balefully at him.

"My mother was human," Leonis said, "but my father is elven and a respected elder in the Wylwoods, where I was raised." His hands tightened behind his back, but he kept his voice even. "In the Wylwoods, we recognize that the land belongs to the forest, and if our elder trees extend hospitality to strangers, we treat them as guests and offer our protection."

The king opened his mouth, but the younger elf next to him stepped forward.

"I am Ayda." Her words held a gentle warmth that seeped in through the branches. Strands of her long, golden hair glowed in the morning light. "And I desire to know why you traveled so far from the mountains."

Leonis paused. "We did not come from the mountains. We traveled from the great river, pursued by those who would harm us, and were driven deep into your lands."

She cocked her head to the side. "You are not of those who eat away at the earth?"

Leonis glanced back at the others uncertainly.

"Do they mine in the mountains?" Serene asked.

Ayda nodded. "And harvest our trees all along the feet of the great rocks. The earth-eaters stretch along the entire border of our woods."

"The Kalesh?" Reese said slowly. "They're mining all the way up the Scales!"

CHAPTER SIXTY-TWO

"WE ARE NOT WITH THE EARTH-EATERS," Sable said, filling the enclosure with the truth of it. "They're foreign invaders, and we want them driven out."

"We're not even miners," Thulan said. "This group has almost no appreciation for rocks or earth at all, and I haven't mined in years. Leonis has his own glowing elf tree that he carts around everywhere." She glanced at the Leonis. "Except right now, obviously."

"Enough," Andolin snapped. "You have been accused of destroying the oak."

The forest was still until Ayda stepped forward again and smiled widely at them. "You have been accused, and if the laws of hospitality were not also revered here, as in the Wylwoods, you would indeed be punished."

The king turned his gaze to her, and Sable expected the young elf to quail, but Ayda merely looked at him with a bright smile. "Now that we have heard what obvious displays of hospitality the elder oak offered, even you, my king, are bound to offer these guests nothing less than she did."

Silence filled the clearing as the king and Ayda faced each other.

"The laws of hospitality bind us." Andolin's voice was like a vice

472

grip around Sable again. "As you have claimed the law, it falls to you, Aydalya, to help them. These travelers are journeying through our land. You will show them the fastest paths back to their own."

A ripple went through the ring of elves, but none objected.

"With pleasure." Ayda turned her smile onto the group in the enclosure. "Let me be the first to apologize for this misunderstanding."

She stepped up and set her fingertips on the branches. A gap appeared next to her hand and spread quickly to form a doorway.

After a short hesitation, Leonis stepped through, and Sable followed. She crossed under the arch of thorns, and the morning freshened. The sunlight brightened, and the trees grew strikingly vivid. Each blade of grass stood out like tiny slashes of brilliant green. A breeze nudged past her, mossy and clean.

Leonis took a deep breath. "I love elven woods."

Sable spun slowly. Aside from Ayda, they were alone in the clearing around the thorny prison.

"Where did they go?" Thulan asked.

"Away," Ayda said absently, focusing on the thorny enclosure.

Leonis glanced around the forest. "How many trees burned?"

"We lost six. Elves aren't particularly good at controlling fire. We rarely use it, and the ones that start naturally in the forest are allowed to run their course. Burning is merely one stage in the life of the trees." Ayda frowned at the brambles. "I don't like this thing."

"Neither do I," Purnicious said.

"Looks like a troll's wart," Thulan agreed.

"Thulan," Leonis said in an irritated voice.

But Ayda let out a peal of laughter. "It does. We should do something about it. These are sweet berry brambles, wouldn't you say?"

"They do look like sweet berry bushes," Reese answered, "except too tall and the thorns are too long."

"I agree." Ayda stepped closer to the branches. "A shame to exploit the thorns in such a way. They chatter like sweet berry bushes. Not a serious thought in their branches."

She knelt and set her hands on the ground. Sable felt a rush of heat surge out of the ground, drawn from the trees at the edge of the clearing.

The branches above Ayda rustled, rearranging themselves into a round bush. In a breath, spring-green leaves unfurled on every branch, followed by a burst of tiny white flowers. The flowers faded almost before they were done blooming, and small round berries swelled in their place.

The group shifted away from the bush, their eyes wide.

"Are they ripe?" Ayda's voice came from under the bush.

The group glanced at Reese.

"Almost," he answered uncertainly.

The berries puffed a little more until they were a rich, deep purple. Ayda crawled out and looked critically at the bush. "That's better. Help yourselves to breakfast while I fix the rest of these." She headed off around the enclosure.

Sable glanced at Serene. "Is it a normal bush?"

Serene touched a branch. "Seems to be."

"Good enough for me," Terrane said. "I'm hungry." He popped a berry into his mouth. His face lit, and he reached for another.

Sable took one, and the berry burst in her mouth, bright and fresh.

When Ayda was finished, they stood next to a lush ring of sweet berry bushes. She brushed off her hands. "That's better."

"Isn't the king going to mind that you wrecked his prison cell?" Thulan asked.

"I *improved* it, but yes, he'll still mind." She shrugged before turning and beaming at the group. "A dwarf, a half-elf, a kobold, and a herd of humans. This is the most exciting day of my life!"

Leonis introduced the group to her while Ayda greeted each of them enthusiastically.

"You're not quite like the other elves, are you?" Thulan asked.

Ayda gave her a dazzling smile. "Not like the ones you saw here." She took a few steps closer to Thulan. "I have never talked to a dwarf before." She reached toward Thulan's beard, but the dwarf pulled back with such a hostile scowl, Ayda's hand stopped. "Is it rude to touch your face hair?"

"It's a beard." Thulan smoothed it. "And no one touches it."

"But I want to," Ayda said.

Thulan crossed her arms. "Too bad."

The elf crinkled her brow, and Sable thought she might lunge at Thulan's beard anyway, but instead, Ayda's mouth turned into a pout. "I didn't get to touch the beards of any of the other dwarves either. The king wouldn't even let us be seen by them."

Thulan straightened. "There are other dwarves here?"

"Well, there were."

Thulan took a step toward her. "Where? When?"

"They skirted the northern edge of the Greenwood several moons ago. I think they knew it was an elven forest. As soon as they got close to the trees who speak, they turned and went along the edge. We weren't supposed to speak to them, but I watched them. They were very easy to follow. Dwarves are noisy, and they smell like—"

"How many were there?" Thulan asked, interrupting her chatter. "What clan?"

Ayda shrugged. "There were a few. Or maybe a bunch. I didn't count. They did all have face hair like you, though."

Thulan gave her an exasperated look. "All dwarves have face hair."

"Even the children?" Leonis asked.

"Of course the children," Thulan snapped. "It's only you humans and elves who think bland, bare cheeks are endearing."

Ayda looked thoughtfully through the trees. "I don't think there were children. At least none of them were particularly small." She gave Thulan a bright smile. "They did leave this behind."

She turned and showed Thulan the back of her head. A clip was nestled into her hair, made up mostly of flowers and some intricately woven strands of greenery, but at the center was a dark piece of stamped leather.

Thulan drew in a breath. "That's Ruulun Clan's shield! What are they doing here? Where were they going?"

"Toward the mountains," Ayda answered. "That's another reason we thought you were with the earth-eaters."

Thulan turned to face the others, her face shocked. "Ruulun is High Dwarf Dirthor's clan. This means they're not all gone. They're...I have no idea what this means. Where were they coming from? Why are they going to the Scales?" She swung back to Ayda. "Do you know exactly how many there were?"

She hesitated. "Some."

"Ten?" Thulan asked, holding up all her fingers. "A hundred?" She gestured to the trees they could see around them.

"Not a hundred," Ayda said brightly. "Less than a hundred."

Thulan blinked at her. "How many campfires were there at night?" she asked with exaggerated patience.

"One," she answered emphatically.

"A small scouting party, then." The dwarf frowned. "What are they doing all the way over here?"

Ayda looked at her with wide eyes. "How would I know? I wasn't allowed to talk to them."

"Did you hear them talking?"

"Yes, but it was all so dull, I didn't pay attention."

Thulan stared at her. "How hard is it to remember what they talked about?"

"It was all homes and rocks and caves, and it was so boring I almost fell asleep. But they did *look* interesting."

"How so? Were they injured? Travel worn?"

Ayda shrugged. "I don't remember any of that. I just wanted to touch their face hair."

Thulan blinked, then looked at the others.

"Steepdale isn't too far from the northern end of the Greenwood," Reese offered. "Maybe someone there talked to the dwarves when they passed."

"Is that where you're going?" Ayda asked. "The city by the big bend in the river? With that tall, pokey wall? If we head straight through the forest, we might get there by sundown."

"Sundown?" Reese said. "How far did you bring us from the clearing last night?"

"Far. They carried you most of the night." Ayda's gaze caught on Sable, and the elf stepped up so close that Sable leaned back a little. Ayda's face was a bit longer than a human's, her skin perfectly smooth, her eyes lively and curious. "You talk like a tree," Ayda said. "Will you walk with me?"

Sable raised an eyebrow but nodded.

Ayda flashed her a glowing smile. "Excellent. Let's be off!" She slipped her arm into Sable's and started toward the trees. The gesture was so much like what Talia used to do that Sable smiled.

Serene fell in next to them, and the others followed.

Ayda looked curiously at Sable. "Where did you learn to talk like a tree?"

Sable glanced at Serene. "I don't know what that means."

"There are two types of voices that an elf can have," Ayda said. "They can speak out of their authority, like the king. His words always feel....inexorable."

"I noticed that," Sable said dryly.

"But an elf can also speak like a tree. Trees always speak utterly truthfully, and it sounds different from normal talk."

"Do they speak in words?" Sable asked.

Ayda shook her head. "No, in ideas. They enjoy how the sun feels, they're curious about the creatures around them, they think a lot about sap."

"I can see why you want to talk to them," Thulan said from behind them. "Fascinating conversationalists."

Ayda nodded seriously. "They are, and you never wonder whether a tree is misleading you. They bravely tell the truth at all times."

"A tree cannot be brave," Thulan objected. "What on earth would a tree have to be afraid of?"

"Dying in a drought," Leonis offered.

"Or groups of people setting it on fire," Ayda said.

"Or trolls uprooting it," Gwen added.

Thulan scowled at all of them. "We're all scared of dying, but fear of death isn't what makes people lie. It's fear of losing something they have or not getting what they want. Things that trees don't experience."

"Maybe," Ayda said. "But their truth still feels brave. It feels substantial."

Sable nodded. "When people speak the truth, it feels different from normal talking."

"When you told the king he didn't believe you were guilty," Ayda continued, "your words felt like a tree's. And so the elves listened." She considered Sable. "That's a rare gift among the elves. Is it rare among humans, too?"

"I think so." Sable glanced at Serene.

"I've never heard of another human who can do what Sable does," Serene said.

Ayda gave Sable an impressed look. "So you hold a position of power among your people?"

Sable laughed. "No. At this very moment, I'm an outcast. We're in your woods because the people in power are trying to kill us and we had to run."

"Why would they want to kill someone with such a gift?"

"To be fair, most of them don't know I have it. Vivaine does, and she's the person leading the hunt for us, but the people chasing us don't know anything—they're merely after a reward."

Serene nodded. "We don't tend to announce when we have gifts like this. They usually bring a lot of attention."

"But trees *can* be brave," Leonis insisted loudly from the back of the group. "Unlike a rock."

"If a tree can be brave, then a rock can be too," Thulan retorted.

"Serene," Leonis called, "explain to the dwarf the difference between a living tree and a dead rock."

Serene slowed, falling back next to the others. "He's right. There's no *vitalle* in a rock."

"Rocks are not dead!" Thulan objected.

Ayda kept her arm linked with Sable's while the discussion grew heated behind them. The elf looked up into the treetops, a crease between her brows.

"The truth is a brave, brazen thing," she mulled quietly enough that only Sable heard. "And so powerful. I can see that it would feel troubling to wield so much power."

Sable let out a little laugh. "It doesn't usually feel like wielding power. It feels like having to see too much of people."

Ayda nodded slowly. "And if you don't tell them you can do it, you can pretend you can't." The elf's words didn't sound accusing. They were quiet, almost to herself. "Because it would change things."

Ayda's last words were warmer than the rest.

Sable looked at the elf. "It would. For instance, does it make you uncomfortable that I know how deeply you meant those last words?"

The elf's brow creased again. "A little," she admitted.

"It makes me uncomfortable too," Sable said.

They walked in silence through the trees. Ayda's arm radiated warmth, not exactly like energy was coming into Sable from it, but like the elf contained more *vitalle* than Sable did.

By that point, the group behind them was firmly split into two camps: rocks can be brave and rocks can't be brave.

"What would it change," Ayda asked quietly, "if we told the world what we can do?"

Sable glanced over at the use of "we," but Ayda's face was so introspective, Sable's question died on her lips.

The elf turned serious, earnest eyes on Sable. "What are you afraid it would change?"

"What am I afraid of? I have no idea." She let her eyes wander through the tree trunks. "But I had a friend who asked that often, and she'd tell me to start talking and I might figure it out." Sable thought for a moment. "I don't know what it's like with elves, but among humans, it feels like people are always trying to control each other. So I'm afraid that if people know what I can do, they'll want to use it for themselves."

Ayda looked ahead, her face pensive.

"What are you afraid of?" Sable asked.

"That they'll think too highly of me," Ayda said softly. "No one expects me to do...anything, really. I'm the king's eldest child, and still, no one expects anything of me."

Sable turned so quickly she stumbled on a rock in her path. "The king is your father?"

Ayda gave her a small smile. "See? Even the humans are surprised." She sighed. "I'm not cut out to lead. It's honestly easier if everyone just thinks I'm completely common."

"And you're not?" Sable asked.

Ayda shook her head slowly. "I can..." She glanced at Sable. "I have a skill—actually every elf has it—but I can do it better. Faster.

Much faster." She shook her head. "It's only a trick, really. And it means nothing. But they won't see it that way. They'll see it as a sign, and then they'll expect things of me."

Sable nodded slowly. "The trees really are braver than us, aren't they? They're unapologetically themselves."

Ayda looked at her with piercing eyes. "Yes. Being a tree is brave. And simple."

Sable shifted under the intensity of the elf's look. "Maybe that's what we're giving up while we're afraid. The chance to be brave and unapologetically ourselves. Maybe what we should be asking ourselves is what are we keeping ourselves from?"

Ayda turned troubled eyes toward the vibrant green forest around them. Clouds scuttled across the sky, sending wide patches of shadows chasing each other across the forest floor. Birds chirped aimlessly to each other, and squirrels chittered from trees or fallen logs, berating the travelers for passing through.

"But if you tell," the elf said quietly, "you can never take it back."

Sable nodded.

The truth is a brave, brazen thing.

"Maybe," Sable said, "if we were braver, we'd never want to."

Ayda let out a rippling peal of laughter. "So we should be trees all the time."

Sable laughed, glancing behind them at where Thulan was still arguing with Leonis. "Or even rocks, apparently."

Ayda's nose wrinkled. "No. Not rocks."

The vivid brightness that filled the elven woods settled into normal sunshine as the afternoon progressed and they traveled closer to the edge of the forest. Ayda traipsed along with them, moving among the group, asking question after question about human life, or dwarven customs, or kobold magic. She gave Reese as detailed information as she could about the earth-eater humans along the mountains in the west. Which, since she knew no numbers, nor had a particularly good grasp of geography if it

480

wasn't related to certain ancient trees, was vague but still troubling.

"I can't believe the Kalesh are so far north," Reese said. "Or I suppose I can. Once you get north of Lord Loren's lands, the base of the mountains is so heavily forested, there are few people. The Kalesh could be there, and no one would notice."

"They cut down many, many trees," Ayda said. "They haven't come into the Greenwood, yet, but they are making a mess of the common forest near the mountains."

"If they're using that much wood, they must be making a lot of mines," Reese said. He glanced at the others. "No one in the north knows this. All of their conversations here are about what they'll do if the Kalesh ever come north. This might be the thing that will actually bring them together. Mining as far north as Ayda says means they're not only on Lord Loren's land, but also Lord Erick's and Lord Darien's. They've trespassed on every territory west of the river."

"This changes things," Serene said.

Ayda watched the conversation closely. "You humans have complicated divisions amongst yourselves."

"True." Jae looked at her curiously. "The elves I've met are all in the Nidel Woods, but none of them seemed particularly interested in human life. Are all your people this curious?"

"No." The elf smiled at him. "Just me. It's my mother's fault, you understand. When she was young, she loved to explore the forest. One night she traveled too far west and was set upon by a pack of mountain goblins. She fought off some, but there were too many. She was wounded and captured, and they took her to a dank, horrid cave. They were preparing to eat her when a human burst into their cave with a long sword. He cut down every goblin and freed my mother.

"His name was Boman, and he nursed her back to health in his cabin. While I don't believe she exactly fell in love with him, he certainly fell in love with her. She found him to be kind and generous, and his human life was so interesting, she stayed with him."

"For how long?" Jae asked.

"For the next forty years until he died."

"Your father was human?" Leonis asked in surprise.

Ayda let out a long laugh. "Do I look like my father was human? My mother and Boman had no children. After he died, she returned to the elves with more knowledge of the outside world than we'd had in many years." She grew more serious. "She married my father some years later, and until her death, she held a position of influence. She only left the forest a few times after I was born and always returned quickly. No one else ever understood her fascination with humans." She glanced around the group. "I can see a certain charm in you all, though."

"Humans are boring," Thulan said. "If you want to see something actually interesting, come see the dwarven caves. The walls glitter with gems."

"But underground you have no trees."

Thulan's brow creased. "Who needs trees when you have rocks?"

A bird cried out overhead, and Sable looked up, catching sight of a flash of light.

"Innov!" she called, running forward to a break in the trees where she could see more of the sky.

The phoenix skimmed over the treetops and dipped into the clearing. Sable held out her arm, and Innov flared her wings, landing in a blinding shower of sparks. Ayda came closer, and strands of her hair caught the phoenix's light and gleamed like burnished gold.

Sable ran the back of her fingers down Innov's chest, and a shimmering fountain of sparks erupted between her feathers. The phoenix's face was sharper, and she stood taller. Her talons wrapped around Sable's arm longer and darker than they'd been yesterday.

Warmth flowed into Sable's arm, filled with something more than just *vitalle*, and a sense of peace and hope settled over her. "I missed you," she said. "I thought you'd left for good."

Innov gazed around the forest in apparent indifference to the sentiment, but she shifted her weight and tightened her grip on Sable's arm.

"A phoenix!" Ayda breathed.

Reese walked up beside them. "She definitely needed fire."

"And sunlight," Ayda said. "They love fire and sunlight."

Sable winced. "We'd had no fires, and I'd been keeping her

covered." She stroked the side of Innov's neck, and the phoenix leaned into her fingers. "It's a wonder I didn't kill you. You should find someone who knows how to take care of you."

Ayda stepped closer to the phoenix. "She's glorious!"

Innov focused on the elf. Ayda held out her arm, and Innov considered her before hopping over to her.

Ayda gazed at the bird, her face lit with wonder. "You're so real!"

"Real?" Serene asked.

"Like the sunlight," Ayda answered, slowly lifting her hand to touch the glowing feathers. "Or like the tiny streams of life inside the trees."

"She is almost bursting with *vitalle,*" Serene agreed. "I've never seen her so bright."

"Is it hard," Ayda asked quietly, almost fearfully, "to have so much inside you?"

Innov blinked at her then launched back into the sky, soaring up into the sunlight.

Ayda drew in a breath and watched the phoenix glide away. "I've never seen anything that alive," she whispered. She turned wide eyes to Sable, then looked around the gathered group. "This is definitely the best day I've ever had."

CHAPTER SIXTY-THREE

THE LONG SHADOW of the Scale Mountains darkened the forest around them as the world settled into dusk. Sable caught a glimpse of light through the trees ahead.

Innov had returned several times during the day and now sat perched on Sable's forearm. Whether from the fact that the phoenix's extra size hadn't added much weight or the trickle of *vitalle* that continually seeped into Sable's arm, it was nearly effortless to hold her.

"So according to the *Ghost of the White Wood* book," Sable told the others, "General Bastian isn't some sort of hero. Instead, he was a captain whom Melia, the Ghost of the White Wood, bested at every turn. She gave herself up to Bastian to save a town and used the chance to get close to Prince Turrn, who was the emperor's son. Then she escaped, assassinated Prince Turrn, and managed to wheedle a promise out of Bastian to not massacre the town that was in danger. All Bastian did was get beat up and then let an entirely false report be sent to the emperor explaining the events."

"So his entire reputation is based on a lie?" Reese asked. "That feels about right for the Empire."

"What does the Empire believe about him?" Jae asked.

"That Bastian is a great hero," Reese said. "That he thwarted a plan concocted by the Ghost of the White Wood and the ruthless Prince Turrn—a plan to assassinate the prince's father, the emperor himself. Bastian was the first to discover who the Ghost was and capture her. He then ended Prince Turrn's treachery by killing him, put down the Ghost's rebellion, and ran her out of the Empire.

"Those events propelled his career forward. The emperor himself gave him some title and made him one of the youngest—and wealthiest—generals in Imperial history." Reese glanced at Serene, then Gwen, then stopped at Sable with a small smile. "Is it strange that the real story makes me like him more? I can relate to a man who was easily bested by a powerful woman."

Sable grinned. "Bastian definitely fits the real story more than the Empire's version. He never struck me as particularly bloodthirsty or ruthless."

"If he is, I'm sure he hides it well," Reese said. "Outwardly bloodthirsty men rarely make good diplomats."

"This man is high regarded among the earth-eaters?" Ayda asked curiously. "But his status is built on a lie?"

"That's more common among humans than we'd care to admit," Reese answered.

They topped a rise, and the forest ended. Below them, hundreds of lights spread out across a plain.

"That's Steepdale," Reese said, impressed. "I can't believe you brought us this far, this fast."

Ayda beamed at him. "Good luck fighting the earth-eaters. It really was terribly exciting meeting all of you."

"You could come with us," Sable said.

The elf hesitated, then shook her head. "That might be too many humans for me."

"It's probably too many humans for me," Thulan agreed.

"We owe you our lives," Leonis said to Ayda. "And I don't know how we can repay you."

Ayda grinned. "Can I touch Thulan's beard?"

"No," Thulan said.

"She deserves something," Leonis pointed out.

"Let her touch your face, then," Thulan said, irritated.

"Gladly," Leonis answered. "But I don't have a beard."

"Reese does," Thulan pointed out. "And Jae."

"Theirs are not as thick as yours," Ayda said, stepping closer.

"Mine is better," Thulan admitted.

Ayda beamed at her and plucked the top off a tall piece of grass. She reached out and ran her fingers down the side of Thulan's beard. "It feels like hair," she said, her voice slightly disappointed.

"It *is* hair." Thulan pulled away from the elf. "What did you expect it to feel like?"

Ayda shrugged. "Something different." She held up the bit of grass, and Sable felt a trickle of *vitalle* flow into it. A little white flower burst from the end. Ayda reached out and tucked it into the side of Thulan's beard before the dwarf could back away. "There! It just needed a little prettiness."

Thulan raised her hand to brush it out, but Leonis grabbed her arm. "She saved our lives," he reminded the dwarf.

Thulan glared at the half-elf but lowered her hand.

With another grin, Ayda turned to the rest of them. "If you find yourselves back in the Greenwood, tell the trees to let me know. I'd be thrilled to see any of you again." She paused. "But don't set anything else on fire." With a parting smile, she slipped back into the darkening woods, and within a breath, she was gone.

"It's creepy how they disappear like that," Thulan said.

"I like her," Leonis declared.

"Of course you do," Thulan muttered, brushing the flower out of her beard.

They moved to the edge of the trees and found themselves standing on the top of a long hill. Below them, a little off to the east, the Black River flowed by, reflecting the rich violet of the sky. Tucked against a wide bend in the river, a city was lit with torchlight and glowing windows. Outside its walls, dark fields were dotted with hundreds of fires.

"What are all the campfires?" Thulan asked. "If that's your rangers, Reese, you lied to us about the strength of your numbers."

Reese studied the lights, his expression pleased. "That's at least five times more people than Tanis has."

"Is it the Kalesh?" Gwen asked.

"No. They camp in regimented squares. These sprawl like northern troops. Steepdale is Lord Erick's home, but this is far more troops than he could rally himself. It looks more like all the soldiers who came south for the summit came back here." He frowned. "No, not all of them. If Perric and Runess were here, there'd be twice this many."

"Then it's the three lords west of the river?" Sable asked.

Reese nodded. "That would be my guess."

"Well, let's hope Vivaine didn't turn them against you two," Thulan said. "Because Sable's pet is glowing like a beacon."

Reese glanced over at her. "I don't suppose you could cover her up?"

"I think that time is past," Sable said. "Maybe she'll just be mistaken for a torch?"

"I'll go down first, boss," Terrane said, "and signal if it's safe."

At Reese's nod, Terrane moved quickly down the hill.

"This could take some time," Reese said.

Most of the party settled down back a bit from the edge of the trees. Sable sat with Innov behind a wide tree trunk while Reese moved partway down the hill after Terrane.

The world had darkened to night before he returned. "Terrane signaled it's friendly," Reese said. "Let's go."

Sable started down the long hill with the others, Innov conspicuously bright on her arm. The noise of the camp grew louder as they approached.

"A whole city that recognizes the Kalesh are a problem..." Sable said to Reese. "It's going to be refreshing to be in a place that doesn't adore the enemy."

A torch waved back and forth a little to their left, and then blinked.

"That's Terrane." Reese adjusted his course.

The big man waited for them at the edge of the camp, smiling broadly. "No need to worry about our reception here. I've found a friend of yours." He stepped to the side, and Innov's light fell on a man with wavy, white hair.

Sable drew back.

"Hello, Sable," Atticus said. He smiled, but it was colored with what looked like regret, or at least resignation.

"I take it back," Sable said. "This place is already tainted."

Reese crossed his arms. "Get out of the way, old man. Terrane, have you found where Tanis is yet?"

"Reese," Atticus greeted him. "It does me good to see the two of you together again."

Reese took a step forward. Atticus wasn't a short man, but he looked old and breakable next to Andreese. "Terrane." Reese's voice was low and angry. "Let's go."

"Ah, I..." Terrane shifted, looking between Atticus and Reese and Sable. "He's the one who knows where Tanis is."

A wide, genuine smile spread across Atticus's face. He leaned around Reese. "Do you see, Serene? I told you. It was no accident finding Sable last year, and Reese—he's part of it. You can tell. It's like she needed a guardian, and one came for her. Almost back from the dead! And now she has a phoenix. An *actual phoenix*." He shook his head, his eyes almost wild with enthusiasm. "This is gold. Gold!"

"It's a coincidence, Atticus," Serene said.

"You always do read too much story into things," Leonis agreed.

"Are we going to stand here all night?" Thulan asked. "Or is there food somewhere?"

"You'd better start explaining yourself to Sable, Atticus," Jae said, "before her guardian makes you understand exactly how angry she is at you."

"I don't need Reese to do that." Sable stepped between Andreese and Atticus. Innov shifted, sending out a burst of embers.

Atticus twitched back, then watched in awe as the sparks disappeared. "Of course you're angry," Atticus said to her, his eyes fixed on the phoenix. "How could you be anything else? But it was necessary." He met Sable's eyes. "I had truly hoped it wouldn't be. But even old men are entitled to foolish hopes sometimes, don't you think?" There was something fragile in the question. Something cracked and almost broken.

Sable ignored it and stepped past him, starting into the camp. "I think you sound like you've lost your wits. We'll find someone else to take us to Tanis."

Reese fell in behind her. She'd passed only a single tent before she came across two men staring at her and Innov, dumbstruck. Sable gave them a tight smile. "Which direction to Tanis's troops? The rangers who've been in the south for the last little while?"

One man opened his mouth, but no words came out. The other pointed mutely deeper into the tents, but neither took their eyes off her.

"Thank you," Sable said.

Reese put a hand on her back. "Let's keep moving."

"I know you don't want to talk to me," Atticus said, hurrying to catch up with them, "but I need to talk to you. So I will take you to Tanis, save you from having to try to get answers from your admirers, and explain myself. If, when we reach the rangers, you are still angry with me, I will leave you alone."

Sable stopped and spun to look at him. "I'm not one of your audiences, Atticus. I know your tricks. You can't spin this in a way that I'll forgive you. I trusted you, and you sold me out to Vivaine because you were blind to what she was really like." She stepped closer to the old man, all her fury at him coming to the surface. "You trapped me under her for a year!"

"I wasn't blind," he said quietly, his words warm. "At least not by the end." He glanced at the growing number of people watching them. "Can we walk. Please? You're drawing a crowd, and we don't really want to be bogged down here. Tanis's tent is all the way in the center of camp."

Sable glared at him. "Lead us straight to Tanis. No side trips."

Atticus nodded and gestured her forward again, falling in beside her. Reese stayed close behind.

"I went to see Vivaine," Atticus said, "not long after we reached the city. I'd been reporting to her for…" He sighed. "My whole life. And you're right, I was blind. When we talked, she showed herself as the same woman I'd known long ago. The one who was a bit lonely and struggling against things she couldn't quite control."

He let out a harsh, humorless laugh. "I'd grown so used to

expecting people to tell me the truth, I honestly didn't expect she'd be any different."

He turned into a different path between tents, heading away from the river. Everyone they passed stopped to stare at Innov, nudging their companions, pulling others out of tents to see.

The phoenix took no note of the attention, but she did twitch her head sharply to stare at any campfire they passed.

"I wanted to tell Vivaine that we'd found the Kalesh razing towns on the Eastern Reaches," Atticus continued, "but she was always with Ambassador Tehl. And while she managed to keep up her lies, he could not. From the things he let slip, I realized that Vivaine knew about the Kalesh in the east. That she knew more than we did and that she was…" He stopped and shook his head. "I admit to feeling jealous of Tehl. He had taken the position I'd always wanted."

Every word he'd said had been true, and Sable found herself almost feeling bad for the man. "So you decided to betray the people who trusted you?" she asked. "In some sort of attempt to win her back?"

"My foolishness doesn't extend that far. When Tehl began to tell me too much, she sent him away, but by then the cracks in her lies had widened, and for the first time, I saw who she really was. She was cunning, manipulative, and, worst of all, desperate."

He glanced at Sable. "She was deeply entangled with the Kalesh, and if our play didn't change the popular opinion, she would side with the Empire, and we'd be branded traitors for daring to question her allies." He looked back at Andreese. "I helped Reese plan the assassination, if it was necessary, in a way that wouldn't implicate you, Sable. But Vivaine was under so much strain and so deeply connected, I was afraid she'd do something drastic. Reese understood that if he were caught, she'd kill him."

Atticus set his hand on Sable's arm and stopped her. "But if she caught you too…I had to make you valuable, do you understand? I had to give her a reason to keep you alive when all she would want to do was kill you."

The warmth of his words filled the air. Sable shook her head, but she couldn't deny the truth of it. The old, hard anger she felt for him crumbled into something raw and wounded.

Next to her, Reese stood with his arms crossed, weighing the man's words.

Atticus held Sable's gaze, his expression pained. "I betrayed your trust," he said, his voice heavy, "because I didn't know anything else that would save you."

"Never again, old man," Sable said, funneling the tangle of emotions into her words. The space between them thrummed with energy. "You don't play with my life. If something concerns me, you tell me, and *I* decide what happens. Not you. No more secrets, no more manipulating the people around you to get the ending you want."

Atticus shifted uncomfortably, glancing around. Movement behind him caught Sable's eye. A crowd of soldiers was watching her, murmuring to each other. She turned slowly to find more men behind her and a trail of them filling the path behind them, cutting off her, Atticus, and Reese from the others.

Reese turned to look warily at the soldiers, but they didn't seem hostile. They looked fascinated.

The brightness of the phoenix on Sable's arm was suddenly terribly conspicuous. "We shouldn't have brought Innov."

"It's not Innov," Atticus said. "Or rather, it's only partly Innov."

Sable's eyes met the eyes of a soldier in the crowd.

His face lit. "Issable!"

The word rippled through the crowd, the sense of anticipation growing.

"It's Andreese and Issable!" someone called from the back.

"Let's keep moving," Reese said, setting his hand on Sable's back.

They started forward, and the crowd in front of them parted.

"Issable," one older man said with slight bow of his head.

She gave him a stiff smile as she passed.

"Andreese," he said warmly.

Andreese nodded and moved to the side so Sable was between him and Atticus as they moved through the crowd.

"Atticus," Sable said slowly, "this looks an awful lot like an audience you've prepped for a show. Is there a secret you'd like to share right now?"

The old man grinned broadly. "I've been telling people about your defiance of Vivaine at the summit."

Sable frowned. "What did you tell them?"

"Nothing but the truth. How could I possibly have improved on you, standing on that outcropping of rock, casting your voice out stronger and clearer than Vivaine's, accusing her of exactly what she was guilty of?" He let out a laugh. "And the phoenix! You took the phoenix from her, and it flew around you like some blazing sign from the heavens!"

The crowd didn't follow them, but as they moved forward, new faces appeared, lining their path.

"This is the first time I've ever felt I couldn't quite do a story justice. But yes, I've told it every day, many times a day, all over this camp and all over the city. They already knew of the play last year, of your speech against the Kalesh, and of the assassination. The two of you were already almost legends. What they desperately need—what we all desperately need right now—is hope. Which you're giving them."

"We've spent the last few days running for our lives after watching a friend be burned alive by Vivaine," Reese said. "How is that hope?"

"Twice now, you two have defied her and the Kalesh." Atticus turned them down a wider street between the tents. "You're still alive, and not only that, you're growing stronger. Last year, you two tried to change the world from a tiny stage in the Sanctuary, with Reese hiding in the shadows. This year, you two stood on a mountainside and demanded the world hear you."

"All I did," Sable pointed out, "all I *wanted* to do, was yell at Vivaine and make her stop. Which I failed to do."

He grinned again. "But no one yells at the High Prioress. You were like some mythological queen with her warrior guardian, declaring the very cliffs your stage, the mountains your backdrop, and living fire your crown." He gestured to the people around them. "And the story has spread faster than fire. It's only been a few days, Sable. I'm obviously not the only one talking about it."

News of their presence raced ahead of them, keeping the way lined with soldiers calling out their names. Atticus led them into a space that was something like a city square, except surrounded by large tents. The throng of soldiers along the edges grew thicker.

"This is the center of camp," Atticus said. "The generals of each army have headquarters here, and their troops branch off in different direction. Tanis's tent is on the other side."

In the center of the square, a bright bonfire lit the faces watching them, and a cheer went up as Sable and Innov stepped into the light.

Innov thrust herself off Sable's arm in a blaze of flames and sparks and dove straight at the bonfire. She hit the flames, and a burst of light shot out across the square.

The soldiers let out a thunderous roar, and Innov soared up into the sky, trailing a stream of glittering embers.

As Innov rose, Sable's heart lifted with her. A fierce, brilliant wave of hope and wonder poured off the phoenix, washing across Sable like a flood, like a purifying flame, burning away her weariness and heartache.

Reese's gaze locked on the bird, and he held his breath as she rose higher.

The soldiers let out a renewed cry. Atticus clapped his hands and broke into a whooping shout. He reached out like he was going to wrap his arm around Sable's shoulders but stopped, his face full of affection and a fierce sort of pride. "Thank you," he said fervently, even as he dropped his hands. "Thank you for coming to us. We've needed hope so very, very deeply."

Amidst the resounding cheers, Sable met the old man's gaze. The familiarity of his expression broke through the last of the bitterness she held against him, and the truth in his words wore it away, leaving only the dull ache of loneliness she'd suffered over the past year.

"I don't expect you to forgive me," he said, and she felt the warmth of that truth, "but I have regretted every day what I sentenced you to."

Tears pricked Sable's eyes, and her throat tightened, but she had no words for him. The pain of the last year tangled with the deep fondness she had for the playwright. The last of her anger crumbled, and she stepped forward, wrapping her arms around him. He enveloped her in a hug, squeezing her tightly.

"I'm so sorry, my girl." His voice broke over the words. "I'm so sorry I couldn't have found a better way."

She buried her face in his shoulder while she took some bracing breaths, then pulled back. "I missed you, Atticus. In a very angry way, but I missed you."

Reese came up next to her, offering the man a slight nod.

Atticus let out a breath and gave Sable a shaky smile. "I've missed you, too. The whole world's missed you."

Sable shook her head. "Don't get your hopes up too high. We haven't actually accomplished anything yet."

His smile grew stronger, and he set one hand on her shoulder and one on Reese's. "We will, though. We will."

He shifted both hands to Sable's shoulders, his face filled with more conviction and passion than she'd ever seen. "I know you don't see it yet, but you are the one who will give us the strength to do what we must. Every day I grow more sure of it."

The heat from his words wrapped around them until Sable could feel Atticus and Reese standing like their own bonfires. Behind her and all around the square, people blazed into vibrant pillars of heat.

Atticus's grip tightened on her shoulders. "I swear to you Sable, from this moment on, any skill I have, any connections I have, any influence I have are yours."

CHAPTER SIXTY-FOUR

SABLE HELD Atticus's gaze as the warmth of his words lingered. Innov soared overhead like a fragment of the bonfire broken free of the rest. Hope and a deep feeling of inadequacy tangled inside her, leaving her speechless.

Atticus looked fondly at her. "That was the moment you should have made a gracious speech of acceptance, but you'll get better at it as more people start pledging themselves to you."

Sable laughed and shook her head. "You're the only person crazy enough to pledge me anything, Atticus. And we'll see if your sentiment lasts past the next time we disagree."

He stepped back and shook his head, smiling. "That was the exact wrong kind of speech."

Serene pushed through the crowd. "I see you two talked things out."

Atticus stepped forward and hugged her. "It's good to see you all!"

Serene grimaced. "Stop being so exuberant," she said, patting his back.

He let go of Serene and slapped Jae on the back. "All of us together again! With new people!" He waved at Terrane and Gwen, who looked at him like he was a mad.

"What's gotten into you, Atticus?" Thulan asked.

"This is a very good day, my friend," Atticus said, dropping a hand on Thulan's shoulder.

"It would be better if we had dinner," the dwarf pointed out.

"Yes! Dinner! Come this way." Atticus started toward the bonfire.

Tanis came through the crowd of soldiers on the far side of the square. "That was a dramatic entrance," he called. "You're usually a bit more subdued than this, Reese." He skirted the bonfire, watching Innov dive back in. She landed on the top of the pile of wood and spread her wings, letting the flames wash over her.

"They're all actors," Reese answered, clasping Tanis's hand. "Even the bird, apparently. It's nearly impossible to get them to do anything subtle."

Tanis laughed, but his gaze strayed to several large tents on the side of the square. "Before any of the three lords show up and try to make your arrival into a political maneuver, let's get you inside." He turned, ushering them toward his tent.

"And your invitation to us isn't at all political?" Sable asked over the crowd.

Tanis gave her a conspiratorial smile over his shoulder. "I'm merely welcoming back old friends. If they choose to see it as a political maneuver, I can hardly control that."

Sable sighed. "I thought maybe we'd have a break from such things."

Tanis shrugged. "You're the ones who made the grand entrance."

At the tent door, Sable looked back an Innov. The phoenix circled up and dove back into the flames. A cheer went up from the growing number of faces lining the square. Sable ducked inside.

Tanis's tent was still the same as it had been in the rebel camp. Large and square, the center of the floor covered in papers. Around the edges, though, benches and chairs had been added.

Tanis drew Reese to the side of the door while the others filed in. "I'm sorry about Tylar," Tanis said, setting his hand on Reese's shoulder. "The entire north is furious." He shook his head. "It took something this horrific and inexcusable before they actually started to pay attention."

"I should have had him come off the island with us," Reese said. "We could have cut the rope from our side and—"

"His death is on Vivaine's head." Tanis's voice was quiet but firm. "Not yours. We all have enough things to feel rightfully guilty for without taking on guilt that belongs on someone else."

Reese shook his head. "I can't stop thinking that there's something else I should have done."

"It wasn't your fault." Tanis squeezed Reese's shoulder. "But it'll be a while until you believe it."

Tanis stepped to the door and spoke with someone outside, then turned to Sable's group, who had filed into his tent. "Dinner is on its way, and sleeping arrangements are being made. Please take a seat."

Reese sat at the end of the bench closest to Tanis, and Sable sat next to him, glad to be out of the crowds and the attention.

Aside from Tanis, only Atticus remained standing. The old playwright stood on the far side of the tent, stroking his fingers through his beard and scanning the group, the same sharp look in his eye that he always had before a performance.

"Welcome to Steepdale," Tanis said to the entire group, "where currently the delegations and troops of three of the Northern Lords are camped. In terms of northern history, they're being remarkably peaceful. But tensions are growing.

"The command tents of all three lords are all right here. The camp is like a giant pie with the square in the center, and each lord's troops are spread out in their own wedge. My people are by far the smallest group.

"When the summit fell apart after the execution, every lord came north. The three western lords, Loren, Erick, and Darien, all came here. Lord Perric and Lord Runess crossed to the eastern side of the river, and my scouts tell me they both went to Perric's capital, Stormfeld."

He sighed. "I thought Vivaine's actions might unite the north, but unity needs a leader. Darien has the largest territory and the most experience and is probably the best suited to lead, but he's not exactly making that prospect appealing, and neither Loren nor Erick are willing to submit to him. Any discussions that look promising are derailed because none of them are willing to give up any of their autonomy."

"It's easy for you to judge us," a voice said from behind Tanis. "You have nothing to give up."

Tanis gave a half smile and stepped to the side. "It took you longer to get here than I'd expected, Darien. I'd almost run out of speech."

Lord Darien stepped into the tent, followed by the tall, thin Lord Erick.

The smaller Lord Loren stepped to where Reese sat and held out his hand. "Good to see you again." They shook while Loren gave Sable a nod. "And you, Issable. It seems you cause a stir wherever you appear."

"Just Sable, please," she said.

Lord Darien stepped around Loren and crossed his arms, standing close enough to Sable that she had to tilt her head up to look at him. "Did you kill the prioress?"

The tent fell quiet, and Reese tensed, but Sable lifted her chin to meet Darien's gaze. He was standing too close, as though trying to back her against the tent wall.

She stayed sitting exactly where she was. "No," she said bluntly.

He studied her, his look verging on skeptical. "You were with her, though, when she was killed."

"Andreese and I were talking with her, eating scarletberries, when someone threw a burning bottle through the window onto the prioress."

"Some mystery person?" The lord's stance was wide and set, as though his feet were rooted to the ground directly in front of hers. As though she had somehow invaded his personal domain.

Next to her, Reese's hands curled into fists, but he didn't interrupt.

Sable kept the irritation out of her voice. "A dwarf, apparently," she answered, still meeting his gaze.

"Like your dwarf friend over there?" Darien jutted a thumb at Thulan.

"Well," Sable said slowly, letting the annoyance bleed into her tone this time, "Thulan *is* a dwarf, but not *the* dwarf who set the fire."

"But she is gonna snap someday," Leonis said quietly from across the room. Thulan jabbed him in the ribs with her elbow, and he grunted. Sable didn't try to hide her amusement.

Lord Darien gave a scornful snort. "It's going to take more than merely your word that you aren't a murderer. I think you wanted to usurp Narine's position in the summit."

The last words were a cold lie. "If that had been my plan," Sable pointed out, "it certainly wouldn't have worked well after she died."

Lord Darien's lip curled. "You cannot hide what you are."

The words were too much like Sable's conversation with Ayda. *Maybe that's what we're giving up while we're afraid. The chance to be brave and unapologetically ourselves.*

Sable let out a laugh. "You think claiming that I didn't kill Narine is hiding what I am?"

"Your hostility toward the other two prioresses was blatant," he continued, looking down at her and ignoring her words. "It makes sense you would feel the same about Narine."

Sable pushed herself off the bench and stood.

Darien was so close her face ended up only inches below his, but he didn't back away. He let out a derisive breath that washed across her face.

Sable set her hand on his chest. "If I'd wanted to kill Narine," she said, "I wouldn't have needed fire. She was frail and weak, and I was with her every moment of every day." Slowly, she pulled just a trickle of warm *vitalle* out of Lord Darien's chest.

The man drew in a sharp breath and pulled back, but she stepped forward, not drawing any more heat but keeping her hand pressed against him.

"Vivaine and Eugessa are heartless, power-hungry predators," she continued, "and they are nothing like Narine. If you can't tell the difference, you're a fool, and your people should be pitied for being led by such a blind man."

His nostrils flared, and the muscles in his jaw tightened as heat traveled up his neck. Sable looked straight into his face, letting silence envelope the tent.

Over Lord Darien's shoulder, Serene watched her with raised

eyebrows. Next to her, Atticus rubbed his hand over his mouth to hide a smile.

"Lucky for your people," Lord Loren said brightly, clapping Darien on the shoulder, "you *can* tell the difference, and you don't trust Vivaine as far as you could throw her sparkly dragon."

Sable patted Lord Darien's chest and, with one more smile, sat down. A few quiet laughs sounded in the tent, and the tension unraveled a little.

"Stop harassing Sable," Loren continued, "and move out of the way so we can sit."

Lord Darien took a step back but held Sable's gaze with a cold look before turning and sitting on an empty bench along the side of the tent. Loren gave her an amused glance as he joined Darien.

Lord Erick remained standing next to Tanis. "It's reasonable for us to have questions, though," he said to Sable. "We know little about you beyond that you served the priories for a long time."

"Longer than I would have liked," Sable agreed.

"And you brought the High Prioress's own personal sorceress here with you," he added.

"Gwen?" Sable glanced over at the Mira, who sat stiffly on a bench across the tent. "Yes, she used to work for Vivaine. And she has more reason to distrust the prioress than any of you do."

"So you say," Lord Darien said, his voice scornful.

Sable didn't turn to look at him, but she infused her next words with a rush of hot, fervent truth. "So I say."

Reactions to the words rippled across the room. Slight nods from Serene and Jae. Lord Darien bristled. Across the tent, Atticus didn't bother to hide his grin.

"That means nothing," Lord Darien said bluntly.

Ayda's words echoed in Sable's mind.

The truth is a brave, brazen thing.

"It does mean something," Sable said, turning to him, "because I can feel when someone is speaking the truth."

He gave her a condescending look. "Why would I believe that?"

"Because I know that you've only lied about one thing since

entering this tent. That you believe I wanted to usurp Narine's position in the council."

Lord Darien's eyes narrowed.

"I'd imagine you're bright enough to know Vivaine was behind that, not me." Sable turned back to Lord Erick. "Both Gwen and I left the priories. Vivaine and Eugessa refuse to see the danger of the Kalesh threat. We came to find people who were willing to unite."

No one answered, and Sable turned to take in all three lords. "Did you know the Kalesh are surveying the Scale Mountains, even as far north as this? That they are searching for gold in the mountains you control?"

Erick's eyebrows rose, but it was Darien who spoke. "How do you know that?"

"The elves in the Greenwood," Sable said. "They've seen the Kalesh logging the edge of the forest, presumably for their mines."

"Why would we trust the elves?" Lord Darien asked disdainfully.

"They have no reason to lie," Erick said, frowning. "The Greenwood lies almost entirely in my territory. While we have few dealings with the elves, I've never heard of them purposefully misleading us. If the Kalesh are in the mountains west of the Greenwood, they're deep into my lands."

"I believe it," Lord Loren said. "My people keep bringing reports of foreigners in the mountains all along my territory. They're trying to be secretive, but they're there."

"Then what are you waiting for?" Sable asked. "The Kalesh are already impinging on your lands. This is not a future threat—they are here now." She crossed her arms. "I thought you were gathered here at Steepdale to unite."

"They're too busy bickering about who gets to lead the unified land," Atticus said. The attention of the room swung to where he leaned against a thick tent post along the wall. "None of them are willing to give up any part of their own power, even if it means risking it all."

There was a brightness in the playwright's eyes that Sable recognized. The old man was enjoying himself. He kept his eyes on Sable, as though waiting for something.

"Then don't give up your lands," she said, exasperated, turning back to the lords. "You need to unite your forces. That's it. You need to take the squabbling armies you've kept to yourselves forever and bind them into one powerful force that can push back the Kalesh. Because if you don't, the Kalesh will come, and they will take the land for themselves and unite it under the Dragon Emperor."

"You're wasting your time, Sable," Atticus said. "They'll never give their troops to another lord. Every step of this process has been cut off at the knees because these men don't trust each other."

Sable took in the three lords. "Don't unite the troops under one of you, then. Choose someone outside. Someone impartial who won't favor some troops over others or use the army for political gain."

The three lords regarded her with narrowed eyes, but they didn't object. From across the tent, Atticus watched with barely controlled delight.

Sable glanced between the three lords. "Someone with experience fighting the Kalesh already?" she prompted.

Erick turned to look at the man standing next to him. "Tanis?"

"Of course, Tanis!" Sable gestured around the tent. "Who else do you know who's been studying Kalesh movements and successfully keeping them from their goals?"

Tanis watched Sable with an unreadable expression, but Reese was nodding next to her.

"Tanis isn't a lord," Darien said, crossing his arms.

"Being a lord is hardly a requisite for being an effective general," Atticus pointed out.

Reese nodded. "You could unite your troops under Tanis until the Kalesh are dealt with. Then the soldiers will return to their own lands, and you can go back to your old squabbles. But at least you'll still have the freedom to bicker over pig herds."

"Says the man who would end up second-in-command," Lord Darien said.

"Andreese spent years studying war in the Kalesh Empire," Loren answered. "He knows more about the empire than any man here. Of course he should help lead."

Lord Darien swung his attention to Reese. "Is that rumor true?"

"My uncle sent me to be trained in a Kalesh school," Reese said. "I lived in the empire for five years."

"Conveniently, your uncle serves Lord Runess and isn't here to verify that story," Darien said.

"*Sasu lipnutu ziata hoc lodust klesanet*," Reese said.

Serene tilted her head, then let out a laugh.

"What was that?" Darien demanded.

"It's a Kalesh phrase," Serene said. "*Only a fool clings to gold while the ship is sinking.*"

"It's what the Kalesh say," Reese said, "about their enemies who are too focused on their own small possessions to even give the empire a fight."

Lord Darien looked unimpressed.

But next to him, Lord Loren nodded. "I trust Tanis, and I trust Andreese. The rangers have been protecting the southern edge of my land for months, and they've never overstepped. I haven't heard a single complaint about them even taking over a farmhouse for their own use." He stood up. "I'll gladly give you my troops, Tanis, if you'll drive the Empire off my land."

Lord Darien shook his head. "You're handing him too much power."

Lord Erick looked from Reese to Tanis. "I've known you for many years, Tanis, and you've never given me a reason not to trust you. If the Kalesh are already moving north in the mountains, we need to push back before they're entrenched. We'll need Perric's and Runess's forces from the eastern territories too, but pulling together the troops we have here is a start. You have my men."

Everyone turned to Lord Darien, who studied Erick and Tanis with crossed arms.

"Your men would make up almost half the force," Tanis said to him. "And they're well-trained, good men. If we are to have a chance, we'd need your army."

Darien didn't answer.

"Are you worried," Sable asked, "that if you aren't looming directly over them in a menacing pose, they won't remain loyal to you?"

Darien gave her a dangerous look, but past him, Sable saw Atticus grin again.

"My men are loyal," Darien answered. "On the condition that we draw up a list of Tanis's exact responsibilities and the limits of his command, my men will join."

Erick nodded and turned to Tanis. "We'll meet tomorrow to pin down the details, but congratulations. Looks like you're the general of the Northern Army."

"A small army that would need the two largest forces in the north to actually be a respectable size," Darien pointed out. "But Perric and Runess have shown no inclination to fight the Kalesh."

"Maybe they will after this." Atticus ran his fingers through his beard. "You've just created an army bigger than Runess has, and one even Perric will take note of."

"More impressive than that," Sable said, "you just managed to have a council that was actually productive."

Atticus laughed. "A true day of firsts."

CHAPTER SIXTY-FIVE

FIRE AND ASH swirled around Sable, snaking back into the root cellar where she crouched. The harsh cry of ravens filled the air. Outside, the Kalesh man raised his sword, and Sable tried to scramble out and protect her mother—but it wasn't her mother. It was Narine's brittle body curled up on the ground, surrounded by flames and whirling ravens.

Derchtu perrot! The Kalesh soldier's sword came sweeping down through the air.

Sable jerked awake and gasped for breath in the cool darkness of the tent. She pressed her hands to her face, as though she could push away the familiar, brutal dream. But even in the stillness of the morning, she could still almost see the flames, still hear the razor-edged call of the ravens. They always showed up early in dreams, their black feathers whipping the fire into a frenzy instead of descending after the destruction to pick at the bones.

Nestled next to Sable on the cot, Innov stirred, casting a ruddy light over the three other beds. Serene and Jae slept against the far wall, and Gwen was curled up on a cot near Sable's feet.

Sable sat up. She put her feet on the rough canvas floor and scooped Innov up onto her lap.

The phoenix had grown in the bonfire last night. She was larger and brighter, her feathers shimmering with an iridescent, reddish sheen. Sable ran her fingers along Innov's back, and stunning orange flames flared out from between her feathers. Sable pulled the phoenix close, drawing in her warmth, driving back the nightmare of ravens.

A question Sable had pushed away since last summer rose to the surface again.

She glanced over, but Serene was still curled up next to Jae sleeping. There was one other person who'd know.

A sliver of leaden sky peeked through a slit in the tent door. "Let's go find Reese," she whispered to Innov, setting the bird to the side and pulling on her boots. "I have a question for him." Sable stood, and Innov hopped onto her outstretched arm.

Outside, mist wove through the nearest dark green ranger tents, fading the ones behind them to ghostly shadows and obscuring everything beyond that. Sable stepped onto the packed dirt road and started back toward the square. Innov lit the tiny droplets of mist around them, casting an orb of reddish light.

Camp was just stirring, and every ranger Sable passed paused to watch Innov. Sable returned the greetings of the few who spoke to her and lengthened her stride until she reached Tanis's command tent.

She stepped inside to find it lit with a handful of lanterns.

Tanis and Reese looked up from where they sat on the floor with three other men. A handful of papers and maps were laid out in front of them.

"Good morning, Sable," Tanis said, motioning her in.

"Good morning," she answered.

The five men all stared unabashedly at Innov, and Sable gave an uncomfortable smile. "I didn't mean to interrupt. I had a question for Reese, but it's not urgent."

A boy slipped past Sable into the tent and handed Tanis a piece of paper. Tanis read it and nodded.

"Loren expects more troops in four days," he said to Reese, "and Darien thinks his first reinforcements will arrive in five. Go get a sense of the troops. Let's see if it's possible to keep our newly unified army from fighting each other."

Reese nodded and stood, stepping around the papers and coming over to Sable. "Good morning." He held the tent flap open for her to step outside, giving her a tired smile.

"Did you sleep at all?" she asked.

He let the flap fall closed behind them. "Tanis was up all night, but I escaped for a few hours. He's had aids from the different lords bringing him information nonstop."

"The man's a fancy general now," Sable said. "Maybe he should get a table so he doesn't have to keep all his important papers on the floor."

"That is an excellent idea."

The young soldier came out of the tent behind them, and Reese stopped him. "Go tell Lord Erick that General Tanis needs a table. A big one. Have it brought here."

The soldier thumped his fist to his chest in a salute and headed off.

Reese turned to Sable, looking indecisive for a moment. Then he shrugged. "Want to walk with me? I need to survey all three armies and report back to Tanis before I get to sleep."

"Lead the way." Sable gestured across the square with the arm Innov was perched on, and a cascade of embers showered off the phoenix.

Reese looked appraisingly at Innov. "So...avoiding fires looks like it was a bad move."

Sable gave a pained laugh. "I know. Poor Innov. Of course, could you imagine trying to hide her if she was this bright? All last night our tent looked like we had a campfire inside it."

He started across the square, skirting the pile of blackened wood still letting off wisps of smoke from last night's bonfire. They walked past the command tents of the Northern Lords and joined a path flanked with rows of tents disappearing into the mist.

Sable's feet crunched through the dead, trampled grass. A few soldiers sat around campfires near the path. Unlike the relaxed clothing of the rangers, these men wore uniforms. On her arm, Innov glowed like a lantern, casting a homey light on the tidy ranks of sand-colored tents and catching every eye they passed.

Sable caught whispers of "Issable!" and "Andreese!"

Reese walked calmly enough beside her, but his hand rested on his hilt and his eyes kept scanning the men around them. When they met his gaze, he gave them a nod, and most of them nodded back. A few put their fists to their chests in a salute.

Sable smiled at the soldiers who met her eye, surprised, somehow, that these troops from the north that she'd heard about for ages seemed so much like the people farther south.

"I'm astonished the lords agreed to unify last night," she said. "Darien especially."

"I'm not," Reese said. "Atticus isn't either. You should have seen him this morning. He came by Tanis's tent long before dawn, almost gleeful. Said this was the turning point. Told me to let as many soldiers see you as possible."

Sable frowned and stopped. "Is that what we're doing right now?"

"Only incidentally," he answered, turning to face her. "I need to get a feel for the troops this morning, and I was planning to go alone. Regardless of what Atticus wants, I don't know what most of these soldiers think of you, and parading you around with a beacon on your arm isn't the safest way to find out."

She tilted her head. "Then why did you invite me? You don't usually mind telling me to stay out of trouble."

A smile curled up the edge of his mouth. "I decided I'd rather have you get into trouble close to me than far away." He gestured down the path. "May we continue? I want to start by talking with Loren's archery unit since I know some of them already."

She nodded, and they started again.

"In Tanis's tent, you said you had a question for me," he said.

Her smile faded. "Ever since my parents were killed, I have recurring nightmares about fire and the Kalesh." She shifted Innov to her other arm. "That night, the Kalesh man spoke to them, and I was wondering if you could tell me what he said."

He winced. "Of course, you'd remember his words."

"I remember everything about that night." Sable ran the back of her fingers down Innov's chest. "I was hiding in the root cellar when the soldiers came into the yard. One was obviously a commander. He came up to my parents and said something like *'Der choo perrit.'*"

Reese's brow creased. *"Derchtu perrot* means *you're hard to find."*

Sable's hand stilled. "I was afraid it was something like that. He seemed to know them. Or to have been looking for them. After that, he said, *'Draconet rachet yolwall.'"*

"Draconek retchhet yoltwelz," Reese nodded. *"The empire reaches everywhere.* It's a greeting of sorts. Or a battle cry. *Draconek* is what they call the Empire, and the emperor."

Innov felt warm against her fingers. Sable drew in the threads of heat. "My father said they didn't control as much as they thought. The commander stopped speaking Kalesh and said they controlled enough. He told my father to surrender." Her hand trembled against Innov's feathers. "My father refused, and they killed him and then stabbed my mother in the stomach."

Reese stopped and faced Sable. He reached out and took her shaking hand.

She turned toward him but kept her eyes fixed on Innov. "I was fifteen, and until that day, I had no idea that these foreigners existed, never mind that my parents spoke their language and were wanted enough for someone to come to a small town on the Eastern Reaches to find them." She lifted her eyes to his face. "Why would the Empire go to that much trouble?"

Reese tightened his grip on her hand but shook his head. "I don't know."

Sable's next question, the real question that had been bothering her for ages, rose to the surface.

"What if I'm Kalesh?" she asked quietly.

He held her gaze. "Then you're one of millions whose ancestors the Empire has absorbed. Their war machine is ruthless and insatiable, but the average people there are just like people everywhere. Some kind, some greedy." He considered her, his brow creasing. "The Empire chased your parents all the way to the Reaches. Whatever they did to deserve that..." He shook his head slowly. "It must have been huge and disruptive."

Innov shifted and flapped her wings, and Reese released Sable's hand. Sable stroked down the phoenix's chest to calm her.

Huge and disruptive.

She saw her mother defiant again, standing in front of the soldiers, refusing to surrender. A fierce pride kindled deep inside Sable at whatever mysterious thing her parents had done.

She looked up at Reese. "Maybe someday we'll make the Empire that angry."

He gave her a smile. "That is the goal."

They were starting forward again when raised voices rang out ahead in the fog. A half-dozen soldiers emerged from the mist, shouting about bread.

Reese strode into the middle of the argument, holding up his arms between soldiers wearing two different uniforms, one blue, the other grey.

"What's this about?" Reese demanded.

"The farmers stole our bread," one of the blue soldiers said. "Nicked it right out of our camp."

"Why would we want bread from a bunch of city boys?" a grey-garbed soldier answered.

Sable stepped up next to Reese, and the men fell silent, every eye focused on her and Innov.

"You're Issable and Andreese," one said slowly.

Sable wrinkled her nose. "Issable is so formal. It's just Sable."

"I saw you call out that dragon priestess when she killed the northman," another said. A few heads nodded.

"I don't like that woman," a blue-uniformed man said darkly.

"Neither do I." Sable looked at the gathered soldiers. "Let me guess, you gentlemen in grey are Lord Loren's troops, and blue is Lord Darien's?"

When no one objected, she turned to study the men from Loren's smaller, more rural territory. They straightened a bit under her scrutiny. She'd expected them to look more like farmers, honestly, but these men looked like soldiers. She nodded slowly. "If this is what farmer soldiers look like, I'm glad to have you here." She turned to Darien's men. "And if this how city boys grow in the north, Immusmala is doing it all wrong."

Both groups glanced between her and each other.

Sable looked around. "Where is the bread magnificent enough to make grown men fight?"

Several eyes shifted to the ground where a loaf of bread was smashed into the dirt.

"Ahh," she said. "A worthy prize to be sure." Sable shifted her arm, and Innov spread her wings, flapping them once to keep her balance and sending out a spray of sparks like shards of fire. They glittered in a slow, lazy arc as they fell.

"Last night," Sable said as the men's eyes followed the lights, "I sat in a tent with your lords, and Lord Erick as well, and listened to them bicker over their own loaf of bread. Meaning you, of course.

"On one hand, I can understand their position. They have land and armies. No one is excited at the idea of handing over control of their own things to someone else. But what I can't understand is you." She looked between the men. "The fights between your territories aren't really between you men. Your farms aren't in danger of the city boys taking them over, and your cities aren't about to be overrun with livestock. It seems to me that the hostility between the soldiers in the north isn't really your own. It's just a continuation of a greedy grab for more land that your lords are embattled in."

She hadn't intended to push any truth into her words, but she could feel the heat anyway, swirling among the group like a warm tendril of the morning fog. The men studied her, their faces ranging from thoughtful to affronted.

"It does the lords good to have you men at odds with each other. They want you to fight each other at the drop of a hat." She glanced at the bread on the ground. "Or the drop of a loaf. But I don't understand why you fight amongst yourselves when you don't have to."

She walked between the men, looking into their faces. This time when she spoke, she filled her words with everything she wanted the men to see. "There is a real enemy. The Kalesh do want to take your cities and your farms. All of you will be conscripted into their army to conquer other lands. At this moment, they're in the Scale Mountains trying to determine if there's gold there that they can take."

The men's brows creased, and they exchanged looks.

"Late last night," Reese said, "the three lords combined all their armies together under Tanis of Stormfeld."

The announcement was met with shocked silence.

"When we meet the Kalesh," Reese continued, "their forces will most likely be stronger than ours. We'll have to be faster and more agile."

"We're going to fight the Kalesh?" one of Darien's men asked.

"The Empire will come," Reese said. "It's inevitable at this point. So, yes, we need to fight."

The soldiers didn't look completely convinced, but they didn't argue.

"This is a new enemy, and we need a new army to face them," Reese said. "By tomorrow, you'll be assigned to new units made up of archers and infantry from all the different territories."

They started to object, but Sable raised her voice. "You're facing a bigger enemy much more threatening than each other. It's time the men of the north started acting like the brothers they are and band together."

She turned slowly, meeting their eyes. "All my life I've heard that the soldiers of the north were the real force to be reckoned with. That if there were trouble, it was the north who would provide help." Her words had formed a pool around them, connecting them all. Innov's heat poured into it as well, strengthening the hope, the latent promise that was growing.

"You've been children up until now, brothers wrestling and bickering over scraps. It's time to grow into what you've always had the power to be. Brothers who stand together and fight together. An army of men who can defy even the mighty Kalesh Empire."

The soldiers met each other's eyes with looks that were more gauging than hostile. Reese surveyed the men, nodding, his eyes burning with a fierce pride.

Sable raised her voice and poured the fervent dream into her words. "The days of fighting over bread are done. Welcome to the true north."

512

CHAPTER SIXTY-SIX

SABLE SANK to the ground and leaned against a large wagon wheel. Atticus's two tall wagons, the bright blue one and the deep red one, were angled against each other, marking out a snug campsite filled with the rich scent of vegetable soup and the hum of conversation.

Reese stayed standing, leaning back against light blue swirls on the wagon wall.

Leonis sat on the roof of the red wagon. The window was flung open on the side, and a large section of the roof folded back to reveal the bright green leaves of Leonis's fairy tree. In the sunlight, the leaves glowed a vivid light green and lit the interior of the wagon with a greenish hue.

"The rumors are," Thulan was saying, "that somewhere between eight and twelve dwarves passed through this area several months ago."

Terrane perched his large form on a spindly stool next to a campfire. With a chirp, Innov left Sable's arm and flew straight at the fire, circling the hanging pot once before landing and nestling into the coals. Terrane grinned at the phoenix. "Nice to see someone else who appreciates fire."

"Did anyone talk to the dwarves?" Jae asked.

"No one here," Thulan answered. "They supposedly passed quickly along the edge of the forest and had some sort of interaction with a farmer. The rumors of that vary from paying him handsomely for a good meal to slaughtering and eating his prize cow." She rolled her eyes. "What sort of scouting party stops their hurried travel to take the time to slaughter a cow and have a feast?"

"Dwarven scouting parties?" Leonis asked, leaning over the tallest branches, plucking off any leaves that were browning around the edges and dropping them to the ground.

Thulan scowled at the falling leaves. "Anyway, as soon as I get reliable directions to the farmer, I'm going to go chat with him." She scratched her beard. "Several people say the dwarves came from the north. Which means they came from the northern entrance of Torren, not the southern entrance we found blocked last summer."

"The north entrance is where you expected to find them last year," Leonis pointed out, tossing down a handful of leaves.

"It is..." Thulan frowned. "Except it's been another year. Digging out a cave-in is slow work, but not this slow. The extent of a collapse that takes more than a year to dig out must be..." She shook her head. "Well, it wasn't natural."

"Why not?" Jae asked. "You said entire mountains shift."

"Of course they do. But in predictable ways. No dwarf with half a brain wouldn't take that into account when tunneling. There are fault points specifically shaped to handle that sort of thing. An earth tremor that collapsed tunnels to this extent would have brought down half the Marsham Cliffs." She pulled her fingers through her beard, and her frown deepened. "What happened there?"

Everyone was quiet. Even Leonis held his tongue.

Serene looked over from where she and Jae were talking to Flibbet. "What have you two been doing?" she asked Sable.

"Surveying the troops." Sable leaned her head back and closed her eyes.

"I was surveying troops," Reese said. "Sable was inspiring them."

"I was keeping them from squabbling." Sable kept her eyes closed. "I hadn't thought it would be so exhausting." The midday sun had burned off the morning mist, and the brightness glowed red through her eyelids.

"Did you move a lot of *vitalle*?" Serene asked.

"There was a lot of truth to be told." She heard footsteps and cracked an eye open to see Serene coming closer. Serene knelt and set her hand on Sable's shoulder. Heat flowed out of Serene's hand, spreading toward Sable's chest and up her neck, driving back the worst of the exhaustion.

"It's true, then?" Flibbet asked. "You can really tell if people are telling the truth?"

Sable nodded.

"She can do a good deal more than that," Serene said, her brow creased. "But you should rest for a few hours, Sable. We need to discuss your limits so you don't exhaust yourself."

"Innov helped," Sable said, "until the last little while when she kept flying off to play in fires."

Serene pulled her hand away, and Sable took a deep breath. She was still tired, but the worst of the exhaustion was gone.

"Thank you," Sable told her.

Leonis searched his tree, but not finding any more dying leaves, he crawled toward the back of the wagon. The moment he moved away from the tree, Thulan scooped up the dead leaves on the ground and flung them back up into the branches. A good number of them fell immediately back out, but several dozen stuck among the other leaves. She grinned and sat back down before Leonis climbed off the wagon.

"How does the army look?" Jae asked.

"Not terrible," Reese answered. "We surveyed Darien's men and half of Loren's. Their biggest problem is that they're bored, but we'll get them training tomorrow."

"Then why do you look so glum, boss?" Terrane asked.

Leonis climbed off the back of the wagon. He walked up to the side of the wagon and, without looking up at it, grabbed the lowest branch of his tree and gave it a hard shake. The dead leaves Thulan had thrown on came tumbling down.

Leonis scooped up a handful and dropped them on Thulan's head before he sat next to her. "You do look like someone just handed you toy soldiers, Reese, and asked you to fight a real war with them."

Thulan brushed the leaves out of her hair toward Leonis.

"I thought everyone said northern armies are strong," Gwen said.

"They are strong," Reese said. "There just aren't enough of them here. Even combined, Loren's, Erick's, and Darien's troops make up just over a third of the soldiers of the north. Even if all three lords gather all their troops here, we'll only be a little larger than Lord Runess's army and not as big as Lord Perric's."

"Once Runess and Perric see what's happening here, though," Terrane said, "they'll have to take notice."

"Notice, yes." Reese looked out over the tents of Lord Loren's men. "But that doesn't mean they'll join us. They have more to lose than these three lords if they stand against the Kalesh. The lumber trade they've been discussing with the Empire would bring in a lot of wealth."

"Until the Kalesh decide it's easier just to take over their lands and claim the trees for themselves," Serene said.

"Hopefully they'll see that," Reese said. "But convincing the rest of the north isn't the worst of our problems. Say Perric and Runess both change their minds and decide they'd like to put their men under Tanis. We're still just the north. The only way any of this land stays free from the Empire is if the south joins us as well. We can't let the Kalesh take over Immusmala. They'd control the only large port along the coast. And if they take over the mouth of the Black River too, it won't matter how many men we have. The Kalesh will have us trapped in the north. They can build up as many troops as they need down south, then come conquer us when they're ready."

"How will having the south join us make a difference?" Terrane asked. "Even if you got all the Sanctus guards, and all the merchant's guards, and all the militias that exist in the towns and cities of the south, it wouldn't add that many to our numbers. Not in comparison to what the Kalesh can bring."

"No, but if we were unified with the south, we could go down there and help. Most of the southern coastline is cliffs. The mouth of the Black River and the port in Immusmala are the only two places low enough to land an army. We have plenty of men to defend those." Reese paused. "Up to a point. If the Kalesh are very set on taking them over, they have nearly limitless soldiers. They could probably still overrun us."

"That's depressing," Sable said.

"It is," Reese agreed. "It's why we need to convince the Kalesh they don't really want us. But right now, they're getting gold from the mines in the south, so being here is easy and profitable. If we could get an army in the south and start making it hard for the Kalesh to reach the mines, we could cause enough trouble that they'd at least have to reassess what they're doing."

"I hope Sable did a better job than this of inspiring the troops," Thulan said.

"So do I," Leonis agreed. "Here we were feeling celebratory about our new little army."

"This army is a good start," Reese said. "We just have a lot left to do."

"Sable!" Atticus's voice rang out. The old playwright strode into the space between his wagons with a broad smile, heading for her. "It's perfect! The true north! Now that's a phrase I can work with!"

"So glad you approve," Sable said, squinting up at him. "I said it just for you."

"No, you didn't." He beamed at her. "That's why it's so good. It is exactly what needed to be said!"

"You're really enjoying all this, aren't you?" Sable said.

Atticus rolled up onto the balls of his feet. "How can I not enjoy this? These are exciting times, I tell you. Exciting times."

"They're thrilling, Atticus," Sable said tiredly, leaning her head back against the wheel. "Terrane, you are killing me with that soup. It smells so good. Is it done yet? I'm starving."

"It'd be better with a bit longer to simmer," Terrane answered, "but cooks get bad reputations if people starve right next to them."

Sable leaned forward, but Reese set his hand on the top of her head.

"Serene said you should rest," he said. "And sometimes she's scary, so you should do what she says. I'll get you soup."

Too exhausted to object, Sable sank back down, letting her eyes close again until Reese sat next to her with two bowls of soup.

Atticus paced back and forth between the wagons. "You two," he said, pointing at Sable and Reese, "did great today. The soldiers respect you, Reese, and they're growing more enamored with Sable and Innov by the moment."

"Atticus," Reese said with a suspicious tone, "why did I have three different men talk to me about the assassination of Ambassador Tehl today?"

"Because it's a great story—" Atticus started.

"That he's been having us tell often for the past few months," Thulan chimed in.

Leonis nodded. "I've told it so many times, I'm sick of it. I want to embellish it, but Atticus is firmly against the idea of you cartwheeling on stage and shooting the ambassador with a flaming arrow."

Reese looked unamused. "How would I cartwheel while holding a bow?"

"Exactly," Thulan said. "It's a ridiculous idea. Mine was better: I thought we should turn Sable's speech into a song."

"No," Sable said.

"Why are you telling that story at all?" Reese asked.

"Aside from the fact everyone loves it," Atticus said, "it's important that the north understand what happened and who was involved."

Reese stared at him. "What if I don't *want* everyone to know that?"

"Too late for that," Thulan said. "Aside from the very new tale of you two defying Vivaine at the summit, the assassination is the most requested story we have."

Atticus nodded. "We started telling it a couple months ago when Tanis began to make some progress against the Kalesh. I figured it couldn't hurt to have the northern folk thinking highly of Tanis's right-hand man. But then you and Sable stood up to Vivaine together! Do you have any idea how perfect that is? Now, the story that everyone knows—that you assassinated the ambassador because the world wouldn't listen to Issable, *and* that you did it in such a way to make sure she'd be free from blame, *and* that Issable sacrificed her freedom to save your life when you were caught—is even better! Because here you are *together*. And everyone wants to know how!" He rubbed his hands together. "I couldn't have planned it better."

Sable pulled out the small book of *Ghost of the White Wood* from her pocket. "Atticus," she said, holding it out, "this is a story you want to read. Aside from the fact it involves the current Kalesh ambassador, the woman in the story, Melia, is exactly the sort of selfless, capable, enthralling heroes you like to talk about."

The playwright's eyebrows rose, and he took the book eagerly. "I do always love a good hero—or heroine." He paused, and his brow creased as he glanced at Thulan and Leonis. "Speaking of which, who's telling the soldiers to call her Sable instead of Issable?"

"I am," Sable said.

Atticus turned back to her and shook his head. "Stick with Issable."

She raised an eyebrow. "I don't want to be Issable."

"Not for your real name," he explained. "Just for your stage name. The name that helps form what the world thinks of you. It's more elegant and sophisticated than Sable."

"I tell you what, Atticus," she said, leaning back on the wagon wheel again. "You tell them to call me Issable, and I'll tell them to call me Sable, and we'll see which one of us is better at influencing an audience."

Atticus narrowed his eyes.

Leonis grinned. "That sounds fun."

"My money's on Sable," Thulan said.

Atticus pointed at the two of them. "You two work for me. You will keep calling her Issable, and keep the stories flowing." He frowned back at Sable. "I have already set weeks of groundwork on your name. You are solidly known as Issable."

She smiled at him. "Then why do you look worried?"

He gave her a flat look. "I'm not worried. You're just making things harder."

"I think it's brilliant," Leonis said. "You've set Issable up as this mythical figure, Atticus, but when she walks among the men, she's relatable, real-life Sable. Makes them think they're friends with the legend."

"Or makes them realize she's not a legend at all," Thulan pointed out.

"Exactly," Sable said. "Because I'm not."

"You didn't see her today," Reese told the dwarf. "They loved her. They definitely think of her as a legend."

Atticus ran his fingers through his beard, considering Sable. "That's a good point. They did love you."

"How do you know?" Sable asked. "Were you following us?"

"Not at first," he said. "But then I found two different groups of soldiers who'd just talked with you two. So I decided to follow your trail." He nodded slowly. "Yes, keep telling them to call you Sable."

She raised her eyebrows.

"I think she was going to anyway," Thulan said.

Atticus waved her words away but moved over to where Leonis and Thulan sat. "*The true north* is good. I have some ideas about what to do with it." He caught Jae's eye. "Interested in telling some stories to the troops?"

"Always," Jae answered.

"If you have room for another storyteller, I'm always up for a good tale, too," Flibbet said, his eyes bright. "Just the unification of three northern lords is bound to go down in history as memorable. Throw in all the other things happening right now, and there's a good chance we're at a turning point in the story of this entire land."

"As long as that story doesn't end with the Kalesh taking over everything," Sable said, "I'll be excited with you."

"That is the big risk," Jae said, "but the more looming and certain the disaster, the better the story."

"On that cheery note," Reese said, standing, "I have more troops to survey."

"I'll come with you." Sable stood and went to gather Innov from where she slept at the edge of the fire. She squatted down next to the phoenix. "Want to come meet more soldiers?"

Innov stirred and shook out her wings.

"You should rest," Serene said to her.

"I know," Sable answered, running her hand over Innov's back, "and I'll be careful. But I really don't want to stay and hear which rumors Atticus is planning to spread about us."

"Rumors?" the old man said, affronted. "These are historically accurate tellings of real events."

"C'mon, Innov." Sable held out her arm, and Innov hopped onto it, shifting and trying to curl up again. Sable tucked the phoenix into the crook of her arm, feeling waves of warmth seep into her. She rubbed the side of Innov's neck, and the phoenix leaned into the motion.

Serene fell in beside her. "I'm coming to make sure you don't overexert yourself."

"Just look at that!" Atticus said gleefully to Thulan and Leonis. "Sable has a *phoenix*! An actual phoenix! She's like some torchbearer! Or a beacon!" His eyes widened. "Oh! I've got it! Sable's a flame! The Flame of the North!"

The white-haired playwright clapped his hands, nearly bursting with excitement.

Sable sighed and glanced at Thulan. "Don't let him go too crazy."

"It's a bit late for that," the dwarf said.

A fortnight later, Sable and Serene skirted the edge of the practice field. What had once been a wide grazing plain for Lord Erick's horses was now trampled to dirt under the swelling numbers of the Army of the True North.

Commanders called out orders, and tightly organized units of soldiers surged forward and planted themselves into one position after another, or flanked bales of hay, or shot volleys of arrows at a line of targets.

"So the dwarves were going to the Scale Mountains?" Sable asked.

"That's what the farmer told Thulan," Serene answered. "Ten of them, and they were an exploration team looking for caves that were 'livable and had the potential for growth.'"

"That doesn't sound like Torren is in good shape," Sable said.

Serene nodded. "Thulan and Leonis are talking about heading up there to see what happened, but Atticus is insistent that he needs them here." She glanced at Sable. "Speaking of Atticus, walk me through the night after the show at the Grand Stadia last year. He's confused on how you ended up in Vivaine's chapel when she found you. He wants me to record the actual story so he can weave it into his retelling. Why did you go into the priories at all?"

"A blue butterfly ring," Sable said wryly, stroking her fingers down Innov's chest.

The phoenix spread her wings and thrust herself into the sky. After two weeks of frolicking in campfires every night, Innov was gloriously bright, even in broad daylight, and she'd almost grown to the size she had been before Narine's death. Her claws and talons now reached halfway around Sable's forearm, and her wingspan was long enough that feathers fluttered against Sable's face every time she took off.

"Issable!" a soldier called out.

Sable looked over and raised her hand in a greeting. It wasn't the wave Atticus wanted her to give, but she refused to give the royal sort of acknowledgment he kept begging for. A cheer went up from the other men in the unit, and several saluted with their fists against their chests.

"I'm hearing more Issables than Sables lately," Serene said.

Sable frowned across the field. "I know. Even soldiers I've talked to more than once are reluctant to call me Sable."

"Flame of the North!" another voice called out from the troops.

"And that's caught on quickly," Serene added.

Sable shook her head. "It's Atticus. There was no chance it wasn't going to catch on."

They moved past the field and started uphill toward the edge of the forest.

Sable watched Innov soar up into the blue sky. "Atticus will like the story of the ring. Eugessa wears it on her pinky finger. It's silver, shaped into the form of a butterfly, and set with several cloudy blue stones. It's sort of ugly and nowhere near as valuable as the rest of her jewelry. According to her, it was a gift from two dying souls who were so grateful for her care and comfort that they gave her all their worldly possessions."

Serene raised an eyebrow. "Only if Eugessa was a completely different person when she was young."

"Apparently she was not. Kiva claims the ring belonged to his mother. He and his parents arrived in Immusmala when he was young. His parents were terribly ill, and they sought refuge in Eugessa's abbey. Overnight his parents died, and Eugessa told him that she'd had their bodies and possessions burned to stop the sickness from spreading. But then last year, he saw the ring on her finger."

"And Kiva wanted you to get it?" Serene asked.

"That was the price of Talia's freedom," Sable answered. "So when the Sanctuary was in chaos and all the abbesses were running into and out of the priories, well…I was already dressed as one. It seemed like the perfect moment."

"You went into the Priory of the Horn?"

"I found Eugessa's room, and she was getting into a huge bathtub, ranting about the night. She took off her jewelry and…" Sable shrugged. "I took the ring and escaped."

Serene let out a laugh. "That was brazen."

"I was a bit desperate at that point. But by the time I got back to the main doors, the Sanctus guards were beginning to lock down the priories. The only way I could get out was through the side, which led me to the Dragon Priory, which led me to Vivaine's chapel, where I was hiding when she found me."

Serene shook her head. "And I thought the first part of the night was dramatic."

"Vivaine knew I had the ring, though." Sable sighed. "I'm sure she was watching me somehow. Anyway, she took the ring back and returned it to Eugessa, who still wears it every day."

Innov flew over Sable's head, winging high over the troops, then soared toward the water, over the dozens of boats choking the Black River.

"It's odd that Kiva works with her," Serene said slowly. "I would think he would hate her too much."

"He definitely hates her." Sable watched another long line of Darien's blue-clad soldiers disembark from a newly arrived flatboat. "I think he might be biding his time. I think, when it comes down to it, he's going to destroy her somehow. He seems to just be using her until then."

"That's charming," Serene said dryly.

"He's a lovely person," Sable agreed.

"Sable!" a voice yelled.

A young woman hurried toward them from the road by the river.

"Callie?" Sable said.

"Sable!" Callie gasped, out of breath by the time they met her halfway down the slope.

"What are you doing here?" Sable asked.

Callie grabbed Sable's arm. "The Kalesh have taken Immusmala!"

CHAPTER SIXTY-SEVEN

CALLIE'S CHEEKS WERE FLUSHED, and wisps of her hair hung loose from her braid.

"The Kalesh have Immusmala?" Serene said, shocked.

"Is Talia all right?" Sable asked.

Callie nodded. "She was when I left. Kiva heard you were here at Steepdale, and he thinks that you might be able to get the northerners to help. Vivaine doesn't want you, of course, but she was so scared!" Her words were tripping over each other, a tumult of warm truth.

"Callie!" Sable took both her shoulders. "Slow down."

"Start at the beginning," Serene said.

Callie took a deep breath. "When the summit fell apart and everyone started leaving, Kiva got a message that there were Kalesh troops landing near Immusmala. We all hurried back down there, but that takes days, and by the time the city came into view…" She swallowed. "The front of the column of people coming back from the Summit stopped at the top of a hill, and none of the rest of us could see what was happening. Then Kiva sent a messenger to bring me to where he and Vivaine and the merchants were."

She shook her head, her eyes wide. "Sable, there were so many

Kalesh soldiers! They were camped in rectangles between the river and the city. Everything near the river gate was blocked in."

"How many Kalesh?" Serene asked.

"The High Prioress said she thought there were almost a thousand. She was scared, you could see it. The merchants were all shocked and scared too. Kiva said between all the merchants and the Sanctus guards, there were only maybe eight hundred men in the entire city who were trained to fight. All the merchants and prioresses were all talking about the hills around the city and the wall and where the bridge over the river was, but I didn't really understand what they were talking about. Because what do those things matter when the army was surrounding the city?"

"They were discussing how much of the area the Kalesh were controlling," Sable said.

"Well, Vivaine seemed mad about everything, but Kiva had me go find a couple that work for him with a letter for Rabbit, since Kiva had heard that Tanis was in charge of the army here."

"Why'd he send you too?" Sable asked.

"Vivaine said that after the summit, the north might be arming itself for a fight. Kiva thought adding me made it look like a family fleeing with other refugees." She swallowed. "But when Vivaine wasn't listening, Kiva told me the real reason he was sending me was that I was supposed to find you at all costs, Sable. To tell you that no matter what you hear from Vivaine or anyone else, that Immusmala needs help. He said he'd heard you had some sway up here." She looked up at Innov. "I thought he was crazy, but...you really stole the phoenix?"

"I didn't steal her," Sable started.

"Where is the couple you came with?" Serene interrupted.

"Giving Kiva's letter to Rabbit." Callie glanced at Sable. "Kiva didn't think you'd believe a letter from him. But he thought you might believe me."

Serene turned to Sable. "*Do* you believe her?"

Sable nodded.

"Then we need to find Tanis." Serene turned and started down the hill.

Sable and Callie followed her, and Innov dove out of the sky and landed on Sable's outstretched arm. They skirted around the first unit of soldiers. A few saluted and called out "Issable!" or "Flame of the North!" and she waved.

"Kiva was right." Callie peered at the soldiers who stopped to watch Sable and Innov pass. "They do love you up here."

They moved quickly through the dusty paths between tents and crossed the square to Tanis's command tent, where the lords and military leaders were already gathered. There was no sign of the two people Kiva had sent. Reese glanced up at Sable from where he stood at the wide table, his face grim.

"How reliable is information from this man?" Lord Darien asked, holding up a sheet of paper.

"Kiva has his own agenda," Tanis answered, "but this does confirm other reports we received that the priories and merchants left the summit in a hurry after we did."

"It needs more confirmation than that," Reese said. "I don't trust the man, and the two messengers never got close enough to the city to see anything."

Rabbit nodded slowly. "Kiva generally does have his own plans, but I don't see a reason for him to lie about this. He knows I could verify it with my people in Folhaven in a matter of days. Lying would gain him nothing."

"Callie saw the troops," Sable said, stepping up to the table and pulling Callie with her. "And she's telling the truth about it."

Callie joined her hesitantly, giving the men gathered around the table a nervous smile.

"How many Kalesh did you see?" Tanis asked her.

"Um," Callie shifted. "There were four rectangles of tents, but I don't know how many that is."

"Sixteen hundred men," Reese said. "They camp in four-hundred-man quads."

Darien held up the letter. "Kiva's numbers are half that."

"Kiva's hardly a military genius," Sable said.

"He may have estimated tents instead of soldiers," Reese said. "Each quad has two hundred tents, holding two soldiers each."

"Can you tell if Kiva wrote the truth?" Darien asked Sable, holding out the letter.

She shook her head. "I have to hear the words, but what sense would it make for him to lie in the letter, then send an eyewitness who would refute it?"

Tanis turned to Callie. "Where were the troops positioned?"

"You know those buildings outside the city wall that go along the road for a little ways? The tents were wrapped around those, then along the wall beside them too. The Kalesh were blocking the road between the river and the city like an ugly, dust-colored scarf."

"We have to go help them," Sable said.

Tanis gave her an unreadable look.

Lord Darien dropped the letter onto the table. "That city needs to take care of itself."

"You know they can't." Lord Loren stood along the side of the table next to Tanis. He leaned forward and pushed papers to the side, revealing the southern edge of a huge map. Immusmala sat on its peninsula, the docks labeled in red. "If the Kalesh gain the docks and the entire city, that's not a foothold they'll give up easily."

"They already have that foothold," Darien pointed out.

"Then we need to go knock their foot off it before they bring enough reinforcements that we can't," Sable said.

"Yes," Lord Erick said. "Let's go free Immusmala from the Kalesh and claim it as our own."

"We hardly have enough men to conquer a city of that size," Tanis said dryly.

"How many do we have?" Sable asked.

Reese glanced at a list on the table. "With Lord Darien's newest troops today, we're at two thousand four hundred."

"That's more than the Kalesh have," Sable pointed out.

"It's more than they had." Tanis turned to Callie. "How long ago did you leave the city?"

"Seven days."

"So the Kalesh had sixteen hundred troops there a week ago." Tanis crossed his arms and looked down at the map. "It would take at least ten days for us to get our troops down there. That's with good weather and no problems. We have no guarantee that their numbers won't grow in that time."

"We should assume they will," Atticus said from where he leaned against a post behind Tanis. "General Goll is in charge of the army. If half the stories about him are true, he'll have planned this out beforehand. He's not going to take over the city without enough troops to hold it."

"It looked like Ambassador Bastian was in charge at the summit, not Goll," Lord Loren pointed out. "I didn't expect this of Bastian."

"Bastian has a darker past than he lets on," Sable said grimly.

Reese nodded. "And the ambassador is only the highest-ranking officer in a time of peace. If fighting breaks out, General Goll becomes the leader."

"We must assume," Atticus said, "that Goll used the opportunity of the summit to take the city while the merchants' guards and the Sanctus guards were gone. But he wouldn't have done it if he didn't have reinforcements available quickly."

Atticus turned to look at Sable, his face troubled and almost apologetic. Sable looked questioningly at him, but he just sighed and nodded.

"It takes weeks to travel from the Empire," Lord Loren said. "How could he get men here so quickly?"

Sable dropped her eyes to the map, her stomach sinking. She leaned forward and slid papers off the eastern edge of the map.

"He couldn't," Lord Darien said dismissively.

"Then where did the troops that this girl saw come from?" Lord Erick asked. "The Kalesh didn't have that many men in the city before the summit."

"They had troops on the Eastern Reaches," Sable said, staring down at the mostly blank section of the map. She looked up to see Atticus nodding.

"We haven't heard any reports of that," Lord Darien scoffed.

"Were you looking?" Atticus asked. "Because every letter Sable sent to Leonis for the past year asked me to find out what's happening on the Reaches, and I've had almost no luck reaching any of my contacts there." He turned to Rabbit. "Have you?"

Rabbit shook his head. "I don't know many people on the Reaches."

Tanis was studying the map near Sable. "We talked about it, but it's nearly impossible to scout the Reaches without a lot of manpower."

"There are vast areas that are uninhabited," Reese agreed, "and the few villages are widely spread apart. It's all hills and valleys, so it's impossible to see any real distance. If the Kalesh are there, they took over villages and converted them to army outposts. A scout might travel for weeks or even months and not stumble across the right valley to find them. And if he actually did, they'd kill him before he could get back and tell anyone."

"Then we have no idea how many troops they have," Sable said, "and we need to move fast." She glanced up at Reese. "This might be a blessing in disguise."

He nodded, looking thoughtfully at the city on the map.

Tanis reached forward and shoved more papers away, revealing everything between Immusmala and Steepdale. He tapped his fingers on the paper, his eyes scanning the map.

"A blessing?" Lord Darien said. "That the Kalesh have taken over a city? And people think I'm the heartless one. You really hate the High Prioress, don't you?"

"I am not fond of Vivaine," Sable acknowledged, "but my sisters and a lot of innocent people live in Immusmala. We can't just let the Kalesh take it."

The faces of the lords and the army leaders around the table watched her with varying levels of skepticism. Tanis shuffled through a stack of papers, pulling out a page with a long list of numbers.

Sable turned to Reese. "If we go to Immusmala and drive off the Kalesh who are there—completely drive them off—we'll prove to Vivaine and the merchants that we are their ally. This is the move we need to unite with the south. They now can't ignore the fact that alone, they can't hold off the Kalesh. But with our help, they could drive out the troops that are there and then protect the docks to keep more from landing."

She leaned forward, pointing to Immusmala on the map. "This is what we've needed." Her words spilled across the table, warm and rich. "We save the city, and we gain the ally we need."

The tent was silent, but Reese nodded. "Even Vivaine won't be able to say no if we save her city."

"It could be a death sentence to our troops," Lord Darien said. "We have no idea what we'll be walking into in ten days' time. We could be vastly outnumbered by a force already entrenched at the city. We might as well just kill all our soldiers here and save them the long walk first."

"Which is why we aren't going to walk," Tanis said. He held up the list. "We'll take the boats. Rowing downriver at this time of year, we can reach Folhaven in thirty hours, then we march the half day to Immusmala."

"We can't possibly have enough boats for that," Lord Darien said.

"It will be tight, but we do." Tanis tossed the paper across the table. "There's a good moon. We'll be able to row during the night as well."

Tanis turned to Rabbit. "Send a raven to your people in Folhaven. We'll need updated reports on Immusmala when we get there." He looked at the faces around the table. "Go prepare the men. The true north has its first challenge. We leave at dawn."

PART V

My Dear Chesavia,

You are correct, during Queen Issable's reign, it fell out of favor to wear white at court, owing to the fact that the queen herself never wore it. Rumors abounded as to why.

Some said she missed the colors and flowers she'd lived among in the south—but only those who'd never visited the south.

Some said she disliked snow—but only those who'd never seen her on a snowy northern morning.

Some chalked it up to the petty whims of royalty—but only those who'd never understood her.

Those who knew her whole story—including me—thought she had too many grim memories of those who wore white.

But she told me the truth late one night, when she'd pulled the royal couch up close to the huge fireplace and talked with me about the early days.

She told me she didn't deserve to wear it.

A year later, when her daughter Narine was born, Issable dressed her in white nearly every day.

-excerpt from a letter from Flibbet the Peddler to Keeper Chesavia,
in the 284th year of Queensland

CHAPTER SIXTY-EIGHT

SABLE STOOD at the front of Tanis's command boat, watching the banks of the Black River move quickly past. The rhythmic splash of oars drowned out most of the conversation behind her on the deck as the commanders discussed strategy. Innov perched beside her on the rail, preening herself and letting the stiff breeze fan her feathers into small flames.

Ahead, the pointed end of Tutella Island rose out of the river, topped by the walls of Aedis. Two monks stood on the wall, looking upstream at the throng of approaching boats.

Tanis's smaller, quicker boat pulled ahead of the others before they reached the island. The vast majority of the river flowed slowly around the east side of the island, and Tanis's boat drew in close until it reached a narrow cove.

Sam stood on the longest of three piers with his arms crossed, watching the dozens of low, flat riverboats row downstream, each one bristling with soldiers.

Tanis came up beside Sable as the boat docked at the pier, and Reese hopped over to join Sam on the dock. "Want to come join a fight? It's for a noble cause."

"We like to stop fights, not join them." Sam looked over the boats that were slowly passing them by. "The summit certainly didn't accomplish what I'd hoped."

"It united a bit of the north," Reese said.

Sam shook his head. "It united their armies, if what I hear is true. I don't think it united their hearts."

"We're still working on their hearts," Sable said.

Sam looked at her, his eyes lingering on Innov. "I'm glad you escaped Vivaine, Sable. I have no doubt she would have killed you." He turned back to Reese and clasped him on the shoulder. "I'm sorry about Tylar, though. He was a good man. We gathered his ashes and buried them in our garden of remembrance. You're welcome to come at any time to pay your respects."

Reese's jaw clenched, but he nodded.

Sam studied him. "Revenge isn't the weapon it feels like. It's a corruption that will eat into you long before you face her. And if you kill her, it will eat into you still."

Reese met Sam's gaze. "The Kalesh are the enemy today, not her."

Sam looked like he might continue, but instead, he turned back to Sable. "We've found out little else about the man who started the fire. He was small and stocky. Perhaps a dwarf, except there were no dwarves that we knew of on the island. He escaped on a boat hidden downstream, and by the time we gave chase, there was nothing to be found. The shore south of here is heavily treed, and there are dozens of places he could have gone ashore and hidden the boat."

"What news have you had from Immusmala?" Tanis asked.

Sam blew out a frustrated breath. "Nothing reliable. There are people fleeing north, but their reports are ridiculous. In just the past two days, we've heard that there are a thousand Kalesh near the city, and we've heard that there are ten thousand Kalesh."

"Let's hope it's not ten thousand," Tanis said.

"Well," said Sam, "that was said by the same man who, despite other reports of soldiers disembarking from boats by the hundreds, declared that the soldiers were actually boarding boats."

"To go back home?" Reese asked.

Sam gave an exasperated look. "Who knows? That man's wife

insisted the Kalesh have giants and wizards and goblins. Oh, and a huge red dragon."

"The Empire doesn't have a dragon," Reese said. "And if they did, they wouldn't waste it all the way out here on a city that has literally offered them no resistance ever."

"That's our thought as well." Sam frowned. "Yesterday morning, I thought there were nearly four thousand troops near the city, but the reports from the last day have been much lower. Sometimes I think the travelers talk amongst themselves and create their own rumors as they walk. Our best guess is that you'll be facing somewhere in the range of two thousand troops." He gave them a grim smile. "We're doubtful you'll find giants, wizards, goblins, or the dragon."

"Two thousand is a number we can work with," Tanis said. "If it's closer to four, we're going to have a bit of trouble."

"No one agrees on where they are, either. Some people say inside the city, some say outside, some say near the city, some say far from the city." He shook his head in annoyance. "It's impossible to know what's true. Most reports agree that the city docks are full of Kalesh ships. In case you were planning on going that far."

"Half these boats aren't seaworthy," Tanis said. "We'll disembark along the river near Folhaven, before we reach the ocean, and walk the rest of the way."

Reese raised an eyebrow. "You sure you and your monks don't want to join our liberation army?"

"Even if I wanted to," Sam said, "we harvested our first crop last week, and most of the monks are out delivering them. The majority won't return until next week. The only ones here are the older ones who can't travel far."

Reese nodded and climbed back on the boat. "Well, we wanted to give you the chance."

Sam stepped forward and set his hand on the rail. "Even if you drive the Kalesh out, they'll be back. There's too much gold here for them to just leave."

Tanis nodded. "But if we drive them back and can ally ourselves with the south, we can guard the docks and the river and make it very hard for them to get to that gold."

"Be wary of the south." Sam's brow creased. "Narine would have liked the idea of allies. Eugessa and Vivaine won't."

"They will if it frees them from being occupied by the Kalesh," Reese pointed out.

"Not everyone sees being occupied by them in the same light as you," Sam said.

Sable shook her head. "The Kalesh will take Vivaine's power away. She won't stand for that."

Sam paused. "Maybe. Just be careful. I think you may be headed down to free one enemy from another. So however that ends, you should still stay on your guard." His eyes strayed back to the passing boats. "I see Darien's, Erick's, and Loren's men. What do Runess and Perric think of the Kalesh invasion?"

"They are undecided," Tanis answered.

"They want to wait and see how this falls out," Reese said, dryly, "before they commit their own men to anything."

Sam looked north, up the river. "Be careful," he said again. "It's risky to be the first to step forward."

The sun was high in the sky and tall clouds piled on top of each other toward the west as Sable walked toward Folhaven next to Reese and Tanis with Innov perched on her arm. The long walk to Folhaven was a welcome chance to stretch her legs. The boat trip had taken all of yesterday, a long night's sleep on a hard deck, and half of today to reach the sandy beach along the Black River.

The packed dirt road through the woods echoed with the tramp of soldiers' feet and the low murmur of conversation. Atticus's wagon rolled and creaked next to them. Tanis and Atticus had argued for hours about using valuable space on a boat for the wagon, and Sable had no idea how Atticus had finally convinced the general to bring it, but the gaudy blue wagon was currently trundling along at the head of the line as though leading a festival parade instead of a long column of soldiers.

Atticus himself had left the boat immediately on docking. He and

Rabbit had taken two of the very few horses that had come south and galloped toward Folhaven in the hopes of finding current news.

A few farmers pulled their wagons off the road, watching the army pass with wide eyes. One younger man on a horse took one look at the soldiers and galloped back toward Folhaven.

"How soon will news reach Immusmala that we're here?" Sable asked.

"In a matter of hours," Tanis answered. "Rabbit's network of spies sends ravens between Immusmala and Folhaven, and I'm sure he's not the only one. Both Kiva and Vivaine will know by the time we pass through Folhaven, I'm sure."

The sun was well past midday when the first buildings came into sight ahead of them, and Tanis strode into the unnaturally empty streets of Folhaven. Faces peered out of windows, but the normally busy road was deserted. They reached the square without passing a single person on the streets and found Atticus and Rabbit sitting on the porch at the Listing Sails.

The inn owner, an enormous man who housed the troupe whenever they were in Folhaven, stood on his porch, gripping a towel in his hands and watching the soldiers pass. "Never thought I'd see you with an army, Atticus."

"Never thought an empire would invade," Atticus said to him. "Did you know, under the Kalesh Empire, you have to have every play you perform approved by the local magistrate?"

The innkeeper laughed. "So that's what it takes to make you go to war."

"Among other things," Atticus answered. He stepped down from the porch, and Rabbit followed him. They fell in beside Tanis.

"News?" Tanis asked.

"Weird news," Atticus answered. "You'll be glad to know that the number of troops near Immusmala is only around two thousand."

Rabbit nodded. "I have several sources who agree on that. There's been a lot of troop movement, which may account for some people thinking there were more, but we've gotten several firm counts in the last twenty-four hours, and they all agree. Twenty-two hundred men, at the most."

"What's weird about the news?" Tanis asked.

"They're not surrounding the city anymore," Atticus said. "All reports say they're on the hills to the west."

Tanis frowned. "Why?"

Atticus shrugged. "That's the direction they'd take to get to the mines, but I have no idea what made them move."

"Are there more troops inside the city?" Reese asked. "We could end up trapped between two armies if there are."

"My people say no," Rabbit said. "The city seems much the same as usual. Only a couple hundred soldiers housed in Dockside. The people are nervous, of course, but there doesn't seem to be an undue number of Kalesh in the city itself."

Tanis looked at them both with a creased brow. "What are the Kalesh doing? If they were trying to take over the city, why retreat back to the hills?"

Atticus shrugged. "Maybe the Kalesh are taking over the mines, not the city."

"Why camp around the city at first, then?" Sable asked. "Why set up a blockade between the city and the rest of the world only to relocate to the mountains? There's no traffic in that direction unless it's going to the mines. A couple years ago, that road into the Tremmen Hills was just a game trail."

"If the Kalesh are making a move to take the mines," Reese said, "they need the docks in the city to move it all back to the Empire. There's no reason to move away from Immusmala."

"I agree," Atticus said. "If they're just trying to keep the north from interfering, all they need to do is keep control of the city and block the bridge over the Lingua River. Then they'd have access to the city and the road to the mines."

"Some of the mines are north of the Lingua River," Rabbit said, looking south as though he could see half-day's travel ahead of them. "But yes, if they controlled the city and the bridge, they'd have access to everything they needed."

Reese exchanged looks with him. "Anyone else feel like we're missing something?"

Tanis glanced back at the army marching behind them. "Reese, tell the commanders to make sure the soldiers are ready. We won't reach Immusmala until this evening, and I'd expected to rest for the night within view of the city and formulate an attack plan for tomorrow. But now…just tell them to have their men ready to fight."

Speculation about the motivations of the Kalesh continued, and before they reached Immusmala, the front of the column had filled with all the commanders, Jae and Serene, Atticus, Rabbit. Sable brought Callie up as well.

"When we reach the point where you saw the city with Kiva and Vivaine," Sable said, "I want you to point out to us where the Kalesh were camped."

"Were?" she asked.

"It seems they've moved over toward the Tremmen Hills," Sable said.

Callie brightened. "Maybe everyone was worried for nothing. Maybe the Kalesh are just bringing troops to guard the mines or something."

Sable raised an eyebrow. "They sent thousands of soldiers on boats from the Empire to secure mines they already owned and were having no difficulty getting to?"

Callie bit her lip. "They why else would they move away from the city?"

"That's what we're trying to figure out."

The sun was starting to drop toward the west when they began the long, uphill climb that would lead to their first view of Immusmala. Callie fidgeted next to Sable, biting her nails.

Reese glanced around Sable at Callie. "Why are you so nervous?"

"Because we're walking up to an army!" Callie's face had grown pale, and her eyes were big. "Do you know how happy I was to go north and get away from that army? And now we're coming back with another army. How are the rest of you not nervous?"

Reese gave Sable a questioning look, but Callie had been telling the truth. Sable nodded.

The top of the hill was drawing closer, and Sable could see the tops of the Tremmen Hills over it. Her heart was beating like she'd run up the hill instead of walked. She ran a finger down Innov's feathers, drawing in some of the phoenix's warmth, trying to sooth her nerves. "We are nervous," she murmured.

They reached the top of the hill, and Tanis held up his hand for the army to stop.

Behind them, the sounds of marching settled into silence.

Ahead of them, the road dropped down toward a wooden bridge crossing the Lingua River. Past it, a wide, grassy field rolled uphill toward the crest of the peninsula. The city of Immusmala sat to the left, covering the end of the finger of land that jutted into the sea. The wall wrapped around the city like a stone snake, edging along the Lingua to the River Gate, where it turned inland, walling off the entire city. The road near the city gate was lined with buildings, but they dwindled away farther from the city, leaving the road to meander through green, summertime grass.

Callie gaped at the city. "They're gone! The Kalesh tents were set in rectangles from the river, around the buildings near the River Gate, and all the way back to the wall." Her words were warm.

Off to the right on both sides of the Lingua River, a wide plain rolled up to the Tremmen Hills. Five quads of Kalesh soldiers camped near the hills, their tents laid out in unnaturally regular rectangles on the rolling ground. Three quads sat on the far side of the river protecting the mining road that wound into the hills. The other two sat on the near side, along a second road.

"What are you playing at, girl?" Tanis swung toward Callie.

"Playing?" She took a step back. "The soldiers were there." She pointed at the buildings near the city wall. "Right there. There were only four rectangles, and they were right there."

Tanis crossed his arms and leveled a cold look at Callie. "You'd better explain yourself immediately. If you tricked us into bringing this army down here, I want to know why."

"Tricked?" Sable asked. "She's telling the truth. She saw the soldiers right there by the..." She stopped and stared at the green grass around the edges of the buildings. A breeze from the ocean rolled over the ridge of the peninsula, sending ripples through the tall blades.

"Does that grass look like it had thousands of soldiers camping on it?" Tanis demanded.

Sable turned to Callie, whose face was deathly pale. "I saw them," Callie whispered. "Right there." Her words were warm and terrified. She looked wide-eyed at Tanis. "I swear to you, sir. The soldiers were right there. So many of them!"

"You saw..." Understanding cut through Sable, cold and sharp. "Vivaine," she whispered.

"Where?" Tanis demanded, spinning to face the city.

"No," Sable said, cold fear spreading deeper into her. "Callie, you were next to Vivaine when you saw the soldiers, weren't you?"

"As close as you are to me," Callie answered.

The reality of what had happened became perfectly clear. "Vivaine twisted the light," Sable said. "That's why the people around you were talking about the hills, Callie, because the soldiers were all on the hills."

"No!" Callie said vehemently. "I know what I saw."

"You saw what Vivaine wanted you to see," Sable said.

Reese crossed his arms and turned slowly to study the city. "But why?"

"Explain yourself," Tanis commanded.

"Vivaine has the power to twist light." Sable tried to keep her words even, despite her rising fear. "She can make something appear to be where it isn't. Obviously, Callie didn't see soldiers by the city. The troops would have trampled the grass if they'd camped there. Vivaine took the image of the Kalesh from where they were on the hills and made it appear to Callie that they were by the city."

"Why?" Callie asked. "And why me?"

Sable looked up at tips of the spires of the Dragon Priory, just barely visible above the city. "Whose idea was it to send you north?"

"Kiva's—" Callie paused. "No, he said Vivaine had told him his normal spies would be viewed suspiciously, and he should send a young woman north with them." She shook her head again. "But Vivaine didn't even want us to go north."

"That's what she wanted you to think," Reese said darkly.

Sable turned to Tanis, the truth settling into a hard knot in her stomach. "Vivaine organized all of this. She manipulated Kiva to send Callie, because Callie would be sure to find me. And Vivaine knew that I would believe whatever Callie believed."

Tanis swore and turned away, his eyes scanning the hills and the city.

"Was Kiva involved?" Reese asked.

Callie looked at them blankly.

"Was Kiva talking about the city?" Sable asked.

Callie shook her head quickly. "He kept talking about the hills and the mines." She gave the Kalesh camp a scared look. "He was talking about those hills. I didn't understand why, but..." She glanced back at Sable. "I often don't know what people are talking about."

Sable sighed. "Which is the other reason Vivaine used you." She turned to Reese. "I think Vivaine used Kiva too. I'm guessing he had no idea what Callie saw."

Callie looked at Sable with wide eyes. "Why did she lie about where the troops were? Why make me think the city was under attack when it wasn't?"

Reese looked over the land in front of them, and Sable could see the wary look in his eyes. "To draw us down here."

Tanis nodded grimly.

"But...why?" Callie asked, her voice small.

Sable stared at the quiet scene below them. "I don't know."

CHAPTER SIXTY-NINE

SABLE STOOD at the top of the hill with Serene, staring at the spires of the priories just visible over the rest of Immusmala. The sun was dropping toward the Tremmen Hills, painting the city in softer, orange tones, leaving it looking deceptively calm.

"What is Vivaine playing at?" Sable asked.

Serene looked severely at the city. "I have no idea."

The road ahead of them was empty, all the way down to the bridge over the Lingua River and all the way to the city gates. Sable caught glimpses of movement among the buildings, and there were guards standing on top of the city wall, but mostly the scene was still and empty.

Even up near the Kalesh camps, there was minimal activity. The shapes of guards could be seen stationed around the quads of tents, but they made no move at the appearance of Tanis's army.

Tanis's commanders gathered at the front of the column, discussing where to stage the army.

"At least there are only two thousand Kalesh," one of them said. "At least we still outnumber them."

"We need to control the bridge," Reese said. "Before the Kalesh do."

"Presuming they want to, I agree." Tanis turned to an officer. "Take two units and secure the bridge. I want defensive positions dug in on both sides."

The man saluted with his fist to his chest and headed down the column of soldiers waiting along the road, calling out orders as he went.

The other commanders threw out suggestions, and Sable half-listened to them, the fear she'd felt at the unexpected situation slowly shifting into anger at Vivaine.

"We should take the position near the city, General," someone said. "If we're here to protect the city from the Kalesh, that's what we should do."

"Even if the Kalesh aren't threatening it?" asked another.

"They have an army camped right there. They're threatening."

"It pins us against the walls," someone objected.

"But it keeps us from being surrounded," Reese pointed out.

"As long as no one comes out of the city."

"There are no Kalesh troops in the city," Rabbit said. "I got confirmation of that. The buildings that housed troops in Dockside still have some soldiers, but they're not full anymore. My people say there are no more than two hundred Kalesh in the entire city."

"We'll put two units on the bridge," Tanis said. "Two more will be positioned there, where the road reaches the buildings. The rest will line up along the wall." The general's body tensed and let out a pained cough.

"Are you all right?" Reese asked.

Tanis waved off his words. "We need to find out what Vivaine is planning."

Sable turned to face them. "I'm going to talk to her."

There was a moment of silence.

"That's a terrible idea," Reese said.

"I can tell if she's being honest." Sable ran her hand down Innov's feathers, her fingers shaking with the anger growing inside her. "Atticus, I need to look like a prioress—no, I need to look like *more* than a prioress."

"That's a dangerous game, Sable," Atticus said.

Reese shook his head. "You can't go into that city, not alone."

"I can't go in with an invading army," she said. "This city has been waiting for Innov to come back. Bringing her in will at least get me an audience with Vivaine."

Reese stepped closer. "Or it will get you killed!"

"I don't think so," Atticus said slowly. "By the time she reaches Vivaine, Sable will own the crowd."

Sable glanced back to where Leonis and Thulan sat on the driver's seat of the wagon. "Can you two make me look impressive?"

Leonis grinned. "Do you want benevolent prioress or conquering queen?"

Sable gave him a grim smile. "Maybe a little of both."

"You don't give us much to work with." Thulan frowned at her. "You look terrible. Have you been rubbing your hair in the dirt?"

"If you're going," Reese said, "then I'm going too."

"No," Tanis commanded.

Reese crossed his arms and turned to the general. "Are you going to stop me?"

"I'm going to remind you that I need you here, with the troops, commanding the ten units that will hold the city gate and the wall along it."

Reese started to shake his head, but the general's face flickered with pain, and Reese took a step toward him. "Are you sure you're all right?"

"I'm fine," Tanis snapped. "But I won't be fine if I lose a commander just when we're getting set for a fight."

"I'll go with her," Serene said to Reese. "Atticus is right. If Sable walks into that city with Innov, she'll win the hearts of the mob before she gets halfway to the Sanctuary."

"Maybe this is all just a ruse to draw Sable down here," Reese pointed out. "A way to get her where Vivaine can reach her."

"This isn't Tutella Island," Atticus said. "The people here didn't see the drama play out there. The momentum Vivaine had there has dissipated. Whatever she's doing here is about more than trying to capture Sable."

"If it were just about me," Sable said, "she wouldn't have wanted me at the head of an army. Something else is happening, and the only way to find out what is for me to actually speak to her."

Reese started to object again.

"I can go talk to the people who live outside the wall," Gwen offered.

The Mira stood with her back stiff, her arms clasped in front of her just like she'd stood a thousand times next to Vivaine. Except now she wore merely a plain, earth-colored tunic and pants. She had not exchanged the haughty look she'd always worn for anything more pleasant.

Tanis frowned at her. "We're still not sure whose side you're on here."

"She's not particularly loyal to the rebels," Terrane said, stepping up next to her, "but she hates Vivaine. You can trust that she's on our side here. I'll go with her."

Gwen half turned her head toward him, her expression registering surprise for just a moment before she schooled her face back into a more detached expression.

"Why would we send either of you?" one of the captains asked.

"Because Gwen has a gift for learning information," Reese said, "and Terrane has the skills to keep both of them safe."

Terrane grinned. "If anything goes wrong and we can't get back, I'll give you a signal."

"We're here to help the city," Tanis said, a note of warning in his voice. "Not burn it down."

"I'll keep that in mind," Terrane answered, his smile still wide. He turned to Gwen. "Spy work! This will be fun!"

She raised an eyebrow at him.

Tanis turned away from them and surveyed the commanders around him. "Make your preparations," he commanded. "We're moving out."

There was a slight sheen of sweat on Tanis's face, and Reese gave him a troubled look.

"Into the back of the wagon, Sneaks." Leonis handed the reins to Thulan and jumped down. "We have a lot of work to do on you."

Sable climbed in the back door of Atticus's wagon, breathing in the dry smell of all the fabric. Crates of costumes and props lined both sides near the back. Up in the front, Leonis's tree sat under the open panel of the roof, coloring the interior a luminous green. Leonis climbed in behind her.

"You want a white dress?" he asked.

"No," she said flatly. "I'm tired of white."

He considered Innov. "How about a cream dress, but we'll give you a black cloak on top of it? Then there'll be a suggestion of the priories, but also, you won't look like merely a prioress. And Innov should stand out beautifully against the black." He pushed a crate out of the way and started rummaging through the one beneath it.

Outside the wagon, the command to march was given, and the wagon rolled forward.

By the time they rolled across the bridge over the Lingua River, Sable was dressed in a simple, cream-colored gown and a long, black cloak with a fur-lined collar.

"If you're not going to take off that ugly sword necklace you keep wearing lately," Leonis said, "at least tuck it inside the dress so no one can see it."

Sable slipped the necklace from Reese inside her dress while Purnicious puttered around next to her legs, adjusting the waistline of the gown and fixing a bit of the fur.

"You'll be hot," Leonis said, "but with your dark hair and that angry look your face is fixed in, it's dramatic." He handed Sable a brush. "Start on your hair. I'll get Thulan."

When the dwarf came into the back of the wagon, she looked at Sable and nodded. "Leonis picked the right clothes for once." She motioned to a crate. "Sit. Your face paint should go fast. You're not really going to be on stage, so we'll keep it subdued. Face the light."

Sable turned, and Thulan dusted her face and eyes with assorted powders, then moved on to her hair.

"Look through that red box while I do this," Thulan told her. "Pick a necklace to wear."

The wagon bumped along the road toward Immusmala, and Sable picked through the selection of necklaces. Even the old, familiar feel of Thulan's fingers in her hair couldn't settle the outrage growing inside of her.

Vivaine had tricked her. But why? Why go through all this effort?

"Purnicious," Thulan said, "can you make those hairpins look less shabby?"

The kobold popped into view and examined three long pins. "I can't do much for gold and gems."

"It's just gold paint and glass," Thulan grunted. "Looks decent from a distance, but Sable should look more polished today even up close."

"Paint and glass I can work with," Purn said happily.

Serene climbed into the back of the wagon and picked up another brush. "If I'm going with you, I figured I should at least try not to look like I slept on a boat last night."

Sable dropped the necklaces back into the box. "What is Vivaine doing? Just trying to draw us into a fight?"

Serene frowned out the back of the wagon at the long line of soldiers crossing the bridge behind them. "More troubling than that, how did she decide the instant the Kalesh came in view that she needed to do it?"

Sable straightened. "She did, didn't she?"

"If Callie is telling the truth—" Serene said.

"Which I'm positive she is," Sable interjected.

"Then within a few moments of finding a Kalesh army camped on the hillside, Vivaine decided to not only create a false story about where they were but figured out how to get that story north. To you in particular so it would be believed."

Sable turned toward Serene. "You're saying—"

Thulan yanked on Sable's hair, pulling her head back straight.

"Ow!" Sable raised her hand to her hair.

"No moving!" Thulan snapped. "And no touching! I do not have time to redo all this."

"If you pull it all out of my head," Sable said between clenched teeth, "it's going to be a lot harder to braid."

"No moving," Thulan repeated.

Sable tried to look at Serene out of the corner of her eye. "Do you think Vivaine knew about the Kalesh army before she got here?"

Serene was quiet for a long moment. "That makes more sense than that she devised and enacted an elaborate plan that involved tricking Callie, Kiva, and you, all in a few moments that should have been filled with shock."

"Then…what?" Sable said. "She planned this with the Kalesh ahead of time?"

Serene shook her head. "I don't have a better explanation." She watched Thulan's fingers deftly weave Sable's hair on top of her head. "Reese is going to insist that soldiers escort us."

"We're not taking any," Sable said firmly. "You and I don't look like prioresses, but I want that general idea. The crowd should see only women and the phoenix. Not a group of armed men marching on the Sanctuary."

Serene was quiet.

"Don't you agree?" Sable asked, shifting her head a little to try to read Serene's expression.

Thulan gave her a warning growl.

"Yes," Serene answered slowly, turning to face out the back of the wagon. "It just feels vulnerable, walking up to the Sanctuary with just you and…me."

A cold thread wormed its way through Serene's words.

Sable straightened. "Did you just lie?" she asked. "To me?"

Serene stiffened but didn't look back at Sable.

"It is vulnerable," Sable said. "But who do you want to come with us? Gwen? I doubt that would keep things calm. And if we bring any men, it'll change the dynamic. Unless you really think Jae or Atticus should come."

"No," Serene said, her voice short. She stood and moved to the door of the wagon. "It *should* be just you and me."

Sable frowned. Those words had been warm. "Then what's wrong?"

"It's nothing." Serene climbed down out of the wagon, the chill of that answer making Sable shiver.

"I know that was another lie," Sable called after her as Serene stalked away out of view. "What was that all about?"

Purnicious looked curiously after Serene. "I have no idea."

Thulan grunted. "She's been weird ever since we caught up with you all in the woods."

Serene *had* been weird. Sable tried to look out the back of the wagon, but Thulan's fingers tightened again.

"I swear to you, Sable, if you pull your hair out of my hands, I will tie it all in one huge knot and you can make your grand entrance looking like a lunatic."

Sable turned her head back forward.

"And pick out a necklace," Thulan said. "That dress is too plain. You need something so you don't look like some baker's daughter who just happened to find a shiny bird."

Sable pulled a necklace out of the box, still thinking about Serene. How scared she'd been about Jae being in Immusmala, how exuberantly happy she'd been to see him, how unreasonably worried she was about the idea of leading Stonehaven now that Merrick was gone. The normally unruffled woman seemed...ruffled.

"Not that necklace," Thulan interrupted her thoughts. "That gaudy monstrosity looks like something a fish mongrel's wife would think was elegant. Pick the gold circle pendant. Or the small, green gem."

Sable dropped the one in her hand and searched for the gold circle. Just as the wagon jolted to a stop.

"Leonis!" Thulan yelled. "Where did you learn to drive?"

"Are you almost done?" Sable asked. Her only answer was some tugging on the hair on the top of her head. A lot of Thulan's work seemed to be on the top of her head, now that she thought about it, even though most of Sable's hair still hung down her back. "What are you doing to my hair?"

Thulan picked up the three long hairpins, which were shinier now that Purnicious had bellished them, and tucked them into Sable's hair, pinning her work tightly to Sable's head. Thulan stepped around her, lifting Sable's chin and looking critically at her hair.

"That'll do. It won't last forever, and it won't survive any undue excitement, so do your best to stay calm." She handed Sable a mirror.

A circlet of elaborately twisted braids wrapped twice around Sable's head. The braids were small enough, and Sable's hair dark enough, that they weren't immediately visible, but they gave a definite impression.

"A crown?" Sable asked.

"You said a cross between conquering queen and benevolent prioress." Thulan took the gold necklace from Sable's hand and hooked it around her neck, smoothing her hair back down over it.

"I didn't mean a crown! It's so…obviously a crown."

"It's subtle," Thulan said.

Leonis appeared at the back of the wagon. He paused, peering at Sable. "I thought we were going for conquering queen. Why'd you make the crown so subtle?"

"It's perfect," Thulan said, gathering up her supplies.

Sable stood, and Innov hopped onto her cream-colored sleeve. Leonis offered his hand to help Sable out of the wagon. When she reached the ground, he kept hold of it, turning her around so he could examine her.

"It works," he said. "You look stunning. Purnicious, you're a wonder. I can't see any of the many, many places this dress has been taken in or lengthened."

Purnicious grinned from deep in the wagon.

Leonis nodded approvingly at Sable. "You look striking enough that the crowd will be besotted."

The wagon was parked off the road, not too far from the line of buildings leading up to the gate of Immusmala. A column of soldiers marched past through the grass, heading for the wall. The soldiers' eyes caught on Innov, and Sable heard "Flame of the North" murmured down the line. She raised her hand in greeting, but the soldiers didn't give the normal cheer. They whispered to each other, turning their heads to watch as they passed.

Sable let her hand fall.

"Looks like the costume is working perfectly," Leonis said smugly.

"Sable!" Reese's voice came from the far side of the wagon. He stormed around the front. "You cannot go into the city. It's too—" He stopped short between her and the passing soldiers, staring at her.

"Yup," Thulan said in a voice as smug as Leonis's. "It's working."

"It's too what?" Sable asked, ignoring them. "Dangerous? Because you're here to fight in a battle. Swords, arrows, men slaughtering each other. So I know you didn't come here to tell me that going to have a conversation is too dangerous."

His brow dove into a scowl. "You're going to have a conversation with the Dragon Prioress, who wants you dead. So yes, I'm here to tell you it's too dangerous. Please rethink this."

"Do you have a better way to figure out what's going on here?" she demanded.

"No. But that doesn't make your idea a good one."

Leonis set his hand on Sable's shoulder. "Doesn't she look stunning?"

"Shut up, Leonis." Sable shifted out from under his hand.

"She always looks stunning," Reese answered, without bothering to give the half-elf a glance. He reached out and took Sable's hand. "Please don't do this."

"She looked awful just a few minutes ago," Leonis said to Thulan.

"You were dumb to ask Reese," Thulan pointed out. "She's like some magical creature out of a myth, and he's a soldier. Of course he's smitten."

Sable gave them an annoyed look, then turned back to Reese. "Vivaine planned this. Serene and I think she planned it even before she returned from the summit."

Reese's scowl deepened. "So does Tanis. This is obviously a trap."

"Yes, but not for me. I think she has some plan for the army, and the faster we find out what that is, the better chance we have of surviving it."

Reese's face stayed stormy, and he shook his head.

"You know I'm right," Sable said. "We need to figure out what she's doing, and no one besides me can know for sure what the truth is."

Reese stepped closer.

"Don't block the soldiers' view of her," Leonis said.

Reese gave him a withering look.

"Maybe we should just leave them in peace," Thulan said.

"Good idea." Leonis took Sable by the shoulders. "Just a bit this way..." He nudged her a step to the side. "Don't want you hidden."

"Leonis!" Reese snapped. "Enough!"

The half-elf held his hands up, looking innocent. "Yes, boss," he said with a grin and started to walk away with Thulan.

"I don't think he used to be that bossy," the dwarf said.

"I don't think he appreciates our skills," Leonis agreed.

"True. That hairstyle could literally save the world."

"Well, not the hair," Leonis said as they ducked around the horses, "but the dress might."

CHAPTER SEVENTY

REESE GAVE SABLE A PAINED LOOK. "Let me come with you."

"How would that possibly help the situation?" Sable asked. "You were banished from this city."

He stepped closer to her, pulling her hand up against his chest. "The idea of you going to her terrifies me."

One of the passing soldiers let out a whistle, and Reese's hand tightened.

"Maybe we should move somewhere a little more private," Sable said.

Reese glanced over his shoulder, and a couple of the soldiers cheered. "Yes, let's." He kept hold of her hand and walked around to the far side of the wagon. They were facing the buildings leading up to Immusmala. It wasn't private, exactly, but the only people they could see were peering out at the soldiers from inside windows and doorways.

The wagon window was open, and Sable held her arm up to it until Innov hopped off. Sable leaned back on the wagon. "Serene is coming with me," she said before Reese could object again, "and she is scary enough that she can probably take care of whatever we come across."

"Even Vivaine's dragon?" he asked, leaning his shoulder against the wall next to her.

Sable paused. "No, but you couldn't take care of the dragon either."

"Which is an excellent reason not to go near it." He reached up and slid a lock of her hair through his fingers. "You do look stunning."

Sable glanced down at the worn leather vest he always wore, the single shirt he owned underneath it. She touched his collar. "You look like you've been living in an army camp for a few weeks." She smiled up at him. "Which is a look I've grown partial to."

"If you mess up her hair, Reese," Thulan yelled, "I will kill you with my hammer!"

"And don't touch the dress!" Leonis added.

Sable sank back against the wagon. "So much for privacy."

Reese leaned closer to her. "I'm so very tempted to mess up your hair," he said with a devious glint in his eye. He looked up at the rows of thin braids. "Except I think it looks perfect." He lifted her chin. "Promise me you'll be careful."

She reached up and pulled his head down. Standing on her tiptoes, she pressed her lips to his. "I promise."

"Reese!" Serene called, her voice alarmed. "Tanis is sick! They need you at the command tent!"

Reese pulled away from Sable.

Serene raced up to them. "He collapsed. Healers have been called, but they need you in the command tent."

Reese swore. "I knew something was wrong with him."

"The Kalesh troops on the hills look to be assembling, too," Serene said. "Sable, we'd better go if we're going to talk to Vivaine before any fighting starts."

"Talk to Vivaine, and then get back here quickly." Reese pointed at both of them. "Neither of you do anything foolish!" He gave Sable one last look before turning and running toward the command tent.

"Is Tanis going to be all right?" Sable asked.

Serene watched Reese, her face troubled. "I don't know." She turned back to Sable. "Do you know what you're going to say to Vivaine?"

"I'm going to ask her what she's doing and listen to her answer."

"And if she chooses not to answer?"

Sable lifted her arm toward Innov, and the phoenix hopped onto it, her now familiar warmth spreading up Sable's arm. "I have a few ideas."

Serene frowned. "Then we'd better get started. We're running out of time to go do something foolish."

The two of them strode up the road toward the closed River Gate. The clouds that had been building in the west had rolled across the sun, dropping the city into shadows. On Sable's arm, Innov glowed brightly, little flames flickering from between her feathers.

Faces plastered against the windows of the buildings they passed. Doors cracked open and people peered out, pointing at the phoenix.

A door farther down the road opened, and Gwen and Terrane stepped out. They caught sight of Sable and Serene and met them on the empty street.

"Everyone agrees that the Kalesh were never camped at the city," Gwen said. "They came in boats, moved through the city, and set up camp on the way to the mines."

"And everyone agrees there aren't many more inside the city," Terrane said. "Aside from the fact that the docks were swarmed with activity for a few days before the prioresses and merchants came back from the city and a few days since, the Kalesh didn't even disrupt much."

"Ambassador Bastian has been seen several times publicly with Vivaine." Gwen's mouth curled at the name. "There seems to be no break in the relationship between the priories and the Kalesh."

"So definitely a trap." Sable looked toward the city gate, which was firmly closed.

"The people here are shocked that there's a northern army here, though," Terrane said. "They got word of it earlier today. Most of the people who live outside the walls ran inside."

Gwen motioned to Terrane. "Let's go report to Tanis." The two started back down the street toward the army. Gwen glanced at Sable and Innov as she passed. "If you get a chance to cause Vivaine any pain at all, please do."

Sable let out a laugh and started toward the River Gate with Serene.

"I've been hoping they will open for Innov," Sable said under her breath. "What do we do if they don't?"

"Knock?" Serene asked.

They got closer to the huge gate, guards watching them from atop the wall.

"We're not going to run into something bad on the other side of the gate, are we?" Sable asked. "Like a Kalesh regiment?"

Serene cast out. Inside the nearest buildings, people crowded up to the windows, their warmth muted by the walls. Up on the city wall, a dozen men stood guard, and past the thick wooden gate came the dim impression of a handful of people scattered in front of the shops on the wide city avenue.

Serene motioned to a Sanctus guard on the wall. "That's Thom." She lifted one hand in a greeting. "He works at the Dragon Priory. Used to guard the library."

"I thought he looked familiar." Sable forced her shoulders to relax.

The guard gave no response to Serene but turned and disappeared out of view.

"That wasn't particularly friendly," Serene said.

"If he's running to the priory, at least Vivaine won't have to wonder who's coming to see her."

Serene nodded. "Since when do Sanctus guards man the wall?"

"There's another one over to the right," Sable said. "I don't recognize that one, though."

They reached the gate and stopped.

"They're not really going to make us knock, are they?" Sable asked under her breath. "What if we have to wait for Thom to reach the Sanctuary and ask Vivaine's permission to let us in?"

The gate made a loud groaning noise, and one side swung back enough for Thom to step through the gap. His eyes scanned the street around them, then came to rest on Sable. "What business have you in Immusmala?"

Sable took a moment to fill her words with enough *vitalle* to reach the men on the wall, the people in the houses around them, and the shoppers on the other side of the gate. "We wish to speak to the High Prioress."

"Why have you brought an army to our gate?" he asked.

"The army of the north is here to offer assistance," Sable said, infusing her words with warmth.

Thom studied her, then nodded. "The High Prioress welcomes you." He moved to the side, offering them room to pass.

"Looks like he already has permission," Serene muttered.

"That's unsettling," Sable answered quietly. She gave Thom what she hoped was a self-possessed smile and walked through the gate.

On the other side, the evening shoppers had turned to the gate. Sable shifted her shoulders, resettling the cloak. The street was shadowed by the city wall, and when Innov stirred, sparks trailed away behind her. A ripple went through the people around them.

"Would you escort us to the Sanctuary?" Sable asked Thom.

Serene gave her a questioning look, but Thom nodded and started up the hill into the city.

"If we're going to gather a crowd, we should look official," Sable said softly.

Several of the shoppers followed them up the hill, and more came out of shops. Before they'd gone two blocks, there were several dozen people following curiously.

"The thief who stole the phoenix!" someone yelled.

"That's not the sort of crowd we want to gather," Serene said.

Sable glanced around. The faces on the street weren't all hostile, but they weren't all friendly either.

A mother pulled her son out of the street ahead of them. "Thief," she spat.

Sable paused and took a step toward her. The woman drew back.

"No one can steal a phoenix," Sable said. "She burns anyone who touches her, unless she chooses to protect them."

Sable knelt down until Innov was at eye level with the boy. He clung to his mother's skirt, but his eyes were wide with wonder.

"That's how I feel about her too," Sable said. "She's magical and beautiful, and I don't really understand her. But she's full of hope. Can you feel it?"

The boy nodded.

Sable looked up at his mother, who was watching the phoenix with a wary expression. Sable could feel the warmth from Innov trickling into her arm, buoying her spirits. "She makes me believe that the best things are actually possible," she said honestly. She looked at the bird, fondly. "She makes me believe that evil won't prevail, that all the things I'm so afraid of for those I love are not certainties but merely fears. That there is real, true good in the world, and I can be a part of it, if I have enough courage."

She stood, and Innov took off, winging over their heads and flying down the street. Every face turned up to watch her, and the glittering bits of fire trailing behind her showered down on the crowd like a blessing. The phoenix was so beautiful, Sable felt an ache in her chest and a coldness on her empty arm.

The mother kept her eyes on Innov as she whirled back around. The phoenix circled above them, showering them in glimmering red and orange embers. The boy let out a whoop of joy and clapped.

Innov shot over the rest of the crowd, and they reached up toward her, murmurs that sounded more excited than angry rippling through them.

Sable watched her fly, then turned and started up the hill again. Serene fell in beside her with an approving nod.

As they wound uphill, the crowd around them grew. There were the occasional mutters, but Innov soared over them all, circling and skimming low over the people as though it was her goal to shower all of them with sparks, and the crowd responded.

By the time they reached the Spine, the large avenue that ran along the highest part of the city, hundreds of people were following them, and the procession felt like a festival day parade. The shops of the wealthy merchants along the Spine emptied as the shoppers joined the throng.

Although the climb had leveled off when they reached the Spine, Sable's heart quickened as they approached the Veil Wall. The gate to the Sanctuary was open, but Vivaine and Eugessa stood under it, flanked by the dragon and Eugessa's black unicorn. A line of Sanctus guards stood several paces behind them.

The sun had dropped below the Tremmen Hills, and the sky was growing darker. In the dusky street, Vivaine shone like a tall, thin star, Argyros glittering beside her. The much wider Eugessa, by comparison, was a dull white, and her unicorn more like a bit of shadow than a live creature.

Sable approached, and Innov swung in a wide arc between her and the gate, leaving a torrent of glittering sparks that momentarily hid the two prioresses.

Sable stopped a half-dozen paces from Vivaine and held out her arm. Innov landed in a burst of embers, keeping her eyes fixed on the dragon.

The crowd behind Sable stopped and fell quiet.

"Have you come to return the phoenix that you stole?" Vivaine asked coldly.

The crowd grumbled at the accusation, and Vivaine's eyes narrowed.

Sable pushed warm threads of *vitalle* toward Vivaine so that her quiet words would be heard by the High Prioress. "Is it a public confrontation that you want? Because Innov has already won over the crowd."

Eugessa straightened and frowned at Sable's voice, and Vivaine studied her.

"You lied about the city being surrounded," Sable said, sending the words to Vivaine. "Shall we talk about why in front of an audience?"

Eugessa cast a questioning look at Vivaine, but the High Prioress paid her no heed.

Vivaine's gaze swept across the crowd, then came back to Sable. Her eyes were cold, but she gave Sable a benevolent nod. "Whatever has motivated you to bring back the phoenix," she said in a rich voice that carried to the people in the street, "we are glad of it. The Sanctuary has been empty without her light."

Murmurs of approval rolled through the crowd.

Sable approached the two prioresses, acutely aware of how near Argyros was with his cold, silver scales. Serene stayed at her shoulder.

"What have you done?" Sable demanded. "Why did you lie about the location of the Kalesh troops?"

"What are you talking about?" Eugessa said dismissively. "No one lied to you about anything. No one cares about you enough to bother to lie to you."

Sable kept her gaze fixed on Vivaine.

"Would you have gathered an army and come if you heard the Kalesh were merely taking over the roads to the mines?" Vivaine asked. Her face had the bland, forbearing look that Sable recognized. Vivaine considered herself safely in control. "I have told you time and time again that I will do whatever I must to keep my city safe."

There was a hint of something almost regretful in the High Prioress's face. "It is not my fault that the Northern Lords you've united have embraced the rebellion that was so hostile to the Kalesh." She paused. "I am vaguely impressed that you managed to unite them. That is no small feat. Had you decided to actually help me, Issable, you could have been a valuable ally instead of an opponent to be destroyed."

Sable glanced down at Argyros, but the dragon showed no sign of the aggression he'd had the day he'd killed Tylar.

Eugessa sneered at Sable. "She could never be an ally. She's nothing."

"Tell me what you've done," Sable said to Vivaine.

"Why? It's too late for you to do anything about it."

Sable's heart beat faster at the warmth in Vivaine's words and the smug expression on her face. Sable's next words stuck in her throat, but she only had one thing to bargain with.

"I'll give you back Innov," Sable said, "if you'll tell me why you lured us here." Sable pointedly did not look at Innov but hoped fervently that the phoenix would agree with this plan.

Serene shifted and frowned at the offer.

"Innov is not yours to give," Eugessa objected.

Sable gave the prioress a flat look and held out her arm. "Would you like to try to take her from me?"

Eugessa's expression soured.

Sable looked back at Vivaine. "I want to know what my men are up against."

"*Your* men?" Vivaine asked with a condescending smile.

JA ANDREWS

Eugessa rolled her eyes. "Even if we believed you'd give Innov back, what makes you think we'll tell you the truth about any of our plans?"

"Vivaine won't lie to Sable," Serene said.

Eugessa's eyes narrowed at the casual use of the High Prioress's name, and she gave an indignant sniff. Her hair was a fluffy cloud of dark brown around her head. Her gown was crusted with pearls, and she wore several necklaces, each hung with a large gem. Sable's gaze caught on her hand, a plan coming together in her mind.

"The price for Innov," Sable said, "is an explanation of what you have planned, and one of Eugessa's rings."

"Absolutely not!" Eugessa said indignantly.

"I agree to your terms," Vivaine said over her.

"I don't!" Eugessa objected.

"Give her a ring," Vivaine ordered her.

"No!" the prioress objected. "I'm not a part of any of this."

"Now, Eugessa," Vivaine snapped.

The Prioress of the Horn glared at the High Prioress, but she started to pull a ring with a large, honey-colored gem off her thick finger.

"Not that one," Sable said. "The blue butterfly ring."

Eugessa's eyes widened in outrage. "No!"

Serene turned slowly to frown at Sable.

"I know where you got it," Sable said, pouring the truth into her words, and Eugessa stiffened. "It's an interesting story. Shall I tell it to this crowd?"

Eugessa glowered at her but shifted to her pinky and worked the ring off, thrusting it at Sable.

"You're nothing but a thief and a snake," Eugessa hissed.

Sable took the ring, the irregular blue stones glinting dully in the evening light, and slid it snugly onto her first finger.

"The phoenix?" Vivaine said firmly. "She belongs here in the Sanctuary, not roaming the wilds with an actress." She gave Sable's dress and hair a dismissive look.

Sable turned to Innov, running a hand down her feathers, feeling the heat rush out from between them. "Go home," she said to the bird, forcing the words. She lifted her arm, but Innov just blinked at her and let out a trilling call.

"I know you understand me," Sable said. "The Sanctuary is in desperate need of something good and pure. It's time for you to go." She pushed some *vitalle* into the words, fighting off the ache that was growing in her. "Thank you. For everything." She ran her fingers down Innov's chest. "Please go," she whispered.

Innov leaned into Sable's hand, then spread her wings and took off, spiraling up into the sky.

The crowd, which had been standing back, milling about, gave a cheer. Sable watched Innov sail over the Sanctuary wall, feeling an emptiness grow in the bird's wake.

She let her arm drop and turned back to Vivaine. "Explain yourself."

"Another detachment of Kalesh troops left three days ago," the High Prioress said simply. "They sailed to the eastern bank of the Black River, where they began their march north."

The warmth of Vivaine's words wrapped around Sable with a smothering heat.

"What?" Serene asked, the word almost a gasp.

"Lords Erick, Loren, and Darien chose to align themselves with the rebels," Vivaine said. "Did you think the Kalesh would ignore that?"

Eugessa stared at Vivaine, her face shocked.

"You..." A deep, horrible dread grew in Sable's stomach. "You lured the northern army down here with the lie that you needed help? So the Kalesh could attack an undefended land?"

Vivaine's eyes glittered with a light as cold and cruel as Argyros's scales. "My city will be safe," she said, the words hot and heartless. "Whatever the cost."

CHAPTER SEVENTY-ONE

SABLE STARED at the High Prioress, hardly able to breathe. Next to her, Serene stood still as a statue.

Even Eugessa had the decency to look appalled.

Tanis's army had pulled every soldier it could from the three territories west of the river. There was no one there to protect the towns, the homes, the families...

"You sacrificed half the north?" Sable's words came out barely above a whisper.

Vivaine met her gaze without a hint of shame. "I offered the Kalesh an opportunity to deal with a faction in the north that was causing them trouble in exchange for their pledge that my city will remain independent."

"When did you make this agreement?" Eugessa demanded. "You had no right—"

"The Kalesh are welcome to the gold," Vivaine said, ignoring Eugessa. "They're welcome to trade and flood the city with their goods. But now, I have guaranteed that they will not touch the priories. They will not take over the merchants in this city. There will be no shrines to the Dragon Emperor. The men of my city will not be taken into their army. We will be left in safety."

"You're a fool to believe them," Serene said to Vivaine, her voice dripping with scorn. "You just betrayed the only people still willing to help you. When the Kalesh come for your priories, there will be no one left."

"I hope they lock you in your own dungeons," Sable said. "How many Kalesh went north?"

"Several thousand," Vivaine answered, unruffled. "You won't catch them—they're days ahead of you. By the time your army returns home, the Kalesh will have established themselves in the western territories of the north. Lord Perric and Lord Runess will have some decisions to make soon. If they are smart, they will create an alliance with the Kalesh as quickly as they can."

Fury rose deep inside Sable. "Were you planning this at the summit? While you spoke to everyone of peace?"

"I have been in conversation with General Goll for a very long time about this land," she said calmly. "We only came to this agreement after you destroyed the sanctity of the summit." She gave Sable a contemptuous look. "You should run along. I doubt the Kalesh troops that *are* still here will take kindly to an army invading the peninsula. You have a bit of a fight ahead of you before you can start back north. You really shouldn't dawdle."

The truth of the words was undeniable.

"Please escort these two back to the River Gate," Vivaine said to Thom, who waited a discreet distance away.

He nodded and gestured toward the still-crowded street.

Sable stepped closer to Vivaine with a scathing look. "We came here to save Immusmala, but you betrayed us. Not only that, you betrayed this city by inviting the Kalesh here in greater numbers."

Vivaine's face stayed impassive, but Argyros let out a low growl.

"This city deserves better than a woman who lies and stabs their allies in the back, while selling her people out to the Empire, just to keep her own seat of power for a little while longer." Sable shoved every bit of *vitalle* she could muster into her next words. "You are done, Vivaine. I'm taking this city from the Kalesh, and I'm taking it from you."

The thin mask of benevolence that still remained on Vivaine's face peeled away. "You think this city will ever follow you?"

"I'm not taking it for myself," Sable said. "I'm just taking it away from you."

Without a word, she turned and strode away from the gate.

Serene followed, her face bleak. The crowd parted for Thom, and they followed him.

"How exactly are you going to take the city from Vivaine?" Serene asked quietly.

Sable glanced at her. "I'm working on it. Let's deal with one daunting battle at a time. Get back to the troops and tell them what is happening. I'm going to get us some reinforcements."

Serene grabbed Sable's arm. "Where are you going?"

The sky above them was fading to a deep blue. Lamplighters moved slowly along the Spine, lighting the lanterns along the avenue.

"I know how to get around this city in the dark." Sable kept her voice low. "Tell Reese that I'll try to get him reinforcements from the city before morning. We need to fight our way out of here as quickly as possible."

"He's gonna kill me if I come back without you." Serene looked pointedly at the butterfly ring. "Especially if I tell him you're going to talk to Kiva. Alone."

Sable shifted the ring. "I'm not thrilled with the idea myself, but Kiva has access to what I need. And one of us needs to go back and tell the army what's happening."

Serene shook her head. "I don't like it. Reese is really not going to like it. Neither is Jae, or Atticus, or Thulan, or Leonis, or our entire army."

"There is absolutely nothing I can do to help the army get ready for a battle," Sable said. "Nothing. Nor can I help them actually fight. But getting them some reinforcements is something I might have a chance at."

"Might? Have a chance?"

"The next street angles down into Dockside," Sable said. "I'll find a way out of the city later."

"The city that is barring the gates because there are *two* foreign armies outside of it?"

Sable grimaced. "True. It might not be until tomorrow morning."

Serene's face was set in a scowl. "Fine. But be careful."

"I'm not the one going out to an army camp," Sable pointed out. "I'll be inside the fortified city." They'd reached the street that headed down toward Dockside. "When Reese starts yelling, remind him he has no right to be mad at you."

Serene gave her one last tight-lipped look but nodded.

Sable pulled her black cloak tightly around herself and ducked into the rapidly darkening shadows of the street, hurrying away before Thom noticed she was gone.

She passed under the bakery's wide awning, which in the daylight was bright blue, turned the sharp corner around the hatter's shop, and moved quickly down the next block.

From the corner of the next street, she could see the looming stone wall separating the harbor and Dockside from the rest of the city. She'd lived in the shadows of that wall for years and never realized how strategic it was. From the top of it, archers could shoot flaming arrows down on every boat in the port.

Sable paused in a shadowy doorway. The familiar streets hadn't changed. She could find Kiva's office in the Broken Mast Tavern even if she were blindfolded.

But she'd forgotten Kiva had changed. He'd transformed himself into a respected merchant who certainly would have moved his headquarters somewhere more reputable.

A little pop by her side startled her.

"Mistress," Purn said, "please don't go to see *him*!"

Sable set her hand on Purn's black hair. The kobold was dressed in her dark purple cape from Reese, which, along with her blue skin, made her look like a piece of shadow in the darkening street.

Sable held up her hand with the ring.

Purnicious's nose crinkled at it. "I know, I was there." Her eyes grew worried. "That was the worst meeting I've ever seen! Vivaine is so evil and..." Her voice dropped to a whisper. "You gave them Innov!" Her voice was full of hurt.

Sable knelt next to the little kobold. "I didn't want to, but I had nothing else to trade. And she was never really mine to keep."

Purn sniffed sadly. "She deserves better than that place."

"It is her home. I couldn't have forced her to go if she didn't want to." Sable looked at her and shook her head. "I can't believe I didn't think that you'd be there. Vivaine made me so mad, I wasn't thinking clearly. You could have taken the message back to Tanis immediately."

"I did," Purn said, "and came back to make sure Lady Serene reached the troops safely. That Sanctus guard was mad that you got away, and he started a search for you."

"I thought he might. But we need help, Purn. What did Tanis say? How fast can we get back north?"

Purnicious looked up, her expression miserable. "Tanis fell senseless near sundown and hasn't woken. The healers say he's weakening fast."

Sable set her hand against the wall to steady herself. "But...who's leading the troops?"

"Reese, for now," Purnicious said. "The lords aren't happy, but Tanis had the other officers pledge their loyalty to Reese when he was getting sick, and the lords could do nothing but agree." The kobold reached up and took her hand pleadingly. "Reese needs your help, mistress. The men need to see you. And...Innov," she ended on a whisper.

Sable gripped Purn's hand. "That's impossible now." The wretched look on the kobold's face mirrored how Sable felt. "I need to talk to Kiva. Then we'll go to Reese. Kiva has a new office, doesn't he?

Purnicious scowled but nodded. "Up this street, at the corner on the Spine. Above the fabric shop."

"On the Spine?" She'd underestimated Kiva again. An office on the main avenue of the city was no small feat.

She started up the street, and Purnicious popped out of view but bumped into Sable's legs often enough to let her know she was still there.

The windows of the fabric shop on the Spine were brightly lit against the growing night. The avenue itself was still busy, although not as busy as it should have been on a summer evening. It was lit with lampposts and lantern light, and most of the stores appeared to be open.

Sable pulled the hood of her cloak up and strode across the street, pushing open the door into Kiva's fabric shop.

Bolts of fabrics were lined up along the walls, glowing with rich colors. Rolled bundles of blues, greens, and deep russet reds stood next to each other on dark wooden shelves. The light from dozens of lanterns caught on sparkles of shining thread woven into them. A long cape of pristine, snowy white silk hung just inside the door, a scarlet, embroidered dragon writhing up the side.

An older man with a neat, black shirt and perfectly combed hair approached her. "What can I help you find, my lady?"

"I'm looking for Kiva." She pushed off her hood.

The man blinked at her and moved to the side, blocking her way toward the back corner of the store. "Kiva is a very busy man, and I assure you that he trusts me completely to take care of your needs. What sort of fabric are you in need of? A new cloak, perhaps? The fur on that one seems a little worn."

Sable leaned around him and saw a thin staircase in the corner. "I see Kiva's even upgraded his guards. Of course, I suppose having Pete or Boone bullying customers wouldn't be good for business." She stepped around a nearby table holding rolls of fabric and strode toward the back stairs.

The older man sputtered and hurried after her, but three bolts of fabric mysteriously toppled off a table in front of him, blocking his path.

Sable shot a smile in the direction where Purn must be. "Kiva!" she called, starting up the stairs.

An enormous man stood at the top, his arms crossed in their familiar, threatening stance.

"Hello, Boone." Sable stopped in front of him. "Beautiful evening, isn't it?"

He didn't move.

"Kiva!" she called again. "Get your thug out of my way."

"Sable?" Kiva's voice came from down the hall, laced with

surprise. "Boone, even your thick skull should know Sable is always welcome here."

The huge man shifted out of the way, leaving Sable enough room to barely squeeze past him. She gave him an annoyed look, and for the first time ever, she saw his eyes widen in surprise.

He grunted and grabbed for his belt, which was rapidly shrinking and biting into his gut.

He fumbled with it, and Sable stepped past him, grinning.

She moved down the tall, narrow hallway, which was uncomfortably like the one Kiva had occupied in the Dockside tavern. Those walls had always felt confining, and while these attempted to do the same, Sable straightened her shoulders and strode toward Kiva's office, leaving enough room beside her for the invisible Purnicious to fit.

She reached the doorway of Kiva's office and stopped. The walls of the office were lined with shelves of dark, carved wood. There were few books on the shelves. Instead, they were filled with expensive-looking trinkets and small chests. The large window was covered with thick brocade drapes in a rich red. Kiva's desk presided over the middle of the room like a fat judge, and the man himself sat behind it with his eyebrows raised.

"My, my," he said. "Don't you look...regal."

Sable stepped into the room. Two chairs sat at the near side of his desk, both short enough that if she sat in them, she'd look like a child. She walked over to one of the shelves, looking at the titles of the stack of books. "You've improved locations."

"I'd say we've both moved up a bit in the world." His voice wasn't quite full of his normal smugness. "You perhaps a bit more than me."

Sable turned toward him and caught him glancing toward the hall behind her with an unfamiliar expression.

She resisted the urge to turn around. Instead, she pushed *vitalle* into the next words. "I have a proposition for you."

Immediately she felt the heat from herself and Purn. A heartbeat later she felt the simmering form of Kiva, but behind her, the hall was empty.

He smiled slyly. "Please say it's a marriage proposal. I have always dreamed of marrying a queen."

She studied him, ignoring his words. He sat easily in his chair, his hands clasped together on his desk. But his knuckles were white and there was that...*something* in his expression. He shifted at her scrutiny, and she realized what it was. Wariness.

In all the years she'd known him, all the times she'd thought she might finally have the upper hand with him, she'd never once seen him wary.

"What are you afraid of, Kiva?" She couldn't muster the gentleness the question deserved. It came out quiet but blunt, and Kiva's hands twitched.

His smile faded. "You." The words were fully, warmly true.

Sable stared at him. There hadn't been even the hint of a lie. "You've never been afraid of me."

"You've never had an army before."

"It's not my army."

He let out a humorless laugh. "You had a proposition for me, I believe?"

She nodded. "Help me run the Kalesh out of the city for good."

"That old goal?" He sank back into his chair and let out a chuckle. "You've been after that for a year, and I've never once helped you."

The shift in the conversation was so stark, Sable could almost feel it, as though the floor had tilted the slightest bit away from her.

Kiva grinned at her, all traces of wariness gone. "Why would I start now?"

She was missing something, but she had no idea what it was, and no time to figure it out. "I've never had the right thing to barter with."

"And you do now?"

"If you help me..." Sable held up her hand, and the silver butterfly caught the torchlight in the office. "I'll give you this."

Kiva's eyes locked on the ring. For a moment, he sat perfectly still. "I'm listening."

CHAPTER SEVENTY-TWO

"I KNOW you're not pleased with the Kalesh army that's here," Sable said. "And you'll be less pleased when you hear that they're here because Vivaine invited them."

His dragged his focus away from the ring and met Sable's gaze. "Vivaine was as shocked and angry about this as everyone." He tried to keep his voice level, but his posture had changed. He leaned forward in his chair again.

"No, she wasn't." Sable turned and picked up a figurine of Amah from Kiva's shelf. Her hands shook, and she set it back down before Kiva could notice, but she kept her eye on the small, silver goddess. She pushed *vitalle* into the next words, making sure Kiva felt the truth of them. "The good prioress made a deal with General Goll. She offered him ownership of the mines and all trade outside of Immusmala." She turned back to face him. The room felt almost hot with her words.

"All trade?" He said the words slowly.

Sable nodded. "Then, she made Callie believe the Kalesh army was surrounding Immusmala so that I'd convince the northern army to come here, stripping three northern territories of their armies. While Goll sent troops north to conquer it."

His mouth fell open in shock. "She...How?"

"She has the ability to twist what you see," Sable said. "It's how she always appears to be so bright." It felt remarkably good to expose Vivaine's secret, even if it was to Kiva.

Kiva sank back and turned to look at the closed window. "I knew her reaction to the army wasn't right." His voice was viciously sharp. "I thought she was trying to act calm..."

Sable stepped up to the nearest chair and set her hands on the back of it. "The northern army came to drive off the Kalesh and unite with the south. Together, we can protect the docks and the river. We can make it incredibly hard for the Kalesh to come back."

Kiva shook his head. "There's too much gold in the mountains for them to give up."

"Then we destroy the roads to the mountains and the entrances to the mines, and we set fire to any ship that comes near the shore."

He let out a laugh. "That's a brazen plan."

"It feels like the time for a little brazenness." She shifted her hand on the chair and saw Kiva's gaze drop to the butterfly ring. "But Vivaine cannot stay in power. I am going to tell everyone what she's done."

"They'll never believe you," he said.

"They will." Sable infused her words with warmth.

Kiva tilted his head to the side. "Maybe they will."

"When Vivaine is gone, there will be a power vacuum. Time to decide where you'd like to be positioned when that happens. Do you want to be known for supporting the Kalesh or helping to drive them out?"

"You still haven't told me what you really want."

She swallowed. "The first thing I want is for you to drive the remaining Kalesh out of Dockside."

A smile twitched at the edge of his mouth. "That would definitely declare which side I'm on. And lose me a lot of money."

"That money is gone. The Kalesh already plan to control everything outside this city. They have no need to pay you rent any longer."

His face stayed mildly amused, and she couldn't tell if he believed her or not.

"I assume there's a second request?"

"The Merchant Guild has every reason to want the Kalesh gone at this point, and I need reinforcements for the northern army at dawn."

He looked at her for a long moment.

"Unless," she said, "you don't have the influence with the Guild to make that happen. In which case I should go speak with someone like Lord Trelles."

He smirked at the barb, but there was a hint of ire in it. "I can get you the merchants' guards."

His words were true.

"But will you?" she asked bluntly.

He leaned forward. "That is a very big price for a single ring."

"The ring is just an extra thank-you from me. What you're paying for is your freedom to keep..." She gestured around the room. "This little kingdom you've built."

Kiva let out a long breath, and a smile spread across his face. "You really are a gem, Sable. All right, I agree."

The words were still warm, but she gave him a skeptical look. "Just like that?"

"I've grown a bit tired of having the Kalesh in Dockside," he said, "and the Guild was chafing at the growing presence of the Kalesh even before this. What they didn't have was a way to revolt. But with your army willing to fight, I can convince them to join."

She sorted through his words, looking for any way he could double-cross her, even though everything he'd said was true.

He leaned forward, watching her with an unnerving intensity. "I don't know why you'd trust me."

Sable flinched at the cold bite of the lie.

He sank back in his chair, his expression guarded. "Three different jays told me you could do that, but I didn't believe them. I thought you were pulling some ruse over on the Northern Lords. Some new act." He crossed his arms across his stomach, looking at her in a hungry, calculating way. "You can really tell if someone's lying?"

She gripped the back of the chair. Telling the Northern Lords had felt freeing. Brave. But the greediness, the predatory look in Kiva's eyes was the response she'd always known he'd have.

She fought back the old, familiar, powerless feeling he'd always given her and met his gaze. "Talking with you has always been unpleasant."

He smirked. "I bet it has."

There was something more than humor in his smile. A bit of the wariness from earlier.

"You look worried," she said. "Anything else you'd like to confess to me?"

He let out a laugh and shook his head slowly. "I did not use you to your full potential, Sable." Those words were very warm, and in them Sable caught a hint of warmth coming down the hallway behind her.

She pushed off the chair, shifting so her back was to the bookshelf and she could see the doorway. "I need the merchant guards at the River Gate by dawn. When will you drive the Kalesh out of Dockside?"

"Dawn sounds like the perfect time," he said, still smiling.

She nodded. "Once those two things happen, the ring is yours."

"I'm looking forward to tomorrow, then."

The person's footsteps rang out in the hall, and Sable straightened. "I'll leave you to your other business. I have an army to reach before bed. Good night, Kiva."

"Good night, Sable," he said pleasantly.

She turned just as Rabbit appeared in the doorway.

"You won't get out to the army tonight." He walked into the room. "The constables have the wall locked down tight. Even my exit's blocked."

"What news from past the wall?" Kiva asked.

"I didn't come to bring you news." Rabbit turned to Sable. "Reese sent me to help you get back."

Kiva's eyebrows rose. "You're taking orders from Reese now?"

Rabbit ignored him. "Serene told us where you were going. But getting back out tonight is out of the question. Around dawn tomorrow, there'll be a changing of the guards, and I've made sure the man guarding my exit owes me. I can get you out then, but I'm afraid you're stuck in the city for now. If you're done here, I can take you somewhere safe for the night."

Every word he spoke was true, and Sable nodded. She turned back to Kiva. He was looking between her and Rabbit with narrowed eyes.

"How will I know that you've taken care of the Kalesh in Dockside?" she asked.

Kiva's mouth spread in a smile that didn't come close to reaching his eyes. "You'll know."

Sable walked behind Rabbit between the rolls of fabric in the shop.

"Reese was...not pleased to hear you'd come to see Kiva," he said as they stepped out into the street. "And by 'not pleased,' I mean he was ready to order a unit to attack the city gates and come find you."

"Who talked him out of it?"

"I did." Rabbit smiled at her. "Although once he hears I can't get you back out tonight, I'm not sure we won't still have the same issue."

"He's not stupid enough to waste troops on this," Sable said.

Rabbit glanced in the direction of the northern army. "You didn't see him."

"I can get word to him that I'm safe," Sable said, wondering how close Purnicious was. "And that we'll be in here all night."

"I sent word that I knew where you were." His voice was warm. "I did not mention you were at Kiva's."

Sable paused. "That was probably wise."

Rabbit nodded. "And I said we'd be here until morning."

Sable considered the man. "I underestimated you when I first saw you in Tanis's tent."

He shrugged. "I wouldn't trust someone I thought worked with Kiva, either."

She frowned at him. "You do work with Kiva."

"No," he corrected her. "I occasionally sell Kiva information and, even more rarely, buy information from him, but I will never willingly work *with* that man again." He glanced down the well-lit Spine. "The Sanctus guards are looking for you, though, so we should get you somewhere safe for the night."

"I have somewhere, and one more person I need to talk to."

He frowned at her but shrugged. "Lead the way."

She raised an eyebrow. "I'll be fine on my own."

"But I'll be dead if Reese finds out I let you head off somewhere alone and something happens to you. And I'm feeling rather at home with Tanis and the north. I'd rather not have to find another place to live."

His words were warm, and Sable shrugged. She headed for a street that would parallel the Spine. "No matter how all this plays out, I'll be leaving the south quickly. I want to see the one sister I can reach tonight."

"She still live at Lord Trelles's house?" Rabbit asked, falling in beside her.

Sable glanced at him. "I forgot you knew her."

"I've met Talia on several occasions." He walked easily beside her, but Sable caught his eyes scanning the shadows and alleys they passed. "I like her."

They moved quickly through the streets, hurrying through the torchlit sections and following as many dark alleys as they could until they came out across the street from a huge house.

"I have some people to contact early tomorrow, but I can meet you here an hour before dawn," Rabbit said.

Sable raised an eyebrow. "If Reese has you gathering information, just worry about that. I spent ten years of my life sneaking around this city at night. I can do it once more."

Rabbit paused. "He won't—"

"Reese isn't here," she interrupted him. "Just tell me where to meet you so we can cross the wall."

He gave her an unhappy look. "The Fallen Gate. Before dawn."

The rarely used Fallen Gate was at the end of the wall near Dockside. "Easy enough. The Fallen Gate before dawn."

"Tell Talia I said hello." He still looked vaguely unhappy as he stepped back into the shadows.

Sable started across the street, feeling Purn's hand on her cloak. "How do we get in?" Sable asked.

"The back alley," Purnicious whispered.

Sable headed there, and Purn took her hand, leading her in

through a dark warehouse to a door at the back of Lord Trelles's house.

"This is the servants' entrance," Purn said. "Wait here." She popped out of sight.

A few minutes later, the door opened, and Talia peered out. "Sable?"

Sable stepped forward, and Talia gave her a wide smile and grabbed her hand to pull her inside.

"Come upstairs! You look lovely! Did that dwarf do your hair again?" Talia climbed up a set of stairs inside the back of the house, through a thin hall, and into a snug little room. Dresses in every imaginable color lined the far wall, a chest of drawers against the nearest wall had jewelry laid out neatly on the top, and a bed was tucked up near the window.

Purnicious sat on a stool, beaming at the two sisters.

"Come, sit," Talia said, dropping down onto the bed. "Tell me everything! You came with an *army*! How did you possibly get an army? And Reese is helping *lead* it?"

Talia's words rushed out, washing over Sable, utterly familiar. Sable sank down, her shoulders relaxing.

Talia shook her head. "What on earth happened since the prioress died?" Her face fell. "I'm so sorry, by the way. I know you loved her."

Sable nodded. "I did."

"I knew you didn't hurt her," Talia said, her voice growing angry. "No one who ever saw you with Narine would believe that you'd ever hurt her. Callie didn't believe it, or Kiva, although you probably don't care what he thinks." She paused. "Why are you smiling like that?"

Sable looked her sister over. Talia's hair was braided into something elaborate and beautiful, and the dress she was wearing was relatively simple but still looked nice enough to belong to a wealthy merchant's daughter. "It is so good to see you, Talia. You're elegant and stylish and everything you always should have been, and I'm really happy about that."

Talia waited with a raised eyebrow. "No comments about working for Kiva."

"I think I've made my opinion on that clear." She took her sister's hand. "No matter what happens here tomorrow, I'm leaving to go back north with the army…and I don't plan on coming back."

Talia gripped her hand, her face taking on a resigned look. "I know. Or at least I was afraid that's what would happen."

Sable glanced around the room. "You could come with me," she said ruefully.

"Maybe someday," Talia answered. "But for now, it feels right to be here."

"I know," Sable said. "But I had to ask."

"Well," Talia said, settling herself more comfortably on the bed, "let's not waste this night talking about Kiva or Vivaine or armies. Purnicious has told me about something much more interesting. I want to know everything about Reese there is to tell. Did you really almost kill him when he kissed you?"

Sable laughed. "I did."

"And?"

Sable scooted back and leaned against the wall next to the window. "You'd like him. He always tells me I don't give you enough credit. He's very impressed with all the things you've done."

"I hadn't realized he was so brilliant."

"And he thinks Ryah is an angel who's too good for this world."

"Why haven't you married him yet?"

"I'm still waiting for Purn's approval." Sable looked up at the little kobold, who was fiddling with a scarf.

"He's growing on me," Purnicious admitted.

"Tell me everything from the beginning," Talia said. "How did you first meet him? What was he like?"

"Grumpy," Purn said.

Sable laughed again. "He had three bruised ribs, and he was very grumpy. He even tried Ryah's patience at first…"

The stars outside the window were fading into the slowly bluing sky when Sable sat up from the mound of blankets Purnicious had made for her to sleep in. Sable had seen the stars creep across the sky, shifting in jolts and bounds across the window as she dozed through the night.

The floor creaked as she stood, sounding loud in the quiet house.

Talia groaned and opened her eyes. "You cannot go looking like that," she said sleepily.

"How can you even see me?" Sable whispered.

"I can see the outline of your head, and it's awful. Hold on." Talia rolled out of her bed and lit a candle on a table. She picked up a brush and motioned for Sable to sit on the edge of the bed.

"I don't really have time—"

"Purnicious told me how all the soldiers rally around you. You're not going out to see them looking like a bird nested on your head."

"But—"

"Sit still. I'll be quick." She tugged at the braids that Thulan had put in and combed out Sable's hair. "You want me to do some face paint, too?"

"Talia, I need to be at the city wall before dawn."

"Fine." Talia picked up a delicate, silver hair clip and pinned it into place with a long, silver pin.

Purnicious shook out the black cloak Sable had worn last night. The fur collar was gone, and in its place the cowl and front of the robe was lined with cream fabric.

"Is that from my dress?" Sable asked.

"You need to wear something different today," Purn said. "The whole city saw you yesterday. I figured Talia would lend you something."

"See if the light blue dress near the end works," Talia told the kobold.

Talia finished, and Sable donned the blue dress, letting Purnicious shorten it to fit.

"I need to go." Sable slipped on the black cloak.

Talia wrapped her arms around Sable. "Be careful," she said into Sable's hair.

"I love you." Sable pulled Talia tight. "And I am proud of all the things you've done. I am."

"I love you too," Talia said, sniffing. "Please be careful." She knelt and hugged Purnicious too. "I'll miss you, Purn. Try to keep Sable out of too much trouble."

Purnicious wiped tears off her cheek and sniffled. "I will, Talia. Please be careful with yourself."

Talia led the way back down the stairs and out the back door of the house.

Sable glanced out the door. "There might be fighting inside the city. You might want to stay inside."

Talia nodded and pulled a thin shawl around her shoulders. Sable slipped into the dark warehouse and back out into the street.

Behind her, the beautifully clear sky was lightening, as though this were just a normal summer morning. As though the two armies outside the city weren't about to maim and kill each other.

As though there were some possibility other than this day ending in heartbreak.

CHAPTER SEVENTY-THREE

SABLE FELT PURN's hand against her leg as they moved into the dark alley, and she hesitated at the first street.

Sable looked into shadows. "I'm terrified about how today will go," Sable whispered honestly, and in the warmth, she felt no one beyond herself and Purnicious. They hurried forward, keeping to alleys just off the Spine, checking each new street as they reached it.

The Fallen Gate, the southernmost gate of the city, sat at the end of the Spine. They were three blocks from the gate when Sable ran out of alleys. She stood at a dark corner, peering down the Spine toward the gate.

The dark blue of the sky showed men patrolling the top of the wall and a handful of guards on the ground at the gate, but almost no one in the street.

"I would really, really like to find Rabbit," Sable said quietly. She felt the heat of a man walking down the avenue and one figure standing in a shadowed doorway closer to the wall. "Purn, can you see if that's him at the second door from the wall?"

There was a pop, a moment of silence, then another pop. "It is him." Purnicious said. "How are you going to get there?"

"The avenue is too wide open to skulk down," Sable said. "Time to look like I belong here, I suppose."

She straightened her shoulders and pulled the hood of her cloak a bit further forward, trying to ignore how quickly her heart was beating. She walked into the avenue, heading toward the doorway where Rabbit waited, hoping he stood there because it was his building and when she got there, they could go inside.

She reached the center of the avenue, and three men detached themselves from the gate, moving toward her. Sable's heart pounded painfully against her ribs.

She kept her gaze forward, hoping they would merely pass by.

"Issable." The Kalesh accent caught on the first syllable of her name, drawing out in a long *ahh* sound.

Sable drew to a sharp stop.

Ambassador Bastian approached, dressed in a dragon-embroidered robe. This one was a light grey with a green dragon twisting up around him. The dragon's head was stitched across his chest, its jaw spread wide, displaying sharp, vicious teeth. Behind him came two Kalesh soldiers in their black uniforms.

She swallowed and attempted to keep her voice even. "Ambassador."

"It is not safe for a *zabat* on the streets this morning." He stopped a few paces from her. His two soldiers moved to flank her.

"It's been a long time since you called me a *zabat*."

"And yet you're acting like one more and more." He met her gaze. "Inciting rebellions, starting fires." He glanced around the street. "Allow me to escort you somewhere safer."

"That's very kind of you, but I'm on my way out of the city."

"I'm afraid I'm going to have to insist. This way, please." He motioned toward the gate.

The soldiers moved behind her, and after a moment's hesitation, Sable fell in next to the ambassador. Rabbit watched her pass from his doorway.

Sable took a deep breath, trying to calm her racing pulse. The ambassador was as non-assuming and pleasant as always, but the soldiers' footsteps behind her sounded heavy in the quiet morning.

"I assume you're not here to escort me through the gate?" she said.

Bastian smiled. "I could, but I don't think you'll be much help to the north on that side of the wall."

They reached the gate, and Bastian motioned for the guards to stay, while he walked toward a set of stairs set into the wall.

"I can't be much help to them on this side, either," she answered.

He waited until they were at the bottom of the stairs before answering in a quiet voice. "No, but you might be a help from the top." He gestured for her to precede him up the steps. "You'll have a great view of the battle and could signal to your people."

She stopped and folded her arms. "I don't think the constables will just stand by and let me signal to my people."

"It's unlikely they will recognize you. They will recognize me, however, and will be happy to let me watch from up there."

Sable studied him. "Why are you helping me?"

"Because, as much as you might not believe it, I do not want this violence, nor do I want the Empire to take over your land violently. I thought I could keep things peaceful, but…"

Sable felt her anger growing. "Your troops are attacking an unprotected north right now!"

"They are not *my* troops. They are Goll's." He sighed. "I recognize that you won't see the difference."

"And you disagree with Goll so much that you'd sell out your people to help me?" she demanded.

Bastian met her eyes, his face full of regret. "Would you believe that I owe you more than I owe the Empire?"

"No," she said bluntly, despite the fact that his words swirled warmly around them.

The world was brightening, and the scar down his face that Melia had given him was stark against his temple. This was the man who had made himself a career off a lie. Who had fought Melia and her rebellion and thought killing innocent people a fair price to pay for peace.

"Were you waiting for me this morning?" she asked.

He nodded. "I know smugglers prefer leaving through the Fallen Gate. It seemed reasonable that you might also." The man was tense, but his words were still true.

Behind her, she was fairly certain Rabbit still waited in the avenue to see if she'd extricate herself. But Bastian was right. If she could get up onto the wall and see the entire battlefield, she could maybe tell Serene or Reese what she was seeing.

The stairs stretched up next to her like the opening to a trap, but it was a trap that might give the northern army an advantage.

"You told me once that I should never underestimate my enemies," she said.

"And you shouldn't. But I'm not your enemy, Issable."

Trusting the warmth in his words, she turned and started up the stairs. Behind her, Bastian let out a small sigh of relief.

Sable stepped onto the top of the wall, and the salty breeze from the ocean pushed past her. To the east, over the roofs of the city, the spires of the priories rose against the brightening sky. The unruffled ocean stretched off to the southern horizon in a dark bluish-green. Sable moved to the parapet along the wall, looking over onto the wide slope rising away from the water. There was no sign of the armies on this side of the hill. The wall snaked up the hill and disappeared over the top in the direction of the River Gate.

"This way." Bastian started along the wall. His robe rustled as he walked, the body of the green dragon glittering around his back. He glanced up at the sky. "Dawn is upon us, and the troops will be mobilizing."

Sable glanced back into the city. The harbor in Dockside was clearly visible, as were the dirty buildings and the wall that separated it from the rest of the city. To the east, the edge of the sun broke the horizon, and Sable studied Dockside. There was no sign that Kiva had kept his promise.

She let out a sigh. It was too much to hope that Kiva would have actually helped. She started after Bastian, keeping her hood up. He paused, waiting for her to catch up.

An explosion shook the wall beneath her feet. Grabbing the parapet, she spun to face Dockside, where a huge plume of smoke rose from the gap where one of the Kalesh buildings had just stood.

Another explosion sounded, then a third. The entire corner of

Dockside was smothered in a cloud of debris and smoke, but the hulking shapes of the buildings were gone.

Sable stared open-mouthed at the destruction.

While she watched, two flaming projectiles were hurled from the Dockside wall, smashing onto the decks of two Kalesh ships in the harbor. Flames shot out from the impact, racing up masts and across the decks. The ships burst into flames, and men flung themselves into the water.

Every soldier on the wall stared toward Dockside. Shouts and cries rose from the city.

Bastian stepped up to Sable's shoulder, and she pulled away from him. However many people had just died in Dockside, they were likely all Kalesh.

Looking at the destruction, his face grew old and worn. "I hate war," he said heavily. He turned away from the smoke and searched Sable's face. "Was that done with or without Kiva's help?"

She toyed with the idea of lying or not answering, but it felt too late to bother with that. "With."

He studied her a moment longer. "Someday you're going to have to tell me how you managed that." There was a note of admiration in his voice. "Maybe you stand a chance after all."

CHAPTER SEVENTY-FOUR

THE RISING sun caught on the column of smoke billowing up from Dockside like a rust-tainted cloud, harsh and savage against the tranquil dawn sky.

Sable followed Bastian along the wall toward the River Gate. Over the parapet, the entire battlefield was laid out. Her gaze caught on the tightly formed units of Kalesh at the far side of the wide, grassy field, near the feet of the Tremmen Hills. The soldiers, dressed fully in black, stood like fragments ripped from her nightmares to be lined up in ominous ranks.

A large command tent sat to the side of the Kalesh troops, soldiers crawling around it like a colony of ants.

"Is General Goll there?" she asked Bastian.

He nodded, striding past city constables and Sanctus guards who stepped out of his way. Sable kept her hood up, and no one made any move to stop them.

She leaned closer to the parapet as they walked, catching sight of the edge of the northern army positioned along the base of the wall. Between the two armies, the wide, grassy plain looked soft in the early light.

Bastian stopped along the wall in an empty stretch between constables. "This is as close as we're likely to get."

Sable leaned over the wall and saw the northern army below her, drawn up in ranks facing the Kalesh. Motion near the bridge crossing the Lingua River caught her eye, and she saw northmen in position at the far side of the bridge facing another two black Kalesh units.

Turning back to the northern army below her, Sable searched until she saw a cluster of officers standing near the center. She caught sight of Reese.

Bastian kept his eyes on the Kalesh forces. "They'll be coming soon. They're almost set. Your men had better be ready." He pointed to the three dark units across the field. "The center company will come first, driving a wedge into your troops."

The Kalesh soldiers were standing ready. There was no way to tell if the center would move first, but Bastian's words lingered warmly around Sable.

She stepped up to the parapet and found Reese again. He was near enough that she could see the tension in his posture.

Bastian gaze followed Sable's. "Ah, the young assassin. I hadn't realized he'd be quite so prominent in the fight." Reese and the other officers were closer to the River Gate, but at least a dozen men guarded the top of the wall in that direction. Bastian shook his head. "I don't think I can get you close enough to him."

This was close enough for her to reach Reese with her words, but with Bastian standing right next to her, she hesitated, unsure of whether her *vitalle* would let the ambassador hear the conversation or not.

Across the field, Kalesh came out of the large command tent and joined the troops.

Ignoring Bastian, Sable leaned over the parapet. "Reese," she said quietly, pushing her words toward him, sending out the *vitalle* in a thin thread.

Standing among the other officers, Reese stopped and spun, looking around. "Sable?"

"Up on the wall," she said.

His gaze snapped up and scanned the wall, locking on her. "Where have you been? I was about to come—" He froze. "Is that Bastian?"

The ambassador looked between Reese and Sable with a shocked expression, clearly hearing everything.

"It is. He's..." Sable glanced at Bastian. "Helping. He says the center of the Kalesh lines will come first, trying to drive a wedge into you."

Reese turned to look up the hill. He called a command to the men around him, and several ran off.

"We can...speak with them?" Bastian whispered. "From this far?"

Sable nodded.

"If that is the move the Kalesh make," Reese said, turning back to Sable, "I'll thank him." He lifted his face toward the towering line of smoke drifting slowly inland. "What exploded?"

"Dockside."

Even from this distance, she saw his jaw drop. "You blew up Kiva?"

She let out a short laugh. "Actually, I got Kiva to blow up the Kalesh buildings there."

Reese was silent for a moment. "That might be even more impressive."

Beside her, Bastian nodded.

"Kiva also destroyed two Kalesh ships in the harbor." She glanced into the city. "He promised me reinforcements, too, from the merchant guards. There should be at least eight hundred men coming at any moment."

Reese shook his head. "Don't trust him."

"He took care of the Kalesh in Dockside like he promised."

"Sable..." Reese's voice was frigid. "Tanis is dead."

Sable stared down at him. "What?"

"A few hours ago." He paused. "His tongue was black."

"Black?" she asked faintly. "Vayakadyn venom?" She saw Reese nod, but she shook her head slowly. "It was Kiva?"

"Do you know anyone else who kills people that way?" Reese asked.

Kiva's fear from the night before suddenly became clear. He'd thought she was there because he'd killed Tanis.

She looked down. "Reese. I'm so sorry."

Reese was quiet for a moment. "Did Serene find you? She and Flibbet convinced the guards to let them in last night. She said if she was never coming back here, there were some things she needed."

A trumpet call rang out from the Kalesh. Down on the field, the black troops of the Kalesh started forward across the grass.

"The Kalesh north of the river are moving too," Bastian said. "Goll's troops will try to drive you away from the bridge. He doesn't have enough men to take it, though, if you hold your ground."

Reese turned to look over the river. "Terrane is there, Sable. Could you tell him?"

Sable peered over the bridge and saw the distant form of Terrane near the front of the northern troops. "He's far away, but maybe."

Reese pulled his sword from its sheath. The Kalesh were drawing closer, and Sable's words caught in her throat. "Reese, be careful."

He looked up at the wall. "Bastian, if anything happens to her, I'm coming for you."

The ambassador nodded. "The central unit is weakest at the center. They want to draw you in to surround you, but if you hit the center hard, you can split the unit in half."

Reese paused. "I know, but thank you." He turned, moving toward the front line of his men.

"How does he know that?" Bastian asked.

Sable turned to face across the river. "Terrane!" She sent the words out, stretching them as far as she could. It was considerably farther than she'd ever tried. "Terrane!" The threads of *vitalle* unraveled before they reached him. She took a breath and focused, pushing the words as forcefully as she could. "Terrane!"

She saw the big man turn. "Sable?" he asked uncertainly.

"I'm on the city wall. The Kalesh are going to try to drive you from the bridge. Hold your ground there."

The huge man was facing the city, shielding his eyes against the rising sun. "I'll pass it along." He paused. "How are we talking right now?"

"Magic, Terrane," she said. "Not all magic has to do with fire. Be careful." She cut off the *vitalle* and found Bastian staring at her.

Ignoring his astonished expression, she turned back to the battlefield. The Kalesh were rushing toward the wall now, approaching the northerners just as Bastian had said. The center was pulling forward like a black spike.

The front lines reached each other with a crash like a horrible ocean wave, smashing metal against metal. Men roared out battle cries or screamed in pain. She searched the line for Reese but couldn't find him in the chaos.

Bastian was watching her, not the battlefield, and she finally turned to face him. "Why are you helping me?" she demanded. "And no vague answers."

He opened his mouth but closed it again, his expression pained.

"I know about the Ghost of the White Wood," she said.

He flinched at the words, and his face paled. "From whom?"

"I know the version that the Empire spreads, and I know it's all lies. I read the book by Soren, bard of the Taken Lands, who claimed to have gotten the story from you and Melia directly."

He blinked at her, emotions warring with each other in his expression. He gave a single nod. "Then you know the true story."

Sable stepped closer to him. "I know you killed rebels. I know you handed Melia over to Prince Turrn. I know you took credit for everything she did, twisting the truth for your own selfish gain. So tell me, what game are you playing? Why are you helping me against your own people? Or do you have a way to twist this to your benefit as well? Are you using me to get rid of General Goll?" She glared up at him. "Why are you helping me?"

Bastian let out a breath that trembled slightly, but he held her gaze. "Because I owe her."

"Who?" Sable demanded.

"The great *zabat*." His mouth twisted in a sad shadow of a smile. "A'Melia."

Sable paused. "Amelia? That..." Something cold gripped Sable's chest. "That was my mother's name."

Bastian nodded slowly. "I swear, you look just like her. The first time I saw you in Vivaine's council, I thought A'Melia had come back from the dead."

Sable took a step back. "Melia was…?"

"She's known across the Empire as A'Melia, the Ghost of the White Wood. The most famous *zabat* the Empire has ever faced. Rebellions rally around her memory to this day. The Kalesh nobles threaten their children that if they misbehave, A'Melia will sneak into their rooms while they sleep."

Sable gave him a stunned stare.

"Prince Turrn—the prince Melia assassinated when I bought her into our camp—his brother is now emperor." Bastian's words were warm. "He believes that Melia seduced his brother, then tricked him into planning the assassination of their father. He hates her. It's been thirty years, and the Empire still can't quell the rebellious spirit inspired by the Ghost. I don't even know if she ever knew how much trouble she caused. It took them years just to track her down."

"They killed her." Sable shoved the words at him. "A Kalesh soldier stabbed her in the stomach while I watched."

Below the wall, the fighting raged on. Dimly, she was aware of the northern army holding their line as the Kalesh threw themselves against it.

"I tried to find her first." Bastian's voice was so quiet she almost couldn't hear. "I volunteered for every expedition I could. I would have warned her, Sable." He stopped, his face almost helpless. "I would have made sure you all got away."

Sable stared at him.

"Tell no one who you are," he said fervently. "Not even those you trust. If the Empire finds out that Melia's daughter not only lives, but is leading a rebellion—"

"I'm not leading it."

Bastian gave her an incredulous look. "If they find that A'Melia's daughter is leading a rebellion," he repeated, "they will stop at nothing to find you and destroy you." Anger and regret and fear warred across his face, raw and desperate. His words were warm enough to drive off the morning chill and block the feel of the ocean breeze. "I failed her," he said, taking a step closer. "I will not fail you, A'Sable."

He reached toward her but stopped. "If I can serve you in any way —if I can help your cause in any way—I will."

"You didn't help Melia's cause when you met her."

His eyes clouded. "I know. Let me atone for that now."

She turned away from him. The battle was a chaos of motion and cries. The field was churned into dark, red-stained mud. She searched for Reese and found him fighting next to a smaller form that must be Thulan.

Sable wrestled with Bastian's words. Melia couldn't have been her mother...

Except Bastian's words had been true. And her mother had owned the elven bow. And the Kalesh had come for her...

"Why do you call her A'Melia?"

"In Kalesh, the A' means ghost, or spirit. Your mother was more than just a woman, she was..." His eyes grew distant, and he shrugged. "She was more. Both in who she actually was and in the way her legend grew and drew people to itself."

"That's what you've been calling me," Sable said slowly. "At the summit, I thought it was just your accent changing Issable to Ah-sable, but it wasn't."

He shook his head. "It had been a possibility from the moment I saw you, but by the summit, I knew you were moving toward some-thing greater, something...*more.*"

The sounds of the battle broke through her thoughts, and her eyes swept along the line, then over to the bridge where Terrane's group still stood strong. The vast number of casualties seemed to be Kalesh.

"If you are the great General Bastian," Sable said, frowning at the battle, "tell me what you see below us. Because it looks to me like the Kalesh are throwing their troops against us madly. They're killing themselves and making no effort to win."

Bastian turned to look over the parapet. "They *are* killing them-selves..." He leaned forward, scanning all along the line. He turned to the bridge, his expression darkening. "What is Goll doing? He doesn't have the men for an attack like this. He has no problem sacrificing

soldiers, but this strategy only works if he's trying to exhaust you for
—" He straightened, his gaze snapping up to the hillsides, tracing out
the edge of the field.

"Maybe Goll is a bad general," Sable said.

"He's a capable general. Ruthless, and capable." Bastian craned to
see north past the river. "He was only stationed here at the far edge of
the Empire as punishment for not controlling his temper well."

"What were you punished for?" Sable asked.

"Nothing. I requested an easy, peaceful assignment where I'd serve
a couple years under Ambassador Tehl, then retire." His brow creased
as he continued to look around the outskirts of the battle. Suddenly he
straightened and turned toward the south, staring at the hill that
blocked their view of the ocean.

"The boats…" he said slowly, "He sent them off in boats." Bastian
turned back to Sable, his face pale. "I didn't know! You must believe
me! I'd have told you if I'd known!"

"About the men Goll sent north?" Sable asked. "We know about
them."

He shook his head. "I don't think he sent them north—not all of
them." He pointed to the hill.

The top of the ridge shifted, and a wave of Kalesh soldiers poured
over it.

A cheer went up from the Kalesh fighting below as the new troops
swept down the hill toward the fighting.

"Reese!" Sable called, pushing her voice down toward him.

"How many?" he shouted.

"A thousand," Bastian said grimly.

"We could use those reinforcements from Kiva!" Reese shoved
himself back from the fighting, calling out orders and pointing up the
hill toward the charging Kalesh.

A low rumble echoed from past the bridge, and Sable turned to see
a cavalry unit of Kalesh gallop out from a gap in the hills, charging
toward the bridge.

Sable held her breath as the horses thundered down, crashing into
the northern troops, driving a deep wedge almost to the bridge itself.

"A'Sable," Bastian said, stepping between her and a city constable running toward them. "Keep your face pointed toward the field."

"What news?" Bastian asked the man, his voice snapping authoritatively.

The man ran up to them. "Sable!"

She shifted until she could see a familiar, narrow face under the round constable's hat. "Rabbit?"

"Vivaine gathered all the merchant families in the Sanctuary." Rabbit's words tumbled out, his breath coming in rushed gasps. "She claims the north is here to sack the city. They have their men guarding their own property. Kiva tried to convince them of the truth, but…" He glanced out over the battlefield, his shoulders heaving and his expression bleak. "Sable, there are no reinforcements."

Despite the truth of his words, a cold fear wrapped around Sable. "None?"

Rabbit shook his head. "The merchants won't risk their own property."

Sable turned to look over the wall. The numbers of the Kalesh were too great. Maybe too great even if the merchants supplied their men and the Sanctuary sent their Sanctus guards, but it would at least help even the field.

Vivaine.

She had lied to the people, again.

Sable leaned over the parapet. "Reese!" she called, shooting out the strands of *vitalle*. He was behind the line with a knot of officers, pointing at the approaching black wave of the Kalesh, but he turned to face the wall. "Hold them off as long as you can. I'll bring more men!"

He took a few steps closer to the wall. He was quiet, then she heard him sigh. "I'm not going to waste my breath telling you not to go anywhere dangerous, but Sable…" He shook his head. "Please, just… come back to me."

"I promise." She glanced up at the approaching army. "Make sure you're here for me to come back to."

He brought his fist to his chest. "As you wish, Issable, Flame of the North."

She gave him the royal wave Atticus always wanted and saw him grin before he turned back to the officers.

Sable cut off the *vitalle* and turned to find Rabbit looking between her and Reese with a stunned expression. He blinked at her, then shook his head. "There are no more men for you to bring."

Sable faced Bastian. "You really want to serve me? Get me close to Vivaine."

CHAPTER SEVENTY-FIVE

BASTIAN SHOOK HIS HEAD. "Vivaine has all of the Sanctus guards and now all the merchants' guards. You won't get close to her."

"I will if you've captured me and bring me to her." Sable turned to Rabbit. "Do you know where Serene is?"

He nodded. "She and Flibbet stayed at my safe house near the gate."

"Can we pick her up on the way? I could use her help for this, and after yesterday's little parade with the phoenix, Vivaine will want her as well."

"This is a bad plan," Bastian said. "If you want the merchants' guards, send someone else."

"I'm the one who can convince them of the truth," Sable said. "You promised to help me."

"I can help you from right here. I can read the Kalesh formations and tell you what to expect."

"So can Reese," Sable said bluntly.

Bastian glanced down at the armies. "So it seems...How, exactly?"

"He spent years studying in a Kalesh school." Sable turned to Rabbit. "Do you have any rope? Can you make it look like I'm under arrest?"

The narrow-faced man crossed his arms. "I agree with the ambassador on this plan."

"Then get out of my way, and I'll get the guards at the Fallen Gate to arrest me and actually take me to the Sanctuary." She pushed past Rabbit. "You can go do something else useful. Like kill Kiva."

Rabbit frowned and fell in next to her. "You saw the explosions this morning, and I know he tried to convince the merchants to come help you."

"Tanis died last night," Sable said. "Vayakadyn venom."

Rabbit's jaw dropped. "What?"

Sable stopped and faced him. "Do you have any rope?" she repeated.

Rabbit let out an annoyed breath and nodded. "This all feels reckless."

"I agree," Bastian said.

Sable pointed down at the battlefield. "It's time for reckless!"

Rabbit pulled a cord off the belt of his uniform and cut off a piece. Sable put her hands behind her back, and he wrapped it around her wrists, tucking the ends into her palms.

"Let's get to the Sanctuary," Sable said. "As quickly as we can."

Bastian, still looking unhappy, started quickly back toward the Fallen Gate, and Rabbit took Sable's arm and followed. Bastian kept up a fast pace, and when he reached the bottom of the stairs, he snapped for a Kalesh soldier to follow them. Rabbit pushed Sable toward the soldier and motioned for them to wait. The Kalesh soldier grabbed Sable's arm with a firm grip.

Rabbit crossed to the doorway he'd hidden in earlier that morning, opened it quietly, and slipped inside. A shout and a crash came from inside the house, and moments later, Rabbit pushed Serene out the door, her hands behind her back.

"This is the other one, Ambassador," he said gruffly.

Bastian nodded. "Get us to the Sanctuary. Quickly."

The soldier shoved Sable down the avenue again, and she stumbled forward.

"I hope you know what you're doing." Serene's voice sounded in her ear, barely above a whisper.

Sable straightened, feeling the strands of *vitalle* coming from Serene.

At Sable's reaction, the edge of Serene's mouth quirked up. "I've been working on replicating your skill."

Sable looked down, hoping the soldier holding her arm couldn't see her smile. "It's working well," she breathed as quietly as she could, sending the words back to Serene and hoping the guards didn't hear.

"Do you have some sort of plan?" Serene asked.

"Expose Vivaine," Sable whispered. "Confront her in front of everyone and get the merchant guards to come help us."

Serene didn't answer immediately. "That would be a goal, not a plan, Sable."

"I plan on talking," Sable offered.

"And if talking isn't enough?"

"That's why I brought you."

Serene gave her an incredulous, sidelong look.

The wide avenue was mostly empty. The sounds of the battle could be heard, muted and distant from the far side of the wall. Down a side road, a group of merchant guards stood outside a warehouse.

"Why are you in the city?" Sable sent the whisper to Serene.

"Flibbet and I tried to get into the Sanctuary last night to see if I could get any more books out."

"Did you?"

Serene shook her head. "The Veil Gate was closed, and at least twenty guards stood outside it. We were going to try again this morning..."

Sable glanced over at her. "Until I got you mock-arrested?"

Serene kept her eyes forward down the street. "My plan was to get in stealthily, not be brought to Vivaine in chains."

"Right." Sable paused. "Sorry."

Serene gave a tiny shrug. "We need the reinforcements more than the books." Her voice was angry.

"It would be nice if Vivaine stopped hoarding all the things we need," Sable agreed.

Bastian strode toward the Sanctuary at a clip so fast it was nearly a jog, and Sable was breathing hard as they drew closer to the Sanctuary.

She caught glimpses of the sun still low in the east beyond the spires of the priories. For a moment, she was stunned at how early it still was.

From inside the Veil Wall, a thin plume of smoke rose into the clear sky.

They reached the wall, and Bastian strode up to the guards at the gate. "Prisoners for the High Prioress."

"Yes, Ambassador," one said, motioning to a guard on top of the wall. In moments, the gate swung open enough to let them through.

The Kalesh soldier pushed Sable through the gate into the huge, walled plaza. The gate thudded shut behind them, and she gripped the ends of the cord in her palms so tightly she could feel her pounding heartbeat in them.

Near the gate, the plaza was empty, but across the wide courtyard, a hundred wagons clustered together near the three huge priories. The wealthiest families of the city milled among them. The women wore brightly colored dresses, and somewhere music played, as though there weren't men dying outside the city walls.

The plume of smoke rose from the front of the Dragon Priory.

"A bonfire?" Sable asked Serene from between clenched teeth. "Did Vivaine invite them to their own festival?"

Serene frowned toward it.

Outside the front door of the Phoenix Priory, abbesses lingered. They caught sight of Sable, and a ripple went through them. One, standing off to the side, straightened. She lifted her veil, and Sable saw Pixy's familiar face. The woman's eyes were wide with alarm, but she gave Sable a small wave. Sable nodded to her, and Pixy dropped her veil and ducked inside the Phoenix Priory.

Bastian strode ahead of Sable and Serene, reaching the wagons, where several Sanctus guards stopped him.

"I have prisoners for the Dragon Prioress," Bastian said.

The men nodded and motioned for him to follow. Several other guards fell in around them as they made their way through the crowd. They came out at the foot of the priory stairs where the bonfire burned.

The guard started toward the steps. Sable searched the raised portico at the front of the Dragon Priory, expecting to see Vivaine's glowing white figure.

The portico was empty.

"She's not here!" Sable whispered, sending the words to Serene.

Serene drew in a breath that sounded like a hiss.

Sable glanced over to find Serene staring at the bonfire. A Sanctus guard tossed three small objects onto it.

"Those are my books!" Serene whispered, her words venomous.

The fire was filled with blackened spines and curled, flaming pages. The pile was as tall as Sable and twice as wide across as she could reach. Another Sanctus guard came down the priory stairs and headed for the fire, holding another stack.

"Stop!" Serene commanded him. "What are you doing?"

He paused at the severity in her voice. "These spread lies about Amah." He held one up.

"That's a history book!" Serene took a step toward him, enraged. "That's Merrick's book!"

The guard shrugged. "Can't read. Just bringing out the ones they tell me to." He tossed it into the fire.

Serene yanked her arm out of Rabbit's grasp, and the cord that had been around her wrists fell to the flagstones.

Rabbit grabbed for her again, but Serene ran close to the fire, peering at the burning books, holding up her hands to protect her face from the heat.

"Get her!" Bastian's soldier cried out.

The merchants and their families turned to look at the commotion.

"Serene," Sable said urgently, "the books are gone!"

Rabbit reached out and took Serene's arm. "Come on," he said, pulling her back.

Serene yanked her arm away and stood staring at the pile, her hands closed into fists, her entire body shaking.

"Why is Vivaine burning books?" Sable looked at Bastian.

"Goll's been trying forever to destroy books that don't conform to the Kalesh regulations..." Bastian stared at the fire. "Vivaine's been refusing."

"You want to burn things, Vivaine?" Serene called out, her voice ringing through the plaza.

The sounds of the crowd around them died, and people craned to see Serene standing next to the flaming books. Faces glanced toward the priory, looking for the High Prioress, but she was nowhere to be seen.

"Then let's burn things!" Serene's voice was low, but it rolled out over the whole crowd like thunder.

The nearest merchants took a step back.

Serene stretched out her hand toward the fire, and Sable felt a rush of *vitalle* as Serene drained energy out of the bushes along the front of the priory. The leaves browned and curled, shrinking down against the branches. The *vitalle* rushed into the bonfire, flaring it higher until the flames towered above the crowd.

Serene twisted her hand, and a slash of air cut through the fire, as though she'd reaped the flames with a scythe. She flung her fingers toward the line of rapidly dying bushes and trees along the front of the Dragon Priory, and the nearest bush exploded into flame.

A cry went through the crowd, and the people stumbled back, pushing against each other.

Serene held her hand out, and the flames spread, lighting a hedge along the front of the Dragon Priory, then hurling itself onto a taller tree, engulfing the branches in an instant, each leaf blazing up before blackening.

A thrashing tongue of flame and smoke blazed up the front of the priory, leaving streaks of black on the white stone walls.

The crowd cried out and started pulling wagons away from the building. Rabbit took a step back from Serene.

Sable's guard tried to pull her back, but Sable yanked her arm out of his grip and took a few steps closer to the fire. Bastian motioned for the guard to hold back.

"Serene?" Sable said warily.

Serene didn't answer but pointed at the other side of the stairs. The flames leapt over the steps in a long, blazing arc to set those hedges aflame.

The fire rushed past the edge of the portico at the center of the

Dragon Priory and dove into the trees and bushes against the front of the building, licking against the first stained-glass window. The smoke dulled the colorful panes, streaking them with soot. With a loud crack, a huge, yellow pane on the window shattered, and the rest of the window cascaded down into the flames.

Inside, the curtains caught fire.

Serene stepped to the base of the stairs, holding her arms out to both sides, still funneling *vitalle* out of the bushes and into the fire, making it grow hotter and faster, until it covered the entire front of the Dragon Priory.

In the vast amounts of *vitalle* Serene was channeling, Sable could sense the heat from all the people close by. Serene herself blazed ten times brighter and hotter than anyone else as the energy streamed through her. Her hands were blazing hot, and her chest, and her stomach. She was like her own bonfire.

Finally, Serene dropped her hands, breathing heavily. The ocean breeze fed the flames, and the fire continued to spread. More windows cracked and shattered.

The priory door flung open, and Vivaine rushed out, three Mira on her heels. The High Prioress shouted commands, and the Mira rushed toward the fire. Sable felt them drawing *vitalle* away from it, pouring it into the ground. The flames shrank down, still burning along the shrubbery but no longer blazing up the stones of the priory.

Vivaine stood at the top of the stairs, her face livid, her white robe blindingly bright. "You," she breathed, staring at Serene. "How dare you attack Amah's house?"

Sable stepped up next to Serene. "This house has nothing to do with Amah." She imbued the words with *vitalle*, spreading them so the whole crowd could hear. "*You* have nothing to do with Amah."

Vivaine's eyes fell on Sable, and she paused. "Here to argue with me again?"

Sable started up the stairs. The firelight caught in splinters of gold, shimmering along Argyros's scales where he crouched behind Vivaine. One of the Mira moved to intercept Sable, but Vivaine held up her hand, and the woman stopped.

Rising the last few steps, Sable stopped a few paces from Vivaine, but instead of addressing the High Prioress, she faced the plaza. Sable saw Lord Trelles near the center of the gathered merchants, Lady Ingred next to him. Sable gave the crowd one sweeping glance, looking for Kiva, but if the man was here, he was keeping himself hidden.

"The High Prioress is using you," Sable said, pushing her voice out so it would be heard throughout the crowd. "You will lose everything when the Kalesh take over, and she does not care. Because she will be safe, still entrenched in her priory."

Sable glanced back at it. The stones were scorched with long, black lines, and inside two windows, fires raged, and she caught glimpses of people trying to put them out.

"This woman," Vivaine said calmly, her own voice easily loud enough to be heard by everyone, "is a traitor and a rebel and has come to this city at the head of a northern army."

Sable could feel the wide, smooth flow of *vitalle* that the Mira closest to Vivaine was casting. It spread out like the surface of a pond, with Vivaine's words flowing across the top like ripples.

Vivaine glowed even brighter, illuminating Argyros too until his scales scattered glitters of light across the platform. "She murdered the good—"

"Vivaine," Sable said, slashing her words across the Mira's *vitalle* and cutting off the rest of Vivaine's words, "doesn't want you to know that there is nothing holy about her."

"This woman tells lies!" Vivaine shouted, but Sable spread her own *vitalle* out in front of the prioress, and Vivaine's words came through weak and muffled.

"Do you want to know how she always knows things about you?" Sable asked the merchants. "It is not through visions from Amah. No, Vivaine has spies. Hundreds of them. They are inside your houses and inside your businesses."

A wave of mutters moved through the merchants.

"The Kalesh forces are outside your city at this moment because she invited them," Sable continued. "She offered them control of the trade routes you've built throughout the south and the north."

"She brought an army to sack our city!" Vivaine shouted. Instead of trying to muffle her voice, Sable filled Vivaine's words with *vitalle*, and she felt the cold lie spray into the crowd like shards of ice.

The merchants straightened. Lord Trelles's expression turned shrewd.

"No." Sable met the High Prioress's glare. "I gathered an army in the north because you lied to me." She poured the truth into her words, the heat rolling out from her. "You told me you were in danger, and the north came—we emptied three territories of men and came to protect you."

Vivaine opened her mouth, but Sable faced the crowd. "And do you know *why* Vivaine made us think the Kalesh were sieging your city? To draw the men of the north here while she and General Goll snuck Kalesh soldiers north to attack the undefended land."

A gasp went through the crowd.

"Lies!" Vivaine shouted. "Do not be taken in, as so many have been, by this woman's lies!"

Argyros shifted forward, moving his head around Vivaine. His slitted eyes pierced Sable, implacable and heartless. He crouched low against the portico, his claws scraping into the stone.

Sable forced herself not to step back. Argyros was no farther from her than he'd been from Tylar, and everything inside her wanted to run down the steps, but outside the city, the northern army was standing against the Kalesh. Reese and Thulan and Leonis and Terrane —they were all standing their ground against a superior force.

Sable planted her feet and turned her back on Argyros, facing the crowd.

Their faces were locked on the dragon, and Sable heard his scales slide closer.

She saw again the fire consuming Tylar, but she shoved the thought away.

"Do you want to know what is a lie?" Sable pushed the words out in a rush, jabbing a finger toward Vivaine. "This brightness. Vivaine can twist light, make it land wherever she chooses. And what does she do with this amazing power? She takes the light around her and focuses it on herself—"

Argyros let out a low growl, and Sable flinched.

"The men of the north need your help!" she shouted. "Go help them drive the Kalesh out of your city! Take back what Vivaine bartered away—"

Argyros's growl deepened, and Sable spun toward him. His sides expanded as he drew in a breath. Vivaine stood at his side, her eyes like shards of ice, ruthless and pitiless.

Somewhere behind Sable, glass shattered.

But she stood transfixed as the silver dragon drew in a deep breath and shifted closer. Sable straightened her shoulders, but when the creature's jaw opened, she stumbled back a step from the horrible brightness she saw deep in his throat.

The scales along Argyros's sides glittered as he thrust the air out. A jet of flames, blindingly bright, shot out, and Sable flung her hands up.

An arc of fire swept in from behind her, and the flames from Argyros slammed into the blazing brightness of feathers and wings.

CHAPTER SEVENTY-SIX

INNOV FLARED her wings to the side, blocking Argyros's fire, shooting it out to the side as though it hit a wall. Vivaine stumbled back from the chaos of flames.

Sable dropped her arms, staring stunned at the flaming phoenix in front of her. The horrible heat of the dragon's fire was washed away by the healing warmth of Innov.

The phoenix's wings spread out, longer and broader than Sable had ever seen. Innov hung in the air, the dragon fire splashing off her like water crashing against the shore or being absorbed into her, brightening her feathers, infusing her with dazzling, blinding light.

Argyros cut off the fire with a furious snarl.

Innov dove at him, her claws extended. He snapped at her with his wide jaw, but she darted around his teeth and gouged her talon across his eye, leaving a bloody trail through his scales.

The dragon let out a roar and sprayed a stream of fire out, tossing his head to try to reach the bird. Vivaine and Sable both scrambled back as Innov dove again, slashing her talons at his other eye.

The merchants screamed, diving for refuge behind their wagons.

"Argyros!" Vivaine called out, her voice desperate. Her robe was a dull white in the shadow of the priory.

The dragon dropped his head and pulled back. Blood flowed down from one of his eyes, and under the other, deep gouges marred his silver scales. Innov let out a wild, triumphant cry and spun away from him, leaving a glittering trail of fire as she circled back to Sable.

Sable held out her arm, and Innov landed on it. The phoenix's chest heaved, and with each breath, flames flickered out from between her feathers. Heat so warm it almost burned flowed up into Sable's arm, pouring into her chest, filling her, lifting the heavy fears of the morning.

"Thank you," Sable breathed.

Innov focused on Argyros, backed up near the priory door with Vivaine, and let out another vicious cry.

Sable turned back to the merchants. "The northern army needs your men. We can drive the Kalesh away, but not without your help." Sable met Lord Trelles's gaze. "Please."

Trelles spared a glance for Vivaine, who was dim and shaken, then nodded. "Gather your men, now!" he snapped. "The River Gate!"

The merchants began shouting orders, and guards streamed toward the Veil Gate.

The women and children clumped together around the wagons, whispering and shooting hostile looks at the High Prioress.

Sable started down the stairs toward Serene.

"You're a fool," Vivaine said viciously.

Sable paused and looked back at the prioress.

"They want our gold, and they will have it." Vivaine took a step closer, and Sable tensed. "If you drive them off today, they'll come back. The force they have out there is nothing. They will come back with numbers beyond count and wipe us from the face of the land." Her glare stabbed into Sable, pinning her where she stood. "You have doomed us all."

The truth of the prioress's words roiled around Sable like swirling flames. The Kalesh would be back for the gold. There was nothing that could change that.

Sable focused on the warmth from Innov, the sense of hope the phoenix always had. "Driving them out is the first step," Sable answered her. "If they come back, we'll fight them off again."

"*When* they come back, you'll die like the rest of us." Vivaine stood in the shadows of her priory, dingy and covered with soot, while smoke from the smoldering hedges cast a brownish hue to the gloom.

"When they do," Sable said, "at least no one will be looking to you for guidance any longer."

Vivaine's face darkened. "Get out of my city."

"It's not your city anymore. Word of what you've done will have spread to every ear in the city by nightfall." Sable glanced at the scorched stone. "Stained black." She nodded. "Fits you better than the pristine white ever did."

Sable turned her back on the woman and strode down the stairs to where Serene and Bastian stood waiting.

Sable ran a finger down Innov's chest. "Want to come see the army?"

Innov merely looked around the plaza.

"I'll take your continued presence as a yes." Sable glanced toward the Phoenix Priory. One of the large windows in the front was broken, and Pixy stood inside it.

Sable sent threads of *vitalle* toward the abbess. "Thank you," she said.

Innov dove at the dragon, her claws extended.

Pixy straightened in surprise. "They'd been keeping Innov trapped in Narine's old room since she came back yesterday, and I thought you might need a friend out there."

"Turns out I did," Sable said. "If you're tired of the priory, come find me in the northern army."

Pixy glanced around the Sanctuary. "I'll think about it." She waved at Sable and disappeared from view.

612

Sable turned to find Serene still glaring at the smoldering pile of books, stretching her very red palms gently.

"You were amazing," Sable said, "and a little terrifying." There was warmth in Sable's own words, and she felt Serene's heat again, as though the woman were still holding more *vitalle* than normal. "Aside from the time Jae almost died, I've never seen you that angry."

Serene glanced at Sable, and one of her hands went to her belly. "I think I was fairly reserved. She burned my books. I want to burn the entire Sanctuary down."

The words were hot with truth, and Sable stared at Serene. Her body burned just like anyone else's, except low in her belly where a flare of heat throbbed.

Sable's stared at the tiny spot of heat, and her mouth dropped open. "You haven't just been weird lately! You're pregnant!"

Serene blinked at her, and a smile spread across her lips. "I've felt a bit more emotional than normal."

Sable laughed and hugged Serene with her free arm. "We've noticed."

Serene hugged her back, not even particularly stiffly, which merely confirmed her condition.

Sable glanced at the gate out of the Sanctuary and sighed. "Let's get back to the River Gate," she said. "And hope the merchant guards aren't too late."

The sounds of battle echoed through the open River Gate as Lord Trelles directed merchant guards toward the fighting.

A line of wounded men lay along the road inside the city gate, and Serene started toward them.

Sable and Bastian hurried up the stairs to the top of the wall. Innov launched herself off Sable's arm and soared up into the sky.

The Kalesh had pressed the northern army back against the wall, splitting the north's forces in two. At the bridge, Terrane's unit was smaller, tucked into a tight cluster at each end of the bridge while the Kalesh continued to batter them.

There were hundreds of bodies on the trampled ground, half-covered in the churned-up mud.

Sable searched the northern troops against the wall and found Reese fighting next to Thulan and Leonis. The dwarf's hammer swung in a wide arc, smashing into a Kalesh soldier's knee and sending him toppling to the ground. Leonis and Reese fought next to each other, their swords slicing out at the nearest black-clad warriors.

The fresh reinforcements from the merchants poured out of the gate in groups of ten or twenty, falling on the flank of the Kalesh forces, sweeping into them and cutting down dozens at a time.

With a shout, two dozen Sanctus guards ran out of the River Gate too. Sable recognized the man in the lead from the Phoenix Priory. He looked up at the wall and raised his sword. Lord Trelles pointed them toward the fighting at the bridge.

As more men streamed out of the city, the tide of the fighting shifted, and the Kalesh fell back.

The northern troops let out a cheer and redoubled their efforts.

Sable leaned against the wall, spent by the morning.

They will come back with numbers beyond count and wipe us from the face of the land. You have doomed us all.

It was true. The Kalesh line retreated again, more black-clad soldiers falling. But this was only the beginning. Sable stared at the still bodies on the ground. So much life spilled out, and the victory would be so small.

Still, it was a victory.

"Why don't they surrender?" Sable asked.

"The Kalesh don't surrender," Bastian said. "They'll fight to the last soldier, and then Goll will either die fighting or kill himself. But Vivaine is right. This will only make the Empire angry. When they return, it will be with a force you cannot stand against."

She sought out Reese again and saw him move forward with the line, pushing the Kalesh farther from the wall, but he moved with a marked limp. His pants stuck to his leg, dark and slick with blood.

A Kalesh soldier rushed forward, and Thulan swung her hammer, crashing it into his hip. The soldier pitched forward and hurled his sword.

Reese tried to spin out of the way, but his leg gave out, and the sword caught him in the side.

"Reese!" Sable yelled, her voice lost in the chaos of the fighting.

He collapsed.

Thulan and Leonis closed in over him, battling back the Kalesh.

"Reese!" Sable shouted, sending out strands of *vitalle* toward him.

She heard Thulan shout for help, and other northern soldiers fought their way over, forming a knot over Reese.

The sounds of the battle blasted her through the magic—harsh, violent clangs of metal on metal, shouts and screams, a deafening, roaring clamor of humanity.

"Reese?" she called, her voice small amidst the noises.

No answer came back.

Thulan shouted out some commands, and two soldiers dragged Reese from the melee, moving him back toward the wall before racing back to rejoin the fight.

He lay where they left him, his shirt covered in blood.

Sable ran along the top of the wall until she was above him. "Reese!"

"Sable," he said weakly. "Stop yelling."

She gripped the edge of the parapet. "Are you..." She paused. "Reese, there's so much blood."

"That's what happens when a sword stabs you." His voice was weak, and he still hadn't moved. "What's happening?"

Bastian came up next to Sable. He looked down at Reese, and his expression shifted into one of hopeless dismay.

A piercing, cold fear shot through Sable. She turned away from Bastian and looked at the battle, blinking back a prick of tears. "The Kalesh are falling back."

Reese gave a grunt of acknowledgment. "You brought more men."

"I stole them from Vivaine. After Serene set her priory on fire."

She heard him give a laugh, but it ended in a wet cough. "You brought more men," he repeated, his voice almost too quiet to hear. "I could kiss you for that."

A dark spot was growing on the ground next to his side, and Sable stared down at it. "You can't handle a kiss from me when you're healthy," she whispered.

He let out another short laugh, but it turned to a gasp. His body twitched, and his face turned toward the wall. "Sable?" The word was raw and frightened.

She waved her hands over the side of the wall. "I'm right here!"

He didn't answer.

"Reese!" she screamed down at him.

His head lolled to the side, and his body lay perfectly still, the ground dark and wet beside him.

Bastian closed his eyes and let out a long, defeated breath.

Sable whirled and looked toward the city gate. "Serene!" she cried, sending her voice down to fill the street. "Reese needs you!"

"Where?" Serene's voice came back, sounding exhausted.

"Outside, along the wall! Serene—hurry!"

A few moments later, the dark form of Serene raced along the base of the wall. She reached Reese and knelt.

Sable glanced back at the fighting. The Kalesh had been pushed back, the fighting shifting ever farther from the wall. The ground was littered with mostly black-clad soldiers, but the Kalesh fought on.

The Kalesh line faltered one last time and splintered, the northern troops and the merchants swarming over them. A shout went up from the field, joined by the men at the bridge.

Leonis and Thulan ran back to where Reese lay, leaning over where Serene still worked.

The cheers of the victorious troops sounded hollow.

Her gaze dropped to the knot of friends clustered around Reese. She could only see bits of him through the others, but he wasn't moving.

Sable pulled the sword necklace out from under her dress and gripped the pendant. She opened her mouth to call down to Serene, but the words stuck in her throat. Instead, she watched Reese's feet, perfectly still on the ground.

Too still, for too long.

Her gaze drifted over all of the other fallen bodies, a wave of dread rolling over her. This was only the beginning. How long did they have until they'd need to fight again? Vivaine had tried to negotiate with them for more than a year, but the more gold that was found, the less chance they'd had to convince the Kalesh this land wasn't worth it.

What would the Kalesh possibly want more than gold?

The answer came immediately, and she flinched.

Bastian stood next to her, looking down at Reese's unmoving body. "I hate war." His voice wrapped around them quiet and vehement and warm.

Sable's eyes found Reese's still legs again.

There was something the Kalesh might want more than gold.

There was also a good chance the bargain wouldn't work. Better than good, really. But what else did they possibly have to barter with?

The question left her cold.

But Reese's body made the answer to the Kalesh problem easier. He'd have never agreed. Now, though...

Footsteps rang out on the wall, and Rabbit ran up, still dressed in the city constable's uniform.

"There are three ships in the harbor," he said, his breath coming fast. "They can take four hundred men each, and they can reach the rowboats we left on the river by midafternoon. We can't beat the Kalesh north, but if we row hard, we can follow fast on their heels."

Bastian nodded. "Goll must have only sent fifteen hundred men north. You'll give him a good fight if you chase him."

Sable took a deep breath and nodded. "Get to the field, Rabbit, and gather enough troops to fill the ships. Every other man able to march starts north. The men on foot can reach the remaining river boats by nightfall. Leave the soldiers who've been wounded here and put the Sanctus guards from the Phoenix Priory in charge of caring for them." She glanced down at Reese. "Rabbit, Reese is...."

Rabbit followed her gaze. "There's a man in the city who can stitch up any stab wound. I'll have him meet us at the ship."

Sable almost told him it was too late and that the space on the ship should be saved for living soldiers, but the words stuck in her throat. Instead, she nodded. "Go. Tell Serene what we're doing—she'll convince the rest to follow you."

Rabbit frowned at her. "Aren't you coming?"

Sable shook her head. "Use my space on the boat for some soldier who can fight. Once the boats are full, get them north as fast as you can."

Rabbit looked at her shrewdly. "What do I tell Reese when he asks where you are?"

Tears pricked Sable's eyes, and she turned back toward the field. "Go, get the men to the ships."

Rabbit hesitated, then ran toward the stairs.

His footsteps died away, and in a moment he raced out of the city gate toward Serene. Officers ran off in several directions, calling out commands, and the northern army began to collect itself again.

Bastian let out a long sigh next to her.

Sable pulled her eyes away from Reese's body and looked up the hill at the Kalesh command tent.

If there was to be a bargain, the time was now.

"What happens to General Goll?"

Bastian glanced down at the northern army still fighting the last few pockets of resistance in the Kalesh. "When your men get organized enough, they'll attack him, and Goll and his men will fight to the death, or else Goll may get impatient and kill himself now that his defeat is ensured." He raised his eyes to Goll's command tent. "Although I think Goll will go down fighting."

"How long do we have?" Sable asked.

Bastian surveyed the last of the fighting. "Not long."

She took a deep breath, pointedly not looking at the people she knew below her.

"Ambassador Bastian, take me to General Goll."

CHAPTER SEVENTY-SEVEN

SABLE'S HOOD WAS UP, narrowing her field of vision to the hill in front of her and the Kalesh command tent drawing closer. There was a flurry of activity around it by the few soldiers still with Goll and a fire out front of burning papers.

She clasped her hands together to keep them from shaking. She'd left Innov perched on the side of Atticus's wagon near Leonis's tree, and her arm felt cold and empty without the phoenix. Maybe the phoenix would stay there, maybe she'd return to the priory, but whatever she decided to do, she certainly shouldn't be near Sable any longer.

Bastian walked next to her, his entire bearing radiating disapproval. Six northern soldiers followed them.

The hill was long, and the northern army felt farther away with each step.

Above them, ravens circled, diving down to land on the bodies of the fallen. One let out a harsh cry above Sable, and she flinched. Ahead of them, over the hills, more black birds winged toward the battlefield.

The crunch of Sable's feet over the trampled grass sounded muffled and grim.

"What changed in you?" she asked, trying to distract herself from the ravens and the death and the coming conversation. "When you captured Melia, you were in support of brutally putting down any rebellion in order to keep peace on a grander scale. And yet, here you are, helping me."

"I would rather be helping you onto one of the boats and sending you north surrounded by soldiers." The scowl he'd been giving the Kalesh tent deepened. "I don't trust Goll to talk to you civilly."

"That's not an answer to my question. Was it the fact that Melia saved your life? Or did you come to believe she was right about the reasons the rebellions were being fought?"

Bastian was silent for a few paces. "Both. She had every reason to kill me, but she didn't. That isn't the story the Empire spread, though. They needed her discredited, so they happily promoted me, proclaiming I'd sent her running scared." He paused. "I was honored with a meeting of the emperor himself. I told myself it didn't matter that he was childish and willful and greedy, because his goal was to make one huge, peaceful Empire. He gave me more wealth than I could ever have imagined, and so...I let him believe that I had driven Melia off.

"I married a beautiful woman, who, if I'm being honest, married my money. Before a year was out, all I could see was a selfish woman who would never give herself up to save a town.

"I began to accept as many missions as I could away from home. I was sent to quell other rebellions that needed someone like the Ghost of the White Wood to give them courage. I gave speeches claiming we were merely keeping the peace, limiting the bloodshed, but the truth is, after Melia, I never believed it.

"When I found out the Empire was still searching for her, I volunteered for those missions instead. My first thought was if I knew she was finally gone, maybe she'd stop haunting me. But before I was two weeks out on my first search, I knew that if I found her, there would be no way I could kill her."

General Goll's tent was getting closer, and Sable concentrated on Bastian's words and keeping her feet moving.

"That was the first time I contemplated betraying my country,"

Bastian continued. "It's the first time that I knew, given the chance, I'd disobey direct orders." He glanced at her. "When I'd heard they'd found her, that she was gone..." His eyes strayed over toward the ocean, just coming visible over the hillside. "I was done. I couldn't go back to leading troops, putting down rebellions that had every right to fight us. I applied for an ambassadorship and have spent the last ten years attempting to keep the expansion of the Empire as peaceful as I can."

"How has that gone?"

Bastian grimaced. "Not well. There are too many men like Goll at the head of the armies."

Someone up near the command tent yelled something in Kalesh, and Sable thought she heard Bastian's name. The commotion around the tent paused.

"We'll wait here," Bastian said, and she stopped next to him. The soldiers with them fanned out on either side.

General Goll strode out of the tent, dressed in armor. "Come to gloat, Bastian?" he called, marching down the hill to them, motioning for his own soldiers to follow. "I've already sent a raven to the emperor of the defeat here. I assume you'll send your own soon too. Unless you've been captured by the pathetic northern army."

Sable pushed back her hood.

Goll's eyes narrowed in scorn. "What are you doing here?"

"I've come to make a deal," Sable said.

"It's too late for that," Goll said. "I've already sent ravens. The Empire will hear of this rebellion. They will return and roll across this land like the sea rising to claim it. You have merely postponed the inevitable and assured that your people will be dealt with harshly."

"So people keep telling me," Sable said.

"I die gladly today," Goll said, stepping closer to her, "knowing you and all your people will be close behind."

"That's very noble and martyrly of you," Sable said. "But what if you *don't* die today? What if you slip away and go back to the Empire and tell them that this land isn't worth their effort? What if you say you found out the reports of the gold were inflated, that the mines are almost empty and the people here continually destroy the mountain passes and collapse the mines? Tell them it will cost you more in blood than you'll get in gold." Sable took a step closer to him. "We will burn the ports and block the mouth of the river. There will be nowhere for your boats to land. The mines that take you months to dig we will collapse in a heartbeat. You will never profit from this land."

General Goll's expression didn't change. "Very nice speech, but we both know you don't have the power to accomplish all that."

"True. But you could tell them we do."

Goll let out a short laugh. "Why would I do that?"

"Because everything I said was true," Sable said. "We will fight you for every inch you try to take. But more importantly, if you take that message back to the Empire, I will offer you a bigger prize than hard-won gold from a handful of mines."

"Sable," Bastian said, a note of caution in his voice.

Goll glanced at Bastian. "What prize?"

Sable took a breath. "You can go back to the Empire with a prisoner —the daughter of A'Melia, Ghost of the White Wood."

General Goll's eyes widened, and he stared at her. "Is this true, Bastian?"

Bastian didn't answer, but the stricken look he gave Sable made Goll's face redden in anger.

"How long have you known?" Goll demanded of the ambassador.

"Since the first moment I saw her," Bastian said. "Anyone who had ever seen A'Melia would recognize her instantly."

General Goll studied Sable, then snapped something in Kalesh to the soldier next to him. The man ran up to the tent and returned a moment later with an older man holding an armful of maps.

"Do you know this woman?" Goll asked the older man sharply.

The man stared at Sable, his eyes widening and his face growing pale. "A'Melia!" he breathed, taking a step back. "They said she was dead."

Goll spun to face Bastian. "You lying, faithless coward," he growled between clenched teeth. "I thought you were merely weak. I wouldn't have guessed you were a traitor." He started to pull his sword out of its hilt.

The soldiers on both sides bristled, and the man with the maps stumbled backwards, out of the way.

Sable snapped her fingers in front of Goll's face. "Pay attention to me, General," she commanded him. "You have a choice. You can die here today, defeated by the 'pathetic northern army,' and have your legacy end in some remote corner of the world that no one in the Empire really cares about. *Or* you can agree to convince the Empire to leave this worthless land alone and return with a prize your emperor will reward you for."

"Sable…" Bastian said again, his voice angry this time.

The northern soldiers muttered unhappily and shifted closer to Sable.

"But," Sable said, "I need your word that you can do this. That you can convince the Empire not to bother with us. I need your word, and I swear to you, I will know if it is true."

Goll ran his gaze over her, as though sizing her up. Then he nodded crisply. "You have my word. I will deliver you to the Emperor and do everything I can to convince him that this land is not worth our trouble." His words were perfectly warm.

"Does he have the power to do that?" Sable asked Bastian.

The ambassador gave Goll a look of loathing. "He does."

"I have safe passage to my ship?" General Goll asked.

Sable nodded.

"If you are my prisoner," he said, "send your men back to their troops."

She looked at the soldier next to her. "Go. Your units are almost ready to leave."

"No disrespect intended, Issable," the soldier said, his voice hard. "But, no."

Sable turned to him. "This is a small price to pay for the rest of you to live in peace. The alternative is a lifetime with a war we can't win."

He shook his head stubbornly. "The general will kill me himself if I leave you here."

"The general is dead," Sable said, trying to keep her voice firm.

The soldier's brow twitched into a frown. "I meant General Andreese."

623

Sable met his gaze. "So did I."

The man's eyes widened.

"Go," Sable told him. "Find Atticus the playwright and tell him what happened here. Then get back to your units. Your families need you."

The soldiers exchanged looks but didn't move.

"Please," she said quietly.

The man beside her gave Goll a venomous look, but when he turned back to Sable, he set his fist against his chest, and the men around him followed suit.

"Thank you," she said.

The soldiers gave the Kalesh one last black look before turning and starting down the hill.

"Go with them," Sable told Bastian.

Bastian planted his feet more firmly next to Sable and crossed his arms. "I didn't come this far to leave you alone."

General Goll turned to the man with the maps and pulled off a cord that had been holding the pages rolled together. He tossed it to one of his soldiers, and the man approached Sable. She held out her hands, and he bound them with efficient, tight loops.

Out of the corner of her eye, Sable could see the northern army reorganizing itself. Her eyes sought out the spot where Reese had lain. It was empty, and she looked away with a hollow feeling in her chest.

"Bastian," Goll said. "You're a traitor, and a disgrace. When the emperor learns what you've done, everything you've earned will be ripped away from you and your family."

"My wife will probably be a better person without the riches," Bastian said tiredly, "and I certainly won't miss that tainted gold."

"No," General Goll said, "you won't."

He drew his sword and thrust it into the ambassador's chest.

"Bastian!" Sable cried, lunging for him.

The Kalesh soldier wrapped his arms around her, holding her back as Goll yanked the blade out, and Bastian crumpled forward to the ground.

He landed face down, one leg twisted beneath him. A wide stain spread across the back of his Kalesh robe, tainting the green threads with a glistening, wet red.

Sable stared at his motionless body, hardly able to breathe.

"Traitors are nothing but fodder for ravens," Goll said coldly.

He turned away from Bastian and snapped out some orders in Kalesh. The men around him rushed toward the command tent.

"Hold the woman," he ordered the soldier still gripping Sable as he followed his men. "We'll burn everything left here, then take her to the boat."

CHAPTER SEVENTY-EIGHT

MINUTES LATER, Sable stumbled after Goll, surrounded by five Kalesh soldiers. The general moved quickly over the hillside that would lead them to the sea.

He didn't spare a glance for the thousands of black bodies that lay near the city wall.

Sable couldn't look away from them.

They lay in heaps or spread out one by one. Some piles shifting restlessly, terrifyingly, until broad, black wings stretched out and ravens rose to circle and drop onto another motionless corpse. Groans and cries came from the entire battlefield, cut through with caws of the ravens.

Sable's feet caught on the tangled grass the Kalesh troops had trampled earlier that morning as they'd joined the fight. She tried to hold her hands out in front of her for balance, but the cords dug into her wrists each time she pitched forward.

They crested the hill, and the salty sea breeze blew past, rolling up the grass from the endless, glittering ocean. Immusmala was stretched out to her left, the city laid over the end of the peninsula like a blanket. In the harbor, the two Kalesh vessels still smoked, but three other large ships were tucked up against the dock.

The wide, gruesome, lifeless battlefield was suddenly merely a patch of death in a vast, unchanging world. The Tremmen Hills rolled off to the north, the coastal cliffs were visible snaking off to the east, and the unbroken, flat ocean ran all the way to the southern horizon. The world itself stood implacably still, unaffected by the horrors of the day.

Sable craned back over her shoulder, looking through the soldiers around her. A line of northern troops moved slowly over the bridge and up the road toward Folhaven. The sight of Atticus's wagon trundling along with them nearly undid her.

One of the soldiers shoved her in the back, and she crashed down onto her knees.

She felt small, invisible hands grab her own before the soldier pulled her back up to her feet.

"Purn," she whispered, clinging like a drowning woman to the knowledge the kobold was with her.

She felt the cords around her wrists loosen slightly and let out a grateful breath.

Most of the coastline ahead of them was cliffs, but there were a few houses crowded around a tiny inlet, and Goll headed toward them.

The northern army fell farther behind them, and an empty chill filled Sable. Immusmala itself, with all its schemes and familiarity, was anchored here, on one small finger of land. Talia and Ryah would stay here, hopefully safer than before. The north would go on squabbling about territories, but they should be able drive out the Kalesh force attacking there now and rebuild.

At least now, no more Kalesh would come.

She focused on the thought, hoping to find some peace, but all it did was leave her feeling smaller and more alone.

Purn's fingers slipped inside Sable's bound hands, and Sable squeezed the bony fingers.

"Thank you for being with me," she said, her voice so low the soldiers wouldn't hear. But Purnicious would hear. She always heard.

Goll hurried them down to the cluster of houses and into a street that wound down to a small dock.

They had just entered the street when a half dozen men stepped out from the buildings around them. They were dressed in rough clothes, their faces unsavory.

More men closed off the road behind them, and Goll's men drew their swords, turning to face the new threat.

"Move," Goll commanded the men. "This is not a fight you want to start."

A huge man off to the side caught Sable's eye, and she stiffened.

It was Boone, Kiva's enormous henchman.

The weasel-faced Kiva slipped out of the shadows of a recessed door. "We'd be happy to move out of your way, General," Kiva drawled easily, "as soon as you hand over the woman."

He stopped in front of Goll, blocking the road to the boat and meeting the general's glare with an easy smile. His scarlet brocade vest shimmered in the sunlight, and his shirtsleeves were glaringly white.

"Get out of my way, Kiva," Goll said. "None of this concerns you."

"Ah, but it does." Kiva leaned around the general. "Lovely day, Sable."

"Get out of the way, Kiva," she said harshly.

He clucked disapprovingly at her. "You shouldn't side with unprincipled men like the general." He turned back to Goll. "You and your men can all die here, and then I'll take the woman. Or you can hand her over, and go get in your little boat, and row your way back to the Empire to report on your spectacular failure. Your choice. But I'm in a hurry, so choose quickly."

Goll took a step toward Kiva, but a dozen more men stepped out onto the street around them. The general glared at them, rigid with fury, then spun to face Sable.

Around them, Kiva's men slid knives out of their belts. And Goll stopped, close enough that Sable could smell his breath.

"I will see you again, A'Melia's daughter," Goll said. "You are no ghost like your mother. You are merely a single powerless woman. We will return and destroy everything you love, and I will drag your corpse back to throw at the emperor's feet."

The heat of his words wrapped around them. Kiva's eyebrows rose at the threat.

The front of General Goll's uniform shifted, and suddenly his collar constricted, tightening around his throat like a noose. He grabbed for the fabric, trying to shove his fingers between the thick band and his neck.

His face turned red, and he gasped, stumbling backwards.

His soldiers started to draw their swords, but almost two dozen blades rose against them, and they froze.

Goll fell to his knees, his face purpling. He opened his mouth, but no sound came out.

Sable didn't bother to hide her amusement at Purn's handiwork.

From directly in front of the kneeling general, Purnicious's voice hissed out of the empty air. "This is A'Sable."

Sable pressed a bit of *vitalle* into the kobold's words, making them spread loudly through the narrow street. A ripple of uneasiness rolled through the soldiers.

"The new *zabat*," Purn continued in a vicious whisper. "Flame of the North."

Goll's eyes bulged out of his darkening face, and Sable saw the threads thinning around his neck.

Every man on the street shifted away from Sable.

Kiva's cheeks paled, and his eyes fixed on the general.

The collar of Goll's shirt tore, and he collapsed forward onto his hands, gasping for breath.

Purn's invisible form backed up against Sable's leg, and Sable pushed gratefully against her.

Goll pushed himself up, stumbling to his feet, facing Sable with heaving shoulders. Behind him, Kiva stood with his eyes locked on Sable, his posture wary.

"Be gone, General." Kiva's voice was not quite steady.

"No," Sable said. "He doesn't leave without me."

Kiva shook his head. "You'll have to choke us all if you want to get on that boat, Sable."

She took a step toward him and Goll, but Kiva motioned to his men, and to their credit, they raised their blades toward her with only a slight hesitation.

"Go, General," Kiva said, "before I change my mind."

Goll shifted away from Sable.

"Kiva," she said, pouring *vitalle* into her words, "he can*not* leave without me!"

The men's weapons faltered but didn't fall.

Kiva studied her for a breath. "Well, then, there's only one solution, my dear," he said simply, "because I'm afraid I cannot let you go."

With a fluid motion, he stepped forward and stabbed a knife into Goll's back.

Sable met Goll's shocked look for a silent heartbeat before the Kalesh soldiers cried out and were attacked by a wave of Kiva's men.

General Goll fell forward to his knees in front of Sable, and she stared at his face as his skin turned ashen.

The fight around her was brutally short, and in moments, every Kalesh soldier lay dead on the ground.

Goll reached forward and grabbed Sable's still-bound hands, his grip strong even as his body sagged forward. She braced against his weight and pulled her hands away, but his fingers were tangled in her bonds.

"It is too late, *zabat*," Goll hissed at her, his face twisted with hatred. "The raven is gone. I sent it before we left the tent. The emperor will learn that you live, and now no one will survive to tell him not to come back. You will soon understand the true might of the Empire." He let out a gasping, savage breath. "You are dead, *zabat*. You and everything you love."

His hand spasmed, and he lost his grip.

She twisted away as he fell face down in the street.

CHAPTER SEVENTY-NINE

SABLE STARED at Goll's body, the last of her hope draining away like more blood on the street. The emperor would learn she existed, and now there was no one to convince the Empire not to come back.

Kiva kicked the general's leg, but the body remained still.

"You've doomed us all," she whispered to Kiva.

"No. I saved your life." He motioned to one of his men, who stepped forward warily and cut the bonds off her wrists. "You're welcome. Now it's time to hurry. You have a boat to catch."

Sable let all the pent-up fear and hope and loss of the day rush out of her in a ragged breath. She rubbed her wrists, her hands shaking with fury.

Kiva reached toward her to take her arm, but she raised her eyes to his, and he stopped. "You were right about the power vacuum, Sable. Vivaine is utterly disgraced. You should hear the city talk about her. Eugessa, by association, is reviled. The merchant guild is in turmoil. I, being the only voice who called for the merchants to fight at the beginning, am being hailed as a hero." He gave Sable a searching look. "Which makes me feel indebted to you," he said reluctantly. "And I do not like to feel indebted to people."

A wave of anger rose in her. "You destroyed everything I tried to accomplish! Goll was going to convince the Emperor that we weren't worth the fight!"

Kiva's look faltered. "No...I saved your life. Which is a lot more than you did for me. The scales are clearly in my favor here."

"If you think," she said, stepping closer to him, filling her words with hot wrath, "that this makes me indebted to you, you are sorely mistaken." She set her hand on his brocade vest and felt his heart beating quickly beneath it.

He raised his knife with a look of warning.

She ignored it. "You don't own me, Kiva." The heat of her words coiled around them. "Not anymore. And I will never feel beholden to you for anything, ever again."

He swallowed but held her gaze. "You miss the point, Sable, as you so often do. I don't expect *you* to thank me for saving your life. You're too stubborn for that. But you have ensured that the north is now a force to be reckoned with—and the north *will* feel indebted to me. I've seen the way the troops talk about you. I have four hundred northern soldiers at the docks right now threatening to burn down the rest of Dockside if I don't get the Flame of the North on that ship. And they will hail me as a hero when I deliver you to them."

He leaned forward, pushing against her hand and setting the point of the knife against her stomach, the old, predatory smile creeping across his lips.

"But better yet, the great General Andreese will be indebted to me. Because *he* will see the value of saving your life, even if you do not."

Sable pulled her hand away. "Reese died on the battlefield." The words tore out of her.

Kiva raised an eyebrow. "He was alive when they loaded him on the ship. Unconscious, but definitely alive."

She stared at him, barely believing his words. "What?"

"They carried him right past me, and I saw him breathing."

Kiva's words were warm, and Sable grabbed his arm as a wave of relief rolled over her.

He gave her a wry smile. "You've never looked at me so gratefully in your life."

Sable straightened and yanked her arm off.

"That didn't last long," he said dryly.

"You're forgetting the glaring, fatal flaw in your plan to woo the north."

He snorted. "Am I?"

His men encircled them, forming a wall Sable could barely see past. But Kiva was barely taller than her, and when she spoke, she felt the anger and warmth of her words swirl in the little circle they were confined in. "How long will the north hail you as a hero once I tell them you killed Tanis?"

Kiva's face darkened. "Why would you do that?"

Sable stared at him incredulously. "Because when he died, his tongue was black."

His mouth opened, and he stood in shocked silence.

"You think you can murder the general of the north without repercussions?" she demanded. "The man they were actually willing to rally under? When they find out, they'll kill you on sight. And then burn Dockside down over your corpse."

"Sable," Kiva said, his voice low, but hot with truth. "I did *not* kill him."

"Who else kills with vayakadyn venom?"

He shook his head. "No one. Someone wanted you to think it was me."

"Me?"

"Who else in the north knows about the venom?" he asked.

"Atticus, Serene, Jae, Andreese...I've told a lot of people about you."

He looked through the wall of his men, his eyes darting around the road. "Someone set me up." He turned back to Sable. "Why would I kill that man when I wanted the north to come help us? I blew up my own buildings to prove I was on your side, Sable. I went to a lot of effort to find you and free you from Goll. Why would I possibly do something as stupid as killing Tanis?"

She bristled against the truth in his words. "Then what were you afraid of last night when I came to see you?"

"You!" he snapped. "You came back to Immusmala at the head of an army!"

She crossed her arms, studying him.

"I have killed plenty of people with vaya venom," he said, still truthfully, "but never anyone as counterproductive as the beloved leader of the group I am trying to ally myself with. I build allies by helping them get wealth and power and whatever particular goal they're after, not by killing them. You've known me long enough to know that."

Sable glared at him. "Then who killed Tanis?"

"There are only two people who wanted the north to lose enough to poison their leader."

"Goll and Vivaine," Sable said. "And Goll would have just killed him in battle."

Kiva turned slowly toward the city. "She used me to get your men down here, then tried to make sure I'd never get the alliance with you that I wanted." There was a note of admiration in his voice. "She's good."

He shook his head. "We need to go. I wasn't lying about the four hundred soldiers demanding you make it on the boat with them."

"I know." Sable cast one more look at Goll's body before turning away.

Kiva motioned to his men and started back toward the city. At the Fallen Gate, Kiva signaled to a constable on the wall. The man disappeared, and in moments, the gate opened.

Kiva moved quickly along the Crest and turned down the street leading to Dockside. They passed under the wall and had to scramble over the edges of the destruction of the three Kalesh buildings.

"How did you blow these up?" Sable asked.

"When I had the buildings updated for the Kalesh to move in," Kiva said, "I added some strategically placed explosives just in case I ever needed to remove the Empire from Dockside quickly."

He led her down to the docks, where a ship waited, its deck crowded with northern soldiers. When Sable came into view, a cheer went up.

Kiva waved away the men escorting them and offered Sable his arm. "May I deliver you to your ship, Issable, Flame of the North?"

She ignored him and started toward the dock.

He kept pace beside her.

Sable reached the wide gangway as the soldiers crowded against the side of the ship to see her. Without a word to Kiva, she started up the gangplank.

"I believe you owe me payment for my part in the battle this morning," Kiva said from behind her.

She stopped. The butterfly ring glinted dully on her finger. She pulled it off and turned, holding it out to him.

He walked up the gangplank and paused. "Let's recap, shall we? You gave me some information about Vivaine that helped raise my status among the merchants, and you're giving me one rather old, worn ring.

"I, on the other hand, blew up two buildings for you, prepared the merchants to feel favorably toward you, and *saved your life* when the Kalesh were taking you." He gave her a piercing look. "Those two lists are far from even."

He reached out, but instead of taking the ring, he took her entire hand, leaning forward and raising it to his lips.

She tried to pull her hand away, but he held it fast, smiling up at her, his face just above her hand. "The north owes me, Sable. And whether you'll admit it or not, you owe me," he said quietly, holding the gallant pose as the soldiers on the deck cheered.

She clamped her fingers around his hand. "You want to put on a show, Kiva?" she asked, her voice low. "I can put on a show. Purn, make him bow."

Kiva's brow contracted slightly in confusion before the bottom of his vest bunched into two wads approximately the size of a kobold's fists, and he was yanked down. His eyes flew open in surprise as he lurched forward, falling to one knee.

Sable tightened her grip on his hand and pushed it down as hard as she could, keeping him kneeling. She felt Purn back up unseen against her legs.

The men on the ship burst out into a loud cheer, and Kiva's face turned livid. "I control this city now," he hissed. "Be careful how you treat me."

Sable leaned toward him. "Vivaine controlled it yesterday," she whispered. "Be *very* careful how you treat me."

He shoved himself back to his feet, pulling his hand away from hers, yanking the butterfly ring out with it.

Sable wiped the hand he'd held on her cloak.

He smoothed out his vest and straightened. "I'm sure we'll meet again. Very soon." He took a step back and gave her a cold, vicious smile. "A pleasure, as always, Sable."

He started to turn, then paused. "Goll wanted to drag your corpse back and throw it at the emperor's feet. Want to explain that?"

"No," she said simply.

He shrugged. "I'll find someone else who knows, then."

"Everyone here who knew is already dead." Sable looked east, but Goll's raven was long gone.

She stared into the empty sky, feeling a growing dread at what that raven's news would ignite.

"Don't worry, Kiva," she said. "Everyone will know soon enough."

He studied her with narrow eyes, then turned and sauntered down the gangplank.

A spark of light arced through the sky, soaring over the city and diving down toward the docks.

Sable held out her arm, and Innov circled her, showering blazing embers.

The cheer from the northmen was deafening. For a breath, Sable could see nothing but the curtain of fire and feel nothing but the vibrant, swirling hope of the phoenix.

Innov flared her wings and landed on Sable's outstretched arm as the sparks around them fell and faded.

Kiva had backed away to the bottom of the gangplank, the lines of his body wary and guarded.

Sable turned her back to him and ran her finger down Innov's chest, letting the flames lick over her skin. "Are you sure you want to stay with me?"

Innov gazed at the cheering soldiers.

"You may regret this." Sable started up the gangplank. Her eyes strayed to the empty sky again. "But we could definitely use your hope."

EPILOGUE

THE RAVEN'S wings flapped in the small opening of the tower, soaring high above the white stones of the imperial palace in Cartelutzia. A young, indolent boy shuffled over to retrieve the message from the bird's leg until he caught sight of its two scarlet bands. His eyes widened, and with a practiced efficiency that belied his former movements, he detached the letter and ran for the tower stairs.

Minutes later, Portus, Chief Minister of the Realm, took a bracing breath and stepped quickly through the tall doors of the imperial study.

Emperor Rolenn Tourris Consur III, First Lord of the Unending Lands, Father of Every Nation, Dragon of the Empire, glanced up from his desk with a slightly irritated look at the interruption.

The minister bowed lower than normal. "A second missive from General Goll, Your Imperial Majesty," he said, attempting to keep his voice even.

Portus kept his eyes fixed on the floor in front of the desk, but he could still see the emperor's quill pause, and the crease between his brow deepened. The Chief Minister remained utterly still and silent.

"You just brought me news that the wretch was defeated on some nameless field in a tiny, barbaric land." The emperor's voice was tinged with a terrifying edge of anger. "How dare you speak his name in my presence?"

Portus remained bowed but held out both his hands, palms up, extending the small roll of paper with the double scarlet bands.

There was a moment of silence.

"Approach."

Portus straightened and set the tiny scroll on the desk.

Emperor Rolenn unrolled the paper.

Your Imperial Majesty,

I address you from my disgrace only out of the greatest urgency.

Amb. Bastian betrayed you, joining the rebels. I left his body on the battlefield.

His faithlessness has its roots in the woman who leads the rebellious north and holds great sway in the south. She surrendered herself to me in hopes of leniency for this land. I bring her to you directly.

But I smell treachery in the air. If I am betrayed and taken, you must know that this woman is no nameless barbarian.

She is A'Sable.

The daughter of A'Melia, Ghost of the White Wood.

Emperor Rolenn Tourris Consur III crushed the paper in his fist.

He stared at his desk, his face darkening to the point that Minister Portus took a half step back.

"Gather the lords," he said, his voice cold. "We have a tiny, barbaric land to destroy."

THE END

FROM THE AUTHOR

Thank you for reading *Raven's Ruin!*

I know, I know. We left Sable in a bit of a lurch. Again.

But you're starting to expect it by now, aren't you? And that makes it better, right?

No?

Ahh. Then I'm a little sorry. (Although not too sorry.)

The good news is that this is a three book series, so by the end of the next book, we shall have our resolution, and poor Sable will earn a happy ending.

Yes, I agree. There's a lot left to deal with in the third book. Future-me is already angry about all the loose ends she'll have to weave together.

Book 3, *Phoenix Rising,* is set to release May 2022.

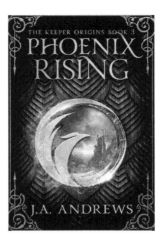

If 2021 turns out to be a better year than 2020 (and we're all hoping it will…) it may be out early. I hope it will be out early.

A review is worth more to an author than an actual solution to the Kalesh problem would be to Sable.
(That might be an exaggeration.)

But, if you enjoyed *Raven's Ruin* and have the time to leave a review, you can do so on Amazon.
     Happy Reading!

Janice

The Ghost of the White Wood has been a thorn in the Kalesh Empire's side for years.

Until Captain Bastian captures her—and she becomes so much more than a thorn.

Get a free copy of the story Ghost of the White Wood at jaandrews.com/ghost

ACKNOWLEDGMENTS

Thank you to you beautiful people who pick up these books and actually enjoy them. I had very little faith that my stories would ever find an audience that enjoyed them, and the fact that you exist makes me endlessly happy. May many blessings fall upon your head.

Thank you to Cheryl Schuetze, Barbara Kloss, and Karyne Norton for your critiques of the messy, plodding first half of this book. I promise book 3 will be written in a more rational way.

Thank you Laura Josephson for being the most flexible editor in the history of this world or any other. I'm sorry about all the misplaced commas.

And most of all, thank you to my husband. The effort you contributed to get this shaky story to actually stand on its feet was Herculean. I love you.

ABOUT THE AUTHOR

JA Andrews lives deep in the Rocky Mountains of Montana with her husband and three children.

She is eternally grateful to CS Lewis for showing her the luminous world of Narnia.

She wishes Jane Austen had lived 200 years later so they could be pen pals.

She is furious at JK Rowling for introducing her to house elves, then not providing her a way to actually employ one.

And she is constantly jealous of her future-self who, she is sure, has everything figured out.

For more information:
www.jaandrews.com
jaandrews@jaandrews.com

facebook.com/JAAndrewsAuthor
twitter.com/JAAndrewsWriter
instagram.com/jaandrewsbooks

Printed in Great Britain
by Amazon

73863212R00388